Margret

P9-DVC-076

"Her strength is as a storyteller. . . . Much of the entertainment of *Family Business* comes from its smartly observed, *roman à clef* references to such powers that be as Katharine Graham, Dolly Schiff, the Binghams of Louisville, and even Rupert Murdoch. Anna Murdoch has kept her *Family Business* all in the family."

New York Magazine

"A big page-turner of a book . . . The romance of the newspaper business and the power it has over the people who work in it."

Toronto Star

"Sex and scandal . . . Enjoyable."

Chicago Heights Star

"Do not miss reading Anna Murdoch's *Family Business*."

California Jewish Press

Also by Anna Murdoch
Published by Fawcett Books

IN HER OWN IMAGE

FAMILY BUSINESS

Anna Murdoch

FAWCETT GOLD MEDAL • NEW YORK

A Fawcett Gold Medal Book
Published by Ballantine Books
Copyright © 1988 by Anna Murdoch

All rights reserved under International and Pan-American Copyright Conventions. Published in the United States by Ballantine Books, a division of Random House, Inc., New York, and simultaneously in Canada by Random House of Canada Limited, Toronto.

No part of this book may be reproduced or utilized in any form or by any means, electronic or mechanical, including photocopying, recording or by any information storage and retrieval system, without permission in writing from the Publisher. Inquiries should be addressed to Permissions Department, William Morrow and Company, Inc., 105 Madison Ave., New York, N.Y. 10016.

Al Dubin and Victor Herbert ''Indian Summer'' © 1939 Warner Bros. Inc. (renewed) All Rights Reserved USED BY PERMISSION

Library of Congress Catalog Card Number: 87-22693

ISBN 0-449-14567-0

This edition published by arrangement with William Morrow and Company, Inc.

Manufactured in the United States of America

First Ballantine Books Edition: February 1989

AUTHOR'S NOTE

This is a work of fiction and does not portray any particular newspaper or newspaper family. However, it would be remiss of me not to admit that the *Aspen Times* was the original "Humdinger," although the events and people written about here are purely my own invention. This book is dedicated to all newspaper pioneers—past, present and future.

God bless the noble art.

—Journeyman's salutation on
entering a print shop. From
ITU Lessons in Printing

FAMILY
BUSINESS

PROLOGUE

NEW YORK
1987

"*S*TOP THE CAR!*"*
        Yarrow McLean leaned forward and rapped the dividing window of the limousine with the rubber tip of her cane.

"Here, Madam?"

"Yes. Stop the car. I want to walk the rest of the way."

The chauffeur raised his eyebrows but he said nothing and pulled over under the next streetlight, skidding slightly in the light snow. There were few cars at midnight on South Street. The street ran like a gauntlet between the shuttered warehouses and vacant lots on one side and the black East River on the other.

"I need some air," she said again in her deep, soft voice as he helped her out of the curbside door. "Give me my stick."

"Madam, it isn't safe."

"There's no danger, Vasik."

"This is not a good area," he said as if she were a child.

She sighed. "You may follow me in the car if it makes you feel better, Vasik. I may be crippled but I'm not an invalid. Not yet."

It was his turn to sigh. "No, Madam."

"Thank you."

Yarrow pulled up the collar of her fur coat. The fresh air felt good. It was only a few blocks to her office and the walk would clear her head. She had felt stifled tonight in the studio, not her usual self. Why she had ever agreed to go on the talk show she could not now imagine. They had appealed to her vanity, she supposed. *"What makes Yarrow McLean tick?"* She must be getting old and rattled, she thought, walking carefully over the rutted sidewalks with her stick. *"Will you sell the* New York Telegraph?*"* Snow hid the traps, covered the unevenness with a thin white lie. She supposed it was good for her character to be on the other side of the questioning for once. A rat scuttled out of a rubble-strewn lot. She could see its distorted shadow in the beam of Vasik's headlights.

Old and rattled, like this city, needing a stick to lean on. Under the sulfuric streetlights, the snow swirled in a yellow fog. Beneath the elevated FDR Drive on her left, sudden showers of snow, ice and dirt sheeted down from the wheels of passing cars. All going somewhere, she thought, as she walked on the quiet roadway beneath. All in a hurry. Perhaps that was it—the interviewer tonight had been in too much of a hurry, trying to rush her, compress her life into the eight minutes he had to fill; so that all questions, all answers had to be short, packaged, precise. What truth was that? How could she answer? Another shower of ice, grit and water drummed down on a parked car. Truth was like that, she thought. Embedded in clusters of other things. And sometimes one heard it, rat-a-tat like a tympany, or sometimes like a gong. And sometimes not at all, muffled, like now, as a drift of snow absorbed the next hail from above.

One of her own trucks passed her, too quick for her to read tomorrow's headlines. She looked and saw that she was almost there and the blank walls of the *Telegraph* faced her like a cliff. Even the first time she saw it, she had found it a very ugly building. Yarrow straightened her shoulders. Flakes of snow were on her hair, fizzed on her lips. She suddenly had a longing for her home in Colorado.

Vasik passed her and parked the car. He had called ahead on the car telephone and the guard was waiting at the door to let her in. She was rather disappointed, for she liked walking in the back door, where the graffiti almost obliterated the gray paint on the walls and she could step through the pressroom over pools of ink and waste paper. There was where the lifeblood pounded through the building. But she thanked Vasik and wished he wouldn't be quite so thoughtful sometimes.

He stood silently beside her in his blue uniform as the elevator rose to the sixth floor. His long Polish face reflected utter patience as he watched the numbers on the indicator.

"Vasik," she said, "go home."

Her father had once had a Great Dane, Sherlock, when he ran the *Journal* in Platte City. In the summer Sherlock would always escape from the yard at home and find his way to the office, sitting panting in the elevator until someone would take him up to see her father. "Go home. Go home, Sherlock," her father would say, pointing dramatically and uselessly toward the doors. Yarrow felt a bit the same now.

"Go home, Vasik." He had been with her for years. She knew he wouldn't.

"I will make you a cup of coffee," he said, standing back to let her out of the elevator.

"I wish you wouldn't. I'm already an insomniac." She stumped along the corridor to her office. Her left leg felt stiff. It always did when she was tired.

"Then a whiskey," he said, unlocking the door of the outer office and switching on the lights. The lights blink-blinked as fluorescents do.

She stepped past him into the room. "That sounds much more like it." She took off a black leather glove while he unlocked the inner door to her own office and as she waited, and her eyes grew accustomed to the change of light, she saw her reflection in the large mirrored windows that looked out over the river. She saw an elegant woman in a dark mink coat thrown open over a classic black suit; the woman's hair was white and dressed severely back into an unfashionable but practical bun. A curly wisp of hair had escaped from under her hairnet and she twisted it back impatiently with her fingers. She saw that the fingers of the ungloved hand were sturdy and short-nailed, more practical than the silhouette would lead one to imagine. And she saw that the gloved hand, under which the bump of rings could be seen, leaned firmly and necessarily on the handle of her walking stick. She was sixty-five years old. She had grown old while she wasn't looking. She wondered if it was that sight in the monitor at the television studio that had shaken her, had made her lift her head so that her chin looked firmer. She had hoped that her eyes would look fresh and youthful and not cynical or jaded as the camera came in for close-ups.

Yarrow turned away from the truth she saw in the window. At the far end of her own office, Vasik moved the photographs of her children and of herself with the ambassador, and put a silver tray, with a jug of water, a glass, and a bottle of Johnnie Walker, on the desk. She slipped off her coat and let it drop on the blue sofa near the door. She did not want to talk to Vasik. She wanted to talk to Elliot. He had said he would watch the program. He had known she would be nervous. She would call him. Like her, increasing age had decreased his need for sleep; what she could have achieved if that had been so when she was young.

"Thank you, Vasik."

"Can I get you anything else, Madam?"

"No."

He withdrew into the outer office and shut the door. She knew, from many nights, that he would take a blanket and a pillow from the closet and go to sleep on the sofa until she called. She wondered at the patience of his wife. But then she had met Irma, and she knew their phlegmatic natures were ideally suited to each other. Not like hers and Elliot's.

Yarrow seated herself at her rosewood desk and leaned her stick against the drawer. It was a walking stick of pale red birch with a gray horn handle and a silver collar. Elliot had bought it for her years ago from Swaine Adeney in London. She poured herself a Scotch and water and dialed Elliot's number. She leaned back in her swivel chair and turned toward the window. But she could not see out with the lights on, only in. She swiveled back to her desk and opened the drawer as she listened to the phone ringing and took out a framed photograph of Elliot. It was much less formal than the photograph on her desk. There was no answer, so she hung up. Perhaps he was still out to dinner. It surprised her because he had not said anything about it when they spoke that morning on the telephone.

"How are you?"

"I'm fine."

"Are you really fine?"

"Yes." He laughed. "I'm really fine."

"Can you watch *Nightline* tonight? I'm on with Koppel."

"Ah, Yarrow. Is that wise?"

Now it was her turn to laugh.

"I've followed your advice. I'll talk if it's live. No editing allowed."

"No *Sixty Minutes*?"

"Definitely no *Sixty Minutes*. They'd tear me to pieces."

"What will you wear?"

She laughed again.

"You never change, do you? I'll wear a black suit with a white blouse."

"Beige."

"Beige then."

"You'll look beautiful. As always."

"Hmmm."

Pause.

"He'll ask you if the rumors are true about Truitt buying the . . ."

"I don't give a damn about rumors."

"But he'll ask you anyway and you must watch what you say or you'll alienate everyone."

"Alienate whom?"

"Yarrow, don't be so obdurate."

"Your friends? The liberal establishment? I don't give a damn about the liberal establishment."

"I know that. I found that out."

Yarrow changed the subject.

"How's Meredith?"

"She wants me to go to the Hamptons this weekend with her and the children. I hate the beach in winter. Where will you be this weekend?"

"Elliot, I believe I hear a note of—could it be—loneliness in your voice?" She teased him.

"Where will you be?"

"I'll be here in the city. I have work to do."

"Can't you come out here? I have something to ask you."

"Can't you ask now?"

"We'll have lunch."

"It will have to be Sunday. I'm too busy on Saturday."

"You never stop. When are you going to stop, Yarrow?"

What makes Yarrow McLean tick?

"Ever since Gary Hart dropped out of the campaign, Democrats have been popping out of the woodwork. There are two new hopefuls coming to see me tomorrow."

"Can't your editor see them?"

"I'm not going to take my hand off the tiller until the last moment, Elliot."

"I was afraid of that."

She hesitated. Presidential campaigns were a sore point between them. "Everyone's running and looking for endorsements. Unless it's my lovely chicken pie from the canteen they all want to taste."

"You need a cook. Who will you endorse? Another Republican?"

She risked teasing him again. "Why not? We haven't done too badly with the last one."

"Yarrow. We will never agree."

"No. But then we never did."

"That's why I love you. I'll watch you tonight. See if you give me a clue. *Have* you made up your mind whom to endorse?"

"No. Of course not. That wouldn't be any fun."

"Who would have thought Yarrow McLean from the little town of Galena would fall in love with power?"

"Yarrow McLean of New York."

"One and the same."

"Are they? Anyway, I was taught by an expert. You."

"I didn't teach you, Yarrow. What you didn't learn from Jock or your father, you taught yourself."

"Oh, stop being so nice. It isn't like you. Listen, I must go. You will watch?"

"Yes, of course."

"I'll call you afterward. See what you think. I love you. Good-bye."

"Good-bye, darling." He hung up first. He always did.

Yarrow sipped her Scotch and dialed his number again. She let it ring but there was still no answer. Perhaps he *had* gone out to dinner. She dialed her own answering service. There were some messages. Nothing urgent. She sighed and got up. She did not feel at all sleepy, yet she was tired.

The question of the future of the paper throbbed in her brain. She would go home soon. She had an early start tomorrow. The senator from Massachusetts was her first appointment. She made a note to herself to remind the editor to bring up Matt Smithlaw. He had written a very incisive piece on the senator's weaknesses last week. No wonder the phone had been running hot from Boston and Washington.

Yarrow made herself a cup of hot milk in the tiny kitchen off her office. She took it back to her desk and poured in a half inch of whiskey. She picked up some of her reading from the desk, put on her glasses and went to the sofa. Yarrow sipped her hot drink and read. She quickly went through her correspondence, marking the margins as she went. She looked at her calendar for the next week. Horrendous. She noticed the note her secretary had made that it was her granddaughter's birthday tomorrow. She circled it with a red pen, wrote "CALL" beside it. Her daughter noticed these things. She read through the pile of clippings she had not had time for earlier; read the late editions of yesterday's papers. She worked quickly, methodically, her pen crossing out, circling, commenting. The discarded pile on the floor grew as the information was transferred to her memory. She ripped out an advertisement from a competing newspaper, marked it for her ad director, wrote "Where's ours? YB" across it and tossed it on the coffee table. Yarrow took off her glasses and rubbed her eyes. If she waited twenty minutes the next edition would be off the presses. She would buzz down and have them send it up. And then she would go home. She pushed a cushion behind her and put her coat over her knees. She placed the extension phone on the floor beside her and kicked off her shoes. How many times had she done this? Countless. In the real sense, *this* was her home. This room, this building reflected who she was, what she thought; told the world what made Yarrow McLean tick. Every day, in black and white, it came out, the answer to that question. Why did they keep asking it? She allowed herself to lie down and shut her eyes for a moment. She put one hand on the receiver of the telephone so that she could answer it instantly. She was very good at covering up the sleep in her voice. As she got older the need for sleep appeared to her to be a sign of some weakness on her part. But she probably wouldn't sleep, just doze. She heard or thought she heard the dull rumble of the presses starting. Visitors never heard it. But she always knew when they were on. She was sure the floor vibrated. She could feel it now through the telephone, four Goss presses pounding out fifty thousand papers an hour. "Forty thousand *good* copies," she would contradict her production manager whenever he boasted of the number. There was nothing about the business Yarrow didn't know. Yarrow listened to the murmur, and listened to it, and it sounded like her heart.

BOOK ONE
- 1922–1939 -

THE FONT

Font: A source, origin or beginning
A complete assortment of type

CHAPTER 1

YARROW MCLEAN WAS BORN IN 1922 IN THE ROCKY MOUNTAINS, just west of the Continental Divide where even in midsummer snow clings to the peaks. Her father and her mother had been born in these mountains; her father, James, in this very house where her mother now stood waiting for the next spasm of labor pains. Freya, her mother, had been born in the Gunnison River region where the old Ute Indian reservation had been. People said that Freya's father, Papa Halvorsen, had Indian blood in him. He had high cheekbones and almond-shaped eyes that, even when he went blind, seemed to see more than most mortals. Whether or not it was true, his Norwegian heritage had held sway, and he and his wife called their only daughter Freya, after a goddess from that other white land.

Freya now stood, wide awake and restless in the early dawn, holding on to the bedpost. She turned her head and her thick braid of pale hair knocked against her shoulder as she glanced at her sleeping husband. He had come in very late last night from the *Gazette* office. He had not tightened the quoins enough on the page form, and when he lifted the form to the flatbed press, the metal type had bellied and the pieces had fallen to the floor. This had happened once to Freya and she had sat down and cried into her apron at all the time and skill it took to put the pieces of type together—now undone in a careless moment. She had to pick up all the pieces, even the tiny little commas that had stuck between the planks on the floor, and sort them out again in their correct boxes in the font, before her husband could set the page up again. " 'Dissing,'' was what James called the redistribution of the type. Freya had another word for it.

She did not want to wake him yet. She wanted to hold this last moment of uncertainty as long as she could. Freya took her shawl from the bottom of the bed and padded to the window. The floor was very cold under her feet and the inside of the windowpane had iced over. She scratched the pane with her fingernail and through the hole she could see, in the soft dawn

11

light, a herd of elk that had come down into their meadow. She saw the elk because of the steam rising from their brown bodies. She noticed it and she watched them for a long time while the restlessness inside her increased and she became aware that forces seemed to be pulling all the skin of her belly forward to one center. Her labor had begun in earnest, and Freya, her suspicions confirmed, put her forehead against the cold pane and called softly to her husband, "James, this is it." Through the gap in the ice fronds on the window her eye fell on some heads of wild yarrow that were somehow surviving the winter and were pressed against the pane. And she thought how beautiful the lacy heads were; weeds she had seen all her life and never really noticed until now. How strong they were to survive the winter in Galena, where nightly the temperature dropped well below freezing and blizzards clawed the skin off one's face. She called out again, "James!" as her own skin gathered more quickly and tautly this time and James shot out of bed and pulled on his pants, and when the spasm of pain had passed she looked up and the elk were gone and the sun was gilding the upper slope of Pyramid Peak.

Freya told her daughter all this. In fact it was the first present she gave her, her own story, about the steaming brown bodies and the lace flower heads. She told her that this was how she had decided to name her Yarrow, and people who had known her family nodded at each other and said they always knew there was Indian blood in the Halvorsens. And Yarrow's father always laughed when Freya told the story and said thank God he hadn't ended up with a daughter named Elk.

Yarrow's grandfather, Jock, gave her a present, too. Since she had done him the great honor of being born on his birthday in November, he signed over to her fifty shares in another newspaper on the eastern side of the mountains. The fifty shares represented half of Jock's interest. There were two other partners in the company. Freya thought it was a worthless gift. "Where's the value in a piece of paper? I want something we can see." Freya had a peasant sense of economics; value lay in things you could hold; things you could eat. But James said his father meant well and told her to hush when the old man came into the kitchen. It was his house after all, though he now lived in a room that led off the porch, with its own outside door.

Jock had bought the house in 1892 when the town of Galena was the star of the Rockies. By then, he had been in Galena ten years. He was prosperous, he had grown a beard, he wore a hat and had a thin gold watch on a chain that he took out of his waistcoat pocket with two fingers as though it were holy bread.

In those days, Main Street was thronged with dark-coated, hatted, bearded men. Prospectors, clutching bedrolls to their shoulders with grimy hands, walked the streets looking for cheap lodgings. Gamblers and faro players fingered their waistcoats and stretched their legs outside the saloons or leaned through the gilt-embossed windows of the bars waiting for their luck to change. There were hustlers, between opportunities, who picked their teeth, lounged against the false fronts of boardinghouses, watching the peddlers, the miners, the expectant faces of the new arrivals. Jock's paper boys darted in and out of the crowds, selling his sheet. Everyone read the *Gazette*—except the men departing; of them, no one took any notice. Disillusionment was an emotion not tolerated in a mining camp.

The *Galena Gazette* did a roaring trade in those days. Silver poured from the mines. When the white metal was king, women followed their men—and with the women came domesticity. It came in the form of beds, and armoires and pianos. They were hauled up the sides of mountains, lashed to the backs of carts and drays. Mud sucked at the shoes of the women and children who walked beside the carts. Houses began to spawn in the ravines and up the hillsides; some were shanties that blew down in the first good storm; some, like gingerbread houses with fretwork eaves and gables, had a feminine gentility that the old log cabins had not. Everyone expected the silver boom to last— and who was to say it would not while the Sherman Purchase Act was in effect?

Jock bought his house on Boomer Street from a prospector who had made and lost one hundred thousand dollars in less than one hundred days. Jock bought the red sandstone house with its lacy wooden fretwork, and the meadow behind, for two thousand dollars. Coin money was rarely seen in the town and he paid for it in silver ore and scrip, with his brand-new wife, Mollie, standing beside him. She had stepped daintily through the stained-glass front door as delicate as a kitten. She was enchanted by the new electric lights installed in the house and kept pressing the switches up and down. "Oh, la," she said. The plume of her hat had brushed against the red cut-velvet wallpaper as she went up the stairs. "Hmmm," she said, "hmmm," trying to hide her excitement from the prospector's wife who sat weeping on the bottom stair.

It was for Mollie he bought the house, thinking his log cabin up behind Red Mountain too rough for her. And besides, as the editor and publisher of the oldest newspaper in town, *Ten Years Young*, it proclaimed on its masthead, he felt a more substantial house was necessary. But he kept the log cabin, where the snow still sifted through the unchinked logs, "just in case." After Mollie died giving birth to James (his only offspring for he never married again), Jock would take the boy up to the cabin and spend nights in winter watching their breath freeze as it fell on their blankets.

This, too, was why Jock still had those shares in the newspaper near Colorado Springs, a newspaper in a little town with the big name of Platte City. He had kept them "just in case." He had got them in return for selling out his share of a grubstake near Leadville.

He was standing on the tailings outside the shaft one day in April 1881, yarning with a stranger from the East. The stranger was sitting on a mule. The thaw had set in early and rain poured from the sky. The ground was a quagmire of snowmelt and slush, and the tailings ran and dribbled their valueless muck down the sides of the hills and washed away the narrow trails that had been hacked into them.

If there was any life more miserable than an unsuccessful miner's, Jock had not seen it.

"I'm sick to death of mining," he said, sucking blood from his scraped knuckles and watching the rain run in a straight rivulet off the man's hatbrim.

"No luck here? What about the other side, near the Matchless Mine? They say Tabor's taking out two thousand dollars a day from that hole."

Jock looked at the man. They were about the same age, but Jock's youthful cheeks had deep grooves from hard labor and poor food. He was twenty-one years old, and when he had arrived he had looked just like this stranger and all the other men who had come. They were suffering from gold and silver fever, so their eyes were bright and greedy; they carried their life savings in their money belts, and strapped their bedrolls and cooking pots behind them on their mules. But Jock didn't look like them any longer.

"You'd be lucky," he said, turning away and picking up his shovel and pickax.

Suddenly the grubstaker next to Jock came screeching out of his hole. "Eureka!" he shouted. He clutched a large nugget of silver ore in his hands. Tears of happiness streaked down his dirty, unshaven face. He did a jig over his pickax.

"Heaven be praised," he said and fell down and kissed the

mud. The stranger was agog. Beads of sweat broke out on his forehead. He jumped down from his mule, making his pots and pans clang.

"For God's sake, man. I'll buy you out now, right here and now, even before you go to the assayer's office."

But the miner was off, skittering down the hill in the rain. A dozen miners came out of their shafts and looked over their tailings like so many gophers.

"You. You," said the man, grabbing Jock by the arm. "Your claim's next to his. Name your price."

"Get away, man," said Jock, shoving him away. But the stranger wouldn't listen. He took off his money belt and tried to fasten it around Jock's waist. He pressed the rope from his mule into Jock's hand. Jock pushed him away, shouldered his pick and shovel and set off down the mountain.

"A thousand dollars." The man came slithering down behind Jock, pulling his mule.

"You'll have to do better than that," said Jock over his shoulder.

"Five thousand dollars." He said it with such vehemence that the mule lost its balance and a pot came loose and landed upright on the track. Jock stopped and went back.

"How much did you say?"

"Five thousand dollars . . ."

Jock screwed up his face as though he were having second thoughts.

"Seven."

A big grin spread over Jock's thin face. He put his arm around the stranger.

"I think we can come to an agreement," he said, rolling his r's. The stranger said something else, but Jock couldn't hear. Instead he heard the steady plinking of the rain in the pot as the cloudburst eased. It sounded like money. It was the happiest sound he had ever heard.

Later that afternoon, when the sun came out briefly only to sink behind the peaks, Jock walked away from the assay office with a bank order for seven thousand dollars, a two-thirds share in a news sheet in Platte City, and a handful of metal type that the stranger had emptied out of his pocket. Jock walked past the children sitting in the gutter sifting the sawdust from the saloon-floor sweepings. His boots almost skipped on the wooden sidewalks as he tossed the children a coin. He walked on to the Pioneer Bar on State Street to split his good fortune with his partner—who by now had washed his face but couldn't quite get the grin off it.

"You're a bloody fine actor for a Cornishman, Max Horace," Jock said, "though I thought you were overdoing it when you shouted, 'Eureka!' "

Max laughed till the tears ran down his face again. They had a few drinks at the bar and then stumbled through the crowds to Tontine's. Max was very drunk.

"What'll you have?"

"Beef and oysters."

"That sounds better than lard and bread in our tent. I'll have the same." Jock slapped the menu down on the table.

"Never thought it would be so easy," said Max.

Jock looked troubled for a minute.

"Well, here's hoping the poor bastard finds something in that hole. He's got as much chance as anyone else in this thieving place."

"Never know your luck."

"Och, if it hadna' been me, it would have been someone else." He got out a little stub of a pencil and a scrap of paper.

"We split fifty-fifty."

"Absholutely."

"Three thousand five hundred to you. Three thousand five hundred to me."

"Right."

"And the shares in the paper."

"Fifty-fifty."

"Right. One hundred to you, one hundred to me."

"Right. Partners."

Jock signed the crumpled piece of paper and Max licked the pencil and did the same. Max tried to arm wrestle on the table and knocked over his drink. "Another drink," he shouted at the barman.

Jock jiggled the metal type pieces in his pocket and put them on the oilcloth.

"I did a bit of printing once, in Pennsylvania. How about you and me going to that paper in Platte City? We could run it together."

"Ish too far." Max lifted his glass. "Anyway, there's a third, a third partner and they said it's worth nothing. This is where the growth is, up here with the miners. Why don't we stay here?"

Jock was attacking his steak. It was the first red meat he had eaten in weeks.

"I don't want to stay in this place any longer than I have to."
He stabbed his knife into his meat.

The food was sobering Max up. He wiped his bread around
the meat juices on the plate.

"What about Galena then? There's a stage leaving tomorrow."

"And I'm not going into another mine as long as I live," said
Jock.

"No, but your other idea—start a news sheet, Jock. But start
it up here, in the mountains."

"Partners?"

"Partners. Fifty-fifty all the way."

Next day they went to Galena where the boom was already on
the upswing. He and Max pooled their money to buy a press.
They had to wait for it to be shipped from Chicago. They hired
an itinerant typesetter and within three months brought out the
Galena Gazette as a weekly news sheet. When he pulled his first
sheet from the press, Jock had never felt so proud. "You little
beauty," he said, holding it up to the light, "you little humdinger." Somehow the name stuck, and even the locals never
called the *Gazette* by its proper name but would ask each other,
"Have you read the latest in the Humdinger?"

Jock soon became as fast as the typesetter, setting three sticks
in an hour, a stick being just over two inches long. He already
knew the difference between Brévier and Bourgeois, Old Primer
and New. Max became the business manager and was out in the
town all day collecting advertisements.

Max Horace was always getting into trouble. Jock knew that
Max loved a scam. It brought out the best and the worst in the
man. Every day Max came in with a new way of making money.
Jock tried to distance himself from Max's schemes. Sometimes it
worked and sometimes it didn't. Max soon had half the town
screaming for his hide and the other half conniving how to copy
him. A deputation of the more responsible citizens of the town
came to see Jock. If Max didn't stop his sharp practices they
were going to make it difficult for the *Gazette*. Jock told Max to
behave himself or get out of the partnership. One night a thief
was shot and hung in Main Street. Pinned to his back was a list
of other citizens who could expect the same. Max Horace's name
was near the top. That night, as usual, Max Horace went out and
got drunk. In the morning he woke up to find he was married,
and the new Mrs. Horace was in bed beside him. He spent every
sober moment of his life ever after trying to remember how it
had happened. Jock got them both seats on the next stage to
Buena Vista and bought out Max's share of the *Gazette*. Max

Horace headed east but he got no farther than Platte City, where Mrs. Horace dug her heels in and said she would stay, and Max looked up the third partner of the *Platte City Journal*, a Colonel Adam Truitt, and introduced himself.

Yarrow McLean loved stories. When she was small she spent hours sitting on her grandfather's knees listening to his tales. It was the only time she would sit still.

"He fills her head with rubbish," her mother said.

"It's harmless," said James. "She's nearly six and she won't listen to him forever. Let them be."

Yarrow liked to sit on her grandfather's knees so that his curly white beard was like a curtain over her eyes. She played with his earlobe with her right hand and sucked the thumb of her left. Under the curtain of hair, her mother could not see her.

"Grandfather, spell Yarrow."

> "Yarrow Parrow
> Nicker-arrow, Coo-farrow
> Barbar-arrow
> That's how you spell Yarrow!"

"Spell Grandfather."

> "Grandfather Panfather
> Nicker-andfather, Coo-fanfather
> Barbar-anfather
> That's how you spell Grandfather!"

"Spell paper."

> "Paper Caper
> Nicker-aper, Coo-faper,
> Barbar-aper
> That's how you spell paper!"

By this time grandfather's saliva was flowing and he would feel the urge to spit.

"That's disgusting," Freya said, hearing the harrumph in his throat. She was washing clothes at the kitchen sink. Grandfather glanced at his daughter-in-law wringing out the clothes and got to his feet.

"Aye, yer mother is right. Jock's a dirty old man. Anyway, I need a smoke. I'll go and have a stogie outside." Freya forbade smoking in the house. He put on his big coat and a hat and his gloves without fingers and went onto the porch. Yarrow and her mother heard the creak of the chair as he sat down. The two younger children were asleep upstairs and the house was very quiet. Yarrow watched the muscles on her mother's arms bulge as she twisted the clothes into thick ropes. A large kettle of water on the Franklin stove began to rock as the water came to the boil. Every now and then the kettle tapped against a big pot of simmering stew. Yarrow listened to the rocking of the kettle, and the hissing, and the squeeze of water from her mother's hands. Then she heard another creak from Grandfather's chair and smelled the fragrance of his tobacco as the smoke drifted through the door.

"Go on with you, then," said her mother in exasperation, pushing back a long strand of blond hair from her forehead with her wrist. She wiped her hands on a towel hanging from her waist. "You'll just be in my way any case in here." She buttoned Yarrow into her heavy wool coat that itched and tied on her cap and mittens and Yarrow skipped through the door into Grandfather's arms.

"Once upon a time," her grandfather told her, "there was a fine young Scotsman from Aberdeen . . ."

"That was you."

"Aye. He was very handsome but very poor because he was the youngest son of a minister who had a great gift for words, and a somewhat lesser gift for saving souls. The minister saw very little virtue in money, and none at all in hypocrisy and consequently the kirk was often empty. You ken what I mean?"

"Aye," said Yarrow, sneaking off her mitten so she could get at her thumb.

"But the youngest son was ambitious. He was not suited for the Church. His mother thought he was too fine to be a tradesman, and *he* knew he was too poor to be a gentleman."

Grandfather pulled Yarrow closer on his knee. His beard tickled her face and she could see his Adam's apple working. Each word puffed out in frozen breaths like Indian smoke signals.

"The youngest son wanted to achieve great things. He wanted to make the world a better place. He wanted to have a say in things. You see he *had* listened to his father all those Sundays sitting in the front pew. But he didn't think his father could achieve those things through his one small voice in that big empty church. His voice didn't reach enough people. So the youngest son begged to get away. He had always loved America. He was born in the same year that Abraham Lincoln was elected

president. He talked his father into letting him join his married
sister . . ."

"Great-aunty Hilda."

" . . . who had emigrated to Pennsylvania. And he joined her
there and got work in the bituminous mines. Because he could
read and write, his sister apprenticed him to a print shop, but all
he listened to were the whispers from miners coming back east
with stories of the new El Dorado. Why, that was a place where
you could pick up lumps of silver off the ground and where
millionaires were as common as mules." Grandfather sucked on
his cigar and the red embers glowed.

"So your grandfather lay on his pallet in Pennsylvania and
dreamed about making his fortune. He dreamed of seeing these
mountains and listened to the stories of cold and hardship, of
men losing their fingers to frostbite, and snowslides that buried
them alive, so that when they were found, mold had grown on
their faces, but nothing would dissuade him. Your great-aunt
wouldn't hear about it. So the young man decided to run away
and he finally made it to Leadville where H.A.W. Tabor made
his fortune . . ."

"And Grandfather made none."

"And Grandfather made none; but"—he tapped Yarrow on
the nose—"Grandfather found something better." He shifted
Yarrow onto one knee and searched in his coat pocket. He took
out a letter that had arrived that day, but he put that back in his
pocket. He went to his other pocket and took out a small slug of
metal from a Linotype machine. "Your grandfather found a
voice," he said, turning the slug so that the raised inverted
letters glinted in his hand.

"You started a newspaper." Yarrow took the metal slug in
her hand, felt the sharpness of it, the weight of it.

"Yes. That's when the Humdinger was born. Right here in
Galena. There were a dozen camps like Galena all over the
mountains; Ashcroft, Ute City, Independence. Thousands of people thronged in hunting for silver or gold. What people needed
was news; they wanted to know where the mining claims were,
what the conditions of the roads were. That's why I started the
Humdinger.

"We nearly didn't get our first edition out. We had to freight
the press over Independence Pass on sledges. I went up to meet
it. It was a big day for me, Yarrow. That press weighed six tons
and the mules panicked on a narrow ledge. We lost the cylinder
over the side and it fell fifteen feet into the Roaring Fork. Of
course we didn't have our Linotype then either—that we didn't

get till after you were born—and over the side with the cylinder went half our print types and all the paper we had ordered from Chicago. The *Rocky Mountain Sun* sold us a bundle of paper for . . .''

"Fifteen dollars and fifty-five cents."

"That's right, lass, and we came out a week late with lower case all over the place and n's for u's and p's for d's . . .''

Freya shouted from inside:

"If you two haven't frozen to death you might come in and have some lunch." Grandfather took a last long haul on his cigar and took the slug from Yarrow's hand. "That's a beautiful thing, isn't it?" he said, holding it up so the sun caught it. Yarrow wiped her thumb under her armpit.

"How moldy were the faces? Were the eyes gone?"

Grandfather put his big finger beside his nose. "Yarrow," he said, "I won't tell about you sucking your thumb, if you don't tell about my stories. Come on or I'll be in trouble again from your mother."

They went into the kitchen and ducked under the washing dripping down from the lines near the ceiling. Freya was a good wife, thought Jock, but like all women she took over all parts of the house. There was no place for a man to get any peace. He pushed through a pair of long johns and went to the table. He thought longingly of his log cabin, where he and James used to spend time, with no women to nag them to keep clean or wash their clothes.

"Are we not waiting for James then?" he asked.

Freya banged the ladle against the rim of the stewpot.

"If we always waited for James, we would never eat in this house."

"The man works hard," said Grandfather, helping Yarrow out of her coat and sitting her on a chair. He wished his daughter-in-law would pay more respect to his son. If only James would speak up more. Mollie had always treated *him* with respect. But then, they'd only been married a year. Perhaps time had something to do with it. Freya ladled up a large helping of beef stew with carrots and dumplings onto his plate and poured him a glass of cider. She gave smaller portions to herself and Yarrow and sat down, thankful that the babies, Nellie and Greta, were still asleep.

Jock bowed his head. "For what we are about to receive, may the Lord make us truly thankful. Amen."

"We all work hard," said Freya, cutting up Yarrow's food. "And we never seem to get anywhere." She looked up at Jock's face and he felt impaled by the direct glance of her large gray eyes. That was the trouble with women, he thought, their eyes follow you all over the house. Never a moment's peace.

"Do we?" she said.

He had not expected that it needed an answer. He chewed on his dumpling and said nothing. She was right, of course. The town of Galena was dying, had been dying since the turn of the century. In the boom when silver was king, the town had a population of six thousand, and double that number of miners and intinerants drifted in and out. There were seven saloons along Main Street between Evans and Berthoud. Three hotels catered to the better-heeled travelers who came in the early years by coach from Leadville and Granite, and later, when the Midland and Denver and Rio Grande railroads arrived, stepped off into the frozen mud from the narrow-gauge railway carriages. It was on Berthoud Street that his first competition had started, the short-lived *Democrat* that he had bought out in 1909. By then he should have seen the writing on the wall. But he had not wanted to see it and had missed the opportunity.

Jock thought about the letter in his pocket. It was from an attorney in Platte City. He wasn't going to tell Freya about it, not yet. He and James could still build something together. But not here. It would break his heart to leave Galena, leave the house and the mountains and his log cabin. Half the town was boarded up now, even the Galena Lumber Supply Store. He'd noticed it this week. They'd given him his first advertisement for bathtubs and plumbing supplies.

"You're not eating," said Freya.

"No, I've lost my appetite," said Grandfather, pushing away his plate and standing up. "If you'll excuse me. I'm going to walk down the road to meet James."

The trouble was, Jock thought, as he put on his coat and gloves, that Freya was right. They were not getting anywhere. He stepped out onto the porch and into the crisp, fresh air of the Rocky Mountains, and as always his spirit lifted when he saw the majestic peaks towering above the town. It was late September and the aspens and cottonwoods on the lower slopes had all but lost their color. A few bronze leaves still clung brazenly to their branches. Jock closed the picket gate and set off down the road.

The house that he had bought for Mollie had once been part of a group of similar gingerbread houses standing on large lots to the east of town. Mollie, however, had been proud that her house was made of stone, while the others were made of wood. Now some of the neighboring houses were closed up, abandoned by owners who found there was no one to buy them. Who wanted to live in a town that was dying anyway? There was always talk of a new mine being opened up. People's hopes were like yo-yos; rumor and gossip were the town's chief industry. The cynics were the ones who laughed and departed; and another yard was overgrown by weeds, another shutter left hanging by its hinges, another merchant left with unpaid bills. Jock hadn't wanted to be counted among the deserters. As for the *Gazette*, two years ago it had stopped publishing every day and dropped the word "Daily" from the masthead. It had been part of the banner since 1885. Now the *Gazette* only came out on Fridays. Poor old Humdinger. He'd had such high hopes for it.

Jock had just got to the corner where the paved road began and Mrs. Brogan's dog always rushed up to meet him, when he saw his son's blue six-cylinder Phaeton coming toward him. Since the paper had gone to a weekly, James had taken over the only car dealership in town, their motto, "A Chrysler for Every Pocketbook." So far he had sold only one—to himself.

"Hello, old-timer, want a lift?" James stuck his head out of the window. He was a big fellow in his thirties, at least a head taller than Jock, even sitting down you could tell that. He had a ruddy complexion from years of living in the mountains, and his dark hair was always unruly. He had two big dimples in his cheeks. You could have taken him for a lumberjack, except for the small round glasses that sat on his nose and a permanent ink smudge on the brim of his hat. What made his face memorable was the sweetest smile, so unexpected in the wedgeshaped face, that people wondered what age he was. The smile fueled Jock.

"Felt like a bit of a walk, son. Going to the train station."

"The train's left already."

"Aye," said his father, opening the door and easing himself in. His breath was coming in heavy puffs that hung in the still mountain air. "I'm buying a ticket for tomorrow." He lifted in his coat hem and banged the door. "I'm going down to Platte City."

James contemplated his father. Jock was a healthy man and wore his years easily. His hair and beard were white, but his chest was like a barrel. There was a time when he could stand firmer and longer than any man James knew. But Jock was getting older. James swung the car around and headed back to town.

"You thinking about the *Journal* again?"

"I received an interesting letter today"—Jock fished in his

pocket and took out a folded sheet of paper—''from Jerrard Fox and Son, Attorneys, Platte City.''

''Never heard of them.''

''Neither had I. But they represent Mrs. Fabiana Truitt of New York.''

''Truitt? Adam Truitt's wife?''

''Adam Truitt's daughter-in-law. Widowed.'' He paused. ''She wants to buy our shares.''

James came to a stop sign and waited to turn left onto Main. A workman was nailing boards across the door of a house that had once been the Maxwell Book Store.

''Dad''—James took his eyes off the workman and began to drive on—''you're not going to sell, are you?''

''No. There's another alternative.'' James swerved to avoid a blowing sheet of timber. Jock exploded.

''Look at this town. Just look at it. It's falling down around us. There'll be nothing left for you, when it's your turn.'' Jock sank his chin into his chest and his beard fanned out like a young girl's hair.

''I think it's time we left. I hate to quit.'' His eyes moved from watching the streets to his son's face. ''But I hate the idea of you as a goddam car salesman even more.''

''Not a very good one.''

Jock was not in the mood for humor. He struck the dashboard of the Phaeton as though he hated it. ''You should be running a bloody newspaper.''

Nellie and Greta had woken up and were sitting in their high chairs at the kitchen table when James sat down to his lunch. Yarrow was helping feed Nellie, who did not like to eat and pursed her lips together tight and turned her head to avoid the spoon. She was making a great deal of noise. ''No. No. No,'' she said. A frown of worried concentration was on Yarrow's face. Jock placed a finger between her eyebrows. ''Whisht, Nellie. You'll give your sister a wrinkle before she's twenty.'' Jock's heart lurched as Yarrow looked up at him. She had Freya's big gray eyes, though they were wider than her mother's, but she had all Mollie's mannerisms and expressions. Even the thick black hair that curled out of her braids no matter how tightly Freya bound them, was Mollie's.

''Here, I'll do it,'' said Freya. ''Greta's just about finished. Yarrow, get a rusk for Greta out of the box.'' Big, blond Greta, two years old, was a placid child who accepted Nellie's usurpation of her mother's attention without a murmur. Greta was a year younger than Nellie. James kissed her on top of her head and placed her on the floor in the playpen. Freya took the bowl and spoon to the double draining board, and then got a clean plate from the wooden dishrack above it and served James his stew.

"The rack needs fixing," she said.

James patted her absentmindedly where her apron strained across her belly.

"You're tired." He always felt guilt when Freya was pregnant. There always seemed too much for her to do.

"Laura will be in tomorrow to help. Nellie, stop bawling." Freya didn't know how she would cope if Laura Brogan didn't come in and help after school. Freya began spooning food into Nellie by making a game of it so that Nellie's little red mouth opened and shut like a soft trap.

Jock sat across from his son and looked at the *Gazette* he had handed him. "Four flimsy pages," he said. He remembered how it used to look when its banner read *Every Evening Except Sunday*, and the display ads cost forty cents an inch.

"We got an unexpected ad from Sadler's," said James, unrolling his napkin from a ring and forking up his stew, "a bankruptcy sale."

"Is that true?" said Freya, looking away from Nellie for a moment. Her husband's glasses had steamed up from the stew.

"Aye, it's true all right," said Jock, answering for him and reading through the paper. Yarrow slipped onto his knee. "Another sheriff's sale," he said. "Who is it this time? Why it's the poor old family of Sandy Allison. 'Judgment rendered in favor of the plaintiffs—for the sum of $2,032.71 cents besides $17.25 costs—all the rights, titles and interests of the defendants, to wit, a one-story, five-room log house, situated on two and one-half acres . . .' " Jock put down the paper and shuffled Yarrow to one knee. Yarrow's small finger was tracing out the letters on the page.

"I remember when Sandy Allison built that house. He came into this town on snowshoes to find silver, and the first strike he got, he built it. When the miners were thrown out of work he sold deerskins to make a living. Poor old so-and-so."

"Grandfather," interrupted Yarrow, "what's a—a piker?"

Jock was astonished. "Is it that you're reading, lass? How long has she been doing this?"

"I've no idea," laughed James, pulling the paper across her. "It's that item you wrote about an out-of-town subscriber," he went on reading from page two, " 'who just can't live through the week without reading his copy of the Humdinger and of course he buys it—doesn't borrow it like a lot of you pikers do.' "

"But what is it?" asked Yarrow. "Is it type, Grandfather? Is it 12-point?"

"Why, no, lass, that's *pica*. A *piker* is just a tightwad who reads someone else's newspaper without putting up the brownies."

"Ah," she said, as though it made sense.

James said to his father, "I'm coming with you tomorrow. I bought two tickets at the station."

"I'd like your company. If ye can come."

James got up and poured himself a cup of coffee. "I can finish what I have to do this afternoon and the paper has a week to go to bed."

He took a screwdriver out of a drawer and tightened the screws on the dishrack.

"Do you mind telling me where you two are going tomorrow?" asked Freya, lifting Nellie out of the high chair and plonking her in the playpen with Greta.

"I'm taking your advice, Freya," said Jock. "About us not getting anywhere in Galena. So we're going down to Platte City to talk to my old friend Max Horace."

"Oh, can I come? Can I come?" asked Yarrow, tugging Jock's beard for attention. She had never been on a train before, never been farther than Jock's cabin. Jock sought approval from Freya with his eyes.

"Aye," said Jock, "if you can really read that label, we'll take you."

"It says, 'Mrs. Winslow's Syrup,' and it's for croup!"

"Oh, she can't really read." Freya laughed, plunging the dishes into a basin of soapy water in the sink. "She's just heard me say it and remembered it."

"I can too! I can too!"

Yarrow jumped down from Jock's knee and picked up the *Gazette*. Her finger underlined a headline that caught her eye. " 'Three Hoochers Sentenced,' " she read. Her father threw her up in the air with a laugh. Her heel caught the big silver reflector of the light bulb, and it swayed above the table. Nellie let out a wail of outrage at her father's defection. Greta let out a burp.

Jock rubbed his beard, and winked at his son and daughter-in-law.

"Well, I think we'll have to take her with us, don't you? After all I do need someone who can read the headlines."

"And," said Freya, "you need the someone who owns half your scrip."

CHAPTER 2

A COLD WIND HAD COME UP AND WAS BLOWING AROUND YAR-row's knees the next morning as they waited for their train. The wind whipped snow free from the peaks so that it looked like mist. But it was brilliantly sunny. Yarrow loved the mountains, the look of them, the air of them. She thought that she would never want to leave them. Freya had packed sandwiches and a traveling rug in a lidded basket, and Yarrow sat on it and hugged her knees, shivering with cold and excitement, watching down the track for the first sign of the train. Her father and grandfather stamped their feet and windmilled their arms to stay warm. Their shadows were squat and dark beside her. Yarrow thought they were like spiders and she, Miss Muffet, as she listened to their talk about newspapers, the *Gazette* and the *Journal*, and about the presses and typeface, and ads per inch and columns per page, and politics and gossip. Yarrow thought the best job in the world must be with newspapers.

The 12:15 train to Glenwood Springs finally rolled in, and once the incoming passengers were unloaded, the family boarded. Galena was on a branch line, and at Glenwood Springs they had to change trains, and they waited half an hour for the Denver and Rio Grande train, roaring in with its Pullman-green carriages and gold lettering above the windows that spelled out "D. and R. G. Western."

The last time Jock had been on this train, he was thinking as James showed the conductor their tickets, was in 1921. It was the year before James was married and Jock had gone to visit his sister Hilda who was ill in Pennsylvania. While in the East he had visited some newspaper offices. He had been astonished at the wealth of some of the publishing houses he had seen. He had visited Curtis Publishing in Philadelphia, "a marble palace on twelve floors," he had sputtered to James on his return. He had visited the *Evening Bulletin* and the *Public Ledger* and even copied the idea of fiction serialization in the *Bulletin* by printing a Sherlock Holmes story in the *Gazette* when he got back to

Galena. He had gone to Boston, where he found the *Transcript*, though the most profitable, the dullest paper."All undigested matter from all over the world," he had told James. "It has no ladder headlines, but long strings of tags like this:

CITY TRACTION COMPANY BUILDS FORTY NEW CARS
They Will Be Running on the Roads Soon"

He couldn't understand why people would read it. But the advertisers loved it. In the silver boom days, one of his short-lived competitors had tried that, and taken the practice to heights never since equaled by announcing its appearance thus:

The Galena Sunshine
is strictly a
Miners Journal
and the only paper printed in Colorado
that keeps its columns
Free from Politics
and aims to be an
Organ of the People
striking fearlessly at all times in defense of
Right, Truth and Justice.
We will be found always ready with our coat off and sleeves
rolled up to vindicate and battle for the most sacred
Interests of the People.

In New York he had gone down to Hearst's main building on Great William Street near the Brooklyn Bridge. Hearst's father had been a miner. Jock found the building to be dirty and shabby but full of energy. He was fascinated by Hearst and his empire. He probed the pages of the Hearst papers, the *American*, the *Evening Journal*, the *Sunday American*, as though they themselves could give him the secret to success. He noted for example that in the *Sunday American*, rather than reduce the number of columns from eight to seven per page, the editor had reduced their width by shaving off a half-em per column. Unfortunately for Jock, no such stratagem would save the Humdinger.

Jock cracked his knuckles as he thought about it, and settled down opposite James and Yarrow.

"We should have gotten out years ago," he said as the train moved out and followed the winding bed of the Roaring Fork River down the valley. River oaks, cottonwoods and aspens shook their leaves down on them as they passed.

"But I owed something to this town. I did a terrible thing to get here in the first place."

James was trying to fit the nubs of his spine between the grooves of the slatted wooden seats.

"I thought you and Max sold your grubstake for a windfall."

"We cheated the man. It was all set up." Jock stared out the window and rubbed it with his elbow as it steamed over. "It haunted me for years. I went back once to find him, but there was no one there. F. W. Shipam his name was. I never forgot it. I thought it was an acronym for Saint Mark eight thirty-six."

"You've lost me now, old-timer."

" 'For what shall it profit a man if he shall gain the whole world and lose his own soul?' The mine was abandoned. Och, that whole hillside was abandoned. There was no more silver there than I had in my teeth."

The train began rocking as it gathered speed.

"So I stayed in Galena. I wrote editorials that fumed and raged at everyone from the mineowners to the state government. I kept hoping that things would change, but they didn't. Every spring, in the snowmelt, a little bit more of the town would trickle away."

"Didn't Truitt know where Shipam had gone?" James always came back to a subject when other people had moved on.

"Never asked him—Max was the one who dealt with Truitt."

James should have left Galena, Jock thought, getting out a stogie and lighting it. James should have taken up the opportunity at the *Journal* long ago. But James was not a self-starter. There was a hesitancy in him that had manifested itself as a stutter when James was in his teens. He had practiced talking with pebbles in his mouth and rid himself of his impediment one day beside the Roaring Fork when he took too deep a breath and swallowed one. Jock declared him cured and that was that. Jock looked at his son as he hitched up his trouser legs and scooted his spine down on the seat. "Going to catch some zees," James said. Jock sighed. James was thirty-five and still acted like a youth. Jock blamed himself. He had never allowed James to have his head, never given him the chance to make his own mistakes. Jock was determined not to make that mistake again in Platte City.

There was no dining service on the train, but it stopped at Minturn, fifty-eight miles east of Glenwood Springs, where the passengers got off to eat at the railroad eating house. James went and bought coffee and milk and they drank it with Freya's ham sandwiches. There was a further stop at Pueblo, but James and

Yarrow were asleep under the plaid traveling rug, and Jock pulled the collar of his greatcoat closer and wished they could have afforded tickets for the sleeping car.

They pulled into Platte City at 4:45 the next morning. Even at that time, the city was beginning to bustle. As James stepped from the train with Yarrow in his arms, he bumped into a woman rushing past with a hatbox under her arm. The box rolled away along the platform.

"I'm terribly sorry," said James, doffing his hat and putting Yarrow down, and straightening his glasses at the same time. The woman turned her head. The high astrakhan collar of her coat hid the lower part of her face. "Don't mention it," she said. Her chauffeur retrieved the box and placed it on the porter's cart. Jock handed down their own luggage from the carriage and the woman and her entourage were swept along with the crowd. The train engine wheezed and sighed, and the great wheels seemed to be shuddering with the effort of remaining still as Yarrow and her father and grandfather walked past it to the exit. Outside they saw the woman in the fur collar climb into a sleek artillery-gray Pierce-Arrow with thistle-green wheels. The car purred out through the early morning traffic.

James shouldered Yarrow again and picked up his bag and with Jock carrying his they headed for the cheaper part of town. The dawn was beginning to light up the mountain range that stopped the growth of the town to the west. To the east, the flatlands of Colorado and Kansas stretched to the horizon. Jock marveled aloud at the changes that had taken place since he had been here last. The city was the terminal point for all goods moving west; not only the D. and R. G. Western Railroad terminated here, but the Rock Island, the Pacific, the Atchison, the Colorado and Southern, the Topeka and Santa Fe, the Midland and the Missouri. They all shunted into the Platte City terminal, deposited their goods and their visitors from the East, and they shunted out again. They carried ore from the mountains and lumber and coal and crops from the Midwest's vast plaza—harvests of barley and blue-stem hay, and millet and wheat and corn and alfalfa. Jock was so intent on watching the activity around the rail terminal that he was nearly run over by an electric streetcar.

They found the address they were looking for, a modest but clean boardinghouse on Eighth Street, and after splashing some water on their hands and faces from the porcelain bowl and jug on the dresser, and after a good breakfast of steak and eggs and coffee, and an extra helping of cornbread, they felt much refreshed and couldn't wait to get out into the city again to see what marvels they had missed.

"Where shall we go first?"

Jock consulted his watch.

"It's too early for the Law, but the Fourth Estate will be awake."

They walked to the office of the *Platte City Journal*. Jock remembered it from his visit seven years before, on his way to Pennsylvania, as a two-story frame building with a Campbell press in the back. There had been a desk with a typewriter on it near the front door. Max and Mrs. Horace had taken turns using the desk. Mrs. Horace had been the reporter, the bookkeeper and the typist. Max had sold the ads, written the editorials and run the press. A compositor had made up the third member of the staff. Mrs. Horace had since died, and Jock was prepared for some changes but not what he saw when they rounded the corner and found the very name on the building had been changed.

Max Horace and the *Journal* were no longer there. They had moved. This was a job printing company now, the young clerk told them at the front desk. The *Journal* had moved to a new building on Stalker Street. Jock thanked the young man and sat down on a wooden bench outside to catch his breath. He was shaken that Max would make such a move without consulting him. He spat onto the sidewalk. "Partners," he said. He wondered what other changes Max had made. James suggested they take a streetcar, but Jock waved off the suggestion with a gruff "save your money." He got out a stogie and bit it thoughtfully, and then put it back in his pocket and patted Yarrow's hand and said, "Come on," and they set off again and after getting lost once or twice they found the *Journal*, in a brick building on Stalker Street with a big plate-glass window at the front, looking much grander and more prosperous than Jock had ever imagined. "Well, I'll be blowed," he said.

"Can I help you, sir?"

The woman who guarded Max Horace's office door observed them through a pince-nez jammed between her eyebrows and her proud Roman nose. Her white hair was cut level with her earlobes and slicked back without a parting. Her age was indeterminate and, to Jock's eye, so was her sex. Max Horace's taste in women had always been a mystery to him.

"I would like to see Mr. Horace," Jock said, holding his hat on his right hip.

"Do you have an appointment?"

Jock began to slap his hat back and forth across his thighs as though he were getting rid of cigar ash.

"No, I don't," he said, "but you just tell Mr. Horace that his old friend, Jock McLean, and his son, James, would like to see him." He stopped slapping his hat. "For a chat."

James, who had taken off Yarrow's coat and hat, had sat down on a brown patterned chair with wooden arms. He gave his helpless smile. "We had trouble finding him," he said.

"Aye, you would think a body would let a partner know when he changes premise."

"Partner, sir? Mrs. Truitt is Mr. Horace's partner."

Something in Jock's face made Pince-nez unsure of herself for a moment, and James realized she was probably much younger than her appearance.

"I'm sorry, I'm new here, but I have strict instructions not to interrupt Mr. Horace."

"Have you now."

She tried again to regain her composure. "He's a very busy man."

Jock leaned forward with his fists balled on her desk. His fists still looked like those of a miner.

"And I'm a ver-ry impatient one," he said.

Pince-nez rose and smoothed her hair, her shirt and her black skirt.

"Well, I'll see if Mr. Horace is in." She nodded to Jock and Jock nodded back and stepped aside as she swished past him and through the door. Jock stared at the glass-transomed door for a moment with its black lettering "Maxwell T. Horace, Editor-in-Chief," then slammed his fist on the table.

"I'll be damned if I'll be cheated and humiliated both on the same day." He got out a stogie and bit on it.

"Aren't you jumping to conclusions?"

"Oh, come on, son. Look at this. Look at this." Jock waved his arm around the room, at the thick drapes, the mahogany furniture, the silver ashtray he thumped with his cigar. "Leopards don't change their spots."

"Mr. Horace will see you now," said Pince-nez, opening the door.

"You stay here," said James to Yarrow as they went through and closed the door behind them.

Pince-nez and Yarrow regarded each other for a moment. Yarrow got down from her chair and went over to stand beside the desk. She clutched her hands together in front of her.

"I'm going to run this newspaper one day."

Pince-nez smiled. "Is that so?"

"Yes."

"Can I keep my job?"

"Can you type? I can't—yet."

Pince-nez lifted Yarrow and seated her on the desk. She opened the top drawer for Yarrow's feet. "There," she said, moving aside some paper clips and rubber bands, and taking out a big box of pink face powder and a swansdown puff. "If we're going to talk about my future, we may as well be comfortable. Would you like to draw?" Yarrow shook her head. "You want to talk?" Yarrow nodded. "Well, fire away. What do you want to know?" Pince-nez examined the pores of her nose through her looking glass. Yarrow leaned forward and looked at her. "How *do* you keep your glasses on your nose?"

"Well, my God, Jock. What a surprise! What a surprise!" Maxwell Trevelyn Horace came forward with his arms stretched out. He was a small man, but what he lacked in height he made up for in rotundity. He shook hands with both hands and back-slapped Jock and James. His sincerity, Jock thought, was as proportionate to his actions as his height was to his girth. He feinted with his fists, punched the air and their upper arms as though they were punching bags.

There was another man in the room, leaning over a desk with galleys of pages fanning out under his hand. Jock had not seen him at first, because the windows let in dim light through their heavy, swagged curtains and a faint haze of smoke rose from an ornate fireplace. He was a young man with a pockmarked face. A red pencil stuck out of the pocket of his overalls.

"You've not met my head printer, have you?" said Max Horace. "Albert Hinton."

Jock heard the word "my" and another grain of dissatisfaction was added to the pile he was building.

"No, we've not."

"He was just about to leave." Hinton rustled together the drying galleys and left without a smile.

"Have a seat," said Max, going to the door and asking Pince-nez for some coffee.

It was an extraordinary room in which they were seated, a room decorated it seemed by the contents of some passing Arab caravan, or perhaps by an interior decorator who, with his outrageous objets d'art had been kicked out of New York or Chicago by disgruntled clients. A carpet on the floor imitated Moorish tiles, and every wall surface was covered with pierced woodwork or patterned wallpaper. Taborets stood about as side tables or chairs, Jock was not sure which, and he narrowly avoided bumping into a tall ceramic pedestal, the use of which was beyond his ken. The two red upholstered chairs in which Jock and his son sat faced the inlaid desk. Jock balanced the sweet Turkish coffee he had been given and said, "Nice place you've got here."

"Ah, Jock. Such changes. Such changes you've never seen are happening here."

"I hope there aren't many more."

Max leaned forward with his old intensity, and for the first time Jock saw the Max he remembered from his mining days. Face-on, Max looked just as he always had, the quick-witted, youthful hustler always looking for a deal; side-on, he appeared as a wary stranger, a banker perhaps, whom Jock would not have recognized if he had sat beside him on a streetcar.

"Only a few. You can't stop progress, Jock."

"Aye, I've noticed that."

"I was going to write to you, but you know how things are. Everything got so busy after Mrs. Horace died. We have more competition. The *Globe*'s got a lot of money to spend, and we had to fight back—or fold. But our circulation went up and our advertising. We grew out of the old shop. Sure you don't want more coffee?"

"Fifty-fifty, Max. That's what we agreed on. We agreed that I'd keep my hands off the *Journal* and be the silent partner. Let you have your run."

Jock didn't take his eyes off Max's face.

"That's what we agreed."

Max's eyes shifted rapidly from left to right. Why, he looks like a weasel, thought Jock, and I never noticed it before.

"Dividends remain the same?"

Max laughed, as if Jock had made a joke, and shot his right arm out. He swung in his chair, offering his profile. "We've had a lot of capital expenditure, Jock. We're using a Goss Comet eight-page press now . . ."

"And this?" asked Jock, putting his cup down beside an object with a tube.

Max's eyes flitted. "A hookah. Jock, the unions . . ." His voice dropped to a whisper. "They are threatening to unionize me. We're small potatoes yet, but it will come. They've already got the *Globe*. The days are numbered when I can pick up a tramp printer when I want to."

"There was a time when we were glad of the unions, Max. That's when we met. Remember the fathom system?"

"The what?" asked James.

"He'll tell you," said Jock, "he's the Cornishman. We worked eight hours a day and hadna' three dollars to show for it at the end."

"It was a system of work payment brought over from the old country. If Jock got into a wide vein of ore he was paid less than if he worked the same distance in a narrow vein."

"We had a strike about it."

"Ah, the good old boys of the Western Federation."

"We took the scabs to the edge of town and Max told them what we'd do to them if they came back. You remember that well enough, don't you, Max?"

Max couldn't take Jock's eyes boring into him anymore and got up and threw another log on the fire under the Moorish tiled mantel. He sighed, warming his upholstered rump to the flame.

"It's not like that anymore, Jock. The International Typographical Union, they've got the whip hand. They employ the people. They make the rules."

"You've changed sides."

"Inevitable," said Max.

"It will never happen to me."

"How's the Humdinger?"

"About to fold—and that's why I'm here. I want James to take up our share of the *Journal*."

"You're going to take an active interest?"

"James will. He can work here, that is if he doesn't have to wear a turban."

"Why, that's—Why, that's wonderful. I welcome you here, James. Of course, I'll have to speak to our other partner about it. It won't do for the word of too much nepotism at the *Journal* to get about." James's face flamed as though the fire had caught it.

"He's a fine journalist and as good a typesetter as that Hinton fellow, I'll wager," snapped Jock.

"You were always overly sensitive, Jock. I'll have to keep Mrs. Truitt informed."

"Does she know about your new premises and the Goss Comet?"

"No, but I'll tell her when I write about James."

"You do that, and tell her he'll be editor and I'll be here to watch her investment."

"Now, just a minute, Jock."

Jock stood up and the two men reared at each other like old bulls. —

"Don't just a minute me. You've been cheating me, Max."

"You're a fine one to talk."

"By God, you've got an evil tongue in your mouth. Fifty-fifty, you said. Partners forever. Loyalty between friends. You're a cheat."

"That's a lie."

"I just have to look around to see it. You've been dummying up the figures. God knows what other shenanigans you've been up to. We've been scrimping and cutting costs to save the *Gazette*, living on the revenue we earned from reporting the minutes of the town council meetings, while you . . ."

"That's enough, Jock."

"Dad . . ."

"You're dead right, it's enough." Jock picked up his hat from the table. "I'm going to find a lawyer." They headed for the door with Max in pursuit.

"There's no need for that, Jock. Let's get this straight . . ."

Jock threw open the door so that he startled Yarrow playing with the typewriter keys at the desk.

"Max Horace, you couldn't lie straight in bed," he said and slammed the door so that the glass shook.

Out on the street, walking fast to keep up with Jock, James and Yarrow had to dodge the billboards on the sidewalks. The billboards advertised "Coal for Sale" and "Trunks for Sale" and "Rooms to Let." Yarrow read them as she skipped around them. Light rain had begun to fall. James kept trying to button up her coat.

"I can't believe it of Max Horace," said Jock.

"That he would cheat?"

"No. That he would take me for such a fool."

"He was never trustworthy. Come on, old-timer, why so surprised?"

Jock stopped abruptly and removed the chewed cigar, which was still in his mouth.

"We were like family. We shared our last crust of bread together. We knelt in ice water in dark mines and clawed like animals to make a living. You don't betray each other after that."

The rain began to fall more heavily.

"Can I get a pair of glasses like the secretary?" asked Yarrow.

"Later," said James. "Dad . . ."

Jock patted his pocket. "I'm going to find this lawyer fellow of Mrs. Truitt's. Perhaps he can help."

"We don't have to drown getting there." James sprinted for a streetcar, and it stopped and waited for Jock and Yarrow to catch up.

In the covered front section of the car, while Jock and her father talked and gesticulated, Yarrow tossed her black braids over her shoulders and rubbed the steam from the windows. She did it in a pattern of flowers; then she drew a house; then she let her fingers obliterate them. She looked out at the street with the streetcar tracks marching off into the distance and the telegraph poles marching along beside them. They were going somewhere, she decided, going somewhere with a purpose. The town excited her, and she squeezed her eyes shut and opened them again and was glad that the town was still there.

"There's money to be made here, James," her grandfather said. "I can smell it. I curse myself for not realizing it sooner." There was a lift in his voice and Yarrow turned to look at him. "Is it our El Dorado?" she asked.

He laughed so she could see his big tobacco-stained teeth. "Well, it just might be."

The streetcar stopped, and a man got on and sat opposite them and opened his newspaper. Yarrow read the headline: HOOVER VICTORY PREDICTED. But she was more interested in the street. El Dorado, Grandfather had said. Yarrow fingered her lips while she said it. There must be gold and silver out there, she thought, buried under the cobblestones.

Fabiana Truitt, the third partner, was also in Platte City as Jock and James discovered when they visited Jerrard Fox and Son, Attorneys.

"She arrived unexpectedly this morning. She's on her way from Los Angeles back to New York," said Mr. Fox Junior, who was on his way to see her at the Broadlands Hotel.

If they cared to have a counter lunch with him at the diner on the way, they could go over her proposal. Throughout lunch, however, Jock and James kept their own counsel.

Now the three men and Yarrow stood outside the door of Mrs. Truitt's suite. Yarrow traced the patterned yellow circles on the carpet with her toe. She had never been in such a long corridor in her life, stretching as it did from one side of the hotel to the other. Through the windows at the end she could see the mountains and wondered what her mother was doing now.

A light step and the door flew open and Fabiana Truitt stood there.

"We met at the st—station," said James, surprised.

"Yes, I remember you and your pretty little girl with the enchanting hair."

She was in her early twenties and Yarrow had never seen such an elegant woman. Her dress was so deceptively simple that one looked for the secret of it. It had a short pleated skirt and a very high collar and tucked into the collar was a purple chiffon scarf that Fabiana wore pulled up across one side of her cheek. Her black hair was swept to one side, too, showing a very white parting (what Grandfather called a "shed"), and fell in glossy finger waves to below her chin. She was tall and slim, and if there would be any fault found in her, it would have been that her nerves were so taut that the intensity detracted from her beauty; her dark blue eyes crackled with interest and her face was seldom in repose.

Yarrow sat beside Fabiana on the sofa. A fern in a pot rested on the table beside a tea tray. She had ordered tea and coffee and milk.

"I will come to the point, gentlemen," she said in her direct way. Yarrow tried to look at her father through the fern. "Mr. Horace is dealing fraudulently with us. I became aware of it only when I was going through some papers after my husband's death."

"A terrible, unexpected death in a fire," said Mr. Fox.

"I'm sorry to hear that."

"My husband was an artist, a very good artist, but he hated detail. It bored him. I handled all his commissions, the correspondence, our travel arrangements. I drove the car. I did everything for him so he could paint." Fabiana poured tea with quick little movements.

"A tragedy," said Mr. Fox, shaking his head.

"I actually met him when he was in Italy, in Porto Ercole, where my family had a summer house. My mother bought one of his paintings."

"Mrs. Truitt's ancestors include a pope."

"On my mother's side. My father was American. My father thought Mr. Truitt was a fortune hunter. He didn't want me to marry him. He only forgave me after my husband died."

"Her family is in steel," said Mr. Fox.

"Please, Mr. Fox," said Fabiana, snapping her fingers at him to be quiet. Yarrow gave up trying to catch her father's eye through the fern and wriggled forward to drink some milk.

"The fact is that I have now come into my own inheritance and I would like to use it. I am going into business."

"The newspaper business?" asked Jock.

"Precisely."

He had only played with his coffee, and now he put the cup down and leaned forward.

"There is one small problem, however, Mrs. Truitt. We are not for sale."

"We'll offer a very generous sum of money," said Mr. Fox, mentioning a sum of money that would have made James whistle if he were alone.

"It's no good," said Jock, his determination only hardened by the amount mentioned. "But you're right about being cheated. I can feel it in my bones, and I know Max from the old days. I'd like to know what that old bugger's been up to."

"I've got facts here, figures," said Mr. Fox, pulling sheaves of paper from a briefcase at his feet. "Mr. Horace has been setting up phony companies and siphoning off the profits. From the books, it looks as though there are no profits, but that's because he's hidden them somewhere else."

Fabiana did not sit back while the men went over the figures. She understood them; it was she who had drawn Mr. Fox's attention to them. She interrupted and explained the figures and played with a gold cigarette case, tapping her long red nails on it. Sometimes she got up and sometimes she sat down. She was incapable of sitting still and James watched her admiringly. Yarrow noticed her father doing so. Once Fabiana leaned over to point out an item on a column of figures, and when she got up the soft purple wool of her skirt caught on the buckle of Yarrow's Mary Janes. Yarrow moved her foot and a long thread came with it and caused a pucker across the pleats. Fabiana tutted as she released it. Her mind was on the business at hand.

"I want this newspaper," she said.

"We think alike, Mrs. Truitt, and quite honestly if I had the money myself, I'd offer to buy *you* out."

"Then we are at a stalemate, and Mr. Horace is in charge."

Jock took out a cigar, sniffed it and rolled it as though it were the problem he was playing with. He didn't light it.

"Not quite. There's another way around it. You and we together can outvote and outsmart Max Horace any day."

"I don't know," said Fabiana, crossing her shiny, silk-covered legs and swinging one impatiently.

"You have no other choice."

"You can trust us. You can't trust Max Horace," said James. Fabiana turned her head sharply to look across at James, and as she did so the chiffon scarf fell and he saw the whole lower part of her jaw and neck was covered with scar tissue.

"I hope so," she said. Her eyes never left his and she forced them up to hers and away from the livid scars by some inner potency she was able to draw on. She carefully rearranged the chiffon, not releasing him yet from her gaze and James felt somehow that what he was watching was indecent. He dropped his gaze with an effort. Fabiana came to a decision.

"We have a lot to talk about then. Mr. Fox—why don't you begin?" She stood up and a dark hairpin fell out of her hair onto the sofa. She tapped out a cigarette from her case. "Your daughter has fallen asleep, Mr. McLean. Why don't you put her in my room while we talk?"

Yarrow had indeed fallen asleep on the big white sofa beside Mrs. Truitt. The night on the train, the excitement of the city, the newspaper office and the hotel, all kaleidoscoped in her head. The last thing she remembered hearing was the *Journal* being mentioned and Mrs. Truitt's throaty voice saying, "Call me Fabiana," and then she was aware of being settled into a bed, softer than any she had known, where the unfamiliar but pleasurable scent of Fabiana Truitt was still present.

CHAPTER 3

"HOW'S THIS?" SAID JAMES, PULLING A PROOF OF THE *Gazette's* front page and taking it over to Jock to read. Jock had sweated over his farewell editorial for hours until he was satisfied it was ready for printing.

They were in the *Gazette* office on Main Street where the Gordon press that had once been lost coming down Independence Pass still dominated the center of the large room. It had first been powered by a foot treadle until Jock and Max Horace hooked it up by a series of line shafts and pulleys and leather belts to an electric motor.

When Jock was first apprenticed in Pennsylvania, he had been taught on something not much more advanced than a Washington handpress. He had worked on flat sheets of paper with one side preprinted: "Dr. Lemon's Magic Elixir for Long Life and Liver Disturbances" and "The Great Morano's Guaranteed Hair Growth

Potion—Money Back in Ten Days If You Are Not Astounded by It.'' When he had set his type in the form, the sheet of paper was positioned on the tympan; then the frisket, a rectangular frame, was folded over to hold it in place. The bed was then cranked under the platen and pressure applied to print the sheet. To take out the paper, the whole process was gone through in reverse; the pressure lever released, the bed cranked out, the frisket lifted up, the printed sheet taken out. Then he started all over again. No wonder Jock loved watching the cylinder of his Gordon press going backward and forward over the paper with ease.

To the left of the press stood the slanted fonts of old type and the high stools on which Jock and the typesetters used to work. Over on the right was the Linotype machine that Jock had bought five years ago. It stood taller than a man with its keyboard below and its matrix magazine above. It had made Jock's typesetting skills superfluous overnight. From the metal ingot suspended over the melting pot, the machine produced the hot metal slugs, or lines of type, that Jock would set up in the page form. Jock never ceased to admire the way in which the Linotype, after casting the lead pieces, automatically resorted the brass matrices that had formed them. He thought of the hours he had spent sorting out his type by hand. Each week, after the paper had been printed, he would break up the page and put every letter and punctuation mark back in its correct place in the font box.

Between the Linotype and the press was the stone, a solid bench on which Jock and James composed the pages and locked them up, and after printing, folded the sheets. Jock still used his old folding bone to help. When the circulation of the *Gazette* was larger, everyone helped with the folding. The taste of ink on their tongues never left them.

The *Gazette* office was an inky, musty, untidy place, with inkstained rags and bundles of paper on the floor, and files of old papers thrown on the top of a cabinet. The ceiling was criss-crossed with the cords of bare light bulbs; drums of ink and buckets of paste were pushed against the wall. Near the front window stood a lone, battered rolltop desk with a Remington typewriter and a telephone, a ledger and a clock. There were a number of nail spikes for galleys and bills, which overflowed to the floor. There was a rack for rubber date stamps on the wall, bought by Freya in a fit of trying to tidy the place up, and a perforated metal holder, which held a ball of string. There was a large roll of brown paper on a stand, so that sheets could be ripped off, a tiered wicker what-not, looking incongruous beside the weight of everything else, and a fat-bellied stove that gave out so little heat that in the winter no one took off their coats inside.

There was a faded chaise, with the stuffing coming out, which had received the bottoms of most of the townspeople at one time or another, and on which each of the McLean children had slept. Freya would come in to fold in an emergency, such as the time when the spring thaw had come with a rush and a foot of cold water sloshed through the building. But the paper had to come out, so Freya perched her feet up on the rungs of the high stool and folded papers with the men. Yarrow, with Nellie then in a basket, watched as her father proofread a sheet, standing in his rubber boots in the water, and then sat down at the Linotype machine to cast a new line, and listened to the clickety-clack as the matrices came up and the liquid metal formed the letters and the line was justified and clickety-clack out came the slug and the matrices fell back into their place.

The McLeans' life was in this place, thought Jock, taking the galley proof from his son and wiping his nose with the back of his hand.

Jock had never learned to operate the Mergenthaler Linotype machine. He had spent too many years setting type by hand, working from the fonts of type directly onto the composing stick. It was James who had slowly mastered the skewed keyboard when they had bought the machine on terms. Jock had concentrated on the headlines and kept his hand in by sticksetting for display ads and any job printing for weddings and posters that came their way.

Now he picked up the last galley from the *Gazette* and read it. James had put Jock's editorial in an appropriately black-bordered box, single three-point rule, across columns three and four. "No wonder they call it a tombstone," he said. It appeared under the date, November 1, 1928:

OUR SWAN SONG

Fellow Galenians, it is our sad duty to say farewell to you with this issue and wish you the best of luck. After forty-seven years in your service as newspaper publishers it sure is like pulling teeth to leave. When we first came to this town it was nothing more than a mud thoroughfare with a town of tents and lean-tos on either side. The hills rang with the noise of men shouting, whistles shrieking, machinery clanking, the boom of powder explosions, the constant thud of the stamp mills. What changes we've seen. We were here in September 1888 when the Rio Grande and the Midland fought for the right to lay their tracks through the town. BABY AND BROAD AT WAR, we wrote.

We were here in 1891 when electric lights went on for the first time.

We were here in 1893 when the bottom dropped out of the silver market and we all thought the town was ruined.

We were here the following year when they pulled a silver nugget from the Smuggler mine that weighed 2,060 pounds. THIS WAS THE GREATEST SILVER CAMP IN THE WORLD and through our pages you knew it.

We gave you all the news without fear. We were lively. We were bold. We told you what happened when a certain politician in this town found his wife had run off with a scoundrel. DUEL AT DUSK. SAVAGE ENCOUNTER BETWEEN A DESERTED HUSBAND AND THE DASHING PARAMOUR.

At one time we had thirty-two libel suits pending against us. NOT ONE COLLECTED.

We have always stood for your best interests, first, last and in between. But for us, for now, the fight is over. We can't run a business on prayers. If the citizens, the merchants and the bank in this town got together to help each other, Galena might be saved.

Until then, so long, good luck and God bless.

THE GALENA GAZETTE
John and James McLean

Jock handed the galley back to his son.

"That will have to do. God knows I hate to see the end of the old Humdinger."

Jock and James had put the *Gazette* to bed for the last time. After the meager print run was over, they folded the paper and put most of the copies aside for direct sale. The remainder they rolled up in brown paper, gummed and addressed, and threw into a laundry basket that hung behind the door for just such a purpose. There were a few loyal readers who still took it by subscription. Jock wondered what they would think about his defection. They carried the basket between them to the post office. Jock couldn't help but ask the postmaster if any late reprieve for the *Gazette* had come in. But no one was interested. Jock handed the postmaster the key to the office. "If ever you want to go in, Ed, just make yourself comfortable and have a drink to the old times."

"Key don't work anyway," said Jock to James as they walked back.

"Well, I've come full circle," he said, when they deposited the empty basket again behind the door. "Or perhaps I've gone downhill. We used to deliver the *Gazette* by dogsled. Now it's just one old man and his son."

*   *   *

A few days later, a week before the family was to leave Galena, Jock suddenly had a compelling urge to visit his old cabin on the back of Red Mountain one last time. All the arrangements for the family's move to Platte City had been completed. The heavier pieces had been sent down by truck before the bad weather set in, and James made a second visit by train to ensure all was well with the new house and Max Horace. The new house was fine. They had rented a five-room house on West Colorado Avenue for fifteen dollars a month. And Max Horace had agreed to sell out. Faced with the threat of prosecution by his two partners, he had taken the easier way out. Fabiana and the McLeans split Max's shares down the middle. They were now equal partners with 150 shares each.

In order to pay Max, the McLeans had arranged a loan from the bank, but Fabiana suggested that she would loan the McLeans the money herself. In the case of default, she would take over control of the *Journal*. It seemed eminently fair to the McLeans, although Jock wondered why Fabiana would bind herself to the McLeans when she had wanted to buy them out before. James was joining the *Journal* as editor on December first. While he was in Platte City, James took Albert Hinton, whom he had met that first day, out for a drink. Hinton said he would stay on. Fabiana Truitt had gone home to New York and left her power of attorney with Jerrard Fox. It had all seemed so easy, James thought. But Jock said women and business didn't mix.

There was no passable road to Jock's cabin on Red Mountain and the last few miles had to be covered on foot or by skis. It had been agreed that Yarrow would go with Jock and James, and Freya packed two large knapsacks and a smaller one for Yarrow. Along with the food, Freya packed a flashlight. She had been unsure of letting Yarrow go, but she understood the importance of the cabin to Jock and James and, besides, she could get a lot of last-minute things done without her lively, inquisitive daughter under her feet. Yarrow was sturdy and had been on cross-country skis since she could walk; "langlaufing" was what Freya called it. So Freya kissed her good-bye and watched them set off in the car early one morning with their Norwegian skis on the roof rack. Nellie cried why couldn't she go, and Freya hushed her and promised next time she would be big enough to see Grandfather's cabin.

The trail they followed in the car had been used by men with burros in the old days. Jock pointed out to Yarrow the sites of the mines he could remember, the Little Maude, the Highland Mary, the Kittimac, and told her what a beautiful and eerie sight it had been when the miners came down after their shifts at night carrying their lamps. There was about a foot of fresh snow and James drove carefully up the razorback ledge they called a trail until he could go no further.

They stopped and changed their boots for leather shoes with metal hooks on the toes and clipped them into the fasteners on their thin birch skis. Yarrow's had been made for her mother by Papa Halvorsen before he lost his sight. James shouldered his canvas knapsack and led the way at a fine pace. Yarrow and Jock found it easier to follow in the grooves he made with his skis. "Like following a streetcar track," said Jock, puffing behind Yarrow. Yarrow was swinging her arms the way her mother had taught her. It was very cold and the sun was weak, scudding in and out behind the clouds, but the exertion of walking had them all so warm and breathing so heavily that James had to stop to take off his coat and roll it on top of his knapsack. Their skis crunched on the snow and their breathing grew heavier as they began to climb. Even Yarrow had to conserve her breath. "Never heard you so quiet." Her father laughed back at her and eased his pace. Yarrow watched the muscles on her father's calves working. She could see them moving under his ribbed woolen socks. They were all wearing baggy knickerbockers and loden jackets. Yarrow had on a colorful woolen hat with knitted braids that bounced against her own. They went up and up, past the bare, pale aspen trees to a height where only firs and pines grew. In summer, the wildflowers here were glorious, lupines and paintbrush vying with cow parsley; but now, in fall, the trees had grown introverted, saving their strength for the winter months to come. Yarrow watched the way her father's jacket strained to one side and then the other. She tried to match her swing to his. In doing so, she toppled over and fell. The snow had drifted thick and heavy here and her upper body sank into a snowbank. "A good place to have a break anyway," said her father, coming back and helping her up. Jock eased his pack off gratefully.

They were beside a stream, still gurgling under and through patches of ice and snow. In a week or a month it would be buried completely. They snapped off their skis and sat on some rocks in among the sagebrush that grew dense and bushy beside the stream. Jock and James had half a tumbler of brandy. "Hoocher's brandy," Jock called it. It had been given them by a subscriber who couldn't pay in cash. Yarrow sipped some hot chocolate from her flask. "Great," said Grandfather, savoring the brandy and sucking it out of the ends of his moustache. He took out a stogie from an inner pocket.

"What's great, Grandfather?"

"This. All this. God's Garden." The sun reappeared and dazzled off the surface of the snow. Deep shadow fell under the pine trees and dappled through the stands of blue spruce. The smoke from Jock's stogie was the same color as the sagebrush. Yarrow widened her nostrils as the cold intensified the smell of both.

"Dad, you'll have no breath left if you smoke that thing." James was rubbing life back into his fingers. Yarrow blew on hers and breathed into her mitts before shoving her fingers back in.

"You know," said Jock, surveying the length and color and width of the cigar between his fingers, "these came over first from Pennsylvania, on the Conestoga wagons that carried freight. You've seen them in drawings, Yarrow. They were shaped like a boat with a canvas top stretched over hoops. That's where the name comes from. Stogie." Jock took another puff and held up the cigar. "And the color, see the color? *Colorado*. That's Spanish for reddish-brown. The Spaniards had explored and claimed this place two hundred years before the English colonists knew it existed. It was not until President Jefferson bought the wilderness from Napoleon that he sent Zebulon Pike to see what was here."

"You can see the mountain that Zebulon tried to climb from Platte City," said James, standing up and flexing his shoulders. "Pikes Peak." He laughed. "The history of Colorado in a cigar."

"We might have to leave the *Gazette*, but we'll never leave these," said Jock, looking at his mountains. "We'll take them with us wherever we go."

From where Yarrow sat she could see the whole slope they had climbed, and beyond it, the distant ranges of the mountains, white and majestic, with bands of red rock and granite pinnacles. Jock pointed out, in the near distance, the crusher plant for a working iron mine. It had closed for the winter and stood like a ghostly reminder of all the other mines that had once been worked in these mountains. Below them on the lower slopes they could pick out the path of past snowslides where pine trees lay like tossed matchsticks. The mountains, Grandfather said, were like a mistress, beautiful but dangerous.

They were on their way soon, it was too cold to linger, and they faced one long last steep climb to the rim of the bowl in which the cabin was situated. James herringboned up the last part and checked his compass, because drifts had obscured the invisible path that he and Jock seemed to be following. Yarrow and Jock side-stepped up behind him.

"We go over there," said Grandfather, pointing to a tall dead tree way down to the right. "White Fork Creek is just beyond it."

It was now getting very cold and they skied down fast to Jock's landmark. Jock was right. From there they could see the broad sweep of the slope down the shoulder of the basin that led to the cabin. Yarrow's father let out a whoop like a boy and set off fast in front of her, making graceful telemark turns down the slope. Yarrow followed in a wide snowplow with her poles between her legs like a brake.

"It's wonderful," she shouted, forgetting how cold she was as the wind rushed into her mouth. The whole white bowl beckoned her like another world.

"I told you, it's God's Garden," shouted Grandfather, sweeping past her in the same crouched stance himself. They were like two witches on brooms swooping down the slope. Grandfather, being heavier on his skis, went faster and straighter. Yarrow, however, went wider and wider off the mark, the deep soft snow making it difficult for her to turn. She ended up a few hundred yards away from the cabin. She could see the men at the door of the little brown cabin.

"Hey, wait for me," she yelled. She did not want them to go inside without her. She was furious that they had got there ahead of her. Her haste made her anxious and she was sweating profusely as she side-stepped toward them. They seemed much further away from her than she had realized, and the basin they were in suddenly seemed very big and desolate. Yarrow came to a narrow ditch, no wider than her height but impossible to cross on skis. It was the snow-covered White Fork Creek, and she saw a log across it, further down. It would be much quicker to take off her skis and walk across than ski all the way along the edge. Yarrow snapped off the skis and pushed them through the loops of her poles to carry them. She stepped onto the log carefully, shoving the snow off with the soles of her shoes as she advanced. It was very slippery and just as she heard her father's voice in the distance shouting, "Yarrow! Wait!" she lost her balance and fell backward and grabbed on to the log with her hands.

The shock of the ice-cold water hit Yarrow immediately. The weight of her knapsack on her back dragged her down. She did not have the strength to pull herself up and hook herself over the log. She felt her fingers slipping down and the water on her neck, as the flow dragged her deeper under the log. She was going to drown. "Daddy!" Her words came out garbled like

Grandfather's word game. The more she struggled to save herself, the more Yarrow lost her grip. Her body temperature had
dropped already to a dangerous level. She had lost sensation in
her legs; they no longer felt cold. Her fingers slipped down
further. She tried to grasp at the log, but her hand just slipped off
and she screamed as she felt herself being sucked under. When
she opened her mouth to scream, it filled with cold water. This is
what drowning is like, she thought, I'm going to die.

"Hold on. I'm here, darling. I'm here. It's all right." Somehow her father, straddling the log, pulled her out like a fish. He
had her knapsack off and his jacket around her in a flash and half
ran, half stumbled with her in his arms back to the cabin.

The cabin that Jock had bought many years before consisted of
one small room with a wide-planked front door and small windows on either side. The ceiling followed the line of the steeped
roof, and at some stage Jock had built a platform under it that
jutted halfway across the small space and was approached by a
ladder on a pulley. On the theory that hot air rises, Jock had
placed his bed there. The area was so small, though, that if one
stood on the edge of the platform and stretched out with one
hand, one could touch the pipe of the wood stove before it
angled out to the wall. And a man with outstretched arms could
touch the stove in the center of the room and any wall of the
cabin. On the hard-packed floor of the cabin stood another small
bed, two hide-covered chairs and a bench that served as a table,
pushed against the wall. There was a shelf above the bench with
a few tin and white-enamel utensils and a string below it on
which fencing wire had been twisted into hooks from which
hung a couple of mugs, a spatula and a frying pan. Under one
window there was a pile of wood.

When Yarrow came to, her father had forced some brandy into
her mouth, which made her sputter and gag, but the trickle that
went down her throat warmed her. She was shivering un-
controllably, and her father had stripped off her frozen clothes
and wrapped her in layers of Grandfather's blankets. He held
Yarrow as they sat in a chair, almost on top of the little rusted
stove, no bigger than three shoeboxes put together. Grandfather
had a roaring fire going in the stove, and he and her father took
turns rubbing her limbs and feeding wood chips into the box.

"Hi, Daddy," she said, her teeth chattering. "Did you pick
up my skis? Ma will kill me if I lose them."

Her father laughed with relief and hugged her so hard the
breath went out of her.

"Oh, thank the sweet Lord," said Grandfather, taking off his flannel shirt and rubbing her hair with it. After a while, the shivering stopped and the one-room cabin was filled with the warmth and aroma of the wood burning. The crisis was over and Yarrow fell asleep while her father rocked her. When she woke she was under what seemed to be a ton of blankets on the little bed near the stove. Her skis leaned against the wall. There was the sound of wood crackling and a dim orange glow from the fire. Grandfather had made some cowboy coffee in a big black iron coffeepot. He had boiled some snow and then tapped in the ground coffee from a can in his knapsack. When the coffee boiled again he threw in a handful of snow and the grounds settled to the bottom. The tapping had awakened Yarrow and she lay listening to the murmur of their talk and watched the steam rise from her drying clothes.

They were talking politics. Grandfather was a died-in-the-wool Democrat. He was not only a Democrat, but a Progressive. He had never gotten over the Republican win when Harding was elected over Cox at the turn of the decade. And after Coolidge won in 1924, Coolidge who had once said that no one had a right to strike anywhere, anytime, Grandfather had been apoplectic. The corruption of the Colorado machine by the Ku Klux Klan the same year caused him to hate the Republican party even more. Now he groaned in despair at the rantings of his own party and their inability to endorse Al Smith, the Catholic New Yorker, against Herbert Hoover.

"Have you listened to Hoover on the wireless?" he asked. "He's lackluster. What does he stand for?"

Even James, a pragmatist when it came to most things, found the Republican nominee perplexing.

"Al Smith's a fine man," said Grandfather, "even though he is a Catholic." From Grandfather these words were a benediction indeed, for next to Sassenachs, those people who lived south of the Scottish border, Grandfather lost no love on the Papists, a distrust ingrained in him years ago on a dim pew in Aberdeen.

It was growing dark outside as Yarrow listened to them talk. One day, she decided, she would live in this cabin, with its smoky, dim interior and sturdy latched door. She would have children and her son would chop the wood for her fire. She would smell nice like Mama, camphor and meatballs, and wear a big apron over her dress. But how could she do that and run the newspaper? She frowned and twiddled the curly hair near her temple. She would just have to do both. She sat up to tell them and her father announced that her clothes were dry.

Her grandfather went out to relieve himself and a blast of frigid air rushed into the room.

"I think we'll have to leave tonight, James," said Jock, coming back in almost at once, buttoning himself. "There's a real storm banking up and we don't want to be caught up here for days. Freya would be worried sick."

"It would be fun," said Yarrow, disappointed that her overnight stay in the cabin was not to be.

"I think Grandfather's right. Are you up to it? I'll carry you if you get real tired."

When they had eaten some reheated beans and sausage and were ready to leave, James fashioned his flashlight into a miner's headlamp by tying it to his woolen hat. There was no moon and the dark was very thick. Yarrow followed her father closely on her skis. She was unable to see his figure but followed the pool of pale light as it picked up the slope, the branches of trees, the drifts of snow that here and there produced a landscape different from the one they had traveled on only a few hours earlier. The night cold was intense and fingers of ice clawed at Yarrow's face as they skied down the runs and climbed up the rises. The night air hardened the surface of the snow so that their speed was faster.

"This is how they used to do it in the old days," said Jock. They had stopped for him to catch his breath. "Travel by night so they didn't sink into the snow. It was once so cold up there in the cabin, that the ink froze in the bottle as I was writing a letter. I had to place it on the stove to keep it liquid."

Yarrow was grateful when they at last reached the car, and she tumbled inside while her father tried to start the motor. It wouldn't catch and he cursed and got out and lifted up the side-opening hood to get to the engine. Grandfather turned the starter again, and at last the engine caught and James ran, freezing, into the car. They had a slow drive home, the snow falling so thick and fast that her father had to stop and get out to push it off the windshield.

Freya was still up when they got home. She soon had potato pancakes in the oven, and hot coffee on the stove. She pulled her wrap around her more closely while they told her of Yarrow's accident. "I should have warned you," she said, "to beware of the water-baby. Papa Halvorsen called him 'pa-ah-a-pache.' He is an evil spirit."

"Oh, shisht, woman," said Jock. "She didna' cry once."

Freya had been sewing when they came in, while listening to the wireless. She had been attaching brown velvet to the under-brim of her old felt hat. She was going to wear it on the train when they left, and began stitching at it again while they ate in the kitchen.

"Herbert Hoover won the election," she said, "but not all the results are in." Grandfather swore under his breath.

"And the *Denver Morning Post* has been sold to Scripps-Howard, and the *Denver Evening News* has been sold to Bonfils."

Jock harrumphed. "How long do you think that will last?"

"Well, it didn't last at all," said Freya, biting off a thread. "The *Post* was immediately suspended and so was the *Evening News*."

"So Scripps-Howard has the morning field to itself with the *Rocky Mountain News*," said James, "and Bonfils has the *Evening Post*."

"Collusion. There ought to be a law against it." James was very silent behind his glasses. "What are you thinking, son?"

James put his arms behind his head and leaned back in the wooden chair. "Platte City," he said, "the *Journal*." He let his chair bang forward as he leaned across the table toward his father. "Now that we've decided to go, I can't wait to get there."

He pushed the plates aside and pulled out a notepad from his pocket. "I've been going over these figures that Fox and Mrs. Truitt gave us. Horace has left a mess, but look . . ." He pulled his chair closer to his father's. "First of all, their subscriptions haven't moved in twenty years. There's a lot of debt outstanding too." He began to go over the figures and doodle diagrams on the pad. Freya put away her sewing.

"Time for bed, Yarrow."

"Do I have to?"

"Yes, you have to." They were walking up the stairs, Freya heavy with her big stomach. Yarrow traced her fingers along the dado under the velvet wallpaper. There was dust on it. There was a big faded rectangle on the velvet where Grandma Mollie's portrait had always hung. The house seemed alien with half its furniture gone and the photographs and paintings removed, as though everything were held in suspension.

"Mama, what will you call the baby?"

"Harold, I think."

"Harold. If I had a son I would call him Zebulon."

"Zebulon?"

"You know, after Zebulon Pike who tried to climb Pikes Peak?"

"Oh, of course."

"Will you always have babies?"

Freya laughed and squeezed her daughter's hand. "I suppose so."

They were in Yarrow's room, a large closet really, next to the girls' room. Freya helped Yarrow quickly out of her clothes and into her long flannel nightgown. The room was very cold. Yarrow jumped into bed between the freezing sheets and brought her knees up to her chin.

"I don't think *I* will," she said.

"Have children? Why ever not?" Freya was so surprised that she sat down on the bed although she had not intended to. "Of course you will. You'll fall in love one day and get married and you'll just want to have them."

Yarrow's dark head turned on the pillow. "But what if I love something else more?"

"Oh, don't be silly," said Freya, smoothing the top sheet under her daughter's chin. "What else could there possibly be?"

Yarrow looked at her mother in the dark.

"Just things." She thought of Fabiana Truitt with her fine thin legs, and the air of confidence that surrounded her like perfume. "The *Journal*, the *Journal*," she kept hearing. She saw Fabiana's slim figure in the purple wool dress; then she saw her mother's lumpy shape in the dark and felt guilty and threw her arms around her.

"What nonsense, Yarrow. Now go to sleep and I'll give you a good wash in the morning when the house is warmer. You've had a terrible fright today."

Freya crossed to the door and stood silhouetted against the hall light. "Good night, child," she said.

"Good night, Mama."

But Yarrow didn't go to sleep right away. She was writing headlines in her mind. CHILD DROWNS IN FORK, or DAD SAVES CHILD'S LIFE. She imagined how she would write her own story and where she would place it on the page. Then she thought about her mother's worried face when she came in and the way her shoulders had hunched narrow under the shawl. She fell asleep dreaming about frozen ink and water and then the cozy cabin and gradually her bed warmed and gingerly she stretched out one leg and then the other and warmth spread right around her.

Freya Halvorsen McLean snuggled into her husband under the quilt on their makeshift bed. She was a contented woman whose ability and role in life were perfectly matched. She gathered people to her as though her capacity to cope were infinite and not subscribed by means, or even the encompassment of her arms. She did not expect a great deal and therefore was always surprised when blessings fell in her lap. She was handsome rather than beautiful. She had inherited the wide shoulders and height of her Norwegian ancestors and her wide, high cheekbones and eyes from her father's people. Her father had taught her many things about the mountains that she passed on to her children. She knew a few words of the Ute language. She had taught Yarrow how to recognize bistort in the high country and to dig up the corms and throw them on their campfire to roast. She knew how to find piñon nuts and which tree had the bark that could be salted and eaten. She had shown Nellie which roots to collect and taught her about the wildflowers.

Once Yarrow asked her if there really was a God, and Freya had told her just to look around and she would find Him, there on Mount Daly when the sun came up, or in the eye of a deer when it raised its head and knew it was being watched. But Yarrow thought God ought to look like Grandfather, and Freya only said, "He's there, too."

"Tell me again about the house," she said to James. "Is it nice? Is it heated?"

"Not as nice as this one, but perfectly comfortable. Warm for the new baby." He patted her stomach. They lay quiet for a minute listening to the creaks of the house, the groan of the wind outside, the muffled sounds of the children sleeping in the rooms above them. "I'll miss it," he went on, he who had been born in this house, "but Dad can't sell it anyway. We'll just board it up."

"We'll come back one day."

"Yes." His voice sounded as though he did not believe it.

"Tell me about the paper again. And the town. What are women wearing? Are there shops near the house? What about schools? Yarrow will be in first grade next year."

"Hold on." He laughed. "One thing at a time," and he began to tell her again about the newspaper office and Max Horace and the new machinery, and Albert Hinton, and about the town and the streetcars and the Broadlands Hotel, and by the time he got to describing Mrs. Truitt, not what she wore, for he could not remember, but the terrible scars she carried from the fire in which her husband had died, he realized that Freya was asleep. He kissed her gently on the forehead and pulled the quilt up over her shoulder, but he couldn't sleep himself and he lay for a long time going over in his mind all that had happened and all that he hoped would and wondered if the one would bring about the other.

CHAPTER 4

*I*T WAS A HOT, DUSTY DAY THE FOLLOWING AUGUST. WINDS FROM the plains swept toward the mountains and swirled in the streets of Platte City. On the terrace of the Broadlands Hotel it rustled fallen pittosporum leaves along the polished tile floor and made the white cloths on the outside tables flap and snap so that white-coated waiters rushed out to save glasses and flatware.

The McLean family was waiting for Fabiana Truitt to join them for lunch. Yarrow was counting the number of Chinese lanterns, which hung like clusters of beehives from the ceiling. She had on her best dress of navy blue piped with white, and a straw boater with a red ribbon. Her mother had brushed her hair until it hurt. Nellie had come, too, and was dressed in a white sailor suit.

"You look nice," said James to Freya. Freya nibbled at a roll. She was not so sure. She was nervous of meeting Mrs. Truitt for the first time and had heard she was a great beauty. She had seen a photograph of her in a society magazine and the scar on her face, always cleverly concealed, only seemed to add a glamorous and tragic dimension to her.

It had been a difficult year for Freya and James, as their son had died at birth. He was born prematurely soon after they arrived in Platte City. James cried for the little boy and told his wife that the move to Platte City had been the cause. Freya said it was probably meant to be, but even she couldn't shake off the sadness. They had christened him Harold after Papa Halvorsen and buried him near his grandparents in Galena. Freya lost interest in the rented house and even in herself, and James asked Laura Brogan, who had come to help in the house, to take her out and buy her some new clothes.

Freya had squeezed her figure into a new side-hook girdle, made of something the manufacturer called "pink brioche." Freya had to laugh, since that was exactly what the girdle made her look like, as she tried to reach an approximation of the

54

hipless style in fashion. She and Laura had chosen a simple dress of fine blue linen with a keyhole neckline, and with her white hat, not quite a cloche because her thick hair would not fit under it, she looked smart. James leaned over and kissed her and told her she looked just fine. Jock took a piece of string out of his pocket and played cat's cradle with Nellie. Yarrow went on counting beehives and swinging her feet under the chair.

"Never knew a woman to be so late," Jock said. He had told James he found Fabiana's nervous manner exhausting. "She's all feery-fary, and then hurry up and wait."

"Perhaps she's not hungry," said Yarrow, and just then Fabiana loped through the tables toward them, holding her son by the hand.

"Of course I'm hungry." She laughed. "I've just played nine holes of golf. Sorry I'm late."

Freya's expression took the place of a sigh as James introduced them. Fabiana looked even more beautiful and elegant than Freya had imagined. She was exceedingly thin, and Freya thought she probably only wore a wisp of crepe de chine under the almost sheer white dress with the pink sash on the hip. A cunningly designed fan collar stood up to meet her ears. Her dark hair hung in a deep wave to one side so that it almost covered one eye and was cut so sleek and tight to her head that it fitted like a cap. Her eyes swept over Freya with a smile that held no warmth, only polite interest, and Freya suddenly felt very matronly in her plain blue dress though she was only a year or two older.

"This is Palmer," Fabiana said, introducing her son. Yarrow and Palmer Truitt eyed each other. They were about the same age, though Yarrow was taller. He was a dark-haired little boy with long-lashed eyes and thin little legs. He wore Italian shorts, a silk shirt and a collarless jacket, and Yarrow thought he was the prettiest-dressed boy she had ever seen. Nellie stroked his hand. She was four years old and thought he was a big boy doll that she had been sent to play with.

At lunch Fabiana chatted away with great charm. She talked about her house in New York and people none of them had heard of. Every now and then Freya would say, "That's nice," and Fabiana would go on some more. James seemed to be fascinated by her.

"I'm going to come here every summer," she said. "I love the dry air after Manhattan."

"You should come up into the mountains if you want dry air," said Jock, who had just been up at his cabin for a week.

"But I love to golf and play tennis. The mountains wouldn't do at all. I've spoken to the manager here and he says he can arrange a better deal on the price of a suite if I guarantee to take it for a few years."

"That's nice," said Freya. Fabiana seemed to her a mass of contradictions. Money appeared to be no object and yet she would say things that showed how shrewdly she accounted for every penny.

"I'm liquidating all my stocks," Fabiana said, "every last dollar."

"Why?" asked Jock. Yarrow saw that the spray of the fountain behind him caused an effect like a peacock's tail.

"Just a feeling." Fabiana gave a shrug. "There's so much rumor about and dire prediction. I listen to everybody and then I take my own advice. Cash, that's what I'm interested in these days." She made a fist motion with her right hand.

Freya cut up Nellie's meat. She had noticed that the collar of Fabiana's dress was whipstitched on by hand. Perhaps when the *Journal* was doing better she could have as fine a dress as Fabiana's. A piece of food fell on her lap and she rubbed the spot with her napkin. This linen dress would have to do her for years. Freya disliked the effect that Fabiana had on her.

Yarrow wouldn't eat her meat. It did not look at all like anything they ate at home; in fact it looked uncooked to her. She hid the pieces under her potatoes and hoped her mother wouldn't notice. The peacock's tail fanned and bloomed and then skewed sideways as a strong breeze blew it.

When the waiter had cleared away the remains of the little lamb chops with the paper frills, Fabiana asked Yarrow if she would like some ice cream.

"Yes, please."

"And Palmer?"

"No." He was sulking and bored. His long lashes caused a shadow on his cheeks.

"You should come and see the newspaper office," said Jock, trying to be kind.

"We went to one yesterday."

"Yesterday?"

"We had lunch with the *Globe* people in Denver," said Fabiana, "purely social. The owner, Larry Schaeffer, knew Palmer's father from the old days."

"Ah."

"I think it's best to keep the lines of communication open, don't you? You never know when it will be useful."

"Fabiana's right," said James.

"You should come home and play with the girls," said Freya to Palmer. "We have a swing and a sandbox."

But Palmer was watching his mother eat. Her lipstick left red marks in the ice cream. "May I have some?"

She pushed it toward him. "I'm quite finished anyway," she said. Freya looked at her own empty dish with guilt.

Palmer ate all around the mound of ice cream so that only the red lipmarks were left. Yarrow respected his fastidiousness and nudged him under the table with her foot. Perhaps they could be friends after all. Palmer looked up from under his long eyelashes. Then he stuck his tongue out at her.

When they had finished their meal they decided to walk in the gardens for which the hotel was famous. As they approached a set of narrow stairs that led off the terrace, Yarrow and Fabiana arrived at it together. Yarrow was about to go forward, but Fabiana stuck out her arm across her path.

"Ladies first," she said. Yarrow looked up at her so that her straw boater fell off her head. When Fabiana bent down to retrieve it, Yarrow ducked under her arm and ran down the stairs in triumph.

"What a little minx," said Fabiana with a laugh and tossed the hat onto her own head where the red ribbon lay on her pale shoulder.

"You're right. I'll have to speak to her about her manners," said James.

Jock went down the stairs with Fabiana, and Freya took the opportunity to whisper in James's ear, "Do you have to agree with her on everything?"

A hot wind blew off the lake, spraying the water from the fountains across its surface. Freya picked up Nellie and carried her.

Yarrow and Palmer ran over a rustic bridge that led to an ornamental island with a Japanese tea garden. "Don't get dirty," called Fabiana after her son. When his mother was out of sight, Palmer lay down and hung over the bridge so he could see the giant carp in the water. There were no railings and the bridge had a hump in the middle.

"Don't do that," said Yarrow. "You might fall in."

"Are you afraid?" he said. "I'm not."

Yarrow had crossed the bridge and stood on the island. "I almost drowned last year. Please come away."

"I won't."

"I can't save you."

At this Palmer came off the bridge and joined Yarrow, who was trembling. He looked at her for a moment.

"I don't expect girls to save me." He looked at her for another moment until she began to think that it *was* an odd thing for her to say. Then Palmer turned and began to run. "Race you to the others," he shouted. Yarrow set off after him, but he had a head start and she was out of breath and out of sorts when she finally caught up with him. She hated to be beaten.

On one of the gravel paths, the adults met Max Horace. He was sitting on a bench with a man in a dark suit and a bowtie. Max jumped up when he saw them and mumbled an introduction. But there was really no need, for James and Jock and Fabiana had instantly recognized the owner of the *Globe*, Larry Schaeffer. Schaeffer's shoulders and lapels were covered in a mixture of cigarette ash and dandruff. He kept flicking his fingers over his jacket as he talked.

Yarrow saw that she was now closer to the bridge than Palmer. "Race you to the bridge," she shouted and set off with Palmer behind her.

James yelled at Yarrow to stop, but she had reached the bridge just ahead of Palmer, and as Palmer lunged to get ahead, he saw that he was not going to win and he pushed her. She tripped but regained her balance, and Palmer overran his objective and fell into the water. Yarrow stared horrified for a second, and then screamed and jumped in after him. With a grateful shock she realized that she could touch the bottom. Palmer came up with weeds all over him.

James was angry as he hauled them out of the water.

"You are a disobedient, headstrong young lady. I told you to stop."

"James," said Freya. "She tried to save him and she's afraid of the . . ."

"Enough. We're going home. Now." James felt he had lost face in front of the others. He frog-marched his daughter to the car. Yarrow could hear Palmer wailing in the background. Served him right, she thought.

"I wonder what that old bugger's up to now," said Jock, wiping the sweat off his brow as they sat in the car. Everyone was silent, except Yarrow who cried as she sat beside Grandfather in the backseat. Her dress was wet and muddy and her hat had lost its shape. Grandfather squeezed her hand. He spoke to James, "He can't keep his cogs clean, that one."

James said something about the *Globe*, and Yarrow was unable even through her sobs to resist asking a question.

"Why are you so friendly with all these people?" she cried as they headed home. "I thought they were the enemy."

James adjusted the rearview mirror and had to laugh at the wretchedness of his determined offspring. "It's never worth it to hold grudges. Keep a little black book, write the names in, and then forget it. Anyway the newspaper business is like one big family—lots of squabbles and lots of making up."

Jock said in disgust, "Just one big happy family."

"Your nostrils were flaring as you spoke to Max," said James.

" 'Keeping the lines of communication open,' I suppose," said Freya.

"That too," said James with a grin, and then patted Freya on the knee. Nellie squirmed in Freya's arms. "Fabiana's a pretty woman but she's too thin for me."

"Bloodless," said Jock. "I don't trust her. She's got grasping hands."

"Pretty legs though," said James and ducked as Freya took a swing at him with her pocketbook.

Jock did not have to wonder long what Max Horace was up to, because Fabiana called James the next day and told him that she had to speak to him urgently. She had just spoken to Larry Schaeffer at the *Globe*. . . . James said to hold it right there and he'd come straight over. He stripped off the black cuff protectors he wore on a "white shirt day"—a shirt day being when he also went out and sold ads, on other days he worked in his undershirt and a coverall—and drove out to the hotel.

He and Fabiana sat in the lounge with its Caen stone walls and painted ceiling.

"Max Horace is starting another newspaper."

"What?"

"He's using my money, our money, to set himself up again."

"That wouldn't be enough."

"Well, I don't know where he's getting the money. Perhaps he took us for more than even we suspect." Fabiana's usual nervous way of speaking was punctuated today by handwaving. "He's bought some equipment from the *Globe* and he says he's going to run us out of town." Fabiana jabbed her cigarette out in the ashtray and started another.

"His timing's lousy. Just as we're getting on our feet . . ."

"And Albert Hinton's going to work for him."

"Not Albert."

"Albert Hinton. What will you do? There's no room surely for two papers in Platte City, is there?"

James took off his glasses and wiped the lenses on his hand-kerchief. "I'm a better newspaper man than either Albert Hinton or Max Horace. If it's a fight they want, they'll get it." His voice sounded more sure than he felt. James, though he couldn't see it, was white to the gills. He thought of all the money he owed, and the likelihood now, with competition, of ever paying it back. Fabiana ordered them both an old-fashioned. She bit into her maraschino cherry.

"What *can* you do?" she asked. James took a breath and folded his arms.

"I'm going to make it work," he said, and was surprised at how like Jock he sounded. He told her about his feelings for the paper and his plans for its future. He had ideas for a column; he was going to bring in more out-of-state news; he could save on newsprint, at least he thought he could. Fabiana listened and pursed her wide red lips, and swung her slim legs with the narrow ankle-strapped shoes. The movement was that of a nervous fidget rather than a flirt.

"I wonder if you will beat Max? I've never heard you so confident."

"Could you afford to lose it?" he asked.

She leaned forward and uncharacteristically touched James on the knee where the crease of his wide trousers fell.

"I have a terrible fear of being poor. My own father died soon after I was born and my mother and I nearly starved. When she remarried, her husband adopted me. He was tough on me. He really didn't think I would amount to much. But I'm going to show him. I'm sure he's watching wherever he is. He probably tipped Saint Peter for the best seat in the house, or Lucifer."

Fabiana looked at James for a long minute between her lashes. He had no idea what she was thinking and he wanted to fill the silence.

"At least we're established and Max's new paper is not. But the *Journal* is going to be pinched; there just isn't enough advertising to go around."

"You know," she said, with her head to one side, "there may be other opportunities for us, too. I keep hearing rumors that there's a paper for sale in New York. Would you be interested in editing it if it was?"

James smiled at her elegant dark head against the yellow stone walls; here they were talking about future possibilities when their present business was in trouble.

"You're a tonic for the spirit, Fabiana."

"Good, because I expect my payments on time."

When James left he still felt buoyed by her confidence. He knew he could beat Max at this game; he didn't doubt himself for a moment.

When he got back to his office, Albert Hinton's resignation lay on his desk. Two weeks later Max Horace produced his new paper, the *Record*, and the war was on.

But larger events in the world overtook their own small battle for survival.

When the Wall Street crash came that October, it took James by surprise. Fabiana had been right, he thought, reading the wire stories of fortunes that had been lost overnight. He was glad that he had never had the money to invest or dabble. Wall Street was a long way from Stalker Street. But after a few months, even the *Journal* began to feel the effect. People began to be laid off and the classified ad market that James had worked so hard to build up began to slow down; the small shopkeepers stopped advertising and soon after them, the retail stores began eking out their advertising dollars. Max Horace and the *Record*, however, still made their presence felt.

"Where is the old bastard getting the money to go on?" asked Jock.

"Probably got it stashed somewhere, Dad, and we'll never find it."

"He must have robbed us blind over the years. Robbed us blind." Jock coughed over his cigar.

The economy tightened like a vise. James began to have nightmares. He dreamed he was running down Main Street, grabbing at newspaper pages that flew past him. They all flew into Fabiana Truitt's arms. He woke up in a sweat when he thought of the payments owed to Fabiana Truitt. He did not know how he could meet them. Before his next payment was due, James went to the only bank in town that had managed to remain liquid. He hoped to convince the bank manager to loan him the money he had once offered. He went over the figures in his head as he parked the car and went in and waited for the manager to see him. But the wait was in vain, for the bank manager laughed at him.

"The whole financial structure of the country is crashing down, because people can't pay their debts, and you come in and ask for a loan for a business that might not make it through the next six months? And in a competitive market? You must be mad," said the bank manager, waving a sheaf of documents in front of James's face. "You know what these are? They're foreclosures, foreclosures for small businesses and farms, and houses and land. You wanna buy some land in El Paso County? You wanna buy it for a dollar an acre? No, of course not. Nobody would. Nobody could. I'm sorry. I'm very busy.''

James felt ill when he got into his car. He put his hands on the steering wheel and put his forehead on them. He knew he was not meant to be a businessman. He knew it now. It had all seemed so easy, coming to Platte City to take up their interest, and then Fabiana loaning them the money to buy out Horace. But now—if they were unable to repay Fabiana, the paper would be hers. They would have nothing. The McLeans did not even own the house they lived in. All James's failures rose like nausea in front of him. He knew he had disappointed his father by not moving sooner to other opportunities. He had not felt the need, and he knew what Jock thought when he turned his head and bit his lower lip in order not to say anything. It had been like that with the car dealership. James had thought it a surefire way to earn some money. What a fiasco that was. And then when they had moved here, the organization and turmoil had overtaxed Freya and she had lost the baby. James blamed himself very much for that. He shook his head on the steering wheel and groaned.

How could he pay off his debt? What would Fabiana's reaction be if he could not? James feared the worst.

"Are you feeling all right, sir?" James's head came up off his hands. A police officer looked at him through the open window.

"Yes. Yes." James started the car and moved on, but he was in a daze. He drove around for a long time; he drove past the entrance to the Broadlands Hotel and sat in his car and watched the golfers in the late autumn sun playing on the impeccable greens. Didn't they have any worries? He drove back into town toward the offices of Jerrard Fox and then changed his mind. He would talk to Fabiana himself. He would ask her to extend the deadline for repayment. Surely she would understand.

Back at the *Gazette* office, the family stood around the stone and talked about it. Freya had come in to lend a hand with the bookkeeping. They laid the little book of debits and assets on the smooth, flat, cast-iron top of the stone. Things looked very bad.

"You should go," said Freya. It was the only way out, to beg Fabiana to ease off. But their pragmatism did not make swallowing their pride any easier. They were battlers, the McLeans. You could see it as they stood there, the hard-working hands, the broken nails and ink ingrained in the men's, Freya's calluses under her wedding ring.

"We'll have to tighten our belts even further," said Jock.

They scraped up the money to buy a train ticket and the next day Freya packed James's bag and he left on a four-day trip to New York.

"Dad?"

"James! How did it go?" Jock stood at the black wall phone and held the earpiece to his ear. Freya came and stood beside him.

"What's he saying?" Jock held the earpiece so she could hear.

"I've spoken to her."

"And?"

"We have breathing space." Freya tweaked Jock's beard and grinned.

"How did you do it, son?"

"Well, she's not real happy about it. I think even Fabiana has been shocked at the losses on Wall Street. One of her father's friends committed suicide."

"But I thought she told us she had liquidated all her stock."

"She's odd about money. She thinks she's close to destitution if even one of her investments doesn't pay off."

"She's a woman." Freya poked Jock with her elbow. "Your wife's beating me up."

"You know she's picked up the *New York Courier* for a song. Funny how there's money for that and not for us." He sounded bitter. "But people are selling everything here."

"Too bad we've no spare cash," said Jock.

"Yes, it is. But at any rate, she's given us an extension on our repayment. Why, I'll never know."

"It's those dimples of yours," said Jock.

"Dad, we can't default."

"By God, we won't."

"But she won't put any more money in. I mean, that's it."

"We can do it, son. Hurry home. Here's Freya."

CHAPTER 5

WHEN YARROW WAS ELEVEN HER FATHER DECIDED TO BUILD A tree house in the plane tree in the garden.

The family had moved by then to another rented house. Freya had taken a dislike to the house on West Colorado Avenue after poor Harold had died. So James found another house, a heavily decorated, solidly built Victorian house with a front porch, six bedrooms, a primitive yard, a resident cat that lived under the crawl space, and a view of Pikes Peak from an upstairs bathroom window.

It was dilapidated and dirty and they got it cheap. Freya rolled up her sleeves and turned her formidable energy toward the task of making it habitable. She sanded floors and painted walls and scrubbed tiles and plastered cracks. She hung her curtains at the windows, moved in her potted plants, unrolled the rugs, polished her furniture and made the house her own. In the spring, when the ground had thawed enough to receive a spade, she began to turn over the yard and put in rye and clover seed and pegged out an area for a tomato patch at the back behind the plane tree. Soon people stopped to admire the work that they had done on the old house on Bellevue Street and Freya was always busy with another project to make it better.

"Pull it up, James," she said, as Jock hauled on a rope and the last sheet of plywood for the children's tree house was hauled into position. With a mouth full of nails and a hammer in his belt, James knelt on the plywood floor he had constructed. The space was too small for him to stand up.

"Will it be ready soon, Daddy?" called up Nellie. Dark little Nellie hugged the cat to herself with delight. She had dressed the cat in doll's clothes. Its claws were leaving white scratch marks on her brown arms.

"This tree house is for you," she said, kissing it on the nose.

"Don't kiss the cat," said Freya. "It licks its private parts."

Nellie listened to her mother and frowned but she only squeezed the cat tighter. She was an intense little girl with a head full of dreams that she never shared with anyone. She held everything to herself as if afraid to let go—even her bowel habits followed her natural leanings. Freya was always giving her cod-liver oil and bran muffins. The cat now scratched her deeply so that she had to let it go, and it jumped from her arms and ran, trailing its doll's clothing, under the house. Nellie took after it with a wail.

Greta clutched her mother's skirt and watched. She twisted the cloth of the skirt around her thumb and rubbed it over her upper lip. She was five and had, since Harold's death, turned from a placid baby into an anxious child. The size of Freya's stomach warned her that another change was on the way.

Freya watched James nailing on the last board. She walked a few feet to see it from another angle and Greta followed her like the little wooden duck on wheels that she pulled along by a string. The duck clacked along behind her, the wooden webbed feet turning like a waterwheel.

"Let me go, Greta, just for a minute," said Freya, releasing the fingers from her skirt. She pushed back her heavy braid of hair and sighed. It was a sultry day. Greta dropped her mother's skirt. Freya went over to hand up some more nails to James. Greta followed and grabbed her skirt again.

Yarrow stood halfway up a ladder that entered a foot-square hole in the floor of the tree house. Freya noticed that her daughter's hem was down and that Yarrow's legs were covered with bruises. Yarrow was a tomboy, always in scrapes. Nellie yelled from under the house.

"Oh, what is it?" said Freya. She was hot and tired and her big, bare feet were swollen in the grass.

"I'll go," said Yarrow, taking charge. She jumped down from the ladder and disappeared under the house. It was dark and cool and the earth was soft and dusty under her feet. It was too small for adults to enter. Nellie had the cat by the tail.

"Let him go," said Yarrow. "Don't you know he hates being babied? He's a wild thing. Look, want to share a secret?"

She pulled one of Grandfather's cigars out of her pocket and a box of matches.

"Are you going to smoke it?" Nellie let go of the cat and it yowled as it made its way farther back behind the chimney wall where no one could reach it.

"Of course I am. That's why I came in here, nitwit." Yarrow bit off the end, lit the cigar and started sucking on it as she had seen Jock do a thousand times.

"I'm going to tell on you."

"Oh, no, you're not," said Yarrow, grabbing her by the arm

before she got past her. "You have to have a smoke, too, or else you can't join the club."

"What club?"

"It's a secret club. Do you want to join?" Nellie reluctantly took a drag and coughed and then Yarrow took another one.

"Now we have to have a blood pact so we can never tell on each other."

Nellie's eyes widened as Yarrow took a safety pin, which was holding up part of her hem, and pricked her finger. A little bubble of dark red blood stood up like a pimple.

"Now you."

"Do I have to?"

"Yes. Go on. Oh, shut your eyes. I'll do it for you." Nellie offered her forefinger and squeezed her eyes shut.

"Ouch."

"Don't be silly, that didn't hurt. Now we join them. The blood has to mingle." They pressed their fingers together. Yarrow made up a few words. "Hokum footle a pa cha nay, spirits witness our pact." She took a pinch of earth between her fingers, placed it on Nellie's palm and squeezed a drop of her blood on it, then she squeezed a drop of blood from Nellie. "This seals our pact. Put it on your tongue"

"Do I have to?"

Nellie followed her sister's example.

"Now, she who lies with her tongue shall die by the words she has broken." The girls smoked the remainder of the cigar in solemn silence.

"What are you two up to?" said Freya from the garden. They could see her bare feet through the trellis of the crawl space.

"Nothing," said Yarrow, stubbing out the cigar, and came out looking innocent. Nellie came out looking green.

"Is the tree house finished?" James was hammering away on the inside of the tree house.

"Soon be done, love," he shouted down. He was feeling mighty proud of himself at this effort. Freya was always criticizing his handiwork.

"You've made a slight miscalculation, son," said Jock from the back steps. "How are you going to get out?"

The hammering stopped and then James swore. He had finished off the upper half of the plywood walls with chicken wire and the only exit was through the foot-wide hole in the floor. Jock and Freya couldn't stop laughing, and James smashed his way out of the plywood floor, threw down his hammer and stalked into the house. Freya looked at Jock with her mouth pursed trying to stop, but it was impossible, and at the sound of their renewed glee, they heard from inside the house a great guffaw as James joined in.

"I feel sick," said Nellie, her face going from green to white, and promptly vomited all over the agapanthus.

"What have you been up to?" said Freya, coming over to her and rinsing her off with the garden hose. Nellie groaned. She could never lie to her mother, and not even the thought of death or her sister's wrath could stop her from bursting out with the truth.

"Yarrow!" But Yarrow had gone. She ran up the street and stayed away for the rest of the day until she thought it was safe to come home. But Freya was waiting for her with the big wooden spoon that she used to stir homemade jelly, and she smacked Yarrow across the calves until it stung.

Yarrow glared at her sister as she went up to bed with her legs smarting, but she never said a word and her father never did finish the tree house.

Laura Brogan came to stay in July when Eric was born. She came for six months and just stayed on. When Freya told her she really could not afford to pay her much, Laura said that was OK and she would leave when she found another job—which was almost impossible during the Depression. When Eric arrived on the scene he was swept to Laura's bosom with as much joy as if he were her own. There was never such a spoiled child as Eric. Even his bedroom was sandwiched between Freya's and Laura's.

Number Eight Bellevue Street had been built when families were still expected to be large and maids were still expected to be plentiful. Thus it had been given back stairs that its new economic level didn't warrant, but in the domestic jumble of Freya's household they worked remarkably well.

The original maid's room downstairs had been turned over to Jock, who preferred to be independent. It was just off the hall, right near the back door so that when he wanted a smoke, and in order to avoid Freya's wrath, he could go outside with little effort. His legs ached now and again. "Rheumatism," said Jock. "Gout," said Freya, taking away his port. He loved to read and piled all his books up on the floor beside his narrow bed and hung the portrait of Mollie outside the door to his room so that she always smiled at him when he went past. James made him a bench that he could use in the summer in the garden, but the first time Jock sat on it, a slat came off and no one fixed it. Besides, Jock preferred to sit in his room or on the back steps watching the birds that swooped in and out of the plane tree. He disliked seeing the neighbors when he sat on the front porch.

On the second floor, Laura and Eric each had a room near the back stairs. The only passage from the front to the back was through two adjoining bathrooms. Freya wondered who could possibly have designed a house this way. But the family got used to it, except they kept forgetting to lock and unlock the doors whenever someone had finished with either room, so that you were always running down the back stairs and up the front when all you wanted was a handkerchief or a book just feet away. If you went into the first bathroom, which you reached from the back stairs, you could go through the door into Freya and James's room, or through another door into the bathroom that served the children. Freya and James lived with three doors in their bathroom and the children gaily banged in and out until James bellowed at the top of his voice; then they stopped for a few days and tiptoed around until they forgot or he was in a better mood.

Yarrow's room was right opposite her parents'. It shared the same view across the street to a row of houses similar to theirs. In the summer you could not see them for the trees had leafed out, but in the winter, with everything bare, then you saw windows and porches and awnings, and half-drawn shades, and lights going on and off, and realized that other people lived there, too. Yarrow wondered if they were like them. She wondered what they read and if one day she could sell a newspaper to them. She oscillated between imagining herself in her father's shoes or her mother's.

Yarrow's room did not have the depth of her parents' because at some stage the room had been halved to make another bedroom at the rear. In this room Nellie and Greta had twin beds. Between the girls' rooms there was another door that led to the attic, which consisted of two box rooms, one of which served as a bedroom for a paying guest. In the early thirties the McLeans needed every penny they could earn.

James had rented out the top floor of the office to a J. F. Smith, Justice of the Peace, and none of Max Horace's Moorish decorations remained except the tiled fireplace and the coffered ceiling. James moved his desk downstairs and built a glass partition between it and the press to break down some of the noise. But when the press was running it made very little difference and you had to shout to make yourself heard even if the door was shut. The door was always being left open anyway, and James shouted at the children when they came in to help, "Were you born in a barn? IN A BARN?"

It was just like being back in Galena bringing out the Humdinger, except the debts were larger and the hours longer as James and the family sweated to keep the paper going. His only hope of paying his debts was for advertisers and subscribers to pay *him*. But as the Depression intensified across the country, a form of barter had become the currency. It was no use explaining to Fabiana or Jerrard Fox that last month's interest payment was late because the *Journal* had no money, but how about accepting a barrowload of potatoes or some cords of wood instead? The Goss Comet press was still not paid for. James and Jock had inherited, not a newspaper, but a bank ledger. Fabiana Truitt's letters of inquiry piled up in a cubbyhole of the desk. James decided not to answer them. An uneasy truce had settled between them, and James surmised that given the opportunity Fabiana would get out of their arrangement like a shot. So he just kept his head down and went on working to pay her off.

James had laid off everyone except for one full-time employee who worked the Linotype machine. It was the first time either James or Jock had had to let a man go. Jock couldn't eat his supper that night, said his throat was constricted.

Three afternoons a week, Yarrow went to the office after school to help. On the other days her mother went. One day Freya was in seventh heaven; she had sold a hundred pounds of potatoes from the *Gazette* cellar to a grocery store. James went straight around to the bank with the money.

Freya took in a new lodger. He was a LEM with the Civilian Conservation Corps.

"What's that?" asked Yarrow, her ears perking up at any word or acronym she didn't know.

"A local enlisted man," George Thringle explained, adding that he trained some of the boys working for Roosevelt's forest army.

The emergency Senate bill had been introduced the year Eric was born to help get unemployed and hungry young men off the streets. They had arrived like flotsam in the towns, crusting around the doors of bakeries or the alleys behind restaurants looking for food. Yarrow had seen some of them, pale and undernourished, hanging around the office window. Her father let one boy sleep in the office for a week when he said he had no place else to go. Each morning James brought him a doughnut and a cup of coffee from the drugstore. One morning the boy was gone. A few days later Yarrow and her sisters were walking near the railway track, something they were forbidden to do, when they found the body of a dead boy. No amount of Freya's warnings had the effect on them that this gruesome discovery did. They said nothing to anyone. When the body was discovered by adults, the children looked at each other knowingly. James did not know if it was "his" boy or not, for many traveled in the boxcars wherever the trains would take them. The children never went to the tracks again.

When the training camps were set up by the Department of Labor, the young men were taken off the streets. Many of the boys were illiterate, and after their daily assignments, whether it was building roads, planting trees or learning about pinebeetle control, they were offered educational or vocational courses. George Thringle was one of the teachers.

There was a camp just outside Platte City, one of two thousand camps that had been set up across the country. George Thringle, or Lem, as the children called him, became one of the family. He was a neat man with one of those smooth-skinned faces that make age difficult to judge. He could turn a lathe or fix a leaking faucet or drain a car radiator. He put James's carpentry efforts to shame. He could hang a gate straight, and open a stuck window. He could paint a room so that there were no blotches or streaks, and paper a wall so that the glue didn't turn brown on the surface after the first week. Laura showed him the broken floor of the tree house and the missing slat on the garden bench, and he brought his tools into the garden one afternoon and quietly fixed them.

He loved to share his skills with his charges and believed in wasting nothing. He talked Jock into teaching some of the Corps boys the old ways of typesetting. Lem was always looking for ways to occupy them. One of the boys Jock taught was from New York. His name was Elliot Weyden, and one day in 1935 he and Lem brought him home for supper.

Elliot was a very thin, tall boy, about sixteen or seventeen, with piercing dark eyes. Yarrow had seen him with her grandfather at the back of the composing room earlier in the week. Grandfather was always surrounded by boys these days, it seemed, standing there in his coveralls—"worn for comfort and from comfort," he said—his back stooped under the frayed collar. He was becoming irascible as he grew older, but none of the boys seemed to mind. They loved his skill with the type stick, and the stories he told as he showed them how job printing was done on an old handpress: how they had to moisten the paper first with a sponge, and then ink the type, and then pull the lever to make

the impression. Yarrow grew resentful when she saw him surrounded by his admirers when she had to do the "real" work,
pecking at a typewriter with two fingers and answering the
telephone. When Nellie came in, she only swept the floor; Greta
put on a show dancing in the window, much to the amusement of
the passersby. But Jock only took in his students when things
were quiet at the *Journal*. Lem was forever grateful when one of
his young charges decided that the printing trade was the road he
wanted to follow.

Elliot Weyden was different from the others. First of all,
Grandfather said, he'd never make a printer; he was too impatient of detail; he had no hand-eye coordination. "You couldn't
set a line of type in a fit," said Grandfather, pulling him off the
stool and putting him to work greasing the bushings of the press.
But for all that, Jock had developed a fondness for this boy more
than for any of the others. He was smart and lively and curious
about everything around him. He had lied about his age to join
the Corps. He never told anyone this outright, but it slipped out
when he made a mistake on his birthdate filling out a form. Lem
said nothing as he scratched out a figure and put in another. No
one was ever sure what his real age was. He was a boy with a
mischievous look in his eye and an inability to sit still, and yet
the center of him was as steady as a ruled line on a page.

When Elliot first came to Colorado, Lem put him to work
moving stones and rubble on the Rimrock Drive. He wasn't very
strong but he pushed with a determination that made Lem wince.
He watched Elliot struggle one day with an enormous boulder
and then organize some others to set up a fulcrum with a couple
of planks of wood and some other stones. When the boulder
finally moved, Elliot somehow was in the way, and the boulder
crushed his right foot, fracturing a bone. Lem then discovered
that Elliot could type. He said he used to help his mother type
out her fees for piano lessons; and he was moved into the CO's
office where there was always a logjam of paperwork. Elliot
attacked his new job with the same enthusiasm as he had attacked rock pushing. Lem told him to try to keep his toes off the
typewriter keys.

Elliot soon discovered he could do the job of CO's assistant
with one hand tied behind his back. It was easy if you were
organized and Elliot was organized. In his quiet moments he
thought of ways to make more money. He earned thirty dollars a
month on the work project. He sent his mother every penny he
earned except for a dollar a week and his canteen book. He
began by buying packs of Bull Durham and tobacco paper and

selling the ready-rolled cigarettes for a penny less than the
canteen did. He cornered the market in Oh Henry candy bars
through a bureaucratic slip when a box of them was delivered to
the CO's office as stationery. Elliot made a small profit and
reimbursed the office for the original costs. Elliot's bookkeeping
was scrupulous. He argued to himself that he was offering a
service, making the chocolate bars available at any time of the
day or night. It was not until a spot check of the sleeping
quarters revealed four boxes of Oh Henry bars and three boxes of
Love Nest candy under Elliot's bed that the CO caught on to his
assistant's game. Lem was brought in to straighten him out.

Lem asked Elliot if he could drive a truck. "Yes, sir." The
thought of being able to go in and out of town fed Elliot's fertile
mind. He had some trouble with the gears on the steep grades
near the camp, and nearly lost a load of boys on a hairpin bend
when he couldn't get up enough speed and they started to roll
backward. "Hey, Weyden, where'd you get your license?"
Elliot crashed through the gears and made it to town in one
piece, though he was white and sick-looking by the time they
piled out at the *Journal* office.

Elliot was different from the other boys in another way. He
was driven by an ambition that was like a fire. He talked little
about it, but it was as though time was burning for him. He
thought a wasted opportunity was an opportunity that was gone
forever. The fever inside him seldom allowed him to relax. He
never took time off, dreaming or goofing around with the others.
He would read feverishly as though he had a whole list of books
that he had to, must, get through that month. He was a loner, but
he was not unpopular. Lem put it down to the fact that Elliot was
born with a tremendous source of energy. He carried it around
like a box of batteries inside him. When his energy flagged, a
few hours' sleep recharged him and all his lights came on again.
Jock thought that Elliot was a natural leader. When Jock had a
group of boys with him, Elliot's attitude determined the attitude
of the group. Elliot himself was too busy to ponder his small
successes; he was seldom given to introspection; that was a
waste of time when you could be achieving something.

In the evening Elliot studied for his high-school diploma. He
and Jock shared a love of books that up till now only Yarrow had
been able to share with her grandfather. She found them sitting
on the back stoop one night when she went out to get some
washing from the line for Laura. Laura was reading a bedtime
story to Eric, who had just turned two. It was early summer and
a soft purple twilight was creeping over the garden and causing

deep shadow under the plane tree. Nellie and Greta were playing hide-and-seek around the house. Elliot was talking about one of his English assignments, a book by Theodore Dreiser. Grandfather said he didn't much care for Dreiser's Russian sympathies, though he understood them, and Elliot said social realism was the thing in contemporary American writing. Grandfather said he ought to read *Babbitt* and *The Great Gatsby* to understand America. Yarrow was unable to enter the discussion because she did not know enough about it, and it made her jealous to see her grandfather sitting there with this thin young man, enjoying his company and ignoring her. She flounced the clothes into the basket and clipped the pegs sharply back on the line.

"Come and join us, Yarrow," said Grandfather, beckoning her with his free hand, as though he could read her mind.

"I'm busy."

Nellie darted into sight and Grandfather's voice pounced on her.

"Take the clothes in like a good girl, Nellie. I want to talk to your sister." Nellie didn't want to, but Greta, always obliging, said, "Come on, it will only take a minute."

Yarrow settled on the step above her grandfather. She pulled up her short white socks and hugged her knees.

"Elliot lives in New York," said Jock.

"In the city?"

"No. Upstate. My father's family came over from Holland long ago when the patroonships were settled along the Hudson," said Elliot. He turned and looked at her and smiled. His voice was as deep and dark as his eyes. It sort of twinkled at her. "My mother still lives there." He did not speak to her as if she were a child. Yarrow blushed and straightened her dress over her lap. Her fingernails were very grubby, she thought. She hid them under her legs.

"Why didn't you stay there?"

"I couldn't get a job." He shrugged. "My mother and sister have to eat."

"What about your father? Can't he feed them?"

"Yarrow," said Grandfather, sucking his moustache, "it's none of your business."

Elliot shrugged again. Yarrow couldn't figure out if he was very offhand or if it was a nervous reflex. His shoulders were very thin.

"My father died." He was leaning against the post of the stoop with one long skinny leg on the ground and one on the step. She wondered what it would be like to lose someone you loved.

"Your wages must be a great help," said Grandfather.

"It's all they've got. My mother was a piano teacher, but nobody wants piano lessons these days. My father was an accountant."

"I can play the piano," said Yarrow.

"My sister can, too. You remind me of her, a bit."

"How?"

"Cheeky questions." He laughed at her.

"Why don't you play for us now," said Grandfather getting up slowly from the step.

"All right. I will."

Later, Yarrow wished she hadn't. She had fumbled all over the keyboard with the piece, her fingers never quite catching up with the speed she thought it should be played at, and she could sense Elliot's amusement as she valiantly tried to capture it. Her cheeks got redder and hotter until at the end she had slammed down the lid and stood up and said, "Well, you do better."

"No. I can't," he said. But when they went in for dinner, across the hall from the parlor, he whispered to her not to worry, that the really important thing was to try. "I like a girl with spunk," he said. And she looked at his dark eyes, with their naughty look, and wondered if there was anything that Elliot Weyden would pass up.

Yarrow's best friend at school was a red-haired girl called Mary-Ellen. Mary-Ellen went to dancing lessons and took piano. In Yarrow's life there was no spare money for such luxuries. But she and Mary-Ellen got on fine. It was Mary-Ellen who had taught her the rudiments of piano playing, and they spent many lunch hours at P.S. 1 in the practice room, with Yarrow warbling "Poor Wandering One" to Mary-Ellen's accompaniment.

Mary-Ellen was an eldest child, too. Her father was a doctor, and her family's front room, which served as the waiting room for her father's office, was always full of strangers—people with lumbago and neckbraces and warts. Mary-Ellen and Yarrow commiserated with each other at how hard their lives were. When Yarrow did not have to go to the *Journal* after school, she often went to Mary-Ellen's house on the other side of town. Mary-Ellen's mother was seldom at home; she went out to work. In the winter Mary-Ellen always cooked up a pan of chopped onions and tomatoes on the stove in the kitchen and they took bowls of it into her bedroom and talked. Mary-Ellen would put on one of her father's Victor records and leave the door open so they could hear the music. There was a new song out by Jerome Kern and Otto Harbach. The girls played "Smoke Gets in Your Eyes" over and over again.

"Isn't it romantic?" said Mary-Ellen as Yarrow leafed through one of the doctor's medical books. Mary-Ellen's house was full of books about the body, whereas *her* house was full of books about the mind.

"Oh, stop looking at those lurid drawings," said Mary-Ellen, grabbing an illustrated guide to venereal disease out of Yarrow's hands.

"But it's interesting," Yarrow wailed as the book was slammed shut.

At school Mrs. Turner's seventh grade, in which Yarrow and Mary-Ellen were prize pupils, was going to put on a play, Shaw's *Pygmalion*. Mary-Ellen, being talented, would play Eliza, and Yarrow, who had no acting talent at all, would help with the costumes, the lighting, the curtain and the program. Casting Professor Higgins was the problem. None of the boys who could play the part wanted to be in the play. In English period one day, Yarrow was caught passing a note to Mary-Ellen. "I know who Professor Higgins should be." She was reprimanded by a teacher substituting for Mrs. Turner, who was ill. Later, in a discussion of words with vowel combinations, the substitute teacher mentioned the word "duo," and so of course words like trio, quartet, quintet, sextet came up, and one wag asked what would you have if you had a group of more than six and Yarrow, who was bored, shouted out, "An orchestra," at which Mrs. Turner would have laughed, but Miss Coyle told her she was insolent. She was to stay in after school and write on the board one hundred times: "I must not be insolent to my teacher."

"But Tuesday's one of my days at the paper! Can't I do this another afternoon?"

But Miss Coyle would not hear of it. Mary-Ellen threw Yarrow an anguished glance as she left when the school bell rang.

Yarrow fumed as the clock hands dragged on. She thought of her father with his lock of hair falling forward over his glasses while he labored on the stone, and of Grandfather filling the ink bucket. Miss Coyle went on correcting books. Yarrow scrawled furiously on the board, squeaking the chalk as much as she could, until she heard a small sound and looked around and saw that Miss Coyle had left the room for a moment. Yarrow took her opportunity and climbed out the window and caught the bus into town.

She felt a little guilty as she puffed into the familiar messy office with the clickety-clack of the Linotype, and her father and grandfather pulling galleys, but she soon forgot because the phone began to ring and a Mrs. Peabody said she had some items for the social page.

The following day Yarrow was up in front of the headmaster and Mrs. McLean had been called in. When her mother asked her why she had done it, Yarrow looked at her with perplexity. "You know the paper comes first, Mama." The end result was that the play the girls had planned was postponed and Yarrow was given class chores to be done at recess for the next two weeks.

There was a metal swing in the garden, behind the plane tree in the backyard. It had an ugly wooden seat suspended on two chains from a tubular frame. It had been left by the previous owners of the house. But for Yarrow, in her fourteenth year, it was a chair to fantasy and dreams. The more she swung on the chair that summer, the dreamier she became; the higher she went, the more the ecstasy. She sang nonsense songs while she swung, going higher and higher, until, with her head dropped back, she could see the chains slacken at the very top, felt the sickening lurch as she began to lose her seat; then she threw her weight forward and returned to earth, where she hung, giddy, head down, toes dragging, until she felt the urge to go up again.

"What do you want to be when you grow up?" Elliot's question startled her. He was lying on the grass, his hands behind his head, while Yarrow swung. Her shadow kept crossing over him. He had a day off from the Corps. They were lifting the old streetcar tracks from Pike's Avenue. He rubbed his thumb tenderly along a blister. The sky was as clear as snowmelt in the mountains. Pikes Peak glistened above them. It was such a high mountain that one always expected it to be much nearer than it really was.

Yarrow was at the top of her swinging again, alternately pumping her legs and straightening them. She waited for the gratifying, death-defying lurch at the top, felt the seat slip from under her, and then threw her body forward and came down.

"I am going to be a lady, and have lots of babies and wear gloves." She was back on the ground, her toes scraping in the dusty circle worn under the swing.

Elliot laughed. "That's not an ambition. That's something you just do. I mean a real ambition, like after college, something you get paid for."

Yarrow's face reddened. She had only recently come around to thinking of her future in the terms her mother had explained. The acceptance of the inevability of it was the result of changes that were taking place in her body; the two bumps that had appeared on her chest, and the sudden swelling of her hips so that her elbows hit them when she was running. Her emotions fluctuated like the tide; she was always either high or low, never in-between, and when she thought at all about her future she saw it, too, as a life of extremes.

Elliot seemed to be waiting for an answer though his body hadn't moved. He was amazingly still today, she thought. He lay like a stick figure on the grass with his eyes shut and a book open, unread, on his chest.

"I might help Dad," she said, twisting the chains of the swing together as she turned in a circle. She watched the patterns her feet made in the dust. "But I still want to have babies and gloves and things." Yarrow lifted her feet and the swing rapidly unwound. "What about you, Elliot? What are you going to be?"

"Me?" said Elliot, opening his eyes and sitting up suddenly. "I'm going to go to college and then I am going to be very, very rich."

Yarrow kicked a cloud of dust toward him.

"You! You only earn a few dollars a week and you send all that to your mother. Grandfather told me. How are you going to get rich? You haven't even got a belt in your pants, just a bit of string."

Elliot only laughed, but his eyes flashed and she took it as a warning. "You'll see," he said. He looked so skinny sitting there, his knees and elbows all sharp angles under his clothing. All the Corps boys wore the same issued clothing, heavy woolen pants, work jackets and work boots. Elliot was so thin, though, that his pants wouldn't stay up and he had long ago sold his suspenders.

"I'll have a leather belt one day."

He was so quiet and sure of himself that she wanted to hurt him. She hated feeling dependent on his moods for her own.

"Yeah, I'm sure. How about a Studebaker that you can ride in instead of that stupid truck? It doesn't even belong to you."

"That too. I'll give you a ride in it one day."

He lay back down, and shut his eyes.

Yarrow got off her swing. She came over and looked down at him.

"How are you going to afford all these things?"

Elliot opened one eye and shot out his wrist and grabbed her ankle. He hurt her. "You bore me, little girl. Go inside and play with your dolls."

Yarrow wriggled and kicked and Elliot let go and closed his eye.

He was no fun when he was like this. Sometimes she did not know what he was thinking at all.

"Well, I'm going in," she said, as though she had made the decision.

Elliot lay still until she was gone. He sat up and looked at Pikes Peak above the back fence and then he got out a pencil stub and a small worn notebook from his pocket and opened it to a page, well creased by his thumbnail, and added to a long list of things:

One Leather belt. Brown

He licked his pencil and thought for a minute and then wrote neatly under it:

One Studebaker. LARGE.

Then he looked through the book at the other entries he had made—the money he sent to his mother in Hudson, and the timetable he had written for his future, and the books he wanted to read. And then he put the notebook carefully back into his shirt pocket and buttoned it in. And then he got up and went to the house next door, where the widow had promised him a dollar-fifty if he chopped and stacked some wood for her, so that when Yarrow came out to ask if he wanted some supper, he had already gone.

The week that Yarrow became a woman, she was sitting at the front desk on a slow day when a tramp came in and asked if he could place a classified ad. Yarrow gave him the form to be filled out and he sat on the wooden bench against the window with last week's newspaper on his lap. He seemed to be taking a long time about it, and Yarrow thought nothing of it until she got up and looked over the counter and saw what she thought was a rubber truncheon in his hand and the newspaper on the floor. Yarrow couldn't think what it was until she remembered what Mary-Ellen had once told her about dirty old men and their things. And as she stared, dumbstruck for once, Grandfather came over from the stone, rubbing his back, and took in the situation at once. Grandfather was galvanized and, with a roar that might have been Gaelic, chased the tramp out of the office, brandishing a galley tray in his right hand. It seemed peculiar to Yarrow that such a thing would happen the very week her menses began, as though men knew she had become a woman. And in truth, Yarrow was changing, though she could not see it.

CHAPTER 6

*S*INCE ERIC'S BIRTH, FREYA HAD GROWN STOUT. IT DID NOT WORRY her because vanity was no longer part of her makeup. There had been a time, before Harold's death, when she had thought a lot about her body and her hair. When they had first moved to Platte City, and she had seen the young women with their crisp, shaky haircuts, she had musingly suggested that she might crop her own. Her hair, thick and the color of honey, wound in braids around her head. James had dropped his newspaper and looked at her over the top of his glasses and said, "Over my dead body." She had looked at Yarrow and laughed and said, "Anyone would think it was his hair we were talking about." But she never did cut it, and Yarrow wondered if perhaps her mother's hair did belong to her father.

Once or twice James teased Freya about her increasing size, but Freya shrugged it off and said she was just a big woman and that she felt good. Indeed she did; her size gave her strength; her energy was unflagging in the care which she lavished on her children, her household and her causes. An observer might have suggested that more time be spent on her husband. But it was as though in losing one son and giving him another, she was off the hook. The guilt that James had once expressed at the death of Harold, she accepted by acquiescence. Freya allowed her body to relax; she bought a larger size of dress, then another. Her love for James became motherly fondness and tolerance; the nights in the matrimonial bed were seldom spent now in the joining of their two bodies, but more often avoided by the feeble affection she offered him with her big, smooth haunches as she turned away.

Freya's lack of vanity was matched by a sense of universal love, and together these two traits of her character were like blinkers on a horse. The more she looked around to see what she could do to help others, the less she saw what was right in front of her.

"James's cronies," as she called his friends, arrived at all hours of the day and night, for meals or refreshments, or just to talk. Freya's work for the PTA or the Children's Hospital fund-raising committee invariably found her sitting at the table in the dining room or, less formally, in the kitchen, or sometimes even in her bedroom, talking to other women, while she breast-fed Eric. Sometimes there was nowhere else for people to sit. James complained that the boy was too old to be breast-fed anymore, but Freya, knowing he was her last, said that she enjoyed it. And she did, even when his teeth came in and he bit her. She just winced and then laughed and wiped the cookie crumbs off the dark areola around her nipple, and put the boy down and went on with what she was doing.

But James was also to blame for the way their lives had begun to diverge. His natural taciturnity increased. As an editor, his silence enabled him to listen; as a father, it increased his distance from his family. The *Journal* absorbed him. As he struggled to keep his paper solvent, he dreamed of expanding. He kept up-to-date with the latest advances by reading about printing presses and type machines offered to big metropolitan newspapers. He wrote the editorials and most of the copy and took over from the Linotype machinist when the man was sick. He did the proofreading, and collected the ads, and bought the paper and the ink, and did his figures late at night and fell into bed at night beside Freya and was asleep before she put out the light.

They were like two streams that had begun to take different but parallel courses. Yarrow noticed these divergences but in her mind she saw the strip of land between them as the Continental Divide. She worried that her parents would part and confided her fears in Nellie. Nellie told Freya, and Freya just hooted with laughter.

Freya and James became more and more involved in the community. James, in spite of himself, was part of the Platte City establishment. Although he tried to maintain a distance from the politicians and the members of the chamber of commerce, he was unable to avoid the ropes that a small town lassoes around its citizens. He found, as Jock had before him, that it was concomitant for a newspaper owner to be a part of a town's life. Through his paper he urged the putting down of roots, the binding together of immigrants. As the Depression receded, he encouraged the spurt toward prosperity and growth and civic pride; these things meant schools and hospitals and churches and an art gallery and a concert hall. They were all signs of the town's sinews and without them there would be no town, no community, no business, no newspaper.

One day James took a call in the office. Yarrow was typing a story that afternoon.

"Morty, what can I do for you?" Morty was a friend, a member of the local council.

"James," Morty's voice cracked. "It's my boy. He's been arrested for that hit-and-run accident last night."

"Morty, I'm sorry." James knew what was coming. His stomach wrenched.

"James, I'll only ask you for one thing. Don't print the story." Morty's voice broke again. "It'll kill my mother. She thinks the world of my boy. Please."

James closed his eyes and squeezed his temples with his fingers so hard that he made a deep crease.

"Morty," he said, his voice soft, "I can't promise you that."

There was a pause and then the phone clicked. Yarrow went on with her typing.

The story ran. It was a big story for a little town where everyone knew everyone else. Ever after, the man and his family cut the McLeans wherever they met. Freya was very hurt. Nellie was cross. All the children in her class had been invited to a party for another one of Morty's children. Nellie was not on the invitation list. James explained to his family that it was a price they must learn to pay if they were to call themselves newspaper people.

"But who was right?" said Yarrow.

"No one," said her father.

James's most pressing problem was to raise the circulation of the *Journal*. The *Journal* and the *Record* were neck-and-neck as far as circulation went. The citizenry watched the two snapping at each other's heels. One day the *Record* was ahead, next day the *Journal*. Down the straight on Monday came the two contenders: A mistake of the jockey here and the *Journal* lost a stride, a slipped stirrup and there went the other. By Friday both horses were back in their stables, readying themselves for Monday's start.

Jock still couldn't work out how Max kept the *Record* going. But Max had always been clever with money, and somehow the paper kept appearing every day against theirs. James redoubled his efforts to help his newspaper as the economy of the town staggered out of the worst years of the Depression. He brought home editors and visitors from out of town and advertisers he hoped to woo.

Just as the children seeped out of the rooms, so James's business seeped out of the office and drowned his home life. He would bring the visitors home for one of Freya's imaginative lunches of smoked fish with potatoes and onions or dumplings with dill sauce and very little meat; and Freya would pat the crying woman who had come in for coffee and comfort because of an erring husband or a child in trouble, would pat her on the shoulder and say, "I'll be right back." Freya would go downstairs and serve up plates full of food with one hand and direct Laura with the other, and pour out some beer and then return to her own waiting constituent. And while she was talking or listening, her hands were never still and she would pick up a sweater she was knitting for an orphan or a balaclava for a homeless man, or take up the weaving hanging from the bedroom doorknob that was going to be a belt or a headband, and say, "Now go on. Where were we?"

At times it was all too much for Yarrow, who needed a space for herself and who earmarked a number of nooks around the house where she could hide. One day, when Laura was springcleaning her room and shooed her out, and Freya had taken over the bench in the garden and her father was in the parlor finishing a business meeting, and Elliot was hanging around playing with Eric and waiting to talk to Lem in his upstairs box room, and Nellie and Greta had sleepovers who were running through the house whooping, and Grandfather had gone to lie down in the quiet of his own room, all Yarrow wanted was a place to read her library book—a novel, *The Passionate Embrace*, by Philomena Smart. She took the comforter from her own bed and with her book, propped herself up on the window seat behind the curtains in her parents' bedroom. She tucked the ends of the eiderdown tight around her and entered her own world.

She had just shut out the sounds of the household around her when she heard the bedroom door open. She shrank back against the wall in case her hiding place was discovered, for she thought it was probably Greta, who had been calling for her all over the house. But when she heard the telephone being used she realized it was not Greta, for none of them were allowed to use the telephone. She was just about to pull back the curtain when she heard her father's voice and something about the way in which he spoke, a stealth in the tone that she had never heard before, caused her to pause, and she heard him ask for Mrs. Truitt and then a silence, and then his voice, soft as a sigh. "Fabiana," he said.

Yarrow froze in her hiding place and thought he must hear the blood pounding in her ears. It was too late for her to reveal herself. She sat on her knees, staring at the reverse pattern of the curtains, as she listened to her father say quietly, yes, he had sent her what she asked for. No, he would not be late. Well, she could come out here if she wanted, but he did not think that would be worthwhile. No, he couldn't come to New York. Did she know how much a train ticket cost? He laughed softly—a youthful sound that sent a surge of jealousy through Yarrow. Her father was flattered at something Fabiana had said. Yarrow heard her father sigh and the phone click. And then she heard the door close, and she practically fell from the window seat as pins and needles attacked her legs, and she rubbed them as she sat on the carpet and thought that her father must be having an affair with Fabiana. He must be, what else could it mean? Yarrow stared at the cover of the romance she was reading. But with Fabiana, with that ugly scar? How had she ever thought she was beautiful? Yarrow threw the book across the room and thought how tame it was when compared with the real thing.

When she was sure her father had gone she came out of the room and bumped into Elliot with Eric on his shoulders.

"What's the matter?" he said. Her curly hair was all disheveled and her face was white. "What is it?" he asked. Just then Yarrow's mother came in downstairs, and at the sound of her voice Yarrow burst into tears and Elliot put his arms around her, though Eric's fat legs got in the way, and hush, hushed her, which only made it worse.

"Racing Patience is a misnomer," said Grandfather as he put down his pen and watched Elliot and the girls shuffling their cards.

"Go," said Elliot and they began to lay out their cards on the floor, snapping them down in rows. Elliot knelt on one knee, as though he were ready to take off on a sprint if necessary. Nellie sat cross-legged and Greta lay on her stomach. Yarrow sat up on both knees and slapped a two of diamonds on an ace that Elliot put down.

"I didn't see it," said Nellie, too late with her own.

Yarrow and Elliot shuffled through their cards fast; one two three, snap, one two three, snap.

"Don't bend the cards," said Greta, tossing back her blond hair over her shoulder.

"Sssh," said Yarrow.

Elliot's hands flew over the cards. Yarrow watched his cards, her cards; she had a jack, queen, king of hearts, and then suddenly he put up a ten of hearts, and Yarrow jumped off her knees and used both her hands to place her cards on the hearts pile. But Elliot was even quicker and slapped down his king underneath her fingers.

"You cheated," said Yarrow.

Elliot was laughing hard as Yarrow tried to wriggle her card underneath his.

"You did. You did."

Elliot couldn't stop laughing. He lay down flat on the cards, holding down the king while Yarrow tried to pry off his fingers.

"Oh, they never play properly," said Nellie, looking at the disarray and throwing her own cards down. Greta had already given up. Yarrow began to tickle Elliot under the armpits to make him move his hand.

"Truce. Truce," he begged.

"Did I win? Did I win?"

"Yes!" His legs shot out in a final spasm and he nearly kicked over the table at which Grandfather was writing.

Grandfather picked up the sheet of notepaper. "And here I am writing this person what a fine upstanding, *mature* young man you are."

Yarrow let go. Elliot sat up, his face red.

"I had it up my sleeve."

Yarrow laughed and pulled her hair ribbon off to redo her hair.

"I knew it. You hate to lose, you cheat."

"It takes one to know one," said Nellie.

"At least I don't tell tales," said Yarrow to her sister.

"Remind me one day to teach you how to play poker," said Grandfather, picking up his pen again.

Yarrow and Elliot found it impossible not to argue. When they argued he would become excessively polite and it exasperated Yarrow when he put on his airs.

"You're only a few years older than me."

"I'm nineteen. I'm a man—you're still a little girl."

"I'm fourteen and a half."

"Then why are you so prickly? I only said that I thought Greta suffers from anxiety."

"Anxiety. What do you know about it? Just because she played hookey from school . . ."

"You're like a picket fence."

"What?"

"A picket fence. Up it comes the moment you think anyone is criticizing your family. You want to keep them all in behind it where you're all safe."

"What's wrong with that? If I want to criticize, I will. You have no right. I will defend my family till the end."

"I wouldn't hurt your family. You've been too good to me but you have to see that Greta seems somewhat—well, lost. All the rest of you are so busy and she wafts about because no one has time to see that she needs help."

"You see? You admit it. You are criticizing her."

"I am not criticizing her. I merely wanted to have a grown-up conversation with you about Greta's avoidance of things."

The picket-fence barb had hurt Yarrow. She imagined herself like one of those naked men in cartoons who wear a barrel suspended from their shoulders by a strap—except in her case the picket fence hung down.

Another time, in the kitchen, when Yarrow was helping Laura with the dinner, Elliot arrived unexpectedly and took off the lid of a pot of stew on the stove.

"What is this?" he asked. "Mystery meat?"

Yarrow flew at him with both hands.

"How dare you," she cried.

He apologized, surprised by her fierceness. "I only meant it as a joke."

But his hackles were just as easy to raise. He, too, would put up barricades when people got too close. Yarrow loved to probe at him and he would become very abrupt. He could not take jokes or teasing about his own ambitions. At first he would laugh, then the little flash would go off in his eyes as a warning. She waited until they were once again in one of their many squabbles and she shot at him.

"You're like an umbrella."

"Yarrow," said Freya, who was listening to them.

"You carry it all furled up until someone gets close, and then, pow, out comes the umbrella and we have to duck to avoid being jabbed by the spokes."

Elliot was embarrassed. The analogy to his own anatomy was too accurate. She was just a child and had no idea what she was saying. He blushed when she kept calling him "Umbrella Head," and Grandfather finally had to intervene and take Yarrow aside one day and explain why she couldn't keep calling him that. It was now Yarrow's turn to be mortified and she avoided Elliot for the next two weeks, always finding an excuse not to be in the house when he called.

*   *   *

At the end of the summer Freya suddenly declared that if she
didn't get up into the mountains and breathe in some fresh air
she would die. It had been a very dusty summer and much as
James wanted to go with her, he could not get away. He and
Grandfather would stay, but he insisted that Elliot should go with
Freya and the children in case of trouble. He arranged with Lem
for Elliot's departure and the family set off in the old Chrysler
jammed with camping equipment and enough food for a small army.

They drove over Independence Pass and down into the valley
of Galena. All the way Freya and the children told Elliot stories
about the old days, and about the silver mining and the *Gazette*
and Mollie McLean who died giving birth to Yarrow's father.
They took Laura to her parents' house, and while Freya went in
for a social visit Yarrow showed Elliot their old house and
wandered through the remains of the town and borrowed the key
to the old *Gazette* office.

"It's kind of sad," he said when they went into the dusty,
musky interior where the smell of ink still assailed the nostrils.

"I like it," said Yarrow, sitting on the stone and swinging her
legs. "I feel it's part of me."

Elliot looked at her there with her proud, defiant hair bursting
back from her forehead; her hair was the color of ink, her skin
the color of paper.

"I wish I'd been with Grandfather when he came here. I wish
it had been me and not Mollie who knew this place when it was
all beginning."

He came over and took up her hand. She had little short nails
and soft fingers. She took her hand away but their eyes held.

She jumped down from the table.

"Mama will be wondering where we are."

Later that day they drove up to the cabin and unpacked. It was
too nice to be indoors, so they camped under the stars. Elliot
started a fire and they roasted marshmallows on the ends of
sticks and burned their tongues eating them. After supper, while
the children lay in their sleeping bags, Freya told them another
story.

"There was once a goddess who was turned into a tree
because she had done a very bad thing. She stood in the center of
a clearing in the forest with her arms permanently held high, for
this was her punishment for breaking her word. After many years
an owl came to live in her branches. He was a beautiful bird and
he grew to be two feet high and day after day he would sit in her
branches asleep and at night he would hunt for mice and other

rodents and bring them back in his great black talons and eat them in among her leaves. And while he was eating she would tell him her life story and he in return would tell her what he had seen on his flights. One day a pair of young lovers were walking through the forest and they came to this magnificent tree which was the goddess and they sat beneath it and she heard all their words of love and promise to each other and she tried to tell them to beware but her words only came out like the sighing of her branches and the owl told her to hush and that sounded like a 'huu-huu.' ''

All the children made a sound like ''huu-huu'' in the dark.

''The tree begged the owl to follow the young couple to see what would befall them and the owl left and did not return. When he had been gone three months she asked the wind if he had heard him, but the answer was no. Another three months passed and she asked the Moon if he had seen her friend, but the Moon replied that he saw a lot of owls and how could he know one from the other? In the ninth month she asked a passing eagle if he had seen the owl. When he said no, she despaired and that night a great storm came and she was so lonely that she invited the lightning to join her, which he did and she was split asunder. The next morning the owl came back. He had traveled far and wide and he had come back too late. While he looked for his friend a long white ribbon from a baby's shoe dropped from his talons. It fell a long, long, long way down from the sky. You can still see the memory of the ribbon in the cirrus clouds over the mountains.''

''That's so sad, Mama,'' said Yarrow. ''Is it one of the stories your father told you?''

''No,'' said Freya. ''I just made it up.''

Yarrow turned over in her sleeping bag. She looked at Elliot lying a foot away in his. His eyes were shut and his hand lay out on the grass, curled and defenseless. A great wave of tenderness swept over Yarrow as she looked at him. Perhaps it was the result of her mother's story. Perhaps it was because he had held her hand that day and she remembered how nice it felt. She realized now that he had been offering comfort. And what had she done? She had pulled her hand away when at the time she had thought his hand was the warmest thing in the world. She thought about her father and mother; how James would sometimes come into the kitchen while her mother was at the sink or the stove and put his arms around her, and how Freya would shrug him off or move away, or glance, embarrassed, at the children. Yarrow saw her father's face and the way he would drop his arms and go out. Elliot sighed in his sleep and Yarrow crept her fingers across the grass toward his hand. She was going to place his hand back under his cover to keep him warm. She touched his wrist and felt the pulse—how delicate it was—and then placed her fingers in his palm. His fingers gently closed around hers and she looked at his face in the firelight and his eyes were open. He smiled and Yarrow felt her heart jump, but she didn't pull her hand away and soon she closed her eyes and went to sleep and felt the clotted stars of the sky gently tumbling down on her like snowflakes on a blanket.

In the days that followed it seemed to Yarrow that she was living in a dream. The weather was warm and sunny and the high country exuded a mist that tinged everything, the horizon, the trees, the very rocks, with a brush that softened all edges. She and Elliot and the children ran through meadows of head-high cow parsley. The thick fibrous stems bent beneath them. When they fell, out of breath and dizzy with the sun and the sweetness of the air, they listened to the sound of birds, saw the wheeling hawks in the sky, found in the shadows underneath the grass, nodding heads of pale rye, deep blue monkshood and harebells, mauve larkspur and lupine.

One day, among the yellow-orange asters and rudbeckia, Elliot said, "I love you." Yarrow saw only that the flower of the rudbeckia hung its petals like a skirt while its cone reached for the sky.

"I love you," he said.

"How can you say that?" She laughed at him.

"I just know it," he said, lying back with his hands behind his head. She tickled his throat with a stem of rye. He got up on one elbow. "You'll have to wait for me. You know I have to leave."

"Why?"

"There are things I have to do. Besides, you're too young. You'll be grown when I come back."

"I'm nearly fifteen."

He tried to touch her cheek, but she jumped up and then she began to laugh and spin away from him like a top through the cow parsley.

Freya was reading to Eric on a blanket back in camp. She leaned against a treetrunk and watched her daughter and Elliot come running back through the meadow. Nellie and Greta were nowhere to be seen. She saw Elliot catch Yarrow and spin her around to him and she saw her daughter's long black hair, released from its ribbon, swinging like a curtain. Freya saw Elliot's face. Yarrow was growing up, she thought, but not as fast as Elliot would have liked. Freya decided to talk to Jock about keeping Elliot more occupied back in Platte City. That night she placed her own sleeping bag on the ground between them.

"Mr. McLean! Mr. McLean!"

Elliot came running into the newspaper office with his jacket flying and his cheeks red. Yarrow looked up. For all the promises of the summer, she had hardly seen Elliot since their return. At first she was puzzled and hurt, and then she was angry and haughty. She heard that Elliot had begun going to the dances that were held in the Salvation Army Hall. Well, she thought, two could play the same game.

It was late fall and the city had already had its first blizzard. Banks of snow were piled up against the office windows and the lights were on, though it was still early in the day. Yarrow's father looked up from his typewriter, his thoughts scattered by the intrusion. Since the summer, circulation and advertising had been improving. His paper was beginning to make a small profit and he hadn't fallen behind in his payments to Fabiana Truitt either. An ominous silence from New York had replaced the previous barrage of letters. In a way he was relieved at the silence.

He was also relieved by the small signs of prosperity he saw emerging in the town—the fragile bones of a new building going up near the old trolley depot, the opening of a ladies' hat shop next to the bakery—and the boys had stopped coming off the freight train. These signs encouraged him to publish a sixteen-page edition on Fridays, which meant printing in two sections and then calling in the family to hand-insert the pages. He had taken on a full-time flyboy, who helped load and unload the press, and he had agreed to let Elliot try his hand at soliciting for ads. Elliot seemed to spend more time out of camp than in. James wondered what stories Elliot told his officers.

"Well, what is it this time?"

Yarrow was clipping and gluing news items for the file at a second desk in her father's office. There was no deadline to meet and it was very quiet in the office. Even Grandfather had given the last squirt of his grease gun into the bushings of the Comet, and gone home to rest. Yarrow clipped a story about a woman who had grown a potato head that looked just like Mrs. Roosevelt.

"Boy, do I have some news," said Elliot, throwing a battered briefcase on James's desk.

Yarrow's father put out his hands to save his copy.

"Have you sold some advertising, Elliot?"

"Yes and no. I was at the lumberyard picking up some copy for tomorrow's paper and there was a guy there buying some piping. I got talking to him, and, Mr. McLean, the guy's a genius. He can make attachments for machinery. He's worked in New York and Chicago and he knows all about Goss presses." Elliot waved his arm in the direction of the floor-mounted Comet. It dominated the outer room and weighed over sixteen thousand pounds. It gleamed powerfully at them through its thirty years of ink and oil.

"What about it?" asked James, his eyes flickering with interest at Elliot's enthusiasm. Elliot opened his briefcase and pulled out some sheets covered with penciled diagrams.

"Look. It's so simple." He came around the desk so fast that he caught his pocket on a drawer handle. Yarrow came over and looked over her father's shoulder.

"You have two problems with this press as I see it. I'm no engineer but I've watched you. You need to print the paper faster to get it out on the street. Your circulation is going up. The Comet is slow. You have to slow it down further to change the reels."

Elliot was right. To change the reels, without losing too much time, the tail end of one reel was used to pull the new one through. Her father would tear off the cardboard core of the expiring reel, mount the new roll on the shaft and plaster a handful of grease on the paper from the grease bucket. The grease worked as an adhesive to pull through the new web of paper.

Elliot's friend had drawn a fair rendering of the Comet, and on the end where the shaft for the heavy newsprint reel was attached, he had designed an iron stand that held three reels at once. The reels could be rotated as the current web ran out.

"What do you think?"

James leaned back in his chair so that the casters swiveled.

"It's not an original idea, Elliot. And it's too big for our needs. This is more suited for a large metropolitan paper than the *Journal*."

"But the idea is sound, isn't it?"

"The idea's sound all right. But it's just not right for us."

Elliot shuffled his papers, nonplussed. His enthusiasm was seldom shaken.

"Plan B," he said, pulling out another sheet of paper.

James laughed.

"OK. Plan B. Folding. If ever you needed anything in this office it's a folding attachment. We spent six hours last week folding the paper and inserting the sections. That's three hours slower than the *Record*. With this, we'll beat them on the streets."

Elliot paused, watching James's face.

"Go on."

"We get a folding attachment."

"Elliot, I can't afford a folding attachment."

"You can. I found one. My friend says there's one available from the *Golden Republican*. Defunct since last Saturday. He has seen it and he can adapt it to the Comet."

"How much?"

"Name your price. It's just sitting there unused. Our costs would mostly be transporting it from Golden to here. Interested?"

"I'm interested," said James, pushing his chair forward again to the desk.

"Plus a small commission for my friend and me."

"Your commission?" said Yarrow, looking at the rough sketches and realizing what a bonus it would be to her father if they could have it.

"Elliot, it's out of the question," said James, putting some more paper in his typewriter.

"No. Listen." Elliot put his hand over the platen so James couldn't type, and began spilling out figures and facts, speed and costs. Yarrow listened in amazement. She had worked for her father and grandfather since she was baby. Ink really was in her blood, and here was Elliot, in and out of the office for the past two years, absorbing technicalities she had not been aware of. She looked at him and saw that the hairs of his eyebrows fanned out where they met his nose. She blushed when she realized how closely she was observing him, but Elliot didn't seem to notice.

"Mr. McLean," he was saying, "it's a bargain. An opportunity that you cannot afford to let pass. You know the *Record* is cutting its ad rates around town?"

"How do you know that?"

"It's all around. Everywhere I go to sell an ad, the *Record* comes in after me and undercuts us. They're running scared, Mr. McLean, and if we can beat them with our deadline, they'll be out of this town within the year. You can't afford not to have a folder. Now this one, my friend says, only needs an angle bar to adapt it to the press. He says the foundry . . ."

"OK. OK. I'll talk to your friend. And you find out how much this will really cost."

"And five percent?"

"Let's see what the cost is first."

"Two-and-a-half on agreement and the other two-and-a-half when we get it working."

"Elliot, just let me talk to the man."

"Deal."

Elliot grabbed his briefcase and wound his scarf around his throat.

"You're looking very pretty, Yarrow," he said, his dark eyes twinkling.

"Oh, really," she said, cool as could be.

He was already halfway out the office, his jacket flying when James shouted after him, "I only said I would talk to the man."

Elliot waved at them through the window, his eyes bright and glittering above the banked snow.

"He always said he was going to be rich," said Yarrow.

"Yes, but not through me, I hope." James shook his head and peered over his glasses at her. "I don't think this town's going to be big enough for him."

Yarrow blushed as she caught her father's gaze. "No, I guess not." She went back to her desk and picked up the scissors.

Her father's voice softened. "Do you mind, honey?"

"Of course I don't mind. I wish you would get it out of your head that I've got a crush on him or something."

"Oh."

Yarrow began clipping and pasting furiously. Her father's typing soon resumed and she mumbled, "I'm going out with Sandy Heartland."

"What's that, honey?"

She shouted, "I'm going out with Sandy Heartland." Yarrow pushed back a strand of thick black hair. How could her father be so stupid?

Sandy Heartland was a senior at Platte High and his sister, Anita, was a sophomore with Yarrow. Anita and Yarrow, along with Mary-Ellen, were honors students and took some advanced-placement classes together. Yarrow had met Anita's brother at their house when she was over there studying for an exam.

Sandy had just got his driver's license, and his father, once in a while, under a great deal of flattery and cajolery, would allow his only son to drive his car. It was a beat-up old Buick that spent most of its time in winter in the garage. Sandy had asked Yarrow if she would come with him to a matinee and see the new movie in town, The Marx Brothers in *A Day at the Races*. Freya said she could, providing Nellie went with them.

Greta was at the front-parlor window watching for Sandy to

arrive. This was Yarrow's first date and for all Greta's excitement one would have thought it was her own. Greta heard the car first, roaring as though its muffler were loose.

"Your boyfriend's here," she hollered.

As usual, Yarrow had left it too late to get ready. She was in the kitchen with her brother on her hip, talking to her mother. Eric had his fingers in her hair.

"Ma, what will I wear?"

"You look very nice to me, dear, as you are. Put Eric down, he's much too big to be carried now."

"I can't go out in this! In a Buick!"

Her mother went on chopping vegetables.

"I don't see why not. Please just comb your hair, Yarrow. It always looks so untidy."

Greta shouted, "He's reversing the car in front."

"Ma!" wailed Yarrow, bouncing Eric from one hip to the other. He grabbed another handful of hair.

"Well, the red dress then."

"The hem's down."

"Then just put on a clean blouse."

"What blouse?"

"The blue one."

"I hate that. The buttons pop open." Eric stuck his fingers in her ears. Yarrow kissed his face in five different places so he giggled. "Again," he said. He was very slow to talk and "again" was his favorite word. Greta came running into the kitchen as though she were trying to hide. "He's here! He's here!"

"Control yourself, child," said Nellie, coming down the back stairs into the kitchen. Nellie had all the superiority of her twelve long years. She loved being the chaperone for Yarrow's first date. "Ma?"

"Well, borrow my lace blouse if you want, but don't spill any soda on it."

"Oh, thank you, Ma. Here, Nellie, take Eric. He weighs a ton." Eric moved like a large limpet from one sister to another. The doorbell rang. Freya wiped her hands on her apron and took it off. Yarrow bounded up the back stairs and shouted from the top, "And Nellie, none of those terrible stories or I'll pluck your eyes out."

Freya and the children trooped to the front door to welcome Sandy Heartland. He was very tall with a broad, fair face, a straight nose and a cleft in his chin. He was on the wrestling team at school, playing at 168, was the quarterback on the varsity football team, and held the school record for the five-hundred-yard swimming relay. Everyone said he was going to win an athletic scholarship to college. Grandfather insisted, however, when he had seen him once at the school, that there was something wrong with his eyes; they were too close together. Freya said Grandfather would find fault with Apollo if he came courting Yarrow. Sandy had soft blond hair that fell over his forehead. There was not a curl in it anywhere, and to Yarrow, who spent hours brushing the knots out of her own curly black mane, it was one of his most attractive qualities.

Sandy shook hands formally with Freya and his hair flopped forward and he pushed it back. The three children sat in the parlor and looked at him while their mother went to get him a glass of juice. Nellie spoke first.

"My sister," she said, "is actually bald. Quite, quite bald. Don't be fooled by all that hair."

"Nellie, that's not true," said Greta.

"It's very sad. She had to take medicine and all her hair fell out." Nellie had been reading one of the medical books that Yarrow brought back from Mary-Ellen's. Greta tried to kick Nellie's ankles but she swung her legs out of the way.

"She normally wears a turban at home but when she goes out she wears a wig."

Sandy Heartland ran a finger around his collar. "How interesting."

"Have you met our Cousin Clara?"

"No."

"Well, she is really bald. I mean, perhaps it runs in the family."

Nellie touched her own glossy dark bangs and got up to look in the mirror to reassure herself. Greta spoke up, "Cousin Clara hates Hitler."

"She's a pacifist," said Nellie, who had had to look up the word when she first heard it. "I'm a pacifist, too."

Freya came back into the room with the juice.

"Are the children being a nuisance, Sandy?"

"Oh, no, very interesting." He gulped down his drink.

"I heard you mention Cousin Clara."

"She's a Baptist."

"No. A Quaker," corrected Freya. "She's a very determined woman and she wants to enter Congress."

Yarrow came into the room in her mother's lace blouse and her hair pinned back from her forehead. Her cheeks glowed with excitement. She looked so like the old portrait of Mollie that Freya blinked. "How nice you look, dear," she said.

"Ma, we must go," said Yarrow, struggling into her coat and throwing Nellie's at her. "Come on, Sandy, or we'll be late for the feature." Her tone was so determined that Sandy jumped up from his seat. He towered over her. Freya thought that although Yarrow might look fragile like Mollie, she had all of her Cousin Clara's strength. Yarrow was well named.

"We won't be late, Ma," said Yarrow as Nellie skipped past her through the door.

"Oh, that reminds me," said Freya, getting to her feet. "Will you drop by the office and tell Dad and your grandfather that we'll wait for them for dinner, so not to be too late?"

"Are they working late? There's no paper tomorrow."

"He's got some new bee in his bonnet for the presses. A folder or something and there's a man working on it tonight."

Yarrow burst out laughing as they ran for the car. It was a clear night but very cold and when she got in the car, with Nellie squeezed in between them, she took out a beret from her pocket and put it on. She felt a tug on her hair.

"Ouch! Sandy?"

"Just checking." He grinned. He made a face at Nellie who shrank into her coat and pulled up the collar.

"Nellie! What have you been saying? Oh, I'll kill you, I really will, one of these days."

A month later Elliot Weyden came to say good-bye. He had been in Colorado more than two years, and for most of that time he had been a part of the McLean household. Freya had accepted him as an older son. It was not that he was particularly useful, but he was nice to have around. Since Jock had spoken to him about Yarrow's youth, he had not come over as often, but when he did, he never arrived without a present. He liked women, he understood them, and would bring a little gift, some wildflowers from the roadside for Freya or a ribbon for Laura that he had bought from a peddler. ("Or traded, if I know him," said Laura.) He loved being with the children and would squeeze and hug Eric and throw him in the air when he thought no one was looking. Freya watched him the last day as she sat in her bedroom writing thank-you letters for a bake sale that had raised money for a scoreboard for the school gym. He was sitting on the floor with Eric trying to teach him to read. Eric smiled when Elliot squeezed his lips into the shape of the words. Eric thought it was all a new game.

"When do you think he'll speak?"

"I don't know," said Freya, dashing off another signature.

"The doctor says he's fine, his hearing's fine and everything, but he just won't talk. Will you, you naughty boy?"

Eric said, "Again," and moved Elliot's fingers back onto his cheeks.

"My mother said all boys start speaking later than girls, at least I did anyway, much later than my sister, Vivienne." Eric had curled into Elliot's thigh as though it were a pillow. He sucked his thumb just the way Yarrow used to. "Don't do that," said Freya, and he took his thumb out.

"What's your mother like, Elliot?"

"My mother? Oh, she's dark-haired. She looks very young for her age. She could have been a concert pianist, she says, if she hadn't had us. She says she married beneath herself when she married my father."

"She says that?" Freya stopped writing for a moment to wipe Eric's nose. Elliot looked down at the curly blond head.

"I'll make it up to her though. It's been tough for her, not having nice things and then Dad dying. He left a lot of debts."

"Jock says he's going to help you get a job back east. You're not interested in newspapers, though, are you?"

"No. I've really liked working at the *Journal*, but even Mr. McLean knows I'm not cut out for journalism. I'd be better in accounting or sales or something like that. Mr. McLean says he'll write to his friends at the *Herald* and AP, see what they have in one of those departments. But he doesn't guarantee anything. He says the *Detroit Free Press* used to give good young staff men a university course. If that doesn't come off, I'll find another way." Elliot watched Freya licking the envelopes.

"Can I tell you something, Mrs. McLean? I don't think there's anything in the world that's going to stop me from getting what I want. I don't mean it to sound—arrogant. I can't explain it, but I feel I can achieve whatever I set out to achieve, if I'm willing to work for it. Could you explain that to Yarrow?"

Freya looked at the thin young man, at the fine hands with the callused fingers that stroked her sleeping son's head. He had changed since she had first known him. He had put on some weight. His skin was a better color. But something else about him had changed, too. He had firmed up inside. He had come knowing what he wanted; now he seemed to know how to get it.

She looked at Elliot Weyden with his brown hair, which still showed a wave despite the short cut, at his jaw and lips, very determined, particularly now when he spoke about his plans. His dark eyes were brooding right now. They were always either mischievous or brooding; there was no in-between. It would be like that with people, she thought in a flash. People would either like Elliot Weyden, or be his enemy. There would be no luke-warm friends. Freya had such a clear vision of his future—not what it contained, but that it would be successful—that she was startled. Elliot laughed when he realized how intently she was looking at him. It was a deprecating laugh, but Freya didn't smile back.

"My God," she said, "you're going to do it."

On the way to the railroad station, Elliot dropped by the office to say farewell to James and Jock. He hoped Yarrow would be there. They had had another one of their ridiculous tiffs yesterday. This time about her father and Fabiana Truitt. Elliot had given Yarrow a small black rabbit for her fifteenth birthday. He had wanted to tell her it reminded him of her hair, but the summer was too painful for either of them to mention. Elliot had been scared off by a firm talk from Jock. Yarrow was so young, Jock had said. It was not right for a nineteen-year-old man to spend so much time with her. Elliot had agreed. The last thing in the world he wanted to do was upset the McLeans. He would come back for Yarrow, he knew that. But now she wouldn't give him the time of day. Besides, what did a fifteen-year-old know about waiting? When he gave Yarrow the rabbit, he was unsure how she would receive it because she had been as cold as ice whenever he came to the house. But the softness of the rabbit unfroze her, and she had blurted out her fears. All the little things that she had stored up for a year, imagined slights from her father to her mother, their coolness and independence from each other. Oh, she hated Fabiana Truitt for what she had done.

"But this, this telephone call happened over a year ago and besides it's, it's preposterous," said Elliot, who of course could not imagine passion in anyone over forty years of age. (James, he knew, was forty-five.)

"Will you please stop stuttering?"

Elliot began to laugh. "You think they're having a love affair because he made a private call from the bedroom . . . ?"

Yarrow's expression froze. He could almost see the hair on her head stiffening, but he couldn't stop.

". . . That he doesn't love your mother anymore?"

Yarrow wished she had never spoken about it. He was not taking it seriously. All her doubts and fears about her own sexuality were mixed up with her feelings about Fabiana Truitt and her father. She remembered when she was a little girl how she had loved the smell of Fabiana's perfume, and admired her clothes and fallen under her spell. She had seen her father fall under it, too. She had just been a little girl, but were all men as weak? she wondered. And she remembered, more painfully, seeing her mother's lumpy silhouette against a doorway and wishing that Freya would look more like Fabiana—and then her mother had lost the baby. Yarrow's eyes brimmed with angry tears.

"For a start," said Elliot, rushing on, "when would your father have the time? He's always here. He's always working."

"They can write."

Elliot laughed. "Sex doesn't work that way."

Elliot had meant to say "love" but he said "sex" by mistake. It was always on his mind these days, he thought. Jock was right to keep him away from Yarrow. Yarrow let out a great shuddering sob. He tried to put his arms around her, but she pushed him away, sobbing harder. He was unsure what to do and so stood there doing nothing. How could he be expected to know that what she wanted more than anything was for him to do just that? She wanted him to hold her; she wanted him not to leave; and all these dramatics were her mute way of trying to keep him here.

And then Nellie came in and accused them of canoodling, and Yarrow rushed off and Elliot puzzled over what they had been arguing about.

"She hasn't come in yet," said Jock after they had said their good-byes and Elliot asked when Yarrow would be in from school.

"You're going to miss your train, lad. You will write to us, won't you?" Elliot gave the old man a hug. He loved him like the father he had hardly known.

"Aye, I'll miss you, too," said Jock, blowing his noise noisily on a big dirty rag.

"Will you give this to Yarrow for me?" Elliot took a small envelope from his pocket and pressed it into Jock's hand. Then he left very quickly without looking back.

When Yarrow opened the envelope later she found he had given her an old playing card. It was the king of hearts. There was no message with it, but when she turned it over she found that he had written across the back of it—"Yours."

CHAPTER 7

"*LEM AND I HAVE DECIDED TO GET MARRIED.*" FREYA NEARLY dropped her stick into the boiler where the whites were soaking when Laura told her. The house was very quiet; all the children were back at school after the Christmas vacation. It was more than a year since Elliot had left to go back to New York.

"We've talked about it for a long time, Mrs. McLean, and well, the Corps is really winding up now. We think it's time to live our own lives." Laura stood in her simple dress with her hands clasped in front of her. Her brown hair was as neat and soft as a pad of wool, her hands like butter paddles that could square pillows and tuck blankets on a bed tighter than a drum. For ten years her hands had never stopped working for the McLeans. Now, as if she couldn't talk without doing something, she began to feed some washing through the wringer. Freya pulled the heavy wet sheet from her.

"Dear Laura, I'm so happy for you." They hugged and soap bubbles from Freya's arms went on Laura's dress. "Let's go upstairs and have a cup of coffee." They were in the basement where the laundry was done, and as they came up into the hall Yarrow came rushing in with her books from school and her thick dark hair flying in curls from under a ribbon. A stream of fresh air flew in with her. It was a very mild January.

"Guess what?" She grabbed her mother and circled her, dancing around and laughing.

"What, Yarrow? Oh, for heaven's sake, what is it?"

Yarrow grabbed Laura and waltzed around her. "I've been offered a scholarship for college. They just told me at school."

"For what college?"

"Concord Academy. I've got one more year to go, but I've got the scholarship! Isn't it wonderful?"

"Yarrow. Oh, congratulations," said Laura, hugging her hard. Freya broke into tears and sat down on the chair in the hall.

"Mama, what is it?"

"I'm losing both my girls at once. This place won't be the same."

"Losing us?"

"Laura's getting married." Freya broke into a new wave of sobbing. "I'm so happy," she said.

Over coffee in the kitchen, Laura told them her plans. She and Lem were going to run a boys' camp up near Galena. In the summer they would run the camp, and in the winter Lem would work as a handyman. There were so many things he could do.

"I'll miss that, too," Freya said, laughing and cutting another slice of apple cake for herself.

"Laura," said Yarrow, "you must get married here, in the garden. It would look so pretty. Wouldn't it, Ma? Oh please say yes."

"This has been as much your home as ours, Laura, yours and Lem's."

"And I wouldn't want to get married in any other place."

And so it was settled, and early in June the house and the garden were so spruced up with flowers and paint that it could hardly be recognized.

On the eve of the wedding, at the ripe age of six, Eric decided that he might as well speak, and he burst forth with a complete sentence. "Laura, I'm too old for you to bathe me," he said and locked her out of the bathroom. Laura ran down the back stairs to tell the family that, miracle of miracles, the child had spoken.

Nellie said, "Now he'll never stop." She had handled the news of Laura's wedding as though it were an intrusion. "What's all the fuss about? It's only Lem and Laura." She was sticking a newspaper clipping about Neville Chamberlain, the British prime minister, on her bedroom door. Cousin Clara had sent it to her from Washington. Cousin Clara was a pacifist. Grandfather said Chamberlain was an appeaser. Nellie said she'd make up her own mind. "Peace in Our Time," wrote Nellie underneath the clipping. Greta saw Yarrow coming up the stairs and trembled. She trembled at any sign of dissension. She was miserable that Laura was leaving her, and had nibbled her cuticles till they bled. Only Laura understood her, Greta felt. Greta could talk to Laura about clothes and dreams and anything that came into her head. She had developed a fear that what she loved most would be taken away from her; she knew it was weird and tried to explain it: Mama went on larding a leg of lamb; "That's nice, dear," she said (there were fourteen coming for dinner and she wondered if there was enough meat to go around); Nellie closed her diary and held it ostentatiously to her chest until Greta had finished, and then went straight back into it as though she had not been interrupted; Yarrow was twiddling with the crystal set she had made and her face lit up when she finally got it to work, and she hadn't heard a word Nellie had said; but Laura had put down her duster and listened and put one of her big flat hands on her arm and said she knew what she meant.

Greta gulped as Yarrow came up the stairs. "It's half my door," said Greta to Nellie, "won't you take it down?" "What is *that*?" said Yarrow pointing to Chamberlain and Hitler. "I will not have that in my house."

Nellie flattened herself against the door. "You will not take it down."

"Fascist!"

"I am not!"

"Please don't argue," said Greta, wringing her hands.

"Appeaser," said Yarrow, her eyes blazing, "Chamberlain lover."

Freya heard the argument from downstairs and said to Jock, "You really shouldn't get the girls so het up about this thing, Jock. It's so divisive."

"It's good for them," said Jock. "They should be aware of the real world."

Freya went to the bottom of the stairs, wiping her floury hands. "Girls, stop. Yarrow, your sister has as much right as you to express her opinion in this house."

"But she's a Nazi!"

"I am not!"

"Stop."

"That's it then," shouted Yarrow. "If she can express her opinion, so can I."

Upstairs, Greta wondered what Yarrow would do. Downstairs, Freya and Jock raised their eyebrows at each other and sighed—but Jock was secretly pleased.

For the wedding ceremony someone found some blue carpet and someone brought extra chairs and Lem took down the old swing and made a bower out of the frame. They strung lights around the trees and hung paper lanterns over the bushes. They pushed the piano to the garden end of the sitting room and opened the window wide so that the guests could hear. One of their neighbors consented to play for them. Freya and Laura made the wedding dress and the bridesmaids' dresses and even Yarrow had lent a hand by stitching some of the hems, though she warned them everyone would be able to see her stitches.

Laura's father gave her away, and when they walked down the

blue carpet toward the minister waiting under the bower, Laura looked sweet and unspoiled on his arm. The girls followed in their flowered dresses. Freya was nervous that their argument would wash over into the activities. But they looked like angels; first came Yarrow, sixteen, with her hair combed so that it fell to her waist in a thick black waterfall, and behind her, Nellie, nearly fifteen, with her high forehead hidden under her straight dark bangs, and then came Greta, who at thirteen had grown into the beauty of the family, walking like a tall blond goddess with a circlet of flowers around her head. Freya burst out sobbing, louder even than Mrs. Brogan, and could be heard, all through the service, gulping and sniffing, until the minister pronounced Lem and Laura, man and wife.

After the service everyone helped set up the tables. Neighbors and friends had all contributed food, and breads and salads and chickens and hams, and corn on the cob, and cheese and wine and beer and angel cake and Jell-o, all appeared on the table under the bobbing lanterns. Yarrow watched a friend of Lem's playing the accordion and another man playing the spoons on the door. She was enjoying the music when someone tapped her on the shoulder.

"Hello, Yarrow."

"Why, Elliot! Is it really you?" Yarrow felt flustered. "You said you'd come, I mean, you wrote that you might. What a surprise. When did you arrive? What are you doing with yourself?"

He put his hand up in mock appeal. "Hold on, one question at a time. How are you?"

"I'm great and you look . . . Has Grandfather seen you yet? Are you working on a paper?" Elliot grabbed a beer, and they moved away from the music of the party and went outside where the lanterns were now yellow against the darkening sky. Family and friends milled around. From all over the house came waves of laughter, and music and gusts of singing. Laura came rushing up, her face shining under her tossed-back white veil. "You came," she said, "I knew you would."

"I wouldn't have missed your wedding for anything in the world. I arrived just in time to hear your vows."

Yarrow looked at him from under her eyelashes while they spoke. She felt awkward and girlish as she watched him. She could not explain why Elliot made her feel this way, for he had always spoken to her as an equal. Yet he always produced in her an uncomfortable sensation of nervousness, of expectation, that Yarrow did not like. It made her say things to him that, when she thought about them afterward, made her wince. He must think she was stupid. Mary-Ellen said that Yarrow had a crush on Elliot Weyden, but Yarrow hotly denied it.

Elliot was talking now to Lem, who had come up and put his arm around Laura. Elliot was saying that he had worked in the finance department of a newspaper in New York but had now switched to an investment bank. He was finishing his degree at night.

"A bank's the right place for you," said Lem, "as long as they check the money's still there in the morning and you haven't cornered another market."

"It's not quite like that. I never see any money around; it's all in paper, it's all ideas."

"Why, that ain't no fun at all," said Lem.

The family were all coming up to Elliot now and Greta finally pulled him away.

"Come and dance," she said. "You promised you would. Could I talk to you about something?"

Elliot laughed and was dragged off to the sitting room, where the piano was being pounded harder than it had ever been in its life before. Yarrow and Mary-Ellen watched them join the dancers. Mary-Ellen was about to say something, but Yarrow said, "Please keep your diagnosis to yourself." She was trying to stifle a twinge of jealousy as through the window she watched her sister dancing with Elliot. Lem came up to Yarrow and asked her to join in, and Laura smiled and pushed them through the door and onto the crowded floor; then Lem cut in on Elliot, and Yarrow and Elliot were dancing. Yarrow felt his hand on her back when he pushed her hair out of the way to hold her. She was so conscious of it that she stepped on his toes.

"Elliot, I'm sorry."

He laughed. "That's OK. You dance just the way you used to play the piano."

When the cake was cut, Eric came staggering out from under the table with a placard on his front that stated "Down with Fascism!" and a placard on his back that said "Support Our Allies!" (Yarrow had paid him well to do it—she would empty the bin in the kitchen onto the compost heap for one month—it was his one hated chore.) Later, after Yarrow had caught the bouquet, and rice had been thrown over the car, and Laura and Lem had gone clanking down the street with tin cans tied to the bumper, Elliot joined the men sitting and yarning in the garden. Yarrow stopped and listened, between helping clear away the streamers and taking glasses and plates into the kitchen. Someone had put a record on the gramophone. Laura's favorite song, "Everything I Have Is Yours," played softly in the background.

Their talk was about war. Even the president, James was saying, gave a fifty-fifty chance that there would be war in Europe. It was incongruous but not unexpected for Yarrow to hear them talk of Hitler and Czechoslovakia, that all the love and happiness of Laura's wedding day should be occurring against this canvas. She shivered and Elliot, seeing her standing against the tree, came over and took off his jacket and put it around her shoulders.

"You're wearing a belt," she said. "It's nice." He said nothing, picking at the bark behind her head. "Do you think we will be in a war?" she went on.

"Yes. I'm sure."

"Will you go?"

"I'll probably have no choice."

"But would you go if you didn't have to?"

"I don't think it's America's war."

"Dad says America's been pacifist too long."

"And what do you think?"

She straightened herself up. "I think we should help Britain, but my cousin says the opposite. She's a congresswoman."

"Who?" he asked.

"Clara Russell, Great-aunty Hilda's only daughter—my second cousin probably. She's at least fifty, and she was elected last year from Pennsylvania."

"And she's a historian?"

"No, a pacifist. She became a Quaker. Grandfather said his sister was furious when it happened. He says you can take the McLeans out of the kirk, but you can't take the kirk out of the McLeans. She's Nellie's ideal."

"Not yours?"

"No. I don't think I have one. I'm too pragmatic."

He poked his tongue in his cheek, as though he had found a hole in a molar.

"Do you have a boyfriend?"

The question took her by surprise.

"Yes. Lots." She regretted it at once.

"Aaah," he said.

James came over and joined them. He had drunk a lot of beer.

"Have you heard about our clever girl," he said to Elliot, "winning a scholarship to some fancy college in the East? When she goes next year, you'll have to keep an eye on her for us, Elliot."

"Yes, sir. How's the folder working out?"

"Good. Good. You did me a favor there, Elliot. I think Max rues the day he started up against us."

"I told you they were vulnerable."

"When are you going back to New York?"

"My train leaves tomorrow. Could I come and see you in the morning?"

"I'd like to hear what you've been up to."

"What nonsense, 'come and see you in the morning.' You must stay here," said Freya. She was walking around the yard picking up the colored streamers and winding them around her fingers for some later use. "Lem's room is empty and you can make yourself quite comfortable. Then we can all catch up with your news at breakfast."

"Well, if you're sure it's not too much trouble."

"Asolutely sure. I almost feel you're one of my own."

So when everyone had gone home, Elliot took his small carryall out of the downstairs closet, and instead of staying at the Y in town, went up into Lem's old room. He laughed when he went upstairs, for Yarrow had strung a message, "Kill the Boche," across the hall from one wall to the other, and he had to duck down to get under it. Chamberlain looked on, a hand frozen in the air. Eric begged to be allowed to spend the night with Elliot, but Freya said no and Eric wailed for half an hour in his room until Nellie went through the two bathrooms and threw her shoes at him and told him to shut up and said she wished he had never learned to speak.

Yarrow tapped on her parents' door. Her father was already asleep, or pretending to be, lying on his side turned away from the light, and her mother sat at her dressing table brushing out her hair. Yarrow took the brush.

"Let me do it," she said. Her mother's hair was still beautiful and fell to her waist. The gray hairs coming in were crooked and wiry within the thick curtain of straight hair.

"Will I ever get married, do you think?"

"Of course you will." Freya adjusted the oval swivel mirror so she could see her daughter's face.

"It seems funny to think of Laura married."

Freya took the brush from her and pulled her hair over one shoulder and twisted it to form a skein. She began to braid it loosely. Yarrow picked up a photograph of her parents on their wedding day.

"How old were you when you married Dad?"

"Nineteen."

"Only two and a half years older than me."

"But old enough to know."

"How did you know?"

"I just felt comfortable with him, as though I could tell him everything about me."

"How did you meet?"

"Mama Halvorsen took me to Galena to visit with some of her old friends. I met your father at one of their houses. Mama Halvorsen thought he was too old for me."

"How did she change her mind?"

"Your father put a very nice paragraph in the *Gazette* about us visiting. And he sent my mother some flowers. She thought he was wonderful after that." From the bed came a loud snort.

"Good night, Mama." Yarrow kissed her mother and went over and hesitated beside her father. She leaned over and kissed him on the cheek.

When Yarrow got into her own bed the house seemed to be murmuring around her. Little eddies of wind crept around the hall and up the stairs, as if they did not want the excitement of the day to end. Outside her open window, the curtains of which Yarrow never closed, the moon played patterns on the windowsill and she imagined the yellow lanterns bobbing against the dark shapes of the bushes and trees. She thought once she heard her mother call out, but she must have been mistaken, for soon everything was quiet and then she must have fallen asleep because a banging door and the smell of bacon frying told her some people were already up.

She pulled a brush through her tangled hair, threw a robe on and ran down the stairs. But Elliot was already gone—he had to catch an early train and Grandfather had driven him to the station.

CHAPTER 8

ELLIOT HAD BEEN RIGHT ABOUT THE FUTURE OF THE *RECORD*, but a little optimistic about the speed with which the paper would fold.

Right after the wedding, total war was declared between the

Journal and the *Record*. Front-page editorials denouncing each other as liars and charlatans appeared with increasing regularity, signed by Maxwell T. Horace, Proprietor, or John Buckley McLean and James McLean, Publisher and Editor-in-Chief.

Jock was in his element. "Just like the old days," he said. He forgot about the rheumatism in his legs and went to the office every day ready to launch another salvo. When Max Horace referred scathingly to the *Journal* as a "rag not fit to be read by a gentleman," Jock thundered back that how could a "moth-eaten mammoth from Cornwall" possibly be the judge? Max paid some boys to steal copies of the *Journal* from their delivery sites. Jock telephoned the *Record* and told them a completely fabricated story about the mayor. When the *Record* published the story and then had to retract it, Max screamed at the maliciousness of his rivals. James ticked Jock off about this, but Jock pushed out his chin so his beard bristled, and said it just went to show that the *Record* never checked its news sources.

It was Jock's policy, and had been ever since his *Gazette* days, never to acknowledge a cancellation. He just threw the cancellation slips away and said that most people forgot they had canceled their subscription anyway and coughed up when the bill fell due. But of course there were some who never paid, whether cancellations were sent in or not. The *Record*, like the *Journal*, had a whole list of unpaid subscribers. Just at this moment in the newspaper battle, Max Horace made a crucial error. He published a list of subscribers who were in arrears. The populace of Platte City was outraged, and not a few of them vowed never to buy another copy of the *Record* again as long as they lived.

"Max never did have much judgment," said Jock, shaking his head in disbelief when he saw the paper. "You'd think Hinton would have stopped him."

That same day, James delivered the coup de grâce. He remembered what Max had done to them by undercutting their rates when Elliot was out selling ads. It was time Max tasted his own medicine. James telephoned all the *Record*'s advertisers and offered them half rates for six months if they advertised in the *Journal*. It was a challenge Max Horace could no longer meet.

But even at the height of the war of words between the two papers, when Jock's vitriolic pen was at its sharpest, James spoke weekly with Max Horace—"keeping his lines of communication open." Their similarities after all were greater than their differences. James would always end his call by saying, "Let me know when you want to quit."

Max would answer, "Never," and slam down the phone.

But one day James was on the telephone with Max and jok-
ingly asked, "Well, Max, are you ready to give up yet?" and he
nearly fell off his chair when Max answered that he was.

That morning Albert Hinton had mangled his hand in one of
the press units. Max was overcome with weariness at the thought
of struggling on until Hinton recovered. Max had never known
his way around the pressroom as Jock had; his beat had always
been the street.

"I'm seventy-six years old and I'm just too darn tired."

"Nor does he have anyone to whom to pass on the *Record*,"
said Jock when he heard the news.

James asked Jerrard Fox to telephone Fabiana—but Fabiana
said she couldn't come to Platte City right now; she wanted
James to come to New York.

"The woman is a menace," James said, folding his shirts for
his visit to New York. "She has no more interest in newspapers
than as something to stuff her shoes with."

"What about the New York *Courier*?" said Freya, handing
him his spare shoes. Freya was looking worn. She sat down on
his bed while he packed. Yarrow's suspicions about her father
and Fabiana were renewed. She put her hand on her mother's
shoulder.

"She's a businesswoman, not a newspaperwoman," said James.
"There is a difference."

"Must you go?" asked Yarrow. "I thought we were all going
up to Grandfather's cabin." Each year, somehow or other, they
all went back to the mountains. For the McLeans it was like
touching a lodestone.

James looked up from his packing at his daughter's tone. He
was elated at the idea of getting rid of Max Horace, but his
daughter's voice brought him down to earth. She had grown
distant this past year and he did not know why.

"I can't. I'll only be gone a few days. Don't forget to help
your grandfather."

"Well, don't get talked into anything. Max Horace has nothing to sell but a clapped-out old newspaper."

"Any other advice?"

"No. I'm just telling you what I think."

"Thank you." He closed his suitcase and pulled it off the bed.

"Be a good girl, Yarrow. Don't get sassy with me."

"I'm not being sassy. I do everything I'm told around here,
and I never get any thanks. I work at the office. I help Ma. I get
a scholarship; nobody thinks that's terrific except Grandfather.
You all use me."

"Yarrow . . ."

"I'm sick of it, you hear? Sick of it." Yarrow burst into tears and rushed out, slamming the door.

"Oh boy," said her father, raising his eyebrows at his wife. Yarrow banged back in.

"I heard that."

"What's wrong with . . . ?"

Yarrow slammed out the door again. Nellie came in to see what was the matter.

"I have to catch my train," said her father. "Find out what's the matter with Yarrow—and help your mother, she looks tired . . ."

"Oh, don't worry about Miss Worrywart," said Nellie when Freya had left the room to go to her eldest daughter. "It's just her monthlies that have upset her hormones. Besides"—Nellie blew a big bubble of gum and let it pop over her lips—"Elliot Weyden hasn't written and that puts her in a foul mood. Have a safe trip."

The following day, while she was working in the garden, Freya added her weight to a lawn aerator that Eric was pushing. She slipped, and the aerator gashed her shin. The gash needed a skin graft, and while Freya was in the hospital, she mentioned to the surgeon that while he was at it he might as well look at a small lump on her breast.

Yarrow was with her mother when the doctor diagnosed cancer. Freya would not let Yarrow call her father.

"Please don't do it, Yarrow. It will upset him more than me."

When James returned, he found Freya in the hospital with her shin neatly grafted and one breast missing. He sat, white and wan with deep grooves showing in his handsome cheeks. He sat with his hand up over his mouth as though he were going to gag. His ruddiness had all gone, and his eyes looked weak and watery behind his glasses. Yarrow hated her father then. She blamed him for being away. He sobbed into the sheets that covered Freya when his big hand couldn't hold his mouth tight anymore. Yarrow was even more disgusted at what she saw as his weakness.

"Why didn't you let me know?" he cried.

Yarrow looked at her father's bent head and her mother's hand with the wedding ring on it. It was a capable hand with short nails and strong fingers. It looked like her own.

"You're here now," said Freya, wiping his wet cheek with the end of her braid. "I need you now."

On leaving the hospital room, James put his arm around Yarrow for comfort, but she pushed his arm off. She couldn't bear to have him touch her.

The house on Bellevue Street was a dismal place while Freya recovered. James would not leave her side until she begged him to please go to the office.

Yarrow was to start college in September and it seemed to her that her life was in limbo. She was neither child nor woman, high-school senior nor college freshman. She took over the running of the house and the cooking, neither of which were up to the standards Freya had set. She fretted over shopping and making beds, and woke up one night to check that all the doors were locked. The one trait of her mother's that did intensify, however, was Freya's penny-pinching economies. Yarrow began rolling up pieces of string; packages that arrived were untied with her teeth if her fingers couldn't do it; rubber bands were wound around cardboard; toothpaste tubes were split with a razor (after they had been rolled up tightly from the bottom and a steam roller could not squeeze out another inch); slivers of soap were collected and put in the wire basket used to make suds to wash the dishes. These economies carried over into the culinary department.

"What is this?" asked Nellie one night, spooning up a meat sauce from the stove. Nellie and Yarrow never got on and, besides, Nellie seldom ate anything put in front of her. She was thin and dark, her bones as angular as her haircut.

"Spaghetti sauce, nitwit. What else?" Nellie did a mock retch and Yarrow threw a plate at her.

"Oh, stop it," said Greta, her big blue eyes filling with tears. "Mama will hear you and be upset." Nellie stormed out of the kitchen, clutching a packet of Oreo cookies, and banged the door behind her. Yarrow burst into tears. Greta put her arms around her. Greta's heart was as big as her beautiful self. She was taller already than Yarrow, and had Freya's wide shoulders and long neck, and her body skimmed down to a little waist before bursting out into the curve of her hips.

"Eric and me will cook the dinner."

"Eric and I."

"Yes, that's right. Eric, come and taste it and tell me what you think."

Eric stuck his finger in the sauce and grimaced. Greta tasted it.

"It isn't too good, Yarrow. What did you put in it?"

Yarrow groaned from the table, "That package of beef in the refrigerator. I don't know. I don't care."

"That was corned beef. You don't put corned beef in spaghetti sauce."

"It took me ages to chop it into little pieces."

"I know just what we'll do." Greta took out the sugarbowl from the cabinet and dumped some into the sauce. She added some chopped tomatoes and garlic. Eric agreed that it was better, though not great, and Greta took over the cooking for the rest of the summer, much to the relief of the family.

The doctor suggested to Freya that swimming would be a good exercise to help regain the strength in her upper arm. She had had a radical mastectomy, and two chest muscles and the arm lymph nodes had been removed. So three mornings a week, or when she was feeling strong enough, Freya would be driven by James or Yarrow to the local swimming pool. She liked to go early when there was no one about. She was very conscious of her lopsided torso and wore a big black swimsuit with wide straps and a modesty skirt that cut across the front of her thighs. She put on a white rubber bathing cap, from which her hair kept escaping, and would go up and down the length of the pool at her own pace. She had adapted her own style to suit her restricted arm movements. It was like watching a very large black tadpole zigzagging along the lanes.

One warm, hazy morning Yarrow waited on the side of the pool, dangling her feet in the water, until her mother finished.

"Won't you swim with me, darling?"

Yarrow shivered. "And let the water-baby get me? No thank you."

Yarrow had left cornflakes and milk on the kitchen table for the others' breakfast. She hoped Greta wouldn't cook; Yarrow hated cleaning up after her. She watched as Freya slowly pulled herself out of the water. Freya had lost weight.

"I love you, Mama," she said, wrapping the towel around her. Her mother's flesh was goose-bumped.

"I love you, too." Freya winced as she pulled off her bathing cap and the rubber caught her hair.

"I'm not going to Concord Academy."

"Yarrow . . ."

"I'm not going, Mama, and that's it. I'm going to take a secretarial course and I can live at home."

Freya squeezed the water out of the back of her hair. It made a big puddle on the warm concrete.

"I feel so bad."

"Do you want to sit down?"

"No. About your college."

"Oh, Mama."

"Your father won't hear of it. He never went to college himself."

"I've made up my mind. He won't change it."

Nellie put her head around the door of Yarrow's bedroom. Yarrow was on the floor reading a book. She had written to Elliot about her mother's illness, and he had replied and sent her a book by Dickens. She had read the letter from him three times but could not find anything in it except what the words said—that he was fine and busy and things were going "swell." Yarrow wondered where he had picked up that word.

"Ma's crying."

Yarrow got up and rushed out of the room and across the hall. The door was open, but she knocked. Her mother was at the dressing table, her face stained and red with crying.

"Mama, don't."

"It's so silly." Her mother wiped her eyes with a handkerchief and took a deep breath. "I can ask them to cut off my breast, but I can't cut my own hair."

Yarrow noticed the scissors in her mother's lap.

"Why cut your hair?" She touched the long braid with her fingers.

"It takes too long to dry." She looked at Yarrow in the mirror and her eyes brimmed again. "I can't put my arm up to brush it." She handed Yarrow the scissors. "Please cut it." Her fingers played with the silver tops of the Victorian glass bottles in front of her.

"What will Dad say?"

"Just do it."

It was difficult to cut because the hair was thick. Yarrow laid the braid over her mother's strong hands. It lay over the hands and against the cut glass and the silver. Freya raised one hand to her neck and rubbed it. Her wedding ring glistened. "It feels light," she said. She saw Nellie in the mirror, standing near the door.

"It's all over, Nellie. I feel much better now."

That afternoon, while Freya was resting and the three younger children had gone to the park on their bicycles, Yarrow joined her grandfather on the back stoop.

"Hello, lass," he said. "Come to talk to me?" His beard and hair were whiter than ever, but thinner, so she could see his scalp. He had lost some teeth and hated his false ones. His body was still sturdy, although the years seemed to have shortened it, and his shoulders were more curved. Even his legs seemed to have bowed. She sat down and put her head on his shoulder for a moment. He smelled the same as before, a mixture of tobacco and printer's ink. Yarrow could never walk into the office without thinking of him. She patted the pocket of his shirt where the familiar slug of metal had worn a hole in the material.

"I had a note from Elliot today. He sent me another book. He said to say hello."

"Is that right? And what's he doing now?"

"He's working at the stock exchange in New York. He started as a squad or something . . ."

"A squad? What's that?"

"It's a clerk, I think, but now he's been taken up by Salomon Brothers."

Grandfather puffed at his cigar, and they both watched the smoke curling up against the horizon of the plane tree, up against the back fence and dispersing against the peaks of the mountains.

"Last time I heard he was at the *Times*, working for the scraparian in the finance department."

"Scraparian?"

"Librarian, Yarrow-Farrow . . ."

Yarrow grinned at the memory of their old childhood game.

" . . . and he saved them one hundred twenty thousand dollars in insurance costs by suggesting they switch to all-metal fittings and shelves."

"Did Elliot tell you that?"

"No. He doesn't blow his own trumpet, you know that. My friend at the *Times* who got him the job told me. He's never met anyone like Elliot. He finished his degree."

"Grandfather, I'm not going to college."

"Aye. Your mother told me."

Yarrow scratched at a mosquito bite on her arm.

"Your mother will be OK, Yarrow. Her prognosis was good— you heard the doctor. She's a very strong woman."

Yarrow sat up against the post. She had a red ribbon in her hair, and her white open-necked shirt made her sun-tanned skin look very dark. Her gray eyes looked at her grandfather.

"I'm not going and that's that."

"Well, I must say, it doesn't surprise me, but I am disappointed."

"You're not surprised?"

"Women put love first."

"Oh, what bosh."

"It's true. Your grandmother did; she put your father before her own health. She should never have had a child. She was warned. Look at my own sister; she left Scotland and everyone she knew to go to Pennsylvania with that turd of a husband.'' Grandfather wiped his beard.

"There's no need for me to go to college. I can get a good job if I had shorthand. Even Dad might employ me if I could take notes. My typing's OK.''

"I wish you were a boy.''

"Thanks a lot.''

"You know what I mean.'' He patted her on the knee. "Do you ever think about the future, Yarrow? Who do you think's going to run the paper?''

"Eric?''

"Well, I ken that he's only seven, so he might come through. But he can't match a button to what you were like at that age. Not a button. And I don't know if he's shown any real interest in the paper.''

"Greta won't want to.'' Yarrow looked at her short fingernails with a sigh. "She won't have to, she's so beautiful. She stopped biting her nails and she's entered the Miss High-School Pageant. I bet she'll win.''

"There's beauty and there's beauty. But I agree, I can't see Greta dirtying her hands with newsprint.''

"Nellie wants to go into nursing.''

"I can believe that. I caught her once giving an enema to that poncy little boy who came here . . .''

"Palmer Truitt?''

"Aye. In the bathroom they all were, playing nurse, she said, the little scamp. Oh, it was years ago.''

"Poor Palmer,'' laughed Yarrow.

"No. You're the one,'' said Grandfather, going back to his original thought. "You can write, you have a good head on your shoulders, and you're not afraid of expressing your opinion. If I could only make you see what a difference you can make. So few people speak out against the consensus. Some people talk about the power of the press—it's all rubbish, you know. The power is only what you make it, but the perception by people that the press has it, well, that's a kind of subtle power. It has to be used wisely or people can see through it.''

"Did you see my story about the fire, the one on Fourteenth Street? Dad put it on page two?''

"I did. You use words like a camera. It's a gift, Yarrow. You mustn't waste it.''

The sun was streaming down on them as they chatted on the steps. Behind them the door lay open to the hall; the hall ran the length of the house, past the portrait of Mollie that hung above the lyre-back chairs, past the door to Grandfather's room and the door to the parlor, to the front door, which stood equally wide open. There was suddenly a great noise of a car and music and young voices, and Yarrow turned to see who it was. The car horn tooted and a wave of laughter accompanied her name being called.

"Why, it's Sandy Heartland. I haven't seen him for ages," said Yarrow, leaving the steps and going through the hall. "Hello, what are you doing here?"

Sandy jumped out of the car. He was a sophomore at Purdue University and seldom came home. People said Sandy did not get along with his father and that his mother had a nervous condition. Grandfather said that was a euphemism for being a drunk. But right now Sandy looked as if he didn't have a care in the world. An Artie Shaw recording was playing on the car radio. The car was full of young people, some of whom Yarrow knew. She saw Mary-Ellen's red hair through the window. Sandy's blond head shone in the sun, his teeth sparkled. They were going up into the foothills and they were going tubing on the river and they wanted to know if she could come.

"I can't, I can't." Sandy's smile was so enticing; he put a hand on her arm. A thrill went through Yarrow that she hadn't felt since Elliot Weyden danced with her last year at Laura's wedding.

"Oh, come on, Yarrow," said Mary-Ellen, putting her head through the window. She was wearing her hair in the new style with a big high wave at the front and the ends rolled under like a sausage. "We'll be back before nightfall."

Grandfather had come up behind Yarrow.

"Why don't you go, girl? It'll do you good. I'll explain it to your mother when she wakes up."

Yarrow hesitated for one more second. She thought of the book that Elliot had sent her. She had been going to spend the afternoon reading it, but the sun glinted off the fender of the car and made up her mind for her. "Give me one minute to get my swimsuit."

Yarrow left Sandy standing with her grandfather beside the car. One of the girls turned up the music.

"Helen Forrest," said Sandy, referring to the singer.

"How do you do, Helen," said Grandfather, shaking hands with Mary-Ellen whom he did not recognize in her new hairdo. Sandy laughed and held his stomach and Grandfather was annoyed, not only that he had made a mistake, but at Sandy's lack of manners. He always thought Sandy's eyes were too close together, Jock mumbled to himself.

When they left, with a roar and in a cloud of dust, Yarrow looked back and saw her grandfather still standing in the doorway. She thought for the first time how frail he was becoming and couldn't pinpoint just when that had happened. She was frowning as she tried to remember, and then Sandy took one hand off the wheel and put his arm around her shoulder. His hand felt so warm and firm that it reassured her of her own youth and she smiled into his eyes. He squeezed her shoulder and she felt that funny thrill again and she thought, Why perhaps I'm falling in love and this is what it's like. And she forgot about Elliot's book, and Elliot, and how she used to feel when he was around.

There was a meeting in Jerrard Fox's office. Jock, James, Fox and Max Horace sat around a board table of polished mahogany and eyed each other over their glasses of water. Fox held Fabiana Truitt's power of attorney.

Fabiana Truitt had come up with a clever idea. She had explained it all to James when he was in New York. Freya's illness had postponed its implementation. If Fabiana and the McLeans issued new shares in their company, they could use that means rather than cash to buy the *Record*. James and Jock didn't like the idea of Max having any new shares in the *Journal*. Hadn't they had the devil of a time trying to get rid of him before? But Fox said it was a simple scheme, and since Max's shares would be nonvoting and since they would issue themselves more shares too at the same time, Max would be in a minority.

Jock said he didn't believe anyone else would want the damn newspaper. "Why do we have to buy it? Why not just let it close down? It's just a clapped-up old pile of junk." James thought he'd heard that somewhere before.

But Max pulled out of his pocket a letter of intent from some bank back east; a letter of intent to buy the *Record*. Jock examined it carefully. He clamped down on his cigar and wondered if he could trust Max, but he kept his mouth shut while he listened. The idea was that the two papers could be printed on the same presses. The *Record* would become an evening paper and the *Gazette* would keep its place in the morning market.

"Max won't go for it," said Jock outside in the hallway where he and James had retired to caucus. But surprisingly, Max Horace said he would—after a little bit of finagling over the finer points. It was then agreed that a percentage of the purchase would be paid from any future profits of the *Record*, and two hundred new shares were to be issued; one hundred nonvoting shares to Max Horace, and fifty each to Fabiana and the McLeans. Jock thought Max must be going soft in the head to walk away without any cash.

But later in the day Jock got a telephone call that set his brain clicking as if it were a Linotype machine. He made a few telephone calls himself around the town and then, clickety-clack, all the pieces fell into place.

"Don't hold dinner for me," he said to Greta as he went out dressed in his suit and hat. "I'm going to be late."

He went into town first and hired a young lawyer. Fox was not the only lawyer in town. Jock went to one bank, where he kept his small savings, and he borrowed some money, and knowing it might not be enough, he went to another where he knew one of James's cronies was on the board. Jock called in all the favors. "Do you think this is wise?" asked his lawyer as he watched Jock's debt piling up.

"I'll get rid of these vipers today once and for all," said Jock.

They took a cab to the *Record* office where Miss Pince-nez, looking not a day older, could not stop Jock from pushing into Max Horace's office. There were other men in there, but Jock said, "Get out," and they did; and then he closed the door and he talked to Max Horace for thirty minutes. The lawyer paced up and down outside, chewing his nails, and then Jock came out, calm as could be, and said they could go home now, and he would see the lawyer at Jerrard Fox's office for the signing tomorrow.

At the signing the next day, the new shares were issued as they had decided; one hundred to Max Horace, fifty each to Fabiana and the McLeans. While Fox was telephoning her in New York with the good news, Jock and his lawyer concluded their deal with Max. Jock asked his lawyer to deliver the papers to Fox the next morning.

It was eleven o'clock in the morning in New York when Fox rang Fabiana. She was just waking up. Fox had arrived at his office in Platte City and had opened up the fat envelope that had been delivered by Jock's lawyer.

"They double-crossed us," shouted Fox over the phone. His voice was nearly incoherent. "The McLeans bought Max Horace's shares. They did the deal that we were . . ." Fabiana screamed and dropped the phone. She had gone to bed owning the majority shareholding of the newspaper and had woken up to find that the McLeans now owned five eighths. Fabiana threw the telephone at the mirror in her bedroom.

"I'll get those McLeans for this, if it takes me all my life."

"But how did you know, old-timer? How did you find out that the company that wanted to buy the *Record* was just a front for Fabiana Truitt?" James was still trying to work out the details of the scheme. Everything had happened so fast.

Jock laughed into his whiskey.

"Elliot found out. Here he is working for some fancy investment company in New York and they send him over to her house to get her to sign the papers. He smelled a rat and called me."

"OK. So how come you got Max Horace to go along with you, and do the same deal he had arranged with Fabiana?"

"Let's just say I was very persuasive." Jock laughed. "I just reminded him of a few things." Like the union scab he had shot a long time ago in Galena. "I know where the skeletons are in Max's past." Jock nearly choked as he drank his whiskey.

"You know, I think this stuff helps my rheumatism. Haven't had a twinge all day."

With Max Horace gone, James decided to amalgamate the two papers to become the *Platte City Journal-Record*. The *Journal*'s old premises were sold, the old Comet broken down for scrap, and James moved in as publisher at the newer plant across town. The *Record* had a new Duplex Tubular press, a unionized shop floor and the still-recuperating Albert Hinton as the union's chapel chairman.

On the first night of their ownership, James came out with a headline, VOTE WILLKIE, which had Jock cursing into his beard.

"The man's a turncoat," he said. "Willkie once voted for Roosevelt himself."

"Turncoat or not, the man's sincere. We're going to support him."

All the family had come to see the first paper with its new masthead come off the press. There was some delay with the machine, which stood like a giant compared to their old Comet, for James had decided to print the paper in two sections and add a tabloid insert. Since the Duplex worked on the principle of a cylindrical printing surface with two plates printing four standard pages each, it was an easy matter of turning the columns sideways to issue a tabloid. Each plate of one broadsheet page, with the type running around the cylinder, now became two tabloid pages with the type running horizontally. James sweated and cursed while the men clamped on the plates and the adjustments were made. Yarrow was up-to-date on the whole process of making the plates and explained to Eric at the stone how the forms, which once had gone straight to the flatbed to print directly onto the paper, were now covered with flong. Flong was like a very wet papier-mâché sheet. Yarrow gave one of the dried, molded flongs to Eric, who made it quiver up and down in front of Nellie's face, but she pushed him away and said she was not interested.

The flong seemed to take forever to dry as they watched it being placed under a ''scorcher,'' a piece of canvas that wrapped the flong around a steam drum.

''If the flong isn't completely dry,'' Yarrow said, ''the hot metal would crack it.'' The flong made a terrible stink as it dried.

''It's the flong that makes the plate,'' said Yarrow while they watched a foundryman ladle molten lead into the mold.

''I know that,'' said Eric.

Jock had brought a glass of whiskey with him into the pressroom. He nodded to Albert Hinton and the union men. He shook his head as he watched the preparations and the hum of activity of which he was no longer a part.

''It's all becoming too removed. It's been a step at a time, but it's happened.'' He touched the metal typefaces in the form and then flicked out his beard so that Yarrow could see he was wearing a tie underneath. She caught his hand and squeezed it, feeling the hardened pads of his fingers. How many times had they picked up the type pieces and placed them nick up, row upon row, in his type stick? Almost without looking, knowing the placement of the alphabet in the typecase, he had transformed his words, his ideas directly into metal. It was his paper from start to finish.

''Not like the old Humdinger?''

''No, not at all, lass.''

One of the men had made Eric a printer's hat from paper, and he wore it when, at last, his father said they were ready to roll the presses. Eric was allowed to push the button that started the great units rolling. Four reels of paper began slowly to turn, and the plate cylinders, and the impression cylinders, and the cylinders that carried the ink began to revolve until the whole thirty-eight tons of machinery began to rumble and spin out the webs of paper, and from the other end, where the family rushed, the blank white paper was magically transformed with its stories and headlines and pictures and columns, all fallen into place, into the new *Platte City Journal-Record*.

They all grabbed a fresh paper as it came off. "Folded," Yarrow shouted at the same time as her grandfather, and laughed. The new *Journal* looked different from the old. James had abolished the use of column rules that Max had liberally squared off all over the place. He had freshened the whole look of the pages by increasing the amount of white space that the eye took in. He had increased the size of the photographs and reversed them where the composition of the page dictated it. He had put in a page of comics near the back (which pleased Eric), and offered free tickets to the local movie house to any new subscriber, an offer boxed in reverse type on the bottom of the front page. He had asked his cousin, Clara Russell, in Washington to write an occasional column headed, "News from the Capital." James was very proud of it, particularly since he had got Clara so cheap. "Look at that," he kept saying, "look at that," turning the pages over. He noticed a misprint on page two and went rushing over to the composing stone to show the compositor.

Grandfather took Eric's hand and led him out to the front office. He felt superfluous here now. He had done all he could. He had gone out with James and upped their borrowings when Fabiana Truitt had ordered Fox to sell her remaining shares. "In for a penny, in for a pound," he'd said. Now they owned it all. It was theirs.

The old name of the newspaper was still on the window. A man was busy scratching off the gold letters with a razor blade. Hanging on the wall on display was an old typecase.

"It's upside down."

"How can you tell, Grandfather?"

"Easy, lad. It's hanging by the handle." Eric giggled. He ran over and picked up a curl of gold shaving that lay on the floor. "Did you know," said Jock, easing himself onto a bench that ran along the lefthand wall, "that the U and the J of the uppercase letters came near the end? I used to think that's how the alphabet really went, JUXYZ."

"That's silly, Grandfather."

"Aye," said Jock, staring at the old, useless case and tipping his head back against the wall. "It was."

BOOK TWO

- 1940–1953 -

THE CHASE

CHAPTER 9

*J*OCK TURNED EIGHTY IN NOVEMBER, ON THE SAME DAY YARROW
became eighteen and James brought out a facsimile of the
first edition of the Humdinger. Jock kept taking out his handkerchief and wiping it over his eyes and beard and mouth.

Yarrow read Eric the stories of the mining camp of 1881, and
their grandfather's first editorial. They were sitting together in
one big armchair in front of the fire. They were listening to the
radio for the result of the elections. The president was running
hard for a third term. James had championed Willkie in his
editorials, but Clara Russell, in her columns, was against him
and President Roosevelt. Clara was an isolationist. Jock said
only a schizophrenic could read the paper and understand it.

"Oh, listen to this," said Yarrow, curling her legs up under
her as they waited for the news broadcast. She had a soft, low
voice suited to reading aloud. " 'A newspaper in a rich and
growing mining camp like Galena is more than an advantage; it
is a necessity. That necessity is twofold, for the newspaper in a
mining camp assumes two duties, the one being to furnish the
camp with the news of the outside world, and the other to
furnish the outside world with the knowledge of the production
and of the strikes in the camp. These two duties the *Galena
Gazette* promises to fulfill, and we promise to make things lively
for the camp and for the capitalists.' Doesn't it sound like
Grandfather?"

"Of course it does," said Jock, coming in and poking at the
fire with his foot. "I wrote it. Read the boy the bit about the
torture of the nihilists."

"Yes, yes," squealed Eric, whose imagination lived on a diet
of gore and detective stories.

"He'll make a good reporter yet," said Grandfather.

" 'The killers of the Czar, Russakoff and Jaliboff, were
mercilessly tortured by electricity in the presence of General
Melikoff,' " read Yarrow. "This is horrible, Grandfather."

"Go on, go on. Don't be so lily-livered."

" 'A *New York Sun* reporter in the best interests of science underwent the actual experience, using a Furdic induction coil.' "

"Does it hurt?" asked Eric.

"Only when he laughs," said Grandfather.

Yarrow threw the paper away from her. "I'm not going to read any more of this."

Jock laughed as Eric scrambled for the paper.

"Read it to me, Grandfather, please."

"Oh, I know it by heart anyway," said Jock, settling into another chair. His big tobacco-stained teeth laughed at Yarrow as Eric scrambled up beside him. Yarrow turned up the dial on the radio. A woman's voice sang into the room: "When the deep purple falls over sleepy garden walls . . ."

"Who is that singing?" asked Freya, coming into the room.

"Bea Wain."

"Hush," said Grandfather as the announcer interrupted.

"President Franklin D. Roosevelt has been reelected with a five-million-vote majority over the former utility magnate Wendell Willkie . . ."

"Whoopee," shouted Grandfather, crushing Eric in his arms. "I told your father Willkie couldn't win."

"Willkie's carried Colorado," said Yarrow, still listening to the broadcast.

"Does that mean we'll go to war, now that President Roosevelt's won?" asked Eric.

"More than likely."

Freya pushed some wood chips on the hearth with the poker.

"I must ring Laura. Lem joined the navy and she'll be worried sick."

"Elliot had to register last month," said Jock.

"Sandy says he's going to volunteer," said Yarrow.

Freya hugged her daughter. "I'm sure if your cousin Clara gets her way, she'll give the warmongers a run for their money."

Jock harrumphed in his throat and waited until the women had gone before he gave Eric a stern lecture on patriotism and said that some things were worth fighting for.

The family did not celebrate Grandfather's or Yarrow's birthday on the day, but decided to wait until New Year's Eve when Laura could come with her baby. Lem was somewhere in the Pacific. Cousin Clara said she would visit, and Elliot, who was in training camp, wrote to Jock that he would come if he could get a midwinter furlough.

Yarrow told Mary-Ellen that she was quite over her crush on Elliot Weyden. It had just been a girlish infatuation. Anyway he seldom wrote; only scribbled inside a book that he sent her now and then; "Beware of Pumblechook," he wrote the last time. She knew he was referring to Sandy, whom he had not even met.

It was bitterly cold on New Year's Eve, so cold that they could not stand outside to watch the fireworks display on Pikes Peak. So a few minutes before midnight they all gathered in the children's bathroom upstairs, the only room with a view of the peak, and perched on the tub and the toilet to drink champagne.

"Put the light out," said Nellie. "We'll all see much better if we do."

"I can't see at all," said Eric and pushed through his relatives toward the window.

"You will if you are patient," said Cousin Clara, planting her feet firmly on the tile floor. She was not very tall, but she loomed against the dark window. She wore a red wig because her hair was quite thin. Cousin Clara was about the same age as James, yet seemed older. She had been a schoolteacher and had never married, having always promised herself to her secret ambition, politics. She had been reelected to the Seventy-seventh Congress of the United States, and her firm chin jutted out a little further now than Yarrow remembered.

Clara had spent one summer with the family when Yarrow was younger. They had all gone hiking around Maroon Bells near Galena. All that Yarrow could clearly remember about her, apart from her sturdy legs, was how at night, when "nature called" as she put it, Clara would set off up the mountain with a shovel, a roll of toilet paper and a lantern. Smaller and smaller grew the light of the lantern. "I can still see yooooou," hollered James through his cupped hands. Clara had been unable to see the humor in the situation.

Jock eased himself out of the corner near the sink and motioned Eric to take his place. It was somewhat crowded in the bathroom. He came over to stand beside Yarrow and Greta near the door.

"Doesn't do to get too close to politicians."

"You told me you once ran for mayor yourself!"

"Aye, and I was defeated, thank God. I didn't say all this wisdom came to me early, Yarrow, only that I learned it the hard way. You can't wear two hats if you're a newspaperman."

Yarrow was half listening to him. She kept turning her head to see if anyone else was coming up the stairs.

"Who are you waiting for?" said Grandfather, knowing very well who. "Elliot?"

"No. Why should I? He didn't think he could make it. I'm waiting for Sandy, if you must know."

The first great wheel of fireworks exploded in the sky. The children and adults aaahed.

"Happy New Year."

"Happy Hogmanay." Jock squeezed the champagne out of his moustache and kissed Yarrow on the cheek.

"I want to give you a little present," he said, reaching into his pocket.

"What is it?"

He placed in her hand the little slug of metal that he had always carried in his pocket.

She held it up to the light from the hallway. "Why, it says 'Yarrow.' I never knew that."

"Aye. It was the first word I cast on the Linotype when you were a year old—and it was the last one. I never could get the hang of it. I've kept it ever since."

"Grandfather." Yarrow hugged him.

There never was such a family, thought Yarrow, for kissing and hugging and touching. Even those not directly related were affected by it, as though close friendship with the McLeans gave one kissing priorities. Laura turned around and hugged Yarrow with such intensity that Yarrow knew whom she was thinking about. Yarrow kissed her back.

"This one's for Little Lem."

Little Lem was asleep in Laura's old room. Greta, with her hair like Rapunzel's, went over and put her arms around her father. Nellie stood beside Cousin Clara as though sizing her up.

"Happy New Year, Clara." Clara, being a Quaker, disdained titles.

"You must come and see me one day in Washington," Clara said.

James embraced his cousin and the front of Clara's starched blouse buckled. James kissed Freya with an extra solicitousness, his hand lingering on her shoulder as he passed in the small crowded space under the pale light from the hall.

The person for whom James reserved most of his affection was his father, giving him a hug so fierce that the old man rocked on the balls of his feet. Yarrow turned away so the others would not see how it affected her and she saw Sandy running up the stairs.

"You said you would drop by," she said, going down a couple of steps toward him. He stood still until their faces were level, and he took her face in his two hands. His hands were icy cold from being outdoors. "Happy New Year," he said, kissing her. It was her first grown-up kiss and Yarrow blushed furiously and they both laughed. He still had his scarf on and his ears were red with the cold. She put her hands on them and they kissed again and just then there was a blast of cold air as the front door opened again and Elliot stood there in his olive-drab army uniform, holding a large box and saying, "I think I'm just a minute too late."

"Yes," she said, "the fireworks have begun. Have you two met?" She felt flustered and blamed Elliot for it.

Elliot put down the box and Sandy went down the stairs.

"Elliot Weyden."

"Sandy Heartland."

They shook hands. Sandy was a few inches taller than Elliot, but Elliot, holding his soft field cap in his hand, was so trimmed down and dark and spruce in his uniform that he seemed like a blackbird with his quick eyes.

"Happy New Year, Yarrow," he said. She allowed him to kiss her on the cheek.

A great whoop went up from the bathroom as a shower of fireworks delighted the watchers. It was almost like the roar of a crowd at a boxing match. Grandfather's head appeared at the door.

"Yarrow, come in, you're missing everything. Why, bless me, if it isn't Elliot. Come up, come up, I'm too old to manage these stairs more than once a day."

Elliot bounded up the stairs past Sandy. His heavy black shoes made a great clatter on the green painted wooden stairs.

"You do my eyes proud, Elliot, to see you like this," said the old man. "Look, everybody, Elliot's here."

"Good evening, sir," said Sandy, coming up behind Elliot while a great fuss was going on. Grandfather waved to him as he kept his hand on Elliot's back.

"Heard any good music lately?" Jock asked. Sandy lifted his eyebrows at Yarrow, and she, being as perverse in character as her grandfather could be, took hold of his hand and didn't let it go, not even when Eric whistled at her. She was surprised that Eric even noticed; he couldn't take his eyes off his hero and kept fingering the small metal letters "U.S." on Elliot's right lapel.

"I won't send you to war," said Clara. "If it comes to the floor of the House, I will vote against it." As the fireworks ended, the older members of the house drifted into the hall and down the stairs.

"I'm sick to death of hearing about the isolationists," said

Grandfather, coming down the stairs slowly. "Britain is bleeding to death."

"And we will, too, if we get into it."

"You've got to fight for something."

"I'll never vote for it."

They were all about to enter the parlor when Elliot said he had brought a present for Eric. He was standing next to the big box he had brought, with a silly grin on his face.

"What is it?" asked Eric, kneeling beside the box while the others watched. A small whimper came from inside.

"Open it and see." Elliot loved surprises, those he gave others, more than anything. His face was almost splitting with glee. Eric tore open the heavy cardboard and inside, among a blizzard of torn paper, was a puppy, more legs than body, that began licking his face with a long pink tongue.

"It's a Great Dane."

"That's the biggest wee dog I've ever seen," said Grandfather as the pup lolloped around them. Eric threw his arms around the pup's neck; it was nearly as big as he was.

"I love him. I'm going to call him Sherlock Holmes."

While the family all admired the new addition to the family, Laura took the cardboard box out to the kitchen to empty out the urine-stained papers. In among the papers was a sharp-edged card. "To Yarrow, Queen of My Heart, Happy Birthday with All My Love, Elliot." Laura glanced back through the hall at Eric and the family surrounding the dog, and at Yarrow standing hand in hand with Sandy. She slipped the card into her pocket. How she missed Lem, she thought.

In the parlor James threw some new wood on the fire and Jock asked him for a "real" drink.

"No more of that fizzy stuff."

"I'll get it." Yarrow went to the sideboard and poured her grandfather a whiskey. Sandy hovered around her, a little put out by Elliot's presence. Eric and the pup lay in front of the fire, getting in everyone's way. Elliot crossed to the window seat, which looked out into the garden, but the striped curtains were closed against the cold.

Clara was pounding a pillow into submission to put behind her back. "If the Lend-Lease deal goes through," she was saying to James, "we will never be paid back. Taft's already said that lending arms is a bit like lending chewing gum—you don't want it back."

"Girl, girl," said Jock, rolling the words in anger, "it's not a question of money."

It had been a long time since anyone had called Congresswoman Clara Russell a girl, and she straightened her back so that the cushion fell out and she glared at Jock.

"Well, if it is not a question of the taxpayers' money, will you at least concede that going ahead with it will guarantee our country being embroiled in this war?"

"We are already in it, Clara."

"Hush, you two," said Freya, looking up from her knitting. She was making booties for Little Lem.

"How do wars begin?" asked Eric.

"Two countries have a disagreement and they fight over it," said James.

"But we're not fighting with Germany, are we?"

"No, but they are fighting with England. And England is our friend."

Eric dropped to a shooting position and cocked his finger like an imaginary gun. "Pow, pow, pow."

"Now suppose," said James, pinching his big McLean nose between his thumb and forefinger, "that you were in the playground one day and some bully came along and hit your sister. Wouldn't you go to her aid?"

Eric squeezed his tongue through his lips and thought for a moment. "It depends," he said.

"On what?"

"Well, how big is this bully?"

Grandfather laughed. "Well, we may have a budding pacifist here, too, Clara."

Clara clenched her fists. "Pacifism has nothing to do with a lack of courage, Jock."

"Will you two stop," said Freya. "You're like a pair of children."

Elliot had moved toward the fire. He had been watching Yarrow and Sandy, who were standing behind the sofa. Whenever he tried to catch Yarrow's eye, she looked away. Sandy was stroking Yarrow's hand. Her cheeks were red.

Clara was oblivious to what was going on behind her. Nellie, who seemed to be very attracted to her, was sitting on the sofa beside her.

"Jeanette Rankin . . ." began Clara. Jock harrumphed in his throat, and Clara addressed herself to Nellie, "was the first woman elected to Congress. *She* voted against the 1917 war."

Jock took his cigar out of his mouth. "And it stopped her political career."

"She's back."

"An aberration."

"We're not all pragmatists, Jock. Some of us have principles."

"I must admit private convictions and public courage are seldom fused in politicians."

Sandy whispered in Yarrow's ear. "Could we go outside for a minute?"

They tiptoed out of the room just as Laura walked in with Greta and Little Lem. Greta loved babies.

"All this talk of war," they heard Laura say as they closed the door behind her, "makes me nervous."

Yarrow and Sandy went through the dining room into the kitchen. Swirling snow was hitting the window above the sink. There was no one there and Sandy pressed Yarrow against the wall, so that the wooden dado below the wallpaper cut into her back. He kissed her again. Yarrow thought he kissed beautifully. Her face flamed and she felt her lips and chin tingle.

"I love you," he said.

She forgot about the dado pressing into her spine. "Do you love me?" he asked.

"I think so."

"Will you wear my class ring?"

He took it off and slipped it over her fingers, searching for one it would fit. But it was too big.

"I'll wear it on a chain."

Freya came into the kitchen with some used drinking glasses. "Why, there you both are." They drew apart abruptly and Yarrow wiped her mouth with her hand. She was sure her lips must show a rash, but Freya seemed to notice nothing. Freya went to the oven for some angels-on-horseback that Greta had made and gave the tray to Sandy with her eyebrows raised. He went off to hand them around and Yarrow gave him an imploring look as her mother set her to wash the glasses.

"He is very good-looking, I suppose," said Freya.

"Oh, yes, isn't he? Look what he gave me, Mama." She took her hands out of the sink and showed Freya the ring in her pocket.

"He's going back to Purdue in a few days. Oh, Mama, I think I'm in love."

Freya looked at her daughter, at the thick dark tumbled hair escaping from its combs, at the eyes that were like a reflection of her own. She had become a woman in front of her and she had not seen it. She pushed a strand of her daughter's hair back behind her ear.

"That's nice," she said.

"Could you be a little more enthusiastic, Mama?"

"I'm sorry."

"What is it?"

"Oh, nothing."

"Go on, say it. It's about Sandy, isn't it? None of you really like him. You don't think he's good enough."

"That's not it and you know it. But I always thought it was Elliot you liked. I thought that was why he came back."

"Oh, Mama. I wish you would all get it out of your heads that I'm carrying some kind of crush for Elliot. He's so old!"

"He's twenty-three!"

"He's like a brother to me. That's all. But Sandy, it's so—so different." Yarrow sighed and her mother flicked a dishcloth at her.

"Come on then, Juliet. Rinse these for me and then it will be time for everyone to go home. Even Romeo."

CHAPTER 10

CLARA RUSSELL ISSUED AN INVITATION TO YARROW TO VISIT HER in Washington later that year. Yarrow was sure that her father's cousin had mixed her up with Nellie. What with one thing and another, it was not until December that Yarrow took the Rock Island train from Denver, wearing a new gray hat and gloves and carrying a clean shorthand notebook. Miss Smithins' Shorthand Secretarial School had raised her writing speed to ninety words a minute, and her typing, too, had improved. Yarrow had begun work as a reporter for her father, which, she told her mother, she had been doing for years; the only difference now was that she was being paid.

Yarrow crossed her legs at the ankles and watched the scenery rushing past as the train roared toward Chicago, across the great white plains of the American Midwest. She had never been out of the state of Colorado before, and had been sent off with admonitions to be careful and not to talk to strangers. Her natural exuberance, now tightly under control, escaped like her hair from under the brim of her hat. The gloved fingers tapped impatiently on the window ledge as the train stopped on its way

across the country; through Lyman and Lincoln and Omaha and
Des Moines and Iowa City and West Liberty and Davenport, as
the states spread out before her and parted like the sea. Yarrow's
high coloring, the red cheeks and the glowing eyes, the thick
black curling hair that sprang from her temples caught many
glances. But she returned none of them, alternating between
haughty disdain or humming to herself as she hugged the thought
of Sandy's ring, hanging on a fine chain around her neck, warm
against her skin, or bumping under her blouse as she made her
way along the rocking corridor to the restaurant car. In Chicago
at LaSalle Street Station, she had to change to the Pennsylvania
Railroad, and it was not until 7:40 on Friday morning that she
arrived, crumpled, tired but excited, at Union Station in Washington, D.C.

But her cousin was not there to receive her; only one of
Clara's two secretaries, an ambitious young woman who com-
mandeered her bags and steered her out of the station and into a
small gray car. The backseat of the car was covered with papers
and pamphlets and folders.

"Sorry about the car," she said. "I haven't had time to clean
it up."

"Oh that's all right." Yarrow was shy of this confident,
aggressive young woman. "Is this your car?"

"Yes. My name's Rebecca and Clara apologizes for not being
here to meet you herself. She's been held up in Pittsburgh where
she was delivering a speech against the war. We'll meet her at
the Capitol later. Is this your first visit to Washington?"

"Yes."

"Then let me show you some of the sights."

In fact it seemed to Yarrow, twisting and turning to see the
monuments out of the window of the car, that Washington was
already at war. When they got out to walk, military men thronged
the streets, and rows of temporary wood and stucco buildings
lined the Reflecting Pool from the Washington Monument to the
Lincoln Memorial. The city was steeped in a great wash of
instability. Trees had been cut down along the avenues to widen
the streets; dismembered trunks lay waiting to be removed.
Traffic poured in from the new National Airport. Instead of the
measured tread of history, which Yarrow had expected to hear
murmuring up from the cobblestones, her ears were buffeted by
the sound of hurrying men; military men and advisers for the
recruitment and training of draftees; men to solve the housing
problems of a city bursting with an influx of five thousand new
residents every month; lobbyists and experts appearing before the

Truman Committee, investigating waste and fraud in the Defense Department; industrialists and businessmen in Washington to lend their expertise in meeting the requirements of the Lend-Lease act; influence peddlers and dollar-a-year men who flocked to the nation's capital to be part of the history they could sense in the making; men moving with the urgency of an impending drama.

Later, in the Cannon House Office Building, the effect of men and power was reinforced. Even the language seemed masculine as Rebecca led her through the Capitol building, past the throngs of congressmen and senators, aides and constituents, tourists and lobbyists who packed the marble hallways and the great Rotunda and whose voices echoed in the Statuary Hall. "There's Senator James Mead of New York," said Rebecca, pointing out a figure disappearing into a room. Yarrow caught a flash of the man's trouser leg. "He's a Roosevelt man but he's on the Truman Committee investigating government spending on the defense program."

"Oh," said Yarrow, realizing how much she did not know.

They came at last to the solemn quiet of the Speaker's Lobby, where an attendant let them in through the wooden doors with the clock set into the glass transom above them. On the blue and brown tiled floor, under the painted ceiling, Yarrow waited for her cousin. She could see her talking animatedly to a very old man. "That's George Norris," whispered Rebecca. Norris was a Progressive who had voted against the 1917 war. "He won't this time," said Rebecca as Clara saw them and came over. She had on the same suit with beading on the lapels that she had worn on New Year's Eve. Over her red wig she wore a black hat with a brim that looked as though she had bowled it all the way from Pittsburgh. Here, in her own setting, Clara Russell looked like she belonged. She was not afraid of voicing her opinion, and, in walking back through the halls toward her office, introducing Yarrow to those who stopped and talked to her, she exuded a confidence that Yarrow recognized was part of her allure as a candidate. She had wondered how anyone could have voted for Clara Russell in her funny old-fashioned clothes and her sturdy legs. But seeing her here, among her peers, Yarrow realized with some shame that Clara's differences were her strengths. Partisanship, Clara explained, had no real place once you got here. She smiled at Yarrow with her funny lock-lipped smile.

Congresswoman Russell lived in a rooming house on the corner of Sixteenth and R streets, N.W., where she could catch a bus to the Hill. She had two rooms, and the sitting-room wall concealed a Murphy bed, which delighted Yarrow who had never seen one before. The furniture was nondescript; a chair, a table, a standard lamp that bathed the room in a false semblance of warmth. But everywhere there were books; on the shelves, on the table, and on the floor, and where there were no books, there were piles of magazines, erudite ones on pacifism, women's issues and foreign policy. Reams of correspondence had to be removed from the chairs before one could sit down. On the wall was a daguerrotype of Clara's parents. Her mother Hilda, Jock's sister, had a little of the look of Jock. She was a small woman with a prominent chin, not hidden by the big black bow that tied on her hat. Yarrow remembered Jock telling her that Hilda had whipped him once with a rope when he was learning the printing trade and had done something to upset her. She looked quite capable of wielding one. Mr. Russell, on the other hand, did not. Where his wife's chin was strong, his receded, and where her eye glinted with a fierce intelligence, Mr. Russell's lacked the glimmer of life. Mr. Russell could never have whipped Jock, and yet Jock had always reserved his criticism for his uncle and thought of his sister with real affection. Yarrow stared and stared at the picture, but she could not bring Mr. Russell to life.

Everything about the city of Washington was exciting to Yarrow. Here, on this street corner, under the leafless tulip trees, she imagined Abe Lincoln's long legs strolling by, and there, on the steps of an old house, the very spot perhaps where Dolley Madison had stopped to talk to a friend. Even the streetlights and the stones of the sidewalk were full of interest.

On Saturday Clara was busy, and so Rebecca took Yarrow to see the Andrew Mellon Collection at the new National Gallery. Yarrow wore a new pair of platform shoes with open toes and her feet ached. That night they went to see Bette Davis in her latest movie, *Dark Victory*. Yarrow disgraced herself by sobbing before the first reel was finished. Rebecca and Clara both thought the movie was sentimental rubbish. "But women put love first, don't they?" asked Yarrow.

"Not so," said Rebecca. "I'm a career woman. I'm never getting married."

"That only means you love something more than marriage," said Clara.

On Sunday it was very raw and cold and Yarrow was happy to stay inside and listen to music while Clara caught up on her correspondence.

"Listen to this," said Clara, picking up a sheet of paper and turning toward Yarrow. "Here's a man who has sent me five dollars to help me 'continue to vote with my conscience.' "

"How else could you vote?"

"Well, I could vote how I think, or I could vote how I think the majority of the electors in my constituency want me to vote."

Clara got up from her desk and went into the kitchenette to make some coffee. The music on the radio stopped abruptly and Yarrow was about to twiddle the brown plastic dials when an announcer's voice said that Japanese planes had bombed Pearl Harbor.

"What was that?" asked Clara, rushing out of the kitchenette as the announcer finished speaking. She was holding a used coffee filter in her hands.

"The Japanese have bombed Pearl Harbor. Where is that?"

"Good God," said Clara and dropped the filter on the floor. She stepped over the spreading brown stain as if it weren't there and rushed to the telephone. She dialed a number, and only then, listening to the ringing tone, did she look up at Yarrow.

"Jock's won," she said. "America will go to war."

The House was abuzz the next morning for a special joint session of Congress. Not a spare seat was to be had, and Yarrow had just squeezed into the press gallery under the wing of a wire-service reporter. By tradition, the front row of stools was reserved for the wire reporters. The press gallery hung over the rostrum where the president would speak, and Yarrow knelt in the tiny space beside her mentor and nervously licked her reporter's pencil.

Below her the great room seethed with emotion and voices.

On the deep blue carpet with its gold abstract design, members and staff were moving into place waiting for the arrival of the president. In the packed galleries opposite, under the temporary ceiling reinforcements, diplomats, officials and visitors jammed into every available space. The photographers' gallery was packed with equipment and people and Movietone cameras. From her position, peering over the balcony of the press gallery, Yarrow saw the Republican members sitting on the left of the chamber. She picked out Clara in their ranks, Clara, in her dark dress with the beaded lapels and the hat with the uneven brim, sitting somewhat withdrawn from her colleagues. She had not gone to bed at all the night before and had still been sitting in her Sunday clothes when Yarrow woke up. Clara had said nothing about her long, lonely night and had tried again to reach Jeanette Rankin, the pacifist from Montana, on the telephone. But Miss Rankin could not be reached.

The Senate, preceded by the vice-president, came in and took their seats. The doorkeeper announced the justices of the Supreme Court, who entered in their black robes and sat along the edge of the well below the rostrum. Then came the members of the president's cabinet and finally, at half-past twelve, President Roosevelt was announced and the whole of the chamber, from the floor to the ceiling, rose to its feet, and after a pause of intense silence, broke into applause that finished only when Speaker Rayburn rapped his gavel. When the President appeared, the applause began again and changed into cheering as he readied himself to speak. Yarrow visualized him standing in front of the bronze motif below her—a mace and a bound column of reeds, surrounded by an olive branch. "Peace Through Strength." Yarrow wondered if Clara agreed with that. She wished she could see the president at the simple rostrum as she scribbled in her notebook and thought how she would report this for her father.

As the lights blazed down on him, Yarrow listened to the familiar voice. The president's war address was constantly interrupted and each time the applause broke out, Yarrow shifted her weight from one knee to another. Her wire-service friend wiped his sweating brow and prayed aloud that the logjam on telephone calls to New York would be cleared by the time he got there. When the president had finished and the joint session was dissolved, Mr. McCormack, the majority leader, asked that the House pass Joint Resolution Number 254 and the clerk was ordered to read it. Yarrow was glad that her shorthand had improved and only hoped that she would be able to read it later.

"That the state of war between the United States and the Imperial Government of Japan which has thus been thrust upon the United States is hereby formally declared . . ."

Speaker Rayburn asked, "Is a second demanded?" and at that Miss Jeanette Rankin of Montana stood up and cried, "I object!"

A hiss went round the chamber.

The speaker said that no objection was in order and repeated, "Is a second demanded?"

Yarrow watched as the white-haired, spectacled woman was ignored, and Miss Rankin sat down. Yarrow looked down at her cousin and could see her nervously clasping and unclasping her pocketbook. For forty minutes Yarrow listened to the impassioned speeches from the floor. They were all for the president, as the bombing of Pearl Harbor had eradicated any partisan differences. The Republicans, Yarrow wrote, wanted to erase any memory of their past objections to Roosevelt's war preparations. Yarrow waited to hear from any of the Colorado congressmen and checked her list of names: Lewis, Hill, Chenoweth, Rockwell.

Mr. Reed of Illinois was the last to speak during the debate, and Mr. McCormack of Massachusetts asked for the yeas and nays.

"Mr. Speaker . . ." It was Jeanette Rankin on her feet. Speaker Rayburn ignored her.

"The gentleman from Massachusetts demands the yeas and nays. Those who favor taking this vote by the yeas and nays will rise and remain standing until counted."

"Mr. Speaker, I would like to be heard!"

"The yeas and nays have been ordered. The question is, will the House suspend the rules and pass the resolution?"

"Mr. Speaker, a point of order!"

"A roll call may not be interrupted."

There were catcalls from the benches and finally one man shouted out, "Aw, sit down, sister," and the roll call began. Yarrow found she was sweating with emotion and tension. Damp patches had appeared on her notebook. She saw Clara go toward Miss Rankin and then change her mind. All through the names, Kirwan, Kleberg, Klein, the yeas rolled on; Pierce, Pitteniger, Ploche, and then Ramspeck, Randolph, Rankin of Montana. Jeanette Rankin spoke up in a firm, clear voice, "Nay," and the man from the Associated Press beside Yarrow wrote down that "a chorus of hisses and boos erupted from the floor and the galleries." Yarrow moved her damp hands and watched Clara. Rockefeller, Rodgers of Pennsylvania, Rogers of Massachusetts, Russell of Pennsylvania . . .

Clara said, "Yea," but she said it so softly that the clerk did not hear her and called her again, and she said, "Yea" again and looked up at Yarrow in the press gallery. It was just the briefest look before she went rushing out into the cloakroom, but there was such anguish in the look that Yarrow thought, "Poor Clara," and her pencil scribbled meaninglessly across her notebook. But when she looked through her notes later while waiting for a free telephone, she found she had written "Had she the courage of her convictions?"

When she struggled through the crowds of people to find Clara, she thought she saw, in a milling group of army brass, Elliot's sleek head. When the man turned his head, she saw it *was* Elliot. He was animated and lively. His dark eyes twinkled as he laughed at something his companion said to him. "Elliot! Elliot!" He couldn't hear her. There was a tremendous crush of people on the stairs and the security was intense. Yarrow tried to reach him; she had not heard from him since New Year's Eve, but when she shouldered her way through a group in front of her and looked for him again, he was gone.

At last she found Clara, or Clara found her. Jeanette Rankin had locked herself in a phone booth in the cloakroom, she said. She had wanted to go up to her and apologize. Clara took Yarrow's hands on the steps of the Capitol. The security people were taking away the barricades.

"I just hope you understand, Yarrow. I had no choice."

"I understand." But Yarrow didn't. She was filled with a real but amorphous feeling of disappointment. Clara had let her down; she had just missed seeing Elliot. She touched the chain around her neck and thought of Sandy. What did it matter?

"You're going to be so busy, Clara. I think I should go home."

Yarrow left Washington two days later and returned to Colorado. All the way in the train, she went over what she had seen and the clacking of the wheels became the sound of the Linotype. Love or business? Love or business? She thought of herself striding through the Capitol building like Clara, with a secretary at her heels. She thought of powerful people coming to her for advice, or leaking information that she could turn into scoops. She could see it now. Her stomach knotted around the realization that she had swallowed a taste of power. Yarrow tried to ignore the feeling and listened to the train. The wheels had changed their lyrics. Love of business. Love of business, they said. Yarrow couldn't wait to get back to work.

CHAPTER 11

LIEUTENANT ELLIOT WYDEN HAD JUST MADE IT BACK TO WASHington in time for the joint session of Congress. He was assigned to General Marshall's staff in Washington, D.C., and he had been on a twenty-four-hour furlough to see his mother. When his mother called him, he knew it would have something to do with his sister, Vivienne. He was right.

"She just went," Mrs Weyden was sobbing. "Without a word

to me. If she had explained or left a note, I would have been able to find her on my own."

Elliot broke a bagel and let his mother go on talking. They were in the sitting room of her apartment on Twenty-eighth Street. He had moved his mother and sister there eighteen months earlier when they had sold their house in upstate New York. It was a walk-up apartment with two bedrooms, the rooms small and crammed with the larger pieces of furniture from his mother's earlier life. A baby grand piano covered with a felt cloth took up all the entrance foyer.

Elliot Weyden's mother was a woman who had worked hard all her life. She had been a gifted child, but in her teens her expectations and those of her parents did not jibe; she had been off course ever since. She had married Elliot's father in a true love match and had told herself that she would give up everything for him; she had not realized how hard it would be. Her musical talent seemed to leave her; she had never been blessed with the steadfastness of ambition, which would have steeled her to sit longer on the piano stool; difficult works or recalcitrant students only increased her longing to put away the music sheets and retire to her room with the shades down. When her husband died, the presence of her two lively and mischievous children, not at all quiet and dreamlike as she had imagined they would be, but more like their dead father, quick and witty and sparkling and headstrong, had only increased the incidence of her migraines. When she felt well, she did not go back to teaching piano, but took work as a housekeeper; she could cook and clean and scrub floors; only the sight of the piano and thoughts of what might have been set off her headaches. But she wouldn't sell the piano; it stood like a big question mark in the foyer where she had to pass it every day.

But it was another aspect of his mother's personality that Elliot found most difficult to deal with; she did not think she deserved any better.

It exasperated Elliot. When he could, he sent her pretty things, a cameo brooch, a lace shawl. He knew she liked these gifts. But they were put away in tissue in drawers and closets. "Oh, it's much too good," she said, and would go out and put her hands in a metal bucket and wring out a smelly floor rag. As he sat opposite the slim figure in the patterned wool housegown and handed her his handkerchief, he understood all her faults and forgave them without rationalizing them. She was his mother. He was there to take care of her. Just as he had sent her every dollar and cent he could from Colorado during the Depression, now he was glad she had sent for him from Washington, because she had known he would come.

"I warned her about this man," his mother was saying, "but she wouldn't listen. She said she met him when she sold him some gloves. Oh, Elliot, if only we hadn't moved here and been so close to Altman's, this would never have happened. I said, Vivienne, a married man wants only one thing from a young woman, and marriage is not what he has in mind. How could she do this to us?" Elliot looked at the gnarled red fingers of his mother's hands. They were quite small hands; he was surprised to realize that once they could stretch to an octave on the keyboard. "Your father would turn over in his grave if he knew. I think she was taken in by his accent. She always was an Anglophile and she said he would help her get on the stage. Get on the stage! Oh, Elliot, she talks to you, I know she does. I'm out of my mind worrying about her. I don't know where to begin looking."

"I know where she is—at least I have a good idea. She telephoned me at the base yesterday."

"Then find her, Elliot, and send her home."

"She may not want to come."

Mrs. Weyden sat up and looked at her son in his military jacket. He had completed officer training and he looked very handsome and capable of anything. She dabbed at her eyes with his handkerchief.

"Elliot, you can make anyone do what you want them to do."

"Except you, Mother," he said.

He had tangled with his sister before. She was stubborn. She was beautiful. She was willful. The idea to sell the house upstate had been Vivienne's.

"Well, I'll see what I can do. But I only have a twenty-four-hour furlough."

"Oh, we're not at war yet."

"You tell General George Marshall that," he said, getting up and putting his hands on her shoulders. She put one hand up to cover his. He squeezed her shoulder. "I'll find her. By the way, where's that rug I sent you?" With the first real money he had made—he had arranged the underwriting in a complicated merger between the Grove Innovation Company and a paper mill and had asked that his fee be paid in debentures—he had bought his mother an antique Kilim rug.

"Oh, Elliot, it's much too good to be used every day. I've put it in the hall closet."

"Mom, I want you to use these things."

"I know, dear. I know. I'll try. I really will."

Elliot shook his head, put on his cap and went out the door to find his sister.

Unlike her mother, Vivienne knew what she wanted and was quite sure she deserved it. She had confided in Elliot that if offered a chance to escape her dismal surroundings, she would take it. Elliot recognized and sympathized with those sentiments, but he had told her to bide her time. When the war was over, he said, he could give her everything she wanted. "When the war is over . . ." she had cried. "What am I supposed to do in the meantime? Just sit here with Mother and grow old? It's all right for you, you can go off and make your mark in the world. I've only got one commodity to sell. I'm not going to wait to become an old maid." She had hung up on him before he could argue with her.

Vivienne was impatient and she had seen her opportunity in the person of a Mr. Clive Basingstoke. Elliot suspected that she had allowed herself to be seduced rather than the other way around. Vivienne had told him that Basingstoke always stayed at the Plaza when he was in New York, and he hailed a taxi and asked the driver to stop first by a brownstone on the way.

When the war is over . . . Elliot thought as he sat back in the taxi. The war could not have come at a worse time for him. He had just begun to make his run on Wall Street and it all had to be put on the back burner. He had made a little money in the few years he had been there, and he chafed at the thought of living on the three thousand dollars a year he would get from the army. He would have to be careful, he thought, as he watched the taxi meter.

"Well, look who's here." The handsome woman who opened the door of the brownstone stood for a moment with her hands on her hips, then threw her arms around Elliot.

"Hello, Mrs. Neil," he said.

"Girls. Girls. Come and see what the cat dragged in," she shouted over her shoulder as Elliot swung her around. A number of young women appeared and squealed with laughter when they saw Elliot. Elliot went to close the heavy door and saw the taxi driver's mouth had dropped open. Elliot was going to pay him, but thought, What the heck, one last fling as a big spender. "I won't be long," said Elliot as the girls pounced on him and he shut the door.

"Well, Mother Mary, this is a surprise," said Mrs. Neil, who had been a Catholic a long time ago, as she swayed into her office and sent the girls back to work. "I thought we would have to let your room again. Do you have time for a drink, soldier?"

"Sure. Why not." Elliot loosened his tie and sat back. He liked to watch Mrs. Neil move. All her clothes seemed to slither over her. Even the most modest dress needed to be pinned over her bosom or it gaped open, and her skirts seemed to climb up her thighs whenever she sat down. He had first met her when he came to New York and was looking for a cheap room to rent. He had walked past the brownstone one hot summer day and she was leaning in the doorway. She was younger then, but the blond hair and the fleshiness were still the same. "You looking for a job?" she had asked. "For a room." "I got rooms. Can you fix a hot-water furnace?" "Sure," he said. He had placed his cardboard suitcase inside the front door and she took him down to the basement and waved her hand at the boiler. "It's all yours," she said. The furnace was like the one he used to fix with Lem, and he saw immediately what the problem was. But he shook his head and said, "Boy, this is going to take me a while. Would you have a glass of milk or a cool drink?" "You sure you know what you're doing?" After a while, when she had gone and he thought enough time had passed, he lit the pilot light, which had gone out. Mrs. Neil was impressed. "We need a man around here," she said. "You look after the boiler and the furnace and fix things when they need fixing, you can have a room for nothing." And so Elliot found a room and he was so naïve and so busy working at the stock exchange as a page, and going to night school, and fixing the boiler whenever it went out, that it took him weeks to realize that the "girls" were not Mrs. Neil's daughters but prostitutes.

Elliot, at eighteen, had done his own share of innocent fumbling in Platte City at the Salvation Army dances. But he was still a virgin when he arrived at Mrs. Neil's and the girls teased him about it. Sometimes they asked him if he would like to come into their rooms, and he had once been smuggled in by a lively girl, Maureen, to peer through a hole at a new girl at work. For weeks afterward he had been obsessed with the idea of his penis entering someone's mouth, and at odd times, usually when it was most embarrassing, his organ would grow hard and it was agony to try to control it and make it subside.

He was too fastidious to use the girls and he was afraid of VD, and would relieve himself by masturbating, sometimes in the bathroom at the exchange when he could not go out on the floor with his trousers bulging. He was ashamed and thought of all his mother's warnings when he was a little boy, that his health would be ruined, or, far worse, that his "dickie," as she called it, would fall off. In fact, he *was* worrying about his health, because he was exhausted. He was taking concurrent degrees in law and commerce and working through the day and studying at night in between calls from Mrs. Neil to fix the boiler or the plumbing or a sticking door or a heater that wouldn't work. But there seemed no other way to keep up with the schedule he had set for himself, and now this urgent need to find release, when he had no time for any girls; and it would come upon him, even when he wasn't thinking about sex and he would have to do something about it immediately.

"Mother Mary," said Mrs. Neil one day when she came upon him in the boiler room with his penis in his hand. "Come and see me in my office, when you can."

Elliot was sure he was going to lose his job and would have to find another room. The ease of not having to pay rent was something he had begun to rely on. But Mrs. Neil had other plans. He found her sitting on her sofa in her pink robe, the one she wore when she was off duty, and she said, "Come here, Elliot," and indicated that he should sit beside her. Some soft swing music was playing on the radio, and just as softly, Mrs. Neil began to talk and ask questions, and Elliot began to relax and Mrs. Neil took his hand and slipped it inside the big satin lapels of her gown. And little by little his hand began to move over the big warm breast, or perhaps she had begun to move imperceptibly under his hand and he had just taken up the rhythm. And then he kissed her, clumsily and roughly, and she let him do it his way until he came, all too fast, the minute his penis had touched her warm, moist opening. She said, as he lay there, "Come with me," and led him to an alcove he had not noticed before, where the whole space was taken up by a bed, and she lay on it and told him to take off his clothes, and then she opened her robe as if her whole body was one pink vulva, and said, "Now, we'll do it my way."

She had been the best of teachers, Elliot thought, as she mixed him an old-fashioned from a tray near the window. She had been a mistress and a mother rolled into one.

"Here's looking at you, Lieutenant," said Mrs. Neil, handing him his drink. He tasted it. It had just the right amount of bitters in it.

"Will you be with us long or are you just passing through?"

"I have a twenty-four-hour pass from Washington. I've come to pick up some of my things."

"The room is yours as long as you want. We miss you around here. We used to have fun, right?"

He laughed.

"Oh, that, too. But when you renegotiated our lease, huh, Elliot?"

"That was my first big case."

"And when you got the girls to hand out leaflets to support the local candidate for the city council?" Mrs. Neil let out a deep laugh as she remembered it.

Elliot swirled his drink in his glass and smiled.

"You got a girl yet? Every soldier should have a girl."

"I'm working on it."

The doorbell rang. Elliot got up, finishing his drink in one gulp.

"I just need to get a couple of things out of my room." The doorbell rang again. Mrs. Neil went to answer it. "I have to make a phone call," he said.

"Go ahead, it's all yours."

Elliot placed a call to the Plaza Hotel to make sure that Mr. Basingstoke was in residence. Then he dialed another number and spoke to a young woman he sometimes took out when he was in New York. Could he see her later? He was making a kissing sound into the telephone when Mrs. Neil came back.

"You *are* working on it," she said.

"Don't be jealous," he said, taking her chin in his hand. "You'll always be my favorite."

"Your first, at any rate."

When they went to the front door, some of the girls came out to hug him good-bye. Mrs. Neil came down the steps with him. At the taxi, as he got in, she said, "Come back sometime, just for old times' sake, OK?"

"Anytime, lady, anytime," said the taxi driver.

"Not you, you jerk. Good-bye, Elliot."

"Whew, what a dame, what a dame," said the taxi driver as they took off uptown. He glanced in his rearview mirror at the good-looking young face in the back. He sucked in his belly where it touched the steering wheel.

"What a uniform will do for a guy. Lucky soldier."

Elliot entered the Plaza Hotel on the Fifty-ninth Street side. He used the house phone, and Mr. Basingstoke, after a moment of hesitation, invited him to come up.

Mr. Basingstoke was in civilian clothes, a dark blue banker's suit with thin white chalk stripes, for which he immediately apologized on seeing Elliot in uniform.

"Bad leg," he said, giving his false left leg a whack with a walking cane. He had thinning hair and a long, intelligent face, but the rest of his body, being round, seemed to belong to another person. He had the manners and ease of an upperclass Englishman, and offered drinks and nuts and comments on the weather, the state of the war, his own business (which was something to do with the City, as far as Elliot could discover); all information offered in a self-deprecating manner in case one mistakenly thought that he took himself seriously. He was, Elliot guessed, about forty-five years old. Elliot realized that Basingstoke was not going to mention his sister unless he did so first.

"Mr. Basingstoke . . ."

"Clive."

"Clive, my sister is nineteen years old. Since my father died she has been my responsibility. I am here to take her home."

"My dear fellow, Vivienne told me she was twenty-one and that she could make up her own mind."

"Is she here?"

Basingstoke's code of ethics would not allow him to lie. His eyes flickered to the bedroom door.

"Vivienne is very special to me," he said. "I would do nothing to harm her."

"I have to think of her future, Mr.—er—Clive, and this episode will do her a great deal of harm." Elliot leaned forward toward Basingstoke's face. "Vivienne was a virgin, Mr. Basingstoke."

This was a fact of which Basingstoke was well aware, but he blushed to the roots of his thinning hair and stood up so suddenly that his false leg clicked.

He tried to recover his composure.

"We live in the real world, Mr. Weyden."

"But my sister doesn't. She is very like my mother. They are innocent of the ways of the world. I will not leave here until Vivienne comes with me."

A small noise was heard at the door to the bedroom. Basingstoke's false leg clicked again as he sat down.

"I did not force Vivienne to come with me. She is very free to return to you if she wants."

At this tiny tremor of defection Vivienne rushed into the room and threw herself on Basingstoke and covered his face with kisses.

"I could never leave you, darling. Never, never." She was like a small pretty butterfly, in a pecan-colored dress with white polka dots. She was wearing a pair of Cuban-heeled shoes with open toes.

"It's all right, my dear," Basingstoke said, stroking her dark hair. She kissed his cheek again. He weakened further. "You won't have to do anything you don't want to do."

"I'll never leave him, Elliot. Never," she said, not taking her eyes off her lover's face. He went on stroking her hair, wiping away the tears that made her cheeks shine.

"You'll never have to, darling," said Basingstoke. Elliot could see the man melting into the sofa.

"Then we have some things to discuss," said Elliot, and Vivienne disentangled herself from Basingstoke and stood up and shook out her skirt and went and sat demurely on an upright chair beside a desk.

"This may take some time," said Basingstoke, "and it is getting very late. Why don't we go down for dinner and continue afterward?" Elliot sighed and looked at his watch. He thought of his date and he caught his sister's eye. "OK," he said.

Vivienne went off happily to powder her nose and then they went down and ate in the Oak Room, and by the time they went back upstairs it was perfectly clear to Elliot that his sister had Basingstoke wrapped around her tiny finger.

By eleven o'clock, Basingstoke had opened a new bottle of bourbon, and Elliot had heard the whole story of his leg injury in the World War. Elliot mentally readjusted his age. By midnight, Vivienne had fallen asleep on top of the coverlet on the bed. Basingstoke went in and put a blanket over her and stood at the door, holding one of her open-toed shoes. This tenderness convinced Elliot to go for the jugular.

He was reminded of the negotiation he had had with the Grove Innovation Company. At the last moment Mr. Grove had decided against the deal. "I can't go through with it." Elliot had grabbed him by the lapels. "Like hell you won't. You sign that damn contract and let's finish what you agreed on." Mr. Grove had signed. There were some men, Elliot thought, who just couldn't come to a decision. Basingstoke was one of them.

By one o'clock Basingstoke had admitted that he and his wife had been separated for years and were husband and wife in name only, and that Vivienne was the sweetest, most endearing human being in the whole world, and how had he ever imagined that he could live without her? By two o'clock the men had their arms around each other and Elliot told him about some of the exploits of Mrs. Neil's girls, and about Maureen, who could stand on her head and do a split in the nude while drinking a glass of water. By three o'clock Basingstoke was calling Elliot his "little brother," and a few minutes later Elliot had him write out and sign a letter of intent—that he, Clive Basingstoke of Sully Corners, Essex, would marry his darling Vivienne within the year. At this he passed out, and Elliot tucked a cushion under his head, put out the lights and left.

When Elliot left the hotel he ran seven blocks to his date's apartment house. He rang and rang the intercom until finally she answered and when she found out it was he, she shouted at him to get lost, who did he think he was standing her up like that? Then she hung up and he stood staring at the locked front door. There were some things Mrs. Neil hadn't taught him.

Elliot had promised to spend the whole day with his mother, but that afternoon, bundled up and walking in from the park, they heard the news of the bombing of Pearl Harbor. He was stunned and knew he had to get back to his base immediately. He managed to hitch a lift back to Washington on a military plane. As he was leaving the apartment, Vivienne returned with the news of Basingstoke's proposal. His mother was not too happy, but at least her sensibilities were protected. Elliot told them that war was inevitable and he did not know when he would see them again. After he left, his mother wept and then she had Vivienne help her lift the rug out of the closet and lay it on the floor beside the piano. Then she thought that the floor could do with a good polish. She got out her tin of lemon-scented wax, a wad of felt to kneel on, and some floor rags and set to work. Vivienne could hear her humming as she herself opened her closet doors and wondered what she was going to pack.

CHAPTER 12

LEM DIED AT THE BATTLE OF THE CORAL SEA IN MAY. Heavy snow still blocked the upper reaches of Independence Pass, and it was not until a month later that Freya was able to drive over the Continental Divide to see Laura. Greta went with her, as Yarrow was working full time at the *Journal*.

One morning in June Yarrow walked into her father's office

unannounced and slammed the glass door shut. As usual, his office was littered with paper; sheets and galleys covered the desk and floor, and tossed and crumpled pieces of copy overflowed from the wastebasket. The increasing prosperity of the *Journal* had not made him any tidier. He was sitting in his wooden swivel chair talking on the telephone. He cupped his hand over the mouthpiece. "Yarrow, what is it? I'm busy."

"I have to talk to you."

"Later."

"Now, Dad."

"Brian, I'll call you back." He slammed down the phone. "For heaven's sake, Yarrow, you're so damn rude and impatient. . . ."

"I have every right to be. I just found out that you're paying that new reporter more than me . . ."

"Yarrow, he's a university man . . ."

"That's not the point. He knows nothing about this business; he can't write a sentence without putting in a word you have to look up in the dictionary; and he's being given all the best stories, while I'm stuck with the opening of a new goddam shoestore. It's just not fair. Why is he paid more than me?"

"He's a young man with a wife to support."

"What's that got to do with it! I put in the same hours."

"Men get paid more. Besides, he'll probably stay with the *Journal* for years."

"What do you think I'm going to do?"

"Women, traditionally, get married and leave. With him, I won't be wasting my time or my money."

Outside in the main office, a few people turned their heads as they heard the raised voices.

"What about my time, and my money? I've worked here for years and now you're giving me this . . ." She waved a handful of copy paper at him, ". . . this crap to work on."

"Yarrow, I won't have you speaking to me like that."

"You won't have to. I quit."

Yarrow threw open the door again and all the heads went down and the typewriters started again. She went to her desk and began throwing her notebooks and papers into her pocketbook. She grabbed the metal slug that her grandfather had given her and that she used as a paperweight and threw that in, too.

"There's steam coming out your ears," said one of her colleagues passing her desk. Yarrow ignored him. She jammed on her hat and stormed out of the office, leaving a stunned silence behind her. She felt coiled tight like a spring. Sandy was still away at college. She would love to have talked to him. When he graduated from Purdue he hoped to be accepted for officer training. He wanted to get married, and the old yo-yo that Yarrow always experienced when she thought about him started going up and down again. She tried to imagine waking up each morning and finding his blond head on the pillow beside her and the thought was comforting. But then she would walk through the newspaper office and hear the hum of people and machines and information and she could feel her hair stand on end with excitement. Why did her father not make it any easier? Well, perhaps he was making it easier for her. He was unable to accept her worth as a reporter—she would always be his daughter, not taken seriously. Yarrow clenched her jaw as she left the building. She would show him. She walked to the railway station and paused, as she always did, at the newsstand. She picked up some copies of the *Journal* and was about to place them on top of a stack of Denver *Globes* and stopped. She stood still for a minute, tapping the stack with her fingers, and then she made up her mind and caught the train to Denver before she could change her mind.

"Mr. Schaeffer, please."

"Who shall I say it is?"

"Yarrow McLean."

Yarrow was ushered into Larry Schaeffer's office. The owner of the *Globe* came forward with a big smile. He was about sixty years old with thinning hair. At least he no longer had a dandruff problem, thought Yarrow, as he brushed some cigarette ash off his jacket.

"Miss McLean, to what do I owe this honor? I haven't seen you since you were so high."

Yarrow sat on the edge of her chair clutching her bag on her lap.

"Mr. Schaeffer, I need a job and I would like to work at the *Globe*."

"I've seen your work. It's good. I saw that story you did on the water board."

Yarrow groaned. "I'd really like to get away from water board stories. I'd like to do a story on the building of Camp Carson. Do you know how much money has been appropriated to build it? Thirty million dollars. That's more than the whole town is worth. Nothing's going to be the same once the army moves in."

"Why don't you want to write it for the *Journal*?"

"Dad won't give me a chance at the good stories."

Larry Schaeffer leaned against his desk with his arms folded. "Does your father know you're here? More important, does Jock know?"

Yarrow swallowed. "Not yet. But they will. Mr. Schaeffer, I'm a very good reporter and I know my way around this town."

"You're not here to spy, are you . . .?"

"Of course I'm not here to spy. I want to work, that's all." Larry Schaeffer walked around his desk and picked up a letter opener.

"I don't know," he said. Larry Schaeffer liked the McLean family and had met Jock and James at a number of functions.

Yarrow stood up. She had on a yellow hat that matched the plaid in her skirt. Her hair billowed back from her face, and her clear gray eyes under their dark arched eyebrows caught Larry Schaeffer's.

"I need one chance, that's all. If you're not satisfied with my work, I'll leave."

Larry Schaeffer looked at the determined young woman. People said she took after her grandfather. Schaeffer had a grudging respect for the rough old-timer. They didn't make them like him anymore. He suddenly remembered Yarrow as a little girl, jumping into the water to save another child at the Broadlands Hotel years ago. She had the same funny look on her face, an expression somewhere between terror at what she was doing and excitement at the idea that she was pulling it off. It was a combination he could not resist. "OK," he said. "We'll give you a try." He pressed his intercom and asked his secretary to come in. "Miss Hines," he said, "take Miss McLean and introduce her to the editor. She'll be joining our staff."

"You don't remember me, do you?" said Miss Hines as they went down the stairs together. Yarrow looked at the middle-aged woman. She was attractive in a mannish way. "You were very little. I used to work for Max Horace."

"Why, Pince-nez. Of course I remember you. What are you doing here?"

"I work here. Shouldn't I be asking you that question?"

Miss Hines threw open the door to the editorial floor. It was a huge room full of desks and people and typewriters and telephones. It hummed with activity; people rushed, phones rang, copy editors shouted. On one side were partitioned offices for the editor and rooms for the proofreaders and the teletypists.

"Welcome to bedlam," said Miss Hines. "Let me introduce you to young Mr. Schaeffer. He's the editor now."

Yarrow followed her across the huge room, a room full of strangers, and all she could think of was, How am I going to tell my father?

*   *   *

"You've done what?"

"I've just told you, Dad. I've got a job reporting at the *Globe* and I've rented a room at Miss Hines's, Mr. Schaeffer's secretary."

Yarrow was standing in the doorway of her grandfather's room. Her father shouted at her. Jock was thunderstruck. He sat up in bed with his frail hair standing out from his head like cotton candy. He was not feeling well. Years of smoking had given him a rattling cough. He went into one of his spasms of coughing now, and Nellie pushed past her father standing beside the bed to offer Jock some syrup. When Jock caught his breath, he only said, "How could you, lass?" and lay back on the pillow. Eric's dog came and laid his muzzle on the counterpane.

"Because Dad doesn't take me seriously. He still treats me as though I'm his little girl. Everyone else gets sent out on stories and I'm sent to get him another cup of coffee."

"That's not true," said Nellie. "You've always had a chance at the office."

"I don't see you rushing in there to work for him. If I'm going to be an editor one day, I have to be given a shot at decent stories and taught how to edit copy, not be patted on the head and shunted to one side."

"Oh, so that's it," said Nellie, putting her hands on her hips. "It's going to be your paper one day, is it? And what about us—Greta, Eric and me? I suppose we're just to go along with you?"

"Nellie, that's enough!"

"Girls, stop! Get out. Get out! I can't stand to hear you arguing." Jock waved them away and started coughing again. Yarrow ran from the room crying, and Nellie squeezed her lips together and followed.

James handed his father a glass of water.

"Are you OK?"

"Oh, I'm all right. Stop fussing like a woman."

James sat down heavily on his father's bed. He felt weary. Yarrow's defection cut like a knife.

"I can't believe Yarrow joined the *Globe*."

Jock shook his head.

"Doesn't she know, haven't we told her often enough, that the family must stick together? You've handled it all wrong, James."

"Oh, Dad, get off my back."

"She's smart but she's stubborn. You should have given her more responsibility."

"You're the one who always said that women and business don't mix."

"Most women. Yarrow's different."

"She's too hot-headed. She will not listen to me. She wants everything at once."

Jock sighed. Outside his window he could see the darker shape of the plane tree against the night sky.

"James, what are you going to do?"

"Oh, she'll be back soon enough. It might be good for Yarrow to work for someone else."

"I mean when I'm gone."

"Come on, Dad. You'll live to be a hundred."

"Most likely not. But when *you're* gone—you have three daughters and one son—who's going to run it? Are you going to pick one to succeed you, or are you going to let them battle it out? We're not talking about the Humdinger now. When the federal government starts pouring money into Camp Carson, it's going to grow. Even the jackrabbits won't recognize Platte City." Jock shut his eyes.

James stood up. He hated to hear his father talk like this.

"We have plenty of time to think about the future and anyway some things have a way of solving themselves."

Jock's eyes flickered back to the window. "The more branches there are on the family tree," he said, "the more likely they are to split."

Sandy's headlights picked out Yarrow's skirt and her hurrying legs as he was turning into Bellevue Street. He had borrowed his father's car and driven over as soon as he got into town.

"Yarrow," he called out.

"Sandy! I'm so happy to see you."

"Honey, what's the matter? You're crying."

She got into the car and fell into his arms. He stroked her black hair.

"I quit my job at the *Journal*. I'm going to work at the *Globe*."

"I don't believe it."

"Oh, drive, drive. I don't want them to come out and see me."

Sandy put the car into gear and headed north. Yarrow went on spilling out her troubles and crying into her handkerchief.

"Everything's going so wrong, and I just want everything to be right."

"Tell me."

"I've argued with Dad and Grandfather, and Nellie hates me. Mama and Greta went up to see Laura. I don't know where Eric is. He'll probably hate me, too." Sandy kissed her hand. "I have missed you. It's so good to see you. I just feel I've had no one to talk to, no one who understood."

They had come to an area north of the town that the locals called the Garden of the Gods. It was an eerie place of huge strewn boulders and rocks standing red and livid out of the earth. It had been a special place for the Indians many years ago, and Yarrow had been here on picnics with her mother.

"Let's stop and walk," she said. She was agitated but she had stopped crying. They walked in among the boulders that towered over them. There was grass under their feet and the sky was clear with a great moon hanging in it.

"I haven't asked about you," she said.

"I've been accepted for officer training." He stopped and held her shoulders in his hands. She looked up at him. The moon made everything very clear.

"When do you start?"

"Soon." He kissed her and smoothed back the strands of curly hair that got in the way.

"I love you," he said.

"I love you, too." He took her face in his hands. All her difficulties seemed to dissolve as he kissed her. Yarrow gave in to it.

"I want to marry you."

"Oh, Sandy."

"I want to protect you and love you and look after you and come home to you every night." He kissed her in between all the words. "I never want to see you cry again."

She put her arms around his waist. "Oh, darling," she said.

He whispered into her ear, "I want to make babies."

"We'd make beautiful babies."

He pulled her against a rock and kissed her hard this time. His hand rubbed over her breast.

"We shouldn't, Sandy."

"If you really love me, you'll let me. Just let me touch you; let me look at you, let me kiss you." He had pulled open her thin summer blouse, loosened it from the waistband of her plaid skirt. His hand freed her breasts.

"Sandy, love. Don't." Yarrow felt herself tensing. She felt in suspension as one part of her seemed to be watching herself. He went on his knees, pulling her blouse and the straps of her brassiere down over her shoulders. Her breasts were free and she felt, for the first time, moon on them and night air and a man's mouth.

"Sandy," she said. "I do love you, but not this now. We should wait." She pulled away from him. He groaned but got to his feet. "You're a cruel woman," he said, helping her slip her straps up. He pressed against her. She was shocked to feel how hard he had grown against her legs.

"Sandy. Stop."

He groaned again. "How will I be able to sleep?"

"You'll find a way." She smiled. "I do love you."

"I'll talk to your father."

"Can you wait till Mama comes home? He's not too pleased with me."

"Your dad and I get along. It's your grandfather who doesn't like me. I rub him the wrong way or something. I wish we could get married now. But I'll need to save. What about a year?"

"Yes. Let's get married a year from tonight. I need a year, too. I've made a commitment to the *Globe*. I can't let Larry Schaeffer down."

She combed her hair in the car as he drove her home. He kept trying to catch her eye in her pocket mirror.

"Say again, 'I love you, Sandy.' Go on, say it."

She laughed. He looked like a little boy with his soft blond hair falling over his forehead.

"I love you, Sandy, I love you, I love you, I love you. Now you say it."

He took his hands off the wheel and made a megaphone around his mouth. He shouted, "I love Yarrow McLean and I'm going to marry her."

When they reached her house she told him not to come in. It was very late. They kissed a long kiss good night. When she came into the hallway, her grandfather was standing at the far end in his striped pajamas. He looked at her with her disheveled hair, and her blouse half pulled out of her pleated plaid skirt. "Good night, Grandfather," she said. But he said nothing, just stared at her with his old white hair standing up and his old blue eyes looking at her, and then she turned and ran up the stairs and her high-heeled backless shoes clicked on the painted wooden steps.

Yarrow worked at the *Globe* for more than a year. She loved it and worked hard. Larry Schaeffer, Jr. gave her more and more leeway and her contact book grew fatter and fatter. Seldom did a day go past in which the by-line Yarrow McLean did not appear in the *Globe*.

Yarrow was working the "lobster shift" one night at the *Globe*. She was on the police beat and nothing was doing. She wandered through to the radio room to chat with the young night editor. He was asleep at the desk with his feet up and his hat cocked over his eyes. A jumble of wire-service cables lay on the floor beside him. She picked one up and rustled it in his ear. He grunted.

"Flash," she said. "Utmosted soonest. The war is over."

Ned Griffin shot out of his seat with his eyes open. He saw Yarrow laughing at him and collapsed back into the chair with a groan.

"Don't ever do that again."

Yarrow perched on the edge of his desk. "I brought you some coffee. Here."

"You're determined to wake me up, aren't you?" he said, putting his feet back on the desk. "You'd think your father owned this paper."

"Just making sure Mr. Schaeffer gets his money's worth." Yarrow sipped her coffee. She and Ned were old friends.

"Are you still seeing Mary-Ellen?"

"We're going to get married."

"No! No one told me. That's fantastic. When?"

"Soon as she finishes college. What about you and Sandy?"

Yarrow ran her fingers through her hair and made a funny face. "We have the longest-running engagement I've ever heard of. First Dad wouldn't agree. And then when he did, Sandy said he had to save more money before we could marry." Yarrow didn't mention her grandfather; it made her ache to think how much he was opposed to her marrying Sandy. He hardly spoke to her anymore. "Anyway," she said, tossing back her hair, "at least Sandy's closer now. He's based at Camp Carson and we've set the date—sort of. I've begun to buy my trousseau."

The Teletype machine began chattering behind them. Ned swung around in his chair and flipped up the roll of paper to read it.

"Nothing," he said. "There's nothing happening in the world today." He stood up and stretched. He was a stocky young man with red hair nearly the same hue as Mary-Ellen's. He was in his late twenties and he had registered for the draft but been rejected. Ned had a congenital heart defect, though looking at him, Yarrow thought he looked as strong as an ox. He began shuffling the papers that lay all over his desk and inserted some copy paper and carbons into his typewriter. "Where's that story you wrote on the murder yesterday?"

"I tore it up. It's terrible."

"It's a good local story. Go and get it."

"It stinks."

"Your writing or the story?"

"Oh, you're so smart. The story of course. It's a beat-up, there's nothing in it."

"Go and get the galley, I want to see it."

He began to type and Yarrow sighed and went off to the composing room. The composing room of the *Globe* extended into a new cinder-block building behind the old office. She walked past the rows of Linotype machines that stood tall and silent with their silver-colored ingots suspended over the metal pots. There were only a few people about. One of the compositors whistled as she went past.

Yarrow looked through the galleys hanging from a hook. She couldn't find the piece she had written. The foreman came over and she explained what she was looking for.

"Just a minute," he said. "Hey, Joe," he called to a compositor sitting idly at one of the machines. "Let's get some of that dead horse out of the way." He jerked his head toward a pile of dried flong stacked in a box near his feet. The compositor swore, but got up and came over and picked up two or three sheets. "There's more than that, old buddy." The compositor picked up another two or three sheets and ambled off, swearing profusely. Yarrow knew why the man didn't want to do it. He was going to set type that had already been used in the paper. The words would all be cast again, the plates for the photographs remade, and when the whole page was reassembled, the foreman would take a proof of it and empty all the metal right back into the hellbox to be melted down. At the *Journal* the same practice went on. The waste drove her father into a frenzy, but there was nothing he could do about it.

Yarrow had been so intrigued by it when she first became aware of it, that she had looked up its origins. The practice of bogus, or dead horse, began in the seventeenth century when the London Stationers' Company had formulated a plan to protect their workers' skills and jobs: "That no work man lend Letter without consent first obteyned of the Master on paine to loose the benefit of Hollydais and Copies."

"I think I'll write a story on dead horsing," she said as she went back to the radio room with the galley of the murder story.

"You'll close us up if you do," said Ned.

A phone was ringing in the reporters' room. Yarrow went over to take it.

"*Globe* newsroom."

"Honey?"

"Sandy. What are you doing ringing me here at this time of the night?" She could tell there was something wrong. His voice sounded high, excited.

"I'm being shipped out. I've just heard."

"Oh, my God." Yarrow sat down on the desk.

"I want to get married tomorrow."

"But what about blood tests? What about the license?"

"That's not a problem. I know someone in the courthouse, we can get our license in the morning and send them our blood tests later. Darling, I love you."

"I love you too, but . . ."

Sandy burst into a line of a popular song.

" 'Is you is or is you ain't my baby?' "

"Sandy . . ."

"I'll pick you up at your place in the morning, and we'll drive straight to Platte City. Eight o'clock sharp."

She hung up and went into the radio room, picked up an armful of wire-service cables off the floor and threw them in the air.

"Congratulate me, Ned. This time tomorrow I'm going to be an old married lady. I'm leaving now to get ready."

"What about my murder story? I need that for tomorrow morning."

Yarrow went up to him with her sweetest smile.

"You can stuff that story, Ned." She gave him a smacking kiss on the lips. "Be seeing you."

The next morning Sandy arrived with a small jeweler's tray with five rings on it.

"Don't ask how I got them," he said. "Just choose one."

Yarrow chose a thin band with a small ruby and a matching wedding ring.

"Will your parents come to the wedding?" she asked as they drove south to Platte City.

"I haven't asked them." Yarrow said no more.

When the license was arranged she went with Greta to buy a hat. She was going to wear a suit from her trousseau, a gold suit made by Jablow with a white ruffled lace blouse. Greta chose a white straw hat, which consisted of a band with two cones on the ends and a stiff black veil. It cost Yarrow twenty-five dollars, but Greta said it was worth it. When Sandy arrived in the afternoon to pick her up and pinned an orchid to her lapel, Freya cried. It

was not the kind of wedding she had dreamed of for Yarrow.
Yarrow stood at attention in front of her. The bones of her knees
were square where the skirt topped them. She looked too thin
and too young to be getting married. "You look beautiful,"
Freya said. Sandy was in his new uniform with the gold bars of a
second lieutenant of the U.S. Army. "And you look handsome," said Nellie.

"I'll just go and say good-bye to Grandfather," Yarrow said.

They stood beside his bed holding hands. He had been bed-
ridden for several months now and needed constant care. A
neighbor sat with him.

"Grandfather, it's me, Yarrow, and Sandy."

The blue eyes that looked at them were bleary. There was no
recognition in them. Yarrow touched his hand.

"I'm getting married today."

The old man blinked. His eyes didn't leave her face.

"Will you give me your blessing?"

The eyes didn't change. She bent to kiss him and he turned his
head to the wall so that all she could see were the deep creases of
his neck under the thin white hair.

"I love you. Good-bye, Grandfather."

CHAPTER 13

ON THE WAY TO CAMP HALE, THE BUS SLOWED ON A HAIRPIN
bend to let a string of laden mules go by. Yarrow had
her window open. There was something odd about the scene as
the bus inched its way around them.

"I hate these corners," said the girl sitting beside her. "How
long you been married?" She had a Brooklyn accent.

"Two weeks—and you?"

"Since last September. We've been stationed at Camp Tanin
near Tyler. But Bud transferred to the Eighty-seventh Infantry.
Says it will be more fun. Hey, hey look at that." The string of
mules had panicked and taken off down the side of the road. The
soldiers with them from the camp ran after them and shouted and
cursed. The mules were silent, though their mouths opened.

"Why, that's it," said Yarrow. "They don't bray. Now how do they teach them to do that?"

"They don't. They operate on their throats. Bud told me."

Yarrow sat silent as the bus lurched forward again. She couldn't wait to see Sandy again. He had had to report to base at 5:00 A.M. the day after their wedding. She blushed when she thought of him. Their first night together had not been successful; he had been impatient; she had been too nervous. He had said it would get better. Yarrow looked out the window and hoped it would, too.

When he got back from tent bivouacking, he had wired her to get on a bus. She could stay at the officers' guest house at the camp for a week or two. He was in barracks. Her whole life now revolved around him, as though she were a leadweight, like a sinker on a fishing line, or a yo-yo on a string being spun around his head. She had not known it would be like this. It was like plunging into a deep well and finding you were in the sea after all; the current carried you along. Yarrow looked at the mountains as they went past; the snow, caught in the dark slopes of moraine, looked like the white markings on whales.

A small city of army huts had been established at the Camp Hale site, where the 10th Mountain Division was training for winter military operations. A pall of smoke hung over the rows of tar-paper army huts as trains shunted in and out carrying coal and provisions for the troops. Sandy was there to meet her and she stared into his face anxiously, as though he might have changed his mind about her in the two weeks they had been apart, but all she could discern was a small patch of frostbite on his nose from camping out at thirty-two degrees below. He showed her to the officers' guest house where she would share a room. There were single army beds, a community shower, a small reception room. He had bought her a foot locker, which she could use as a chest. Meals would be served in the officers' club.

"What do you think?" he said.

"I love it."

She saw little of him, and when she did, it was not enough. She and Lisa—Bud's wife whom she had met on the bus—shared a room and spent their days playing bridge in the little reception room. They were not free to walk about the camp, but it seldom mattered because it was very cold. There were days when the snow swirled and they could not leave the hut at all, and they rinsed out their lingerie in the corner basin and washed their hair and sat and smoked cigarettes and curled their feet

under them and talked. There were nights when the sky was so
clear that the moon seemed as close as the top of the nearest
mountain. Yarrow felt she was in heaven. When Sandy was off
duty they sat talking in the reception room with the radio on
softly; Lisa withdrew discreetly to her room, and he told her how
the Mountain soldier carried his rifle on his back and his skis at
"right shoulder" while marching, how he gave the "ski salute"
and learned to stack his skis and take them down by numbers,
and all the time she listened but was conscious only of her small
foot in his hand, of how he rubbed the instep with his big thumb.
They had little time alone together, but for Yarrow this was the
best time of her marriage, for they could not see enough of each
other. She overstayed her visit at the guest house, as did Lisa,
both of them expecting at any minute they would be told to
leave; but April went and then May, and they were still there.

Then Sandy had an overnight pass, and they went into the
historic mining town of Leadville with its wooden sidewalks and
stayed a night at the Vendome Hotel and made love in a four-
poster bed. Perhaps her body had softened because his entry was
not so painful. He came quickly and she was glad for him, but
she puzzled over what all the fuss was about and how any
woman could enjoy the sex act. In the morning they walked up
the dirt track of Seventh Street to the little wooden hut that had
once guarded the Matchless Mine, where Tabor had made his
fortune. Tabor's wife, Baby Doe, had died in poverty there ten
years before. Sheets of rusted iron boarded up the windows and a
small chipmunk scuttled under the rotten wooden walls. Yarrow
wrote to her grandfather about it, but she did not expect a reply.

One morning in early June, Yarrow was eating breakfast with
Lisa in the officers' club. The radio was on and some POWs
were painting a mural of a mountain scene on the inside wall of
the hut. Suddenly the Germans began talking excitedly to one
another. One man waved his brush around and a splash of blue
paint landed on the wooden floor. "What is it?" asked Yarrow.
"What's happening?" The Germans were agitated. Sandy came
in looking for her and ordered the guard to take the POWs
outside.

"It's D Day," said Sandy. "The Allies have landed in
Normandy."

Yarrow was overcome with relief; she thought that the war
might now be over and Sandy would not have to go, but he only
showed frustration at not being in the thick of the battle. She
knew he had a temper; she had watched him one day working
with the troops when he had bawled out a private on the firing

range, but she had put it down to his frustration at being held at Camp Hale too long. They had their first argument about that time, too. It was over a trifling thing. Sandy had managed to get hold of a car—an unexpected luxury—for another overnight pass in Leadville. He drove fast around the bends and she gripped her seat as the wheels hit the gravel on a treacherous turn.

"That was close."

"You're a nervous passenger."

"You're driving too fast, Sandy."

"Look, if you want to drive, I'll stop right here."

"I don't want to drive, I just want you to slow down."

"OK, I'll stop right now. Right now, here. You can take over."

She looked out the window, unable to understand how they could be arguing like this. Her breathing was irregular. They didn't speak the rest of the way and when they got into their room she pulled her cardigan around her—she could feel her shoulders were still tense. He came over and put his arms about her. She pushed him away.

"What is it now? Christ, you're difficult."

"Me difficult? You act rude and boorish all the way here and now you want to forget it as if nothing was said."

"A spat. Honey . . ." He came to her again, began unbuttoning her blouse.

"Leave me alone."

He kissed her hard. She could feel his clenched teeth. The muscles on his neck and shoulders were tight.

"I'm sorry," he said. She was still angry. He had hurt her feelings and had made her feel in the wrong. But she could see he was excited; his pupils were dilated, he wanted her. Yarrow was confused; to her, anger was incompatible with lovemaking. But not to Sandy. He was aroused and she tried to respond. But in bed she could feel the tension rippling in her like electricity. When he touched her he scratched her with a hangnail on his thumb. She wanted to scream with frustration as she felt him come, but he, who had caused the argument, curled over when he had his release and slept, innocent and content as a baby.

"I've written to your father," he said one afternoon when they were eating apple pie à la mode in the officers' club. At least Sandy was eating. Yarrow only played with the salt and pepper shakers.

"I've asked him if I could have a job there when this is all over."

"That would be wonderful, if you came into the business."

"You wouldn't object?"

"Why should I?"

"Oh, I just thought. Well, you're funny about the newspaper, you know?"

"What do you mean, 'funny'?"

He raised his shoulders to his ears and then dropped them. "Proprietary, I guess."

"I can't be all that proprietary. Remember, I worked at the *Globe*."

"I guess there's not much difference between one newspaper and another."

Yarrow felt as though some powdered pepper had got up her nose.

Bud put his head in the door. He came over to their table. "It's on," he said. "I've just seen the orders. We're moving out for Texas en route to Italy. But we've got to take those damn mules with us."

The men went on the troop train to Bastrop, Texas, in July, and Yarrow and Lisa and another wife drove there in a car. It took them five days and when they got there Yarrow was as sick as could be. "It's just the heat," they said, but Yarrow knew it wasn't. I'm pregnant, she thought.

"I've got to call my mother." It did not strike her as odd until many years later that she had wanted to share this news first with her mother and not with her husband.

Freya's voice sounded distant when she got through.

"Oh, darling," she cried, "I've been trying to reach you for days. Jock died on Friday and we buried him yesterday."

Yarrow heard her mother sobbing on the telephone, but Yarrow didn't cry. She felt he had left her months before on her wedding day when he had turned his face to the wall. She didn't want to think of him dead; she only wanted to remember him in his old boiler suit with the frayed collar, working on the stone in Platte City, fanning out his beard with his fingers when something caught his fancy.

"Are you there, Yarrow?"

"I'm still here, Mama."

That afternoon as she stood out in the garden behind the rented house under the noon sun, she realized she had forgotten to tell her mother her own news. The house made an intense shadow across the yard, one side deep in shade, the other side white with heat. Why is it, she thought, that when the sun is at its greatest height, the shadows are the deepest?

She didn't cry until much later that night when the mournful sound of a freight train pierced her room and made her realize how much she would miss him.

Sandy was overjoyed at the news of the baby. He fussed over her, scolded her when the others drank rum and Coke and she wanted some. Whenever he could, he came and picked her up from the house she rented with Lisa. They drove to Lake Austin and went swimming and ate Mexican food on the way home. When he finally left for Naples, on the *U.S.S. West Point* from Newport News, in Virginia, it was already early January and she had gone home to her mother to await the birth of her baby.

Yarrow felt sleek and fat as a cow while she was pregnant. Her skin glowed as her stomach blossomed and she padded around her parents' house with her hands like a sling under her bundle. Her mother laughed.

"I never thought you'd be the earth-mother type. I always thought it would be Greta."

"Greta's grown so svelte, she'd hate to be this fat. I love it. I think I'll make another hot chocolate."

"Greta can't afford to put on weight now she's working as a mannequin. I can't tell you what they're paying her in New York. A fortune. There's a picture of her in that magazine beside your bed." Yarrow picked up the magazine and looked through it. They were in her old bedroom and Freya was painting the baseboard, "for the baby," she said.

"It is Greta but, my goodness, it doesn't look like her."

"She's had her teeth fixed. Nellie's envious of the money Greta makes. She says she's working for slave wages as a nurse."

"Nellie's always envious."

Freya sat back on her heels and surveyed her work. "I wish you two got on better."

Yarrow flicked through the magazine. "Nellie's hard to get on with. She's always so adamant that she's right about things. She reminds me of Clara."

"Clara's a broken woman. Since she lost her seat in the House, she writes the most pathetic letters to your father."

"Justifying the position she took?"

"Don't be harsh on her, Yarrow. She paid a terrible price."

"Good heavens. Here's a picture of Elliot Weyden in Europe!"

Freya said, "Help me up," and Yarrow gave her an arm. "Your father received a lovely letter from Elliot when your grandfather died."

Yarrow was still staring at the picture of Elliot in uniform. He was standing with a woman wearing a hat with a stuffed bird on it that tilted over one eye.

"What's he doing now?"

"He was in England. He didn't say much about himself."

"Cool, quiet Elliot. He never changes."

They were in the kitchen sipping hot chocolate when Eric came home from school. Freya's kitchen was hung with dried herbs and the shelves overflowed with plants being propagated. You could hardly see the snow outside for the plants crowding the window. Bulbs and cuttings at different stages of growth stood in pots and containers on all surfaces. An attempt at air-layering a pittosporum stood on the floor. Eric nearly knocked it over as he came in.

"It's like a jungle in here."

He was twelve years old, and was grabbing a sandwich before going to do his stint at the newspaper. He picked up an egg carton with seedlings growing in it.

"What's this?"

Freya took it from him. "Thunbergia. Take your hands off."

"I nearly ate it."

Freya made him a tuna fish sandwich.

"They've got me doing all the crummy jobs," he said as he wolfed it down. He dropped a crust on the floor for Sherlock. Eric was very like his father, big and raw, with a lock of hair falling over his forehead. "Why can't they let me write some stories?"

"Just as well they don't," said Freya when he and his dog had gone and she was pinching out the tops of a trailing ficus, "he can't spell for beans."

Yarrow's baby gave a kick so that a little bump could be seen under her smock.

"That must be his heel," she said.

"His?"

"I'm sure it's a boy. I can feel him urinating inside me."

Freya took off her daughter's wedding ring and plucked a long black hair from her head. She tied the ring to the hair and suspended it over Yarrow's stomach. The ring began to oscillate, then it went round in circles.

"You're wrong," she said. "It's going to be a girl."

"Sandy will be disappointed. He's already thinking of getting him on a football team."

"He'll put up with it."

The ring fascinated them as it glinted in the pale sun poking its way through the plants at the window.

"I wonder how Sandy will do as a newspaperman," said Freya.

Yarrow caught the ring in her hand. "Haven't you got a way of telling me that, too?" She laughed.

Freya went to the sink as though she were about to rinse out their mugs, but she looked out through the little green vines of the stephanotis and the wandering Jew at the window to the white cold beyond. The vines were like a web, like a network of veins on a membrane. A leaf fell into the sink and all she said was, "They need misting again."

"Besides, Mama," said Yarrow getting up and waddling over to put her arms around her, "Sandy's got me. What more help could he have?"

Freya laughed. "Yes, I suppose so. I was forgetting that."

Yarrow's daughter, Lily, was born in March, a healthy, long, noisy baby with straight blond hair that hung like monkey fur from a tonsure. She was the most beautiful thing Yarrow had ever seen. Yarrow breathed into her baby's mouth and smelled the returning breath, sweet and pure as milk; she examined the little crease behind her daughter's ear and felt the strength of the tiny fingers clutching her ring finger. Yarrow wrote to Sandy to tell him of his daughter's arrival, but she had no idea when he would receive the letter. His own letters to her, passionate but censored, arrived in batches. They told her everything and nothing.

Yarrow had fallen in love all over again with Sandy through his letters. He wrote well and graphically and his own image in her mind grew in stature so that she ascribed to him mythical qualities that perhaps he possessed in mere human quantities. He also displayed a ribaldness in his letters, which, she admitted to herself, excited her. She put out of her mind their disappointments in bed and determined to try harder when he returned to her. Reading his letters after the birth of Lily (when she felt at times that her femininity had been compromised), she believed that Sandy saw her both as a madonna and a whore.

She ached to hold him in her arms, wanted to see him with Lily in his. He sent her his allotment and she bought war bonds with it. He was glad, he wrote, that she was staying with her parents, but he wanted to support her himself. One day he would show her, he wrote.

She was breast-feeding Lily in the spring, sitting on the window seat in her mother's bedroom, when she received a telegram that Sandy had been wounded in action. She was distraught for days and could feel the tension in her body. Lily had difficulty getting enough milk and screamed with hunger. Then a letter came from him in the hospital. He was OK, he had been wounded in the head, but apart from a few scars he was the same as ever. Lisa wrote to her from New York that she had heard from Bud that Sandy had gone AWOL from his hospital bed to join his troops. Again Yarrow couldn't get her milk to flow, and Freya suggested they bottle-feed Lily.

Yarrow spent hours under the shower trying to disgorge the milk that had swollen into her breasts and would not flow. She cried as she pumped the milk out and grimaced at the pain and watched the thin, milky stream fan out over her. Why wasn't Sandy here? Why did she have to cope with this tired, cross baby who wouldn't take the bottle, who kept turning her head to her nipple? Yarrow stood in the shower, squeezing the milk out like waste and watched it dribble down over her breasts of stone and her stomach of jelly. Men's lives were so different. She felt ugly and unwanted and used. Pity washed over her. And then she thought of Sandy being wounded and she felt ashamed.

"Greta doesn't want to make decisions," said Nellie, typing up a paper that was due on Monday. She was studying for her nursing certificate. It was a late Saturday morning in July, and texts and notebooks lay on the dining-room table around her father's old Olivetti. "What's that word?" she asked, peering at her notes.

Yarrow leaned forward, holding the baby upright on her knees. "Inguinal hernia, I think."

"Thanks." Nellie went on typing and talking. Her shiny dark hair bobbed as Yarrow talked. "Greta forces others to make decisions for her so that she doesn't have to blame herself if things go wrong. I've been studying psychology," she said.

Yarrow rubbed Lily's back. The baby brought up a contented burp.

"Poor Greta," Yarrow said. "She's so easygoing"

"Not easygoing. Indecisive. Chronic p-r-o-s-t-a-t-i-t-i-s. There. Finished." She turned the platen knob up fast so that it made a zipping sound. "She's living with this photographer in the Village." She lowered her voice. "And he's old enough to be her father. Dad would have a fit if he knew."

"That doesn't sound too indecisive to me."

"Well, it is. She told me it just sort of happened. She stayed there one night after a late shoot and every day she just takes one more of her things over—one day her hairdryer, next day her bain-marie . . ."

"Her what?"

"Her bain-marie. She's taking a French cooking course in case the modeling doesn't work out. She wants me to make up her mind for her—should she stay or should she leave—I told her she has to decide herself. I don't want her crying on my shoulder if things don't work out."

"What did she say?"

"She says she'll think about it. She's hopeless."

"She's lovable."

"Oh, you've gone soft in the head since you had a baby."

"So will you."

"I doubt it." Nellie stood up and stretched. Her arms were still as skinny as they had been when she was a little girl. She had on a striped sweater with square shoulder pads. "I have one more year to go before I get my diploma," she said, tugging down the short sweater to meet her slim hips. "I'm going to do two years of working at a rehabilitation hospital and then I'm going to take on some private nursing where I can travel and see the world. I'm so tired of Platte City and bed baths."

Their father came in with the mail. He had slept late, and wore a big striped dressing gown that still seemed too small on him.

"Three letters for you, Yarrow," he said. "How about some coffee, Nellie." Yarrow snatched up the letters and her father took Lily. Lily lay against James's shoulder, sucking her fist.

"What on earth does he mean?" said Yarrow, reading quickly through the ripped-open letters. "He says to 'take his summer uniforms to Indiana.' I don't know anyone in Indiana."

"That means he's coming home, you goose," said James, stroking his granddaughter's wisps of hair. Yarrow shrieked and kissed him. She hadn't kissed him so warmly for years. She ran into the kitchen and danced around Nellie, holding up the coffee-pot and filters in her hands. "He's coming home. He's coming home." Then she burst into tears.

"Well, of course he's coming home. Didn't you always think he would?"

"Oh, no, Nellie. You don't understand. I'd made up my mind that the chances were that he never would. Then I knew I could accept whatever happened."

Yarrow arrived in Indiana a week before the war was over. She heard the announcement on the radio as she drove with her old Camp Hale friend, Lisa, to the Fort Wayne railway station. It was only twenty-five miles from the boardinghouse where they were staying, but it took them forever to get there. People were going crazy. Cars were honking their horns. A woman came out of her house carrying a goldfish bowl as though she had forgotten what she was doing when she heard the news. At the station Yarrow lost Lisa almost immediately in the crowd, and every time a soldier came through the barrier, she thought it might be he. And then Sandy was there, taller than she remembered, stronger, crushing her into his arms, so that her little brown wool Moulton hat fell off. She took in everything about him at once, the cropped hair, the angular cheekbones, the wound that had left a slight indentation on his left temple. There were wrinkles around his eyes; had they been there before? She held him tight. It was good to have him home.

"Oh, hello," he said, "oh, hello, little mother."

CHAPTER 14

*A*FTER THE VE DAY CELEBRATIONS IN LONDON, ELLIOT DROVE TO his sister's house in Essex to spend the weekend. His discharge was imminent. He had been with the U.S. Ninth Army, which had been the first to reach the Elbe, he had come through the war unscathed and he was grateful. He was twenty-seven years old and he was hungry and eager for life to go on.

Elliot's dark, handsome eyes flashed as he drove through Epping Forest and turned up the road to Sully Corners Farm. There had been a morning rain, and the air and grass were fresh, as sporadic drops of water fell from the elms and the hedges along the road. A small flock of black-faced sheep scurried across the drive as he approached the house. He couldn't quite place the sheep with Vivienne's old persona. He hadn't seen her since the war began. He pulled up in front of the two-story stucco building, a solid house with some Georgian pretensions and healthy Garrya ellipticas growing against the front walls. Vivienne flung open the front door as he opened the trunk to get his luggage.

"Darling," she said, hugging him, "you haven't changed. Yes, you have, you've grown better-looking. Did you leave any broken hearts over there?"

He laughed and kissed her. She looked well, she looked happy. She was just the same irrepressible girl; yet something in her, something American, had been toned down. He couldn't believe that she and Basingstoke could be so comfortable together, he thought, as he followed her up the stairs to his room. There seemed no sign of strife or boredom. "Don't underestimate Clive," she said as though she had read his mind. She hugged him and told him to come down for lunch as soon as he was ready. And at lunch, taken at a small table in the bay-window area of the dining room, with Basingstoke huffingly present in his tweed weekend jacket, he could not pinpoint any discord. It baffled him. Not that he was disappointed by the absence of any discord—in fact he was relieved because he felt that he had railroaded Basingstoke into this marriage. He had thought the odds against it working would be high. There was just no telling.

"You two must have lots to talk about," said Basingstoke, getting up soon after lunch. He kissed Vivienne on the forehead as he took his leave. "I'm off to see a heifer our tenant farmer wants me to look at."

"Let's go for a walk," said Vivienne, pulling her brother up. "The rhododendrons are beautiful now." She put on a headscarf and rubber boots, and the old Vivienne was completely transformed into an English squire's wife. He laughed. She caught sight of herself in the hall mirror and saw the joke.

"You'll be giving me bubble-and-squeak next," he said.

"You guessed what's for dinner!"

He put his arm through hers and they went out. "Americans always judge the English by how they sound—the more sincere, the more they gobble up every word. In fact, the opposite is true. You should listen to an Englishman most closely when he is being a fool and take no notice of him at all when he is pontificating—that is when he is pulling your leg."

"A matter of psychology, Viv?"

"No, a difference in humor."

Then she told him all about "her" war, as she called it, her work for the Girl Guides, and the Harvest Festival at the church, and Clive's stepchildren, "who hate me," and about her garden. She pointed out the espaliered fruit trees on the brick wall and the herbaceous border she was planning and the fact that there was not a garden faucet in the whole green lawn. "We do it all by bucket if the rain doesn't come." She stood with her arm up, shading her eyes as the weak sun glinted off the morning's pools of water. "There's a rook's nest," she said.

"You're happy."

She took his arm and squeezed it, and they set off down some shallow, wide steps that led toward the pond.

"Wouldn't you be? I'd like to see you settled like me. A house, a wife, a garden—then you'd be happy."

"I am happy."

"Bachelors only think they're happy. You won't know the real thing till you marry and have all these things."

"I don't need things."

"Oh, no? What about that little book you used to carry around?"

"How did you know about that?"

She jumped over a puddle. "I spied. When you went out of your room, I used to read it. All about Mrs. Neil," she teased.

"Christ," he said.

"And Yarrow McLean . . ."

"Old married lady now."

She put her arm through his again. "Is there anyone now?"

"No." He laughed. "Just you."

"Good. Because I've got someone for you to meet tonight."

"Vivienne, don't matchmake. Not everyone is as lucky as you."

"One good turn deserves another."

Just before he went down for dinner, she came into his room and sat on the edge of his bed while he did his tie.

"We lost some friends in the war. Did you?"

"Yes."

"Do you want to talk about it?"

"No."

"Oh."

They could hear the door knocker being banged downstairs.

"I'll get it," shouted Basingstoke from the hall. They could hear the first faint click of his leg as he went down the stairs.

"Are you all in one piece?" she said, as though the sound of her husband's leg put it in mind.

"Just the same as ever," he said as they left the room, and she switched off the light. "Except," he whispered, "for one atrophied testicle."

"Good heavens," she said, stopping short and gripping the banister. "Were you badly wounded, darling?"

"No," he said, "just a bad case of mumps I caught in Germany."

"And you're neither . . .?"

"Sterile nor impotent."

"Well, that's a relief."

"Yes, you may introduce me to all your female friends without worry. In things matrimonial I am A one."

"Do behave yourself tonight, Elliot."

"How staid you've become."

"The vicar will be here."

"Does he have a daughter?"

"A number, but none of them is your type. No, I have just the person. She's perfect for you."

When she opened the door of the drawing room, where the fire was lit and Basingstoke was already offering sherry, Elliot's eyes sped over the women for his sister's choice—but the first person he recognized was Fabiana Truitt.

"Have you met?" asked Basingstoke, introducing her.

"I haven't had the pleasure," said Elliot. There was no way Mrs. Truitt would remember a young Wall Street clerk coming to her before the war to sign a piece of paper.

"Mrs. Truitt," said Basingstoke, "owns the *New York Courier*."

"She's Mrs. Newnom now," said a thin birdlike man coming up behind her and shaking Elliot's hand. Elliot had heard of Richard Newnom's firm on Wall Street. He was probably the most powerful man in New York's financial circles. Certainly the richest.

"Congratulations are in order then," said Elliot. He thought Fabiana Truitt Newnom was a fine-looking woman. She wore a thin silvery sort of dress that showed her arched collarbones. It was not at all the kind of dress that English women wore. Basingstoke introduced him to the vicar and his wife, and there was another couple, an English major with a widow on his arm. The widow had large breasts and a handsome profile, and Elliot raised his eyebrows discreetly at his sister but she shook her head. There was a group of young people, some in uniform, standing near the fireplace, and Elliot was introduced but could not distinguish one from the other.

Newnom came up and said, "I've been doing some business with your brother-in-law. He tells me you want to get back into Wall Street."

"Yes, sir."

"Do you have anything lined up?" He was a concave man who had probably once been taller in his youth. His neck thrust forward and his shoulders were bent. He wore a double-breasted suit jacket that flapped about him. Yet the whole effect was elegant and reeked of money, from the wavy silver hair that swooped back from his forehead to the handmade shoes on his narrow feet. Every detail seemed to have been put together with great care and then treated with even more indifference. His voice was high, and instead of saying "er" or "um," he would make a little smacking noise with his lips.

"Use your contacts," he went on, without waiting for a reply. "Everyone uses the network. Take my advice. When my mother took me to America she couldn't speak a word of English. When she gave her name they couldn't understand her. 'Noname,' they wrote down. Newnom I became. But what's a name anyway, eh? Like money it is only a symbol. It's nothing compared to ambition and determination." He gave a cackling laugh high up in his throat. "I found a friend, and he had a cousin and he had a barrow and that's how I began in Mulberry Street."

"Daddy, are you telling that old story again?" said one of the young girls, peeling off from the group at the fireside. She was a slender pale girl of about sixteen. "Has he told you about the secondhand books he hawked? And how he made his first million dollars before he was twenty-one?" Her blue eyes looked straight into Elliot's. Then she blushed and lowered them.

"Blanchette, let an old man have his fun." Her father went cackling off to Fabiana, who towered a head above him.

"No," Elliot answered, "but he was about to."

"Are you interested in money, too, Lieutenant Weyden?" She pronounced it "leftenant" the way the English did.

"Of course, aren't you?"

She thought for a moment and then said, "No." She shook her head so her pale hair looked golden in the firelight.

"Then you grew up with it and don't know what it's like to be without it."

"Yes, I suppose that is a luxury he gave me. That—and other things."

"Like what?"

"Oh, things like—safety. I was at school here when the war started, so he moved me back to New York."

"I thought you had a funny accent."

"Oh, is that so?"

"Are you English or American?"

"I have an American passport."

"That begs the question."

"My mother was English. Shall we sit down?"

"Yes." She had long, awkward legs like a gazelle's. Her cheeks had retained their blush so that, in certain lights, she looked almost pretty.

"What will you do, now you've left school?"

"Why do you want to know?"

"I'm curious which country you'll choose."

"You're so chauvinistic."

"England, I'll bet."

"If you must know, I'm going to study fine arts here in London."

"Aaah."

"Why aaah, Lieutenant Weyden?"

He nodded toward his sister talking animatedly to the vicar.

"My sister was an Anglophile and look what happened to her."

"She looks very nice to me."

"Not like your stepmother," he whispered in her ear.

"Fabiana looks very—bare," she said and then blushed furiously to the roots of her pale hair.

He laughed. "Can I get you a drink?"

"Yes. A Manhattan."

He laughed again. "You're not old enough, and besides, Basingstoke's only serving sherry."

"Well, I'll have one of those, but don't let my father see it."

"Isn't she perfect?" said Vivienne as he went to the drink tray and poured out a drink.

"She's just a baby," said Elliot, looking at his sister with shock.

"She'll grow up. And she'll give you polish—and as for their contacts in New York . . ." Elliot winced at his sister's social ambitions.

"Vivienne, I won't need to marry a rich man's daughter. I'm going to get it on my own. Ambition and determination, that's what Newnom says I need."

"Well, a rich wife won't hurt," said Vivienne, floating off to her other guests.

Elliot took back a glass of mineral water for Blanchette.

"Ooof," she said, "I had more fun than this at the Brearley School."

At dinner Vivienne had sat Elliot between Blanchette and her stepmother. Fabiana was glowing. She was animated and witty and her voice sparkled like her dress. He asked her about her business and was impressed by her replies. He said he would like to visit the *Courier* when he was back in New York. He didn't mention Colorado and neither did she. She seemed to like the way in which her husband's glance sometimes caught hers across the table. She raised her glass to him once and then turned and smiled at Elliot.

"You are looking at a happy woman who has found a man who allows her to be as she is."

"Is that so difficult?"

"Harder than you would imagine. Some men want mothers. Rich, thank God, knows he already had one."

Elliot was about to reply when he felt Blanchette's knee press against his. He forgot what he was about to say to Fabiana.

"You seem familiar, Lieutenant Weyden," Fabiana went on. "Are you sure we haven't met before?"

Elliot demurred.

"Well, I feel I do know you from somewhere."

"The war is full of men in uniform." Blanchette's knee began to rub up and down against his.

"Excuse me," he said to Fabiana and pretended to drop his napkin. He whispered furiously to Blanchette as he bent down. "Stop it, you little urchin." Blanchette gave him an innocent look and broke into a burble of laughter.

All through dinner he squirmed as Blanchette teased him. He tried to talk to her father, and her stepmother, and he could feel her long thigh against his, and once, when her hand rubbed against his leg, he jumped as though he had been touched by a red-hot poker.

"Is there something the matter?" said Fabiana, steadying a glass that nearly went over.

"The leg," he said.

"Yes, the leg," said Blanchette, leaning forward. "It's a Duncan Phyfe table."

"Yes, the legs always get in the way," said Elliot.

"You ass," said Blanchette a minute later under her breath. "Duncan Phyfe tables don't have legs. Only pedestals."

Elliot couldn't wait for dinner to be over. Under other circumstances he would have enjoyed sparring with Blanchette, but her age terrified him. Her father, the most powerful and richest man in New York, beamed at him across the table.

"We sail for New York the day after tomorrow," said Newnom. "I want you to call me when you get there." He scribbled a number on a piece of paper he tore from a small pad in his pocket. He twiddled the gold pen in his clawlike fingers. "I'm told you can smell a deal a mile away."

Elliot silently blessed his brother-in-law. "Sir," said Elliot, his ears burning as he heard Blanchette whispering to her neighbor that she had a "thing" for men in uniform. The widow, who was next to Newnom, looked straight at Elliot, then licked the edge of her glass with her tongue. There was no mistaking the message there. She told the table at large that she would not be driving back to London tonight, but would be staying at the Crown and Feather in the village. The major looked crestfallen and checked his lapels to see if perhaps he had spilled some soup on them. The widow managed to slip a box of matches, with "Crown and Feather" written on it, into Elliot's hand as she said good-bye.

After dinner, when everyone had gone home and he was undressing in his room upstairs, Elliot found a second slip of paper in his pocket. "Blanchette," it read, and it gave her telephone number. He groaned as he fell onto the bed. Between Vivienne and Blanchette he felt he was a goner. He thought of Blanchette, the way she'd blushed when he tried to patronize her before dinner, and the way she'd got back at him throughout the meal. He began to smile again and then he began to laugh. "Little minx," he said, and picked up the slip of paper and looked at the phone number again. Then he thought of Richard Newnom, whose firm was showing the older ones, like Morgan Stanley, the back of its heels; Newnom's was a dealmaker, bigger than Salomon Brothers, cleverer than Goldman Sachs, hungrier than Lazard. Elliot wanted to work for Newnom. Until he had the capital to start his own venture business, he had to work for someone else. Newnom was the best; from Newnom he could learn. Elliot felt his mind burning with the possibilities. There was money to be made now that the war was over. Pots of money, if one only recognized the opportunity and ran with it.

He got up from the bed. He was restless. His mind pounded with ideas. He looked at his watch. Two A.M. The room was cold. He wrapped the comforter around himself and sat down with some sheets of paper at a table in front of the window. He blew on his fingers. He saw the matchbox he had tossed into the ashtray when he came in. For a moment he thought about the widow with the big bosom waiting at the Crown and Feather, but Elliot shook his head. He wasn't going to give Newnom a chance to forget him. He would see him tomorrow—today rather—and if he was going to sell himself to Rich Newnom, he had some work to do.

He halved the page in front of him with a bold stroke of his pen. On one side he made a list of the investments he already had. He headed it with "American Car and Foundry." On the other side he began to put down some of his ideas. He had worked out a scheme for buying properties that were still valued at pre-Depression prices. Through a number of separate sales, Elliot proposed to sell them again at less than their book value.

Under the existing tax structure the companies would show a book loss—but Elliot would have a tax-free profit to reinvest—because he planned to purchase the stock of the companies that owned the properties as well. He knew it would work. He hoped Newnom would think so, too.

New York
1945

Dear Blanchette,

I hope this letter finds you well and still enjoying London and your course at the Victoria and Albert. Thank you for the scarf. I will wear it in the winter and think of you. You ask what I do with myself. Well I live with my mother as you know. I have got into a routine that suits me well. I get up every morning between four and five and I work until seven at night. No, I do not take vacations. No, I do not have a girlfriend. How do I make money? Well, mostly I agree to lend money (that is, usually your father's, sometimes that of banks and institutions), and then I go out and sell convertible debentures in the company. As my fee I keep some debentures. Later I can convert these into stock. No, I don't have to go out every day to do that. I work the telephone. My left ear has grown as big and red as a cabbage from listening. I take risks. I gamble. Yes, I get lonely. Little Blanchette, you do not know what love is. Go out and meet some young men.

                                                                    Elliot

New York
1946

Blanchette,

This is getting ridiculous. You are seventeen years old. I am flattered that you have proposed to me but I cannot accept. Thank you for the cologne. I cannot keep the gold cuff links and am returning them to you. Your whole life is ahead of you. Pursue it.

                                                                    Elliot

New York
1946

Blanchette,

I did not mean to hurt your feelings. You are a very attractive young woman and you have many talents. My refusal of you has nothing to do with my pride. OK, in a way, it has. Of course you can continue to write to me. I enjoy hearing about the art and the furniture. You are educating me. No, there is no one else. I have little time for romance.

                                                                    Elliot

London
1946

Dearest Elliot,

 Daddy says you have made a big killing on the public utilities
breakup—whatever that is. Does this mean you will be very rich soon
and able to take a wife? I am coming to New York next month—by
plane!—my first transatlantic flight, isn't that exciting? Will you be
there to meet me? Did you get the book I sent you on Fragonard?
They are very beautiful paintings. When we are married we will hang
one in our drawing room. Don't fight it, darling. I will make you very
happy and Daddy would be pleased.

                                                      I love you,
                                                      Blanchette

"Mrs. Neil?"

"Elliot! What a loyal friend you are. I thought you would
telephone, not come in person."

"I felt like a walk."

Mrs. Neil stood at the door of her brownstone.

"It is a lovely day. I'll get my hat and join you."

Mrs. Neil, Elliot observed when they set off downtown, had
become a handsome, stately matron. Only the dangling glass
earrings that shivered as she moved gave a clue that perhaps she
was not all that she seemed.

"You're kind," she said, taking his arm with her gloved
hand. "I don't believe all the stories I hear about you."

"Hear about me?"

"That you've become ruthless, mysterious—Byzantine, someone said. That you cultivate people and secrets . . ."

"Me? I'm an open book. The Street is just a peddler of rumor."

". . . even that you're no fun anymore."

"I have a lot of fun."

"Girls, Elliot. Romance."

They went into Schrafft's on Broadway for ice cream, but
Mrs. Neil changed her mind and ordered guava jelly on nut-
bread. She always ate guava jelly when she was worried.

"What's the trouble?" asked Elliot as he sipped his black
coffee.

"They're going to close me up. I can't get my lease renewed." She began to cry. "I don't really care for myself. I've
got enough to retire on, but my girls. No one will look after
them the way I do. I always ran a straight house, Elliot. Clean.
Looked after my girls. Remember Maureen? She married a bum.

Promised her everything, came back to me with her nose busted and a kid with rickets. Who else would take her on?''

"I'll see what I can do. Do you want more coffee?"

"No thanks. How can I thank you? Can I send a girl over? Very discreet. Mother Mary, you'd think this one came straight from the convent. You could take her to meet the cardinal and he'd never know." She paused for a moment, "The monsignor might, though."

Elliot laughed as Mrs. Neil regained her composure.

"I'm all right in that line. Besides, I've got a young woman who says she's going to marry me. She's been telling me for two years and she's got me accepting it. She's worn me down."

"You don't sound very enthusiastic about it. Do you love her?"

"I like her—a lot. I admire her. She'd be good for me."

Mrs. Neil looked disapproving.

"You're so handsome and so successful and so damn stupid."

They got up and Elliot paid the bill and they went out into the sunshine and traffic of Broadway.

"What happened to that little girl you used to talk about—the one in Colorado?"

"Yarrow? I heard she just had twins. Her sister keeps me in touch." They passed a shop window with a cardboard advertisement propped up inside, showing a beautiful girl smoking a cigarette. "That's Greta, her sister." They stopped, and the lunchtime crowds bumped into them.

"You see her picture everywhere," said Mrs. Neil.

"She's dating young Palmer Truitt," said Elliot as they went on. "His mother is my . . ." He was about to say "my future mother-in-law," but checked himself. ". . . my boss's wife."

"Oh, Elliot, you and your connections," said Mrs. Neil as they turned into her street. "You won't forget, will you?"

"It's done already." He waited until she had reached her front door and then walked back to the corner where his car and driver were waiting. He glanced at his watch. "The airport," he said. "We're going to meet Miss Newnom's flight. But first just drive east on Forty-sixth Street. I want to look at the slaughterhouses."

He had heard a rumor that Webb and Knapp, a development company, had been offered the old meat-packing companies' land that bordered the East River and extended south to Tudor City. If it was true, Mrs. Neil's brownstone and all the other houses in the depressed area would be valuable once development took place. Right now nobody wanted them, for the stench from the slaughterhouses was unbearable when the wind blew across the river. You could pick up property here for four or five dollars a square foot, while in midtown the price per square foot was anywhere from one hundred to two hundred dollars.

On the way to the airport Elliot wrote out a scheme to help Mrs. Neil. He would buy the property. He had noticed there were a number of other brownstones on the street that looked as though they had seen better days. He made a note of these and thought he would set up a separate company to invest in real estate. He would need more capital from Newnom. They could make a big killing if they moved fast. Wherever he looked Elliot could see ways of making money.

He had the car stop at a florist and he went in and bought an orchid corsage for Blanchette. A big vase of red and white roses at the exit reminded him of Yarrow. He had not thought about her in years. Greta had told him of the twins' arrival and he had sent her some roses. Yarrow had written a short, formal note of thanks. In the back of his air-conditioned limousine, Elliot thought about Yarrow; not as a flesh-and-blood woman, but as an embodiment of the warmth he had known in the McLean household—the fire crackling, the cooking smells, the children's voices, the arguments, the laughter, the joy. He imagined Yarrow at the center now of the same such scene.

Elliot thought of his own life: the small cold apartment he owned, the long hours on the telephone, the hours at his desk, the meals to consummate deals, the shrill women and tough men he now called his friends. It would be nice, he thought, staring blindly through the window, to come home to someone, to have a child, to give him the things he had not had. He imagined Blanchette in that role. She would carry it off admirably. He could now afford a rich wife. His pride would not be compromised. He had proven that he could make money to himself and to her father. He, Elliot Weyden, had made Rich Newnom and the firm even richer. He would soon be able to move out on his own. He even had a name ready for his own company—Phoenix. He needed one more break and then he could begin. He had gambled enormously on the falling share price of public utilities. He had gambled when the Supreme Court upheld the power of the Security and Exchange Commission to break up the giant companies. The share prices had tumbled and he had bought and bought and bought. He had gambled everything, and now it was all working out.

He could not have thought of a way to make more of an impression on Blanchette. She had no idea he was coming to meet her, and she flew into his arms, a pale young woman of eighteen in a blue suit. In the privacy of the car, with the glass partition up, he closed his eyes and kissed her. "I love you, Elliot," she said. She longed to hear him repeat it, but he didn't.

He held her chin with his fingers. "You've grown up," he said. When he took away his hand she could still feel the impression of his fingers. Blanchette sighed. She put her nose to the corsage he had given her, but there was no scent. Still, she considered herself the happiest of women.

"You wanted to see me on a private matter, Elliot," asked Rich Newnom, settling into a leather Chesterfield in his library.

The Newnoms' pied-à-terre was a large duplex on Fifth Avenue that overlooked the Metropolitan Museum. During the day, light flooded the room through the large windows. Now at night, while Elliot had waited for Newnom to finish his dinner and join him, he had watched the lights of the apartment houses on the West Side flicker on until the whole dark sky was starlit to the ground.

Elliot heard male voices and went to the door into the hall to greet Newnom. He saw a diminutive man with large ears and a wide mouth leaving through the front door. Newnom did not introduce him. He came in with his usual elegant, casual way and folded himself into the Chesterfield. Newnom lit a cigar and offered one to Elliot. Elliot declined.

Elliot pulled up a chair. He noticed it was a cross-legged Regency bench with a buttoned cushion—Blanchette's lessons were paying off.

"Two things," said Elliot, pressing the ends of his fingers together hard. He told Newnom about his ideas to buy the land around the abattoirs. Newnom watched him shrewdly through the smoke. Elliot suggested they would use three or four brokers to buy up the mortgages around the slaughterhouses. There was no point warning people what they were up to—the prices would jump before they were in place if that happened. He knew, said Elliot, that there was no way he could cut into the deal that Zeckendorf of Webb and Knapp had with the owners of the packing companies. But they, Elliot and Newnom, would be sitting pretty on some valuable property when the prices went up—as they inevitably would. But Elliot saw this as his deal, he made this very clear to Newnom; he wanted Newnom to come in as a partner, Elliot wasn't just going to take a percentage on this one.

"How much do you need?"

"Half a million dollars."

Newnom agreed so easily that Elliot was surprised.

"What's the second thing you want to talk about?" said Newnom.

"It's about Blanchette. I guess you know how I feel about her and we—I—that is, would very much like her hand in marriage."

Newnom let out one of his cackles, which left his thin body heaving and shaking, and Elliot realized that he, Newnom, hadn't been surprised at that either.

"So she got you in the end, eh? No, no, no, Elliot, don't be offended. I couldn't want a better match for Blanchette. I'm delighted. Delighted." He rang for the butler and ordered some champagne. "Thank God she's chosen a real man, not like that ne'er-do-well of Fabiana's. Christ what a dilettante. How can such a smart woman be so blinded by a boy? But you, son, you"—he wagged a finger—"I've watched you. I've admired you. You can negotiate. You are creative. You have judgment." He smacked his lips and puffed on his cigar.

"You love her?"

"Sir, she means more to me than any other woman. I'll protect her, and look after her."

"But don't let her get the upper hand, eh? Otherwise your life will be hell." He let out another cackle. "Go on, go on. I know you want to go up and see her. She's been in bed with a cold. Tell her you have my blessing."

Elliot excused himself and took the stairs up to the next floor three at a time. Blanchette was peering around a doorway in her robe. She could tell from his face that her father had said yes. She threw open the door as he picked her up and whirled her around. "Yes, my beauty, yes," he said as he kissed her and she held his head between her hands.

"Are you ill?"

"No. Dad had someone he wanted to dine with and I wasn't very welcome."

"The little man I saw leaving?"

"Yes, that's him. Mansky, Lansky, or something."

"Meyer Lansky?"

"Yes. Do you know him?"

"No. But I'm surprised your father does. He's a mobster." Meyer Lansky's picture had been all over the *Courier* a few months back when he and Frank Costello had seen off Lucky Luciano who had been deported to Italy.

"Oh, forget about Daddy and business. Look at me." She kissed him full on the lips.

He put her down on the pink and white bed and took out a sapphire ring from a box in his pocket. Blanchette began to cry.

"What's the matter?"

"I don't deserve it." She snuffled into the sleeve of her robe.

"You sound like my mother."

She put her arms around him and snuggled into him like a kitten.

"Are you happy?" she asked.

"Yes."

"Will you stay with me?"

She put one leg over his like a coil. He turned and laid her on the bed so that her arms were pinioned above her head by his.

"No," he said. He kissed her long and coolly with his eyes open. He was thinking of all the telephone calls he had to make. He did not want to waste any time starting on the East River venture. "We'll wait," he said. "Wait and I promise you it will be worth it."

"Oh, Elliot," she said, "I love you so." Her eyes brimmed with tears again. Elliot was moved. He kissed her along the cheekbones and found a little pulse under her right eye. He lingered over it.

"I am going to love you," he said. "I am going to love you."

He got up abruptly and left, blowing her a kiss from the door. When he had gone she still felt the weight of his body on hers, the wool of his trouser leg on her bare skin. She put her hand down between her legs and felt that she was as moist as a beaver in a pond. It had never happened to her before and she withdrew her hand in shock. And then, slowly, her hand crept back down again and found the place and stroked. Oh, Elliot, she thought, Oh, Elliot, my darling.

CHAPTER 15

"ELLIOT WEYDEN," READ YARROW, "THE WHIZ KID OF WALL Street, married Miss Blanchette Newnom in a ceremony held at the bride's home in Larchmont, New York. Miss Newnom's father, Richard Newnom of Newnom, Farkas and Weyden, gave the bride away.'' Yarrow shook the clipping at her children. "Ah ha! Who's Mr. Pumblechook now?'' Lily didn't even look up from her drawing. She was two years old and used to her mother speaking to herself, but the twins both smiled at her. "Thank you, my darlings,'' said Yarrow. She was sitting on the floor breast-feeding one twin while the other lay propped against a pillow on her knee. They were five months old and she adored them. True to her childhood dream, she had named one boy Zebulon and the other, as though she had run out of originality, John.

"You,'' she said, glancing again at the clipping and the picture of Elliot and his pretty young bride, "have achieved what you said you would. I, on the other hand, have achieved—nothing.'' John burped up at her and she took him off the breast and rubbed his back in circles, "Oh no, darling, not nothing. Babies.'' A spill of milk ran down her blouse. She rubbed it with her finger and then switched the boys over. She took out the other breast. "I blame it on Motherhood.'' Zeb's little mouth popped onto her nipple with satisfying greed. She watched his little cheeks going in and out and felt the strong surge of sexual excitement that feeding them always produced in her.

"Motherhood robbed me of ambition, Zeb. It happened surreptitiously; it began with your daddy's warm hand on me in the Garden of the Gods, and then you and your brother and sister with your little, little mouths sucked more out of me. Do you know that, Lily?'' Lily looked up and laughed as she heard her name mentioned. Her hair was thin and almost white in color. She had Sandy's wide face but her mother's eyes. "Yes, you're adorable but you destroyed me. And then you two, why you tore any last remnant of ambition from my shoulder. It fluttered free and flew away.''

Yarrow lay back and lifted Zeb high above her head with her elbows locked. He squealed and gurgled and then she put him down with his brother and they squirmed around her like cubs in a litter.

Today she felt like a sow. She always knew when she began to talk aloud to the children that she was becoming self-pitying. Cabin fever, Grandfather would have called it. Yarrow jumped to her feet and tucked herself in. "A fat old sow,'' she said. But she was harsh on herself. Her breasts were large with milk but her waist had come right back. She was so busy looking after the three children that her weight had dropped to what it was before. Her figure was womanly and had she known, she would have realized that her body had improved. Her face, too, had filled out and softened, and men noticed in her eyes a voluptuous awareness that had not been there before the birth of the children. And yet behind it, in the look of her eyes, there was a yearning for some explanation, like the loud ticking of a clock in a room that waits.

Sandy noticed it, too, and it made him jealous. When men's eyes followed her, their admiration only fed his own feelings of inadequacy. He could take no comfort from the fact that he was Yarrow's husband. When they got home after an evening out and she had been the object of someone's admiration, he would take her and be impatient, rough, abrupt. Love for him was an aggressive act. Even with the children he could be short and bored. She could not understand why he was like this. She had begun to realize that anger and confrontation with Sandy only made her own life more difficult. In her day-to-day dealings with him, she grew more submissive; she noticed it within herself and hated the person she was becoming. In bed she became more passive in his arms. Her inertness enraged him and he would become even quicker, even more insensitive to her needs. The dry friction hurt her, there was no joy, and she would wait for it to be over and when he soon fell off her, they would both be dissatisfied. He would lie with his arm over his eyes and she would wait for a polite minute or two and then get up without a word and go into the bathroom to wash him off her.

And yet, Yarrow wanted her marriage to work. Shame and pride were intermingled with her determination to make a go of it.

"All right, enough," Yarrow said, picking up the babies from the floor and putting one on either hip. "Let's go for a walk." When she got like this she needed adult companionship. She missed the office, and the excitement and the camaraderie. Her father had made Sandy assistant editor. Yarrow wished it had been she. She changed the boys and dressed them and put Lily's jacket on and got out the old perambulator her mother had given her, strapped the boys in and put Lily on a seat on top. Once outside the house she felt better and began to walk the long distance to her father's office.

She loved the fall. It was her favorite season. It had all the elements of sadness that appealed to Yarrow's romantic nature, and yet the crisp air made her feel more than alive. Even the children felt it. Their little cheeks glowed like apples. Yarrow kissed the dimpled knuckles of her daughter's hand. Leaves and paper swirled about her legs as she walked.

Eric's dog, Sherlock, greeted her with glee in the entrance

hall. Sherlock escaped from the yard as soon as Eric had gone to school each morning and padded across town to see James, whom he adored. Now the Great Dane covered her coat with fresh horse manure as he put his paws on her shoulder to lick her face. Sandy was annoyed when she came in breathless and laughing with the children and the dog, the perambulator and the stink of the outdoors on her clothes. "I couldn't help it," she said, collapsing into one of his office chairs and bouncing Zeb on her knee.

"His nose is running," Sandy said.

"He has a cold," she said, wiping his face with a bib. "What are you writing?"

"Your father asked me to write an editorial on . . ."

"Lily, don't touch the pencils on your father's desk. Sorry, you were saying?"

John woke up and began to cry.

"Yarrow," said Sandy, "I'm really busy."

"Oh, that's OK, I just thought you might like to see the children. Sometimes you're home so late, they're all asleep." She stood up, put Zeb back in with John, put the seat back on for Lily. Sandy came around the desk and pulled the collar of her coat up and kissed her on the forehead.

"I know, I'll try to be early tonight."

"Promise?"

"Promise." He patted her on the fanny as she went out, pushing the children. She passed a sleek female reporter and gave her a wave. She thought she detected a note of sympathy in the girl's replying smile.

She pushed the perambulator along to her father's office and stuck her head in the door.

"Hey, remember me?"

Her father was looking worried but he brightened when he saw her. "Come in, come in." He kissed her and brushed her coat with his hand. "I see Sherlock's back again. Can you send that dog home when you go down?"

She laughed and he kissed the children. "Stay for coffee," he said. Lily squirmed around the floor looking at magazines. Yarrow fell into a chair opposite the desk. She watched him make some instant coffee on a crowded credenza behind his desk. They got on so much better now that she was married. She supposed it was because she was no longer a menace to him.

"What's happening? I miss all this," she said.

He took off his glasses and rubbed his eyes.

"We're going to have a strike and I can't see any way to avoid it."

"The journalists?"

"No, the press room. We've had a number of paper breaks which makes me suspicious—I found some chewing gum in the running presses yesterday. Of course the men deny it. Hinton says we bought inferior paper. We've got trouble with the mailers too—they won't work overtime."

"How is Hinton?"

"He's smart, honest, ambitious—and impossible."

"I wish I could help. My fingers get itchy when I see this place."

"Nothing can help. The ITU hates the Taft-Hartley Act because it outlaws the closed shop. They want to force us to comply with union law. Christ, I'd comply with anything if I was dealing with a reasonable cause. But what does Hinton want?"—her father ticked off on his fingers—"a closed shop, the old priority rules, and the continuation of setting bogus type."

"Dead horse," she said.

"Yes. I'm glad your grandfather's not here to see it. It would break his heart."

He popped a couple of pills into his mouth and swallowed them with a glass of water. "A touch of indigestion," he said. "Got to watch it."

Two days later the strike was on. Both the *Journal* and the *Globe* were struck and Albert Hinton, head of Local 82, had come into his own.

Albert Hinton had become a printer at the age of seventeen. He had completed only two years of high school when he saw his father thrown out of work. There were times when the family had gone hungry and Albert Hinton knew the powerlessness and fear of unemployment. He had seen his father, a proud man, a printer, reduced to an impotent raging drunk when he could not get work. The union, for young Albert, had become his salvation. He had taken to heart its axiom, best expressed in a poem in his book on trade unionism:

> What man would be wise, let him drink of the river
> That bears on its bosom the record of time;
> A message to him every wave can deliver
> To teach him to creep till he knows how to climb.

Hinton was a man who had learned how to wait. He trusted nobody and he particularly did not trust newspaper publishers. In his book the only way to deal with them was to beat them over the head with an iron bar and truss them up at a negotiating table. He had not trusted Max Horace when he went to work for him, and he did not trust James McLean or Larry Schaeffer either, for that matter. He hated all employers. But he kept this to himself, offering an affable and polite public demeanor while inside he seethed with resentment. So Albert Hinton had learned to wait and year by year he had built up his own fiefdom within their very walls.

When he had lost two fingers years ago working for Horace on the old *Record* he could no longer follow his trade. He threw himself into the organization of his local union. He had been elected president of Local 82 five years ago. Now with a new contract up for negotiation, he saw it as a way to attack the power of the employers, to protect his fellow workers and to draw the attention of the parent union to his own skills.

The first meeting was held in the board room of the *Globe* two days later. The *Globe* pressroom was under a different jurisdiction, but it had been agreed that Hinton would speak for both printers and pressmen in the negotiations.

Neither the *Globe* nor the *Journal* had been able to publish. Larry Schaeffer of the *Globe*, and his labor lawyer, Pilcher, was there and James McLean and Sandy Heartland of the *Journal* with their own counsel, Woodard. "You may as well learn about this the hard way," James had said to his son-in-law. There were four union participants, including a member of the pressmen's local. On the table was a proposal from the publishers for a new contract, but Albert Hinton wouldn't look at it.

"You're not negotiating in good faith," he said when he finally walked in thirty minutes late. (Hinton knew all about psychology.) He placed his hands on the table so that the chopped-off fingers of his left hand were in full view. A gold wedding ring was on one of the remaining fingers. No one could look at his hand; it always worked—made the bastards uncomfortable.

"What do you mean?" asked Pilcher.

"You've already violated the contract by employing nonunion workers on Varitype machines—even women! These operations commenced before the contract terminated."

"We have every right to protect ourselves," said Pilcher.

"You're goddam liars."

"We have not violated the contract. We have not produced any newspapers these last two days."

"You are preparing to produce them."

"That's different. Aren't we entitled to protect our own interests?"

"Put some additional money in the pay envelope and we will continue to try to reach an agreement."

"We can't make you a money offer until the ITU policy is changed."

"You don't even want to make us a wage offer. You don't want to negotiate any part of our proposal."

"Christ, Albert, we can't negotiate on these terms. Take this sixty-day termination clause—what security does that give the publishers?"

"You don't want to make deals at the local level."

"That's not true. We have no quarrel with you. It's the policy of your International that's keeping us apart."

They broke up without any further meeting being scheduled. James popped a couple more pills in his mouth. Confrontation always made him ill.

That night Freya and James went over to Yarrow's for dinner. Her father did not look well. He couldn't take his mind off his worries. He did not have the resources of the *Globe* to take a long strike. He was still paying the journalists and the mailers and the clerks every day without any money coming in. He couldn't eat. His skin was a gray color. Freya took him home early.

The following day, entering his office, he had to cross a picket line. He knew most of the men by name and he was just about to greet one of them when a big ripe tomato was thrown at him. He looked down at the red stain like blood that ran down his trouser leg. He felt he was bleeding to death, like his newspaper.

The following day Hinton proposed a meeting. That night they all met again at the *Globe* office.

He began strongly. "We can settle this right now, quickly and cleanly. We do not want to evade or violate any laws, but you know, and I know, that we've all ignored laws for many years." Hinton was referring to the backlog of dead horsing, or bogus printing, that hung on hooks at both newspaper offices. It had always been left to the local chapel chairmen and the employers to work out a solution on bogus.

"There is no reason why, if money is laid on the line, that this cannot be resolved immediately," he went on. "Just don't throw things on the table that mean nothing to us."

"This is just a repetition of what you said to us the other day."

"You've made suggestions and we're answering you. You've never yet approached a problem with any give in it. Nothing will be settled without wages being discussed. Nothing."

"Is the principal obstacle the question of wages, then?"

"Absolutely, because your persecution of us, of our men, cannot be taken away from the minds of this union."

"We've been trying to arrive at a contract within a certain framework—that is, the tying of conditions to wages. That has been procedure."

"Procedure. You're all procedure. Let's talk money."

"The last night before the strike, the mailers wouldn't work overtime."

"So?"

"We asked you to bring pressure to bear on them. We're disturbed about the obligations of your men. A contract sets up obligations on both sides. Now you're trying to tell us that the union has no way of making men work."

"I can't do anything about making the men work if they don't want to. Unless the wage issue is resolved, it will get worse. The members will not listen to me."

"Albert, you must understand our apprehension. We are concerned that whatever framework we work out here will eventually be extended to the mailers."

"Don't keep bringing the mailers into it."

"We must bring the mailers into it. Your men are skilled, the mailers are not. The mailers' union has been unwilling to give us enough men—even with overtime they will be short of help. How is it going to be supplied without running into your closed-shop condition?"

They broke at four-thirty for lunch, each team going off in different directions. James was surprised to see that it was still daylight. He ate a cheeseburger with a side order of onions.

"That won't help your indigestion," said Sandy, wolfing down a ham and Swiss on rye.

"I can't even taste it," said James. "That damn Hinton has taken away my appetite."

They went back into the negotiation room and picked up where they left off.

"You fear," said Woodard, "that we will fill up the shop with the mailers and vote out the union men. The jurisdiction problem is with us now. Two unions are claiming the right to do certain work. These are the problems we are trying to solve at this table."

"We've always resolved these problems in the past. What you

want is perfection. Perfection for you—nothing for us. This is just another red herring you are putting on the table."

"Nevertheless, these problems are of concern to the publishers because if we give you the protection you ask, the same thing applied to the mailers will give us trouble."

"I'd have had the mailers with us if I'd known you were to bring this up."

"Then, how can we avoid difficulties?"

"All I can say is the problems will be met."

"Why can't we agree to something?"

"Because the Taft-Hartley law makes it impossible for us to guarantee anything of the sort."

"Can we assume that any extra men must come in at time-and-a-half?"

"I can't promise you that."

"How are we going to get the papers out?" asked James.

"I can't tell you how to get them out." Hinton smiled sarcastically. "Maybe I can get the answer from the mailers tonight."

"It's already morning," said Larry Schaeffer, looking at his watch.

"I think you ought to start talking money—we've been through all this for hours," said Hinton. He scratched his nose with his mutilated fingers.

"We would like to have an answer," said James.

"I told you we weren't going to give any answers till we talk about wages."

"If you got a proposal on wages attached to that, what would your answer be?"

"We might refuse. I don't know."

"What do you suggest we submit this with—a schedule of wages?"

"No, I don't think that fast. I say we've got to talk wages under any circumstances."

"We need a framework before we can talk wages."

"Then you've got to change that procedure. We've talked to you about framework for days now—shouldn't you begin to talk to us about money?"

"This is where we were two days ago," said James.

"If we talk about money without any framework, you'll post the money in your Conditions of Employment and forget about the rest. We think the publishers are entitled to an answer," said Woodard.

"You want to know what the framework is now?" said Hinton. "You're in a hell of a fix. Anyway what difference does it make—you're going to print newspapers anyhow."

"What's wrong with our proposal?"

"We do not want to agree that we will approve all but one point and then have to bargain with you on that."

"What difference does it make?"

"Collective bargaining has always been a give-and-take proposition."

"You haven't given that impression."

"We will give our answer after we have studied the whole proposal . . ."

"Then go ahead and study it!"

" . . . but you won't get an answer until wages are on the table. To be quite frank about it, we have to call up our expensive lawyers to discuss this before we can answer."

"You'll be telling us to sell our newspapers for seven cents or eight cents next."

"If they were worth five cents a year ago they are worth seven cents or eight cents today. The reason they aren't is because you newspapers won't raise your prices on account of competition and that's your problem, not mine."

"Christ, I'm tired. It's four A.M." said James.

"Let's stop now," said Schaeffer.

"When shall we resume? Do you want some time to consider this?" said Woodard.

"I've nothing to consider until you get over the hurdle of wages."

"What's wrong with following the usual procedure? You've got the proposal in front of you—you always went down it item by item before—what's wrong with following that here? We can discuss it that way now."

Hinton got up and stretched.

"I suggest ten-thirty in the morning. Good night, gentlemen." The meeting was adjourned.

James crawled into bed beside Freya. He was exhausted. She heard him get up an hour later.

"James? Are you all right?"

"My pills," he said. "Indigestion . . ."

She heard a crash. "James!" She put on the light. He lay on the floor in his striped pajamas. Freya got out of bed and ran to him. "James, what is it?" But he didn't move.

"Oh, my God. Oh, my God," she said. "What have they done to you?"

James was dead. She knew it but couldn't accept it. She kept trying to talk to him and she began to cry. After a while she got up and went to the telephone.

"Yarrow? Sandy? Come over. It's James. I think he's gone."

CHAPTER 16

A CONFUSION OF CHRYSANTHEMUMS SPILLED FROM A FAT BLUE vase in the hall. Yarrow pushed one more in and stood back for the effect. She took great pride in the flowers she grew and arranged. She thought it made up for the lack of talent she had in other domestic areas.

"Are you celebrating the end of the strike?" asked Mary-Ellen Griffin, who had dropped in for a cup of morning coffee. Her two girls were playing in the yard with Lily.

"It's twenty-two months since the strike began. We have just a few people coming in, some of the secretaries who've been working the Varitype machines."

"I can't believe it's that long since your father died," said Mary-Ellen, putting her coffee cup down on the hall table and pushing aside some mail and books and a child's sweater and a metal pail. "What's this?"

"Oh, Grandfather called it a 'gadhunter.' He used to take it down the mines." Yarrow put it back in place. She liked to think of it lighting her own way, but she didn't say this to Mary-Ellen.

"Greta looked so beautiful when she was here for the funeral," said Mary Ellen as they stepped over some toys and went outside to watch the children play. "I'm surprised she's never married."

"Because she fell in love with a jerk who won't marry her, that's why," said Yarrow.

"Palmer Truitt?"

"The same."

"Fancy Nellie marrying before her. Did you know that when she came over for the funeral?"

"No, she kept it to herself."

"I didn't even know she'd moved to California."

"That I knew. She's working in a private hospital."

One of Mary-Ellen's girls fell over and Mary-Ellen rushed across to pick her up.

Yarrow went around the hall tidying up. It had taken her months to be able to talk about her father without her throat closing up. It even seemed her mother had recovered more quickly from his death than she. In the lawyer's office a few days after the funeral, it had been Freya who grasped the situation right away. Under the conditions of James's will, the family shares were divided equally among his four children. Provisions had been made for Freya, and until Eric reached the age of twenty-one, Freya would be a director of the company and able to vote his shares.

Freya had told Yarrow that she had hoped that James would pick one of the children as his successor. Admittedly they were all young—Yarrow was twenty-five when James died, Nellie was twenty-two, Greta twenty-one, and Eric only fourteen. Freya had mentioned it once or twice to him, but James never wanted to think of the future. He was, after all, at the peak of his power; he had been only fifty-five years old when he died. Picking a successor would be like digging his own grave. And what wife wanted to keep harping on what would happen when her mate was gone?

James had believed he had all the time in the world to put things in order, thought Yarrow, rolling up a ball of string that was twined around the newel-post. He had been grooming Sandy to take over, that was obvious but, true to his character, he had balked at choosing one over the other and had left the decision to be worked out among them.

The estate taxes had been in excess of forty thousand dollars, and their lawyer, C. K. Pierson, had suggested that the widow and family might be better off selling the paper and investing the money.

Freya and Yarrow had looked at him with horror. "Never," they said.

"Then who's going to run it?"

"It's always been a family business and it will continue that way," said Freya. "Sandy can manage it and we will continue to support him."

They sold off half the land that surrounded Jock's mountain cabin and arranged to pay the rest of the taxes in installments.

"Sandy knows nothing about running a business," said Nellie.

"He'll learn," Yarrow said, jumping to Sandy's defense.

In fact Sandy had thrived on the opportunity. The family had granted him the title of Publisher and Editor, and he had slipped into their father's shoes as though they had been made for him. He had made a deal with Schaeffer to help each other while the strike was on. Women were employed to set the type on justifying typewriters, and the two papers shared the costs of photocopying and engraving. The blocks were driven up and down the highway between the two cities, and sometimes the drivers were attacked. Of course the papers looked a bit muddy at first—they were still trying to get the hang of photographing the copy and then engraving it. They put out some very amateurish-looking papers those first weeks, but gradually they improved.

"Isn't it strange," said Yarrow as she sat on the front step with Mary-Ellen, "that we are going back to hot metal again? I mean, what on earth was the strike for? What did we gain?"

Mary-Ellen shook her red hair. "Ned asks the same question. Did you see that Albert Hinton is going to New York as head of the Big Six?"

"No, I didn't."

"Ned is thinking of moving, too. With Larry Junior at the *Globe*, he doesn't see much chance for advancement. He's been offered a job in California."

Lily came over with a lovely pile of mud in her hands. "This is for you," she said, "and this is for you." She was wearing the most unsuitable dress for making mud pies—a fine lawn with pintucking all around the skirt.

"Greta sent it," said Yarrow with a sigh. "She sends them all the most beautiful clothes and if I don't use them up they grow out of them too soon. The boys are asleep in the most exquisite little blue velveteen pantaloons right now."

Mary-Ellen picked up her youngest daughter. "You need help, Yarrow. Why don't you get a young girl to come in?"

"Sometimes I wish I could find another Laura."

"Look at you. Look at your hair. Remember how it was?"

"Oh Mary-Ellen, don't pick at me. I don't have time anymore." She ran her hand through her curls. Her hair stood out like a frizz. "One of these days I'm going to chop it all off."

"Oh, don't do that. Remember how upset you were when you had to cut off your mother's hair?"

"I always thought she would be the first to die. I never thought it would be Dad."

Mary-Ellen kissed her on the cheek.

"I'm not being critical, really I'm not. But I hate to see you looking so—so tired."

"I'll be fine, really," said Yarrow, waving good-bye and

going in to prepare the children's lunch. She was sitting down with them in the kitchen eating peanut-butter sandwiches when Freya arrived.

"I thought we were going to plan out that back section of the garden today," said Freya. Freya's energy was still unflagging. Little wrinkles had appeared around her eyes that had not been there before, but her eyes were clear and calm.

"I forgot. Come on, kids. Out we go. I'll clear up this mess after." Freya winced. The remains of the breakfast were still in the sink. But she said nothing and as they went past the yellow chrysanthemums in the hall, she said, "How beautiful your flowers are, Yarrow." Yarrow smiled at her mother, with her lips pressed together.

They pegged out an area for a new flowerbed. Freya held a stick near the wall while Yarrow crawled around with a string in her hand.

"Further," said Yarrow as her mother unrolled some more string, and she curved the line more and tapped in another stick to hold it in place. Zeb and John were playing together in the sandbox. Lily was dunking a doll in a tub with water that leaked down from a drainpipe.

"They're angel children," said Freya. Zeb had curly dark hair like Yarrow's. It stood up around his head like that of a Botticelli cherub. John's hair lay like a smooth cap with only the lift that a double cowlick gave it at the front.

"Lily, don't do that, please," said Yarrow, jumping up and pulling Lily away from the water. Lily let out a wail. "It frightens Mommy."

Zeb toddled over to the string and gave it a twang and the stick holding the string popped out. Yarrow snapped at him and grabbed his little arm.

"You're tired," said Freya, calmly tapping back the stick with her foot and picking up Zeb to comfort him. "You need some help with the children."

"Oh, not you, too."

Yarrow sat back on her heels. She was wearing a floral skirt and an old, long cardigan with a droopy hem. Her hair had escaped from a rubber band. She felt old and miserable. She had tried so hard to be the perfect wife, the perfect mother, but things got in the way. The best-laid plans were so easily veered away from. The children and the house and Sandy's needs distracted her from everything. But the truth was, she was not happy with her life. There was a void inside her that was not being filled. It was as though she had once been a stick like the

one she was holding, and the fire stick had been removed before
a spark had caught, leaving only a dimple. It was the navel of
her inner self.

"OK, Mama. Perhaps you're right."

"Good. I'll put an ad in the paper today."

A week later Yarrow had hired a girl of whom even her
mother approved. She had no better recommendations than any
of the others Yarrow had interviewed, but when she walked in,
she picked up some toys from the floor and put them in a box
near the door. Yarrow's eyes lit up. And when the girl let John
crawl all over her on the sofa and pull her hair and examine her
teeth without any qualms or complaints, Yarrow knew she was
the girl for them and hired her on the spot.

Apart from that, Belinda was pretty, she was eighteen years
old, and she chewed gum and wore white socks and sneakers and
tight sweaters and pedal pushers. On her hours off, a series of
young men would show up to take her out. Yarrow and Sandy
would roll their eyes at the giggles and scuffles on their front
porch when the young men brought her home. "Come to bed,"
said Sandy, as though the girl's presence and that of her swains
aroused him, too. But it never aroused Yarrow and their frustra-
tions in the bedroom only continued. He would get up afterward
and she would listen to him go downstairs and open the refrigerator door. She would hear the pop of a bottle being opened and
hear the squeak of the kitchen chair as he pulled it out from
under the table. Then she would fall asleep and not notice when
he came back to bed.

"Darling, here's a brownstone for sale on Sixty-fourth Street,"
said Blanchette Weyden, looking through the real estate section
of *The New York Times*. She was sitting in an armchair, still in
her dressing gown on Sunday morning in their suite at the Plaza.

"Too far uptown," said Elliot, also in a silk dressing gown
but working at the telephone on the desk. He had already called
London, Los Angeles and Florida this morning and taken nu-
merous calls offering him bauxite mines and avocado farms from
Australia to Brazil. It was not a day of rest for Elliot, and it was
not Sunday everywhere in the world. There were times when he
felt like a marriage broker putting client and client together.
Whatever happened to the ventures, Elliot, as the middleman,
always made money.

"Elliot, it's only six blocks north of here. We've been living
in this hotel for three years now. It's April, darling, 1950. Aren't
we ever going to have a place of our own?"

"I like it here," said Elliot. He did most of his work from an adjoining room and besides, he enjoyed the anonymity of a hotel. It was the one sore point between them, this question of a "home." Elliot was afraid of the domesticity of owning the kind of place Blanchette wanted. He did not want to be encumbered with possessions. Everything he bought, pictures, rugs, ornaments, could be packed up, rolled up and taken with him. It gave him the illusion of being a gypsy. He liked the feeling of freedom it gave him.

"Hello? Jules? Yes, it's me." Elliot leaned back in his chair for a long telephone conversation. Blanchette sighed. It was no use trying to talk him into something he didn't want. He was the kindest of husbands, the most generous. He lavished her with presents, some valuable, some not, and given at any time because he liked to do it. She knew he did the same for his mother, and his sister and countless other women he called his clients. He worked hard and long hours at his desk. There was no such thing as a day off, a holiday. Elliot loved what he did. If the phone didn't ring for an hour he wondered if he had been forgotten. She had heard him call someone once and petulantly ask what he had done wrong to be treated this way? Another time he had telephoned the hotel switchboard to check if his own phone was in order; it had not rung for twenty minutes. When she went to her gynecologist (she was having difficulty conceiving), he went with her and sat in the waiting room, working out deals on the backs of envelopes, on the margins of newspapers until she returned. "No news yet," she said. He would squeeze her arm under its sable throw. "We'll try harder," he said.

For her twenty-first birthday he had taken over the Rainbow Room and filled it with friends, freesias and roses, and they had danced until dawn. Everyone said it was the best party they had ever been to. Blanchette knew she should be blissfully happy but one small nagging doubt like a toothache always bothered her. She knew she loved her husband more than he did her. She was insanely jealous of any woman who came his way and she knew it was unfair to him. She didn't make scenes. She considered herself too well brought up for that, but she would be aware of her teeth shaking and her stomach knotting if she allowed herself to think of him with another woman. And then she would outdo herself to be kind to him, so then she was worried that she was annoying him, that she was too cloying, too suffocating and that he would leave her anyway. Blanchette looked at him now, the sleek head leaning back against the leather chair as he talked into the phone, his long bare legs sprawled out, slipperless, under the desk. She knew what she would do.

Blanchette got up from her chair and went to the bathroom for a bowl of soapy water and some towels. She brought out her manicure things, clippers and emery boards and creams and nail brushes. She took the bowl back, and she knelt down and put her husband's feet in the warm water. Elliot sighed, glanced at her for a moment, and went on talking into the telephone. Blanchette knew he was a sensualist. She felt like Mary Magdalen as she worked on his feet (she had been reading a lot about the Catholic Church lately), taking first one foot, then the other out of the water and massaging them with cream. She allowed her hands to creep up and massage his firm calves and the narrow knees, and then she heard him say, "Jules, I'll call you back," and she smiled.

"What are you doing?" he said, pulling her up onto his lap. She curled into him, and then he kissed her and picked her up and took her to their bed. He had just undone the knot of her belt when the telephone rang. He tried to ignore it for a moment and then gave up and rolled over and answered the phone on the bedside table. He sat up suddenly, pulling his own robe closed.

"God," he said, "I totally forgot, your stepmother's coming up now to see me."

He rushed into the bathroom and she followed him petulantly.

"Why is she coming here, Elliot? On a Sunday?"

"I've no idea. She said it was personal. Quick, be a love and order us some coffee in the other room and let her in."

By the time he had changed into a gray suit of the finest silk and wool (he always dressed formally, even on Sundays), Fabiana was sitting drinking coffee in the adjoining room that he used as his office. Blanchette slipped away tactfully.

"It's about Palmer, my son. Will you help me?"

"I'll try. What is the problem?" But of course he knew, since his telephone kept him in touch with all kinds of rumor and gossip, which he converted into money, power and knowledge.

Fabiana was more agitated than usual. She stood up, her body still slim, a hat hugging her head in such a way that only the initiated knew it hid an ugly scar on her jaw and neck. "I can't talk to Rich about it. Rich has no time for Palmer. Palmer's a good boy but he has got in with the wrong crowd."

"What is it?" He would make her say it.

"He's on some kind of drugs." She passed her hand over her eyes. "I've tried everything. I've threatened him. He lies to me. Oh, he's such a good liar. He has stood in front of me and sworn he won't touch anything and a cellophane package of white powder has fallen out of the newspaper he was carrying. Oh, Elliot, what can I do?''

"Cut him off.''

"How can I? He's my son.'' She paused. "Anyway, I tried. He steals from me. When he comes to the house there is always something missing. Rich has forbidden him in the house now. He must steal from Greta, too—or she gives him the money to support his habit.''

"Greta McLean?''

"Yes. He lives with her sometimes. You know the McLeans from Platte City?''

"Yes. During the Depression when I was in Colorado. They were very kind to me.''

"You've never mentioned it before. They weren't very nice to me. They double-crossed me on a deal.''

Elliot said nothing and wondered if behind her dark blue eyes she knew that he was lying.

"Anyway,'' she said, "they did me a favor. If I hadn't lost out to them in Platte City I might never have bought the *Courier*. Elliot, you've advised me very well in the past. Will you help me now on this—will you help my son? He won't answer the phone when I call anymore. If Greta could help him, I would be glad of it, but Greta's not strong enough to deal with him.''

"That I know.''

"He might listen to you. If you could talk him into going to a sanatorium. Here''—she reached in her bag and took out an address book—"it's in Connecticut. There's a very good man. I've spoken to him.'' She wrote down the information on some paper on his desk. "Here's Greta's number, too. Please, Elliot.''

"I'll try.''

"And don't say a word to Rich, will you? He thinks I'm just a pushover where Palmer is concerned.''

When she had gone, he placed a call to Greta. He was just about to hang up as the phone rang and rang, and then Greta answered. She sounded numb, out of things, not like her usual placid self.

"Palmer's not here,'' she sobbed. "He's not here. Oh, what am I to do?''

"Greta, shall I come over?''

"Oh, no. It's nothing you can help with.'' He could hear her struggling to control her emotions. He did not wish to intrude.

"If Palmer comes, you will let me know.''

"Oh, yes. Yes. Good-bye, Elliot.''

When he had hung up he was still troubled. So much so that he sat down again and thumbed his way through his address book. But he had to call directory assistance.

"Hello? Hello, Yarrow? Yes, it's me. How clever of you to recognize my voice after so long. Yes, it must be nearly ten years. Yarrow, I'm afraid it's about Greta. I think you should come and see her in New York."

Late the next day, Yarrow was in New York. It was a glorious spring day and the magnolia blossoms on the bare trees were as big as plates. The magnolias were like a promise that spring would really come and that the trees would leaf out again and the grayness of winter would be over. But Yarrow hardly noticed. She took a taxi straight to Greta's latest apartment, which was in a newish building on the Lower East Side with a view across the river to Queens. She had tried to telephone her after Elliot's message but there was no answer and she had organized the children and Belinda as best she could and got on the first plane available.

There was a Spanish-speaking doorman on duty, but he said Miss McLean was not in.

"Of course she's in," said Yarrow, pushing past him and getting into the elevator with her bags. "She's expecting me."

She knocked and knocked on the door until finally she heard Greta's voice. "Go away. For God's sake, go away."

"Greta. It's me. Yarrow. Let me in."

"Yarrow?" There was a slow shuffling noise and then she heard the chain being taken off the door and then the door opened and Greta fell into her arms. "Oh, thank God someone came."

Yarrow staggered back with her sister to her bed. The sheets were covered with blood. Greta had collapsed on the floor. Her face was white and shiny-looking. There was blood on her nightgown and on the floor.

"Greta. You're hemorrhaging. Greta?" Greta had passed out. Yarrow lifted her sister up onto the bed, how light she was, and covered her with blankets. Her face was a ghastly gray, yet her body burned with a fever. Yarrow rinsed out a washcloth in the bathroom, where more bloody towels and sheets lay on the floor. She wiped her sister's face gently and placed the cloth on her forehead and then telephoned Elliot.

"Elliot, I'm sorry to bother you so soon. I need a discreet doctor—urgently. Greta is bleeding to death." She could hardly bring herself to say the word that horrified her, but she knew without a doubt. "Greta's had an abortion."

While the doctor was with her sister, Yarrow looked around for the first time at the apartment. It was really one large studio room with the bed to one side and a huge double-height window. It looked as though Greta had furnished it directly from a Platte City furniture store with the heavy practical furniture that they had both grown up with. There was nothing to indicate the life of a sophisticated photographer's model until she went to a wardrobe and a whole spill of beautiful clothes in brocades, taffetas and tulles burst out when she opened the door. She jammed in her one change of clothes and shut the door.

The doctor came out from behind the screen that hid the bed. He shook his head and went to the bathroom and washed his hands. He had cleaned her up, he said, and given her a shot that would help her sleep. She had an infection. It had been a bloody, botched job. He would leave some pills to take the fever down.

"She'll probably be all right, but she'll never have children now. Why do women let this happen to them?" Yarrow bit back an angry retort. Men had something to do with it, too.

"How old is she?"

"Twenty-three."

The doctor shook his head again. She supposed he did not mean to be callous. He gave her a brown bottle of pills and a phone number. "If she continues to hemorrhage, call me at this number. Her fever should go down. I'll be back at eight in the morning." He stopped at the door. "Give yourself a Scotch. You look like you need it."

Yarrow pulled a chair up beside the bed and wrapped herself in a blanket. It was late afternoon. She must have dozed off, for she was suddenly aware of Greta groaning, and the apartment was in total darkness except for the winking of a Pepsi-Cola sign across the river. She put on the bedside light. "Water," said Greta. Her sister's lips had disappeared into the whiteness of her face and her lips were so dry a crust had formed. It reminded Yarrow of her babies' milk blisters, which she could peel off with her fingers, and she began to cry. She lay with her head on the bed beside Greta and her arms across the flat barren stomach. She remembered Greta as a little girl, how she had loved to play with dolls, how she adored Laura's little Lem, how she sent the most inappropriate presents to her own children. Greta had always been the placid child, the one they had never had to bother about. Perhaps that was it. Perhaps if she had demanded more, they would have paid more attention. Would that have made a difference, would it? Would she have been a different person if she could have said, I need help. If only she had said it. If only she had called out. If you don't want the baby, Yarrow would have told her, I will adopt it, bring it up as my own. Never say a word—why intensify the pain by offering what might have been an option?

Greta was delirious. Her eyes were not quite closed. Yarrow wondered what they saw. She got up through the night and changed the washcloth, wiped her sister's brow, stroked her hand, made the soothing noises she had once heard her mother make, had used with her own children. Nonsense sounds that replaced superfluous words for all they meant repeated over and over again was, I love you.

At dawn when the great city of New York was bathed in a sunrise as beautiful as any Yarrow had seen in the mountains, Greta's fever broke. Her breathing became easier and slower and her skin cooled down. Yarrow slept on the chair and at eight the doctor was there. When he had gone she brought in a cup of apple tea. "Hello, little sister," she said, placing the mug in Greta's hands.

"Oh, Yarrow. Don't tell Mama."

"Of course not."

"Don't tell anyone, please."

"Only I know—and Elliot. He had to know. I had to find a doctor."

Greta lay back exhausted on her pillow.

"I had to do it. He didn't want me to have it. He told me to get rid of it. He threw things at me. I made an appointment with this sleazy man. I was going there when Elliot called me. It was horrible. Dirty. I could have used a coat hanger for all the good it did me." Greta and Yarrow sobbed together. "I had to bring cash. It hurt when they did it. Oh, God, Yarrow did it hurt. They tore it out of me. This was not something apart from me—this was part of my body. I don't know how I got back up here." Her eyes shut. "Have you seen Palmer? Did he call?"

Yarrow shook her head. He had run, like the skunk he was. I should have let him drown when I had the chance, she thought.

"It's the drugs, don't blame him. He hid it very well from me at first. Then he got bolder. He tried to get me to join him . . ."

"You didn't . . ."

"No." For the first time a smile crept across Greta's face. "I'm still the little girl from Platte City. Can't you tell?" She motioned around the room with a limp arm.

"I'm going to give you a sponge bath," said Yarrow, getting up. "You'll feel much better." After she had helped her change into a clean nightgown and changed the sheets again, she took some talcum powder and sprinkled it through Greta's hair, then she went to work with two brushes. As she brushed they talked. They talked about when they were small and men had not come into their lives.

"Remember when Grandfather taught you how to box? You came to my defense for something or other at school and a boy knocked you down," said Greta.

"How could I forget? 'No air in the fist,' Jock kept telling me, 'and line up his nose with your knuckles.' I think I kayoed him." Greta laughed and her eyes closed. Yarrow pulled the covers up higher and spread out her brushed hair.

"I'm going to have a shower now," whispered Yarrow; she was still wearing the clothes she had traveled in.

She scrubbed herself and washed her hair until she felt clean. This whole sordid affair of Greta and Palmer had left her feeling soiled. She dressed in the blouse and slacks she had brought with her and was putting on some lipstick when the doorbell rang. She thought it was the doctor coming back and when she opened the door expecting to see him, she had half turned away and then her eyes swiveled again and she took in the man at the door. Elliot—standing there with a gentle smile on his face and holding a big bouquet of flowers in one hand and a thermos bottle in the other. "Chicken soup," he said. "My mother says it cures everything."

She took his beaver hat and his coat and hung them up and then he hugged her and she clung to him like a long-lost friend. He held her at arm's length and looked at her. Not a flicker in his eyes, not an atom of change in his demeanor showed that he saw in her anything except her old self. And yet she knew she was tired and older-looking, and her clothes felt shabby. But he took in every hair, every thread, every fiber of her being. It was like being swallowed whole.

Greta slept on. He sat on the edge of a chair near her, with his elbows on his parted knees. He wore no jewelery, Yarrow noticed—she noticed everything about him—no rings, no watch, no tiepin. She was glad. She would hate to have found him foppish. He talked quietly to Yarrow and then he got up to go.

"Can I do anything for you?" he asked as Yarrow helped him into his coat. It was of the finest cashmere and it slipped under her fingers like silk.

"No. You've done enough."

"I'll come by tomorrow then." They shook hands. "I've not said a word to Blanchette, or Fabiana," he said. "They don't have to know."

"Thank you." His brown eyes held her own for a moment longer, then he touched the brim of his hat and was gone.

The next day he returned, about lunchtime, with a brown paper bag of groceries and a parcel under his arm. He was pleased to see Greta sitting up in bed. She thanked him for telephoning her sister. He waved her thanks away.

"I've brought food for the stomach and food for the soul," he said.

"Can you stay for lunch?"

"Yes. I've given my secretary the number. We'll have a picnic. Deli food. New York has the best in the world." He delved into the bag, "Pastrami on rye, Black Forest ham with Swiss, egg salad, cream cheese and lox on an onion bagel. Who wants what?"

When they had settled around the bed, with coffee and paper plates and squares of waxed paper laid out like placemats, he unwrapped the second parcel. "I bought it this morning for my office," he said, "but I thought you might like it here for a few days." It was a small picture in an ornate gilt frame, a painting of walnuts and an ivory-handled knife on a creased white tablecloth. On the tablecloth there were also a chrome nutcracker and some deep purple grapes on a blue-edged platter. He mentioned the artist's name but it meant nothing to Yarrow. He propped the painting up on a chair where they all could see it and they contemplated it while they ate.

"It's so serene," said Greta. "It's beautiful."

"I thought so, too," he said. "Blanchette keeps telling me to look into things, to see the heart of them. She's taught me a great deal about art but mainly she's taught me to trust my own instincts. Good things jump out at you. Don't you feel you want to pick up one of those grapes and eat it?"

"Yes," said Yarrow.

The phone rang. It was for him. Yarrow watched him switch like a train onto a different track. He was clear, abrupt, concise, cold. When he came back to the lunch, he had switched again.

"I've spoken to Palmer," he said after a while. "He's agreed to go into a sanatorium. What will you do, Greta?"

Yarrow looked at her sister. She was still pale and there were dark rings under her eyes, but she was again as serene as the painting.

"I've had an offer for a screen test on the West Coast. I

thought I might give it a try. What do you think, Yarrow? I could stay with Nellie.''

"I think it's an excellent idea.'' Anything to get her away from New York and Palmer Truitt.

"Do you have an agent?'' asked Elliot.

"No. Do I need one?''

"Everyone needs one out there.'' He scribbled down a note to himself. "I'll find out for you and tell you tomorrow.''

"Oh, why don't you take Yarrow out for lunch tomorrow? She's never been in New York before and all she's seen are the backyards of Queens from this window.''

"Oh, no, I'll stay with you.''

"I'll be fine, really. In a few days you'll be leaving. Please, Yarrow.''

"I'll send the car for you at twelve-thirty then,'' he said, his brown eyes flashing. "I'll show you the prettiest restaurant in New York.''

When he had gone, Yarrow tossed the crumpled papers into a wastebasket across the room. She could not look her sister in the eye.

"You love him, don't you?'' said Greta.

"No. Yes. Oh, I don't know. I can't think when he's here.'' She paused. "Have you met his wife?''

"Yes. She's—friendly, I guess.''

Later, when they were sitting listening to the radio Yarrow said to her sister, "If Palmer walked in that door right now, what would you do?''

"I'd cry.''

"And?''

"I'd go to him.''

"Greta, how could you? After all this? Where's your pride?'' Greta looked at her with pity.

"There is no pride where love is concerned.'' She got up from the bed painfully and walked doubled-over to the window. "It's just as well I'm leaving for Los Angeles, isn't it?''

Yarrow wept on her shoulder.

"Hey,'' said Greta, "we have to find you something to wear. You can't go out in that tomorrow. You can borrow something of mine.''

He had indeed picked a pretty restaurant, a French one in the old tradition with red-velvet banquettes and a mural of some allegorical nymphs painted on one wall. Fresh flowers sat on the pristine cloths and he ordered fish and wine for them with an ease she admired.

"You look beautiful," he said.

She had borrowed a red suit that belonged to Greta. The waistband of the skirt had had to be turned over to reach the proper length.

"You should wear red more often."

"It's such an obvious color," she said.

"What's wrong with being obvious? You were never so retiring before."

She remained silent while the waiter filleted their fish. When he had gone she said, "You're right. I've been feeling as flat as—Kansas."

"Not nearly as flat," he said. His eyes went over her admiringly. It was a long time since anyone had flirted with her. She blushed.

"You make me feel good." Sitting with this attractive man in this restaurant made her feel good. New York made her feel good.

"You deserve it. Don't you always feel good, Yarrow?"

She paused with her fork halfway to her mouth. "No." And gradually she began to tell him about the children and about Sandy. She did not tell him all about Sandy because it made her feel disloyal. She made excuses for him. The ITU strike had been long and hard. Whatever his faults Sandy had worked and slaved over their business to keep it going. Besides, to allow herself to criticize him made her sound like a fool, or worse, self-pitying. Yarrow glossed over the problems with her marriage. But Elliot was sensitive enough to read between the lines. It was what she did not say that spoke most eloquently to him. He endeavored to cheer her up, and soon the confident Yarrow of the old days burbled up at him between the rocks.

"I don't know why I'm telling you all this," she said.

"I don't know. Why?"

"You're an old friend. You know more about me than almost anyone probably."

"The old owl in the tree?"

She smiled, surprised that he remembered.

"Are you happy?"

"Of course I'm happy. I have three beautiful children, a husband . . ." She choked. What he heard was that she was miserable.

"Why don't you go back to work?"

"Are you kidding?"

"I'm serious."

"Do you know how busy I am with three kids?"

"You said you've got this girl now . . ."

"Belinda. Sandy would hate it. He believes in the old, traditional, caveman role. He brings home the bacon, the wife cooks it."

"But what do you believe? If you're unhappy, Yarrow, you have the means to change it. Ah, here's Blanchette. She said she might join us for coffee."

Blanchette had been unable to resist coming to see Elliot's old friend. "He's told me so much about you," she said. This morning he had asked her to join them for lunch, but she had said, no, they would have too much to talk about, she would only be in the way. But he knew how jealous she was, so he had said, Well, this is where I'll be, if you change your mind. She had fought with herself all morning about coming and now, finally, she had arrived, and he, cool as the wine in his glass, didn't bat an eye.

Blanchette settled her full-skirted dress with the nipped-in waist carefully on the banquette beside Yarrow. The gunmetal color of her outfit played up her pale skin and hair. She was not beautiful, thought Yarrow, looking at her, but she was elegant and pleasing to the eye. She had on a broadtail stole, which was too heavy for the weather, and her light blond hair was clipped and curled neatly on her head in the height of fashion.

"Is your sister feeling better now? Elliot said she has been very ill."

"Yes, thank you."

"What was it. . . ?"

"Pleurisy," said Elliot. "I told you that before, Blanchette."

"Oh, yes. Of course. No, just a coffee and a petit four," she said to the waiter. "I am sorry I was late but I was looking at houses."

Elliot smiled and looked up at her from underneath his heavy eyebrows. "And?" he asked.

"I found a darling house, double-fronted Federal in the Seventies. It needs some work, the kitchen is out of the dark ages, but it would suit you perfectly, Elliot."

Elliot put his strong brown hand over her pale one. It could have been taken as a quieting motion, an admonition or a sign of tenderness. "I don't want a house, Blanchette."

Yarrow poured cream into her coffee over the back of her spoon. She watched it float on top of the dark coffee. Marriage is like this, she thought, smooth and bumpless to the outsider, dark underneath.

"We're going to start a family," said Blanchette, smiling at Yarrow. When she smiled her face lit up. "You have children?"

"Yes. Three."

"Good heavens, you don't look old enough. How lucky you are. But at least you could explain to Elliot that it would be impossible to have children in a hotel."

"It would be very difficult."

"He's afraid of having a house, of the domesticity of it. If this goes on, I'm going to have to buy a house for myself and visit Elliot in his hotel room."

The skin tightened around Elliot's eyes, then he smiled. He kissed his wife's hand. "Don't push me," he said.

"I must get back to Greta," said Yarrow, gathering up her gloves and bag.

"Yes, we must run, too. When are you going back to Colorado?"

"Tomorrow or the day after."

"Well, it was so nice to meet you." Her hand was very soft and cool.

"Can we drop you off?" asked Elliot outside, standing beside his limousine.

"No thanks. I'll get a taxi. Elliot, I can't thank you enough for calling me about Greta."

Elliot kissed Yarrow on both cheeks. She could smell the faintest aroma of after-shave on his skin.

"Let's not lose touch," he said. When he got into the car and she bent down to say good-bye to Blanchette, she saw that Blanchette's hand had already crept over Elliot's knee. She stood on the sidewalk and watched the car pull away. It's time I went home, she thought, if I'm beginning to think the way I shouldn't.

She had fallen in love with New York City; the hustle and bustle, the people and the cars, the cyclists who defied the rules of the road, the sidewalk vendors with their chestnuts and pretzels, the steam that rose from the manholes in the street, the newspaper stands, the men pushing racks of clothes between the traffic on Seventh Avenue. She had never realized how the adrenaline would pump after an infusion of Manhattan air. She bought a whole bundle of newspapers at the corner, all eight of the dailies that were sold in Manhattan. It was crazy to think about it, but she wondered if there would ever be an opportunity, if—well, she shook her head. Too much wine probably, better to get back to good old Platte City and get the *Journal* right. Elliot had whetted her appetite again for the business she loved. She *would* go back to work. She only had to tell Sandy about it.

CHAPTER 17

*Y*ARROW CAME BACK FROM NEW YORK WITH A DETERMINATION to reorganize her life. Greta's inability to do it with her own galvanized Yarrow into action, and Elliot's belief in her encouraged her. Before she lost her nerve she told Sandy that she wanted to start writing again and—she took a deep breath—she was going to go to college. Sandy was appalled, but she said he would adjust and enrolled part time at the university for a bachelor's degree in liberal arts. It had come to her with an increasing sense of shame that she knew little about anything.

Two years went quickly by and Nellie wrote that she had given birth to a son—Justice, she'd called him. Yarrow thought the name must be "Justin," and it was just Nellie's poor handwriting.

Yarrow was busy writing a column from home about television and its impact on news. She had written extensively about the Kefauver Committee investigation into organized crime last year. "Trial by Television" she had called it. Now she was writing about Richard Nixon and his dog.

She seldom went into the office. It was difficult with Sandy being the boss; it was as though he resented her there. He said that although he was a member of the family, in fact, he was not. He was a paid chief executive—an employee like anybody else and this fact rankled with him. Since the strike, too, Yarrow had walked through the composing room only once. There, where she had felt so much at home in the past, she now felt like a stranger. She did not like it. She missed the old camaraderie. But writing at home and doing her college courses were compatible with her "duties as a mother." Those were Sandy's words, once he had accepted the inevitable.

She typed: "September 23, 1952. Richard Nixon, the Republican vice-presidential nominee, made a stunning comeback in his speech on television last night. Whatever President Eisenhower might have thought of the accusations of Nixon's secret 'slush fund,' he has surely lost the battle to dump Nixon from the ticket.'' Yarrow paused and looked at her notes again. The telephone rang. It was Sandy.

"You know we have people coming for dinner tonight?"

"Yes. I know. I've asked Mrs. Hillier to come in and cook."

Mrs. Hillier was the best professional cook in Platte City. Yarrow had given up any pretensions of expertise in the kitchen. Between Belinda and herself, the household staggered along from one domestic crisis to the other. Meals appeared on the table and the house was cleaned periodically. Yarrow spent most of her time at her desk in the house or at the library. She and Sandy had reached a stage of neutrality in their marriage. It was not a particularly happy stage, but neither was it an unhappy one.

Sandy had changed, she thought. He had grown a moustache; it hung like a thick, blond fringe over his upper lip. He was as busy as she was. Their anger only flared up at times when neither was watching it closely enough. One day his picture appeared on the front page beside an editorial he had written. The *Journal* was running a campaign against corruption in local government.

"Did you have to put your picture in?" she asked him that night.

He looked at her sharply. "Didn't your father or your grandfather ever have their picture in the paper?"

"Only in their obituaries," she said.

Another time when she had remonstrated about some expense at the office, he had shouted at her, "What the hell am I? Only another goddam employee around here?" She was afraid of his anger. He had thrown the telephone book he was holding across the room at her and she had gone into Lily's room and spent the night in her daughter's bed with Lily's soft, skinny little arms around her. She worried about the effect their relationship was having on their children. But she thought anything was better than a divorce. Oh, she'd thought about it. But no sooner had the disloyal thought entered her head than she would pull herself together and tell herself not to be so damn stupid. Who wanted to be alone at thirty with three children in tow?

What kept her going was her writing and her college courses. Yarrow felt much better having a job to do. She liked spending time in the library at the university and coming home to the children and sighing with relief that Sandy was not yet home.

Lily was so independent now, as smart and sassy as she herself had been. Zeb and John went to kindergarten. Zeb was always getting into scrapes. If there was a dangerous tree to be climbed, he would be up it.

She had found him one night up on the roof of the house in his pajamas. "What are you doing up there?" she asked, getting the ladder and climbing up to him.

"I was being Zebulon Pike. I wanted to get to the summit."

Once he picked up a hot poker beside the fire and the flesh had been burned from his palm. He would always carry the scar. He put his fists through a glass door (eleven stitches), and swallowed some glass when he crunched down on his breakfast juice. He had thought it hilarious to have his stools examined for any slivers that his mother had not managed to wash out of his little bloody mouth. And yet, he was not a violent boy. It was just that his body seemed to need more space than the volume it took up.

His twin, John, on the other hand, was quieter. He was moody and deep; a follower rather than a leader; he was like a little night shadow of his brother. But the boys were inseparable. Sandy had built them a play area in the back part of the garden, where a few trees and rocks had defied Yarrow's horticultural plans. The boys called it "the wilderness." They were always running off together in their little Oshkosh B' Gosh overalls to some new adventure. "Me first, me first," she heard over their shoulders as their five-year-old legs hurled them toward the rubber tires and ropes that Sandy had put up.

Yarrow felt they were getting the attention they needed. She was busy and proud and happy at the way things were working out. She could feel her professionalism coming back to her and her self-confidence returning day by day.

"Well, I'll be home by seven," Sandy was saying. "The governor's arriving at seven-thirty."

"Don't worry," she said. But once she had hung up, she sighed, looked at the paper in her typewriter, and got up to check out the kitchen. Mrs. Hillier was already there. She was a great cook, but she had a terrible temper. She had a missing front tooth, which she had not replaced.

"There's no saucepan for the crepes, Mrs. Heartland," she said now, with her hands on her hips. Her words hissed through the tooth gap.

Yarrow rummaged through the cupboards. "Won't this do?"

Clearly, from Mrs. Hillier's expression, it would not.

"I'm sure you'll find something that will work, Mrs. Hillier. I have great confidence in you." Yarrow fled into the dining room. Belinda had set the table and Yarrow had done the flowers. She checked the napkins and glasses and went into the drawing room. "Will you help serve tonight, Belinda?"

Belinda had been morose lately. Yarrow suspected an unhappy love affair. There had not been quite so many callers for Belinda in the past few months.

Belinda shrugged. She had on a big full skirt with petticoats to make it stand out. She wore a red elastic belt and blue hairclips were holding back her ponytail. She was sitting cuddling the new, yellow Labrador puppy that Sandy had given the the children.

"I don't need another child in this house," Yarrow had cried when she saw it. But Rufus was there to stay. He proceeded to pee all over the carpets and curtains. "He's only establishing his territory," Belinda had said.

Belinda got up, and Yarrow plumped up the cushions on the sofa, checked the ice bucket, the flowers, the nuts, ran into the guest bathroom, checked the soap, towels, toilet paper. Why did entertaining take up so much time? It was time to pick up the children. She heard Belinda get the car out, and she went back to her desk for another hour, tiptoeing past the kitchen in case Mrs. Hillier heard her and came out to complain about something else.

At seven o'clock, with the children fed, bathed and in bed, Yarrow went into the kitchen. There was a great sense of foreboding in the air. It touched Yarrow with an icy hand as soon as she opened the door. It was thirty minutes before the guests were to arrive.

"Is anything the matter?" asked Yarrow.

"I'm not going to do those, Mrs. Heartland," said Mrs. Hillier, folding her arms across her bosom. Belinda had left a stack of children's dishes in the sink.

"Of course not, Mrs. Hillier. That's Belinda's job."

"Well, I don't think she and I can work in the same kitchen. I'm not used to being treated this way. I can't cook for twelve and clean up and not have the right equipment and be expected to do my best."

Perspiration had begun to gather on Yarrow's brow. This dinner was very important to Sandy.

"Mrs. Hillier . . ."

"As for the dog. How can I work in a kitchen with that dog under my feet? And look. It's crapped under the table. I'm not going to clean it up."

Yarrow groaned, "Mrs. Hillier, please . . ."

"I just won't do it. I can have my pick of jobs in the community. I don't have to come here. The Schaeffers always give me extra help. They even send a car for me to drive me to

Denver. If I'd known how much I had to do, I wouldn't have accepted . . .''

Yarrow had picked up a pot. If only the woman would shut up! She was trying to think of the menu, and what she would do if Mrs. Hillier walked out.

"As for the oven—this thermostat didn't work the last time I was here. I asked you to fix it before, Mrs. Heartland . . .''

Yarrow screamed, "Stop!" and threw the pot at the kitchen door.

"Well," said Mrs. Hillier, "I'm certainly not staying now." She banged out the kitchen door into the hallway. Yarrow panicked. Cripes, crepes, she thought. Brandy sauce. She rushed into the pantry and picked up the bottle of cooking brandy. Her hands were shaking. Back in the kitchen, she thought, I'll just take a quick gulp to steady my nerves. She pulled out the cork with her teeth and just as she was drinking from the bottle, Sandy walked in.

"What the hell's happening? We've got the GOVERNOR arriving in fifteen minutes. There's an irate cook out in the driveway, Belinda's in tears in the drawing room, there's, what's that? DOG CRAP on the floor, and my wife's swigging brandy in the kitchen? Christ, Yarrow, can't you run a damn household?"

"Shut up, shut up," she said, riffling through the pages of a cookbook. "Crepes, crepes, crepes Suzette."

"You can't cook! You can't boil an egg. Mrs. HILLIER." Sandy went running out the back door. "MRS. HILLIER!" The doorbell rang. Yarrow took another swig of brandy and went to the front door, wiping her mouth on the back of her hand.

"Oh, Governor, how nice to see you again. And your wife. Charmed. May I offer you a drink? Belinda, could you hand around the nuts, please." Yarrow was cool as could be. "Will you excuse me for a minute?" she said. "I have a small crisis in the kitchen."

When she got back into the kitchen, Mrs. Hillier was back at the sink. Sandy was on his knees, cleaning up the dog mess. Mrs. Hillier ignored Yarrow. "Don't ask me what I'm paying her," whispered Sandy, pulling Yarrow out of the kitchen. "Just DON'T ASK. Stay out of here. Get Belinda to go in and apologize."

To her credit, Mrs. Hillier cooked a superb meal for the Heartlands and their guests. Yarrow sat through dinner, saying charming things of which she had no recollection once she uttered them. She vaguely registered Sandy remarking that the Supreme Court had ruled in favor of the printing union, that bogus setting was not an unfair labor practice—but that was all. She kept listening for some crash from the kitchen, which would announce that Mrs. Hillier had given up, and she watched Belinda pout as she handed around the vegetables and hoped she wasn't going to spill broccoli with cheese sauce all over the governor's wife. When dinner was finally over and the guests had left, she fell on the sofa and left Sandy to deal with Mrs. Hillier.

"I guess she won't be coming back again," said Sandy returning from the kitchen.

"You have to admit it was funny," said Yarrow, who began to laugh. Sandy was enraged. It only made Yarrow laugh more; tears were running down her face as she looked at Sandy and his impotent fury. It was all so important to him. So important. It was so funny and sad at the same time.

"Oh, let's not have a dinner party ever again," said Yarrow. "I don't think I can take it."

A small sound woke Yarrow in the night. She sat up in bed, disoriented. Sandy was not beside her. Surely he wasn't still upset about this evening. She got up and put her robe on and went down to the kitchen. The light was on but he was not there. She stood puzzled for a moment, and then she heard a soft murmur from Belinda's room. Realization hit her like a bucket of cold water. She clutched her robe to her and went to the door and listened. The blood drained from her face. She tried to open the door. It was locked. "Open this door, Sandy." She began to pound on the door. "OPEN THIS DOOR." She didn't care who heard her. "Oh, for God's sake," he shouted from inside. She heard her own voice shrieking.

He opened the door, ashamed but assuming a bravado that made her hate him even more. He was wearing a pair of pajama bottoms. He was tying the cord. She hit him on the chest with her fists. "How could you? With her, in my house, with the children asleep upstairs?"

"Your house. Your house. Everything's yours, isn't it, Yarrow? The business, the kids, the house. Well, not me, honey, not this little old boy. You don't own me." He was thumping her with his finger, bruising her shoulder. Belinda sat up in bed, horrified and pale. Yarrow rushed to her and began pulling at her hair. "You whore," she said, "looking after my kids and humping my husband at night. Get out. Get out."

"Come on, Belinda," said Sandy. "I'll drive you to a hotel."

"You can go with her and stay with her," cried Yarrow. She ran up the stairs and opened the closet in which they kept their suitcases and she pulled them out and threw them down the stairs. "Don't bother to come back." She heard the door slam. "And take that damn dog with you."

It was a month later. There had been a sudden cold snap and the whole of Colorado was caught in the early, icy grip of winter. The ponds had frozen over and icicles hung from the eaves of the houses.

Sandy had called her a few days after she had found him in bed with Belinda. She hung up on him, but he had kept calling. He begged for her forgiveness. She had to understand how lonely he felt. She was so busy. They never made love any more. And Belinda had been there, and, well, it happened. He swore it never happened before. He had been upset about the dinner party and how she had laughed at him. "You know how to make a man feel small," he said. He had gone down to the kitchen for some milk and Belinda had come in and "God, Yarrow, you're human," he said. "We're not all perfect."

She listened to him in silence. She did feel guilty about her own interests. Her writing and studying took up a lot of time. She was aware of her own failings, how tired and bad-tempered she could be, how insensitive she was to his needs. She had failed in her obligations to him in the sexual side of their marriage, too. She thought she was probably the only woman with three children in the state of Colorado who was still a virgin. To him the silence seemed both an admission of guilt and a promise of forgiveness, and he asked, "Do the children miss me?"

"Yes."

"Can I come home?"

She hesitated. They seemed to be tied together in so many ways; the office, the house, the children, their own comfortless vows. What had she vowed? To love, honor and obey. Which one of those had she broken first? Which one had he? But she believed in the institution of marriage; she believed when making those vows that through sickness and in health she would uphold them; as tenuous as they seemed now, she would not admit defeat. Perhaps it was pride. What was it Greta had said? There is no pride where love is concerned. But Yarrow knew she did not love Sandy. She loved someone else. Someone she could not have. She realized it now with all her heart. Her pride was wrapped up in something else.

"Yes, come home," she said.

She was determined to make their marriage work. She spoke

to no one about her difficulties. Not to Mary-Ellen. Not to her mother. Greta was abroad, making her first film. And Nellie was not the most sympathetic of listeners. One day Yarrow dialed Elliot's number in New York. She heard him answer, "Hello? Hello?" but she lost her nerve and hung up. She had no idea what she was going to say to him anyway.

This weekend a paper was due for her philosophy professor. Lily had gone to Mary-Ellen's house on a sleepover, and her mother had taken John for the day on Sunday. Zeb had been going to go, too, but he woke up with a cold, so she kept him home. He was whining and he kept asking her to take him to see the Garden of the Gods. He had devleoped a fascination for it through a project at school.

"Honey, I'm busy," she said. "I promise I'll take you next week." But he kept at her, getting in her way. Each time she sat down to write, there he would be, pulling at her sweater and sucking his thumb. "Don't do that," she said gently, hearing her mother in herself. "Sandy," she said. He was watching football on the television. "Won't you please take him out?"

"I thought he had a cold."

"Only a little one. He's driving me crazy and I must finish this today." Sandy grumbled something.

"Oh, for heaven's sake," she snapped. "I'm only asking you to look after your son for a couple of hours." Sandy switched off the television set with bad grace. He dressed Zeb and collared the dog and they went out. He slammed the door, and she took a deep breath and tried to concentrate on the thesis statement that was due. She read the statement over:

> "So the final causes of all social changes are not to be sought in the minds of men, in their growing insight into eternal truths and justice, but in changes in the mode of production and exchange; they are to be sought, not in the philosophy, but in the economics of the epoch in question." Discuss Engels's statement.

Yarrow opened her annotated copy of the contract that had settled the twenty-two month strike of the ITU. She knew all about the issue of production and exchange. She opened her textbooks, rolled paper into her typewriter and began.

It was about five o'clock when the telephone rang. It had become dark while she was writing. She had lost all track of time and was surprised how late it was. Sandy and Zeb should have been home by now.

"Hello?"

"Mrs. Heartland?"

"Yes?"

"This is Doctor Epson at the county hospital."

Her heart began to pound. "Yes?"

"I'm afraid I have bad news. Your husband is here with your son."

"What happened?"

"Will you come straight away, Mrs. Heartland? You know where we are? The emergency annex. We'll be waiting for you."

Yarrow had no recollection of how she got to the hospital. She had not even bothered to put on a coat or boots, and she left the car engine running and the door open when she ran into the emergency annex. She was met by Doctor Epson. "Mrs. Heartland?" She thought he must be a fool—how many other wild-eyed women were running into the hospital without their coats when it was twenty below?

He took her into a waiting room, where she saw Sandy sitting on a chrome-legged, plastic chair. Sandy's head was down between his knees as though he were fighting off a fainting spell. Yarrow spoke to the doctor. "Where's Zeb? What happened?"

"He's gone, Mrs. Heartland. If we'd got him out of the water a little sooner, we might have been able to save him. But he was under the ice too long. I'm sorry."

Yarrow sank down on a chair. Her stunned mind tried to take it in. Her mouth was agape, her eyes uncomprehending.

"Zeb? Drowned?" She didn't look at Sandy. Didn't reach out to touch him.

"I want to see my son."

"Are you sure?"

"I want to see him now." They took her into a room full of equipment and monitors. He was so small on the high bed. But he looked so peaceful. Why, he looked as though he were only asleep. She expected him at any moment to turn his head and say, "Hi, Mom." She touched his hand. It was as cold as the ice that had claimed him. His skin was blue. "Zeb. Zeb!" she cried. She knew the terror he had felt being sucked under the water, how it had been when it went into his mouth, filled his nose and ears. "Oh, God," she said, "why couldn't it have been me? Why did you have to take him?" Her heart was breaking. She kissed her son for the last time and they led her from the room.

In the waiting room, her anger began to take over.

"How could you?"

"Yarrow . . ."

"How could you let it happen? You took him out for a goddam walk!"

She let out all the ugliness of which she was capable as though it were the only way to release the hurt and anger. She allowed her eyes to throw at him all the hate and loathing she felt.

"You killed him, you careless bastard!" she shouted. "What were you doing? Flirting with some other bitch in skirts?" The waiting-room door was open. Someone shut it from the outside. She didn't care if people heard her. The pain was too much for her to hold in.

Sandy hadn't moved from his chair, but he put up his hand to ward off her words. He had begun to cry, not closing his eyes or anything, not wiping them, but staring at her, his face white against the institutional green of the wall.

"It happened so fast. I told him, Zeb, don't go too far out, but you know Zeb. One minute he was beside me on the ice with his sled, and the next he was gone. I couldn't get to him, I was too heavy. I told him to hang on. Hang on, old buddy." Sandy began to cry. They were unable to comfort each other.

Pok. Pok. Pok. Sandy pushed the buttons on the radio console beside their bed. What is he doing? Yarrow wondered. She had taken two of the pink sleeping tablets the doctor had prescribed to help her sleep. It was a week since Zeb had died. She had been unable to sleep. Grief kept her awake. She hurt. She needed. She had gone in and kissed the other children good night. They had lain so very flat in their beds that they, too, seemed not to exist. She avoided looking at Zeb's bed and staggered into her room and collapsed on her own. The patter of a radio show washed over her without making any sense. The green light on the radio dial glowed.

Sandy got in beside her and touched her hand. It was the first time he had touched her and she had not pulled away. She looked at him with indifference. Grief made him a stranger to her. She looked into the stranger's eyes and there were tears there. Anger struggled up in her mind and then succumbed, washed away by a heavy apathy. Those are my tears, she thought, and felt her own eyes fill with self-pity. She looked at the man whom she had promised to love forever and ever and despised him. And then she saw, not her husband, but a man who had lost his son, a man who cried and ached, who suffered as much as she. And Yarrow felt pity and she lay back on the pillow and let the tears rain down as the stranger slipped her nightgown off her shoulders and began to lick her breast into his mouth as though he might find succor there. And she thought, Oh, poor man, and she opened her eyes and looked at the color of his pale hair in the green light. Oh, Zeb.

CHAPTER 18

*S*PRING CAME AND WITH IT EASTER, BUT YARROW WAS FILLED WITH a great numbness. It sat like a rock within her. She had been feeling ill. Her hair was stringy, her skin gray. She was lethargic and had stopped going to classes, stopped writing her column. When things were really bad, Mary-Ellen appeared like a guardian angel to comfort her.

Yarrow was always cross with John. He reminded her so much of Zeb and she knew it was unfair to him. He was clumsy and dropped things. One day, just before lunch, he begged to be allowed to have a bowl of cereal in front of the television set. Yarrow had just had new carpet installed and banished Rufus from the house.

"No, John," she said. "You'll spill it."

"I won't."

"All right then, but if you do, you are going straight to bed." She watched him carry his Cheerios and milk into the drawing room and she sat down to open her mail and had another cup of coffee. A minute later he was back, standing in the doorway.

"Excuse me, Mom," he said, "where are my pajamas?"

Freya saw that Yarrow was taking out her grief on the children. She suggested that she go and stay with Laura for a few days, and so when Lily's school let out for the vacation, Yarrow put the two children in the car and drove up over the pass to Galena.

Laura and Little Lem, whose real name was George, welcomed her with hugs and big bowls of fried chicken and mashed potatoes. For the first time since Zeb's death Yarrow slept through the night without a sleeping pill. Under the crocheted blanket on an old bed that Laura's parents had slept in, she had settled into the hollow in the middle as though it were a pair of arms encircling her. The following day she accompanied Laura and the children to the small shop that Laura had opened at the base of the mountain in town. A towrope had been set up for skiers using parts of old mining equipment. Men from the old 10th Mountain Division had not forgotten the wonderful skiing they had experienced here. Since the war they had begun to come back. The sun shone on the snow, sparking a thousand diamonds from the surface. In the shop Laura sold ski wear, mitts and hats and woolen socks and sunglasses.

"I have plans," she said. "Here at the back, I'm going to set up a ski repair shop. George is just like his father. He can repair anything. We can wax the skis and sell boots and things."

"It's wonderful," said Yarrow, looking at thirteen-year-old George showing Lily and John how to buckle their bindings. Her eyes filled with tears for no reason. Laura put her hand on her arm.

Yarrow said, "I need to get away."

"When Lem died, I did the same."

Yarrow looked up at the mountain peaks. "I'd like to visit the cabin, have a few days to myself."

"Why don't you then? Lily and John will be fine with me. We've got lots of things to show them. They can use the towrope and ski with George."

"Laura . . ."

"Go on. We can equip you very easily."

So Yarrow set off for her grandfather's cabin that afternoon. She drove until the road petered out, and then put on her skis and shouldered her pack and by nightfall she was at the cabin. She set a fire in the shoebox of a stove and brought in a lot of wood to feed it through the night. She brought in a bucket of clean snow and put it on the stove to melt. She huddled in a chair, sipping coffee while she watched the fire. She was not hungry, did not need anything. The dearth of things took want away from her, and with everything so stripped down and bare, it seemed to Yarrow that she could approach and deal with her sorrow. It stood there alone like a monolith in the moonlight. In the dark, under her sleeping bag on the old camp bed that her grandfather had made, Yarrow opened herself to the pain. There were no children around to hear, no children to protect, no need for self-control to stop the lamentation. There was no husband here, no need for her to worry that her mourning would only increase his own guilt. Yarrow opened herself more. It was a release she had never allowed before, and the pity she felt for herself, what was wrong with that, for if one cannot pity oneself, from whom can one accept forgiveness? The wind shouldered its way through the pine trees at the rear, whispered around the old cabin and blew the snow like plumes of smoke off the roof. It blew gently at first through the chinks in the logs and then began to sift the finest snow, like mercy, onto her blanket. And Yarrow cried and the more she cried, the louder the wind grew and in that state of exhaustion which any emotion allowed without rein finally brings, Yarrow fell asleep.

She woke in the late morning and got up, stiff with cold. She broke the ice on top of the water in the bucket and splashed her face. Her eyes were swollen from crying but within herself it seemed as though something had begun to move. "And they found the stone rolled away from the sepulcher," she thought. She started the fire and put the kettle on top of the stove to heat. Then she dressed herself warmly and went for a long walk. The sky was clear and still and blue. She went down to the stream where years ago she had almost drowned. She thought about Jock, and about her father and about her son. She had been brought up without religion: A weak sort of humanism had been extended by Freya after the early prayers and bits of Bible Jock had taught them all. And yet it seemed to her that customs and ritual were what she needed to comfort her now; they would help her get through her period of mourning. She had once asked Freya if there was a God, and did He look like Grandfather? And Freya had said, He's here all around you. This valley, this was Yarrow's church. She watched the burbling water running under the fallen logs and branches, felt the thick, soft snow, so dry in this climate that a snowball could not be formed. She listened to the water and she sat so still that a bird came over, a black bird with a blue breast and a black stiff ruff of upright feathers on its crown. She recognized it as a Steller's jay. She put out her gloved hand and it flew away.

That night the moon was so high that she wanted to sleep outdoors. The wind had dropped and it was not as cold as the previous night. She remembered camping outside with her mother and Elliot years ago on this very spot. Of course it had been warmer then, but she wanted to do it now: She did not want any walls between herself and nature. She built up a huge fire. She made it the way the Laplanders do, the way her mother had taught her.

She hauled a great log that had been split by lightning to her campsite—she was sweating under her parka by the time she got it there—and she laid a fire all along its length, and then she sandwiched it with another split log. She toasted some bread on a stick and ate some slices of meat that Laura had provided. She lay down in her sleeping bag with her hat and gloves on and put her boots inside the bag way down at her feet so that they would not freeze in the night. She watched the glow of the fire, the logs falling in on themselves, and listened to the sounds of the forest; not much animal life—too cold, but creaks of trees, snow falling off overladen branches. She lay there in the dark, Yarrow, who had never been alone in her life, and she thought about it. Of what was she afraid? What made her heart thump listening to the great outdoors? What made her imagination run wild with thoughts of her own body being hurt, being destroyed? What pain could be greater than that which she had already experienced? What loss could match it? Her breath froze on the edge of the sleeping bag, it scratched her chin. Yarrow pulled her head under the sleeping bag and breathed in her own smell. This was all there was, wasn't it? Just one's self and one's belief in that self, and from this small center of the universe one could find all the courage one needed. The navel of the inner self was how she had once thought of it. Yarrow's mind began to drift and even the iron-cold ground that froze underneath her could not stop her from falling into the most forgiving sleep she had ever had.

In the morning a small pika woke her up. It stood perfectly still, a tiny guinea-piglike creature, unafraid on her chest. In its little paws it held some grass it had collected where the fire had melted the snow. She knew that it built small haystacks of grass among the rocks where it lived. It was unusual to see one while snow still lay on the ground. Yarrow and the pika stared at each other, its little beads of eyes frozen onto hers, its round ears back and alert. She would not be the first to move, she decided, and for a long moment her gray eyes and its black ones looked into each other while the first lick of sunlight crept across the frozen ground. With a squeak it shot off into the safety of its rocky home.

Yarrow laughed and then groaned when she tried to move. Her whole body ached and seemed bruised from lying on the ground. As she got up, she saw the pika sitting on a pile of rocks that showed the path of an avalanche. Then the pika was met by another, smaller one. The bigger one gave a sound of warning to the other, a funny little bark, unlike its earlier squeaking, and then they both fled. The sight of the two creatures made Yarrow think as she stood, with her hands supporting her lower back, and tried to work the stiffness out of her hips. It was the breeding season, she supposed, and then she stopped. I'm pregnant again.

The realization, which had been growing on her for weeks, made her so weak that she lay back down again and laughed. She had missed two periods, or was it three? but she had thought it was from the stress of Zeb's death. Now she knew. How strangely the world turned. To take one child and give her another. And this child conceived, not in love, but in pity. Poor creature, she thought, placing her hands on her stomach. But she would love it enough for both Sandy and herself, for he would not be around. She had made up her mind, had come to a decision up here in this high country that she loved. She would make her life what she wanted. She had tried living by other people's expectations and it had not worked. It was not enough. She had thought, in her simplicity, that by willing things to happen, they would be so. But mere willing didn't make things happen.

She would make it up to this little fish of life that swam within her for bringing it into the world; for bringing it in through a conception that had neither love, nor ego, nor a sense of mortality behind it. And because of this, this baby would be special to her. She could no more have thought of Greta's solution than cut off her own hand.

"I'm ready to go home," she said, and the picture of Lily and John waiting for her filled her with happiness. She stood up and cupped her hands around her mouth and shouted out, "I am coming home. Are you ready?" and she listened to the echo—ready, ready, ready—bounce off the walls of the bowl around her and she remembered that her grandfather had long ago called this place God's Garden.

BOOK THREE

- 1953–1961 -

THE PRESS

CHAPTER 19

*I*T WAS TWO WEEKS LATER, AND ON THE WINDOWSILL OF YARROW'S kitchen some hyacinths were turning from green to blue. Outside, the thaw had set in and there was a constant trickle of water from the icicles on the eaves.

"Sandy, I want a divorce."

"What?"

She was making breakfast. "One egg or two?" she asked.

"Yarrow, what is this? You've been back a week and I don't know you anymore."

She held the eggs high above the frying pan and squeezed them. "Two," she said. The shells and the eggs fell into the pan. She fished out the bits of shell with a spatula.

"You see, Sandy, this is the real me. I've decided not to go on pretending. It's been over between you and me for years but neither of us would face it. I'd like the divorce to be amicable, but that's up to you."

"This is about Belinda, isn't it?"

She pushed the eggs around. "Do you like them crispy?"

He got up from the table, came over and grabbed her hand.

"Will you stop this stupid game?"

"Look, it's not about Belinda, although that added to it."

Neither of them mentioned Zeb.

"I'm pregnant again."

He let out a harsh laugh. "Oh, great. That explains everything. Now you want a divorce so our kid can have a really happy home."

"It hasn't been happy for a long time, has it?"

He sat at the table and and ran his fingers through his hair. How she once had loved the way it flopped down straight across his forehead.

"I don't understand you," he said without looking up. "I don't understand you and I never have. I thought you loved me when we got married and ever since then, even the Camp Hale days, we've been fighting each other. I've tried, honest to God,

227

I've tried, Yarrow." He thumped the table suddenly. "Why can't you be a proper wife, goddam it?"

She put the eggs on a plate and looked at them. They had turned into lacy, crispy brown things. "You want them?" she asked. He shook his head. She slid them into the garbage can at her feet in one easy movement.

"You wanted too much. You wanted every bit that made me who I am. You wanted to take that away, destroy it. You nearly succeeded. You took my pride away, my ambition."

"Oh, your ambition. We're on that again, are we?"

"You see? You can't accept it, Sandy. It's a joke to you, all that side of me."

"The newspaper."

"Yes, the newspaper." She would not lose her temper.

"I can't take this."

"You won't have to. I'm going to see Pierson. I think you should do the same."

He got up angrily, spilling his coffee over the front page of the *Journal*. AIR FORCE ACADEMY TO CHOOSE SITE, the headline screamed.

"And what about me?" he shouted. "What about me?"

Yarrow rubbed her arm where some fat had splashed on it.

"I said I wanted it to be amicable. But I'm going to take over the running of the paper. I'll give you time to find something else."

"Time! I don't want time working for you. It's been bad enough working for a stinking wife, let alone for one who's divorcing me."

He stood breathing heavily at her across the table. She broke the silence first. Her voice was quiet. "That's how you really feel, isn't it? The resentment you've always had. Don't you think I've been aware of it? Don't you think I've watched you sleeping, looked at your lips, and known they've lied to me?" She turned away from him. "I don't want to see you, Sandy. I don't want you to come back here tonight." She waited, listening for what he would do. He broke out in a burst of swearing, and then she heard him slam out the door and the engine of his car started. The gravel spurted up as he accelerated away. She called her mother. "Could you come over and spend the night with me?" Eric was away at college so Freya was a free agent now.

"Is there something wrong?"

"I'll tell you when you get here."

Yarrow sat down at the table. John padded in in his bare feet. She tried to take him on her knee but he resisted.

"Did you have another fight with Daddy?"

"Did you hear us? I'm sorry."

"Don't you love him, Mommy?"

"I did when I had you. Oh, but we love you, John. We'll never stop loving you." His eyes accused her.

She fed him a piece of toast, and then while he ate his cereal she read the paper. She dabbed the front page with a paper towel. "Your father spilled it."

"Daddy's clumsy, like me," John said.

She was full of guilt and she tried to read the paper. The USAF was rumored to have picked an area of land south of the city for its new academy. There had been a number of speculations about which area they would pick. Some people hoped to make a killing second-guessing the air force's choice. Yarrow suspected that most would have their fingers burned, but she had no idea until later that afternoon that Sandy might be one of them.

She was in Pierson's office when he said, "Did you know Sandy is in debt over this land deal?"

"What? How?"

"He's been buying land he thinks the state of Colorado will buy for the air force academy. He's paid top dollar for it."

"Where is the land?"

"Twelve miles north." Pierson had read the morning papers, too. "Doesn't look like there's going to be an air force academy up there."

"Oh, my God."

"But you must have known, Yarrow."

"No. I didn't know."

"He used the newspaper as collateral. I've got the deeds here. You've signed them. You're the major shareholder."

Yarrow felt sick as she looked at the papers. It was her signature. She remembered signing it, now that she saw it. She had been busy and distracted, and Sandy had given her a whole bunch of things to sign at once—their tax returns, a mortgage payment. He had held open the pages and pointed to where she had to sign. It was careless of her. Stupid. She would never be so trusting again.

She walked out of the lawyer's office in a daze. But then her bewilderment turned to quiet rage. How dare he jeopardize the *Journal*? Sandy had never understood the family's commitment to it. He had once told her he thought one paper was just like another. How could he think that, not understand that the life-blood of her paper flowed through her veins? She saw the *Journal* as a continuation of Jock's first venture, the old Humdinger. The whole history of her family was wrapped up in those pages, the years Jock and her father had sweated over the stone, it was all caught up in there. And even though the composing room had been wrested from their grasp, it was still theirs. Her mother had stood and folded papers with the rest of them; and the children, her sisters and brother, coming in after school and typing, or greasing, or folding or bundling. Had he no idea what it meant to them? It was like another sibling in the family. It was the important one.

Yarrow was angrier than she had ever been. She vowed, however, that she would not lose her temper. Sandy wasn't worth her losing her dignity. She walked through the dripping streets where melting snow revealed patches of flat brown grass. The gutters and drains ran heavy with water. She went straight to the *Journal* and into Sandy's office. It was her father's old corner one, with a big window that showed Pikes Peak in the distance.

"I want you out," she said. Her voice was shaking with rage.

"Could you lower your voice?"

Her voice was cold, hard. She made it stop trembling. "You cheated me as a wife and you cheated me as a business partner. I want you to leave now, today, this minute."

"Are you talking about the land deal?"

"Yes I'm talking about the land deal."

"I thought it was a wonderful opportunity. I was thinking of you and the kids."

"So that's why you didn't explain it to me? Little stupid wifey doesn't have to know the details? Do you think I am a complete fool?"

His mouth was open. She had never noticed before how like a toad he could look. His secretary put her head around the door.

"Can I help?" she said.

"Yes," said Yarrow, "you can call a meeting of the staff, right now in the editorial room."

"You're going to do one more thing for me, Sandy, one last thing as editor of this paper . . ."

He interrupted. "Yarrow, you must listen about this land I bought."

She put her hands up over her ears. "I don't want to listen to your land deal. I'm not interested. We run a newspaper, not a real estate office."

"OK, OK, but if Pine Valley works out you'll have to eat your words."

"The only words I want to hear are from you, out there—you're going to come out there with me and you're going to resign. I don't care what excuse you make, but you're going to tell them that as of tomorrow, I will be in charge."

"Shit," he said.

Sandy was ashen. God, he was weak. They went out into the hubbub of a small company in which there were no secrets. Sandy said the ritual words and left. Yarrow could not be seen above the heads as the staff craned for a view, so she stood up on a table. She made a few conciliatory remarks and said she would see them all tomorrow. When she got down, she heard one man say to another, "She'd better be careful she doesn't get her tit caught in a typewriter."

She wheeled around. "You," she said, extending her arm and raising her voice so that everyone could hear her. "You're fired." When she left the room everyone thought she was at least six inches taller.

Sandy's secretary approached her. "Mr. Heartland has asked me to work for him. I don't know what to do."

Yarrow thumbed through some correspondence that Sandy had left on the desk.

"Do what you want."

"Well, if you don't mind, I would be uncomfortable remaining." She stood there wringing her hands.

Yarrow nodded. "I understand." She wondered how many others would feel the same way. "Will you stay on for a week with me, just till things get straightened out?"

The girl's smile showed her relief. "Oh, sure." She left.

Yarrow surveyed the room. She did not know where to begin. She picked up the telephone book and found a number.

"Hello, Miss Hines? You won't believe who's calling. Yes, Yarrow McLean. Listen, remember once I asked you if you'd like to work for me one day? Well, now I'm really asking. Would you come and help me? I'm the new editor and publisher of the *Platte City Journal*."

The next morning Yarrow put on her plainest dress—a black linen that Greta had sent her—which she hoped minimized her bulk. She always gained a lot of weight early in her pregnancies. She put on a pair of low-heeled, sensible shoes because her back ached, and she pulled her black hair back into a bun. It made her look much older, she thought, as she looked at herself in the mirror. But that was the effect she wanted this morning. She was very pale and rubbed some rouge into her cheeks and tied the brightest scarf she had around her throat. As she surveyed herself, Lily came in, dressed for school. Yarrow had given up dressing Lily when Lily was three years old.

Eight-year-old Lily asked, "Where are you going?"

"To the office, darling."

Lily put her small hands on her hips. "Are you going to do this *every day* of your life?"

Yarrow saw her own reflection and her daughter's side by side in the mirror. It dawned on her that that was exactly what she was about to do.

"Why, I suppose I am, Lily. Does that bother you?"

"Who's going to look after me?"

"Grandma's going to stay."

Yarrow escaped from her daughter's merciless gaze. Lily could see right through her: She hoped that others couldn't see through her quite so easily. She was going to the office now as the publisher, not as Sandy's wife. She sucked in her stomach behind the steering wheel of her station wagon as she drove into the parking lot. She saw the parking space marked "Mr. Heartland," and she drove out again and parked along the street. She stopped the car and burst into tears as an attack of nerves hit her. I can't do it. I can't do it. She blew her nose and thought of her grandfather. She adjusted the rearview mirror and checked her lipstick and then started the car and drove back. She drove straight into the parking space and nodded to the security guard as she went in. He was a new man. She hoped she looked strong.

"Good morning"

"Good morning," he said. "Your name?"

"Miss McLean," she said.

"You have a pass?"

"No."

"I can't let you in without a pass." He was a big black man with beefy arms. He folded them and stared at her. The elevator door opened and the secretary came rushing out.

"Tyler," she said, "this is our new boss, Mrs. Heartland."

"Miss McLean," said Yarrow as she followed her into the elevator. She kept her eyes on the floor indicators as the doors slowly closed. She could feel Tyler's eyes on her and knew she had not passed muster.

Her first visitor was the company accountant, a small, flour-faced woman with chipmunk cheeks and myopia. She handed in her resignation. She had a Texas accent.

"Ah wish Ah could stay, but Ah jist cain't work for a woman. No hard feelings."

"None," said Yarrow, and waited for the next blow to fall.

The next morning Yarrow drove to her usual spot, burst into tears, fixed her lipstick and drove back into the parking lot again.

"Good morning, Tyler."

"Your name?"

"Miss McLean."

He flicked through his personnel list.

"You can go right up," he said.

The assistant editor resigned that day and Yarrow went home with a headache that would slay a bear.

On the third day she did not want to leave the house. Her stomach had knotted into a fist; her legs and her back ached. She caught sight of herself in a mirror. She looked like death. Her mother stared at her as she kept making excuses not to go the office.

"What's your problem?" asked Freya.

"I can't do it, Ma. Can't you see that? I've set myself up for the biggest fall in my life."

Her tone was belligerent, but Freya was not fazed.

"So?"

"You expect me to go back in there? You don't know what it's like. They're all leaving me. I don't know what I'm doing and they know it!"

"Are you a McLean or a mouse? Are you a woman or a girl?"

Her mother threw her the metal slug that spelled her name. Yarrow had been using it in the kitchen to prop shut her toaster.

"Mama, how can I do it?" Yarrow stared at the metal slug. "There's so much to do, so much I don't understand."

"You do it bit by bit, one day at a time." Her mother handed her her pocketbook. "Get going."

Yarrow was about to drive past the entrance to the parking lot and then swung into it before she could change her mind. She dragged herself out of the car.

"Good morning, Miss McLean," said Tyler, holding open the elevator door for her. "Nice day, isn't it?" He leaned in and pressed the floor button for her.

Yarrow went up to her office. The janitor gave her a nod. The secretary had her coffee ready. Yarrow placed Grandfather's slug on her desk and the secretary came over with her notepad.

"Number one," said Yarrow, settling into the chair, "please

have the name on my parking space changed; number two, send my mother some flowers and put this message on it, "You little Humdinger," and sign it Yarrow Halvorsen McLean."

There was a knock at the door and Miss Hines stood there, wearing a felt hat with a hatpin as big as a knitting needle stuck in it.

"Where's my desk?" she said. "I'm ready to begin."

Yarrow stood up and said, "So am I."

It was August and one of the hottest months ever recorded in Platte City. The city room was stifling.

"What is this?" asked Yarrow of a young reporter sitting at his desk in the office.

"Copy p—paper," he stuttered. "Carbons." She had picked them out of his wastebasket.

"Yes, I know that," she said, "but they're unused." She threw them on his desk. "Don't waste paper. I can't afford it."

She strolled through the office, stopping at desks, inquiring about stories. She looked over their shoulders and listened to their telephone calls. She passed her brother Eric, who was working as a junior reporter that summer. He was twenty years old.

"Jean, can I call you back? Yes, I love you, too." He hung up. "Oh. Hi, sis." He scurried past her with some telexes.

She posted "Private telephone conversations are banned" on the bulletin board. Another day, "Waste not. Want not" went up. This notice went everywhere, even in the bathrooms, where she was appalled at the number of cakes of soap, toilet rolls and quantity of water being used.

"All expense sheets must be accompanied by requisition slips" was another edict. "They must think I'm Croesus," she remarked to Miss Hines, walking back to her office from her daily tour of the editorial floor.

She pored over the account books for weeks with Miss Hines and a new accountant she had hired. Each question unearthed another horror. They were in debt; more money was going out than coming in. She rearranged financing on the money the company owed, but the debts still hung over her like dark clouds. "We're going to have to nickel-and-dime this place," she said. She canceled plans to paint the office; canceled orders for new typewriters and desks.

"The chapel is having a meeting this afternoon," said Miss Hines one day.

Yarrow groaned.

"It's about that reprimand you gave the composing room about Mr. Johnson's obituary." Yarrow sighed and picked up her letters. She had had a lot of flak about that. Across the bottom of some copy about Mr. Johnson (a man she knew slightly but didn't like), she had scribbled a comment meant only for one of the reporters who had worked on it, "This silly ass is dead." The obituary had appeared with her comment neatly printed on the bottom.

"You have to remember that the composing-room axiom has always been," said Miss Hines, "follow the copy even if it flies out the window."

"They were late getting out yesterday."

"They blamed late copy."

"Well, it wasn't my copy. Who's coming in for lunch?"

Miss Hines flicked her notebook. "Mr. Elliko from FinPap. You want to be reminded to ask him why he's selling the same quality paper to the *Globe* as he is to you, but they get it at a better price." Miss Hines closed her book with a flip. "He'll deny it. He'll tell you they ordered it last year and had a fixed price on it. That won't be true. He can divert other paper to you here if you're tough with him. He's also very susceptible to flattery."

"What would I do without you, Miss Hines?"

"You'd be incapable of functioning." Miss Hines went out and buzzed her only a minute later. "Your mother's on the phone."

"Anything wrong, Mama?"

Freya had moved into Yarrow's house and taken over. Lily was ecstatic about it. Yarrow wondered how a child could be born such a complete conservative. Since Freya's arrival, meals appeared on time, floors were cleaned, shoes were repaired. The only chore that Yarrow insisted on doing, and it was not a chore, was arranging the flowers and working in the garden.

It was a great relief for Yarrow to have her mother with her, and for Freya it meant her life had purpose again. Eric only came home on long vacations and she had been rattling around in that big empty house all on her own with too much time on her hands.

"Everything's fine. I was just calling to make sure you were resting. You shouldn't be on your feet so much now, Yarrow. Your time is nearly due."

"As a matter of fact, Mama, I am sitting at my desk with my

feet up." She put one slim, well-shod foot up on the desk, which was awkward considering her stomach.

"Then I'm happy. John is in a play this afternoon, at summer school. He's playing Rip Van Winkle. Can you come?"

"I'll try." She worried about John. He had not gotten over his brother's death or his father's departure. His introverted personality pushed these defections, as he saw them, even deeper into a layer that no one could reach. Yarrow had tried; she tried to touch him, but even if she took him on her knee, he stiffened like one of those cheap stuffed toys that one won at a fair. She would kiss him and let him go.

Her lunch meeting with Mr. Elliko went like a breeze. He reacted just as Miss Hines had said he would, and Yarrow was ready with her figures. After a while Yarrow told him about her own northern heritage, embroidering only a little, and searched her memory for more of Freya's stories. Mr. Elliko was charmed. They came to a mutually acceptable price over the tuna fish sandwiches and soup that Miss Hines had sent in from a local delicatessen. When he had gone, Yarrow got up and went into Miss Hines's office. "I'm going to walk through the composing room and see what those bastards are up to."

She bent down to pick up a paper clip from the wooden floor. One of these days she would be able to have a nice wall-to-wall carpet in here, she thought. Suddenly a sheet of water ran down her legs.

"Good heavens. I've lost control of my bladder."

"No, you haven't, dear," said Miss Hines, rushing around and pushing her into a chair. "Your waters have broken. You're going to have the baby."

"But I can't. I have to hear what the chapel meeting decides. If I turn my back the foreman will be asking for more men or time-and-a-half, which we can't afford. Besides, I've got to write tomorrow's editorial."

Miss Hines was already on the telephone for an ambulance.

"Don't worry, everything will be fine."

"Well, take this down." Miss Hines flipped her notebook open. "The Colorado legislature yesterday stamped final approval on a bill . . ."

It seemed that the ambulance men arrived with a wheelchair almost immediately.

"Hello, Mrs. Heartland. How are the pains?"

"Careful with her going down the stairs . . ."

". . . an academy to rival West Point and Annapolis . . ."

"Can you lift that end up?"

". . . the civilian payroll alone is estimated between one and a half and two million dollars a month, the advantages of which. . ."

"In you go, Mrs. Heartland. We have to close the door now."

". . . delete that last phrase. Oh, drat. Miss Hines, get in. Yes, of course she has to come . . . through the new withholding-tax system, the state income taxes from construction workers . . . aaah ooooh."

"Shouldn't we stop now? I can get one of the reporters to finish this off."

". . . it is expected that the population of our great city will increase threefold in the next twenty years . . ."

"It's just *one* population increase I'm interested in now. Mrs. Heartland?"

"Yes?"

"Hold my hand."

CHAPTER 20

YARROW DELIVERED A BIG, BOUNCING BABY BOY, NINE POUNDS TEN ounces, that afternoon. He was much bigger than either of the twins had been, much fatter than skinny little Lily, who had been all head and legs. He had not a thread of hair on his head, and when he yawned his mouth made that perfect baby O shape that melted Yarrow right down to her toes.

"What are you going to call him?" asked John when her mother brought the children in to visit that night.

"Buckley. That was your great-grandfather's middle name."

"I like it. Can I see him?"

"Only through the glass, I'm afraid, but when we get home you can help me feed and wash him."

"Is he instead of Zeb?" Yarrow looked at her six-year-old son standing in his jeans and T-shirt beside her bed. His hands were clenched like knots beside his legs.

"No, darling. No one can take the place of Zeb."

"If I died, would you have another baby instead of me?"

"No. You're not going to die. I need you, John. You're the

man about the house. One day I'll need you at the newspaper, too." It sounded so trite. She did not have the words to console John and ease his fears about his place in her life.

"Hey, I'm sorry I missed you as Rip Van Winkle. Did you wear a beard?"

They talked about that for a little while and then Freya, seeing Yarrow was getting sleepy, took the children home.

A nurse popped her head around the door about ten that night.

"Are you awake?"

"I am now."

"Your husband's here to see you." The nurse gave her a soppy grin. Yarrow thought, Well, that's nice of Sandy to visit us; she had not been at all sure he would, but then the door opened and Elliot Weyden stood there, looking embarrassed in his dark city clothes with a big brown teddy bear in his hands.

"I'm sorry," he said. "I told them I wasn't your husband, but they were determined. They wouldn't have let me in probably."

"Elliot Weyden," she said. "What are you doing here?"

He leaned over and kissed her on the forehead and she realized she must look a mess. "Could you hand me my mirror?" she asked. He took it from the bedside table. "You look lovely," he said. "Maternity suits you."

She smiled. It was very hot in the room, so he took off his jacket and hung it over the back of a chair. He sat on the bed. Her hair was all around her shoulders. He lifted a strand of it. "You look as though you just woke up from a beautiful sleep. How's the baby?"

She told him, and then he said, "I was sorry to hear about you and Sandy."

"How did you hear?"

"Your mother writes to me, and Laura."

"Did they tell you to come here and see me?"

"No. Although I would have. No, I'm here on business—it's a happy coincidence. The place has changed, hasn't it? I have a client who has a lot of land. He wants to see where it lies in proximity to the new air force academy. Do you know what site they've picked?"

"No, but everyone says south of town."

"That's not what my client thinks."

"I'm sick about that academy. If the academy goes south, Sandy's busted. I wish you'd been around to advise him." She told him of Sandy's debt. "He can't pay it off on his salary. He's working at the Globe as—wait for this—the finance editor."

"Perhaps I could rearrange financing. Would that help?"

"Can you do that?"

"I might be able to." He paused and then said, "I'm going up to see Laura tomorrow."

"Why?"

"I have a . . ."

". . . client."

He laughed as they spoke in unison. He took her hand. "Galena's changing, too. You know all that snow and stuff they have? That's the fortune up there, not what's in the ground."

"What are you talking about?" She was not listening properly, was thinking about his hand in hers.

"Skiing. It's going to be a great resort with hotels and a ski school and a music festival in summer. It's all possible."

"There are only five hundred people there."

"In a few years, wait and see. You ought to think what you'll do with the old *Gazette* office."

Yarrow burst out laughing at his enthusiasm. "You're incorrigible, Elliot."

He laughed, too, and his face reminded her of the boy she once knew, the twinkling, naughty eyes, the thick brows that fanned where they met his nose.

"Would you do me a favor? Would you hug me? Full length?"

He lay on the bed beside her and put his arms around her. He didn't kiss her, just held her very firmly, so she could feel his chest beating against her own. She felt his shoulder blades, the width of his back under his shirt. They didn't speak, yet when they released each other something unspoken was understood.

He stood up and put on his jacket.

"Is the teddy bear for me?" she said.

"No, for . . ."

"Buckley."

"Yes, Buck." The night nurse bustled in. Elliot leaned over to say good-bye to Yarrow. "I'll try to come in and see you tomorrow." He looked in her eyes for any hesitation, and then he kissed her, a gentle kiss on the lips, but one that lingered.

Then he was gone.

"Oh, he's so handsome that husband of yours, Mrs. Heartland. All the nurses are swooning over him."

"He's not my husband," said Yarrow, patiently accepting the nurse's pummeling and straightening of sheets and pillows.

"Oh, I'm sorry," said the nurse. "I misunderstood." She placed the thermometer under Yarrow's tongue and took her pulse. Odd, the nurse thought, as she watched the hand on her pocket watch go around slowly, odd how those that look like a perfect couple never are the ones. She would have sworn she had never seen two people so much in love, but there you are. She took the thermometer out, gave it a good shake and patted Yarrow on the shoulder.

"See you in the morning."

Yarrow was sitting on a rubber doughnut on top of her bed when Sandy came to see his son the next day. The temperature outside had climbed to a hundred, and an electric fan beside her stirred a hot breeze around the room. It lifted the paper that surrounded the grapes he had brought her.

They were uncomfortable together and spoke in stilted sentences.

"Have you seen him yet?" she said. "I'll take you." She got up slowly and he helped her into a robe and slippers. Her stitches were very painful, but she hobbled out into the hallway and shuffled up to the window of the nursery. The nurse saw her and brought Buckley, wrapped up, to the window.

"Isn't he beautiful?"

She made motions to the nurse to unwrap him a bit so his father could see him.

"He's got the McLean head," said Sandy, "but the rest of him is all Heartland. He's going to be a football player."

"How can you tell?"

"Look at those hands—look at that neck." Sandy had a silly grin on his face. Yarrow looked at him and realized that she held no bitterness toward him. They should never have married in the first place. The only thing they had in common was the three children. Whatever went wrong had gone wrong from that very first night. Rancor would receive short shrift from her. She felt—she felt sad about Sandy, as though something had been wasted. Their youth? Their innocence? She wasn't sure.

"John misses you," she said as they walked back to her room. "I worry about him. He needs you more than Lily does." She didn't add, and much more than me.

"I know. If I had a place of my own, I'd see him more often." He didn't say, though she knew, that he was living with Belinda.

"I'll go by the school and pick him up today if that's all right. I have something I want to tell him."

"Oh?"

"I'm moving," he said.

"Where?"

"I've been offered a job as assistant editor in New York. On the *Courier*."

Yarrow was stunned—Sandy, working for Mrs. Truitt, or whatever her name was now. How would Mrs. Truitt know of an obscure editor in Colorado and offer him a job? She thought it was all part of a plot, a vendetta that Mrs. Truitt was conducting against her family—what a perfect way to humiliate Yarrow—employ her ex-husband. She half listened to him filling in the details. Somehow, although she didn't want him, she still felt possessive. It was a strange emotion, not one she thought she would have. A sharp pain went through her as she crawled back onto her bed.

"Be gentle telling John. It will break his heart."

"Yarrow, about that land deal . . ."

"Oh, don't tell me about it."

"It may just come off. You must listen to me. If the air force does go where I think it will, half the money will be yours."

"And if it doesn't?"

"If it doesn't, I'll repay you. I swear."

He stood there, taking up most of the room, looking contrite under his thin summer jacket.

"I don't hate you," he said. "I sometimes think if it hadn't been for Zeb . . ."

She turned away from him abruptly and the sudden move tore at her stitches. Her eyes filled with tears. When she was in control again, she glanced back at him. He looked so abject. The fan beside her bed lifted up his hair.

"I just wanted you to know," he said.

She nodded, not trusting her voice. She supposed she ought to think it noble of him.

"You will let me see the kids often?"

"Of course."

"Good-bye, Yarrow." He bent and kissed her on the top of her head. When he moved away, his moustache tickled her temple.

When he had gone, she called her mother and passed on Sandy's news. "I wish I was home. Will you make a fuss over John tonight, Mama?"

"You stay there and get your strength back. John's much more resilient than you think."

Yarrow sighed. "I had a visitor last night—Elliot."

"Oh, Yarrow, he called me not ten minutes ago. He tried to reach you at the hospital but there was no answer from your room."

"I was probably down the hall with Sandy."

"He said he had to go up to Galena but would drop in and see us on his way back east in a week's time."

Yarrow felt slightly abandoned. She didn't realize how much she was looking forward to seeing him again. She hung up and went through some correspondence that Miss Hines had left with her this morning. There was a letter from Clara Russell hoping that her pregnancy would go well and then, her last paragraph: "I have been writing a few articles for my local paper, and am sending them to you for you to read. You know how I loved doing those columns for your father before the war. I would love to do something similar now that you are editor, if you thought they were suitable. I realize that you and I parted ways after your visit to Washington those many years ago, but I can only say that your disappointment in me was not as great as my own in myself. Love, Clara." Yarrow read the pieces; they were quite good. Clara's background and training gave a richness to her observations. They were not unlike the columns Yarrow had been writing about television, but Clara's were much more erudite.

The nurse brought Buck in to be fed. Rather, it was just putting him to the breast, for Yarrow's milk had not come in yet. She compared the pads of his little pink fingers with the whorls on her own, noticed the one long crease in the palm of his right hand. Forgiveness was written there, just as it was in the big blue vein that stood up on her breast as he tried to nurse. "Well, what do you think, young Buck? Shall we give the old girl another try? And shall we forgive your daddy? Let's call this our first joint executive decision."

Over the next few days Yarrow had a lot of time to think about her newspaper. She had been taking notes, reading many other newspapers that Miss Hines brought in from Denver and Chicago and New York. She read through stacks of them, dropping them on the floor as she finished. She read some cover to cover, first going into the stories, the editorials, the philosophies behind the editorials, and then looking at them critically, asking herself which one looked better, why was this paper more easy to read than that one, which more lively, which more bold. It was a learning process. She looked at back issues of the *Journal*. She thought that under Sandy's tutelage the paper had become too gray, too masculine. She wanted to liven it up, use bigger photographs, condense some of the articles. There was a lot she could do without spending extra money. She telephoned Miss Hines to set up a lunch each day in her office with two of her staff. She wanted to get to know them all, know their strengths, know their weaknesses. She was still tripping over old feuds and congealed attitudes in her dealings with them. The editorial people hated the advertising people; the circulation department (an amusing term for one elderly man and his son) disliked the composing room. Yarrow had no idea that running a business would be so political. She had to deal with everyone prudently until she knew the lay of the land.

On the fourth day she went home, and John and Lily had crayoned a big "Welcome Home" sign across the front door. Three days later, after feeding Buck and handing him over to her mother, she went into the office for two hours. The editorial people all stood up and clapped as she came in, and one of the women presented her with a big bunch of wild flowers. Yarrow was touched. "Just because I'm thinner doesn't mean I'm going to be any easier to deal with," she said and then fled into her office before she broke down in tears.

"Postpartum blues," said Miss Hines, handing her a box of tissues.

"How do you know so much about it?"

"I read a great deal and I observe." Yarrow went over what she had to do quickly with Miss Hines, then held the editorial conference at which everyone hashed out their ideas.

There were two or three good people she was beginning to watch, a couple of sassy younger ones whose spunk she admired but whose enthusiasm had to be watered down. There was also the usual number of deadbeats for whom Yarrow had no time. She would quietly go over all contract agreements with Miss Hines in the privacy of her office when she had time. She did not mind if people didn't like her. She knew there would be some tough decisions to be made. But not yet.

After the conference, when stories had been decided upon, which ones to follow up, what new angles there were to a running story, a couple of human interest stories, she dismissed the staff and turned to Ed Greene, who had been running the paper in her absence. He was an older man with a blotchy face and broken capillaries from too much booze. She wondered if he was going to last with her. She wanted to test him and asked him to continue writing the editorials. They discussed possible topics and then he left.

Her buzzer sounded. "A Mr. Weyden here to see you."

Elliot came in, still in the same suit or perhaps an identical one.

"Shouldn't you be at home?" he asked.

"I'm going there now. But can I show you around? You will see the changes we've made."

"By the way," he said as he followed her out, "I've arranged the refinancing—you can save three percent on your interest payments."

"Elliot." She squeezed his hand.

"And that land, by the way, it may be OK. I've advised my client to hang on to it."

"That would be one for the books, if Sandy finally did something right."

She gave him a quick tour of the office and told him her plans. "One day I'm going to start a Sunday edition. We can't afford it yet. But we'll need a new line of typesetters there—I have to expand the wall a bit. We'll have to put them in because the town is going to grow. It's very exciting, isn't it? Anyway, the plant is underutilized on weekends. You'll see. This is a new Teletype room we've added. Hello, Joe, how's your wife doing? Oh, I'm so glad. This here"—she pointed at a big coffee machine—"is the canteen. There's a move afoot to put in a sandwich bar, but we can't do it. Not yet. And this is the radio room, not as big as the *Globe*'s but we manage."

"Are you in competition with the *Globe*?"

"Some of our areas dovetail. Their chief competitors are in Denver."

They walked back toward her office. She was tired. "You gave me an idea about the old Humdinger the other day. I'm going to start it again. I don't know what it's going to take, but I've got one man here I think would jump at the chance, Alan Craig, he's an old-timer with a printing background and he knows the mountains. There he is, he used to know Jock. Alan, I want you to meet Elliot Weyden. Elliot worked part time for my grandfather at the old *Journal* building in the thirties."

They circled back to her office and she said as they went in, "Alan's the kind of person I could trust. He told me he doesn't like the pace here, would like to work somewhere smaller. What do you think?"

He put his hands out, his palms open. "I'm impressed, Yarrow. You look as though you've been doing this all your life."

"Well, I have been in a way."

She sat down and began signing letters that Miss Hines had typed up.

"I've never seen you with your hair up like this."

"Keeps it out of the way. Do you like it?"

He paused. "It's you. It's another part of you that I'm just beginning to understand."

She sat back and folded her arms and said nothing, smiling at him just because she was happy he was here in the same room with her.

"Yarrow," he said, "I have no right to ask you this." He stood up, paced, stopped and then sat down. "Blanchette has moved to Virginia."

Her heart began to pump. "Moved?" she repeated calmly.

"We've agreed to live apart for a while. She's always wanted something I wasn't willing to give her—I don't know—perhaps I misled her. Perhaps I did think I wanted the same things she wanted. A house. A social life. Children. She miscarried again last year."

"Oh, I am sorry." Yarrow felt her own fertility glowing out of her skin.

"I finally agreed that if she wanted a house so badly she should buy one. It became her obsession, buying this house. She went all over, looking at houses in Connecticut, Long Island, Pennsylvania. And then she fell in love with Virginia, a house near Charlottesville. She says it reminds her of England. Oh, it's beautiful all right. But I don't want to be there." He leaned across the desk and took her hand. "I don't want to be with her. I want to be with you."

Yarrow's heart stopped. Her mouth went dry. She could feel her breasts swelling and tightening as they did now under any emotional strain.

"Elliot . . ."

"I have no right to ask. Yarrow, tell me if I'm exaggerating your feelings toward me. I love you. I don't want any other man to have you. Will you wait for me till I'm free?" His eyes never left her face, but he lifted her hand and kissed it on the knuckles. She still wore her wedding ring, he noticed. "I want this to be mine," he said.

"I . . . I don't know what to say, Elliot."

"I've spoken too soon."

"No. Yes. Well, yes. I've just given birth to a baby—everything is too emotional for me right now . . ."

He kissed her hand again, came around the desk without letting it go.

". . . And the *Journal*, I'm just finding my feet here."

He pulled her to her feet and kissed her gently, touching the curls at her temple with his fingers.

"I'm in no hurry. I can wait. But I just have to know you're mine."

"Elliot, I've been yours ever since we were children, except I didn't know it."

"I should never have left here."

She laughed softly at him. "You had to. Dad said Platte City was too small for you even then."

"I should have sent for you. Shouldn't have let Pumblechook steal you away."

She laughed. "Poor Sandy."

"The timing's not been good, has it—the war, Sandy, Blanchette, my business, now your business."

They held each other.

"I've got to go," he said. "I'm flying to Chicago tonight."

"I know you can't stay."

"I love you."

"I love you, too."

He turned at the door, "Did I tell you you are quite beautiful?"

"Yes, you did."

"I'm thirty-six years old," he said. "How old are you?"

"You know very well. I'm thirty-one. Is that OK?"

"Perfect age for a woman," he said. "Just perfect."

He gave a salute as he passed Miss Hines. "Look after her," he said. Miss Hines looked at Yarrow. Yarrow couldn't stop the crazy happiness she felt from shining out of her. Her cheeks glowed, her black curls were escaping all over her head. She was wearing a pale blue summer dress with no waistline. She would soon have her figure back and belt the dress in.

She took out a hand mirror from her pocketbook to see what he had seen. "I'm overweight, I've just given birth to my fourth child, there's a varicose vein behind my right knee, and this wonderful man says he loves me. Oh, Miss Hines, you are looking at the luckiest woman in the world." Then Yarrow began to cry. She reached for a tissue, and then she swung Miss Hines around in a circle.

"Don't get cross. I am going home now. By the way, when Buckley is christened, will you be his godmother?" She kissed her assistant on the cheek and left.

Miss Hines got out her handkerchief and blew her nose. There was obviously dust in this room or something, she thought, that made everyone who came in have to resort to handkerchiefs.

She stuffed hers in her sleeve and went off to find the janitor.

CHAPTER 21

*E*LLIOT FLEW TO CHICAGO AND HIS THOUGHTS WERE FULL OF Yarrow.

He had loved her since he had first met her in Platte City. He could still see her the way she had looked the first time when Lem had taken him to the McLean home for dinner—a small vivacious girl with a mass of black hair and the reddest lips he had ever seen. He had waited for her to grow up, but he had waited too long. He had put his ambitions before his heart—but never again. Never again, thought Elliot looking out the window as he buckled his seat belt. He would go to Virginia this weekend and tell Blanchette he wanted out. He had never loved Blanchette. He had never lied to himself about that. Blanchette had probably known it all along and it had fed her insecurities. Yet she had wanted him enough to put up with that imperfection. There were no children involved, yet it would be painful. Poor Blanchette. She had pursued everything in her life with a fierceness that astounded him. She had wanted to marry him, and she had mounted a campaign that had succeeded. Wherever he turned, she had been there. In the end, she had won. She had wanted a house. She was going to have it, and she had persevered until he agreed. She had found Coakley, a magnificent old mansion with three hundred acres of rolling hills in Virginia. And she had gone there to live. She was gambling on the fact that eventually he would give in on that, too, and take up the life of a southern gentleman.

But more than anything, Blanchette wanted a child. And the more she wanted one, the harder it was for her to conceive. There was nothing physically wrong with either of them, said doctor after doctor. Her rhythms were monitored; every morning she took her temperature and charted it on a calendar; when her temperature went up, she knew her ovulation had begun and that she was at her most fertile. When she knew the time was right, she would appear and he would perform. It had been amusing at times. She had arrived once in Boston unexpectedly, when he

247

was staying at the Ritz Hotel. He was negotiating a deal in his suite with the chairman of the Bank of Boston Securities when she came in, her pale hair hidden under an enormous gray hat, dressed in a gray suit, the jacket with a single button cinching in her tiny waist. She had pulled him into the bedroom, undoing his shirt.

"Honey," he whispered, "these men, I'm about to sign a deal with them for two hundred thousand dollars, they'll leave . . ."

"They'll come back. This is my time. *I* need you." She had waved a thermometer at him. So they had made love, she with a pillow under her backside, and after he withdrew, she stayed in the same position, with her legs raised, holding her vagina up as though it were a cup, and she had smoked a cigarette and said, "Thank you." Increasingly he felt that he was a mere sperm donor.

He wondered how different things might have been if they had had a child. He had not seen her for weeks. He disliked Virginia, disliked the friends she had made down there. It was too far away from his work. He had tried living there for four days and had nearly been driven insane by boredom.

The plane banked over Lake Michigan on its approach into Chicago. Elliot gathered his papers together and put them in his briefcase. He clipped a small picture of Yarrow to a pocket inside the lid.

"Nice wife," said the man in the seat next to him, seeing him pick up the photograph. "Your first?" It took Elliot a minute to understand the man was referring to the fact that Yarrow was very pregnant in the picture. Elliot hadn't noticed it till now. He grunted and locked his briefcase and stared out the window. It would not be easy to tell Blanchette about Yarrow, he thought. She was a possessive woman, used to having her own way. He dreaded telling her that he wanted a divorce.

Elliot got through his morning appointments quickly. He had lunch with some people from the board of trade and he hired a young man, Dixon Dwyer, who worked as a floor dealer in the pit. Dwyer was a genius at trading in futures. Elliot watched him in the pit later that day, an average-height guy with a paunch from eating too many meals on the run and an uncanny ability to foresee the way prices would behave. Elliot was pleased that he would work for him. As Elliot became more successful he found he was spreading himself too thin. He wanted to open an office in Chicago, and Dixon Dwyer he felt was the man who could run it.

That night Elliot attended a dinner in honor of Governor

Stevenson. Elliot was one of the speakers. He spoke about Eisenhower's administration, attacked it for its "do nothing" attitude toward business. He praised Adlai Stevenson, a man he personally admired, and gave a short interview afterward to the local press. The report the next day was flattering to Elliot, and it did not go unnoticed among the Democratic bigwigs who had been present at the dinner the night before.

By Thursday Elliot was in New York. Friday he spent the day in Washington, and Friday night he drove from Washington to his wife's house in Virginia. He always thought of Coakley as Blanchette's, although he had paid for it.

The manservant, Abraham, took his bags. "It's nice to have you home. Mrs. Weyden is on the porch with her guests." Elliot groaned inwardly and went through the house, past the antique furniture, the glowing pictures, the old rugs on the floor. He went out onto the porch, a true southern porch with pillars and a view across the rolling Virginia hunt country. Candles flickered inside hurricane lamps, and a waft of perfume and cologne from the assembled guests was released by the humidity in the air. The men were in white cotton or seersucker suits. Elliot's dark suit looked as out of place as an easel-shaped coffee table would look in Blanchette's drawing room. He never felt so Yankee as he did when he came to Virginia.

"Darling," said Blanchette, getting up and offering him a cheek to kiss. "You know Lyle Moss, Ginger . . ." Blanchette was ever the gracious hostess. He shook hands all around, unsure who half the people were. Abraham brought him a large sourmash bourbon on a silver tray, and Elliot sat down beside Ginger and the cane sofa creaked as it took his weight.

Abraham brought around hot cheese sticks and tarts stuffed with some kind of tomato and anchovy mix. Elliot ate two or three; he had missed lunch that day. The anchovies made him thirsty, so he had another bourbon. He seldom drank, and then usually only wine, but the bourbon tasted good. Elliot relaxed. It was a hot, late-summer evening and the fireflies were out. The conversation droned around him.

They talked of Simone de Beauvoir's *The Second Sex* (though few had read it themselves), which had just come out in English translation. De Beauvoir had written that for man, woman was just an amusement; for woman, man was "the justification of her existence." Elliot looked at Blanchette and wondered if this was true. He rubbed a gnat from his forehead.

"The pursuit of happiness has become the pursuit of materialism,'' he said. Ginger stared at him. Elliot sank back into his chair and had another bourbon.

He thought about what he had just said. It had once been his guiding philosophy, but now something that was rampant across the country disturbed him. There was a conformity about everything; just like the cars they all drove—Buicks with fins and chrome. It was the same politically, he thought: conformity; McCarthyism. McCarthy made him sick. Elliot thought of the Rosenbergs' execution in Sing Sing in June. What was happening to the world?

It had been a long week and Elliot was getting tired, but Blanchette had just ordered another round of drinks for everyone. Elliot knew he had had enough. ''If you'll excuse me, please,'' he said, standing up. ''I'm going to bed. Enjoy your dinner.''

Blanchette shot him a look that would have made a weaker man quail. Elliot bowed to her. ''Madam,'' he said. The South or the bourbon was getting to him. He withdrew. He could hear Blanchette making excuses for him as he walked back through the drawing room and up the curved mahogany staircase to their rooms above. He went into the smaller room that served as his dressing room. Like everything Blanchette touched, the furnishings were exquisite. He flung his tie and shirt over the Louis XVI bergère and padded across the Aubusson carpet to the bathroom. Abraham had already laid out his pajamas on the antique sleigh bed that Blanchette told him had once belonged to a mistress of Napoleon. Elliot couldn't care less. He pushed the pajamas onto the floor and slipped into the cool sheets naked as God had intended. He was asleep well before the guests downstairs had started their sherbet.

He awoke feeling wonderful, the depression of the night before gone, his thoughts on Yarrow and the future. He wrapped a towel around his waist and went down to the pool that Blanchette had built within the walls of an old rose garden. He imagined, as he thrashed up and down the length, what this place had been like at the time of the Civil War. Coakley was surrounded by great battlefields where American had once killed American. Perhaps that was why everything was so green, so lush, fed with the blood of boys. When he had showered and put his head in the door of Blanchette's bedroom, he saw she was still asleep. He was ashamed to realize that he felt relieved. He went whistling down to a breakfast that Abraham's wife made for him in the kitchen—fresh-squeezed orange juice, pancakes and bacon, maple syrup and coffee.

Elliot finished his coffee and then he went for a good walk around the stables where Blanchette kept a few horses, and then to the perimeter of the farm where Blanchette said she was going to build some horse jumps

It was all so beautiful, all so carefully planned. He had to hand it to Blanchette. She had taste. She knew exactly what she wanted. She was very much her father's daughter. Rich Newnom had been ill lately. Some scandal had touched him about his connection with Meyer Lansky during the war. Elliot had asked him about it, and Newnom answered that all he had done was invest Lansky's money. There was nothing wrong with that, was there? Was he supposed to check everyone's credentials before he did business with them? Besides, hadn't the U.S. Navy dealt with Frank Costello during the war to keep the wharves in New York open? Lansky had been in on that. If the government could deal with the Mafia, why couldn't he? Elliot wondered if Newnom's money, Mafia money, had built Blanchette's swimming pool. Each month a set amount of money went from Elliot's bank acount to Blanchette's. He assumed there was enough to run Coakley, for she had never asked for an increase. She was a woman of independent means and he had never inquired what she spent her own money on.

It was nearly lunchtime when Blanchette woke up. She came downstairs and out onto the porch where he was sitting reading the newspapers. He had scribbled figures all over the pages of the stock market prices. Bold, black arrows, drawn and redrawn, underlined his sums. Blanchette was wearing a pair of light-colored slacks and a white blouse. She had put on a little weight, he thought, as she sat down and Abraham brought her a tray.

"Good morning," he said. "I'm sorry about last night. I was too tired to do anything but sleep."

Her voice was very quiet as she buttered a piece of cornbread. "You humiliated me last night, Elliot."

"I did not."

"Yes, you did. All my friends, whom I had asked to come to welcome you home—well, it was rude to them, too."

"I didn't mean to be rude. I apologize. But there was no way I was going to sit up and talk to a bunch of old farts who get up every day at midday. I work, Blanchette."

She started on another piece of cornbread.

"I wanted it to be special for you last night. I even ordered champagne. We were going to have a toast with the meringue." Her eyes were red. He looked at her, puzzled. "Don't you look at me anymore? Don't you really see me? Can't you tell?"

She stood up.

"Oh, Elliot. Can't you see?" Her hands went down over the small curve of her stomach. "We're having a baby."

"Is it true?"

She came over to him and stood with the sunlight falling on her thin arms. "Yes, it's true. I waited and waited this time before I asked the doctor to confirm it. I spent the first ten weeks in bed. I didn't want to tell you until I was well along. Are you happy?"

"Why, Blanchette. Of course I'm happy." He stood up and she put her arms around him.

"It's what we've always wanted, isn't it?"

He was too overcome with shock at what she had told him to respond.

"It's due in December. I thought I would have the baby at home, here, at Coakley."

"Of course," he said. Of course, she was pregnant. He had thought there was a difference in her, but he imagined she had just put on weight. She had always been so painfully thin. He seemed to be surrounded by women at different stages of fecundity. When she went inside with her tray to organize lunch, he leaned against the white balustrade of the porch and gazed out unseeingly at the verdant hills. He thought about Yarrow. He had asked her to wait for him. He had promised to free himself. But now? How could he leave *Blanchette*, leave a wife in her pregnancy, go off with a childhood sweetheart? It was impossible. It was unthinkable. If only—oh, what's the use of thinking if-onlys? It *was*. He was about to become a father. And his wife's name was Blanchette. Blanchette. He said it over, trying to blot out the other's name. Trying not to think of her darkness against Blanchette's pale image. How could his life change so drastically in the space of a few minutes? He had worried about how to tell Blanchette he was leaving her; now, his only thought was how to tell Yarrow he could not.

In late September Yarrow went to a parents' meeting at her children's school. Mary-Ellen was visiting her for a few days from California and said she'd come with her. They sat with their knees up to their chins in the too-small chairs and listened to the teachers being introduced.

"It's funny, isn't it?" said Mary-Ellen, in a lull in the proceedings when they went to get some warm cherry punch (nonalcoholic) and some curled-up cheese on biscuits from the refreshment table. "Funny how your life and mine diverged."

Yarrow tried to find a piece of celery that didn't bend like rubber.

"I mean," said Mary-Ellen, munching on, "I was the one who went to college and was going to have a career. And you rushed off and married Sandy overnight."

"Well, the war did put an urgency on things."

"Yes, but look what happened. Yarrow, you surprised me. I never thought you'd leave Sandy, not when you were pregnant. I mean, people don't do that. I mean, I just can't imagine me leaving Ned at a time like that." She began to warm to her subject, and Yarrow had the sense that Mary-Ellen had been saving up these observations for a long time. "I feel that a woman really derives her sense of—of being from her husband. It is your duty to stay at home, to help the man, and nourish the children. That's work, isn't it? You don't have to go out of the home to receive that sense of worth. It's all there."

"I suppose it is for some," said Yarrow.

"For most of us," said Mary-Ellen. "I'll bet there's not one other woman in this room who goes out to work. They're all too busy with the Boy Scouts, and the PTA, and the Colorado Young Leadership Group."

"They are all worthwhile, Mary-Ellen." Yarrow realized that her decision had threatened Mary-Ellen. She had not considered that before and it surprised her. She looked at Mary-Ellen anew, saw the neat, short hairdo, the conical breasts that the new bras gave everybody. Yarrow had not thought that she was laying new guidelines when she left Sandy, or rather when she asked him to leave her. She had done what she thought was right at the time. The decision to take over the newspaper was the same—it had felt right. She was glad she had decided not to confide in Mary-Ellen about Elliot's proposal. She held the secret within herself like another pregnancy. And she was afraid that if she spoke about it, something might jeopardize it.

When they came out of the school about nine o'clock, it had begun to snow lightly. Yarrow pulled a scarf over her head, and as they turned out of the school gate, she saw Elliot waiting for her.

"Why, you sly old fox," said Mary-Ellen, putting two and two together immediately. Yarrow blushed. It was useless trying to keep any secrets from Mary-Ellen.

"I'll go and get the car," said Mary-Ellen. But something about Elliot made Yarrow say, "You take the car home. We'd like to walk." She rushed to him.

"Elliot, you turn up like a ghost. How are you?" Under the

streetlight his face looked older. The grooves in his cheeks had deepened. She wanted to ask him if something was wrong, but instead, seeing his face struggle to control some terrible emotion, she bided her time, took his arm, and they began to walk.

Something had gone very wrong, she knew. He gripped her arm tightly as they walked slowly under the light, wet snow. They left a trail of dark footprints behind them.

"It's about Blanchette, isn't it?" she asked, trying to help him. "She said she wouldn't divorce you."

"Oh, Yarrow, I wish it was that simple." They trudged a few more feet. "I didn't ask her. I couldn't, Yarrow. She's having a baby."

They stopped. He faced her. "Yarrow, my darling, I swear I wanted to end this marriage. I waited so long for you that when I heard you and Sandy had parted, I saw my chance. I didn't want to lose you again. I shouldn't have spoken to you about us until I had cleared up my own marriage. But I couldn't take the risk. And now—now."

"Oh, don't." she said. They were near a bus stop and she felt suddenly weary. "I don't think I can walk home now." A bus was coming along the street. She hailed it and got on. Elliot scrambled on behind her, digging into his pocket for change.

There was no one else on the bus and the harsh white light was merciless on their faces.

"Yarrow," he said, "I'm sorry. I don't want to hurt you. God knows that's the last thing I want to do. But how could I leave her? I can't. And I don't think you would want that." He could not get a response from her. He took off her gloves and kissed her fingers.

"This is my stop," she said. "Please don't come with me."

"Yarrow, please. I beg you . . ."

"Beg me what? You have no right to beg me anything." The driver had stopped the bus. He looked up in his mirror at them.

"You getting off or not, lady?"

Elliot still held her fingers in a fierce grip.

"Let me go, Elliot. LET ME GO!"

"Hey, mister . . ."

Elliot released her hands. Yarrow stumbled off the bus into the snow. She felt her heart had broken in two. If only he had not spoken to her in August, if he had not opened her up to the joy it would be to have him, to hold him, to be his. In having done so, he had made her vulnerable. It was a risk, like playing the stock market, she supposed. You put your money out, speculated, and if the stocks came home, you were a winner; if they didn't, you lost. She had lost. How could she have been so foolish to think it would be easy, that he would just walk into her life and everything would fall into place like a happily-ever-after fairy tale? She opened her front door and went in and hung up her damp coat. Her mother was sitting up with Mary-Ellen watching Milton Berle on television.

"Buck's still sleeping," said Freya without glancing around.

"Can I get you anything?" said Mary-Ellen, dying of curiosity but knowing Yarrow would give nothing away.

"No, I'll do it." It was nearly time for Buck's ten o'clock feed. Yarrow made herself a hot chocolate in the kitchen and took it up to bed. She took Buck out of his crib, felt the solid little weight of him and brought him to bed with her. When he began to suck at her breast, she started to cry. Little drops of salty tears fell on his head. He blinked once or twice, but nothing stopped him. He was hungry. His fists were clenched, as tight as a boxer's. No air in the fist, huh, Grandfather? she thought.

"It's you and me, baby," she said. And then she stopped. That was not true. Buck would not remember this moment. His life would be made up of different memories. She was the one who would remember the airplane pattern of his little pajamas, the fuzz on his bald head, the yellow baby blanket with the hole in it. She would remember all of tonight. Buck would remember nothing. "Then there's only me," she whispered. "Only me."

CHAPTER 22

THE NEXT NINE MONTHS WENT QUICKLY FOR YARROW. SHE WAS SO busy with the paper and her children that she had no time to mope. Necessity took the place of indulgence. Whenever her thoughts did turn to Elliot, there was always a meeting to go to, a decision to be made, or someone to see that enabled her to put him out of her mind. "Let's get on with it" became her motto; "it" being life, the *Journal*, her children. The nights were the worst. Then it was not so easy to deceive herself that all was well. She was lonely. She was a young, attractive woman with normal sexual impulses. She wanted a man. She wanted Elliot to make love to her. Her own inadequacies in that area with Sandy no longer haunted her. She knew she was a woman whose sexuality had not yet been touched.

On June 24, 1954, a windfall came her way when the air force at last announced that it had decided to erect its new academy in an area north of Platte City, near Pine Valley. Yarrow let out a whoop that could be heard across the city room when the news came through. Sandy had done one thing right. The seven hundred acres he had bought (that *they* had bought) for $120,000 was now worth three times that much. Yarrow sent him a telegram of congratulations and, by mail, a drawing of herself eating a string of typefaces. Yarrow took Sandy's success as an omen for the future of Platte City. She knew that as the city grew her current press capacity would not be enough. She ordered four new units of a Goss Universal press and a folder. She hoped by the time of delivery to have the money to pay for them. But in fact the *Journal*, along with the city, was beginning to boom.

In July, when Eric turned twenty-one, he became a director of the company and Freya came off the board. Yarrow thought this was a good time for the family to get together and talk about the future. Her own was so tied up now in the success of the *Journal* that she wanted it understood that she was the boss and she wanted to know that the family was behind her.

Freya was excited about everyone coming home. Her children had been scattered from one coast to the other by career opportunities and marriage. She thought of them as seeds that had been carried by the wind from their source. Now she made plans for a celebration. Nellie and her husband, Jack, whom they had not met, were going to stay in the house. They would sleep in Lily's room, and Lily went back in with John for two nights. Greta said she would stay in a hotel. She said she had a surprise for them. Eric was bunking out on the summer porch.

Nellie arrived first in the same rattling Plymouth she had driven to her father's funeral seven years earlier. This time, though, she came with her husband, Jack Hoggart, a schoolteacher with a moustache and a long, sensitive face, and her two-year-old son, Justice. Every part of Jack Hoggart was long as he unbent out of the car—long legs, long arms, long fingers. The back of his shirt hung loosely from his shoulder blades as he picked up the suitcases. "Where do you want them?" he asked. Nellie unstrapped her son from the back. "Little Justice needs a wee-wee," she said, letting him relieve himself, with a little help from her, on the driveway. Yarrow was surprised but held her own counsel. This was going to be a nice family weekend, no arguments and no dramas.

Yarrow showed them up the stairs to Lily's bedroom. She had pushed the two little beds together in the pink and white bedroom and borrowed a cot for Justice. "I hope the bed's long enough for Jack," she said.

"Oh, we're used to that," said Nellie. "Jack can never find a bed that lets him lie with his knees straight. We've been all over the West Coast and we've never found a motel that caters to anyone over six feet tall."

"You do a lot of traveling in your business?" asked Yarrow. "I thought you were an English teacher."

"It's a long story," said Nellie. "We'll tell you after dinner. Now where are those kids? I want to see them."

Jack followed his wife down the stairs. He seemed to carry a weight across his shoulders, as though at some time he had been espaliered and his shoulders and arms had not forgotten. Yarrow thought there was something infinitely sad about him.

Freya was delighted with her new grandson. Justice was a strong-looking little lad with the same long limbs as his father. He climbed quite happily onto her ample lap as she fed him bits of apple pie in the kitchen.

Just before dinner was ready, Greta arrived. She wore an aqua silk suit and her hair was cut to shoulder length. They all met her at the door, and she flung her arms around everybody with little squeals of delight. Behind her, in the dusk, stood a man carrying a number of paper parcels. "This is my surprise," she said with a wide smile. Her teeth were perfect. Yarrow couldn't remember them being quite so straight. But it was the same smile they had all seen on billboards across the country. Greta pulled the man into the light of the hall and Yarrow stopped in shock. "Here he is. This is my surprise. Palmer and I got married two weeks ago."

"Palmer Truitt. Well, I never," said Freya.

"We met again two months ago, and we just decided to get married," said Greta. She gave her new husband a hug.

Yarrow wondered at Greta's forgivingness and impulsiveness. Greta, imperturbable Greta, the one to whom things happened, was a risk-taker. Yarrow gave her sister a second warm embrace and shook Palmer by the hand. She could still see in the handsome, dark countenance the face of the little boy she had known long ago. But the face had coarsened; there was a meanness around the mouth.

Freya was ecstatic. She saw Greta's recklessness as romantic in the extreme. She knew nothing about the sordid episode five years ago when Yarrow had rushed to New York to nurse her sister. To Freya, Palmer was a handsome, well-to-do man in his thirties whose mother had once been a partner in the *Journal*. Freya clapped her hands together. "This calls for champagne."

"Mama," said Yarrow, "we don't have any."

"Oh, yes, we do," said Lily piping up, and then to her mother, sotto voce, "the good housewife is always prepared."

Nellie laughed. "She sounds the way I used to."

"I think I'll get her to write a column on home advice for the paper," said Yarrow in a wry voice. Sandy would be pleased with his conformist daughter. He would approve of her as a candidate for a "proper wife."

The men then began to ask questions about the paper. Yarrow was wary of Palmer Truitt's inquiries. She could not forget that he was his mother's son. By the time dinner was ready, however, everyone was in full conversational swing. Even Eric, who could be shy at times, opened up to these new brothers-in-law. He'd been to L.A. once and met Jack, but he had not met Palmer before. Eric admired the elegance of the man. He wore his hair longer than most men did. It curled, black and oiled, behind his ears. He wore a big gold wristwatch of a kind Eric had never seen; he supposed this was because he had never seen a real gold watch before. His grandfather's old fob watch was so thin and fragile that it hardly compared with this one, which was as thick as a slab of butter on Palmer's wrist.

"At long last," Palmer was saying, "I've got a regular job on my mother's paper, the *Courier*. In management, of course."

"Why do you say, 'of course'?" said Yarrow, bridling at his tone. It was as though he thought other sides of newspaper production were dirty or detrimental to one's health. Yarrow was fierce in her defense of her business. She was proud of every aspect of it from the mixing of the ink, nine parts oil to one part pigment, to her reporters typing out a late-breaking story with a cold cup of coffee at their elbows.

"I dislike journalism," he said. "I hate the gossip that goes on, and the way reporters take themselves so seriously. The newspaper business is a business like any other business. The only difference is we sell news, not paper clips."

"Nothing to do with freedom of speech?" said Jack quietly.

"The power of the press is exaggerated," said Palmer. "There was once a time when the newspapers might have mattered. In the thirties, their power was already being usurped by magazines."

"Political power?"

"That's the only kind of power there is. And now the magazines are slipping. Look at *Collier's*, *Life*, *The Saturday Evening Post*, they'll all go. I hear *Collier's* is about to fold any day now. Mass-circulation picture magazines will be a thing of the past."

"Why's that?" Yarrow was interested. Although she did not like Palmer, there was a great deal of sense in what he said. He had his mother's instinct for making money.

"Television. That's where the power is."

"McCarthy's finding that out," said Jack with a lugubrious face.

"And that's where the money will be," said Palmer. "If I could get out of newspapers I would. Television." He let out a stream of smoke through his lips. "But they're all riddled with unions. If I could get rid of every last unionist on this earth I would."

Jack gave him a melancholy look but held his tongue.

Eric was enjoying himself. He had been so surrounded by women since his father died that he had felt big and clumsy in the house. Now he looked at these men and he liked it. He liked men's company and their voices and their questions and their self-confidence. He had always felt a bit overwhelmed when Yarrow and his mother got going. Eric was like his father. Now he relaxed. When the wine bottle went around the table again, he took another glass, and when he saw his mother raise her eyebrows at him, he saluted her and gulped it down.

The three sisters offered to do the dishes while the others went into the drawing room. Yarrow was a bit ashamed of her kitchen. When she and Sandy had bought the house, it was a new house in a new suburb of Platte City. They had bought it with the help of a GI loan and the government bonds that Yarrow had bought through the war. With the cash she had saved, they bought a box-spring bed, a coffee table, an end table, a dinette set, a radio and a record player, all for nine hundred dollars. Yarrow thought wistfully of the first Christmas she and Sandy had spent in this house when they made eggnog in the washtub. Everything had held so much promise then. The house, too, had seemed big and solid—well, big anyway. Now it looked merely shabby.

"Why don't you paint it?" asked Nellie, when she mentioned it. "And why don't you get a dishwasher?" said Greta, looking at her hands. Yarrow threw her a pair of rubber gloves.

"Stop complaining, you two. I have other things to spend my money on."

"Are you pleased about Palmer?" asked Greta.

"I'm pleased for you," said Yarrow, hating herself for being so specious.

"I was such a dud as an actress that I went back to modeling in New York. But I won't do it for much longer, I'm getting too old for it."

Yarrow and Nellie looked at each other in disbelief. Greta laughed.

"But it's true. I'm twenty-seven. That's ancient in this business. Besides, I was never much good at photographic work."

"We see you everywhere!"

"It may seem like that. But my cheekbones aren't prominent enough. Not like Mama's or yours, Yarrow. That was half the problem with film acting. The camera puffs me up."

"So Palmer has rescued you from an early demise, given you the easy way out?" said Nellie.

"Something like that."

"Do you see much of his mother?" asked Nellie.

"No. I don't think she approves of me. She came over for a drink after the wedding, though." She pulled the plug out of the sink and ripped off the rubber gloves.

"Elliot came, too," she said, blowing into the gloves to turn them inside out. Yarrow went on putting dishes away.

"His wife had a little girl on New Year's Day. They called her Meredith."

"Are you still in the same apartment?"

"Palmer likes it. He even likes my taste in furniture, he says." They all laughed at that. Greta's own elegant exterior didn't extend to her taste in home furnishings.

"You're just an old-fashioned girl," said Nellie. "When are we meeting with Pierson, Yarrow?"

"Tomorrow morning."

"Can Jack come along?"

Yarrow was annoyed. She was worried that Palmer would come along, too. She did not trust any Truitts. "No. This is family business, only the shareholders."

"Jack is family now."

"Nellie, if you want to give some of your shares to Jack, then he's a shareholder. We can talk about all this tomorrow."

"He's had a tough time. You know he was one of the teachers in California who wouldn't sign the Levering oath?"

"What oath?"

"It's part of all this hysteria about Reds and Communists and McCarthy's witch hunting. All civil servants had to sign."

"Why not sign a loyalty oath? Jack went to the war, didn't he? He must have signed then?"

"Yes, but this oath has an added paragraph asking you to state if you've ever been a member of the Communist party or any other organization."

"And?"

"Jack says that's against his constitutional rights of free speech. Loyal dissent and all that stuff. Anyway he wouldn't sign. So now he can't get a job."

"He can't teach?"

"Every time he fills in an application form for a position, he has to give the reason for his last dismissal. 'Refusal to sign the loyalty oath.' He's a very principled man."

"Couldn't he just have signed?" asked Greta. "Everyone has to sign things like that and it doesn't mean anything."

"To Jack it does. He says the oath goes against the very thing it's supposed to be defending."

"So what does he work at?"

"Menial things, clerical jobs. He's writing a book."

"What subject?"

"Backaches."

"Oh."

Yarrow looked at Jack with new eyes when she went back into the drawing room. Was he principled? Or just stubborn? Her own pragmatic nature was puzzled by him.

Young Justice had gotten up out of bed and unexpectedly toddled into the room. The night had turned unseasonably cold for early July, so Freya had lit the fire and pulled away the screen. Justice went over to the fire, and Freya was about to jump up and pull him back when Jack said, "No, Freya. He must learn. Justice, come here." Justice swayed on the balls of his little feet. "Hot," he said. For a moment it looked as though he were going to topple into the fire. Everyone held their breath, frozen in fear. Except Jack; his voice was calm. "I said, come here, Justice, away from the fire. You'll get burned if you don't." The boy laughed. He saw all their eyes on him and he made a quick motion with his hands toward the flames and then ran to the safety of his father's arms. Everyone let out a sigh of relief and Freya hurriedly replaced the screen.

Stubborn, thought Yarrow, to risk burning his son because of a principle. Stubborn, she thought, and probably principled and suffering from backache, too. Greta and Palmer got up to leave. They were staying at the Broadlands. Yarrow saw them out to their car.

"Thank you for the lovely presents for the children," she said. Palmer bundled Greta into the car.

"You'd better watch that brother-in-law of yours," said Palmer.

"Why?"

"The guy's a goddam pinko, that's why."

" 'Bye, Yarrow," said Greta, tugging her husband by the tail of his coat.

When Yarrow went inside, she heard Jack saying to Nellie, "You'd better watch that brother-in-law of yours, he's nothing but a goddam union basher."

Well, this will be interesting, thought Yarrow. How am I going to keep them apart?

The directors' meeting was held in the board room of the office. It was a room that Yarrow seldom used, for it had no windows and it was paneled with plain dark wood. Atop the paneling were opaque glass transoms that gave the room a Japanese feeling. There was a central light fixture of dark orange-colored glass, an oval wooden table with an inlay, and twelve chairs. An ugly clock with a loud ticking mechanism was the only ornament in the room. It stood on a mantel over a fireplace that had never been used.

"And you complain about my taste," said Greta with a shudder. Her white suit and blond hair made her look like a large pale ghost in the somber room. Yarrow wore a navy and white pinstriped suit with a white piqué collar. Nellie had on a dark red dress and flat-heeled shoes. She must only come up to Jack's bellybutton, thought Yarrow inconsequentially. Young Eric had put on a tie for the occasion.

On the table, Miss Hines had laid out pads and pencils. Mr. Pierson was there with one of his assistants. Freya was not there, and Yarrow and her two sisters and her brother sat on both sides of the table facing each other. Mr. Pierson sat at the head of the table, and his assistant sat beside him.

For the first time in her life Yarrow felt uncomfortable with her siblings. She was aware that from now on they would be dealing with each other not just as brother and sisters, but as business partners. It would be a totally different situation in which their personalities, ambitions and differences would be judged not against a background of love, but against a background of money.

"Shall we begin?" asked Pierson with a smile.

"As you all know, under your late father's will, Eric is now a director on reaching his majority." Pierson looked over his glasses. "Congratulations, Eric." He coughed and went on. "It was your father's wish that you four children would come to an agreement among yourselves on the disposal of his assets. Under Yarrow's care, I'm sure you will agree with me, these assets have increased substantially. Of course, so have some of the debts. Apart from the cabin and land outside Galena, and re-member we sold a hundred acres to pay some of the estate taxes, there was no other property of your father's, except the office and plant of the *Galena Gazette*, which had no value, and the newspaper here, the *Platte City Journal-Record*. As you are also aware, you each control an equal amount of shares, one hundred twelve each to be exact, except Yarrow, who has fifty extra shares given by your grandfather when she was born—" he looked down at his notes—"thirty-two years ago. Perhaps this would be an appropriate time to go through the figures of the company. Yarrow?"

"Yes." Yarrow gave out copies of the figures she had pre-pared with Miss Hines and the company accountant. They showed clearly the value of the assets in the building, the land itself, and the profit-and-loss figures for the paper over the past seven years. She explained the figures as carefully as she could and answered her sisters' questions. Then she told them what her plans were.

"I believe that the *Journal* is on the way to becoming a big profit earner. In fact, I'm so confident of that I've ordered new presses for delivery early next year. Because we've plowed profits back into the business, the paper is in pretty good shape." Yarrow cracked her knuckles then and took a deep breath.

"I want to state very clearly and plainly that I love the *Journal* and I love my family. But I have made this paper my career. I want you all to support me. I want to feel that in anything I do to improve the paper or, perhaps one day, expand our company beyond Platte City, that you will be behind me."

"Well, of course," murmured Greta, her big blue eyes open-ing wide as she looked at her sister.

Yarrow went on, acutely aware that Greta's husband would make her next remarks even more timely.

"Don't you trust us?" continued Greta.

"Familial loyalty is not enough. I would like to increase my share of the company to fifty-one percent."

Nellie gasped.

"Please put yourself in my position," said Yarrow. "I work here. I have the ideas. It is my blood, my livelihood that pounds through this building. You are all busy with your own lives. A committee of four can never run anything as well as one. There will be decisions to make, risks to take and I will be more willing to take them than you. My losses or profits should reflect my beliefs. I would like to buy from each of you enough shares to increase my control of the company to fifty-one percent. It would be up to Mr. Pierson and ourselves to come to an agreement of what we thought those shares were worth.''

"What about Eric?" asked Nellie, folding her arms. "What about my son, Justice, in the future?"

"Well, the next generation is one we have to think about when we work this out," said Mr. Pierson.

"Eric," said Yarrow, "you've been very quiet. What do you think? What do you want?"

"He is the man in the family," said Nellie.

"I'm well aware of that," said Yarrow, "but I'm the publisher."

"I want to do what Grandfather did," said Eric, leaning forward on the table. His face had reddened when he had to speak, but his voice was strong. He looked very like their father, thought Yarrow, watching him with sisterly attention.

"One day I might want to run the *Journal*, but I'm not ready, and from what Yarrow says, none of us are getting the push. We'll still be sitting around this table voting in ten years."

"I hope not," said Greta.

"I want to do what Grandfather did," he repeated. "I want to go up to Galena and start the *Gazette* again. It would be good training, wouldn't it, Yarrow? I could be my own boss, make my own mistakes, not have all of you breathing down my neck. Besides, if Yarrow bought half my shares, think what I could do with the money. I could buy a car."

Yarrow sat up in her chair. She had been thinking of sending Alan Craig up there to start up the *Gazette*. Alan and Eric would be a far better solution. Alan could teach Eric and Eric was no slouch.

"I think that could be done," said Yarrow. "Greta?"

"I'm upset. I don't see the reason for these changes—why can't things just go on as they have been? It's worked well up until now." Greta's lip trembled.

"I'm only trying to consolidate my position, Greta. This is not personal—it's not against you."

"Well, it seems that way. And Palmer's in this, isn't he—somewhere in your thinking?"

"No, I was planning this before I knew you had married Palmer. I am trying to protect the company from any outside takeover. Look at us—look at how different our lives are now.

One of us should be in charge. I want to keep it in the family. It's imperative that we organize it this way."

Greta nodded and sat back, but Yarrow could see suspicion in her eyes.

"Nellie?"

Nellie was thinking about the money.

"I'm so torn," she said. "I want to keep this opportunity for Justice one day. Who knows what will happen in twenty years' time?"

Yarrow shrugged her shoulders. "You'll either have an enormous share in a very profitable company, or we'll all be broke and this will be moot. There's plenty of space for all of us, but someone has to be the boss."

Yarrow touched Nellie's hand. It was a hard-working, square hand. She had never got on as well with Nellie as she should have.

"Jack could write full time," Nellie thought aloud. "He'd like that. Sometimes we dream about starting our own literary magazine, you know, a pamphlet type of thing with poetry and good writing, political stuff." Yarrow thought that would be an ideal way to send a lot of money very quickly down the drain, but she said nothing. "I'm sorry, Yarrow, I didn't mean to disparage what you've done with the *Journal*. It's very good, actually." Yarrow ignored Nellie's condescension.

"But OK, I think it's for the best," Nellie said.

"Great," said Eric.

"I'm not sure," said Greta. "I don't know what to do."

"Oh, come on, Greta," said Nellie, "make up your mind."

"I knew I should have had Palmer here to help me."

Nellie was exasperated. "He can't help you and I'm not going to tell you what to do. You know what I want—now you decide what you want."

They all looked at her and finally Greta spoke up, "Yarrow has always been the one who loved this business most, and she has been the one who's put in the hours to make it profitable." They all waited patiently while Greta convinced herself.

"I agree," said Eric.

"But I still feel it's hardly necessary to cut us out."

"You would not be cut out," said Pierson. "You three would still be major shareholders."

"I'd always be loyal to Yarrow," said Greta.

"I know that," said Yarrow.

Nellie was thinking about Jack and what they could do with some money instead of just sitting around dreaming about what she was worth on a piece of paper. She thought of the times she had written to Yarrow about the possibility of receiving some dividends. She wondered if the others had also asked. But then none of them had had to face her hardships. She wished Greta would come to a decision.

"Between us three we would still have forty-nine percent?" asked Greta.

"Yes," answered Mr. Pierson.

"Then Yarrow can have her way."

It took them all a moment to realize that Greta had finally accepted.

"Thank you," said Yarrow, and Pierson and his assistant began shuffling papers.

"How much do you think our shares are worth to you, Yarrow?" asked Nellie.

"About one hundred thousand dollars each."

Eric let out a low whistle. Mr. Pierson raised his eyes over his half glasses to look at Yarrow. He thought she was giving away too much information. "We still have to work it out," he said.

But Yarrow knew she was in the ballpark with her figures. She was about to take the biggest gamble of her life. To borrow the amount of money she needed, her interest payments alone would be over twelve thousand dollars a year. She had done her homework, and she was gambling everything on her ability and hard work and her knowledge of the business. She knew that her newsprint prices would be stable—as far as anyone could be the judge—and union differences at the moment were settled; so she could see no immediate problems there. She knew that she would have to increase her portfolio so that she could pay the interest rates and reduce the loan. All this depended on the biggest gamble of all. More than 80 percent of the *Journal*'s sales were home deliveries. Yarrow planned to raise each subscription by fifty cents a month. Would people cancel?

When they all left, Yarrow went to her office and shut the door. She stood at the window and looked out; below her she could see the scurrying lunchtime crowds. They were her salvation or her downfall. She looked down at two young office girls sharing a sandwich from a paper bag as they enjoyed the midday sun. What do you want to read? she asked. What is it you want to know? If she found those answers, and Yarrow believed that she would, she had nothing to fear from the future.

CHAPTER 23

Y ARROW HAD NEVER WORKED SO HARD IN HER LIFE. SHE WAS seldom home; she resented any time not spent at the office as wasted. Some nights she would talk to the children on the telephone, and then would work at her desk until well after dinner. In the morning she would be gone before the two older ones got up for school. She felt guilty about her lack of time, her rushed answers, her preoccupation. She could feel young John growing more and more distant. She tried to explain that she was working for him, but he did not believe her.

However, the hard work was paying off. The next two years were years of expansion for the *Journal*. The population of the city exploded, just as the statisticians had predicted. And these people had money to spend. Yarrow was ready. Her people canvassed the new suburbs as they opened up. No longer was her circulation department one old man and his son. New people meant new readers. The *Journal* became their paper. "We Support You!" was the slogan Yarrow splashed across her delivery vans. She increased the availability and ease of putting in small ads for houses, sublets, automobile sales. On Mother's Day she opened up a whole new section of personals and read the tributes with glee while her mind calculated the tinkling profits.

She poached a new sports editor from Denver. She knew nothing about sports, but sports were important to her readers. And pictures. She badgered her photographic staff to give her better and livelier photographs. Hardly a day went by that someone didn't comment on the photograph on the front page of the *Journal*. Yarrow was not afraid to blow up the picture to half the size of the page if it warranted. Babies with toothless smiles, doggy pictures did well. The photographers would bet on which picture their editor would pick. Invariably they were wrong, and invariably Yarrow was right. She had her finger on the pulse of the population. There were so many requests for copies of the *Journal*'s photographs that Yarrow had to create a clerical position to cope with the demand.

Her foresight in increasing the number of Linotype machines paid off well. In 1955 the first four units and a folder of a Goss Universal press had been installed. The old Duplex couldn't handle the number of papers and the speed that were needed now. The changeover was a nightmare, but at last it was done and the *Journal* came out without missing an edition. Yarrow sent a case of whiskey to the foreman in gratitude. The circulation had doubled; she employed over one hundred people at the *Journal*. She had started the *Sunday Journal* with some trepidation. It increased her costs and she was as nervous as a dieter in a candy store.

But the *Sunday Journal* was a goldmine. Yarrow knew this was partly due to Ed Greene, the editor. He flourished under his own wing. What he lacked in managerial skills, he made up for in editorial style. He could smell a story coming, but more important, he knew who his readers were. He identified completely with them. He started a television foldout in which he gave previews of *The Colgate Comedy Hour* on Sunday nights and reported interviews with Lucille Ball of *I Love Lucy*. He wrote a piece about Jimmy Durante and why he was so appealing. (Every time Yarrow heard "Bye Bye, Blackbird" she felt sad because it made her think of Elliot.) But her editor could be serious, too. When Rosa Parks, a black woman in Alabama, refused to move to the back of the bus, he saw the story as a harbinger of the future. In a number of stories that the *Journal* ran on the civil rights movement, Elliot Weyden's name cropped up. Yarrow wondered about Elliot's increasing politicial activism. There seemed no end to his ambition.

Everything Yarrow touched these years turned to gold. Eric and Alan Craig were even running the *Galena Gazette* at a modest profit. Yarrow thought her grandfather was looking down from somewhere with a big grin on his face and his wide teeth clenching a cigar. She hoped her father was doing the same.

One of her own innovations had been to employ Greta in New York to write a gossip column from her regular seat at El Morocco. She lunched often at The Stork Club and The Colony. Since Greta had given up modeling, she dined out and gossiped a great deal. Her "Oh gosh, gee whizz" style endeared her to readers; each woman could visualize herself sitting on the zebra-striped banquette or talking to Sherman Billingsly. Greta seemed to know everybody in New York.

When she telephoned her copy through, there was always a great deal of noise and chatter in the background. Yarrow took the copy down once herself as a joke on her sister—she also wanted to see if her shorthand was still up to it. Greta, unaware of whom she was talking to, rattled off her items, one of them being about that "ultra-rich Elliot Weyden, who was seen dining at El Morocco with a lady who was not his wife." After that, Yarrow handed the headset back to the teletypist. It was better to live in ignorance. But the information piqued her interest. She was always picking up bits of news and information about Elliot. In the past two years he had increasingly come on the national scene as a critic of the Eisenhower administration. There was never any mention of his wife.

"Miss Hines," said Yarrow one day in June in 1956, "I'm going to ask Ned Griffin if he'll come back from California and take over as editor. What do you think?"

Miss Hines was still the same thin, spinsterish woman that she had been when Yarrow first met her. The years hardly seemed to have touched her. Her hair had always been white, her Roman nose had always been too prominent to make her face beautiful, and yet in profile her face was noble. The pince-nez had long ago been replaced by glasses. Behind them a pair of shrewd eyes and a lively intelligence took in the world around her. Right now her gaze fell on the stack of correspondence on Yarrow's desk.

"It would certainly help with the workload around here."

Yarrow ran her fingers over her dark hair. She had never cut it and still wore it in a twisted thick bun at the back. Now she loosened some pins, and her hair fell down as she wound it around her fingers to pin it up again. She looked impossibly young with her arms up and the thick black hair escaping from her fingers, thought Miss Hines.

"I haven't got time to read as much as I want, or understand what's happening across the country. Do you realize I've only been out of Colorado twice in my life?" She walked to the window with her hands clenched deep in the pockets of a black woolen jacket she often wore. She looked out at Pikes Peak. "There must be something more than Platte City."

"Of course there is."

It was a sunny June day and thin clouds streaked across the sky like carded wool.

"Perhaps you should go and ask him directly," said Miss Hines.

"Who?" said Yarrow.

"Ned Griffin. Aren't we talking about Ned Griffin?"

Yarrow came back to her desk with a pale pink blush on her face.

"I think I'll go then. I'll leave tomorrow. Can you make the reservations? Do you think you and Paddy can run this place?"

Paddy was her assistant editor, a competent forty-year-old journalist from back east who had come out to Platte City to enjoy a winter's skiing and never left.

"You bet we can."

Yarrow stopped shuffling papers and stilled her hands. "Paddy might be put out. I think he wants the editor's job."

"You can worry about that later."

"You're right. I can't deal with problems I don't yet have." She dropped the papers and went back to the window.

Miss Hines shook her head. Yarrow was never as vague and unsure of herself as this. Today she was very—well, vulnerable, thought Miss Hines, tidying up the desk.

There were a number of letters to be answered that had nothing to do with the day-to-day running of the *Journal*. Yarrow's dual act as publisher and editor was the reason for her frantic schedule. Miss Hines picked up one such invitation to attend a speech to be given by Mr. Adlai Stevenson on June 5 in Los Angeles. "Shall I accept this, since you'll be in L.A.?" she asked.

"Oh, yes," said Yarrow, "I may as well go."

Miss Hines nodded, and as she added the letter to the growing pile of correspondence under her arm, she gave it a quick glance and noticed that Mr. Elliot Weyden, the philanthropist and Wall Street wizard, was going to be the introductory speaker. Ah hah, she said to herself, Ned Griffin indeed.

"I do hope he likes what you have to say," she said.

Yarrow glanced at Miss Hines, but her face was inscrutable.

"I hope so."

"It will be warm in Los Angeles," said Miss Hines, looking at Yarrow's jacket, which had seen better days. "You're going to need new clothes."

"This will be fine."

"Miss McLean" (She still found it hard to call her that, but Yarrow had insisted on being known by her maiden name once her divorce came through.) "You will be representing the company. Besides, men prefer blue." Miss Hines left and Yarrow leaned against the window and laughed softly. There was nothing she could hide from Miss Hines.

"You are in Bungalow Number Forty-four," said the desk clerk at the Beverly Hills Hotel, handing Yarrow her key, "We hope you have a pleasant stay." The bellboy carried her small

suitcase and led the way along a corridor, papered with great
green palm leaves, into the garden. Everything seemed exotic
and different.

"Your first visit?" he asked. Yarrow nodded. Beverly Hills
was glorious, she thought; the waving palm trees, the balmy air,
the thick banks of bougainvillaea and plumbago that spilled and
splashed colors onto the rich dark green of lawns and ivy. She
already felt she was on vacation. The bungalow was charming
and luxurious, and she waved the boy away with a tip so she
could explore it on her own. There was a bedroom, a bathroom,
a sitting room, her own small private courtyard. There was a
white sofa in the sitting room. Yarrow squealed with delight and
fell on it and called Miss Hines back home.

"There's a WHITE sofa in my room," she said. "I feel like a
movie star. But you've overdone it, this is far too expensive. I'll
have to ask them to move me."

"Don't worry," Miss Hines voice came back, "They've given
it to you for the same rate as a room. Power of the press, you
know."

Yarrow laughed as she hung up the phone and pulled off her
black jacket. She unpacked her bag and put away her clothes.
Now, why did all her clothes look so funereal? The phone rang.
It was Mary-Ellen.

"Welcome to California," she said.

"How are the girls? How's Sally?" Sally was Yarrow's god-
daughter. "I can't wait to see you. Tonight. I'll expect you and
Ned here for cocktails. About six?"

Yarrow made a reservation at the Polo Lounge and then took a
car to Wilshire Boulevard. Miss Hines, as always, had been
right. She definitely needed some new clothes.

Ned Griffin was unhappy at the *Los Angeles Times*. Mary-
Ellen had told Yarrow that, but Yarrow pretended it was news to
her as she helped herself to some more guacamole in the bar of
the Polo Lounge.

The Griffins had grown large since they had moved away.
Mary-Ellen, whose dark red hair had faded to a soft ginger, was
now a handsome matron. Ned, who had always been stocky, had
become even more so. His square frame, solidly packed atop a
pair of small feet, would have looked exactly like a box except
for his buttocks, which jutted out, pushing apart the vent of his
jacket.

"There's Mike Todd," whispered Mary-Ellen as Ned went on
talking. Yarrow peered through the dim room.

"It may be different when Otis takes over . . ." said Ned.

"Where? I can't see him."

"Third table over."

"What I would like to see is more diversity of opinions in the paper . . ."

"Do you think he's good-looking? Could I have another daquiri?"

". . . but I'm not the editor and I'm nowhere in the running. It's so frustrating . . ."

"What do you think is in this guacamole?"

"Chili sauce?"

"Onion?"

"Here we have the California campaign in full swing, Kefauver in town and Stevenson speaking, and politics is my beat, so what am I covering? They've put me on . . ."

"I'm going to hear Stevenson tomorrow. What do you think of him, Ned? What about Nixon?" Ned's eyes brightened. If there was anything he liked doing more than eating it was talking politics. Yarrow pumped him for gossip over the small, round marble table. She wanted to sound him out. She didn't want to hand over her baby to someone with whom she couldn't agree. Ned was firm but not inflexible. He leaned more to the Democrats than the Republicans. They talked about foreign policy and the cold war, and in the end Yarrow was convinced that Ned and she could work together.

They moved into the dining room, and halfway through dinner Ned was called to the telephone.

"I have to talk to you," said Mary-Ellen the minute he was gone. "I'm having an affair and I can't seem to end it. I'm terrified Ned or the children will find out. But whenever I tell him we must stop seeing each other, he calls me on the telephone."

Yarrow looked at Mary-Ellen in astonishment.

"How did it begin?"

Mary-Ellen helped herself to another glass of wine.

"I was lonely. He's a friend of Ned's. He was always in the house and then he began coming over when Ned was working late." She gripped Yarrow's arm. "I've become so reckless, it frightens me. Sally came home unexpectedly the other day and we had just made love on the sofa. I could see my panties under the chair while I was talking to her. I know it must stop, but I just can't help myself."

Ned came back and Yarrow was still sitting looking stunned at Mary-Ellen's revelation. Mary-Ellen, however, recovered quickly and powdered her nose; plain, housewifely Mary-Ellen who could lie without blushing.

As they were ordering dessert, Mary-Ellen saw Elliot Weyden. He was working the tables like a professional politician or a movie star as he made his way toward the door. There was a woman behind him. A little current like electricity seemed to precede him, as though his power were an aura that surrounded him. People sat up straighter; women primped, men were glad to be seen shaking his hand as if some of his magic might rub off on them. Yarrow had never seen Elliot like this before, had never experienced his effect on people. As he came toward their table, his eyes swept over them and then back to Yarrow before greeting the people at the table next to them. Yarrow couldn't tell what his reaction was, and then suddenly he was there, looming over their own table. He was not a tall man, yet his presence suggested that he was. He was on his way out with an extraordinarily good-looking blonde—a Hollywood blonde, Yarrow said bitchily to herself—who clung to his arm. He mumbled an introduction, kissed Mary-Ellen, shook hands with Ned, whose work he said he knew and admired, and smiled at Yarrow. Of course, it was hard for him to greet her across the table, she thought. She hadn't seen Elliot since they had parted on a bus in Platte City three years ago. He was still as sleek and trim as ever, though his chest had filled out more. She found herself looking at him as though she were a wife parted from a husband for some time. Was the hair longer, thinner? Had he put on weight? Did he look well? Oh, Blackbird, she thought.

The others were talking around her and she realized she hadn't heard a word.

"Yarrow's going to hear you speak tomorrow," said Mary-Ellen. Elliot's eyes flashed to Yarrow's. She felt a shock as something within them connected.

"Everyone's going to hear Stevenson speak," he corrected Mary-Ellen. "I'm just the guy they send on to warm up the audience. I'll leave your name at the door," he said to Yarrow, "to make sure you get a good seat. Where are you staying?"

Cool, clear-eyed Elliot, she thought. "Here," she said. He just smiled, and the blonde on his arm purred something, and then he moved on.

"Well, is that guy running for office or what?" said Ned. "Did you see his effect on this room? Did you feel it? He could put half the candidates in the shade if he ran."

"He's never held public office," said Yarrow. "Could he run?"

"Remember Willkie? Nineteen-forty election. He never held public office either. There were Willkie Clubs all over the country. Draft Willkie, and they did, on the sixth ballot at the convention."

Mary-Ellen looked bored. Ned's political memory was phenomenal.

"Ned," said Yarrow, also realizing this, but finding it a bonus. "Would you come back to Platte City and be editor of the *Journal*?"

"You're giving up being editor? Why?"

She drew lines on the tablecloth with her fork. "I love it, but I have too much else to do. I don't think I'm giving it the time it needs. We've been too successful. Do you know how many people come to me now, with papers for sale, or magazines, or radio stations? There are many things I want to do. You would be great, Ned. What do you say?"

"Oh, Ned, it would be nice to go home." Yarrow understood the fervency in Mary-Ellen's voice.

Ned was thoughtful. His big square chin rested on his tie. He had tightened his lips so they disappeared into his face.

"I want you to think about it," said Yarrow, signaling for the check by making a writing motion in the air. "You'd be the big fish in the little pond in Platte City."

She signed the bill. "I'll pay you well, Ned. Call me in the morning and we'll talk."

As they left the restaurant and walked past the false fire roaring behind glass in the reception lounge, Mary-Ellen said, "Have you time to come and see the children? Sally is eleven now and Katherine is thirteen. She's already had her first period." Mary-Ellen burst into tears.

Ned handed his wife a handkerchief. "She always starts crying when she thinks of the kids growing up," he said.

"Of course I'll come," said Yarrow. They kissed good night and Yarrow walked back to her bungalow. She got into bed and called her mother and the children. The children were already asleep, her mother said. Buck fell off a swing today, but apart from a cut on his knee he was fine. Yarrow worried about Freya getting tired looking after them. But her mother wouldn't hear of help. "I'm only fifty-four," she said. Apart from her bout with cancer all those years ago, Freya's health was superb. Yarrow touched wood as she hung up. Then she called the *Journal*, her other child, and spoke to Paddy and hearing that the presses were running on time, she hung up with relief. No sooner had she done so than the phone rang.

"Yarrow?"

There was no mistaking his voice.

"Yes."

"How are you? That's a stupid question, I know. You looked wonderful tonight, more lovely than ever."

"Thank you."

"Are you here on your own?"

"Yes. Are you?"

He laughed. She could picture him laughing with his head back so his Adam's apple wobbled. She pictured him lying down because his voice sounded soft and intimate.

"That was Amanda," he said. "We're just good friends. How's the paper doing? I hear good things about it."

"It's going well. I've doubled the circulation."

"*Will* you come and hear me speak tomorrow?"

"Of course."

"Will you give me good coverage in the *Journal*?"

"It depends if you say anything worthwhile. Anyway, what are you running for?"

He laughed again. "I'll tell you tomorrow. I'm free in the afternoon. Would you stay behind after the lunch? I'd love to talk to you."

"Yes." There was no hesitation in her voice.

"I liked you in that blue dress tonight."

"How can you remember what I was wearing?" Miss Hines had been right, she thought.

"A boat neckline," he said. "White satin collar, deep blue dress."

Now it was her turn to laugh. She was flattered.

"And tomorrow—what will you be wearing?"

"Red," she said, "bright red." She heard a rustle, as though he had turned over or sat up. He whistled softly into the telephone. "You'll be hard to miss." Then he hung up. She looked at the receiver for a minute. He had always hung up first, she realized. She wondered why he did it. Then she thought about tomorrow. She was acting like a girl; she felt like a girl again. She got out of bed and stood in front of the full-length mirror on the bathroom door. She took off her nightgown and examined her figure as objectively as she could. She was curvy; she always had been. Her breasts had improved with childbirth, her rib cage sloped in to her small waist, and then her hips swelled out. If she had been as small as Nellie, she would have been too hourglass-figured for modern tastes, but she had a little added height and the extra inches were in her legs, so that the curve of her hips

smoothed out to her knees. She turned sideways and held in her
stomach. She could see a silver stretch mark on her skin. She
had had only one man before, her husband—Sandy. Somehow
these stretch marks had been his stretch marks, too, but now as
she thought of Elliot, they troubled her. Her figure was not
perfect but it was good. "Gudrun," she thought suddenly. In
Norse mythology Gudrun was the daughter of a king who lured
Sigurd away from the Valkyrie Brynhild.

But Gudrun had a secret potion to do that, thought Yarrow,
climbing into bed. She thought about Mary-Ellen and her in-
fidelity. Yarrow had not asked Elliot about Blanchette, nor about
their daughter, Meredith. But he hadn't asked her about her
children either. It was as though they were back at the same
stage as years ago in Platte City, when they had teased each
other over cards. But in those days, they had been unencum-
bered; no amount of wishful thinking could bring those days
back. Were they fated to go on teasing each other all their lives?
she wondered.

The applause was deafening after Elliot spoke. He spoke well;
he looked good on the podium. He started speaking as if all the
power and charisma were contained within his suit, and then,
first quietly, then more firmly, as the rhythms of his speech
became more pronounced, some of the energy was allowed to
escape, then he pulled it back in.

Yarrow was mesmerized. Elliot had a gift. But today he was
not the principal speaker and he held his powers in check; he
lifted the audience to that pitch at which they were most re-
ceptive and allowed the applause to swell into a welcome for the
candidate. People stood up and cheered. Elliot wiped his face
with a handkerchief as he came off the podium. Yarrow listened
to Stevenson. He was a more formal speaker. He attacked Richard Nixon and asked for fifty million dollars a year to match
state funds to increase teachers' salaries. Yarrow thought that
Jack Hoggart would be pleased.

Elliot was beside her, his eyes glistening with vitality.

"Come on," he said, "let's get out of here." It took them
some time to make their way out of the hall, for people kept
coming up to him, slapping him on the back about his speech.
He had a word for everyone, recognized many of them. Outside,
a car waited but he said, "Wouldn't you rather walk?" It was a
beautiful day, and so he dismissed the car and told the driver
where to pick them up. He took her to an art gallery where he
said he wanted her advice on a picture.

It was a painting of a nude woman. The gallery owner hovered around them until Elliot waved him away.

"What do you think?" he said.

"I don't know anything about art." She was embarrassed because, not being used to art, she was unable to get rid of the thought that she was standing here beside him looking at a nude woman. The woman had voluptuous hips. Yarrow thought of her own.

"You don't have to know anything about art in order to like it or dislike it," he said.

He began to explain the picture to her, how the artist had turned the figure, the expression in the eye of the woman, the color of her skin. See the bit of landscape in the background? What about the ring on her small finger? What did it mean? he wanted to know. Yarrow had never spent so much time studying a painting. She found she enjoyed it. She ventured an opinion.

"The woman has just had a bath," she said. "Her skin has that rosy color, but the artist has a cruel eye."

"Why?"

"He shows the marks where her corset has pressed. Perhaps he doesn't like women."

"Perhaps he does, and the marks don't matter," he said. "What about this?" He pointed to a landscape, a quite small drawing that was so harmonious she smiled. "I like it."

"I do, too," he said. "You have a good eye. That's a Fragonard." He nodded to the gallery owner and they left.

"Who was the nude by?" she asked.

"Degas." She looked at him.

"Even I've heard of Degas. And you let me dismiss him like that."

"But your point was perfectly valid. Perhaps he didn't like women, perhaps she had just had a bath." They discussed it all the way to a coffee shop where they sat in a courtyard under a huge magnolia tree. The underside of the leaves was cocoa-brown. A big leaf fell and skittered across the tiles like a soft leather shoe.

"Will you join me tonight?" he said when the car picked them up. "It may be very dull—a group of local Democrats."

"They might find out I'm a Republican," she said.

He squeezed her arm. "You'll be pleased to know that we Democrats do believe in forgiving original sin."

In the afternoon she went to see Mary-Ellen; Ned was still thinking about the move to Platte City and Yarrow told him she would have to know soon. She talked with the children and then left for the hotel to change for dinner.

She wore a red off-the-shoulder dress with a pattern of white leaves on it. She was not sure it was grand enough when he picked her up, but when they got to the ballroom where hundreds of other people were gathered, she felt she was as well dressed as the others. He was very attentive to her and sat beside her and brought her drinks and introduced people to her and talked about politics and art and business and the world—everything except about themselves, and then he drove her back to the hotel and kissed her hand good night. She was devastated. She thought she had bored him, that he found her unattractive. In the morning he called and woke her up. It was a Saturday.

"I'm going out to the beach," he said. "Would you like to come?" She had been about to call the desk and make a reservation to return home.

"I'd love to," she said.

This time he himself drove. He had rented a convertible, and she put a scarf around her head and let the wind blow into her face. At Malibu he turned north and they came to a place called Paradise Cove, where they parked near a modern-style gray and white house.

"Can we park in this person's driveway?" she asked as she got out, the wind from the ocean blowing her skirt.

"Not only park," he said, "but we can change. I have a key." He opened the door for her. "It belongs to a client—a Republican, unfortunately. I've lost him for the cause."

"I thought you were a businessman," she shouted through the door of the room where she changed, "not a politician."

"I am but politics is like breathing. I'll meet you on the beach."

When she came out, she picked up a towel and ran down the few front steps onto the sand. She saw him ahead of her plunging into the breakers. She followed him in, but he swam out too far. Since she could not swim, she stayed near the shore where her feet could touch the bottom. When he came in, they lay on the sand and talked, and then they went for a long walk on the beach, miles in each direction.

"I've always thought of the mountains as my sea," she said. "I hadn't realized how noisy the ocean is; it's as though it's marking time. I don't feel that in the mountains."

They were on the terrace watching the rollers breaking on the sand beneath them. "Such a pity to leave," she said, "just as I'm getting to know them."

He was standing beside her and now he touched her hand and then he took her in his arms and kissed her.

"You could stay," he said. "We could go back tomorrow." His lips had a salty taste, she noted, as he kissed her again.

"Yarrow, please," he said, "won't you spend one night with me in my whole life? Did I hurt you too much?"

His eyes were so beautiful, so pleading. She leaned against the balustrade; she felt so weak. He took her silence as hesitation.

"I won't touch you if you don't want me to. I just want to know you're with me, in the same house, that in the morning when I wake up, the first person I see will be you." He dropped his arms.

"I'd like to stay, very much." She was shivering in her wet bathing suit. "But I'm going to have a shower and then we can talk."

His smile was so ravishing that she was tempted to stay outside with him. But she went and showered and changed back into her skirt and blouse and left her hair down so it could dry. The wind lifted curls of it while it dried and she kept pushing them back from her face. He had changed, too, and was barbecuing on the terrace when she came out. She came up and slipped her arms around him. It was their first sign of intimacy, and they both knew it.

"I never knew you could cook," she said, slipping away from him and pouring some red wine from a bottle. She held his glass up to him to drink. He was having fun, tossing tomatoes and lettuce and garlic in a big bowl beside the barbecue. She sat with her legs tucked under her on the grooved wooden bench that ran around the gray terrace. They seemed to talk about everything; there was no subject they could not discuss. She found some candles and a tablecloth and napkins, and when they sat and talked, the candles got lower and lower and the sea became just a rushing noise that ebbed and flowed. The white breakers were like dim shadows as they creamed up along the beach. When the moon came out, they were still there, and Elliot had twined one arm around Yarrow's where she sat opposite him. His fingers stroked her arm under her shirtsleeve.

"You're getting cold," he said. "Shall we go in?"

"Elliot," she whispered, "I'm scared."

His fingers never stopped stroking her. "I am, too."

They rose together and they walked into the house with their arms around each other. He had picked up a candle and as she went to switch on the light, he said, "We don't need that."

In the candleglow they walked to the room where she had

changed. He placed the candle on the bedside table where it
flickered. She sat on the bed and he knelt down in front of her
and unbuttoned her shirt. When he quietly opened the buttons,
her breasts were naked, proud and womanly and roseate like the
painting he had shown her. He kissed them and Yarrow wished
he had been there when she was a girl and it had not been Sandy.
He undid her skirt and the zipper snagged and then he pulled it
down with a little abrupt movement, so that she knew he was
fighting his own impatience. She lifted herself a little with her
hands behind her so that he could slip off her skirt, and then he
stopped. Her small white panties covered the triangle of dark
hair. She unbuttoned his shirt and took it off and she felt his
smooth, smooth skin. There was a patch of hair on his chest and
she saw there were hairs around his nipples and she drew a circle
around each with her finger. Then she leaned forward and kissed
them, his nipples, as though he were a woman, and her hair fell
forward over them both.

He stood up and slipped out of his trousers. He was a graceful
man, and when he stood naked before her, she knew that she
loved him and that he was not disappointing to her. There was
nothing about him that disappointed her. She pulled him to her
and he cradled the back of her head, his fingers like a comb
lifting the hair from the nape of her neck; they fell back on the
bed and then he bent down to take off her remaining clothes and
she felt, fool that she was, she felt herself freeze and he sensed
it.

"I'm sorry," she said.

"No, don't be sorry. Lovers have all the time in the world."
So he came back up to her lips, and he kissed her and licked her
and caressed her lips with his own and she felt herself respond-
ing and knew for the first time in her life the tenderness that went
with male love. He found her beautiful, he told her that again
and again, every bit of her, she had nothing to fear, and under
the candlelight she felt herself grow more beautiful. He slipped
his hand down and she quivered and then her last vestige of
clothing, the little wisp that didn't matter, was gone and she had
opened herself to him, slid deep down so that he could enter her
and it was as though for the first time someone had found the
key that unlocked her heart. She thought from her experience
that it would be over soon, but he didn't come. When he thought
that he would lose it and she wasn't ready, he withdrew. He
moved her with his hands, his legs, his arms, he used every part
of him to bring her to the same level of readiness as he. And
then when she felt her body ready to respond, when she thought

that she would come without him entering her again, he sensed it. He plunged into her, her darling Blackbird who had left her, and swooped her away into the sky. He was here, he was hers. This was what heaven meant.

Her skin was oiled with sweat when they were through. Even her hair felt damp. He moved her up on top of him as though she weighed nothing, and he looked at her.

"You are mine," he said.

"I know."

He traced her breasts with his fingers, moved her so her hair swayed.

"I can't have enough of you," he said.

She fell onto his mouth and kissed him, and somehow she fell asleep with his tongue inside her mouth. She did not want him to stop touching her; having a part of his body in hers was her lifeline. She dreamed she would die if the connection was broken, and she awoke to find that she was wet and his tongue was not inside her mouth but inside her vagina, and the pearly dawn was breaking across the Pacific sky.

CHAPTER 24

YARROW WOKE AGAIN LATER THAT MORNING TO THE SMELL OF coffee. She put on a robe that hung on a hook on the door and found Elliot preparing breakfast. She went to hug him and he pulled open her robe so that she could feel the cool length of his body against her. He had just come in from the sea.

"Juice, coffee, bacon?"

"After fornication?"

"My sweet Yarrow," he said, "I am no more married than you are."

"No?"

She sat on a high barstool at the kitchen divider, and popped some bread in the toaster.

"Blanchette and I live separate lives. She never leaves Virginia and I only go there to see Meredith. She's two now." He was silent. She sensed that he was unsure how much to tell her.

"I don't love Blanchette," he said. "I stopped loving her long ago, and even when I did love her, it was not the way I feel about you. It was more of an agreement—we gave each other something in return—our marriage was like that: Her father was powerful and could help my career; I was ambitious; Blanchette wanted me as her husband. There are worse contracts. She won't let me go, Yarrow. She is the mother of my child."

Yarrow listened and knew what he was saying; he was saying he would always remain with Blanchette. He was warning Yarrow that their time together would always be fragmented, always taken from others. In their deceit he wanted not to lie. He wanted her to be under no delusions about their future. It hurt her, sitting there with the sun pouring into the white and gray house, the white and gray interior, amorphous like their own relationship; it hurt her because she wanted him to love her so much that he would leave Blanchette for her. But she would never say it; she knew that he understood and was explaining why it could never be.

"Will I see you again?" she asked.

"You will always see me, my darling. You are mine as much as Blanchette is." He kissed her over the countertop. "You do trust me on that?"

She was thinking that she must be a fool. Here she was, a mother with three children, a successful businesswoman, a woman able to make decisions, able to drop things when they didn't work, a woman—a fool, knowing that she was about to accept an imperfection because she could not have him any other way. It troubled her. She did not want it to be this way. She wanted to be open about him, share her pride and pleasure and joy in him with other people. She could see along a whole valley of years how it was going to be; not perfect, not at all.

"I love your eyebrows," she said, stroking them outward with her thumbs and then running her fingers across to his ears. She dropped her hands. "I must go back today, you know."

"I'll drive you to the airport." They were both businesslike.

She called her office.

"My God," she said, putting her hand over the mouthpiece. "We had a fire in a press last night. They tried to reach me at the hotel."

"How bad was it?"

She listened to Paddy on the other end. She hung up, she was worried.

"We were late getting out and lost some sales. Damn! I should have let them know where I was."

"What could you have done, Yarrow, from here?"

"Nothing probably." She gave him a wry smile. "But at least I could have given them some support."

They picked up her luggage at the hotel and in the car, on the way to the airport, he said, "You know the story of the name Yarrow?"

She shook her head.

"The Latin name for Yarrow is Achillea something or other. Some people think of it only as an obnoxious weed."

"Thank you," she said.

"Hard to eradicate, stubborn." He lifted her hand beside him on the leather seat and kissed it without taking his eyes off the road.

"But Achillea—people say that Achilles used the flower as a medicinal for his soldiers in ancient Greece." He squeezed her hand. "You're my Achilles' heel." He kissed her fingers again.

At the airport she didn't want to leave him. They kissed long and tenderly and then she had to get on the plane. She wept into her handkerchief on the plane. The stewardess was sympathetic. She offered Yarrow an aspirin. How could Yarrow explain that she was filled with a mixture of delirious happiness and sadness at the same time, a potion even Gudrun would have recognized as her own?

"Mr. Weyden? Mrs. Weyden? She's awake now. You can come in and see her." The doctor at the Washington Children's Hospital held open the door to their daughter's room.

"Hello, darling," said Blanchette, throwing her arms around the tiny form that lay on the bed. The safety bars got in her way, so the nurse dropped them down for her. Meredith smiled, her china-blue eyes, like her mother's, crinkling at the corners.

"Hi, Popette," said her father, coming around the other side of the bed and stroking back her blond hair. He avoided looking at the ugliness around his baby's mouth. "You are a brave, brave girl," he said, "and we love you very much." It was her third operation, for Meredith had been born with a cleft lip and palate. Blanchette was talking to her about her dolls and her little dog waiting at home. Meredith's eyes never left her mother's. Elliot spoke quietly to the doctor at the back of the room.

"It was very successful," said Dr. Glaston, looking pleased.

He had operated first on Meredith when she was four days old, cutting and using black silk to stitch her upper lip into the semblance of a human mouth. It had taken two operations. He had left the asymmetrical nose with the flaring nostrils until later. Now that she was two years old, Glaston felt the time was right to close up the opening in her palate. He had explained precisely to Elliot what he would do. The palate, he said, was formed of bone plate, which in Meredith's case had not closed, and then there were layers of mucosa and the oral linings and muscles of the mouth. There had been enough material for Glaston to lift the tissue up to create a flap, which he had sutured down the middle of the palate to form a roof for the mouth. It had been a long, tedious operation.

Elliot's eyes filled as Glaston explained some of the details.

"This won't be the last operation?"

"No, it won't. We'll see how it heals. You know she will always have a speech impediment, Mr. Weyden?"

"I don't care as long as she's OK. What about the nose, can you reshape it later?"

"We can reconstruct the nose when the time comes; the results are most amazing and quite good looking." He patted Elliot on the arm. It was always more difficult for the fathers, he thought. "Let her rest now."

Elliot took his wife's arm and they went out into the corridor. Blanchette wiped her eyes now that her daughter couldn't see her.

"She's going to be fine," said Elliot, putting his arms around her.

"Are you sure?"

"Of course I'm sure. Dr. Glaston is the best there is. She'll be the belle of Virginia when she's older."

Blanchette blew her nose and smiled at Elliot.

"Thank you," she said, as though they were strangers. "Will you be coming home tonight?"

"No, I can't," he said gently as he took her out to her car. "I have a business dinner at the Hay-Adams, and I'll stay there. I'll be here at the hospital in the morning. You know you can call me at the hotel if you need me."

He closed the car door as she got in. It made a soft luxurious thunk as he did so. She settled back on the blue upholstery and wondered if he would be with a woman tonight. She and Elliot had come to an arrangement in their marriage in which their duties to each other were defined by social circumspection. As his wife and the mother of his only child, she would be cherished and looked after in all material ways; she would be given respect in her status as Mrs. Elliot Weyden. He would not embarrass her in any way. It was assumed that she would not embarrass him either.

If only she were more European, Blanchette thought, she might be able to accept the arrangement more easily. But she was American, brought up to believe that romance and marriage went together into happily-ever-after sunsets.

Blanchette looked out the window as the car crossed the Potomac River and sped out of Washington into the countryside. Perhaps she had overplayed her hand with Elliot. But then she always had. She had pursued him relentlessly and when he agreed to marry her, she thought she had won. But she had not won his heart. When she bought Coakley House, she had believed he would soon tire of living in hotels on his own—he told her he had moved to the Carlyle now—but he had not. In fact what she had not realized was that Elliot was a loner; he did not need companionship. Although Elliot had many acquaintances, he had few close friends.

And then there was Meredith, blessed Meredith, who had come at the right moment and saved whatever vestige of feeling Elliot still felt for Blanchette. He was besotted by his daughter. Blanchette knew he would have stayed with her even if Meredith had been born perfectly formed. But he would not have stayed if Blanchette had remained barren. Blessed womb, she thought.

Blanchette was taking instruction in the Catholic Church. Ever since Meredith was born with that horror of a lower face, Blanchette had turned to religion for comfort. Her father, who had become an Episcopalian when he became an American citizen and changed his name, understood. Sometimes, she talked to him about it on the telephone. At times, Fabiana told her that he was unable to talk to her: Rich Newnom had had a series of strokes.

Blanchette switched on the little reading light over her shoulder and opened a small black Bible she carried. Abraham drove steadily through the dark countryside to her beautiful empty house. " 'Women are strongest,'' she read, ''but above all things Truth bareth away the victory.' ''

The Republicans swept the country in the November elections that year and Elliot felt personally crushed by Stevenson's defeat. He had invested a great deal of money and time in the Democratic campaign. He went to Virginia for Thanksgiving and licked his wounds in the solitude of Coakley. He received a call from the governor of New York asking him to join a nonpartisan commission investigating crime in New York. Elliot said he would think about it.

Meredith had one of her many colds. Holding her in his arms, reading to her, Elliot felt humbled by his daughter's disability. If there were anything he could have done to save her from the pain and humiliation she was going through, he would have found a way to do it. Blanchette took herself off to New York for a few days' shopping, and he spent the time with Meredith, reading to her and trying to understand her speech. When he was traveling, the telephone was a poor substitute for intuition; he could sense the child's frustration as she repeated what she wanted him to hear. When he was with her, though, other clues, her toys, her facial expression helped him understand her.

At Thanksgiving Yarrow once again played host to her family and this time Ned and Mary-Ellen and their brood joined them. Ned had taken over as editor from Yarrow and it was as though a burden had been lifted from her shoulders. Mary-Ellen told her that her affair was over and waited for Yarrow to unburden her own secrets. But Yarrow kept her secrets to herself, and Mary-Ellen felt miffed.

Between Thanksgiving and Christmas, Yarrow and Elliot had arranged to meet for a long weekend in the mountains. Jock's cabin had been given a minor facelift—a wooden floor had been put in and some insulation installed in the ceiling. Yarrow said she was going up there to check that everything was all right. Freya urged her to go. She had seen a change in her daughter that pleased her. She had worried about Yarrow's life being so empty of male companionship. Freya noticed the brighter colors Yarrow wore and the toss of her head and the spring in her step. Once or twice Yarrow had mentioned Elliot in passing and Freya had put two and two together. Her daughter, after all, was thirty-four years old. It was not for Freya to question her.

The cabin was bitterly cold when they arrived after driving from Denver.

"It's enough to freeze a man's balls off," said Elliot, getting a fire together in the old stove.

She hauled in the food and rations and blankets and things she had brought from Platte City in the car. There was a road now up through the pass and they no longer had to ski in.

"We could be snowed in," she said.

"I'm praying for it."

"Don't say that," she said. "We both have too much to do." Each had brought a briefcase of work. Modern times, thought Yarrow, modern romance. "I must be back on Tuesday. We've got our big pre-Christmas issue that day. Our first color ads. Elliot, are you listening to me?"

He was unpacking the bags of groceries she had brought.

"What are you planning to do, cook all weekend?"

She pulled his hand away from the bags. "I want to show you that I *can* cook."

"I've heard otherwise. Besides, that's not why you're here. Come here."

"No. Unpack first. Elliot. Please. Elliot!"

He didn't wait to take off his boots. It was still so cold in the cabin that they coupled with their clothes on. When they were finished, her hair was disheveled and her face red.

"You look ravishing, and ravished," he said, helping her up. "My wild Yarrow. Do me a favor?"

"What?"

"Don't put your hair up this weekend. Leave it down."

She unpacked the groceries while he carried more things in from the car. She had brought a portable phonograph with some records. He looked at her choice. "I didn't know you liked opera," he said.

"There's a lot about me you don't know." She picked up a book he brought. "I didn't know you liked poetry."

He put on *Lucia di Lammermoor.*

"What do you think of the hydrogen bomb?" he asked from behind her, putting his arms around her. She was busy with the pots. "Do you like Patti Page? Have you seen a movie in Todd-AO? Do you know who said, 'Come in the evening, or come in the morning, come when you're looked for, or come without warning'?"

"Are you being vulgar?"

"It's nineteenth-century poetry! I don't think Davis meant to be vulgar, but it depends how you read it. He was more interested in couplets."

She threw a string of sausages at him.

"More food!"

"It's for a cassoulet," she said, kissing him on the nose as he pulled up a chair beside the stove. "It's going to take me two days to cook it."

"I hope you know what you're doing," he said as she took out beans and pork and streaky bacon and onions and garlic and lamb and a can of bread crumbs. Lastly she held up a pig's trotter.

"The secret ingredient," she said. She had him take the meat outside and hang it on a beam out of reach of predators.

While he was outside Yarrow propped up the cookbook behind the string along the shelf. She had telephoned Greta twice to make sure she understood the recipe. She put the beans in to soak and then they went out in the late afternoon to ski.

The temperature was way below freezing, and he had never skied cross-country before. He had been once or twice to Gstaad, he said. They spent most of their time falling and laughing and picking themselves up, and when they got back to the cabin the window, glowing gently from the stove light, welcomed them in. He pumped up and lit the kerosene lamp and under its hiss they dined on bread and cheese and drank red wine. And then they went to bed with the fire crackling in the stove and the light of the lamp flickering out and the smell of kerosene and firewood in the air.

In the morning she woke first and the stove had gone out. She could hardly bear to put her feet down on the new, cold floor. The earth floor might have been warmer. She ran across and started the stove again and put the water on to boil and jumped back into bed with him.

After breakfast she had him bring in the meat and she chopped up the streaky bacon and put it in a pan with the herbs and spices and the garlic and the onion. Then she went outside to drain the beans and added them to the other things in the pan. She covered everything with water and put the pan on to boil. She felt that everything she was doing was a little "I love you." She heated up a small Dutch oven that sat on the stove and put in the lamb and the bits of pork to bake. He watched her hunkering down over the stove.

"Why do women always want big kitchens," he said, "when you can do everything on a stove that's smaller than my briefcase?"

Then they went skiing and she told him all the things she could remember Jock telling her: how he had staked out ten acres here for mining and then put in other claims to add to his parcel; here was where the Kittimack mine was, and here a shaft to the deepest mine this side of the Rockies and not an ounce of silver in it; and that tree there was where a bear nearly took him once. Jock had staked out his newest parcel and gone back to walk around it the next day, and he had found great claw marks on the trees following his line. It was as though the bear was marking out its own boundaries. Sure enough, he came across the bear and he had climbed that tree as though his pants were on fire. Jock spent all night up there waiting for the bear to leave.

When they got back to the cabin, Elliot put on some music and sat and read while she cut up the cooked meats and sausages and layered them with the drained beans in a big, deep earthenware casserole. She imagined she was a pioneer woman—she stopped layering as she thought about it. There wouldn't have been the music, but the fire would have been the same, the smell of cooking, the man home, sitting in his chair, the snow outside. How simple life might have been then. She was glad that she and Elliot had this opportunity to share the simplicity.

"Talk to me," she said when everything was put on to simmer for three hours. It had begun to snow outside. He put his book down and she sat on his knees. He told her about himself. He told her about Blanchette. He told her about Meredith, which was the hardest to tell, because it meant that his seed and Blanchette's had not been perfect. He made this discovery in telling Yarrow. The fire crackled, and she got up and put on some more wood and checked the liquid level in the pot. Then she came back and sat on his knees again and told him about Sandy, and about her inadequacies (in some ways, she still blamed herself), and then she told him about Zeb, and she couldn't stop the tears that rose in her eyes. You just never get over it, she said. Then she told him about Lily and John and Buck, and outside the snow got thicker and the swirl of it against the wooden logs made them feel even more secure. It got dark and Elliot brought in some more wood and pumped up the kerosene lamp and lit it.

There was no running water in the cabin; they used snow they melted on the stove. At nightfall, before they ate, Yarrow wanted to wash. "Turn away," she said. He laughed but turned his head and watched her shadow on the wall, watched her raise her arms one by one and heard the trickle of water falling back into the basin, watched the cloth move over her breasts, watched her squat and wash between her legs. He watched her brush her hair, her long, pioneer-woman hair, and listened to the quiet, the deep, deep quiet, with only the hiss of the kerosene lamp punctuating it. He could hear the sound of the brush moving through her hair.

She opened some red wine and then they ate. The cassoulet was delicious. It filled them with a torpor that was irresistible. They fell asleep in each other's arms, full of love and wine and meat. Their cabin was a cave in which they were safe from everything that could hurt them.

He was restless the next morning. He went out and chopped some wood and then they went skiing. It was snowing thick and fast, and within an hour of leaving the cabin they were skiing in a whiteout. There was a small steep slope of which Yarrow was unaware; she had turned her head to make sure that Elliot was behind her and suddenly the ground seemed to fall away under her skis. She tried to right herself, but a tree loomed up and she twisted to avoid it, but the tip of her ski caught on it and she heard her leg go *crack, crack, crack* as it broke. Yarrow passed out with the pain.

"Oh, my God, Yarrow." Elliot could see from the way her leg was twisted that it was broken below the knee. "It's going to hurt to move you," he said. "I'm sorry, darling." He was glad she was unconscious. He took off her skis and dragged her inch by inch up the slope. It took him forty minutes to get her back to the cabin.

"Yarrow, darling?" Her eyes opened. She was inside and warm. Pain raced through her body like heat. He gave her some brandy.

"Your leg's broken, Yarrow."

"I'm accident-prone up here. I'm sorry."

"Stop apologizing." He was worried, the weather had closed in. There was really no way he could drive the car down to Galena.

"We're going to have to sit it out, Yarrow. As soon as it clears I'll go and get help."

She smiled wanly. "At least we have plenty of leftover food to eat."

He half laughed and cried and leaned over to kiss her. The slightest movement caused her to break out in a sweat. He stoked up the fire and sat beside her. "I'll put some music on," he said.

"That would be nice," said Yarrow and passed out again.

The phone rang.

"Blanchette?"

"Yes?"

"This is Fabiana. Your father is fading fast. They say to come—it's only a matter of hours."

Blanchette tried to reach Elliot, but even his secretary, Lainie, did not know where he was. Blanchette wondered if Lainie was covering for him. She caught the shuttle to New York and was beside her father's bed within hours. The apartment on Fifth Avenue was glowing with light. It was incongruous that he should be dying on such a light and beautiful day.

The stroke had incapacitated him. He could not speak. Even when Blanchette held his hand, he could not squeeze it in response. But his eyes opened every now and then, and she knew he recognized her. He seemed to be agitated. It was a feeling no one else picked up. She sat beside him, the two of them alone in the room.

"Daddy," she said, "is there something you need?"

His eyes locked onto hers.

"Oh, if I could only understand." She stroked the liver-spotted hand. It had always been clawlike. Now it seemed even more so. "Is it about me or Fabiana? The will or something?"

She spoke slowly, went through everything she could think of, pausing each time and watching him. Only when she took out her little Bible and thought to comfort him by reading did she see something in his eye that stopped her. She looked at the Bible in her hand. He had taken up the Christian faith when he was a boy. Now death loomed in front of him.

Blanchette leaned forward and whispered to him:

"Daddy, do you want a rabbi?"

A tear trickled down from one eye. She wiped it for him, but the tears kept coming.

She went out and spoke to Fabiana and then went back into the room. "He'll be here, soon," she told him. She put down the Bible and sat holding his hand until the rabbi came.

"Mommy's with a man."

"That's not true," said John. He bit his lip and looked at his older sister. They were on the bus coming home from school. It was only a few blocks but it was snowing.

"She is," said Lily. "They were off skiing and she broke her leg. That's why she's not home. She's in the hospital."

John lifted up his bookbag from the floor of the bus, and they got off.

"Who was it, then, if you're so smart?"

"Mr. Elliot Weyden, if you must know. He's rich. You see his picture in the paper all the time. He's got his own airplane."

"You're lying."

"It's true. He has a plane and he flies all over the country. It has a bathroom in it."

John shouted at her as they banged through the door. "It's not true about a man!"

"Oh, grow up," she said. John ran to his room and locked the door.

Freya came out from the sitting room. She had been resting with her feet up. Her varicose veins were hurting.

"Lily, what are you teasing him about now? You used to be so nice together."

"He's not nice anymore. He's so moody, I can't stand it. He's in trouble again at school, he didn't do his homework."

Lily went off to find something to eat. Freya stood looking up the stairs for a moment and then went up. She knocked softly at the door.

"John? Honey? Can I talk to you for a minute?"

"Go away!"

"Honey?"

"Get lost, Gran! Can't anyone leave me alone!"

Freya tried the lock on the door. There was no sound from inside. She sighed and shook her head and went downstairs slowly. John needed a man around the house. He was too much for Freya to cope with.

Yarrow spent weeks in the hospital in traction. The fibula and tibia of her left leg had both been broken. It was a bad break, compounded by the fact that they had been unable to get help as soon as it happened. The leg, they told her, would never be quite the same again. She told Elliot that she felt that it was her "Scarlet Letter." She was so serious about this that he was annoyed, and they had their first argument since becoming lovers. Then he sent his plane to move her from the small hospital in Galena to the one in Platte City, and he came and visited her and the tiff was forgotten. When he brought her children presents, Lily looked at John with her eyebrows raised as if to say, See, what did I tell you? John felt he was being bribed. He hated this man who was taking his mother away. He felt it very strongly. He hated his mother. He threw a brick through the window of the school cafeteria.

"Mrs. Heartland, er, Miss McLean." The headmaster did not like this feminist stuff; he was uncomfortable with it. "John is a disruptive element in our school. Does his father see him very often?"

Yarrow sat in the headmaster's office with her leg in a cast and her crutches beside her. She was annoyed at the question. What did Sandy have to do with this?

"No. He goes to New York sometimes to see his father, but he lives with me."

"I have the school psychologist's report here on John. It suggests the boy needs a strong male presence in his life." The headmaster paused. Yarrow blushed. What the man was saying was that she couldn't cope with her son.

"The boy has expressed an interest in living with his father. Do you know that?"

"John said that?" He had never mentioned it to her, but then she had never asked.

"Why don't you talk to John about it," said the headmaster, getting up. "We can't keep putting him on probation." When Yarrow hobbled out of the room, he thought, if only women would get back in the kitchen where they belong, we wouldn't have these delinquency problems.

Yarrow took the matter up with John that night. They went to an ice-hockey game. He was crazy about sports. She sat on the end of a row so her cast could stick out. She offered him some popcorn. He wouldn't take it.

"Honey, do you miss your dad?"

His antennae went up like a periscope.

"Why?"

"Well, you seem to be so unhappy here with me . . ."

"You want to get rid of me."

"John, that's not true. I'm trying to help you. Would you be happier living with your father?"

John watched the players chasing after the puck. The home team scored a goal and a great cheer went up. But his mind was on something else, so he didn't cheer. She didn't love him, that's what she was saying. She wanted him to leave, so she could have that baby, Buck, all to herself. And her lover. Yeah, well, he didn't care. He was nine years old. He could be tough.

"I love you, John. If I could only reach you."

He didn't look at her. His dad had said he loved him, too, and he left. There was another home goal and the stadium erupted in joy. John got up.

"I want to live with Dad." He wouldn't look at her. She couldn't look at him. She had all this buttered popcorn over her fingers. She was hunting for a tissue. "This is boring," he said, "Let's go home."

CHAPTER 25

THE FOLLOWING SPRING YARROW TOOK JOHN TO NEW YORK TO live with his father. She had been planning to wait until the end of the school year, but he began stealing things, small things, money, combs, baseball cards, from other children's lockers. Her excuses, to herself, to the school, to her mother, that John's problems were mere pranks were wearing thin. She had lost control of him. There were times he drove her to tears, and times she thought she would kill him if he didn't behave.

"I've failed," she said to Sandy on the telephone. "And now I'm passing him on to you."

"Why do you always do that?" he said.

"What?"

"Blame yourself?"

"Do I?"

"Even us. You weren't to blame."

"Why, thank you, Sandy." This was a new Sandy she was hearing.

"Your dissatisfaction wasn't with me, but with our marriage. You expected too much from it. You're too romantic."

Yarrow looked at the phone and thought that at least Sandy's ego was still intact.

"Are you through psychoanalyzing me?"

"I wouldn't attempt that." He paused. "Your boyfriend has made a big splash on that crime commission here."

She was cautious now.

"My boyfriend?"

"Yarrow, everyone knows about you and Elliot Weyden. He's too public a figure now for people not to talk."

"I'm a single woman now, Sandy."

"Yeah, but I always hoped—well, what does it matter what I hoped." He changed the subject. "I heard something today you might be interested in. There's a radio station for sale on Long Island. It's small but you might want to look at it while you're here."

"Why don't you buy it?"

"It's too expensive for me. Besides, I'm not the entrepreneur. You are."

"I'll look at it. About John—Sandy, he's lazy and he needs pushing. Can you get him a job as a copy boy or a delivery boy somewhere?"

"Yarrow, lay off the kid."

"I have high hopes for him, Sandy, but he needs to be pushed."

When she hung up she thought about what he had said about her. He believed her commitment was to her work, yet she knew that when they married all she had wanted was children and family, nothing more. Was he right, or had he come to this conclusion as a rationalization for his own behavior? Yarrow could not be sure. And the gossip about herself and Elliot— reporters were notorious gossips—would hurt Elliot if she and he were not more discreet.

The weight-bearing cast was finally taken off her leg, and although the leg was completely healed, Yarrow was afraid to put her weight on it and walked with a cane. She kissed Buck and Lily good-bye when she and John left for New York. The children were so busy, Buck with kindergarten and Lily with piano and ballet lessons, that Yarrow felt she could leave her mother with them for a few days.

Sandy was at the airport to meet them. He had hardly changed. If anything, maturity had improved his looks, taken away a certain weakness that she now noticed in their old photographs. He was rather blustery with his son, but she thought that would soon wear off. Yarrow was ashamed at her feeling of relief that Sandy was taking some responsibility for John. But the relief only tinged the heartbreak she felt at letting him go.

"It's us two men together," Sandy said in the car as they drove into Manhattan. Yarrow sat in the back and John sat up front beside his father. Sandy had not married again—Belinda had faded into oblivion.

"Here are those figures on that radio station I told you about." He handed her a sheaf of papers in a manila envelope.

"How's the job?" she asked.

He made a grimace.

"Fabiana Newnom retired when her husband died. Palmer's running the show now. That's how I heard about this station for sale. He asked me to look at the figures and see what I thought. Me! I'm a newspaper editor, what would I know about broadcasting?" He laughed, not pleasantly. "He probably thinks I'm still in the family. Story of my life—I leave one job where I worked for my wife and I end up working for her sister's husband."

"You don't like Palmer either."

He paid a bridge toll and said, "He's a real Simon Legree. He's OK as long as he leaves me alone. The first time he tries anything on me or undercuts my authority, I'll quit. He's a mean bastard."

He tapped his finger against his temple. "But I've got to say he's smart. He's ambitious, too. Tough with the unions. We've got problems there."

"The *Courier*?"

"All the papers. One day we're late, the next day we have unexplained paper breaks; the chapel keeps meeting. Now we have complaints about ink droplets, and excessive noise. Albert Hinton's got a whole list of complaints he can run his finger down at any time and stop us with. Half of it is blackmail—and he knows it. He plays one publisher against the other. Eight of us are out here on the streets every day. Eight of us. We get our paper out despite our staff, not because of them.''

Yarrow was surprised. She had not heard Sandy quite so vehement before.

"You sound impatient.''

"Yeah, well, I am. It's not just the printers' union; try dealing with the Teamsters. At least the printers aren't corrupt. I get so damn frustrated dealing with them, though. We can't move new technology in. Why are we still printing with hot metal?'' He looked at her in the mirror. "Remember in the forty-seven strike? We were using phototypesetting then; hot-metal type-setting is an obsolete craft. But every time you try to talk about it, they dump a few more reasons why you can't change it into your lap.''

"I guess that's what Hinton worries about.''

"You cannot have a society in which you keep men on jobs that don't exist. The bubble's got to burst sometime.''

He looked at his son. "Hey, John. I thought we'd see a basketball game this afternoon at Madison Square Garden. We can sit in the press box.''

John's eyes lit up. "Neat,'' he said. Yarrow smiled at him. She hoped she'd made the right decision.

Sandy dropped her off at the Plaza Hotel where she was staying. Greta had asked her to stay with her, but Yarrow did not want to spend more time with Palmer Truitt than she could help. She would never forgive him for what he had done to her sister. She wondered if they were still happy. She kissed her son good-bye. He went as stiff as a little board. His hair had dark-ened from its baby blondness and had picked up some of her curl. It used to look like a smooth cap. She wanted to ruffle it now, but he would have died of embarrassment.

"Good-bye, darling,'' she said. She felt a wrench as the car pulled away and she thought how casually he had let her go.

When she got to her room she dialed the Carlyle, but Elliot's line was busy. Next, she telephoned Greta, but her sister had an afternoon appointment, could they see each other tomorrow? Yarrow made her other business calls. She wanted to see a number of newspaper people while she was in town. She liked to feel the pulse of the city. She telephoned the radio station in Long Island and made an appointment to see them the day after tomorrow. The idea of beating Palmer Truitt out of something he wanted was an idea she could not resist.

She sat down at the desk near the window, took out her stack of papers, and opened up the audit and audience breakdown figures that Sandy had given her. It was early afternoon on a sunny spring day. There was a great view along the whole length of Central Park from south to north, but she never looked up and two hours had passed before she realized the time and telephoned Elliot again.

His line was still busy. She banged down the phone and went and changed into something cooler. New York's spring seemed more like summer to her.

She dialed again as she zipped up her dress.

"Well, hello," she said. "You're a hard man to reach."

"Darling," he said. "Come over."

"Oh, good, for months I've been thinking this whole affair was going to be played out over the telephone."

"That won't do for what I have in mind. How's your leg?"

"All mended. I'll be there in half an hour."

Elliot's apartment at the Carlyle was entered through a separate doorway from the main hotel. The first thing she noticed when his secretary opened the door was the Degas nude they had seen in Los Angeles together the year before. He came out of his office when he heard the doorbell and took her in his arms and kissed her. The secretary left discreetly. She was a middle-aged black woman with an intelligent face. When she had gone, he kissed Yarrow even more firmly.

"I've missed you," he said. He looked at her and took her cane away from her. "Turn around," he said. Her dark hair was back in a bun, but she had cut some wispy bangs, which he noticed immediately. "I like it," he said. She had on a simple sleeveless pink dress with a short jacket over it. The hemline was short. Her legs were still beautiful, he noticed, though one leg was thinner than the other. The skiing accident had not damaged them, though she walked with a slight limp. "Can't we toss this cane away?" he said.

"Not yet. I've missed you, too."

They went into his office together. The desk overflowed with papers and files. There were three telephones on it. From the windows, which faced south and east, she could see the whole skyline of Manhattan.

"I've got a few things still to tidy up," he said, "and then we can go to a Broadway play tonight and a party afterward. I want to show you off."

"What should I wear?"

"Let me buy you something new." He buzzed his secretary. "Lainie," he said, "call that girl at Bergdorf's, they should still be open, to send over some evening clothes for Miss McLean to select." His eyes moved over Yarrow's figure. "Size six," he said. He hung up, and she wondered how many times he had done this before.

"I didn't say I had *nothing* to wear, I just said I didn't know *what* to wear." She had forgotten what it was like to be with Elliot. He smiled and was back on the telephone before she had finished. I am not going to be jealous, she said to herself. I am not going to be jealous of his work, or any previous women he's had. She sat in an armchair with some books and newspapers while he was on the telephone. She half listened to him while she read and absorbed the newspapers. The *Courier* she read with interest because of Sandy's work on it, and she was critical. It was too gray, she thought. Too wordy. Typically Sandy. She wondered if he'd recognize the *Journal*.

She began to make a list of what she would do with a paper in this city.

1) Identify the market.
2) Tight, concise editing.
3) Anglo-Saxon words. Active verbs.
4) Cut the number of runover stories.
5) Cut the fancy artwork. Simplify typefaces.
6) Inform.
7) Entertain.

Then she scribbled all over her list. Pipe dreams, she thought. She could never afford a newspaper here. And after hearing Sandy's list of woes, she wondered if anyone in their right mind ever would.

Elliot had totally forgotten she was there. He was leaning back in his chair, talking away and staring out the window. The secretary, Lainie, came in half an hour later, and beckoned her to come out into the other room. As she rose to go, his head snapped around. "Where are you going?"

"To try on some clothes," she mouthed at him.

The dresses were beautiful, but she was shocked at the prices. She picked the least expensive one, a red beaded affair with a low neckline. There was a little sequined pillbox hat that went with it. She knew he'd like that. The great thing about being with Elliot was that he noticed everything. He soon came to find her. He admired the dress and told Lainie she could leave. It was obvious to Yarrow that Lainie adored him, although in everything she seemed extremely proper.

Elliot took Yarrow upstairs to the living quarters. He poured two drinks, sour-mash bourbon for him, white wine for her.

The room was plain but sensuously furnished with leather and soft lights. Nothing was allowed to vie with his paintings. But Yarrow took him in more than she did the room.

"You look tired," she said. "You're working too hard."

"Just a busy time of year. I miss you." There were fine lines under his eyes she had not noticed before.

"I wish I could be with you more to look after you," she said. "Who comes in here and cooks and cleans for you? Who sends out your laundry?"

"That's the beauty of the hotel. They do it. I don't need very much." He roused himself from where he had been slumping in a chair. "I'm going to have a shower," he said. "Come with me. Talk to me."

She laughed. She remembered how she had once thought meeting him was like being swallowed whole. It was still like that.

He stripped and shaved unselfconsciously in the bathroom while they talked.

"Do you do all your work from here, just one secretary and a bank of telephones?"

"Most of it. I keep an office downtown, but Lainie handles nearly everything. I'm only selling ideas," he said. "I don't run a day-to-day business like you do. My staff is very small." He told her what his schedule had been over the past few weeks and what it would be like this week. In three days he was off to Illinois, Texas and California. He was going all over the country making speeches, seeing people, attending board meetings, putting deals together. "I'm just a marriage broker," he said, "on a fast plane."

"Why are you doing this to yourself?"

"Because I enjoy it." He was in the shower. She watched him through the glass door, and when he was finished she had his towel ready.

"Why don't you stay here?" he said. "Why do you have to stay down at the Plaza?"

She dried his back. "Because I have children. Because I run a business. Because you're married."

"It's because you're stubborn." He walked naked into his dressing room and threw open the floor-to-ceiling wardrobes. "Look, there's plenty of space here." He walked into the bedroom and switched on the light. "Plenty of space here, too." He picked up a menu from a table. "And room service," he said. "What more could you want?"

"Are we going to this show or are we going to stay here and argue?"

"Let's stay here and argue and then make up." But he threw on some clothes and combed his hair.

"Put your hat on," he said.

"Elliot . . ." She had thought it would be too much.

"Put it on," he said, "and take down your hair." He watched her as she did so. Her dark hair was like a cloud under the sequined hat. She looked good; she could see it in the mirror. He nodded approval and then he escorted her out.

"I won't let you off easily," he said. "I'm not going to your hotel after the party and coming back here in the middle of the night. I'm getting too old for that caper." She glanced at him quickly as he helped her into the limousine. He knew he had put his foot in it. He decided to win her sympathy before she attacked.

"It's my birthday today anyway," he said as he got in the car. "That's why I'm feeling old."

"How old are you?"

"Forty."

"Darling." She gave him a long, wet kiss as the car eased through the traffic.

"Was that given in the spirit of sympathy?" he asked.

She was thoughtful. "I didn't know your birthday was in April," she said. "I always thought you were a Leo."

"Hmmm." He kissed her again so he wouldn't have to reply.

The show was amusing, but Elliot said it wouldn't last. He had been talked into putting money in it. He seldom acted as a backer, he said, he thought it was a sucker's game. "I should have taken my own advice," he said.

At the party afterward at a nearby restaurant, he introduced Yarrow to the playwright. He was a homosexual whose brilliance was all channeled toward the words and moods he could create onstage. In other respects, he was foppish and sycophantic.

"Miss McLean," he said, on being introduced, "I've heard so much about you."

"How could you? I live in the boondocks."

"Fame travels far. And as for Elliot—he's divine. I mean he's not only good-looking, he's smart. You know, we all hope that he's secretly running for president? But he's a dark horse. Doesn't it suit him? Ah, there's my dearest friend over there. I must run. So nice talking to you." He rushed over to someone else and

Yarrow heard him say in a loud stage whisper, "Why, she's positively homophobic! Don't go near her. You might catch something."

Yarrow suddenly felt very unsophisticated despite her glittering clothes. She looked around for Elliot, but before she could go to him, someone came up, a small woman with lips painted outside her natural mouth line.

"I'm a fellow backer of the play. You must be Elliot's friend." The woman's eyes were shrewd yet friendly, and under the brassy New York talk, Yarrow sensed a kindred spirit. "My husband used to be mayor," she said. "This is a crazy city. But you'd love it if you knew it. Elliot knows this city better than anybody. He can move from one level of society to another quite easily. Not all of us can do that. But he's like a chameleon. I saw he was in court the other day with a madam who works down on Fourteenth Street."

"Elliot was?"

"Yes. And last night he spoke at yet another fund-raiser for the Democrats. What about us poor Republicans? We're not all rich like Rockefeller. Excuse me, there's Averell Harriman. I need to have a word with him."

The crowd swirled and there was Greta coming toward her, tall and blond in a slinky white dress that left nothing to the imagination.

"Sweetheart," said Greta. Somehow her sister looked vulnerable in this crowd. Her eyes had a glassy look. "Palmer's here, somewhere," she said. "Have you seen him? I'm supposed to meet him here. Oh, there he is. It's so great to have you in New York." She was shouting over the hubbub of the crowd. "I'm seeing you tomorrow, right?" The crowd swirled her away and just as Elliot came over to take Yarrow's arm to introduce her to some people, she spotted Palmer Truitt with the playwright in a dim corner of the room. Palmer had just made a gesture that shocked Yarrow, yet it was so innocent: He had raised his hand to take a feather off the playwright's lapel. The man must be right about me, thought Yarrow. "Do you know your friend thinks I'm homophobic?"

"Well, aren't you?" he said.

"No!" Then they were in another group and at some later stage, Elliot looked at her and said, "Had enough?" She nodded and they left within minutes, just melted out of the crowd without saying good-bye.

"What's it to be," he asked, "my place or yours?"

"You know damn well it's going to be yours."

"You're a woman after my own heart," he said. "Desirable, intelligent and extremely sensible."

"Providing I do what you want."

"Of course."

"What if I didn't?"

"Why wouldn't you?"

She leaned her head against his shoulder. "Right now I can't imagine."

He made love to her as she had dreamed he would, and then they fell asleep. A siren woke her about two and with no more thought than just expressing her affection, she held him and stroked him and soon they made love again, a sweet sleepy joining in which all their limbs and lips were so relaxed they were as one. Sleep. A small noise. It was Elliot getting up. She looked at the clock, 5:20 A.M. She groaned and turned over and shut her eyes.

The distant noise of traffic honking woke her up. Elliot had gone, leaving a note under the clock beside the bed: "Sleep tight. See you at seven P.M. My place. Get the key from Lainie. Love, Elliot."

She put on his silk dressing gown. It smelled of him. She ordered some breakfast and decided to explore the apartment. It had only one bedroom, a study and a more formal room with *boiserie* cabinets on each side of a marble fireplace. All the tones throughout were muted browns. A door closed off the stairs to the office below. The bathroom was fitted out with cream-colored marble and mirrors. She looked at Elliot's razors and soaps. He liked to shave with a shaving brush, she remembered, working the soap up into suds. She thought it was old-fashioned, but there was much of him that was.

After breakfast Yarrow threw some fragrant bath salts into the deep tub and ran the hot water. She looked for a shower cap and opened some drawers and cupboards to find one. In a bottom drawer she found a cap and when she took it out she saw some cosmetics and her heart stopped. There was a vivid red lipstick, not the color she thought Blanchette would use. Yarrow's jealousy made her feel unworthy. She rummaged through the drawer and came across a small drawstring bag. She knew what it was before she opened it. It contained a woman's diaphragm, carefully talcumed and put away. Her heart rose to her mouth. All his talk about love. Oh, she was a fool. A fool to love him so completely. He didn't want that. He wanted her when it was convenient. There were obviously others, other women he had when she was not around. Yarrow threw the thing into the toilet with disgust and flushed it. Then she took the red lipstick and wrote on the mirror "NO!" The diaphragm bobbed up obscenely in the toilet bowl. Let him put his hand in and get rid of it, she thought.

She dressed and left, her heart thumping, halfway between fuming with anger and dissolving into tears. She put out the "Do Not Disturb" sign on the door as she used the upstairs exit. She wanted him to find it just the way it was when he came back.

Yarrow spent the day seeing the people she had to see. She was glad she was kept busy going from one appointment to another. She visited the *Post* and the *World-Telegram* and had lunch at the *New York Herald Tribune*. Then she caught a taxi to Greta's apartment and went up to see her.

Greta had stopped writing her column when Palmer took over the *Courier*.

"He doesn't want me to do anything," she said. She had taken up smoking. She puffed on a cigarette in a long holder.

"So what do you do with yourself?"

"Oh, I go to the hairdresser. I have my fingernails done. Do you know you can get a fungus under your false fingernails? I shop. I like to shop. Hey, how about a drink? It's nearly five o'clock."

"Greta."

"Yes?"

"Just a soft drink, thanks." Yarrow was worried. She remembered Greta's eyes last night. Her sister was drinking too much.

"How's Palmer?" she asked. Greta was shaking up a martini on the bar that stood to one side of the room.

"Great. He loves the paper." She concentrated on pouring her drink and carefully carried it over. Yarrow realized she had already had a few.

"We're going to the Bahamas this week."

"Just the two of you?"

"No—no—with some friends. Palmer has lots of friends."

"What about your friends? Darling? Greta, look at me. Who do you talk to? Do you have a friend?"

Greta's big eyes quivered and filled with tears. "No." She was like a big blond baby, thought Yarrow with exasperation.

"Yarrow, can I tell you something I've never told anyone else? You won't say anything?"

Yarrow nodded and waited. Greta took another drink.

"We don't have sex anymore. Not real sex. He—he only wants me to—to douche him. And then—he does it to me. That's not normal, is it?"

"Well, I guess anything is normal if you both want it. But you don't want it, do you?"

Greta began to cry. "He frightens me. He doesn't love me at all. It's as though I stand for something. It's not me he hates. It's us." Yarrow put her arms around her sister.

"For God's sake, leave him, Greta. Walk out. Get a divorce."

Greta sat up and pushed back her hair and wiped her eyes with her fingers. Her mascara had smeared. "Yes, yes, I guess I should." She stood up and looked in a mirror. "Why, just look at me and I have to get ready to go out."

Yarrow looked at her sister, the beauty of the family. Greta's face was smeared with mascara and she stank of booze. Yarrow could kill Palmer Truitt for doing this to her. Hadn't he done enough?

"Don't go. Let me stay with you."

"No. No. I'm fine really. He'll be home soon. Please don't be here when he comes. He knows you don't like him."

"Greta, if you're afraid . . ."

"Oh, no. He'd never hit me. Go. Go." Greta almost pushed her out. Yarrow walked through the busy, darkening streets, past the corner greengrocers with their fruit piled high on outside displays, past the lines of people standing at the check-outs of all-night delis and supermarkets, past the cars and buses and trucks rushing by. Yarrow thought about what she could do to help Greta. She felt so inadequate. Why did Greta stay with Palmer? She decided she would telephone Nellie. Nellie was close to Greta. Nellie was a nurse. Yarrow stopped abruptly in the street as the thought struck her. A taxi driver put his head out and screamed at her. Yarrow gave him an absentminded obscene gesture with her fingers. She felt she was becoming a New Yorker. Damn Nellie, thought Yarrow, she started all this, with her games when they were children. Douching little Palmer. Could that be possible? It would be funny if Greta weren't so frightened.

Yarrow walked to the hotel and picked up her key at the front desk. There were some messages for her. Most were from her office, one confirming tomorrow's appointment on Long Island, several from Elliot. He had called every five minutes since seven o'clock. She went up to her room and kicked off her shoes and switched on the television set. What she saw was a ten-second shot of Elliot speaking at a luncheon of Americans for Democratic Action. She switched off the television in a fury. There was no getting away from him. The phone rang and it was he, and she hung up. She decided to have dinner downstairs in the hotel restaurant rather than be pestered by him.

She was walking through the Palm Court when she saw him. Rather, he saw her. She turned away but he grabbed her arm.

"Yarrow, please. Let me explain."

"Leave me alone. I'm going to have dinner." Their voices were both very calm and polite. They were not the kind of people who made scenes.

"Darling, don't do this. Those things—I don't know how long they've been there—you have every right to be angry, but you could give me a chance to explain."

"There is nothing to explain."

"There is, there is everything to explain. I love you." He held her arm very tight. A woman going past tittered and smiled at them. Yarrow walked through the revolving doors of the hotel and went down the stairs. She wanted to run but her leg wasn't strong enough. A line of horses and carriages used mostly by tourists, stood waiting for customers on Fifty-ninth Street. Yarrow went to the first one and got in. "Through the park," she said. Elliot jumped up beside her. They were silent as the carriage lunged forward and then steadied to a walking gait. The woman driver flicked her whip once or twice and settled her head into her shoulders as they turned into the park. The plastic seat covering was cracked and a few plastic carnations in a small vase decorated the front of the carriage. There was a smell of horse manure, not unpleasant, and young buds and leaves were coming out on the dark trees around them. It was suddenly like being in the country.

Elliot let out a deep sigh. Yarrow glanced at him out of the corner of her eye. He was deep in thought, a frown, or at least a look of resignation, had settled across his face. The dark, heavy brows were lowered, and in the darkness she could only see his face now and then when the carriage crossed a pool of lamplight.

"What can I say," he said, "except that I'm sorry. I had no idea anything of—anything was there of another woman's. I didn't think you'd go looking through those drawers."

Yarrow was ashamed. "I shouldn't have. It was wrong of me. I was—I was just so damn hurt, that's all. I just feel so insecure about you."

"Oh, Yarrow. If only you knew." He hesitated and then kissed her and she melted in his arms. "Please, darling," he said, "don't ever let this happen again. If you think I've neglected you or hurt you, talk to me about it. Don't just go off like that."

"I'm sorry."

"I thought I'd lost you." They held each other, and then when they reached the Upper East Side, where the carriage would turn and roll back down Fifth Avenue, he paid the driver and they got off and walked toward his hotel. They had their arms around each other and he began to laugh. It started slowly at first, and then it caught him, so he had to stop and laugh till the tears came to his eyes.

"What's so funny?" she asked and then she began to laugh, too.

"That goddam diaphragm," he said, "I keep seeing it floating in the john."

CHAPTER 26

THE CONTRAST BETWEEN HER TIME IN NEW YORK AND HER LIFE back in Platte City made Yarrow restless on her return. She told the children all about Central Park and the horses and carriages she would take them on one day. They asked about John, and she told them, more gaily than she really felt, that John was enjoying his new school on the West Side and going to sports events with his father. She told them about the restaurants and the parties and the Broadway show she had seen. What she couldn't convey to them was the vitality of the city, the surge of adrenaline it always gave her. Platte City was very dull by comparison. She heard soon after her return that her bid for the radio station on Long Island had been rejected. Palmer Truitt was the successful bidder. It depressed Yarrow more than she would admit. She had thought that perhaps the radio station would be a way for her to be in New York more often. She had even discussed with Elliot the possibility of moving to New York. He had been thrilled with the idea. He could not get to Colorado as often as he wanted to see her.

At work, Yarrow missed the day-to-day involvement in editorial decisions. She sat in on some of Ned's meetings and knew he was in complete control. She was afraid that if she interfered too much she would undermine Ned's authority. So she drew back purposely from making some decisions and let her staff work out the problems. She knew it was time for her life to move on, but where and in what direction she did not know. All she knew was that she was ready for a change.

One bit of excitement happened before the end of the year. Ned was running a story about a case against a local attorney, Q. B. Shield, whom Yarrow knew socially. The judge in the case was a woman called Skolly. The *Journal* had once attacked the judge for being too lenient with offenders. A disciplinary action was taken against Shield, and he fought back by saying he would file a petition with the Supreme Court.

Yarrow was at her desk when Miss Hines came in and said there was a man outside who would not give his name but had something he could only hand to Miss McLean personally. Yarrow was intrigued, her old reportorial senses alerted. The man handed Yarrow an envelope. Inside was a copy of the petition to be filed. Yarrow gave it to Ned to use, and the next day after its publication she was subpoenaed to appear in court.

Judge Skolly, who brooked no nonsense in her court, asked Yarrow to divulge the name of the person who had given her the petition. Yarrow refused, invoking the First Amendment. Judge Skolly immediately sentenced her to a thirty-day jail term. Yarrow's lawyer, the ubiquitous Mr. Pierson, leaned over and whispered to her, "What do you want me to do? I can ask for a stay to be granted and you could be placed under a bond."

"How much?" said Yarrow. "She's a . . ."

"Careful, she can slap another sentence or fine on us."

"Yes, and I'll bet she can lip-read."

"I would guess five hundred to one thousand dollars."

"OK."

Pierson got up. "I humbly ask the court for a ten-day stay on Miss McLean's sentence, and that Miss McLean be placed under a bond."

The judge said, "In view of the leniency of this court, of which Miss McLean is well aware, I grant a ten-day stay on the sentence and post a bond of five thousand dollars."

"What?" Yarrow was outraged. "I won't pay. Come on, Pierson, tell her I'd rather go to jail."

Yarrow was taken out of court. While she was being fingerprinted, she said, "Now, Pierson, don't you dare pay this bond." She watched her fingers being rolled over the sticky black ink. "It's a good story for tomorrow's paper. PUBLISHER INVOKES FIRST. Can I use the telephone?"

Yarrow was put into a cell overnight. It wasn't too bad, except it stank of urine. A drunk was put into the next cell and made a terrific racket and crooned Irish songs to her until he fell asleep. Freya came to see her.

"Why do you have to be so stubborn?" she said. "Mr. Pierson says if the bond was paid you'd be out now."

"Skolly is a witch. I won't come out of this badly, Mama, she will. Don't pay it. Now come on, kiss me and tell me how the children are taking it."

"Lily burst into tears and said all her friends called to tell her her mother was a jailbird."

"Did you explain to her why I'm here?"

"I've tried but I'd rather you did it. We've even had a television camera crew at the house. You're on national television, Yarrow; that impressed Buck. And Sandy rang from New York and wants an exclusive interview."

"What a nerve! I wouldn't give an interview to the *Courier* if it was the last newspaper in the country."

Yarrow was preparing to spend her second night when a guard came along with a big grin on his face and let her out.

"What's this?" she asked.

"Your bond's been paid."

Yarrow groaned. "And I'll bet I know who did it."

She went to the office, where to her surprise she was met by some out-of-town reporters and a camera crew from one of the networks. It gave her a funny feeling to be on the other side for a change. She realized it was much more difficult to answer questions than to ask them. She kept reiterating the same sentence, "I felt there was a principle involved."

When she had typed up her own statement for Ned to use in the paper, she asked Miss Hines to get Elliot on the phone.

"OK, you wise guy. Why did you pay that bond? I don't need you picking up the pieces for me like some personal guardian angel."

He laughed.

"I didn't realize you were enjoying it so much. I would have left you there."

"I wanted to show that old buzzard up for what she was"—she searched for the words—"a—vindictive liberal."

Elliot laughed again and then he grew serious.

"I wasn't going to have my woman in jail."

"I know you were worrying about me and I do thank you."

"I miss you. Can't you get away? Can't you steal a day for me?"

She flicked through her diary. "What about you? Can't you

come here? I want to be with you but I hate taking any more time away from the children.''

"What about after Christmas? Blanchette's taking Meredith to England to visit my sister, Vivienne. Why don't you and the children spend spring vacation with me?''

"All of us? In New York?''

"No. We'll go somewhere warm. Jamaica.''

They met Elliot and John at the airport in New York. Sandy brought John, and they waited, talking to Elliot, until the plane came in from Denver. Sandy had accepted Elliot's place in Yarrow's life. In fact he admired Elliot's success and followed his career with more than casual interest.

The children were excited. Even John's sullenness seemed to have lifted. They flew to Kingston and then transferred to a flight to Montego Bay. They would spend one night in the hotel and then drive along the north coast to a house they had rented right on the sea. Buck kept repeating, "right on the sea,'' as though it were a phrase that held a magic charm.

Montego Bay was in total darkness when they arrived since the whole town had a power shortage. Their car driver giggled as he drove them up to their hotel. They were met by the hotel staff holding candles, and the children and Yarrow were enchanted. They ate on the balcony of their room overlooking the bay; they could not see it, but they could feel the soft, scented Caribbean breeze blowing off the water. The children were asleep the moment their heads hit their pillows, and Yarrow fell into Elliot's arms as softly as a frangipani blossom falls to the ground.

The first week was blissful. While Elliot worked on the telephone, Yarrow would take the children and walk along the beach hunting for seashells. She couldn't swim; she had never got over her fear of drowning, but she engaged the housekeeper's son, a big strong boy called Billy, six feet two and nineteen years old, to teach Buck. She sat on the shore under a big straw hat and tried to hide her anxiety while the three children and Billy frolicked like dolphins in the sea. They bought fish early in the morning from the fishermen who hauled their nets up on the beach. Buck got covered with a rash at one stage from a branch he had been poking into crab holes in the sand. The Mercurochrome with which she covered his whole body made him look even worse. Elliot took John out snorkeling on the reef. Elliot didn't fuss over John's moodiness, and the boy came to respect him grudgingly, though he could never admit it.

Lily sat on the beach with her mother. She was a very

feminine young girl, but her ideas were so entrenchedly old-fashioned that Yarrow wondered where she had gone wrong. Lily's hair was almost white and very fine; her face, broad at the brow like Sandy's, had grown heart-shaped. She had her father's blue eyes and her mother's eyebrows. She was twelve years old, and already small mounds of breasts had appeared and a few long hairs grew under her arms. Yarrow wondered when her period would start.

"Do you love Elliot?"

Yarrow put down her book. She had been waiting for this, too. She wanted to be completely honest and wondered how honest she could be.

"Yes, I do."

"He's married."

"Yes, Lily, he is."

"So you're living in sin, then."

"Where did you hear that phrase?"

"It's all the girls talk about at school. Lana Turner's daughter stabbed her mother's lover to death."

"I don't think Elliot is anything like Johnny whatsisname."

"Stompanato. No. I like Elliot, I really do. But I'd rather you were married." She dug with some shells in the sand.

"I would like it, too, darling."

"Then why doesn't he divorce his wife and marry you?"

"Well—he also has a little girl, about Buck's age. Besides, what does a piece of paper mean? I know this is hard to understand, Lily, but sometimes I feel I am married to Elliot. Even if he did divorce Blanchette, I wouldn't feel any more confident that I was his and he was mine." Yarrow paused; she tried to examine what she was saying. Is it true, what I just said? Does it not bother me? "Lily, one day you'll fall in love and you'll get married and you'll be happier than your dad and I were. I didn't have that luck."

"You're his mistress."

"I'd rather you didn't use that word."

Lily seemed to get bored with the conversation. "Mom, could I have my ears pierced? All my friends have their ears pierced."

"When you're older."

"How older?"

Yarrow picked up her book again. "Oh, when you get your period, I suppose."

When Elliot came in from the sea with John, their shoulders were burned. Even Elliot's deep tan couldn't fight the fierce Jamaican sun. She didn't tell Elliot about her conversation with

Lily. She didn't know if she had handled it properly or not. She did not want to be a hypocrite; neither did she wish to bring up her children thinking she was a woman of loose morals. But in most people's eyes she would be considered that. And yet she loved Elliot Weyden, as purely and monogamously as if they were indeed married. His own marriage was a sham, an edifice to protect his daughter. *This* was his marriage, this relationship with her. She watched him walking along the beach with John. Elliot's skin had darkened like an Indian's. His chest was thick, it had broadened with age. He was still slim in the hips, his stomach was flat. But she knew she would still love him when all that went. Thank God, she had this time, this gift of time with him, to cherish him and know him and love him. She would take any crumb that fell off Blanchette's table.

Elliot came up to her. "Billy's taking the children to visit an old sugar plantation. I've given him the keys to the car." He put out his hand to pull her up. "We have all afternoon to ourselves."

"I've been planning this all week," he said, taking her into their cool bedroom with its marble floors and the big old tropical fan that whirred quietly above the bed. "I love your children but they do inhibit me."

"I hadn't noticed."

He laughed, pulling off her bathing suit, and they fell like teenagers onto the big bed. The untanned areas of their bodies made them look as though they were still partly dressed. He made love to her so expertly that she came well before he did. He winced when she touched his shoulders, so she got up and gently rubbed some cream on, and then he thought that was rather nice and she rubbed some cream on the ribs of his back and then down his spine and around and around on his taut, white buttocks. Then he turned over and she was able to take him in her mouth, and she imagined that her teeth were like the little pads of a centipede moving along a thick, smooth branch. And the centipede came to a smooth, round knob with a slit and the centipede became a tongue that explored the slit and the length of the branch and its root. And all the time the tree it grew from trembled and groaned until at last it could no longer take the centipede-tongue and erupted so fiercely that its sap exploded from the branch and the branch withered away and died.

"You are a wicked, wicked woman," he said, cradling her lovingly.

"You've made me wanton," she said. "You know, we've never made love outside?"

"We tried it once, remember, above Lake Powell?" Yarrow

laughed. They had tried to push the bed in their hotel room through the sliding doors onto a balcony. Yarrow had wanted to make love under the moon. They had given the bed one last heave and it had crashed through the thin wooden railings and ended up in a ravine below.

"How could I forget," she said. "I never knew how you explained that to the hotel manager."

"I didn't. We left a check and sneaked away in the middle of the night."

When the children came back, Elliot and Yarrow were sitting in the garden chairs under a tree on the beach. Yarrow had put on a caftan. She had told Elliot her body was so swollen from lovemaking that she couldn't bear any kind of pressure between her legs. He kept glancing at her from his papers as though he couldn't concentrate.

"Mommy," said John, "Aunt Greta's staying at the hotel down the road. We saw her at the plantation. She's asked us for dinner one night."

Yarrow sighed. "I'll have to telephone," she said. The last thing she wanted was Greta and Palmer's unhappiness to sully her pleasure.

"I'll do it," said Elliot. "I'll be stronger than you." Yarrow listened to him on the telephone. "Yes," she heard him say, "tomorrow night, fine." He looked at her sheepishly. "I'm sorry, I couldn't get out of it."

That night, when the children had gone to bed and they had put out their own lights, Elliot told her to come with him. She was about to pick up her robe—for, being lovers, they slept naked—when he said, "No, come as you are." He took her hand and they stepped out of the door into the garden and over the creeping roots of couch grass that grew in the sand, under the tree onto the beach. He had brought a towel and he laid it down and the moon came out and they joined together as two silver fish would in the sea. Yarrow had never felt as free, nor, paradoxically, as bound, as she did then to the man with her.

Billy took them in a boat to a cavern where the locals swam. They walked into a cave over rocks made soft and slimy by the chemicals in the water. The water was green and silky. They all went in except Yarrow, and they held their hands in a chain and dived down under a rock ledge to an interior cavern. Yarrow could hear them whooping and hollering at her from the secret place, their voices echoing all around her. When they came back, Billy put some salt on the leeches they had picked up, and the leeches shriveled and dropped off.

"Leeches are hermaphroditic," said Lily, showing off.

"How do you know?" said John. He hated his sister when she thought she knew everything.

"Because we studied them at school," she said.

"Does that come from Hermes and Aphrodite?" asked Yarrow.

"I suppose it does," said Elliot, and whispered to her, "What a waste."

All good things come to an end, and the next night, their last night on the island, was to be spent with Greta and Palmer. They ate outside on a terrace that hung over the sea, and a Jamaican band played calypso music and ballads and people danced under the colored lights that were strung across the dance floor like a fairy web. They were a handsome group—Greta with her chic, blond New York look, Palmer, a pretty man rather than a handsome one; Elliot, trim, muscular, with a face that made women turn around; and Yarrow with her black hair down and pinned to one side with a yellow hibiscus. Yarrow excused the children, who went to sit near the band and ordered fruit drinks decorated with pineapple chunks and little paper umbrellas.

Greta was very drunk.

"You know we been here five days an' this is the first time Palmer's with me? Where you been Palmer boy?"

"Oh, shut up, Greta."

"Greta," said Yarrow, "why don't you let me take you upstairs?"

"Why? What's the matter?"

"Greta, you've had too much to drink. Come on." Yarrow got up and put her arm under Greta's arm. Greta wouldn't move. Elliot got annoyed.

"Palmer, take your wife upstairs."

"Stay out of this, Elliot," said Palmer. He turned to Greta. "Go away, you lush." Greta staggered to her feet.

"You wanna go up and play water games, darlin'?"

Palmer got up and, before anyone could stop him, he punched Greta in the face. Greta staggered back. The other diners looked on, horrified. The band lost its place in the music. Palmer drew his arm back to hit Greta again, but Elliot lunged forward and flattened him with a punch that threw him five feet backward. Palmer sprawled over an adjoining table with blood spurting from his nose. Two waiters rushed up and grabbed him.

"I apologize for this disturbance," said Elliot to the diners, whose food had been scattered. "I'll pay for any damages. Yarrow, get the children. Greta, you're coming with us." He picked Greta up in his arms. She was a sobbing mess with a closed black eye and a split lip. Yarrow and the children followed him out. None of them looked at Palmer. But he looked at them. An ugly sneer crossed his pretty features. He threw off the restraining hands that held him. He picked up a napkin and dabbed at his nose.

"Bastard," he said. "I'll get him."

CHAPTER 27

YARROW CAME STRAIGHT BACK INTO A STRIKE AT THE PLATTE CITY *Journal*. It was the first one she'd had since she took over the paper. There was no love lost between management and unions, but neither had she thought there was a great deal of animosity.

It was a Thursday, the day in Platte City when the *Journal* carried most of its retail ads. Most people received their paychecks on Fridays and the food stores advertised their specials the day before.

Ned Griffin called over a copy boy. "Take this in to the foreman." It was a report from the courthouse of a murder trial.

Ned sipped his coffee and went on marking proofs. They were running up to press time.

"He won't do it, Mr. Griffin."

Ned looked at the copy boy.

"What do you mean he won't do it?" He grabbed the copy from the boy and strode into the composing room. He went straight to the foreman, Joe Bellini. He and Joe were wary of each other. Bellini was younger; he was a printer who talked tough and looked after his men.

"What is this, Joe?"

"There's no one free to print it."

Ned looked around the room at the men at various stages of composing the paper.

"Who are these guys?" He walked up to one man in blue overalls casting a line on the Linotype. "What about him?"

"He's going on his lunch break."

Ned went to the next man in line. He was an apprentice printer, a young lad whom Ned wished had come into the management side of the business. "Hello, Mr. Griffin," the boy said.

"What about this lad, is he on lunch break, too?"

"Yes, he is, Mr. Editor. So's the next guy if you want to go down the line."

"I want to get this damn paper printed, and I want someone here to print it. Are you telling me you won't let them print it?"

"Are you telling me these men should go without lunch?"

"Yes, goddam it, they can postpone their lunch break and get this work done."

Bellini folded his arms across his belly. "We'll have a chapel meeting about this. This is our turf and my men are entitled to have their lunch."

Ned swore under his breath. "You don't have any grievance here Joe."

"We do now. You have no jurisdiction in here. I'm calling a meeting now." He turned on his heel and the word went down the line and across the room in a matter of seconds. The noise stopped and the men trooped out after the foreman. The silence was eerie after the clickety-clack of the machines and the activity around the stone. Ned glanced at the clock. They had missed their edition now. He went back to his desk and called Yarrow.

Thirty minutes later Joe Bellini made a formal complaint to management about the incident. It was unfair, he said, and not part of their agreement that men should have to postpone their lunch break. The men were unanimous in their vote and refused to do the work.

"We are perfectly within our rights to ask you to do this, Mr. Bellini," said Yarrow. " 'Chapel meetings are not to be held at such times as they will delay an edition.' Those are rules that are also part of our agreement."

"I can't force the men to work."

"Then, Mr. Bellini, you are discharged."

Bellini left Yarrow's office. She waited tensely by the telephone. In five minutes Ned called her. "The printers have walked out. They're on strike." Yarrow went out through the editorial floor. People were gathered in small knots around their desks.

Yarrow felt sick to her stomach. "Make sure all the doors are locked," she told Miss Hines, following along behind her. "We'll need more security to protect the machinery. Please arrange it."

She wouldn't leave the office while the printers were on strike. Some of the others wouldn't cross the picket line. She understood that and told Ned to forget about trying to put out the next day's edition. She made up a cot for herself in her office and had food brought in. The first night, a brick was thrown through a lower window. She felt her heart jump in her mouth when she heard the glass shatter. She ordered another guard to patrol the machine room. When the staff changeover came in for the *Sunday Journal*, she waited to hear what would happen. The Newspaper Guild, which seldom supported the printers, decided to work. The mailers went out in sympathy with the strikers.

Larry Schaeffer of the *Globe* telephoned. His printers were threatening to go out in support of their colleagues at the *Journal*. Larry Schaeffer said the *Globe* had had a number of skirmishes and slowdowns this year. The printers were very "antsy," he said.

"It's all so stupid and senseless—we asked three printers to postpone their lunch break."

"Then call it off," said Schaeffer. "None of us can afford this."

"I hate to give in to them," said Yarrow.

"We all do. But they've got the power—we don't control our papers anymore."

Yarrow thought it over. What Schaeffer said was right. Trying to run the newspaper these days was like trying to run something with your hands tied behind your back. She hated to lose face, but this time it was not worth the fight. She called Ned and told him she was going to reinstate Joe Bellini. Ned didn't want her to do it, but Yarrow persisted. The word went out and in twenty-four hours, the *Journal* was back on the street.

But the incident left a bad taste in Yarrow's mouth. Ned was surly because she hadn't supported him. But she couldn't—in this war she had to pick which battles she was going to win and which ones she could afford to lose.

The rest of the year slid by quickly and without trouble, and then suddenly in December Elliot called Yarrow with the news she had been waiting for.

"There's a paper for sale in New York. Are you interested?"

"Which one? How much?"

"Why don't you fly here? I'll arrange for you to meet the owner."

The paper for sale was the *New York Telegraph*. Elliot took Yarrow and the owner, Burt Reamington, to lunch. Reamington was one of the Philadelphia Reamington's who owned the *Philadelphia Bugle*.

The *Telegraph*, along with the other major daily newspapers in New York, had been struck by the newspaper mail and deliverers' union.

"We are now in the second week of this strike," said Reamington, "and I don't think I can open again. You know what this thing is costing me? Do you know that eighteen newspapers closed permanently last year in the United States? Eighteen. This year may be worse. I don't want to be a statistic. Miss McLean, we're not the *Times*, we're a marginal paper, we can't take strikes. I can't afford to keep the paper open and I can't afford to close the paper down."

"What do you mean?"

"I mean that the Newspaper Guild has severance pay contracts." The guild, which employed the journalists and clerical workers, had become the dominant union in newspaper negotiations. The ITU, Albert Hinton's union, had been trying to wrest its power back for years. Reamington wiped his brow. "It would cost me too much to close down."

"How much?"

"One or two dollars."

It took Yarrow a second to realize he meant one or two million dollars.

"Money I haven't got," he went on.

"Neither have I," said Yarrow, wondering what she had gotten into.

"What Burt is suggesting, Yarrow, is that you would take over his debts. His creditors would become your creditors and Burt can walk away," said Elliot.

"Somethin' like that. Of course, there's the plant and our goodwill. They're worth something. But, sure, what I need is a signature that someone is going to take over."

Yarrow made a mental note to herself that if she didn't get the voting stock for nothing, she would walk away from the deal.

They went down to The *Telegraph* office on South Street after lunch. Reamington took her through the plant, and she asked him questions all the time. He sweated though the empty floors and up the stairs in front of her. They went through the composing room with its rows of Linotype machines and past the stone, a series of metal trolleys like so many tall, empty tea carts, on which the pages were made up. They went through the two-story pressroom with its lines of Goss presses and catwalks of ink-stained perforated iron. On the lower level, she stepped over the rails which men used to push the heavy reels of paper onto the machines. She looked at the number of reels stacked in the back and asked Reamington about those, too; how many did he have in stock, how many ordered that still had to be paid for? She looked at the giant bins of wastepaper and reel cores, and tried to judge the amount of waste. She looked at the stereo room, where the plates were made, and at the photographic equipment. There was a big old camera, its bellows the size of a coffin, that was still used to magnify or reduce photographs. Reamington didn't know how old it was. He took her through the editorial floor, which looked like any other editorial floor of a newspaper office with its utilitarian desks and chairs and typewriters and telephones, and upstairs to the executive suite, a long, thin corridor with doors leading to offices on either side. They even looked in the gentlemen's john and in the ladies' washroom.

After they had been through the whole establishment, Yarrow asked Reamington to send her his figures. He promised they would be at her hotel that night. Yarrow said she would call him in the morning.

"What do you think?" she asked Elliot as they got in the car.

"Don't touch it," he said. "I had no idea the paper was in so much debt."

Elliot had to go to Wall Street, so they swung south on the Drive, and she dropped him off first and went to her hotel, deep in thought.

It was a tremendous risk. The building she had seen was old. It was a converted warehouse, and there were damp courses along the lower walls. She found out later that when the river rose after the rain, the basement always flooded. The whole newspaper industry was in strife right across the country. Strikes were the norm at newspapers these days; there was nothing resembling arbitration. The old bugbears of the ITU were still there, too—forget about the guild for a minute, forget about the deliverers—the ITU still argued about their area of jurisdiction and that old headache, the resetting of local ads that had already been completed. "Wasteful practices." She could hear her father saying it now. And then there were the demographics of New York; eight papers vied for readers in a city that saw its middle class increasingly fleeing to the suburbs. The effect was exacerbated by television.

But Yarrow wanted a foot in New York. There might not be another opportunity. She could only buy a newspaper that was in trouble. She did not have the capital to buy a healthier one, or, heaven be praised, buy a monopoly newspaper in another city.

The *Platte City Journal-Record* was a monopoly and it was going to have to pay for the *Telegraph*. How much could she let one bleed for the other?

She telephoned her accountant in Platte City to fly in first thing in the morning, and then asked Pierson if he would come also and advise her. Elliot said there were plenty of good lawyers and accountants in New York, but Yarrow wanted people around whom she knew and could trust.

When they went over the figures with her the next day, they both gave her the same advice—don't touch it. "It's a money pit," said Pierson. Yarrow thanked them and they went off to have lunch, shaking their heads.

Yarrow sat in her hotel room for a long time, thinking. Then she called Elliot.

"I want the voting stock for nothing. I don't care what Reamington bandies about—he can say I paid whatever he likes—I won't comment on it."

"Are you sure you want it, Yarrow?"

"Yes, I'm sure."

He hung up, and half an hour later, when she was getting out of the shower, he called her back.

"You've got a deal," he said. "I don't know whether to say congratulations or commiserations."

"Elliot, be nice."

That night about six o'clock, she, Elliot, Pierson and her accountant went to Reamington's apartment. It was all very friendly and merry, though Pierson looked as though he had a permanent toothache. Reamington had some champagne on ice, and when Yarrow signed the papers presented by Reamington's lawyers, he popped the cork and she was the new owner of the *New York Telegraph*. Reamington received a call from his office. He handed over the phone to Yarrow. "It's all yours," he said. The caller said the strike of the mailers and deliverers was over. Yarrow took it as a good omen.

It was an exhilarating feeling. It had begun to snow outside, but she couldn't sit in a car. She was too excited. She and Elliot walked to his hotel. She was bubbling with more than champagne. She was full of ideas. It was all a matter of perspective. She could make economies. She could improve the paper—God could she improve it—but the editor might have to go. If that happened, she would bring Ned in from Platte City. He would jump at the opportunity. She would make Paddy editor of the *Journal*, he was ready for it now. Oh, she had so many plans.

She looked along the streets at the steam rising up from the manholes, cars and buses snaked around eight-foot-tall red-and-white-striped tubes, also emitting steam. It was as though they were vents from some underground hell. As a child she had thought of gold and silver lying under the cobblestones of Platte City; now she wondered what alchemy was taking place beneath her feet in this one. She looked at the looming shapes of the apartment houses and the skyline of tall, jagged buildings; lights lit every window, thousands and thousands of them. She looked at the people hurrying along the sidewalks, jumping over backed-up water at the curbsides; thousands of people, people of all races, shapes and sizes. And every one a potential reader, she thought. How could anyone not love this sight, not be excited by it? And now she, Yarrow McLean, the little girl from Platte City, Colorado—Yarrow McLean owned a part of it.

It took Yarrow a few weeks to organize the move to New York. First she had to tell Freya and Miss Hines and the children.

"Mama, how would you feel about moving to New York?"

"Well, for heaven's sakes, Yarrow. Is that what you've been up to?"

"Mama, I can't tell you how exciting it is." Her mother was sewing a pair of Buck's pants in a seat near the window where the light was good. Yarrow squatted down beside her. "It's an opportunity to move our business into something much bigger, more important." Freya bit a thread off with her teeth. She had put on the weight she had lost when she was ill. Her legs swelled now, but her face still had the softness and the fine skin it had when she was a girl and James had fallen in love with her. Her gray hair was short and her wide cheekbones shone with health.

"Why not?" she said. "It sounds like an adventure. Besides, I take it you're going anyway and what would I do here without my kids to look after?" Yarrow hugged her.

"Thank you, Mama. None of this would be possible without you."

"Go on," said her mother, picking up a shirt that needed a button. "What does Buck do to his clothes?"

Buck thought New York sounded exciting, too. He drew pictures of skyscrapers and cars and people and stuck them up in his room. He was always drawing; he was observant, a gentle boy who cared for animals and wildlife. His room resembled and smelled like an animal laboratory. "Can I take my white mice?"

Yarrow sighed. "I guess so."

"Then I'll come."

Lily was another matter altogether.

"But my friends," she cried, "I'll have no friends there. Who wants to live in a dirty old city anyway? What about my ballet?"

"You can take lessons there."

Lily was crying. "You're so insensitive, Mommy. It's all right for you. You'll have Elliot there. I'll have no one." She ran dramatically from the room and thundered up the stairs.

At the office, Yarrow asked Miss Hines to come with her to New York. Miss Hines was torn about leaving.

"I can't, but I'll miss you," she said.

"I wish you would reconsider. I do need you there. I would help you with an apartment."

"Thank you. I—I need to stay here. Platte City is my home. Anyway, I'll be able to help Ned run this place when you've gone. I'm the only one who knows where the nuts and bolts are kept."

"I know why you have to stay—but I don't know what I'll do without you."

The telephone rang. It was Lily calling from school.

"Mommy, I can have my ears pierced now."

"What? Lily, please, is this a joke? That's not important enough to cut a class."

Lily's voice lowered and she said slowly once again, "Mommy, I can get my ears pierced now. Remember? In Jamaica?"

Yarrow racked her memory, and then she realized what Lily was saying. Her daughter had become a woman.

"Darling, you mean . . . ?"

"Yes! But I can't talk, you know?"

"Are you OK?"

"I just had to tell you. I love you, Mommy."

"I love you, too."

"It's OK about New York."

"Lily, I know you're going to love it."

Miss Hines stepped out of the office a few minutes after Yarrow. She never left before her boss did. Tall and slim in a blue hat and coat, she had been in her mid-twenties that day when she had first met Yarrow and picked her up and sat her on her desk. Miss Hines was now in her mid-fifties. She had never married and her life was the office. She drove her car to a small, neat brick house where she had moved with her father when she came to work for Yarrow.

Her cat met her at the door.

"Hello, Prince," she said.

"Is that you, Ariel?"

"Yes, it's me, Dad." She went into the darkened sitting room. He never noticed when it got dark. She pulled on the little knob of a reading lamp.

"Did you have a good day?" she asked.

"Yep. Mrs. Reeves came over and sat with me for lunch. We listened to that new radio show, oh, I forget what it's called, a variety show, a really nice girl singing, Patti Page."

"That's nice, Dad. What do you want for dinner?"

He got up. He was as tall as she was, his hair the same kind of white, the nose the same shape. It was as though their heads had been cut out with the same cookie cutter.

"I've peeled the potatoes," he said as he walked into the kitchen. He walked with no hesitancy. He never bumped into anything as long as everything was placed in the same position. It had taken him a while to adjust when they left Denver to come south. She couldn't move him again.

"How was your day?"

"Fine. Miss McLean is going to live in New York. She asked me to go with her."

Her father's hands were moving over the pots. There was no hesitation in them. He salted the potatoes and put them on to boil.

"Of course I said no." Her father turned toward her voice. His sightless blue eyes looked past her shoulders.

"I'm sorry, Ariel. Perhaps, perhaps I could manage on my own."

"Oh, don't be silly." She patted him on the arm. "Go on, put on some music and I'll join you in a minute."

He nodded and went out. "I've set up the trays," he said.

"Yes, I see that. Thanks."

Prince jumped into her arms.

"Did you miss me today, too?" she said into the soft fur. Prince purred. Miss Hines let him drop to the ground. He stalked off offended, with his tail in the air.

Miss Hines blew her nose and then opened the back door to let the cat out, and stood outside. It was cool and damp. It would soon be Christmas. She would have to buy a tree, and then there was the turkey, and the cranberry recipe that her father liked. She called for Prince but he didn't appear, so she went inside and washed her hands and got out a pencil and began to make a list.

CHAPTER 28

*I*N FEBRUARY YARROW FLEW WITH HER MOTHER AND THE CHILDREN
to New York. There was a snowstorm in Denver, which
delayed their departure by three hours, so it was not until the
early hours of the morning that they arrived at Greta's apartment.
They would stay with her until Yarrow found a place of their
own.

"I thought we could live in a big hotel," said Buck, "and
order room service."

"That's exactly why we're not," said Yarrow. "Greta has an
apartment with a huge window that lets in all the light. We're
going to have to camp there for a few days."

"Camp? Inside?" said Lily.

"Why are you both acting so spoiled?" said Yarrow. "You're
lucky we're going to stay with Greta at all."

Greta had set up a bed for Freya and Yarrow, and the children's sleeping bags were placed in the corner of the room where
they would not be in the way.

"You look marvelous," said Yarrow to her sister when the
children had rolled into balls, asleep on the floor, and Freya was
reading in her bed against the far wall. They were drinking
camomile tea at the table near the window.

"I'm going to AA," said Greta. Her eyes were clear and her
skin had lost its coarseness. "I haven't seen Palmer since—since
Jamaica. We communicate through lawyers. He's getting married again. Can you imagine? He was two-timing me all along.
Anyway, I've fallen in love."

"Greta! Who with?"

"Oh, no one you would know. I met him at one of our
meetings. He's an alcoholic, too. Silly big Greta, yes?"

Yarrow leaned over and kissed her. "No, big-hearted Greta.
Now, tell me, what's the plan for tomorrow? I have to find a
place to live so you can get your own room back."

"Oh, I like this," said Greta, looking around the one huge
studio room with the extra beds and sleeping bags on the floor.

"It's like camping used to be with Mama, remember? But I've lined up a few things for you to see. I didn't know whether you wanted to rent an apartment or a brownstone, so we can look at both."

"It depends on what fits—and what I can afford. I've stored the furniture until I have somewhere to put it."

"Did you sell the house?"

"Yes—to a young engineer and his family. They're building a dam outside the town. The air force academy has made the place boom."

"Were you sad to sell the house?"

"You know something? I wasn't. I felt I was taking all my family with me and that's what made it easy—and I can see more of John now."

The next day Yarrow and Greta went around Manhattan with a broker. They saw apartments and brownstones from the Upper East Side to the Village; they saw apartments that had not been cleaned since George Washington crossed the Hudson; they saw brownstones with so many latches and locks and iron bars on the windows that if Yarrow had lived in any of them it would have been like being in a prison. She was so depressed when she got back that night that even the children could sense it. Sandy came over later with John and took the children down to Luchow's for dinner. Freya and Greta went to a movie, and Yarrow went over to spend a few hours with Elliot.

"I want you to meet someone," he said. "This is my mother." A woman with fine features and Elliot's dark eyes came forward to greet Yarrow. She was very thin and her hands were small. She was dressed in lace and wore a necklace of colored stones so beautiful that the gems looked edible. She held Yarrow's hands for a minute, looked at them and then smiled.

"You have working hands," she said. "I like that."

Yarrow was immediately ashamed of her hands. She must have a manicure, she decided.

"I've been trying to get my mother to stop working for years, but she won't do it," said Elliot. "Any housekeeper she hires, she tells not to come in, she'd rather do it herself."

He gave Yarrow a drink and sat down beside her on the sofa.

"You exaggerate, Elliot," said Mrs. Weyden. "I get pleasure out of doing things myself." The phone rang in the next room and Elliot left to answer it.

"I went to England last year to stay with my daughter. Have you met Vivienne? You would like her." She sipped her mineral water and flashed a look at Yarrow that was very like Elliot's. "I know my son is in love with you, Miss McLean. It's very difficult, isn't it? He's a very honorable man and he's caught in this situation between you and Blanchette. But it's not really Blanchette. It's Meredith. Have you seen her?"

"No, we haven't met."

"Come here." Again, that glimpse of Elliot in her manner. "Sit beside me. She's a beautiful little girl and they have done wonders with her." She took out some photographs. A little doll, about five years old with blond hair and brown eyes, smiled out at Yarrow. On the upper lip were faint traces of scars and the nose was not quite symmetrical. "Blanchette wants to take her back to England to live. She's found a very good speech therapist in London. Blanchette is half English, you know. She still has family there."

A waiter came in wheeling a dinner cart. "Shall I set it up?" he asked.

"No, we can manage," answered Mrs. Weyden. When he had gone, she began placing things on the table near the window.

"Elliot doesn't want Blanchette to take Meredith away. He's heartbroken about it."

"I didn't know."

Mrs. Weyden put a vase with a rose in it in the center of the table.

"Elliot keeps a lot to himself."

"What do I keep to myself?" he asked, coming back into the room and filling it immediately with his male presence. "Sorry about that call. I've got about ten things happening tonight."

They had a pleasant dinner, and Yarrow enjoyed hearing Mrs. Weyden talk about Elliot as a small boy. It made him seem even more real to her if that were possible. Then Yarrow told Mrs. Weyden what Elliot had been like in Platte City when she had first met him.

"That was a sad time for all of us," said Mrs. Weyden.

"I can't remember it as being sad," said Yarrow. "It seemed to me to be a time when everyone helped each other. Money didn't seem to matter as much then. My father used to get paid in potatoes."

"You were fortunate," said Elliot. "You never went to sleep with your belly empty, wondering if you could find something to eat the next day."

"Is that what drives you?"

He laughed. "I don't know. It's probably more complex than that."

"It's past my bedtime," said Mrs. Weyden. "I must go

home." Her glance lingered over the table as though she longed to do the washing-up. She couldn't bear a mess. Elliot helped her up. "Don't worry about the dishes, Mother," he said. She sighed and shook Yarrow's hand. "You're very pretty," she said. "Very pretty." She patted Yarrow on the cheek.

Elliot took his mother down to the car. When he came back, he said, "She likes you."

He sat beside her on the sofa and took her in his arms. She kissed him as though it were the last thing she would ever be able to do for him. He was surprised by her intensity.

"What is it?"

She couldn't explain that seeing the photograph of his daughter had upset her. It had made her realize that other people had a call on him. She, Yarrow, had no rights over him. No matter how much she deluded herself, their love was not enough.

"Nothing, darling. I'm just tired. My leg aches. I've been all over town looking for a house."

He slipped off her shoe and began massaging her leg.

"What did you do today?" she asked.

He smiled, a secret smile, and then said, "I was approached by some people about the possibility of running for office."

"Elliot! You'd like to, wouldn't you?"

He bit his lower lip as he massaged her calf.

"I remember when I was in Washington assigned to General Marshall's staff, I loved the excitement, the camaraderie. I felt in my own way that I was being useful—that I was doing something of importance for my country. When the president declared war that day in the House—I never felt so proud or so alive."

"I saw you that day. You didn't see me. I was staying with Clara—remember, she promised never to vote for war?"

They were both silent, thinking of what was, what might have been, what would come.

"I called out to you, outside the chamber, afterward. You didn't hear me."

"Things might have been different."

"Yes." Yarrow looked at his dark eyes, which she knew so well but would never fully comprehend. But she understood now when the flicker of political ambition had been fanned.

"You want to run, don't you?" she said again. "And you want to run for president."

"I keep telling them there's not a hope in hell of me winning, but they're not convinced."

"Who's 'they'?"

"There are different factions within the Democratic party—each wants to support its own candidate. It's the way the system works—then the power groups fight it out."

"It's hardly democratic."

"Oh, yes, it is. The Republicans are no different. In my case, not having held office before, I need the support of the system."

"Ned Griffin says Willkie never held public office either, but he had the support of Henry Luce and his magazines."

"In spite of which, he didn't win."

"So you won't be supporting Adlai Stevenson again—you'll be running against him?"

"Stevenson says he is not going to run again."

"But the election's not till 1960—the end of next year."

"The preparation is interminable and I would have a lot to do. Anyway"—he patted her leg—"nothing may come of it. I'd be a rank outsider, a dark horse."

"A blackbird," she said, kissing him. The phone rang. She groaned. He loosened his tie as he went into the other room. She took this as a sign that he would be a long time. If he ran, she thought, there would be no role for her. Their relationship would compromise him. This realization had come over her like a bolt of lightning while he talked. He would have to leave her. How could she exist without him? Had he thought about that?

She fell asleep on the sofa and woke much later not knowing where she was. She looked in at him through the open door. His head was down in deep thought while he talked on the telephone. He did not see her. She tiptoed out and caught a taxi back to Greta's. They were all in bed. She called him on his private line.

"Hello?"

"Elliot."

"Where the hell are you? Just a minute." He left the other phone and came on the private line. "I thought you were still in the sitting room. I went in to check."

"I'm here, with Greta."

"I'm sorry. I—"

"Look. Don't. I'm very tired. I'll call you tomorrow."

"I love you," he said.

She was about to say, I love you, too, but he had hung up. His other calls were waiting.

"This is the fifth house we've looked at this morning," said Yarrow. "I don't think I can bear to look at another place."

They were parked outside a brownstone in Murray Hill. It had seen better days. There were three steps leading up from the

street and a basement that could be entered through a separate
door. The steps were crumbling. Yarrow was using her cane
today. Her leg was aching. The broker let them in with a set of
keys that she jingled like a jailer. They entered a small, narrow
hall; immediately to the left was a kitchen, but beyond, the room
opened out to the width of the whole house. The broker drew the
curtains back, and light from a tiny garden flooded the room.
There were three floors above, one with a large sitting room, the
next two with bedrooms. Yarrow looked out the main bedroom
window, and there was a tree, bare now because it was February, but a squirrel scampered along a branch and jumped onto
another. The branch quivered in the winter sunlight. Yarrow could
see the tree clothed green in the spring, she could see Buck
playing underneath it in the summer, and Lily enjoying it after
school. She turned from the window.

"I'll take it," she said. "I can make a home of this."

Yarrow took it unfurnished, and Greta found a painter who
came in and covered everything with a layer of white paint.
Yarrow arranged to have the furniture sent from Colorado, and
then she went to look at schools for the children. Rather, the
schools looked at her and the children, for like everything else in
New York City, competition was the game. The children had to
be tested; the children had to be interviewed. Lily thought it was
fun, but Buck was shy and resisted any attempts by strangers to
draw him out. At one notable private school, she had to haul him
out from under a sofa in the waiting room to go in for his
interview. He was six, but big for his age and people expected
him to behave better. To her surprise, the school thought he was
a delightful boy. "Artistic," they said, and took him.

On Monday, while they were still waiting for the painters to
finish and the furniture to be moved in, Yarrow went down to
her new office for the first time.

She was met at the front door by Burt Reamington, who took
her up to the fourth floor and introduced her to the new team.
Burt had offered to stay on for a week or two to show her the
ropes, but she declined his offer, saying it was best she stood on
her own feet as soon as possible. When most of the editorial
staff were on duty, she went down to the editorial floor to meet
them. The editor, Mike Edwards, was an unknown quantity to
Yarrow. Reamington had said he was a good technician and left
it at that. Edwards was a handsome man with a thick shock of
gray hair. He was about forty-five years old and had come to the
Telegraph from the *Chicago Tribune*. After Reamington spoke,
Yarrow stepped up onto a chair.

"I know you are all curious about me, but not half as curious as I am about you. I want to know everything about you and this newspaper. I'm going to be around. I'm going to be learning from you what makes this paper tick. You know that the paper has been falling in circulation for some time. I want to bring it up. If you're willing to help me do it, we're going to be great friends. Any questions?"

A male voice shouted from the back, "Are you married?"

There was congenial laughter. Yarrow knew she cut an attractive figure. "The answer is no. I hope this is not the level of reporting for which the *Telegraph* is known."

"What changes are you going to make?"

"I don't know yet. But you'll soon find out."

"Will you put out a *Sunday Telegraph?*"

"No. Too expensive."

"Will you cut the staff?"

"I don't know. I think it hardly likely. There are lots of other places we can cut first. Yes? You." She pointed to a woman in a black dress near the front.

"We hear your paper in Colorado is conservative. Will you change the editorial policy of the *Telegraph?*"

"I don't even know what the editorial policy of the *Telegraph* is," said Yarrow. She joked about it because she wanted to deflect that question for a while.

"Bolshevik," shouted someone.

"That we'll change. No more questions? Thank you." Reamington helped her down to a smattering of applause.

"Who was the lady in the black?" she asked as she went out.

"Gladys Greenhouse, she's VP of the guild," said Reamington.

"Aaah," said Yarrow.

Her first day was spent trying to get a grasp on things. She interviewed Reamington's secretary, Margaret, who was willing to stay on as her assistant. She was younger than Yarrow would have liked, though Yarrow knew she herself was not much older. Margaret was divorced. She had no children. She admitted that her shorthand was not up to scratch, but she was efficient and smart. Yarrow was loath to take on someone new who did not understand the newspaper business, so she asked her to stay on. Margaret proved herself to be adept, and the more Yarrow worked with her, the more she grew to appreciate her qualities. Margaret was acutely aware of the sensitivities in the office, and although she was not as discreet as Miss Hines (who was a master at getting messages across without divulging sources), she was invaluable to Yarrow in these first few weeks.

Elliot telephoned. "What about dinner?"

"I can't, I'm too busy. I'm taking out some of the people to get to know them. Could I see you Saturday?"

"Saturday? Yarrow, this is Tuesday, how can I wait till Saturday?"

"You'll have to. Just imagine I'm back in Platte City."

"But you're not. You know what I want to do with you . . ." He lowered his voice as though he were an obscene caller. "I'm going to take you into the bathroom and take off all your clothes and cover you with soap and . . ."

"Elliot, you're far too busy yourself. Besides, when I am with you you're always on the telephone. You didn't even know I'd left last time."

He laughed.

"I'm sorry about that, darling. I was so involved. I was talking to someone who wants to introduce me to Clark Clifford in Washington."

"He's a powerful Democrat. He knows people."

"I suppose you could call him a lawyer of the elite."

"Speaking of lawyers, you were right. I need a good lawyer here. There's a company lawyer, but he's Reamington's man and he's moving on. Any suggestions?"

"I'll call you back. I love you."

Elliot introduced her to a man he knew only slightly but whose reputation was sound. Marvin Rifkin, of Rifkin, Goldstein, Purvey and Klein, was in his fifties, thinning hair, tall and a bit too heavy for his health. He had a great sense of humor and a quality that Yarrow recognized instantly—he was someone she could trust. Yarrow transferred all the *Telegraph*'s business to his firm.

About the fourth day, when Marvin Rifkin was in her office, they were visited by a representative of one of the unions. He had asked for an appointment and Yarrow assumed it was just a courtesy call. He was a big man with black hair and eyes and a dark complexion. His stomach bulged over his trousers. He was no sooner seated than it became clear that he was trying to blackmail Yarrow about the future deliveries of the *Telegraph*.

"You won't have any trouble if you just slip a little cash this way. You can mark it off as payment for a couple of extra drivers. But you won't need them. We'll take care of everything. Of course, if you don't, I can't promise your arrival in New York will be as sweet."

"Would you mind just repeating that, sir," said Yarrow. "I'd like Mr. Rifkin to take that down on tape, so that if I do have any trouble the authorities will know who is responsible.''

The union representative was quite unperturbed. He got up and took his leave, just as though he had made some proper business proposal that had been rejected.

''I've never heard anything so blatant,'' said Yarrow when he had gone.''What do you think he'll do?''

''I think it's just a bluff.''

''I hope so.''

''You were very strong,'' said Rifkin with admiration and surprise in his voice. ''Most people would have been intimidated.''

''Threats I can handle,'' said Yarrow, ''flattery I find much more difficult.''

Yarrow studied the overall budgets for the paper. The more she read, the more she was appalled at how desperate the situation was. She had the editorial budgets brought to her and asked to see Mike Edwards.

As he sat opposite her, she thought that although he was very handsome he was rather supercilious. He found it difficult to hide his arrogance, and she assumed it must be merely because of his looks, for his work certainly didn't warrant his having such a high opinion of himself.

She was blunt.

''We have to save money or we're all going down the river. I'm setting up a new budget for your department and we can't go above it.''

''We've always worked on a very tight budget for Burt. I don't know where we can pull in more.''

Yarrow picked up some sheets in front of her. ''You put on two new reporters last month. Did you have that authority?''

''We were understaffed. Burt had no idea . . .''

''You didn't have the authority. What about this? You sent a reporter to Minnesota to interview Hubert Humphrey. Why didn't you just use the telephone?''

''That's never as good as face to face.''

''Then wait until Humphrey's here, or, when he's in Washington, let one of the bureau staff do it. Don't spend money unnecessarily.'' Yarrow felt it was like talking to a brick wall. Mike Edward's smile didn't shift from his face.

''Why do you think the Democrats would nominate me?'' said Elliot.

He was sitting in his office, with the view of Manhattan

behind him, and there were four men seated on chairs around him. He knew all the men very well; he had worked with them over the years on Democratic causes, first as an onlooker able to sign checks; then, as his own name became more familiar to the public, they had helped set up speeches and organized rallies. He had worked with them on the Stevenson campaigns, had followed them through exhausting and harrowing primaries, when he had had the time. The game of politics fascinated Elliot. He was intrigued by the whole Byzantine puzzle of it. Intellectually, he had watched the striving for power, the toll it took, the rewards one could reap, and had enjoyed it. But his other half, the poor boy from the Depression who had made good, stimulated him to enter politics from another aspect. He wanted to help others; he had watched people lose everything in the Depression; he could still identify with other people's sufferings. He believed in the American system and he wanted to bring about change through that system.

One of the men, Murray Bates, who was a senior senator in Washington, sat forward with his hands on his knees. "We believe the Democratic convention in 1960 will be a deadlocked one—we believe you can be the candidate of compromise."

"Look who's going to run—at least as far as we can tell at this early stage," said Lew Haniman, a soft-spoken but powerful back-room Democrat from New York. "Hubert Humphrey—everyone loves Hubert but who knows him outside Minnesota? Stuart Symington from Missouri—"

"Would he enter the primaries?"

"I doubt it. He'd go for the power brokers. Lyndon Johnson—a southern candidate? He might carry the southern delegates, but not the whole convention. John Kennedy—a Catholic from Boston—"

"—Is Stevenson definitely not running?"

"Even Stevenson doesn't know the answer to that. We have to assume he's not, since he says he's not."

"What about Governor Brown?" asked a man who had been quiet up till now. He was Deke Smith, a lawyer from California with contacts to the labor unions and black voters.

"Another Catholic. If there's going to be a Catholic up there, it's going to be Kennedy."

"Look, I hate to act coy," said Elliot, "but why me?"

"You can appeal to businessmen, you can cut across the party lines and pick up all those Republican voters who will never vote for Nixon. You've got a good record within the party; you've supported Stevenson openly, you've supported enough civil rights and liberal social policies to be on record there. You're good-looking and you're young. Those Democrats who still want the old New Deal, they can have it with Humphrey, but you'll appeal to the younger ones.''

Elliot gave them his own list. "I'm unknown; I have no political office to fall back on; I couldn't win in the primaries."

"Those are pluses as far as I'm concerned because you owe no favors. You won't enter the primaries; we work on the delegates and you work on the press. We work toward a Draft Weyden movement on the convention floor.''

"You think he can get away without entering any primaries?" said Deke Smith.

"If he's going to be the candidate who heals at the convention, why go out there making enemies for a year before?''

They were all silent for a moment, and then the last man spoke up. He was Mel Gavins, the head of a public relations firm that was increasingly becoming known as the "Kingmakers." He packaged politicians.

"What about your wife, Elliot? Will she campaign with you?"

"No. But she won't campaign against me."

"I have to ask these questions. I'm sorry, but there's no privacy under the national spotlight. Are you planning a divorce? Because that would kill your chances.''

"There will be no divorce," said Elliot.

"What about Miss McLean . . .''

"Oh, for Christ's sake, man, leave Yarrow out of this.''

"Elliot, it's common knowledge.''

"We have an understanding. There will be no compromise there.''

The four men looked at each other. Each in his way thought that in this convention, this 1960 election coming up, they would have a share of the glory. Eisenhower and the Republicans had been in power since 1952. They believed that the old wheelers and dealers of the Democratic party again would be out in force, pushing their candidates, their views. This time they wouldn't win. These men, Bates, Haniman, Smith and Gavins, saw a chance for a new beginning. They all liked and respected Elliot Weyden. Some of them had been watching his rise to national prominence longer than others. He had some name recognition through his professional stature and had not harmed himself by having sat on the panel investigating corruption in New York last year. He had received good television coverage. But they knew it would not be easy to make his name a household word across America. This was their strategy. They knew Elliot had a political charisma, a presence in front of an audience that was almost erotic. They wanted to harness that power. Among them they had the ability to reach and influence a multitude of people. It was a risk they were willing to take. They nodded their heads in agreement. Elliot Weyden was their man. Now they had only to convince him to run.

Mel Gavins stayed behind after the others had gone.

"You've got to want this badly."

"I know."

"The press will scrutinize every part of your life; even your bed won't be sacrosanct."

"Christ, Mel, you've got a way with words."

"They'll be watching every move you make. They'll stake out your apartment if necessary."

"They didn't talk about Roosevelt. They don't talk about Kennedy."

"No—but they may not treat you the same. You must be prepared for dirty pool. Do you want to take your wife and Yarrow into that? Can you take the heat?"

Elliot chewed on his lower lip. He could taste the possibility of power like salt in his saliva.

"What would you suggest I do?"

"Stop your affair with Yarrow McLean."

"Deke—this woman—we've been together for years. I wanted to marry her."

"Elliot, you're a married man. You're going to run for President of the United States. You can't have a reputation as a womanizer.

"I'm not a womanizer."

"One woman outside marriage is one too many. Your mistress. Do you want to see that splashed all over the front page of the *Telegraph*? How about the *Courier*? God—she's a publisher—and she's a Republican!"

"Would her being Democrat make it any better? I have as much hope of switching Yarrow's political allegiance as you have of making me give her up."

Mel pulled at his hair.

"You're running a risk. We can only cover up so much."

"I'll hardly see her. I'll be discreet—but I can't stop it all together. I won't lie about it, Mel."

"But you'll be lying to the American people. They'll see that. It's a remarkable and awesome thing this game, because it's all up to them—us—We the People. If it comes out, you'll be shown as a hypocrite—your judgment and your character will be questioned. Sleep on it, Elliot, will you? I'll call you tomorrow.''

''Mommy says she's taking me to England to see Aunt Vivienne again. Will you come with us this time, Daddy?''

Elliot was on a horse at Coakley in Virginia, with his daughter sitting in front of him.

''Turn the horse's head, darling, a little more firmly, tighten the rein, that's it. Now I'm going to make him trot. Shorten the rein, hold on with your legs.'' They trotted a few yards and then slowed to a walk. Meredith's blond curls escaped from under her black velvet riding cap. She chattered on a mile a minute. Her diction was very poor. There was a glottal stop in her speech which made her difficult to understand. One had to listen carefully and concentrate. Sometimes Elliot missed what she was saying.

''Will you come to England?'' she repeated, and he understood.

''I will, if you go, but how can I let you out of my sight?'' She giggled as he tickled her, and then they turned back for the house.

''There's Mommy. Let's trot back and surprise her.'' Elliot almost lost his seat as Meredith urged the horse forward.

''You little minx,'' he said as they came to a halt in front of Blanchette. Meredith laughed and he jumped down and lifted her off the horse. Her nurse came down from the veranda and took her inside. Elliot handed the horse to a groom.

''You used to call me that,'' said Blanchette. She was dressed in pale floaty chiffon with a scarf around her neck. It was spring in Virginia, but the humidity was high today.

He strode onto the veranda and eased himself down onto one of the white cane sofas with floral cushions. He had on a pair of yellow riding breeches, and his legs in their polished knee-high boots stretched across the veranda onto the balustrade.

''I don't want you to take her to England,'' he said.

''I know you don't, but I would like to spend a little time there so she can get to know my side of the family.''

''You went last year. Can't you just make it a short visit?''

''Elliot.'' She had sat down opposite him. She was quite a pretty woman, he supposed. She folded her hands on her lap. ''There is nothing for me in this country anymore. When Daddy died I felt my ties with America were really cut at last. I went back last year to—to test myself. I'm still English. I want to go home. If you and I, well, if things were different, if I thought there was a future for us . . .''

He was ashamed for her. He felt that no matter what was between them, he did not want to hear her supplicate like this. Neither of them spoke of Yarrow. He was unsure how much Blanchette knew. He did not know how she would know—there had never been a mention of it in the papers—but people talked.

"You do have a future here," he said. "Meredith is our future. I'm her father."

Blanchette sighed and leaned back against the wicker chair.

"I don't think it's enough, Elliot."

"I want you here. It's important to me." He had sat up. His sleeves were rolled up above his elbows. His arms, under the dark hair, were very tanned.

"Your ambitions," she said. They had spoken over the months of his idea of running. She was not against it.

"You have ambitions, too. In that we are alike, Blanchette."

"I don't understand American politics," she said. "They seem so messy. Why can't you have a plain old parliament so everyone knows who's the leader of the party and who's the leader of the opposition?"

"We had a war to straighten that one out." He laughed.

"I won't campaign."

"I wouldn't expect you to."

"I want an apartment in New York."

He glanced at her. Her cheeks were flushed.

"You can have one," he said.

"And I can go to England when I want."

"Without Meredith."

"I'll think about it." She got up and went inside without looking at him.

He worked for the rest of the day in his study. That night they ate dinner quietly with Meredith, and afterward he listened while Blanchette read to their daughter. Blanchette was full of fairy tales and children's stories that he had never heard—about Tiggy-winkle and Farmer Giles. Blanchette was a good mother. She had devoted herself to their daughter. For that, Elliot would be forever grateful. The word "divorce" had never been mentioned between them.

When Blanchette went up to bed, she saw a small red jeweler's box on the pillow of her turned-down bed. She opened it and took out a large blue sapphire shaped like a teardrop. It could be worn as a pendant. She held it in her hand and began to cry. She heard Elliot come upstairs and enter the room next to hers. She walked toward the connecting door. She heard the lock click. Blanchette fell on her knees beside her bed. Oh, Lord, she prayed, help me understand. But the only answer she received was the coldness of the beautiful stone. She pressed it to each of her eyes. This was all. This was all.

In the morning when she went down to breakfast, which she seldom did, the first thing he noticed was the pendant hanging from her neck. He said nothing and neither did she, but she put her hand up to it where it hung against her breast, and she turned it so the winter light glinted on it. It looked to Elliot as big and all-seeing as an owl's eye.

CHAPTER 29

F OR THE MONTH OF AUGUST YARROW RENTED A SMALL HOUSE near the beach at Amagansett on Long Island. She installed her mother and the children there and a young housekeeper she had engaged.

Yarrow spent the first weekend settling them in. The house was reconstructed from a number of old barns—its beams and walls were weatherbeaten to a pale, splintered gray, and a cottage garden had been planted where old potato fields once flourished.

Yarrow was in the garden with a trowel, weeding a bed of spiky yellow gazanias, when Mel Gavins drove up. She had met him two or three times before, once with Elliot, and she was convinced that he distrusted her. She knew this was not a social visit—she did not know Mel well enough for him to drop by casually.

"Hello, Mel. Can I get you a cool drink?" It was a hot, sunny day.

"No thanks. Mind if I sit down?"

"Please." Yarrow eased her skirt up where she was kneeling on it and inched forward to the next section.

"Nice flowers," said Mel, sitting on a beam that separated the driveway from the bedding plants.

"I dislike them," said Yarrow. "All spikes and show but shallow roots. Nothing else will grow here."

He took off a Panama hat, wiped his balding head with a handkerchief. He leaned forward, twirling his hat in his fingers.

"You're going to hurt his chances."

She didn't look up, went on digging and rooting with her fingers.

"Did he send you here?"

"No. He won't do it for himself."

Yarrow dug up an old potato with a spade mark like a scar across it. She sat back, holding it in her hands.

"What do you want me to do?"

"I want you to leave him—at least while the campaign is on."

Yarrow bent her head under her straw hat. Her hair was tied back with a ribbon at her neck, and the long, curling mane hung like a wave down her back. They could hear the children shouting as they played in the sand dunes.

"I hate asking this," said Mel. Yarrow kept turning the potato over in her hands. After some time Mel went away. She waited until she heard the sound of the car engine fading away before she raised her head. The sunlight made her eyes water. She threw the potato as far as she could, but it only landed on the other side of the flowerbed.

Yarrow got up from her knees. She felt a hundred years old. She wouldn't think about it. She wouldn't. She left the trowel sticking up in the sandy soil and walked down to the dunes to see the children.

"Won't you stay with us, Mommy?" asked Lily. "You never have time to do anything anymore."

"I'm sorry, but I'll be out every weekend."

"You promised to take me shopping." Lily loved shopping; Yarrow hated it.

"I promise I'll take you next Saturday."

"Promise?"

"Promise. Now you get on with John this time—don't give your grandmother trouble."

Yarrow drove away from the house and the sand dunes with a heavy heart. She waved at the children in her rearview mirror. Nothing seemed to be going right. She worried about not seeing enough of them. She worried about the newspaper. She worried about Elliot.

She would love to have spent time with the children this summer, but she didn't dare take her eyes off the *Telegraph*. She knew she had trouble with Mike Edwards, but she kept hoping it would work out.

When she got in she called him and the assistant editor, Jim Burroughs, up to her office to talk about yesterday's edition. Mike came in with his usual supercilious smile, and settled himself deep in the chair opposite her. He put his feet up on her desk.

"Take your feet off my desk," she said.

"Sorry." He took them down very slowly, and she tried to concentrate on the copy of the *Telegraph* in front of her and not on how irritating and rude she found him. She went through the paper page by page.

"How many people are interested in the spending in Albany?"

"Many people. It's our money they're spending."

"But front page? I think it's boring. It makes the paper look boring. It should be more snappy, it should have a hook. Why do we have to have another picture of the governor on page four? Is he that interesting? What's this picture of Mamie Eisenhower doing with this story? I've seen this block for the last eight years. There must be other pictures in the library. I'm sick of seeing that hat."

"Did you read the editorial on Khruschev's coming visit?"

"Yes. That was quite good. At least we've stopped being apologists for Stalin."

Jim Burroughs guffawed. He was as opposite in appearance to Mike Edwards as it was possible to be. He was short and his face was plain; he looked like a farmer from the Midwest. Yarrow infinitely preferred him to Mike.

"I want more balance in the paper. It's grim, Mike. This is summer. People don't want all this heavy navel-searching. Get some light into it. Beach shots. What about a pretty girl?" Mike rolled his eyes to the ceiling. Yarrow stood up and they left.

She wished she was at the beach with the children. The humming air conditioner gave her a headache. Outside she could see a sailboat tacking down the East River under the Williamsburg Bridge. It gave her an illusion of summer in the city. She turned back to the pile of work on her desk.

After she had tackled her correspondence and Margaret had gone off to type it, Yarrow went through a stack of overseas newspapers. She liked to keep up to date with what was happening, and she admired a lot of Fleet Street's newspapers. She liked the energy of the tabloids; she was amused by the pomposity of the others. She worked through them, making notes to herself, ripping out articles that had some relevance or that she wanted to show Edwards, if he would even look at them before dumping them in his wastebasket. She came across a picture of

Elliot arriving in London with his wife and child. PRESIDENTIAL
HOPEFUL, said the caption. What a handsome family they
made, thought Yarrow. Even little Meredith had been caught at
an angle that showed how beautiful she could have been if not
for the capricious, cruel whim of nature. Yarrow missed Elliot.
She had not seen him for months. Ever since his mother had
shown her the photograph of Meredith, Yarrow's head and her
heart had been at war with each other. Mel's visit to her had only
compounded what she had already decided to do. She had avoided
Elliot and he knew it. He telephoned her constantly. As though
on cue, her telephone rang now. It was him, calling from
London.

"I've just been looking at a picture of you in the *Times*," she
said.

"I've been thinking about you, too. What are you doing?"

"I'm trying to get through all the letters I haven't been able to
answer for the past six weeks. At least in August everyone
leaves town and I can get my work done."

"I miss you, Yarrow. What is it? I feel you're moving away
from me. Do you still love me?"

"I do. But it's wrong, darling. Not wrong to love you, but
wrong to want you. You don't belong to me. I kept trying to
pretend you did. Your wife and child were just—well, it was
easier for me to deal with them if I thought they were just
figments of my imagination. It was not until I saw Meredith—
knew what Blanchette has been through . . ."

"Darling . . ."

"I saw a picture of your daughter. Your mother showed it to
me. It made me think of Lily and how I feel about her. It made
me think that I was taking you away from Meredith—and
Blanchette."

"I don't know what to say. I don't want to lose you, Yarrow,
my darling. Don't leave me."

"I don't want to see you anymore, Elliot." Yarrow hung up.
It was the only time she had ever done that before him.

Margaret came in with some letters for her to sign. She saw
Yarrow's face and the red-rimmed eyes.

"Are you all right, Miss McLean?"

"Yes," she lied. "I just heard about a death in the family.
I'm upset, that's all."

But it wasn't really a lie. It was a death, and she suffered from it.

Fall came. Winds blew along the concrete canyons of Manhattan, hurling scraps of paper and grit before them. The garbage

swirled in eddies around doorways. Yarrow pulled a sheet of paper away from her legs as she entered the corner newsstand near her house.

"Hello, Miss McLean," said the man at the counter. He was a cheerful young Armenian with a dark moustache.

"We sold twenty more *Telegraphs* yesterday than usual. Good business, yes?"

"That is good. I hope you've ordered more for today and tomorrow."

"Lady, I'm just a little guy. When I call up, they don't take any notice of me."

"I'll fix it." Yarrow went to the back of the store to select some party things. She had missed Buck's birthday in August and had promised him a party when school began. She picked up paper plates and balloons and ribbons and loot bags and party favors and jammed them in a plastic shopping basket. Buck was six. Sandy was on vacation and John was staying with them for a month. For the first time in many years she thought of Zeb. She didn't think about him when she saw John anymore, but now, picking up the little-boy favors, action figures and gumballs and baseball cards, she saw him standing there before her. You never get over a loss like that, she realized, you just learn to live with it. It made the things you had more sweet.

Lily came bounding into the shop on her long gazelle legs. She was in a panic. "I thought you'd be here," she said. "Something's happened to Grandma." Yarrow dropped everything on the floor and ran out of the shop like a maniac. "What happened?" she kept asking, "what happened?"

"She fell down the stairs, I don't know."

Yarrow found Freya on the first floor. The ambulance men were already there. They were taking turns thumping on her chest.

"You can't die, Mama. You can't leave me." Yarrow began to sob, then she saw Lily's stricken face. "Oh, baby, I'm sorry, I don't mean to frighten you." She hugged Lily and held her own emotions in check.

Yarrow went with Freya in the ambulance. They had got the heart going again. "She's a fighter," said one of the attendants.

"Yes, she is," said Yarrow. She called Greta from the hospital, and her sister was with her in twenty minutes. They sat with their heads together in the corridor, waiting for news. At midnight the crisis was over and Freya was able to recognize them.

"Didn't think my ticker would fail me," she said slowly. "I always thought it would be, you know . . ."

"Oh, hush, Mama. Thank God you're OK."

Yarrow hired a nurse, Edith, when her mother came home. Freya had lost the use of her right side and had to learn to walk again. Her speech had been affected somewhat, and she forgot things. Edith, the nurse, was a big, strapping Australian girl with an infectious laugh. The children took to her immediately, and even Millie, the timid little maid who had always been under Freya's thumb, blossomed under the Australian's booming friendliness.

"She'll be right, mate, with old Edith here. A good old sponge-bath and you'll be as good as new, won't you, Mrs. Mac? Here, Lily, hold up your grandmother for me while I pull out this sheet."

"What we need here, Miss McLean, is a bit of organization," said Edith one day, coming in from the kitchen.

"Yes," said Yarrow, looking up from her papers at her desk. The room on the ground floor was a catch-all living room. There was one big table in the middle and an old sofa with a loose cover on it against the wall. In the winter they lit the fire and the children did their homework at the table. They also ate at the table and Yarrow did her work at one end.

"When Mrs. Mac recovers she still won't be able to use the stairs. Why don't you convert the basement into a flat for her? It's only a few steps down from the back here, she could manage that. I could fix it up for you. It only needs a bit of work."

"Oh, would you?" said Yarrow. "You're sure it won't be too much trouble?"

"Bob's your uncle," said Edith. "I'll get some spackle and paint at Janovic's tomorrow. Millie's going to help me. Aren't you, Mill?"

Yarrow looked at the young Filippino maid, who had never said a word before in her presence.

"Millie's going to help you?"

"Yeah. She's a dab hand at carpentry. She helped her father build a boat. Right, Mill?"

"Right, Missee Edith."

"And John here's going to burn off the old paintwork. Now, don't you worry, Miss McLean, we know what we're doing."

Yarrow retreated to her coral-colored bedroom and shut the door with relief. Edith inspired everyone with confidence. If only she had a few more like Edith around her office.

Mike Edwards sent up an editorial that Yarrow thought was terrible. It was a platitudinous piece about a city councilman whom everyone knew was on the take.

"Look," said Yarrow, "if you had one fresh or original thing to say about this man I would let this piece stand, but it's dull." She had gone down to Mike Edwards's office, and thrust the copy paper down on the spike on his desk. "No," she said. "I won't run it." She was aware of all eyes on her as she left the room. She heard the buzz as she waited for the elevator to her floor.

That afternoon she went over the budgets for each department. Most of them had kept within the guidelines she had called for. Some areas had trouble. She spoke to each of the different department heads and listened to their explanations. Some she accepted; some she did not. She blew up at the overrun costs in the machine room. She screamed about the overtime that had been racked up. "I can't keep this going," she said. "This is not a charity we're running here."

The last budget she looked at was the editorial budget. Yarrow nearly burst a blood vessel. Mike Edwards had gone way over his jurisdiction. In spite of all her warnings and pleading, he had hired another journalist—and had promised to pay him above the going rate.

Yarrow was about to rush down to the editorial floor to pull his hair out, but then she stopped. She forced herself to think calmly. She thought of all the problems that lay before her in this building. She had grown to love the building and the paper. It had a vitality of its own. She thought of the newspaper sometimes as a gutsy woman clinging to a raft that was speeding toward a waterfall. Somehow, always, there was a branch, a rock that the heroine managed to clamber onto. Yarrow knew it was she who had brought the vitality into this place. She was damned if she was going to let the Mike Edwardses of this world pull it down. Yarrow picked up the slug of metal that always stood on her desk, the one her grandfather had given her. What would he have done in this situation?

Yarrow felt utterly alone as she stood at the window of her office and looked, unseeing, at the view. She could not turn to Elliot. She could not ask Freya for advice. Her sisters and brother were too removed from the business to be of help. This was her decision.

"OK, Grandfather, I've procrastinated long enough," she said as she put down the slug carefully on the blotting paper on her desk. She buzzed Margaret to have Mike Edwards come up.

She was very calm when he came in. When he sat down, she handed him the offending account sheet with the budget overrun circled in red ink. She said nothing. He began to explain.

"It's too late for explanations. We've been over this many times. I want your resignation, in writing, on my desk in one hour."

The smile slipped off his face, and for the first time she saw the meanness that the superciliousness had covered. He would make trouble, she knew. He was a rat.

Jim Burroughs was in her office, where she was asking him if he would take over as acting editor, when the security guard rang to say that a television crew had arrived outside the front door. They wanted to go up to the editorial floor.

"What?" said Yarrow, grabbing the telephone. "Who asked them to come here?"

"They say they have to see Mr. Edwards."

"Like hell they do," said Yarrow. "Not in my building. Shut the doors. Don't let them in."

It was just before the local six o'clock news. Yarrow switched on the television set, and there was Mike Edwards, striding out of her building, carrying his briefcase and papers, and declaring to the public how his publisher had interfered with his editorial freedom. A claque of journalists stood around him outside the door and applauded. Yarrow made a note of every one of their faces.

The announcer solemnly declared the importance of the First Amendment. Yarrow switched off the set.

"You still want the job, Jim? I'm not offering it to you permanently. I want to see how we get on together."

"I'll give it a try."

"Thank you."

When Yarrow left the building an hour later, the television crew was still there.

The television reporter pushed a microphone into her face. "Miss McLean, what do you have to say about your editor's complaint that he resigned because you stopped an editorial in tomorrow's *Telegraph*?"

"No comment." Yarrow stepped into the rental car waiting. Smart girl, Margaret, for realizing she would need one tonight.

"Is it true that the journalists have threatened a strike in support of Mr. Edwards?"

Yarrow shook her head. "I have nothing to say." She told the driver to move on. While the car made a U-turn on the road, she found she sympathized with the reporter. He was only doing his job. But then, so was she.

She arrived home just as Buck was getting out of his bath. Millie handed her the towel. It was a long time since Yarrow had seen his naked little body. His skin shone and glistened like a seal while she rubbed him dry.

"I saw you on television," he said. "Why were they asking you questions?"

"Oh, the editor and I disagreed about a number of things. I guess he's upset because I asked him to leave. I brought home the late editions for you. Can you read the headlines?"

"I told you, Mommy, I'm not going into the business. I'm going to be an artist."

She helped him into his pajamas and combed his hair. "I can do that," he said.

"I forget you're growing up," she said, getting off her knees.

"Could you tell Lily not to spoil my buildings?" Lately Buck had been constructing fantastic castles from wooden blocks and toilet-paper rolls and egg cartons. "She glued beads all over the last one."

"I'll talk to her," said Yarrow. "I'm going upstairs now to see your grandmother."

"Edith says she'll have Grandmother's new flat ready soon. What's a 'flat'?"

"That's just a short Australian word for apartment." Yarrow went downstairs and made a drink for her mother and herself.

"Are you going out again?" asked Lily, looking up from the table.

"Darling, I wish I didn't have to. By the way, please don't stick things all over Buck's creations. It's very annoying."

"Oh, he's such a baby. I made it look better."

"That's not the point, Lily. It was his building and you weren't supposed to touch it."

Lily reached for another cookie from the package beside her.

"And don't eat because I'm reprimanding you—you'll get fat."

Yarrow put her hand on her daughter's shoulder to soften her words. "I am sorry about tonight. I've been trying to get this account for the last nine months, and tonight of all nights, the man's in town."

"I'm never going into business," said Lily, throwing back her hair. "It's too much trouble."

Yarrow kissed her on the forehead. "Sometimes I think you're right. But now I have all these people depending on me at the office. I have to go. Wouldn't you do the same?"

"I would put my children first."

"Oh, Lily. You do know how to hurt. Don't you think I'm doing this for your future, too?"

Yarrow took the Scotches upstairs to her mother's room. She put a straw in Freya's drink and sat down with her.

"Cheers," she said. She held the glass up so that Freya could drink through the straw. She was getting stronger, but the motor control in her hands had not come back. The doctor suggested that the right side never would recover.

She told her mother everything that had happened that day. Freya nodded and, between nods, Yarrow gave her sips of her drink.

"Did I do the right thing?" asked Yarrow.

"I think it's what Jock would have done."

"I hope so."

"Where's Elliot?"

"I told you, Mama. I don't see Elliot anymore."

"Elliot should be here with you."

"I have to go and change," said Yarrow. "I'm meeting an advertiser at the Twenty-one Club." As Yarrow bent to kiss her mother, Freya's trembling hands came up and held her head for a moment. When she released her, Freya was holding a long gray hair in her hand. Yarrow took it and wound it around her finger.

"Thank you, Mama, that really makes me feel better."

Yarrow's advertiser was a brewer from Denver. Her advertising manager had been trying to get the account for months, and finally they had agreed, pending their bosses' decision. Yarrow met J. C. Calloway in the foyer of the restaurant.

"Just call me Cal," he said as they shook hands.

"Your usual table, Miss McLean?" said Tony, showing her to a banquette on the left.

Cal was a pleasant dinner companion, Yarrow found to her surprise. She had been ready for some boorish, beer-drinking out-of-towner, but instead Cal was urbane and funny. He was a gray-haired widower, about sixty years old but trim and vital-looking. She was glad she had changed into a black velvet dress and a frivolous cocktail hat, which she put on after her mother found that gray hair in her head. She had needed to put on something to deny she was growing older. Heavens, she was only thirty-six—no, thirty-seven. Yarrow laughed. She had been so preoccupied lately that she had forgotten it was her birthday.

"Today's my birthday," she said.

Cal ordered some champagne. Yarrow was so delighted to be with an attractive man again that she forgot to talk business. Whenever she remembered, Cal would say something funny and she would forget again. He was flirting with her. She asked him to order the wine, and he did—alcohol after all was his field. He ordered a superb red wine.

"Here's the best way to taste it," he said. "I used to be an altar boy, so that might have something to do with it." He speared a piece of roll on a fork, dipped it into his wine and offered it to her.

"I've got friends in your business back home," he said. "They've got trouble with cross-ownership of television and newspapers, and the FCC is breathing down their necks. Are you interested?"

"Of course."

Cal put the roll into her mouth as if it were Holy Communion. Yarrow took it from his fork and as she put her napkin up to her lips, she turned to her right and saw Elliot at a corner table looking at her. He was with a group of people, some of whom she recognized. Yarrow lost her appetite after that. She felt as though she were doing something wrong, which was ridiculous. She did not belong to Elliot; that was all over. The sooner she could forget him, the better it would be.

When she and Cal got up to leave, they had to pass Elliot's table. One of the people at his table called to her. She went over and introduced Cal and shook Elliot's hand as if he were a stranger. Cal was impressed to meet Elliot Weyden, whom everyone was talking about as a possible presidential candidate. He enthused about Elliot's achievements as he was introduced. Yarrow was embarrassed. How could she have thought anyone could measure up to Elliot? When they left she felt as if she were leaving the scene of a crime.

In the rental car, Cal made a pass at her. He slipped his hand inside her dress and tried to fondle her.

"Please, Cal, don't do that," she said. He apologized immediately and said he'd had a lot to drink. He asked if he could come into her house for a nightcap.

"No," she said. "My children are asleep. Good night, Cal. The car will take you home." She slipped into her house before he could prevent her.

Inside, Yarrow leaned against the door. Oh, hell, she thought, for sure she had lost that account. It was all she could think of.

But the next day Cal sent a bouquet of roses to her at the office. "Happy Birthday to one swell little lady." Yarrow looked at the card and laughed. She called her advertising manager, who said the contract had been signed.

"I think I've got a beau," she said to Margaret as she put the flowers in water.

* * *

Yarrow discovered that Jim Burroughs was a better number two than editor; he couldn't seem to grasp the overall picture of what the paper should look like. So she decided to go to Platte City to ask Ned Griffin to come work for her in New York. First, she had to make sure that other management people were in place at the *Journal*. She could not afford to threaten the success of the *Journal*.

Miss Hines greeted her with real affection. The paper was running smoothly. Ned and Paddy had done a great job.

"Ned," Yarrow said, as she sat in her father's old office, "I want you to come to New York. That paper is going down the drain and it's going to take us with it if I can't stop it. Do you want to think about it?"

"Yeah. Give me two minutes. OK, I'll come."

Yarrow laughed. "Well, that was quick. Don't you want to talk to Mary-Ellen about it?"

"That's my problem. But what about the *Journal*?"

"I'll make Paddy editor, but he can't handle the publishing side." She got up and strode about the room. She had on a plain, black suit with a straight skirt that had become her uniform in the office.

"I've got a crazy idea and I want to try it on you first. I need a strong manager here, someone to handle the labor negotiations, the printing side, the shop management."

"Yes, but who?"

She turned to him and watched his face.

"Joe Bellini."

Ned nearly fell off his seat.

"God, Yarrow. That's like putting the fox in with the chickens. Joe Bellini, the union foreman?"

"Yes, but he'll know what all the other foxes are up to."

"It's your paper."

"Yes, but what do you think?"

"I think you've got guts."

Yarrow paced up and down again.

"It wouldn't work if you were remaining here. You two have never gotten along. But with Paddy it will be different. And they'll both report to me."

"Then do it. I'm glad I don't have to work with the bastard." He got up. "When do you want us in New York?"

"How about the end of January?"

"OK."

Yarrow came up and put her hands on Ned's shoulders.

"Ned, how can I thank you?"

"How can I resist when you ask me with that smile?" He grinned at her and went out. Yarrow felt good about Ned and Mary-Ellen. They had never let her down, had stood by her in all kinds of crises. When Zeb died, seven years ago—how the time had flown—it was Mary-Ellen who had moved into Yarrow's house to comfort her.

Yarrow had a gut feeling about Joe Bellini. She judged him to be an ambitious man who used the system to get ahead. The only problem was, he was in the enemy camp. That didn't mean that she hadn't watched him and appreciated his qualities of leadership and honesty. Within the union rules of dealing with management, Joe Bellini had always dealt fairly. Even that ridiculous lunch-break fiasco, which had cost her three days of profits, had been within his understanding of how the game was played. Fair was fair. Yarrow decided to ask him to join her management team, but she wouldn't ask him here at the office. She wanted to do it on neutral territory. So she asked Miss Hines what was the best Italian restaurant in town, and invited Joe Bellini to have lunch with her there the next day.

That night, Cal came in from Denver and took her to a basketball game. They ate hot dogs and relish and stamped their feet on the polished wooden floor of the gym. Yarrow hadn't had so much fun in a long time. Cal was a model of discretion; when he took her back to her hotel, he kissed her hand and released it.

"I'm falling in love with you," he said.

"Oh, Cal . . ."

"I'm not going to rush things, don't worry. But I want you to know what I'm thinking."

She watched him leave the hotel; a decent, good man, but a man she knew she was not at all in love with.

Between the antipasto and the spaghetti at Prego's Italian Restaurant, Yarrow told Joe Bellini what she wanted. Between the spaghetti and the veal, Joe Bellini told Yarrow what he wanted. Over the zabaglione and the coffee they both came to an agreement. They finished off the bottle of Chianti, and Yarrow had a new member of her management team. She also thought afterward that she had added five pounds to her hips—but it was worth it. She left Platte City feeling positive that her intuition about Bellini was right. It was a bold move but one that proved again that some risks are worth taking.

* * *

On her return to New York, Yarrow announced that Ned Griffin, the editor of the *Platte City Journal-Record*, would be taking over as editor of the *Telegraph* on February first. A flurry of concern began percolating through the building as the guild geared up for its annual tearing of hair.

Yarrow had ignored the reporters' murmurings after Mike Edwards resigned. A coterie of them had handed in their resignations at the same time. Yarrow accepted them without pain. There were many she didn't want anyway. There were one or two she was sorry to lose.

But the most damage was done by reporters on other publications who related with glee the problems at her newspaper. She saw them as a bunch of hyenas gloating around a corpse that one day might be their own. Every now and then a story would come out somewhere, blasting her for her political philosophy, or her interfering management style, or her inability to understand the glory of the journalistic profession. Yarrow hardened. She read the stuff if she thought she had to, but more often dumped it in her wastebasket. She refused interviews on television and other publications. What was the use? She would only be pilloried and she felt time was on her side. She watched with dry amusement as Mike Edwards was hired by one of her rivals to be the editor of a new *Manhattan Style* insert each week. Yarrow gave it six weeks. The insert lasted eight, and Mike Edwards went off somewhere else, sharpening his knives.

Christmas came and went. Eric came down from the mountains and joined them in New York. He brought his girlfriend with him. She was a tiny, feisty girl called Yanna. She was a great skier and had written a ski piece for the *Gazette*. She wrapped hulking Eric around her little finger. Eric was twenty-seven years old, and he said he was doing what he wanted to do for the rest of his life. When the snow was good, he put up a "Closed" sign and went skiing. People just dropped their ads through the letterbox, he said. Yarrow wished it were like that in New York. But she knew she would be bored with Eric's existence.

Nellie and Jack and Justice had gone on a trek to Katmandu. Yarrow supposed they were searching for new poetry for their monthly paper. The publication was very earnest and was called *Soul Seeker*. It was printed on recycled paper. Yarrow thought its philosophy was recycled, too, and found it unreadable. Greta had gone on a honeymoon with her new husband, a Seventh Avenue clothing manufacturer, given to gold chains and Gucci loafers. Before she left she telephoned Yarrow to say that Clara Russell had died. Greta was the recipient of most people's troubles. She had taken over where Freya left off. Yarrow had written to Clara to come for Christmas, but she'd been too ill to travel. Yarrow now wished she had done more for her.

The basement apartment was ready for Freya. Edith had done a splendid job with it. Yarrow wouldn't have thought it possible that the dark rooms could be so transformed with white paint and colorful fabrics. John and Eric made a chair with their arms and carried Freya down to her new quarters. Edith had hung herbs and dried flowers around the one-room apartment and Freya was delighted with it. Edith made no mention of leaving now that Freya had recovered somewhat, and Yarrow never mentioned it either for fear that she would. Edith had gradually taken over the running of the household, and "fair dinkums" and "true blues" and other antipodean phrases floated through the rooms. Once Yarrow heard Millie arguing with a delivery boy. The diminutive Filipino maid came in later, shaking her head at Yarrow. "He's just another pommy bastard," she said.

Yarrow's family had settled into a routine that she found to be infinitely supportive. Without all of them, she realized, she would not have had the courage to go on.

On New Year's Eve, she telephoned Miss Hines, and then she phoned all the executives who worked for her and wished them a Happy New Year. When she finished, it was late. Edith and Millie had gone out for the evening. Yarrow opened a bottle of champagne. The cork made a lonely sound as it popped. She poured herself a glass and went out into her tiny terrace garden. It was very dark but the weather was mild. She stood breathing in the still night air. Behind the protective row of houses she could hear the sounds of the city, a siren, an occasional car horn, a distant rumble of traffic. She looked up and she saw on a terrace across the way, a woman standing in a white bathrobe. A man came out and joined the woman. He untied her bathrobe and slipped his hands inside it as they embraced each other. The sight filled Yarrow with longing. She raised her glass to them. "Happy New Year," she said, "Happy Hogmanay."

CHAPTER 30

THE GRAND BALLROOM OF THE WALDORF-ASTORIA WAS ABLAZE with lights at eight o'clock in the morning. Two thousand people were eating breakfast of orange juice, scrambled eggs, coffee and croissants. Outside on Park Avenue, February rain streamed down on pedestrians hurrying to work.

There was one long main table at the front of the ballroom near the stage. No one sat at it: all the occupants were working the room, shaking hands, meeting old friends, placating old enemies. A tumult of information and gossip poured from the mouths of two thousand people; it boiled over the struggling waiters in their short red jackets as they maneuvered trays of hot coffee and eggs between the crowded tables; it rose above the cream and gilt walls, passed the chandeliers and hung from the ceiling, where a silver unicorn raced across a gilded sky. It was power and excitement and part of the political way of life in New York City.

"Ladies and gentlemen. Ladies and gentlemen." A man with a gavel pounded away on a podium on the stage. To his right was a felt-covered table with four chairs; behind him a banner stretched across a blue curtain, proclaiming, "New York Democrats Welcome Elliot Weyden."

"Ladies and gentlemen, if you would please take your seats, we could begin." There were more bangs of the gavel, and then some people appeared on the stage and sat down behind the table and poured themselves glasses of water.

People began to drift back to the main table; they were the politicos, the power players, in the greatest city in the world. Some of them had been elected to power—the mayor, the borough presidents; others had not, having created their own power, wrested it from positions of prominence, bought it or been appointed. They handshook their way back to the main table. Sometimes they used both hands, as though the hands offered them by the seated guests were a rope on which they pulled themselves upward.

Yarrow sat with some of her press cohorts at a table on an upper balcony near the stage. She watched Elliot take his seat at the main table and gulp down a cup of coffee. The words of the master of ceremonies flowed over her. She had not spoken to Elliot since last summer except for that brief meeting at the "21" Club. She feasted her eyes on him as any woman does who loves a man. And on another level, as a newspaper publisher, she looked at him candidly as a man seeking the highest office in the land. Someone tapped her on the shoulder. It was Mel Gavins, the public relations maven, who masterminded Elliot's campaign. He crouched down on the floor beside her and spoke so only she could hear. "He knows you're here. He wants to see you afterward."

"No, Mel. I made up my mind."

Mel nodded. He squeezed her hand; there was no need for words.

"Mel, tell him good luck." Mel nodded again and crept away through the tables as though he were blocking the view.

". . . Elliot Weyden," the voice continued through the microphone, "a hero of the Second World War who, without thought of his own life or limb, saved his men from a machine-gun attack by the Germans." The crowd roared as if on cue. "Elliot Weyden, who was so poor he stuffed paper in his shoes to fill the holes; the son of immigrants, who suffered under the greatest depression this country has ever seen and rose above it to claim the American dream; Elliot Weyden, a self-made man, a millionaire, who has never forgotten his humble roots, and has shown that business has a human face." There were more cheers. "A man who, as co-chairman of the Governor's Committee to investigate Organized Crime, fearlessly investigated the corruption rampant in our city; a man whose humanity has led him to establish a foundation in Washington for research into birth defects. Ladies and gentlemen, may I introduce New York's favorite son, Elliot Weyden." A roar of applause and foot stamping shook the venerable ballroom.

Elliot bounded up the stairs at the side of the stage. He shook hands with each of the men at the felt-covered table, and then stood at the podium with his hands up until the hall quieted down. He leaned forward into the microphone. "My name is Elliot Weyden and I'm running for president."

The room erupted again and Elliot grinned until the hubbub settled down.

"Why would anyone run for president? What does it say about a man's ego to admit he strives after the highest office in the land? My fellow Americans, I love my country. It is you who put this burden on me. It is a burden I pick up gladly. Here in America we live free, and we live free because we have the courage to believe in the people. We believe in the people's ability to think. We believe in the people's ability to vote. We believe in the people's ability to feel compassion. There will always be Americans willing to stand for office, willing to strive, willing to work and fight for what we believe in. We believe in peace in the world and compassion for our fellowman. It is time we got rid of a Republican administration. The Republican party believes, as Calvin Coolidge said, that the business of America is business. I believe that the business of America is people.''

Yarrow had stopped listening to the words. She was mesmerized by Elliot's performance. All his passion and enthusiasm were conveyed by his voice. His body was very still. He was like a conductor, and his voice, the orchestra, and she, only part of an audience watching some extraordinary performance. His voice rose and swooped. She realized he spoke in a different pitch when he was speaking publicly. It was not unpleasant; it was different. It had become a powerful tool which, when taken together with his strong and handsome body, his fine head and brooding eyes, amalgamated the listeners. She felt its effect and she shivered. He had begun to come down now, she realized. She could tell from his voice, the intensity of the message was now over. He told a little joke. It relieved the tension. The room rocked with laughter. It was not that funny a joke, but Elliot had the audience in the palm of his hand. The two thousand people in that room were in love with him, Yarrow thought. She had never heard a demagogue speak before. It shocked her to think that Elliot had become one.

She ducked out quietly while the questions began. She thought about Elliot as the taxi made its way downtown to her office. She was a registered Republican, she believed people should help themselves. But she was not an ideologue. She voted for candidates as often as she voted for platforms. Elliot was different; he believed that his Democratic dogma held the cure for his country's ills. He had an answer. Yarrow was not partisan. As a newspaperwoman she did not think that was too bad a thing to be. The danger was that such an attitude left one either too pragmatic to be trusted or too cynical to be wise.

In her office Yarrow wrote up her impressions of Elliot's speech. She knew Ned had a reporter working on Elliot's fight for the nomination. Humphrey had declared in December, and

Kennedy had announced his candidacy last month. Johnson had been running since way back, and no one knew whether Symington would run. As for the Republicans, Governor Rockefeller had pulled back from the race and Vice-President Nixon hung in limbo. The Democratic runoff was the exciting story of the year, and Yarrow had instructed Ned to go all out for it.

Cal came to town again in March, and Yarrow asked him home to have dinner with the children. He was pleased, and came bearing a pair of silver earrings for Lily and a red eighteen-wheeler truck for Buck. Buck, aged seven, thought the truck was too young for him. Lily's avariciousness, a trait that Yarrow worried about, was sated by her present. Lily seemed to have transferred her cravings for food into cravings for trinkets.

After dinner they went upstairs to the formal sitting room, where Yarrow lit the fire in the grate. She offered him a brandy and sat down. Edith's sturdy legs could be seen thundering up and down the staircase past the door. Yarrow got up and closed the door.

"You're a beautiful woman, Yarrow," Cal said.

"Thank you."

He sat beside her on the sofa. Buck came in to say good night.

"Can I watch half an hour of television with Edith and Grandma?"

"Buck, it's late."

"Just one half hour, one wee half hour?"

"Don't 'Jock' me," she said but his charm had won. "OK, one half hour only." Buck left in a flash, not to miss a minute.

"Buck's learned to manipulate me through flattery," she said with a sigh.

"Perhaps it would work for me."

Yarrow looked at him. He was an attractive man, he was successful in his own field. But she couldn't imagine herself being in love with him, couldn't imagine it at all. She thought of Mary-Ellen's long-ago affair in California, of her kicking her panties underneath the sofa. Yarrow shook the thought from her head. It would be like being unfaithful to Elliot. She tried to force herself to see Cal as an attractive alternative, but it didn't work. He had taken her hand.

"It's a long time since I went courting. I never looked at another woman while Mary was alive. No sir. But I get lonely. You must get lonely, Yarrow?"

"Yes, I do."

"I admire you very much. You're different from most women

I meet—widows, friends of Mary's—some of them seem lost. I know how to handle women like that—but you? What I'm trying to say is, I respect you, Yarrow. I'm sorry I came on so strong when we met the first time."

"Oh, I've forgotten that."

"I'd like to see you when I come to New York, take you to dinner, to a show, not just for business."

"Cal, I want you to understand. I'm not looking for a husband."

"Oh, hell, I know that. But companionship, friendship. And who knows, one day somewhere down the line, you might learn to love me."

He put his brandy down very solemnly and turned to her and kissed her. His lips were warm and tasted of the cognac. But nothing happened inside Yarrow.

"Let's just be friends first," she said. She held his hand.

"Friends," he said.

Deke Smith's office in California lay just north of Wilshire Boulevard. Through his window he could see the sun beating down on exclusive boutiques and restaurants, women, dressed in pantsuits and light dresses, sauntering into Elizabeth Arden for beauty treatments or into Nate 'n' Al's deli for a pastrami sandwich. Outside, the pace was slower than New York's, but inside Deke Smith's office, the pace was frantic. You could not tell which side of the continent you were on, for a battery of people and telephones was hard at work.

It was April and Deke at last had the OK to start setting up an official Draft Weyden campaign. Elliot had already poured thousands of dollars into the cause, and now Deke was marshaling his forces to urge contributors to support Elliot's run for office.

In twenty states across the nation, there were little groups of Weyden supporters. In each of these, Deke wanted the excitement to swell. He had carefully orchestrated a number of speeches and rallies that Elliot would attend. He had managed to buy spots on television and taken out newspaper ads to get his candidate's name known. It was all a matter of fine-tuning—to move too soon would be as disastrous as to move too late. If he overspent now, the coffers might be empty when they needed to make their final push.

"Yes," he said into the telephone, "yes. Listen, cut the red tape, will you? I want the balloons up, and I want you to get those people out there in the arena before Weyden arrives." He hung up the phone and grabbed his coat, talked to his chief-of-staff while he ran out to his car.

Deke's law practice had gone down the tubes since he had started running this campaign. But he loved it. He loved Elliot Weyden. The man had an integrity and decency that Deke admired. Elliot had not been touched by the cynicism and compromise that tainted many others Deke had worked for. At first Deke had wondered if Elliot had the toughness to undergo a rigorous year of campaigning, but once he had made up his mind to run, Elliot had thrown himself into campaigning with an enthusiasm that was infectious. Each day began with breakfast with his advisers; they talked strategy, finance, press coverage. He traveled, he smiled, he spoke, he made statements, he cajoled, he lunched, he flew, he answered questions, he refused to be drawn into personal vendettas against the other candidates. So far he had not made a wrong move. Every day, wherever he was, Elliot placed a call to his daughter, Meredith. Elliot Weyden was the loneliest man Deke Smith ever knew.

Deke arrived at the sports arena well ahead of Elliot. The whole gambit today was to get Elliot press coverage. There would only be a few hundred citizens there, and the thrust of the event, carefully orchestrated, was a presentation of an award by the NAACP to Elliot in recognition of his support over the years. Deke was happy to see that the press almost outnumbered the people who had gathered. The stalwart Democratic volunteers had already set up a great array of balloons that spelled out "Draft Weyden" in black on white. Deke realized that the balloons were on the wrong side of the arena floor, and wouldn't be seen by the viewers at home.

"Move them. Move them," he said. He wished Mel Gavins was here. He knew more about this kind of thing. But Elliot's national organization was still thin, and Mel was in Scranton preparing for Elliot's visit there on Friday.

Deke had just finished coaching the few people who were to speak. There was a leader of the black community, a Baptist minister with frizzy gray hair, and a woman with a baby in her arms. A little girl of four or five was going to present Elliot with some flowers.

"OK," Deke said, "you all know what questions to ask. I don't want you to look at the camera, and I don't want you to get between the camera and Mr. Weyden. Just be natural." The little girl nodded and smiled. Just then Elliot arrived with his advisers. He looked handsome and youthful. Some women screamed as though they were still bobby-soxers. Elliot took it all in stride. The church choir in their crimson robes began to sing "Amazing Grace," and the little girl with the bouquet of flowers froze in her seat. She was unable to move and even when the minister urged her forward, she was unable to do so. Elliot came over and picked her up in his arms.

"You remind me of my own little girl," he said. The cameras clicked and whirred, and although the presentations were made and the little speeches were given and Elliot's responses were recorded, this was the picture and the words that were used. The message beamed into people's living rooms that night; here was a candidate with heart, who loved children, who acted in a natural way. No matter that no one heard his ideas on foreign policy or defense or even domestic issues; his name recognition was being reinforced and the papers the next day carried the same picture.

Deke was delighted. "Good," he said afterward, before rushing back to his bank of telephones, "trust your own instincts, Elliot. They're always the best."

Palmer Truitt hated the publicity that Elliot was receiving.

Every time he turned on the television, or opened a newspaper, there was a glowing interview with Elliot. Palmer had never gotten over Elliot punching him in Jamaica two years ago. No one punched Palmer Truitt and got away with it. He was the publisher of the *Courier*, for Christ's sake. Some local Jamaican rag had even published a picture of him with his nose bleeding after he left the hotel. His divorce from Greta had cost a fortune in alimony—but then Greta had become a drag. Thank God she had remarried and the alimony payments had stopped. Now his wife, Nancy, was on him about Elliot Weyden. She thought he was "cute." "What?" he'd asked. "You know, cute—a gentleman," she'd said. "He doesn't use street language like you do, Palmer." Well, what did she know. Her judgment was impaired, being pregnant for the first time and all.

"I'm going to get that son of a bitch," he said to Sandy as he threw the *Courier* across the desk in his office. "Why are we being so nice to this shitass?"

"No more than anyone else. He's a viable candidate and he's a New Yorker."

"Well, he can't be that clean. I want you to find out everything you can about him. I want to know what he ate for breakfast, I want to know who he sleeps with, I want to know everything about that bastard."

"Don't you have any loyalty? He's married to your stepsister."

"I don't give a damn about that. Is he still banging your wife?"

Sandy got up and threw a punch at him. Palmer ducked. "You dirty bastard," Sandy said.

Palmer screamed as Sandy drew back his arm again.

"Don't hit me."

"I'm not going to waste my time."

"You're fired!" Palmer shouted, finding his courage.

"Don't worry," said Sandy, "I don't have to work for scum like you."

But outside Palmer's office, Sandy began to shake. He had a mortgage to meet, car payments to make. He paid support for his three children. He stood rubbing his thumb on his moustache for a few minutes until he calmed down. One thing was sure, he wasn't walking back into Palmer's office and asking to be hired back. Palmer Truitt would trample his own mother if she stood in his way.

It was at a press conference in Scranton, Pennsylvania, that a reporter first asked Elliot about his father-in-law. Elliot had been barnstorming the state. He'd received good press coverage, what Yarrow would have called "ink," and it was his last night in the state. In Scranton anthracite and coal mining had once dominated the economy; now there was unemployment and things were grim. He had just finished a prepared text about his plans for helping the industrial areas of the northeast when a male reporter lobbed him the question.

"Is it true, Mr. Weyden, that your late father-in-law laundered money for the Mafia?"

"Not true," said Elliot. "Where did you get that information?"

"Wasn't your wife's father an intimate of Meyer Lansky, the Jewish gangster?"

Elliot glanced at Mel Gavins, who had started up from his seat.

"I have no comment on that."

"That's it for tonight, ladies and gentlemen," said Mel, coming forward and pulling Elliot away from the group.

"Will you have a comment tomorrow, Mr. Weyden?"

Mel rushed him out of the conference room and into an elevator.

"What was that all about?" said Elliot.

"Muckrakers," said Mel. "Come on, we're going to have to find out who's spreading it and you've got to tell me the truth."

"I always have."

"Elliot, if you've got any other skeletons I should know about, tell me now so I'm prepared."

Mel wiped his handkerchief over his bald head. He was sweating profusely.

Elliot met his gaze as only an honest man could.

"I can't think of a damn thing."

Palmer Truitt lounged against the door in his mother's bedroom.

Fabiana was very ill, but anger had given her strength. She lay in bed, her tea tray abandoned beside her thin form, and she rattled the *Courier* at him.

"How could you write this filth about Rich?"

"He was filth."

"He was not. He was an honorable man. You knew he had business with many people. This—this is a total distortion of the facts to meet your own ends."

"He was a scumbag."

"Your language is as disgusting as your morals."

Palmer played with his gold watchband. He was enjoying himself. Already half the press was picking up his story on the Real Elliot Weyden and quoting his newspaper.

"You say that Rich paid for Elliot's house. What about this house? Are we living on Mafia money? How can you do this to your own family?"

Palmer laughed. He looked around the room at the walls lined with blue watered-silk taffeta, at the Piranesi prints that hung on either side of the marble fireplace.

"The Newnoms are not my family. My name is Truitt. And aren't you living on the old duffer's money? Rich never let me in this house, so that's just too bad for his memory. You want to remember him as a nice old man who looked after you. He was an old miser who wouldn't let you give me an allowance, wouldn't even let me in the house when I needed help."

"You deserved the way he treated you. You abused his kindness."

"Stop playing Lady Forgiving, Mother."

"Why do you want to destroy Elliot? What did he ever do to you?"

He came forward, his pretty face twisted into a grimace.

"Because to me he is a McLean. This is the way to hurt them."

"I don't understand you."

"You of all people understand revenge. You made me this way. You filled me with anger, you told me about the McLeans, and how they cheated you way back and how you'd never forgive them. Why do you back off now when I've got them where it hurts, right by the short hairs?''

"You married Greta. Didn't you love her?"

"No. It was a game—but it was no fun after a while, because she didn't fight back."

Fabiana lay against her pillows. "I don't know you anymore, Palmer. Something in you has snapped." She rang a bell beside her bed. Her maid came in. "See Mr. Truitt out, please." She turned her head away. She didn't want to let him see her cry. She wasn't crying for him. She didn't know him anymore. She was crying for the little boy with the long eyelashes she had known a long time ago.

Yarrow was in Platte City on one of her six weekly visits when she read the wires about Elliot's so-called Mafia connections.

"Oh, no," she said. She called Ned in New York.

"Is it true?" she asked.

"True or not, this man is running for president. We have to print it."

"But what evidence do you have?"

"The *Courier*'s been digging deep."

"Ned, don't you see? It's a vendetta against Elliot by Truitt."

"Are you telling me not to run it?"

"No, I'm not. How are you handling it?"

"It's a big story. I've splashed it across page one." He waited for her to say something. The silence stretched on the telephone. Everything in her screamed to stop the story: I don't want to run this story—oh, Dad, you never told me how it would hurt.

"You have to use your own judgment, Ned," she said. "I'm not objective on this one."

She hung up. She felt as though she had put a knife through Elliot's heart. She tried to reach him on the telephone, but she couldn't get through. Every paper she picked up, every radio news service and television news led with the story. A TV crew camped outside Blanchette's house in Virginia. There was a fleeting glimpse of her driving through the gate in her car and then a panoramic shot of the Coakley estate. Yarrow felt sick as she switched off the television set in her hotel room. Elliot was due to speak in Denver the following day.

The next day she drove in heavy rain up to Denver where she was looking at a television station, KMZO-TV, which was for sale. Cal was taking her out to dinner that night, and he told her he would meet her at the station. He knew the owners well, he said.

Yarrow met with the station directors in the afternoon, and after touring the facility and walking through the studios, they went into a control booth to watch the nightly news being telecast. Cal came in while she was watching. He squeezed her shoulder. The station manager was saying something about the ratings for the program. Yarrow was looking at the set and watching the cameras moving on their dollies when the news commentator began:

"Further revelations have come out today about Mr. Elliot Weyden, one of the front-runners in the Democratic race for the presidential nomination. A report in today's *New York Courier* claims that Mr. Weyden was the owner of a brothel on East Thirty-eighth Street, and has been since 1947. A meeting of the . . ."

An assistant put his head in the door and spoke to one of the directors. "We've got Weyden live. The crew is at the stadium where he was going to make his campaign speech."

Yarrow was on her feet. "Cal, please, take me there as fast as you can."

He didn't ask questions, and when they got to the stadium, she waved away his offer of an umbrella and he took her through the gate. On their way in they passed some reporters leaving. It had stopped raining and the stadium was a sea of mud. The camera crew was finished, but the bright arc lights were still on. Bedraggled paper and streamers, with their colors running, lay abandoned over the bleachers and the stage. Yarrow saw Elliot as she had never seen him before, sitting looking dejected and aged on a folding chair, oblivious to everyone.

"Cal . . ." she began.

"You don't have to explain," he said. "I think I always knew. If you need me, you know how to reach me."

She pulled her Burberry around her and thrust her hands in her pockets. She watched while people left; they passed her, intent on their own business. Scraps of words came to her:

"Finished, poor bastard."

"Did you get that last shot?"

"Does that mean his campaign is over?"

"What do you think?"

There were only two or three people left now. Elliot hadn't moved. Yarrow walked forward slowly. Mel Gavins and Deke Smith saw her. She ignored them; her eyes were only on him. She went up the few steps where the gaudy paper decorations had ripped.

"Hello, Blackbird," she said. He didn't look up. She stood in front of him and he looked at her shoes. With a sob he threw his arms around her hips. She stood over him, protecting him, holding his smooth dark head against her belly. "They'll never get you again," she said. "Never give them another chance."

CHAPTER 31

*F*ABIANA TRUITT NEWNOM WAS DYING. SHE LAY ON HER BED. THE once perfect skin now the color of graying foie gras. Her hair was still very black, for she had continued to dye it, and it hung so that it covered one side of her face.

"Do you have a cigarette?" she asked in her husky voice. "Silly nurses won't let me have them. It won't make any difference now. They should have stopped me years ago."

"No. I don't smoke," said Yarrow.

"There are some hidden over there in my dressing table drawer—would you mind?" Yarrow was uncomfortable going through the personal things, the scarves and letters and hair bows in Fabiana's drawer. She was uncomfortable being in this woman's bedroom. She found the box and some matches and gave them to Fabiana.

"Would you mind opening the window?"

Yarrow crossed the yellow and blue rug and opened the double-glazed windows over Fifth Avenue. Fabiana lit up and inhaled with great relief, and then fanned away the smoke with her hand.

"Thank you."

Yarrow sat down again on a Savonarola chair.

Beside her, on a commode, a small black and white television set soundlessly showed the inauguration of President John F. Kennedy. It was January 20, 1961. President Kennedy wore a top hat.

"I must be honest. I didn't want to come," Yarrow said.

"Yes, I know. But I had to ask you. I am dying. Oh, please, no false sentiment, but I felt I owed you an explanation about Palmer and Elliot."

"Palmer destroyed Elliot."

"Elliot's a survivor. He will go on to other things. But what Palmer did was—was ugly and I am to blame."

"You?"

"I've heard of Elliot and Palmer's contretemps a few years ago—over Greta, yes? But that wasn't it. It goes much further back than that. Back to your grandfather."

"To Jock?" Yarrow sat forward on the sling seat of the chair.

"I hated your Jock. As my mother hated him. He swindled my father out of his inheritance. My father was the original partner of Colonel Truitt in the *Platte City Journal*. But he sold it out for a worthless silver mine and a balloon of dreams."

"Your father was Shipam." Yarrow made it a statement. She was stunned, trying to absorb the information Fabiana was giving her.

"Yes. Fabian Wallace Shipam. How do you know that?"

"F. W. Shipam. I remember Grandfather telling me it was an acronym—'For what shall it profit a man if he shall gain the whole world . . .' " Yarrow's voice trailed away.

"I blamed Jock for so many things. He was the repository of everything that went wrong for me. In that way I didn't have to blame myself. And yet, if he hadn't taken my father's money, and if my father hadn't died trying to get silver out of that mine, where would I be now?"

Fabiana began to cough and Yarrow said, "Shall I call the nurse?" But the nurse had already put her head around the bedroom door. Fabiana dropped the hand holding the cigarette down on the far side of the bed. "Go away," she said imperiously. "I'm talking." The nurse withdrew.

"You can't 'what-if' all your life," she went on. "My mother did. She was determined that if she couldn't get even with Jock, I would. Jock McLean would pay. All the McLeans would pay. And I tried to do the same with Palmer." She blew out some smoke.

"To be fair to Jock," said Yarrow, "he did go back and try to find your father. The whole area was devastated and empty."

"I'm not surprised—typhus broke out in the camp soon after he got there. My father died of it, and my mother and I were left destitute. There were times we didn't eat; we lived on the street; she sang for pennies; she took in washing when we had a room. Get even, she said. Don't get mad, get even. She developed a whole new persona for herself and me when she married again."

"You mean, no popes in your background? No Italian holidays?"

"None. All invented. Do you know what my mother showed

me, years later when we had no fear of starvation anymore? She kept a can of sardines at the bottom of her pocketbook. She had it all the time when we were begging on the streets. Things never got so bad, she said, that she felt she had to use it.'' Fabiana laughed. ''There were nights when I went to bed crying with hunger when I was small, yet she never took it out. She never threw it away.''

Yarrow was silent, but her mind churned with questions. Her ideas about Fabiana were undergoing a tremendous upheaval. Yarrow had envied her, had felt guilty about that envy. She had been living on a diet of lies and half truths about Fabiana that she now knew to be false.

''I once thought my father was in love with you,'' she said.

Fabiana's eyes widened and for a moment she looked hauntingly beautiful, like her old self. ''There was only one woman for James, and that was your mother. I flirted with him but that was only to make mischief.'' She coughed again and then smiled. ''Oh, this is cathartic. I should do it more often.''

''What about Max Horace—why didn't you blame him as well as the McLeans?''

''Because I knew I could use Max to hurt Jock. He was a weak man who would do anything for money. When I couldn't buy out your family I went to Max—''

''—*You* underwrote Max Horace and the *Record*?''

Fabiana shrugged. ''Yes. It was all part of a plan.'' She lay back, looking very tired and said, ''But it's all gone too far. I poisoned Palmer. I feel terrible about Greta. I had to tell you. Please tell Elliot. He wouldn't come to see me. They keep saying he is still out of the country.''

The nurse came in and whispered to Yarrow, ''You'll have to leave now. Mrs. Newnom must get her sleep.''

Fabiana's eyes fluttered.

''It's such a pity,'' she said. ''You and I could have been friends, Yarrow McLean.''

It was a frantic day in April. Even the wind outside the office window seemed to be in a hurry to get things done. The traffic on the Brooklyn Bridge raced across in sun-flashed streaks of metal and glass. Yarrow's phones had not stopped ringing since she arrived. Margaret had taken on an assistant to cope.

''Why don't you just say no to all of this?'' said Yarrow, lifting a wedge of invitations and inquiries from her desk. ''Or dump it in the wastebasket?'' Margaret looked horrified. Yarrow said, "Well, at least it would cut down on your filing. What's all this stuff? I'm sinking in a sea of information I don't need."

"You do too much," said Margaret. "I have no control over the mail that comes in."

Yarrow read through some of the pieces of paper.

"An invitation to speak at a medical college in Ohio—attend the American Jewish Congress dinner to honor Abe L. Rubin—who's he?—a ball at the Metropolitan—be chairman of a fund for a doggie home—co-chair the restoration appeal for the concert hall. I have to run a business! How can anyone cope with all of these? No, no, no. Send a check to this one, say I'm out of town here."

"You have to go to this one, Miss McLean."

"Why?"

"You've already accepted to be head of the committee. Your name's at the top of the invitation."

Yarrow groaned. "I hate asking people for money. Why do I get on these things?"

Margaret gathered up the offending pieces of paper and said nothing.

"Get me Mrs. Griffin on the phone. Perhaps she can rustle up some names of big givers. I've already been through all the people I know. I can't keep going back to the same ones. And Margaret?"

Margaret was going out the door. "Yes, Miss McLean?"

"Next time I agree to go on a charity committee or make a speech, chop my phone line."

Yarrow's eyes felt gritty as she waded through her correspondence. She had four meetings today and a luncheon uptown which she could not get out of. She felt she was not seeing enough of Freya these days; she had wanted to sit with her mother and talk to her about the old times. Ever since Fabiana had told Yarrow about Jock's deceit, Yarrow had wanted to talk to someone about it. Elliot had gone to England months ago to deal with his despair in his own way. When he telephoned her, which was seldom, it was as if he were grieving. They did not talk about the things that meant the most to them. With an effort, Yarrow put thoughts of Elliot and her family out of her head. She read, she dictated, she worked on the telephone.

"Mrs. Griffin on line two," said Margaret.

"Mary-Ellen," said Yarrow, "I'm glad you're home."

"Well, if it isn't Miss McLean calling the old home guard, remembering her old buddies."

Yarrow's antennae pricked up, but she laughed politely and

said, "I'm sorry, I've been so busy. How are you? How are the children?"

"Apart from the baby having conjunctivitis and the dog being mated right now as we talk, I'm fine. As for the other children, they are all quite well, thank you."

"Mary-Ellen, I need help right now with a charity I'm involved with. I need some names. You know lots of people."

"Not as many as you."

"You and Ned go to a lot more functions than I do. Would you have a list of people, you know, a charity you've worked on, who could buy some tickets?"

"You mean rich people."

Once again a warning signal flashed in Yarrow's brain.

"What is it, Mary-Ellen?"

Mary-Ellen sighed, then her voice sharpened. "Look, I'm as busy as you are. I'll see what I can do."

"Thank you." Yarrow hung up. She was not insensitive to other people's moods. Mary-Ellen's attitude troubled her, but before she could go over the conversation again in her mind, it was time for her next appointment and Margaret was pointing at her wristwatch.

At the end of the day Yarrow put on a pair of flat-heeled black shoes and walked through the building. She liked to see what people were doing, wanted them to see her. She was leaning on the city editor's desk asking questions about a page three story when his phone rang. It was Margaret. Could she transfer Lainie, Mr. Weyden's assistant? It was urgent.

"Lainie, what is it?" Yarrow cupped her hands over the mouth and earpieces to cut out the noise of the typewriters and ringing telephones.

"I'm worried about Mr. Weyden. I think you should come over."

"He's back? I thought he was still overseas?"

"Mr. Weyden has been back a week and he hasn't seen or called anyone. I hope I'm not being disloyal, but I thought I should call you. He keeps saying that Mrs. Weyden has taken Meredith away from him. You know how he loves that child."

"You did the right thing. I'll be there in half an hour—forty minutes—whatever it takes me."

Yarrow waited impatiently for the elevator to take her back up to her office to collect her briefcase. When the elevator door opened, a scruffy messenger boy was lounging against the push-buttons, picking at a zit. He held a bicycle wheel in one filthy hand. His appearance and manner offended Yarrow.

"Who the hell are you?" she said. The boy stood straighter and began stuttering. "You're a disgrace," said Yarrow. "Look at you. You represent me and my company when you go out looking like that." One of the clerks from the accounting office got in at the next floor. "Bill," said Yarrow, recognizing him, and giving him a hundred-dollar bill from her pocketbook, "take this boy and pay him off. One week's salary, whatever it is. I don't want to see him in this building again."

She got out at her floor.

"Who was *that*?" said the messenger boy, playing with his oily nose and then taking the money Bill offered.

"That's the boss. Now what department are you with?"

"Me?" said the boy, pocketing the money as he got off the elevator. "I don't even work here. I'm just delivering a parcel."

"He's in there. He's been drinking pretty heavily. He hasn't eaten for days."

"Thank you, Lainie. You go home now. I'll look after him."

"Are you sure you can manage, Miss McLean?"

"Yes."

"Well, I do have my kids waiting for dinner. Good night."

Yarrow opened the door to Elliot's study. It was dark, save for the twinkling lights of Manhattan through the black windows. She stepped forward, and glass crunched under her foot.

"Lainie, is that you?"

She hardly recognized Elliot's voice. It sounded hoarse and cracked like an old man's.

"No, it's Yarrow."

He let out a long groan. "Go away," he said.

"Can I put on the light?"

"NO."

She felt her way toward the voice. There were glass and pillows and papers on the floor. She groped over to his armchair, and then as her eyes became accustomed to the gloom, she saw him sprawled out, his silhouette turned toward the window, his head sunk into his chest, the white reflection of his shirt giving off a faint glow in the darkness. He had no shoes on. She sat down on a pouffe beside him and was silent.

"It looks pretty, doesn't it?" he said. His voice was slurred. "All those pretty lights of the city. It looks as though the whole place works; that it's good, that it's a good place to be, you know? From this distance it looks like that."

"Yes. It does."

"That's what we need—distance—to make it seem like that.

Don't get too close, because if you do, it will DESTROY you.'' He smashed his fist into the side of his chair.

She was silent.

''The newspapers stink,'' he said. ''Journalism stinks.'' He turned and looked at her. ''You're in a rotten business.''

She could see his eyes glistening.

''You build people up,'' he went on, ''and then you tear them down. You people, you're all the same, you don't know about loyalty or decency. You know that word?'' He leaned forward and she smelled the whiskey on his breath. ''Decency.'' He spoke with venom. She touched his cheek. Thick stubble scratched her fingers.

''Sure, I owned a brothel, but I had nothing to do with it. God, I had forgotten all about it. I bought it to help a friend, a woman who was kind to me. It could be a grocery store now for all I know.'' He ran his hand over his face. ''We sold most of that land when the UN was being built. I let Mrs. Neil rent her building for as long as she wanted it. Did I really do something so very wrong? Their business is sordid but what I did, was it wrong?''

''Living on immoral earnings,'' said Yarrow quietly.

He sighed again. ''That's what they tried to say about Newnom, too. The man had one client whose money he invested.'' He laughed. ''I'm sure there were things that Newnom did that were much worse. But that's not why he was pilloried. Where does guilt begin and stop? Can you tell me that?''

''I don't know.''

''Yarrow,'' he said. It was the first time he had used her name since she came in. ''Would you have published the story—if you'd gotten it first, if one of your reporters had come up with it—*and you're my woman*—would you have published it?''

''I don't know.''

He suddenly grabbed her wrist and twisted it and held on.

''Answer me!''

Yarrow looked into his eyes and saw the pain there. But she loved him too much to lie to him.

''Yes,'' she said.

He released her arm. ''I thought so.''

''I love you, Elliot.''

He laughed. ''You and the *New York Telegraph* and all your noble colleagues.''

She stood up and kicked the whiskey bottle that stood beside his chair across the room.

"Well, we don't cry when we're down. We don't sit around and pity ourselves when someone hurts us. We fight back."

"Oh, spare me."

"It was the truth! The truth. I can't help it if it hurt you. Oh, you can complain about my newspaper, and you can tell me that I have a bunch of sleaze bags working for me and you can hate my guts. But that's what I'm there for and you just have to live with that because if I kowtow to every poor bastard who thinks he's getting the rough end of the stick, I may as well print out toilet paper."

"I already think you do."

She stood breathing heavily and watched him. He shook his head and dropped his gaze.

Yarrow's pulse was pounding. She felt dizzy and wanted to end this. Could he separate the woman from the publisher?

"Anyway," she said, controlling her voice and softening it with a great effort, "you're the one who stinks now. You reek of booze and sweat. How long have you been sitting here?"

"I don't know. Yesterday? Two days? Four? Who cares?"

"I care. You're going to come home with me. I can't stay here and you need me."

"I do not."

"You damn well do."

"You're not going to walk in here and fix my life now that you've broken it."

"Just you watch me. Where are your shoes?"

"Don't have any shoes."

"Here they are." She slipped them on his feet while he complained. "Can you stand up?" He tried to move but he was too weak to stand. Yarrow telephoned the front doorman to send up her chauffeur. She took out her comb and brushed Elliot's hair, and made him sit forward so she could slip his jacket on. He was shivering, though it was not cold. She fetched a blanket from his room and put it around his shoulders. "Mr. Weyden has been very sick," she said to Vasik, the chauffeur, when he came. "We're going to take him home—to my place."

Yarrow was shocked when she saw Elliot in the bright light of her bathroom. He had lost fifteen pounds and his face was haggard. When she took off his clothes to help him into the bathtub, she saw that the skin on his belly sagged and there were wrinkles where his buttocks met his thighs.

"I hate you to see me like this," he said. She soaped him with a washcloth and used a loofah on his back.

"This isn't you," she said. She shaved him with her razor and found an old nightshirt of hers that fit him. By the time she led him to the bed, the warmth of the bath had relaxed him and he fell into a deep sleep before she had lifted the covers over him.

She had never had a man stay in the house before, and when she went up to say good night to Buck, he said, "Is Uncle Elliot staying the night here?"

"Yes. He's sick and I have to look after him."

"In your bed?"

"Yes, Buck. You know I've always loved Elliot."

"Are you going to have sex with him?"

Not tonight, thought Yarrow.

"Buck, if you love someone very, very much, then sex is how you let that person know that, but sex isn't the reason you love them."

Buck thought for a moment. His room was full of gerbils and white mice and hamsters that sniffled and moved and squeaked in the dark.

"My garter snakes don't have sex," he said. "At least I haven't seen them at it." He jumped out of bed. "Have you seen them eat? Look." He scooped up a live goldfish from a plastic bag of water and placed it in a water receptacle in the snakes' tank. Immediately both snakes attacked each end of the fish and began to lash their bodies around the glass walls. "The one that takes the head always wins," said Buck. Yarrow led him back to bed.

"How observant you are."

"I like Uncle Elliot."

"I do, too. Go to sleep."

Yarrow switched off the bedside light and went downstairs to the kitchen. Edith had picked up Elliot's dinner tray.

"Mr. Weyden didn't eat much, did he? I never saw a man so thin." Edith sucked in her own large frame, as she thought about it. "We'll fatten him up again, don't you worry. Lamb's fry and bacon, tripe and onions, toad-in-the-hole. Oooh, and suet pudding, that'll put a weight in his belly."

"A lead weight," said Yarrow. Thank God, I have my family, they always pull me back to earth.

Yarrow picked up an apple. "Edith, how do snakes have sex?"

Edith went bright red. "I beg your pardon, Miss McLean?"

"I just wondered," said Yarrow, "I thought you might know." She went upstairs, munching her apple. She had forgotten how prudish Edith could be; besides, to Edith who had grown up in the Australian bush, the only good snake was a dead one.

Yarrow nursed Elliot for a week before she began to see signs that he was returning to normal. It was not that he was suffering from any kind of fever or disease, but as though he were in mourning for something that had died, something in himself that had been destroyed. At night, she would put her arms around him and go to sleep holding him as if he were a child. They did not make love in the accepted sense of the word, but every glance, every brush of one against the other, every thought of comfort was a statement of that condition.

In the morning, after she had breakfasted with the children, she had Millie take all the papers up to him and leave them on the table beside the window. They would be untouched when she came home at night. He would not leave her room, and Lily and Buck would knock and come in shyly and see him sitting in a chair beside the empty fireplace, dressed in their mother's coral-colored terrycloth robe with his wrists out and his shins showing. Yarrow had sent for his clothes, but he did not have the energy or the interest to change into them. Freya, who could not climb the stairs, sent him up a potpourri for his bath from the herbs she grew around the basement flat.

"Freya's here?" he asked one Saturday, as though he'd had a memory lapse.

"Of course," said Yarrow, then she hesitated. "Do you know where you are, Elliot?"

"Platte City? No. No. New York, yes?"

"Yes. New York."

"Is—is Blanchette here?"

"No, not here. You're with me."

He became agitated. "Where's Meredith? Is Meredith all right?"

"Meredith's with her mother. Shall I get them on the phone?"

She had no idea where they were. She hadn't thought about Elliot's family since she had moved him in. He nodded and she left the room and telephoned Lainie.

"I think they're in London," said Lainie. "They all left together months ago and then Mr. Weyden turned up here on his own. But I can find her."

That night, while Yarrow was sitting beside Elliot telling him about her day, waiting for the old spark that she would recognize and know from it that he was mending, the telephone rang from Paris. Yarrow recognized Blanchette's voice immediately.

"I wish to speak to Elliot."

Yarrow handed the telephone to Elliot. She watched his face, the grooves in the cheeks from which she had scraped the gray stubble, the cracked lips from which she had kissed the dried blood.

"I'm much better now," he was saying. "May I speak to Meredith? No. Please don't lie to her, Blanchette. You'll frighten her." He paused and then he closed his eyes and tears flowed down his cheeks. "Hello, darling," he said, "how's my Popette?"

Yarrow stood up and left the room. The light on the telephone glowed for a long time, and when it went out she went back upstairs to see him and he had fallen asleep with a smile on his face. When she slipped into bed with him later, he put his arms around her for the first time since he had been ill. Oh, my love, she thought, as she nestled there and listened to his deep breathing, welcome home.

BOOK FOUR

- 1962–1988 -

FACSIMILE

Facsimile: A copy
A printing process in which the image
of the newspaper page is produced on
a cathode-ray screen

CHAPTER 32

"*M*ARGARET, WHAT'S HAPPENING?" YARROW FLUNG HER
gloves, her black crocodile bag and her walking
stick down on the sofa in her office as she went to her desk.

It was early December, the height of the pre-Christmas advertising season and ad pages were up at the *Telegraph*.

McLean Publishing's other acquisitions were doing well: Yarrow and Larry Schaeffer had started a magazine together, *Mollie* magazine, and it was a success; Yarrow had bought the television station in Denver (Cal had helped arrange the financing and was a junior partner), KMZO was leading the ratings; the *Platte City Journal-Record* and the *Sunday Journal* went from strength to strength. The company had started paying dividends to the family shareholders.

Yarrow wanted to expand her company further, but she hesitated to follow her own instincts. She was still unsure how much she could take on, what she could accomplish. This uncertainty was twofold. Elliot's spectacular fall from grace had shaken her confidence. If the mighty could so easily be toppled, what about jackstraws like herself? Yarrow shuddered as she thought about it. She had no illusions about her own worth or influence. Her chief assets, she knew, were that she wasn't afraid of hard work and her credit rating was good. Apart from those, all was ephemeral.

Secondly, the *Telegraph* was proving harder to turn into the black than she had thought. There was a limit to the amount of money Yarrow could keep losing on the paper—and every labor rumbling, every increase in the price of newsprint made Yarrow wonder how long she could keep it going. The Newspaper Guild had struck the *Courier* earlier in the month, and Yarrow, watching the *Telegraph* slowly inching its way forward, nibbled her nails with worry. When things got really bad and a free-floating anxiety seemed to envelop her, she would sit down and make out a list of problems. This, Greta had told her—Greta who knew all about anxiety—was the way to deal with it. Yarrow found, however, that her list of problems spilled over the pages, and she gave up and decided to attack each problem as it arose. "If it ain't broke, don't fix it," Grandfather had said. Yarrow often found herself talking to him in her head.

Margaret came in with her steno pad.

"You had a call from Mr. Marx at KMZO in Denver. I said you would return it as soon as possible."

"He's up early. What else?"

"Your first meeting is at ten o'clock with the *Mollie* magazine executives about the new monthly." The *Mollie* venture was so successful that Schaeffer was eager to start another. Yarrow picked up the dummy of *Belle*, the pasted-up prototype that Schaeffer wanted to finance jointly with McLean Publishing. It was to be thick and glossy and unashamedly narcissistic. It was going to do what Eugenia Sheppard did so brilliantly in the fashion pages of the *New York Herald Tribune*. Yarrow had looked at those features with envy—not envy for the clothes, but envy for the resources that the other newspaper had. The *Telegraph* was very low on the totem pole.

"What else?"

"Mr. Heartland called from Washington—could you call him as soon as possible? Mr. Weyden called. He left the number he can be reached at in Paris. Mr. Griffin called—his wife had a baby girl."

"Good old Mary-Ellen. I forgot she was even pregnant. Is that the fourth or the fifth?"

"Fifth." Margaret read on through a string of messages and placed them on Yarrow's desk.

Yarrow hadn't seen Mary-Ellen for months. "Can you send Mary-Ellen some flowers? See if I can visit the hospital on my way home tonight."

"Your guests are due at seven-thirty."

"All I seem to do is eat," said Yarrow, making a note to call Edith about the menu, "but it's impossible to talk business through an opera." She was already dialing when Margaret left the room. She looked around the room while she listened to the dial tone. "Eat and talk on the telephone," she thought. She moved a small bunch of tight pink roses that stood in a jar to one side of her desk. Her office was not extravagant. In fact it was downright shabby; damp patches showed on the walls. When Margaret had pointed them out, Yarrow said they would ignore them. She refused to paint the room; there were more pressing needs. She had bought an eighteenth-century partner's desk and had hidden the Naugahyde chairs until she could afford new ones.

"Sandy," she said, sitting up abruptly when he answered the phone. "How's the job? Written any good speeches lately?"

"I think two of my original words were left intact last week—'and' and 'the.'"

"Oh, yes, I picked up your distinct style. Was it you who suggested we bomb the Russians out of Cuba if they didn't take their missiles out?"

"I'm a changed man, Yarrow. I've mellowed."

"That must be Washington; turns real men into jellyfish."

"I called you for a reason. I'm getting married on Saturday."

A jolt went through Yarrow, similar to that she had felt when he told her he was going to work for the Truitts.

"Congratulations. Do I know the young lady?"

"No, I met her here. John likes her. I wondered if Lily and Buck could come down for the wedding? They could be back on Sunday night."

"I'm sure they'd love to. What do you want for a wedding present?"

He laughed. "Well, don't send anything for the kitchen. Willie can't cook."

"Willie?"

"Yeah. Wilhelmina. Just like you, can't boil an egg. She's a journalist assigned to the White House beat."

Yarrow hung up slowly. It was strange. Sandy's announcement made her feel that one part of her life was finally over; the cutoff was much cleaner than the divorce had been.

Margaret buzzed. "Lily on line one."

"Mommy." Lily's opening was a statement. She was a freshman at Columbia University.

Yarrow's heart always sank when she heard that tone in Lily's voice. It meant Lily wanted something—or wanted to get out of something. Yarrow decided to get in first.

"I'm glad you rang, Lily. I wanted to talk to you. What are all these parking fines I've been sent—three hundred dollars?"

"I can explain about those."

"No need. I'm going to take it out of your allowance."

Lily groaned. Yarrow heard her tone change. "I called you because I have a paper due on anthropology. Do you have any old pictures of yourself I could borrow?"

"I'm forty years old! I'm hardly old enough to be a study for anthropologists."

Yarrow took a mirror out of her drawer and examined her

hairline as they talked. A gray streak had begun to appear above her right temple.

"Are you still depressed about turning forty? I'm relating something Margaret Mead said to our own family history."

"What did she say?"

"That 'the most aggressive girls in the village were the daughters of prominent widows.' "

"Well, try to keep some family secrets safe. This 'widow's' ex-husband called. Your dad's getting married."

Lily squealed on the other end of the telephone, her financial woes forgotten for a moment.

"He wants you and Buck to go down for the wedding on Saturday. You could take the shuttle down on Friday night and come back on Sunday."

"Will you pay?"

"Of course I'll pay."

"Great. There's the neatest boy I met who hangs out in Washington. Can I call Edith to hunt up those photos?"

The light on Yarrow's other phone was flashing.

"Yes."

"Excellent. 'Bye, old lady." Yarrow winced and picked up the other line.

"It's Tom Marx, the station manager from Denver," Margaret said as she came in with a cup of coffee for Yarrow. "Mr. Weyden's holding on the other line."

"Yarrow, this is Tom Marx. We got our rating figures yesterday and I wanted to be the first to tell you. They're good. We're up there."

"Tom, that's great, but when are you going to increase the length of the evening news?"

She could almost hear Tom shift in his chair. He was an old newspaper hand and she liked him, but he was as stubborn as a mule when it came to making any significant changes. They had been arguing for months now about the length of the news broadcast—Yarrow wanted it doubled, to thirty minutes a night. Tom thought that was too long.

"People won't sit through thirty minutes of news, Yarrow."

"Of course they will, but you have to make it snappy. Boom, boom, boom, like a magazine, a gossip column. You don't keep some boring old face up there talking all the time—it's got to zip. News was made for television . . ."

"I thought television was made for news."

"And entertainment. You can still get the message across without being dull."

"One thing at a time, Yarrow."

"Tom, don't wait for the networks—we'll lose our initiative—we're on a roll with the station. I want to do this now."

"Let's talk about it."

"I'll be out next week, but then I want to see a pilot, OK?"

"OK, Yarrow, whatever you say." Yarrow knew as she hung up and picked up the other phone that he wouldn't do a thing. But she was pleased with the station. Tom ran a tight ship and the oil industry in Denver was booming. KMZO made money.

"Elliot? How are you?"

"I'm just fine, but I'm frustrated. I've been here for days and I still can't get anyone to make a decision." Elliot was staying at the Ritz Hotel in Paris, where his office was acting as intermediary in a deal between the French government and the nuclear industry. Millions and millions of dollars and francs were involved.

"How did Meredith's operation go?"

"Her mother says her teeth look great. Poor little Meredith. She's nine years old and she's had as many operations. You know, she says she wants to be a doctor?" A little trace of pride could be heard in his voice, subtle as spice in a sauce.

"Then she probably will be one day. She sounds determined enough. But I'm worrying about you." To most people, Elliot seemed to have recovered from the debacle of his nomination attempt. There were many people who believed he had been the victim of a smear campaign and that the accusations against him were despicable. He had begun to accept a few speaking engagements, his old clients had rallied around him with only one or two defections. There were some who shunned him, some society people who dared not delve too deeply into their own pasts who stopped asking him to dinner, but Elliot's good manners, his modesty and kindness, won more admirers than he had lost. To Yarrow though, who loved him, his eyes never again had that confident, mischievous glow. Sometimes she would see him gaze off into the distance and she would want to snap him out of it. It was not her old Elliot, but someone wiser, someone hurt.

Yarrow picked up her favorite paperweight and warmed it in her hands. "You sound—low."

"I was trying to hide it."

"What is it?"

"I didn't want to tell you. I asked Blanchette for a divorce and she said no. She'll fight me for Meredith."

Yarrow was silent, swallowing her own disappointment.

"I miss you," he said. "I suppose you can't come over and join me?" Yarrow heard the discordant tone that had not been present in the old Elliot.

"I can't, Elliot. I'm too busy."

"We could walk through the Bois de Boulogne. I could feed you sea urchins at a grand old restaurant."

"Oh, Elliot. I can't."

"Come," he said.

Yarrow looked at her calendar, which was filled with appointments.

"The sun pours into my suite in the mornings. It's not at all cold. I want to show you Montmartre on Sunday. We'll have coffee on the sidewalk and watch the people, and then afterward we'll visit Notre Dame where candle smoke fills the cathedral with the most incredible diffused light."

"Elliot . . ."

"The organ music is marvelous and the scent of incense burning—oh, come over, Yarrow. And afterward we'll stroll back to the hotel, over the bridge, with our arms around each other. And then we'll come upstairs here and make love in this wonderful bed . . ."

"Are you lying down?"

"Yes. You've never been made love to in a French bed before. They have this six-foot-long bolster behind the other pillows."

Yarrow looked out at the December darkness that hung over the East River. She thought of being in Paris with Elliot. She thought about the children being away with Sandy for the weekend.

"Oh, to hell with it. Yes, of course I will."

"That's wonderful." His voice became cheerful. "I'll have Lainie call with the details. I love you." He hung up.

Yarrow smiled as she made her last few calls. She could see by her clock that the Schaeffer people were already waiting in the reception room. But she felt buoyed by the fact that she would be with Elliot in a few days. She had never been overseas. She was as excited as a child.

On the morning of the day she was to leave for Paris, Local 6 of the International Typographical Union struck four of the New York daily newspapers. Yarrow got a phone call about two in the morning. She switched on her light and squinted at the clock.

"What's going on?"

It was Marvin Rifkin, her lawyer, who now handled labor negotiations full time at the *Telegraph*.

"They're out. Hinton and the Big Six have struck the *Times*, the *News*, the *Journal-American*, and the *World-Telegram and Sun*."

Yarrow was now wide awake. She sat up and pulled her comforter up around her shoulders.

"I guess that means we have to suspend publication, too?"

"Yes. You're a member of the Publishers Association; one out, all out."

"Solidarity working on both sides. What about the other craft unions—the pressmen, the mailers and so on?"

"They've pledged support to the printers, as have the stereo-typers, the paper handlers, the photo engravers . . ."

"And the guild?"

"Everyone. Twenty thousand people. There's a publishers' meeting at ten A.M. this morning at the Commodore Hotel. Will you be there?"

"I'll be there." Yarrow depressed the cradle of the telephone with her fingers. The Paris trip was off indefinitely. She called long distance and soon she had Elliot on the telephone and told him the news.

"It's going to be a long strike. Albert Hinton said so."

"What do they want?"

"Ostensibly, more money, but Hinton really wants power—he wants the Big Six to have the power it used to have in New York. It's been piggybacking on the deals made by the guild over the last few years."

"How did they allow that to happen?"

"Just a consequence of the calendar—the expiration dates of the guild's contracts came before the others, so they made the deals and the others usually followed suit."

"But no longer?"

"No. Hinton's been wanting this one for a long time. It's so depressing. Not all the papers are healthy—certainly not mine. I don't know if I can take a strike, Elliot. I don't make money from the *Telegraph* yet."

"You may have to sell or close down. Have you thought about that?"

"Of course. But I'd do anything to save the paper. It's my own flesh and blood."

"That's the commitment Hinton's counting on."

"I'm sorry I can't come to Paris, darling. I was looking forward to it."

"I was, too. I bought you something for your birthday."

"What is it?"

"You'll have to wait and see."

"I'd better get some sleep before tomorrow's meeting. Stay in touch, darling?"

"Good luck."

When Yarrow walked into the Publishers Association meeting at the Commodore Hotel the next morning in her black Chanel suit, she was very conscious of being the new girl on the block.

There was the power group—and then there was she. This was not a perception based on who was or was not losing money—the *Herald-Tribune*, after all, was bleeding to death—but it was a question of the influence each newspaper wielded. Sometimes the power came from the individual who owned the newspaper; the *Herald Tribune* was kept going by massive intravenous shots of money from its owner. The *Journal-American*, the *Mirror* and the *World-Telegram and Sun* were owned by chains. The *Times*, the *News* and the *Post* were all represented, too, when Yarrow took her seat with Rifkin beside her. Palmer Truitt of the *Courier*, who had been named publisher when Fabiana died, sat opposite Yarrow. She ignored him after a perfunctory nod.

"The printers," a counsel for another newspaper was saying, "are demanding an increase of eighteen dollars and seventy-five cents over the next two years. We have offered a weekly wage rise of eight dollars over the same period and a fourth week of vacation. We are in for a long strike, but we are not going to accept Mr. Hinton's blackmailing techniques, or what he calls 'negotiations.' "

"He wants forty-eight changes in the contract," said a man from the *News*. "You know what that would cost us? Ninety-eight dollars and four cents per man, per week." A murmur went around the room.

"But they've cut their demands since then. Hinton now says thirty-eight dollars a week—that was at four minutes to two this morning—right before the strike deadline."

"He doesn't want to negotiate; he wants to kill us."

"We made a counteroffer to the printers of a nine-dollar twenty-cent weekly package. Now we wait. Mr. Bradford?"

Amory Bradford, vice-president and general manager of the *Times* and chief negotiator for the Publishers Association, began to speak.

Yarrow looked at the typewritten pages that were handed around. They gave a breakdown of the union's demands and the counteroffers made by the publishers. There was a list of the demands of the other eight nonstriking unions that would have to be dealt with. Also included was a page dealing with the machin- ists' and electricians' contracts, which would not expire until March. There was a list of subcommittees with various newspaper publishers and their counsels represented on them. Some of the publishers would be part of a negotiating team, some would deal with automation. Yarrow read that the *Courier* and the *News* were represented on a smaller committee. The chairman was now going through other parts of the agenda.

"Excuse me," said Yarrow. "I think there's an omission— there's no mention here of the *Telegraph* being represented on a negotiating committee."

Bradford raised his eyebrows at one of his own advisers, who spoke up.

"Miss McLean, we've put you and your counsel down on an advisory committee. See item seven. Now, I was saying . . ."

Yarrow took a deep breath. "I'm sorry, but this isn't good enough. I think it's only fair that I, or my representative, should be appointed to one of the teams working on the negotiations with the Big Six."

"Miss McLean, there is nothing in the rules of the Publishers Association that says that the *Telegraph* has to be represented on any of the committees."

Yarrow's face flushed. "There's nothing in the rules either that says that the *Telegraph* has to remain a member of the association."

"It is extremely important that we publishers keep a united front. Together, solid, we can beat these printers."

There was a strained silence around the table.

Yarrow held the man's gaze. He sighed.

"Can we take a vote that the *Telegraph* be appointed to one of the negotiating committees? Unless of course you have already decided on which one you wish to be represented."

"As a matter of fact I have. I would like to be on the committee with the *Courier*. We are both afternoon papers."

The adviser looked around the table.

"Agreed? Agreed. Now may we continue, Miss McLean?"

"Of course. I'm quite satisfied." Yarrow stole a glance at Palmer Truitt. Dark red patches had appeared on his cheeks. He was livid. Good, thought Yarrow. She had him where she wanted, right where she could see him, and he couldn't play any nasty tricks. She didn't trust him one inch to negotiate anything on her behalf. She looked down at the pencil she held and saw that her hands were shaking.

*   *   *

Yarrow went through the pickets in front of her office that afternoon. She recognized some of the men with the placards on their chests and backs. It was bitterly cold, and they stamped their feet and clapped their hands to keep warm, but when her car drew up they began jeering. She realized she was no longer a person to them, but a symbol; just as to her they no longer were John and Joe, or Hank Birley whose father, he had once told her proudly, had worked at the *Telegraph* for forty years, but had become a mass, impersonal and hostile.

The building was like a tomb. She shuddered as the security guards took her through it. Inky footsteps from the composing room threaded throughout the editorial floor. Nothing was immune to the all-pervading ink; it smeared the handrails and the elevator doors, smudged its way up to the executive floor and along the carpeted hall; like blood, it was impossible to clean it off completely.

Yarrow locked herself in her office and put on the lights. She told Margaret to hold all calls. Yarrow had a bad feeling about this strike. Her intuition told her it was going to be long and nasty. She had seen it on the men's faces outside; she could read it in the statements of Albert Hinton, whose intransigence punctuated every sentence. She picked up an out-of-town paper that had interviewed Hinton.

"The only thing that counts is muscle. If disputes were settled by reason or justice, there wouldn't be unions." In answer to a question about the viability of sick newspapers, Hinton said, "The papers don't let us see their books. The only time one does is when it's down and out. Things are not as dire as they say. The number of dailies is dwindling as a reflection of voluntary consolidations and efforts by publishers to reduce competition. In any case, we can't take the position of being a partner to the sick papers and the antagonist to the rich ones."

Yarrow tossed the paper aside and looked at the latest figures of the *Telegraph*. The numbers this week were all in red. How very apt that the ink here was indeed the color of blood.

She was restless and got up and went into the bathroom. She looked at herself in the mirror. Her black curly hair, worn back in a chignon, was turning gray. She was a beautiful woman with large, clear gray eyes and a face that needed little artificial help. The black eyebrows winged across a proud bare forehead. But Yarrow saw none of this. She saw a terrified woman carrying debts she could not afford, a woman masquerading as an executive. She was the mother of three children. She should be at home. She had a mother who needed her, a lover she never saw, books she never had time to read, closets that needed to be cleaned. She had a varicose vein behind her right knee, and she sometimes needed a cane to walk with. She got tired and angry and frustrated because the day was too short. She had little time with her children; they accused her of always being preoccupied—with some justification. Only this morning Buck had complained about her lack of interest in him. He was playing on the football team at school and she had never made it to a game. As for Lily, when was the last time she had really talked with her daughter?

But more than anything, her debts haunted her. What am I doing here? Who am I kidding? Am I really up to this? Yarrow stared at herself in the mirror, but there was no answer. She switched off the bathroom light, went out and said to Margaret: "I'm beginning to talk to myself in here so I'm going to watch Buck play football. I'll be at home later if you need me, but I don't think there'll be anything happening today."

She went through the corridors to the back elevator and out through the pressroom. Vasik was waiting for her, and the pickets were, too. She moved a blue and white police barricade and stepped into her car. A man spat at the window as the car moved off. She watched the saliva slip down the glass as they headed toward Randalls Island. A light, sleety rain began to wash the spit off the window.

It took her a while to pick out her son on the team. They all looked alike in their white football pants and blue and white shirts with numbers on them. The shoulder pads and helmets made them all look top-heavy. Buck longed to win a star for his helmet. The coach awarded one only to those who made a touchdown. Then she picked him out, a skinny, shivering nine-year-old with his knees knocking in the cold. He saw her and came over grinning through his face mask with the mouthpiece dangling.

"Hey, Mom. How'd you get time off? Boss let you out?"

"Wise guy," she said.

"McLean. Get over here!" screamed the coach. Buck jogged back across the field. She watched Buck as he played wide receiver. He was hopeless, she decided. He had inherited none of Sandy's coordination. It was John who was the athlete. Buck, well—she winced as she saw him tackled by another boy. He would never get that star at this rate.

"Come on," she shouted. "Come on!"

She was stamping her feet in her thin leather boots to keep warm. The wind whipped across the river and bowled unimpeded over the flatness of Randalls' playing fields. There was another

parent there—few came on weekdays—and the man brought her
a weak hot chocolate from a vending truck. She put a scarf
around her head and sniffled, her nose red, and ignored her
watering eyes. She and the other parent stormed up and down the
sidelines as they followed the play. Then, astoundingly, she saw
that Buck had the football at the thirty-yard line. Yarrow shouted,
she screamed, she waved her arms. She ran along the sidelines.
"Go! Go! Go!" Buck made a touchdown. It was better than the
NFL championships. Yarrow flung her arms around the other
parent. "Oh, I'm sorry," she said as she came to her senses.

"That's the warmest thing that's happened to me all day." He
laughed. Yarrow got back into the car and rubbed her frozen
feet. When Buck came over she wound down the window and
asked him to get his things and climb in.

"Uh, Mom. I want to go back with the guys, you know? You
don't mind?"

"No, I understand." As he pulled his head out of the car
window, banging the top with his helmet, she said, "Buck, you
helped me today. Thanks."

"How? What did I do?"

"You made a touchdown."

"Yeaah." He grinned.

"See you at home."

Yeaah, thought Yarrow, as she settled back and opened her
briefcase. Buck made a touchdown. Nothing's impossible.

CHAPTER 33

T HE SMELL OF ROASTING TURKEY WOKE YARROW ON CHRISTMAS
morning. Greta must be here already, she thought, slipping into her robe and padding down the two flights of stairs to
the kitchen. Greta was divorcing her second husband.

"I couldn't take the clank of his gold chains any longer," she
had said, "and I was sure he was going to slap a status label on
my forehead if I stayed around—he had them on everything
else."

"We let you sleep late," said Greta now, handing her a mug

of coffee. Yarrow stared bleary-eyed at Greta and Edith and Freya working in the kitchen.

"It's eleven o'clock," Freya said. She was stringing beans, using her good hand. It didn't matter how slow she was at it, said Edith, because she must be made to feel useful.

"What time did you come in?" said Edith. "It must have been well past one."

"About three," said Yarrow, sitting on a stool in the crowded galley kitchen. Greta was making a broth at the stove. Edith squeezed some orange juice for Yarrow.

"We talked for eighteen hours yesterday," said Yarrow, shutting her eyes and trying to blink them open. "And we have yet to start talking about the fundamentals. Where are the kids?"

"Millie took them to a Filipino Christmas Mass. Lily said she was going purely for research; John went because Lily said he had to; Buck went because he said he's been before and liked the music."

"I've been a failure as a mother," said Yarrow, drinking down her orange juice and waving a muffin at Edith to put it in the toaster. "I should have sent them to church more often when they were small."

"You can't send them," said Freya slowly. "You have to take them."

"It was easier in the mountains, wasn't it, Mama?"

"That is true."

Yarrow watched her mother slowly pull a long string from the side of a green bean. If it were not for her mother's stroke they might all have gone to Galena for Christmas and stayed with Eric—of course they couldn't now with the strike on anyway.

"Did Eric and Yanna arrive yesterday?" Yarrow was so involved in her troubles that she had not kept up with everyone. Eric and Yanna had finally tied the knot last summer in a quiet ceremony no one had been invited to. Freya had been hurt and Yarrow tried to explain that young people did things differently these days.

"Yes," said Greta. "They're staying at a friend's apartment and the Hoggarts are with me. They'll all be here by one. Take your hands off that, Yarrow." Greta pulled away a bowl of stewed cranberries that Yarrow had just put her finger in.

"I was just going to taste it," said Yarrow.

"You have no taste buds. You'd oversweeten it or something." Greta retied the strings of her apron firmly around her waist. Greta's blond hair waved upward from her forehead.

Under her apron she had on a chic little red jersey top with long sleeves tucked into a pair of houndstooth-checked stirrup pants.

"Aren't your pants a little tight?" said Yarrow as her sister turned around.

"Out," said Greta, pointing at the door. "How can we cook with you around?"

Freya was smiling, trying to say something. "Noth—nothing changes," she said.

Later in the day, when they were all replete with lunch, Yarrow asked if anyone would like to come down to the office with her. Greta and Nellie said they would, and Eric and Yanna came, too. So did all the children, except Nellie's youngest, Thimi. Thimi had been conceived sometime during Nellie and Jack's visit to Katmandu four years before. Jack would stay home with her. Besides, he said, he would not cross a picket line.

"I understand," said Yarrow as she wrapped a scarf around her throat. "I'm not antiunion just because I'm on the other side."

"Have you tried to deal reasonably with Hinton?" asked Jack, bending down dolefully in her narrow hallway as they all streamed out. "Perhaps if you just met the man yourself, without intermediaries, you might be able to come to some agreement."

"Jack, first, they haven't struck me—technically, this is a lockout. Second, it's not about money, regardless of what the PA chairman says, it's about power. Hinton doesn't want to talk yet. We haven't suffered enough."

Jack nodded his head over his daughter's little dark one. Yarrow could see that he did not believe her.

When their cars pulled up, it was getting dark and there were no pickets at the back door. The familiar smell of ink and paper met them as they walked into the pressroom. Eric wanted to show Yanna, who had never been in a large newspaper office before, all over the pressroom. She had never realized the size of the machines, the double-story system of presses and paper webs that was like something out of Dante's *Inferno*. The printer's devil, the nickname for a printing apprentice, had always struck her as a good one, thought Yarrow. Eric guided his tough, little pregnant wife carefully up and down the iron stairs. The four children clanged happily along the perforated walkways on the first tier.

Yarrow and her sisters stood below, watching them. Lily would be eighteen in March. She was as slim and pale as her name. She had the same straight hair, like Oriental silk, that Nellie had, only blond. Under each light on the walkway it flashed like a beacon. The trouble with Lily, thought Yarrow, was that her ambitions and confidence did not match her abilities. It saddened Yarrow that this was so. Lily liked to think she was mature, but she was constantly in trouble with her checkbook. Lily was an inch taller than her mother and had borrowed a navy blue skirt to wear today.

"I wonder what they'll grow up to be?" said Greta, putting into words what they were all thinking.

"John's grown up," said Nellie, folding her arms and watching Yarrow's eldest son as he slouched behind the others with his hands in his pockets. His hair had darkened from its baby blondness and a cockscomb of waves centered on his forehead.

"I wish he would walk with his head up and fix his hair," said Yarrow as she looked at her fifteen-year-old. As if on cue, John stopped, took out a comb and combed back the sides of his hair. Buck, walking behind him, bumped into him and knocked over an empty grease bucket.

"Watch it," said John, giving him a shove with the flat of his palm.

"Oh, lay off," said Buck, shoving back. Justice, their eleven-year-old cousin, ignored them. He was walking as though on a balance beam, carefully placing one foot in front of the other with his arms out at shoulder height. As he approached Buck and John, he began to wobble as if he were teetering on a high wire. He executed a nerve-racking turn, bent his knees carefully, straightened up and walked back the way he came.

"Perhaps they should all join the circus," said Yarrow as Eric and Yanna returned. Yanna was tired. The baby was due in a few months.

They went up to Yarrow's office, where Justice did cartwheels and Buck showed everyone who would look where he had chipped a tooth making his touchdown last week. Yarrow put the kettle on to make some instant coffee in her kitchenette and then got on the phone. All the publishers called each other. Some of them were more friendly than others. It was like a game of tick-tack, the sign language bookmakers use at racetracks, in which odds were being passed on; a federal mediator was being sent in; the mayor was making noises; the governor was threatening to establish a board of public inquiry. It was all tick-tacking, all sleight-of-hand. Nothing was really happening. There was a meeting scheduled for tomorrow. "Nothing will come of it," said Yarrow. "I'm quite convinced of that."

"Next year we should all spend Christmas in Galena," said Eric. "I want to show you what we've done with the house."

"I miss Galena," said Greta.

"Why don't you come and live there?" asked Eric.

"What would I do back in Galena?" said Greta.

"Cook!" said Eric. "Open a restaurant. I can't tell you what the old town is like. It's jumping at this time of year. You know they've got sleigh rides through the streets now?"

"Jock would feel right at home," said Yarrow.

"It would cost a lot of money to open a restaurant," said Greta. "Do you think I really could?"

"Sell your shares to Yarrow," said Eric. "She'll buy them."

Greta crossed her legs in their tight pants. She made her sisters look matronly. "I'll think about it," she said.

"How you've changed," said Nellie.

"You know," said Eric, leaning back and putting his arm around Yanna, "I didn't want to mention it in front of Ma, but the old cabin is falling to pieces. We went up there the other day, and if we don't save it, there's going to be nothing left. I don't get up there enough. I have no use for it."

"Yarrow or Greta should take it," said Nellie. "We're not skiers."

"I'd be scared up there on my own," said Greta.

"But it's Ma's," said Yarrow.

"But you used to dream about that cabin," said Nellie. "How you were going to live there with your children when you were married."

Yarrow laughed. It was good to think of the old days. They seemed such carefree times in which any problems that did exist could be swiftly dealt with and put away.

"We'll see," she said.

When Greta went back to the car with Eric and Yanna and Lily and Yarrow, she was asking Eric all kinds of questions about Galena. Yarrow wondered if Greta would take up Eric's challenge. The three boys squeezed in the front with Vasik, turned on the radio and rolled up the window divider.

"How's Elliot?" said Nellie as the car made a U-turn and headed up the East River Drive.

"He's fine," said Yarrow, looking at her sister. A small furrow had appeared across her forehead, which used to be hidden by her bangs.

"You've changed your hair," said Yarrow.

"You're changing the subject. Why doesn't he marry you?"

"Because he's married."

"He should get a divorce."

"Nellie."

"It's unfair to you, Yarrow. If he's not going to divorce her, you should leave him."   —

"I don't want to."

"You should have gotten pregnant. I did."

Yarrow stared at Nellie.

"I couldn't get Jack to come to a decision, so I made up his mind for him."

Nellie had used her body to get Jack; Greta had abused hers to keep Palmer.

"I couldn't do that."

"He's using you."

In the back of the car, Yarrow wondered who was the "real" user. She had always thought Justice had been named in honor of Jack's political beliefs. Now she wondered at the subtleties of Nellie's mind.

"Elliot wouldn't do that. Nellie . . ." Yarrow put her hand on her sister's arm. The questions hurt. They were not new, it was not as if Yarrow had never thought about them herself. But she had never been tempted to use any strategy on Elliot to see what would happen. Instead, she had accepted that she would probably never have Elliot, that they would never marry. She thought perhaps that the very looseness of their bonds held them to each other. If she were to tighten those that she held, he would escape, like a wild stallion caught for a night in a corral. Nellie did not understand: Yarrow had come to terms.

"I worry about you," said Nellie. Her fingers fiddled with her gloves. She seldom spoke about affection or family ties. These things were shown by deeds, not words.

"I know."

"I was listening to Eric, about Greta selling her shares? I'm thinking of selling some of mine. We lost a bundle on the stock market. Jack wants to buy a ranch. We could live on it and Jack could write his books and lecture."

"Let me know when you're ready." Yarrow made a mental note to call her banker in the morning. She could buy only if she could borrow.

She lowered the divider and the boys' music blasted into the back. Vasik's neck remained stoically stiff, though his ears had turned red. "Turn it down, boys," said Yarrow. "What is it?"

"Dion and the Belmonts."

"My God," she said, raising the window. "I must be getting old."

*   *   *

Yarrow propped up the small Cézanne still life, or *nature morte*, that Elliot had given her for her birthday. It stood on an easel that usually displayed a plate.

"The fruit doesn't look edible," she had said when Elliot asked her, honestly, what did she think of it?

"But that's precisely the point," he had said. "He has moved the beauty of the objects away from what they are. He wants you to look at the planes, to feel the tension in the shapes."

"I'll never understand painting," Yarrow had said and placed the painting on her bedside table so that she could study it more often. "Give it time," Elliot had said.

Yarrow lay back on her pillow and stared at the painting. She was bereft without her paper to occupy her. She couldn't sleep. It was five in the morning and she was waiting until it was time to get up. She felt helpless in the current situation; helpless and frustrated because she believed that the cost to all of them, all the newspapers and all the unions, would be enormous and it would be for nothing. None of them would attack the central problem of automation. They would circle it, and their egos would get involved and the language of law would get in the way, and all the historic resentment, the prejudice and the bitterness would remain.

Yarrow couldn't sleep. She stared at the apples, but didn't see them. She got up and went into the bathroom. She looked terrible. Her eyes, she thought, looked like those of a whale. They peered out, subhuman, from the puffiness of her face. Yarrow splashed cold water on them and then showered and put on her black suit. She went downstairs to the kitchen and put up some coffee. She called Elliot. He was in London, staying at the Savoy, and it was five hours later over there.

"I feel sick," she said, "I feel sick to my stomach and suicidal. Elliot, what am I going to do? I could lose everything." She sipped her coffee and listened to his soothing voice. She would shut her eyes and imagine he was beside her.

"This is already the longest blackout in the history of New York newspapers. I don't trust any of them, not the printers, not my fellow publishers. I'm caught. I'm absolutely caught." She clenched her mug so fiercely that she slopped some coffee on the countertop.

"I can't help you, love," he said. "You've got to do what feels right for you. Sell out, if you have to."

Yarrow put her head in her hands. "If only it were that easy.

But so many people depend on me." They were both silent, but the communication was not broken.

"Did you have a nice Christmas?" she asked.

"Yes. I wish I was with you."

"I can't see the apples yet."

He laughed. "Oh, Yarrow. You're wonderful."

"No, I'm not. I can't appreciate art and I can't run a newspaper."

He spoke gently. "Stop it," he said. "We don't cry when we're down. We fight back."

"Thank you, Miss McLean," she said. "You have a wicked memory, Elliot."

"Only if it helps."

"I love you."

"I love you, too. Call me if you need me."

She took a cup of coffee down to her mother. Freya was always awake early. Only with her mother and with Elliot could Yarrow show that there were still things that terrified her in this world.

Freya had aged a great deal since her stroke. Soon, Yarrow thought, holding her mother's liver-spotted hand with the soft, wrinkly, shiny skin, there might only be one person left for her to confide in. She dreaded the day her mother might return to being only another child.

"Would you hold me," she asked her mother, since the thought had become unbearable, "hold me like you used to?" Freya's heart had always been big. She didn't question now, but just held her daughter, this grown-up woman, in the smart suit with the pearls at her ears and the gold rings on her fingers, held her with her one strong arm and rocked her as if she were a child and made those crooning noises she had made long ago when Yarrow had a nightmare.

The meeting was held at the Commodore Hotel on Park Avenue between the Publishers Association and the ITU representatives. They all shook hands cordially enough and sat down facing each other across the polished table of an anonymous-looking conference room.

Yarrow couldn't bring herself to look into Albert Hinton's eyes. She still blamed him for her father's death. He was the same age now as her father had been when he died. She wondered if Albert Hinton knew that. Hinton was now a ruggedly good-looking fifty-seven-year-old with a pock-marked face.

"Shall we begin?" asked Amory Bradford. Everyone nodded.

The chairman of the PA leaned forward, with his arms crossed and his shoulders hunched.

"Are you ready to negotiate then, Mr. Bradford?" said Hinton.

"Mr. Hinton, we are ready to move toward an agreement when your union comes to a meeting ready to modify its position and effect a reasonable solution."

"Our proposal was made," said Hinton, "with that very thing in mind. It's merely a basis for negotiations."

"Well, if you would begin to demonstrate that by your actions instead of just talking about them, we might be able to make some progress."

Yarrow was looking at Bradford as he spoke, and then, to everyone's surprise, Hinton simply got up and left the room with his advisers. Everyone sat looking shocked.

"Was that it?" said Palmer Truitt. "We've been here less than fifteen minutes." An aide rushed out of the room to follow Hinton. He came back minutes later.

"Talks are off," he said. "Indefinitely."

"Bastard," said Palmer Truitt.

Yarrow was stunned.

It was going to be worse than she expected.

Over the next few weeks she moved through a blur of meetings. By January 12, neither party had budged an inch and there had been fifteen meetings. On Saturday, the printers lowered their demands from nineteen dollars to eighteen dollars, and the publishers raised their package to just over ten dollars. On the fourteenth, eight thousand strikers held a mass meeting outside the *Times* building on West Forty-third Street. They voted to continue the strike.

At a further meeting between Hinton and the publishers, Yarrow and her counsel, Rifkin, began to lay out the publishers' terms.

"We would like the right to use perforated tapes," said Yarrow.

"But we've been over all this before," said Hinton.

"These tapes, as we are all aware, are supplied by the AP and UPI services and can be fed directly into automatic Linotype machines. They provide stock-market tables, sporting-event results and some other things. They are already available to other newspapers and are being used. But not in New York. You won't let us."

"Because we have a contract clause prohibiting it."

"Is there room for negotiating here, Mr. Hinton?"

"I'm not opposed to automatic typesetting, Miss McLean,"

said Hinton, playing with his truncated fingers, "providing we get adequate job security and that we share in the increased productivity that results."

"Well, the *Times*," said its spokesman, "doesn't regard automatic typesetting of stock tables as much of a money-saver. It would save us time—it takes twenty men two hours to set the late-afternoon stock tables. If you agree to our use of the tapes, we will agree not to lay off those men, but reassign them."

"What's your opinion, Mr. Hinton?" asked Yarrow.

"I haven't got one until I hear an offer. I haven't heard an offer yet."

"You're not negotiating in good faith, Mr. Hinton."

"Oh, don't give me that. Talk money and I'll start to hear you."

"You know our final offer on that. Now we are trying to deal with the changes that you suggest should be made in the existing contract. You can't expect us to negotiate and not get something in return."

"What in return?"

"Bogus."

"Ah yes. The publisher's bogeyman."

"Under the existing contract the publishers have seven days in which to set up this bogus type—seven days before you penalize us," said Rifkin.

"We don't penalize you. It's in the contract. Read the contract."

"I have read the contract."

"The union insists on retaining the seven-days clause."

"The publishers would like to reduce the volume of bogus, and to do so we want to go over your definition of what is a local ad."

Yarrow closed her eyes. Her head pounded. They were getting nowhere fast.

"You know what a local ad is as well as I do," said Hinton. "That clause is our protection against subcontracting. We shouldn't lose jobs because of that." Hinton stood up and stretched. "We've been here eight hours already. I have to caucus with my colleagues. I'm not coming back unless you have something substantive to say." He made an almost courtly sort of bow in Yarrow's direction and left. They all got up and stretched when he left. Yarrow swung her arms and touched her toes. Palmer Truitt smirked at her. "Enjoying yourself?" he said. Yarrow ignored him.

"How does Hinton stay so fresh?" she asked. No one answered. Palmer Truitt sprayed some Gold Spot freshener into his mouth. Yarrow left for the powder room, but she saw Hinton talking in the hallway with some reporters. She dawdled in the ladies' room until the men had gone and Hinton had walked into another room and shut the door. He was quite alone. Yarrow waited a few minutes and looked over her shoulder guiltily. She walked to the door of the room into which Hinton had disappeared. It was an anteroom of some sort. She turned the knob quietly and opened the door. The room was absolutely bare except for a blanket on the floor under which Albert Hinton was sound asleep, on his back, snoring his head off.

Yarrow went and found the hotel's night manager. "The security in this building," she said, "is nonexistent."

"Yes, Madam?"

He was well aware of who she was.

"There are a number of very angry people involved in this dispute and it is your hotel that would suffer if someone irresponsible caused something to happen."

"Madam?"

"Every door on the floor we are meeting on should be locked. Don't you agree? There are some disreputable types hanging around, sleeping on the flor, sneaking in."

"I will see to it right away." He went off to find the housekeeper with the keys, and Yarrow went back to her own group. She left the door open to the hall, and after a few minutes there was a ruckus and then the shambling figure of Hinton was seen being escorted past by the hotel manager. They seemed to be bowing to each other and apologizing. Yarrow smiled. Hinton wouldn't be so fresh the next time they met. But after that episode, Hinton refused to meet the publishers face to face and insisted that both groups meet through a mediator.

Everyone tried to get into the act. Like Yarrow's brother-in-law, Jack, some thought they would be more patient, more reasonable, more just, more understanding than the two groups involved. A number of unofficial meetings went on, too. Hinton met with Thayer, president of the *Herald Tribune*, in the board room of CBS on Madison Avenue, but nothing came of it. The publisher of the *Washington Post* flew up and met with Hinton and took notes for hours and rang the president and nothing came of it. One of the president's aides flew to New York that month and met with Thayer at the Gotham Hotel. They got Hinton in, and he began reciting a whole new list of demands, tougher than the ones he had originally asked for, and nothing came of it. It would all have been funny if the consequences were not so serious.

By the end of January, the mayor had stepped in and the publishers and printers agreed to start using him as a mediator at City Hall. On January 28, separate meetings were held for thirteen hours. There was no progress. On January 29, February 4, February 9, the talks dragged on. Elmer Brown, president of the AFL-CIO ITU, flew in from Colorado Springs. On February 12, after eighteen hours of negotiations, the talks broke down completely. The union officials claimed the publishers were arguing among themselves. The publishers claimed the unions were doing the same. There was a great deal of disgruntlement on both sides.

"I'm sick and tired of coming down here for these meetings," said Palmer Truitt one day at City Hall. "I'm wasting my time."

"Then why don't you leave?" asked the mayor's chief negotiator. "Because if you don't, I will. I have better things to do with my time."

"Oh, boys, stop it," said Yarrow.

"I'm leaving," said the negotiator and walked out. It took two days and a visit from the *Times* representative to stitch the PA back together again.

The unions had formed a unity committee in order to stay up to date and share information as it came in from the negotiations between the printers and the publishers. Some of the unions had already accepted terms from the publishers before Hinton took his men out. These union members had now been without pay since December 8, and there was no end in sight: The rank and file were restless.

On the night of February 19, Yarrow sat with Buck and her mother and watched Hinton and Thayer on television. They appeared on the same program but separately. It began to dawn on Yarrow as she sipped a glass of wine, that she was being left more and more out of the real negotiations. As she listened to both men talking about the contract expiration date, and the use of perforated tapes, she realized they had moved on. Some decisions had obviously already been made. She had been shunted aside, fobbed off with Truitt and kept busy at exhausting, time- and energy-consuming confrontations. The more she watched them on TV, the more certain she was she'd been sold out.

On the twentieth, the publishers met with the eight nonstriking unions. The talk was about shorter hours. Yarrow was not asked to attend. Six days later the talks broke down again and Hinton called for a federal antitrust investigation into "the callous lock-out" of employees by six newspapers. "This is not only an offense against public morality," he said, sounding like an

American Alfred Doolittle, "but also a criminal violation of the antitrust laws. Decent American citizens," he went on, "will want an independent grand jury to scrutinize this scandalous news blackout."

At the next publishers meeting, Yarrow waited until business was almost completed and then interrupted.

"I would like myself or Mr. Rifkin appointed to the negotiating committee."

"Miss McLean, you are already on one."

"It's a sham, and you know it. Dryfoos, Flynn and Thayer are doing it all. I insist as a member of this organization that my views be heard."

"Shall we take a vote, then, around the table that Miss McLean be appointed to the *News* and *Tribune* negotiating team? Ayes?" Not one hand went up. "Nays?" Up went the hands. "I think the nays have it, Miss McLean."

Yarrow was furious. She picked up her bag and ground her teeth together to stop shaking. She stood up.

"Then I resign from the Publishers Association. I am going out right now to telephone the news of my resignation to Mr. Hinton. Good morning, gentlemen."

Yarrow went straight to the public telephone in the hotel foyer. Truitt rushed after her.

"You can't be serious about this."

"I am." She rummaged through her bag. "I haven't any change. Can you lend me a dime?" He gave it to her and she turned her back and flicked through her personal phonebook and called Hinton.

"Let's have lunch," she said. "I've resigned from the PA."

"I don't believe you."

"One o'clock? The Pierre."

By the time she got there, he was already waiting outside with a long face.

"The restaurant's on strike," he said. "We'll have to go elsewhere."

It was too perfect for words—the union boss and the renegade lady publisher being turned away from a restaurant on strike. Yarrow leaned weakly against the wall and laughed.

"All right, Maestro, you've got the baton. Where can we talk?"

"There's a Chinese place right around the corner."

CHAPTER 34

A CROWD OF REPORTERS AND CAMERAMEN WAITED IN THE FOYER of the Commodore when Yarrow returned with Albert Hinton. Yarrow had called Rifkin, who had arranged to hold a press conference at the hotel rather than at the *Telegraph* building, since Hinton would not cross picket lines. Hinton promised that the pickets would be removed that afternoon. Yarrow took her place in front of the crowd and spoke simply. The bright lights of the television cameras made her look pale. She sounded much more confident than she really felt.

"I have resigned from the Publishers Association of New York and will publish the *Telegraph* on Monday."

A barrage of questions hit her.

"Miss McLean, why did you resign?"

"The strike has gone on long enough and I don't see any end in sight."

"Was the *Telegraph* in danger of closing permanently if the strike continued indefinitely?"

"I've never made a secret of the fact that the *Telegraph* doesn't make money. There's a limit to how much, how long I could sustain these losses."

"Miss McLean, it's being said you have a 'sweetheart deal' with the printers' union. Do you have a separate deal?"

"No. The printers will be returning to the *Telegraph* under the terms of their old contract." She glanced at Hinton beside her. He spoke up.

"We will reach agreement on a new contract later when all this is over."

"Miss McLean, how do your fellow publishers feel about your defection?"

"I think they're somewhat unhappy."

Hinton laughed at this understatement.

"Mr. Hinton, this must make your hand stronger. How do you feel about this development? What do you think of Miss McLean's resignation?"

"I think she's the only publisher in New York with balls."

"Strike that from the record," said Yarrow.

At the front door of the *Telegraph* building on South Street, the men were already tearing up their placards. They gave a cheer as she went in. "They would have cheered if I'd been guillotined," she said to Rifkin.

"You were great," he said. He put his hand on the small of her back as she went into the elevator.

Already the building was beginning to hum. She could sense it. The first shift of printers who had been contacted was streaming in, and some members of the advertising department were already at their desks. Yarrow disdained the elevator and walked through the departments greeting those who had heard the news early and come back to work. Ned Griffin was holding an editorial meeting with a few reporters in his office. Yarrow stopped for a few minutes there and then went upstairs to her own office.

She called a meeting immediately with her production people. The presses had not run for eighty-five days. She went back down to the pressroom when they said they were ready to run a test. Yarrow stood with her arms folded as the great presses shuddered into life. As the roar of the machines reached a crescendo, she turned with a grin and raised her thumb at the press foreman. Yarrow loved her machines.

"What about the newsprint?" she shouted above the noise. She knew the newsprint had been stored in an unheated warehouse and that the chances of paper breaks on the runs would be high.

The foreman put his mouth near her ear. "It's brittle but we'll do our best," he said. She nodded; that was all any of them could do.

Back in her office, Margaret gave her mournful news. "Macy's has announced they won't advertise in the *Telegraph* until the dispute is over."

"I wonder who got to them," said Yarrow. It was what she had feared most—that in breaking ranks with the other newspapers she would be punished by the advertisers. She knew Palmer Truitt would not hesitate to threaten any of his advertisers if they came in with her. Yarrow jutted out her chin. Well, she would hang tough. Her advertising manager came rushing along the hall.

"What's happening?" she asked as they went into her office. "Coffee," she told Margaret.

"Do you want the good news or the bad news first?"

"I heard about Macy's."

"There's more. Gimbels has canceled four pages now that they've heard Macy's won't advertise."

Yarrow threw herself back in her swivel chair and picked at her lower lip. If she were a cursing or smoking woman, this was when she would have let out or lit up. Instead, she looked at the little paperweight that had come off the first Linotype machine her family had ever owned. Courage and stamina surged through her as she looked at it. She was a survivor. She was through the worst. Having made the decision to go out on her own, she knew she could face any criticism, any derision. She had spent sleepless nights thinking about the worst that could happen. Nothing she could conjure up was as bad as the nightmare of closing down the *Telegraph* completely.

"It's lousy," she said using one of her son's words, "but we'll get through it. How many classifieds?" Her telephones were lighting up like a Christmas tree.

"So far, six pages." That was two more than their normal ratio.

"We're planning to print a ninety-six-page paper on Monday," she said. "Go to it."

On Monday Yarrow was down in the pressroom to take the first warm issue of the *Telegraph* off the press. They were printing 750,000 copies, nearly double their normal circulation. She watched with pride while the folded papers jostled and shifted on the wire tracks, the copies interleaved, as they made their way down to the room where they would be bundled and distributed. There were ten pages of classifieds, six pages from A & S, the department store, and four pages from S. Klein's. "It looks good," she said. Yarrow knew she had made the right decision to "publish and be damned."

When she went back to her office, there was a statement waiting for her. The *Herald Tribune* had printed half a million copies. Its headline read: IF MR. HINTON'S OFFER IS GOOD ENOUGH FOR THE *TELEGRAPH* WHY ISN'T IT GOOD ENOUGH FOR THE *HERALD TRIBUNE*? It went on to say that the *Telegraph* had been permitted to publish under the following terms:

> Whatever demands the other papers finally settle on must be accepted by the *Telegraph*.
>
> The *Telegraph* will have no voice in determining that final settlement.
>
> If the *Telegraph* can't afford the terms of the final settlement they'll simply have to go out of business.
>
> The *Tribune* was offered the same deal. We rejected it. For the privilege of publishing today, we'd risk sudden death tomorrow.

*   *   *

The knives were out, thought Yarrow. Margaret came in and switched on the television set. "Mr. Hinton's being interviewed."

Hinton was being asked about the *Herald Tribune* statement.

"I've no commitment with the *Telegraph*," he said. Yarrow watched him as he spoke. As he had at their luncheon, he impressed her. They were totally apart on most issues, and he was a difficult, stubborn, infuriating man to deal with. No wonder her father's heart had given out. The strain of negotiations took its toll. But she had come away thinking that Albert Hinton was fair, he was intelligent, he was not corrupt. They had cracked their fortune cookies together and come away with a grudging respect for each other. Yarrow's cookie message said, "Do not judge a man until you have walked two moons in his moccasins."

"That Chinaman must have had Ute blood," said Yarrow.

"The primary objectives," Hinton was saying, "are to get a common contract expiration date with the Newspaper Guild and the other unions, to resolve the automation question and to get a reduction in hours. When the strike is over we will negotiate with the *Telegraph* management. We may seek retroactive pay for the men now working or we may not, or we may seek the same contract or not." Hinton wasn't going to be hogtied, Yarrow could tell.

Ned Griffin, the editor, had put two of his best reporters on the strike story, which Yarrow continued to watch from the sidelines. It seemed at first that her defection from the Publishers Association had forced them all to work more urgently for a settlement. The mood outside the picketed newspapers was increasingly ugly. It had been a long, cold winter. On the morning of March 6 the mayor announced that the publishers and the union officials had come to an agreement. It had only to be ratified by the union membership. Wages had been upped to $412.27 a week over a two-year period, and a thirty-five-hour week had been agreed on. The publishers had also agreed to a common expiration date for all union contracts, the date to be the day on which the papers resumed publication. The guild, of course, still had to have a say in that decision. The publishers, too, still had to come to an agreement with the other unions on strike. The machinists' and electricians' contracts had expired at midnight. The stereotypers said they were now on strike. The mailers also had to be dealt with. Yarrow rubbed her forehead until it ached and wondered when it would all end. She switched on the television while she did her work. A spokesman for the publishers was being interviewed outside City Hall. She could see Hinton in the background, waiting his turn to speak.

"This package," said the publishers' spokesman, "will cost the papers $18,500,000 during the life of the two-year agreement. The unions have agreed to the use of outside teletype tape." Yarrow raised her head. "That of course helps with the setting of the financial tables of the New York Stock Exchange and the American stock market. The pact also provides that printers and substitutes who held jobs the day the strike began cannot be laid off as the result of the use of the tape. But those workers do not have to be replaced when they leave the newspapers."

"Which side won?" asked the reporter.

"We did," said Hinton. "We got our three principal items."

"Did you make any concessions on your side?"

"Yes. We should have gotten more money."

There was no mention made of bogus. Yarrow wondered if the publishers could afford the deal. She wondered particularly if she could.

Next there was an interview with Gladys Greenhouse, vice-president of the guild, who worked as a political correspondent at the *Telegraph*. The guild, explained the reporter, represented six thousand editorial and commercial employees.

"We are about to meet," said Mrs. Greenhouse, "at the Hotel Vanderbilt with the publishers to discuss our contract."

"You came to an agreement last November with the publishers, didn't you?"

"Yes, but things have changed since then. We believe we deserve some compensation if we agree to extend our contract as the printers and the publishers would wish."

"You mean you want more money?"

"I suppose you could say that money is a consideration."

Yarrow paused with her pen in her hand. She wondered if she would still be sitting at this desk two years hence when the contracts came around again for negotiation.

In the next few days, while the unions met with the publishers, Yarrow began to hear rumors that various printers' chapels were voting to turn down the package. The members were angry. But a subtle shift had occurred; their anger was directed now at their own leaders. Yarrow heard that the *Journal-American/Mirror* chapel had voted 451 to 2 to reject the offer. The *Mirror* had the second largest circulation in the United States and was owned by the Hearst Corporation.

Yarrow called Albert Hinton to fish for information. She wondered if he knew what he had unleashed.

"I'm going to tell my members that I reluctantly favor this deal. It's in their own best interests to accept it."

"You don't sound too confident."

"They must understand we've been told by the other unions that if we want to continue, we'll have to go it alone."

Yarrow felt sorry for Hinton when she hung up. She never thought she would. She called the *Telegraph*'s industrial correspondent and had a long chat with him. She had him rewrite the lead story on the strike, based on what Hinton had told her.

On the seventeenth she listened to Hinton pleading with his members for thirty minutes. She was driving to Connecticut with Greta. Greta was involved with a drug and alcohol abuse rehabilitation center and had asked Yarrow months ago to come as a guest speaker. But Yarrow had a cold. She hadn't wanted to leave her office while so much was going on that could affect the paper's future. She couldn't get out of it, however. Each time she phoned Greta, her sister would ask breathlessly, "You're still coming, aren't you?" So Yarrow couldn't say no.

Under her coat, Greta was wearing a miniskirt and a top with holes cut in it.

"Isn't that a bit skimpy?" asked Yarrow. "It's freezing outside." She sneezed into her handkerchief.

"It's Courrèges," said Greta.

"I wouldn't have the courage to wear it."

As Yarrow listened in her car to the radio, her handkerchief twisted in her fingers, she could hear that the mood at the Manhattan Center where the ITU was meeting was ugly. Hundreds of printers were being turned away and the doors locked by the fire department. Hinton was repeatedly booed and heckled.

"This is the most pathetic deal anyone ever came up with," shouted a printer. "Why don't you throw the book at us, too?" The booing had begun when Hinton strode down the aisle to take his seat. When Elmer Brown of the ITU arrived the heckling increased. Men stamped their feet and jeered. Each time the union leadership rose to speak, the catcalls increased.

"I won't be intimidated by catcalls and booing," said Hinton in his quiet voice. "You'll have to hear me out."

"Oh, shut up." A shout went up for Mick Fitzgerald, a committee chairman who opposed the package. "Fitz. Fitz. Fitz." The call was punctuated by footstamping.

"Sit down, Mr. Fitzgerald," said Hinton. He tried to go on speaking, but his voice was drowned out. He obviously gave up the floor to Fitzgerald, for a great cheer went up and Fitzgerald began to speak.

"We oppose the mayor's formula." Cheers. "We oppose it as a threat to our job security by giving too many concessions to management; because it abandons the welfare gains sought to restore health benefits lost through rising costs; we oppose it because too many of these gains are to be postponed to the second year; we oppose it because this package was put together by outsiders; we oppose it because the total amount of dollars we are being offered is ridiculously small." More cheers sounded. "After a fifteen-week strike this union has only been able to up the ante seventy cents over what the publishers were willing to pay on December 7 last year."

The hall erupted again and then Hinton's voice, angrier this time, came on: "We've won our three basic demands. We have the thirty-five-hour week. We have the common contract expiration date. We have an agreement that we'll share in savings made through automation." Booing broke out. Hinton shouted over it. "That's our lifeline to the future."

"You've sold us out," yelled a voice.

"What about the teletype tapes?"

"Yeah, what about the tapes?"

"We knew we couldn't put it off forever, just like you knew you couldn't hold off the Linotype machine." The men cried out again and Hinton raised his voice. "The computer is here and automation is going to grow. You can't push it away. You've got to learn to live with it."

"He's lost," said Yarrow, shaking her head as the car sped through the greening countryside. The signal began to break up. Vasik fiddled with the dial, but they did not learn until they got home that the vote had been defeated by a sixty-four-vote majority.

The next day Yarrow's cold was much worse, so she stayed home in bed. She had lost her voice. Rifkin rang her that Elmer Brown had threatened to stop strike benefits to the printers. He was reportedly furious at having been booed by the rank and file at the meeting yesterday.

"He said," said Rifkin, "that one hundred thousand printers across the country are paying a strike assessment total of four percent of their wages to the Big Six strikers and that every day pressure is mounting to stop the support."

"How much are the strikers being paid?" whispered Yarrow.

"About one hundred and twenty dollars in strike benefits, but that includes fifty dollars in unemployment insurance."

"What's going to happen now?"

"I think they'll have to have another Big Six meeting. I heard the mayor's offering Madison Square Garden for it. They can fit more printers in that way."

"What else is happening?"

"The guild has voted to extend the contract as suggested."

"Good."

"And the stereotypers have also ratified their agreement. The mailers are still negotiating and the photoengravers' union has voted to call a strike if they don't get a satisfactory contract by four P.M. today."

"It all makes me feel like Chicken Little, I keep looking up to see if the sky is falling on my head."

"You should be drinking chicken soup."

"You haven't talked to Edith. I've had so much chicken soup I'm pouring it in my plant. The leaves have gone yellow but its throat is fine."

"I'll call you tomorrow," Rifkin said. "Look after yourself."

Edith came in with a big bunch of red roses that Elliot had sent. He was abroad again. She watched Edith place the roses on the table in front of the window. She wondered what it would be like to have him, or a husband, in the house all the time. She imagined sharing her room with him, sharing her bed and bathroom. She had grown accustomed to being on her own, she realized. Her belongings were spread throughout the room. She slept in the center of the double bed. Feminine toiletries crowded the vanity beside the washbasin. The house reflected her; the seating around the fireplace was her; the coral wallpaper, the cream carpet, the Chinese lamps were her. It would be difficult, she thought, to give it up. There was a degree of independence that she would no longer have. She was the boss, here and at the office. No man sat at the head of her table, she did. She had become accustomed to being on her own, had become accustomed to making her own decisions. She wondered if she could give up this hard-won independence. Could she give it up for Elliot? But then, he had never asked her: He had asked a young woman in Platte City, a young woman who had just given birth and who was soft and feminine and dependent, to be his wife. Yes—she had fluttered her wings, she had taken over her inheritance from Sandy—but she hadn't really taken flight. Now Yarrow felt like a great eagle that could expand its wings and soar. She could feel the little upturn of her wingtips. Even with the state of things in the printing industry right now, Yarrow knew that her confidence in herself had never been greater.

On the day of the vote at Madison Square Garden, Yarrow

was back in her office. She wanted to go up to the Garden to watch the vote, but she would have been lynched if she had been discovered. Besides, any direct interest on the part of the publishers themselves was seen to be a sign of weakness. Because of that she had had to overcome Rifkin's own reluctance to allow her to sit in on the original negotiations. Yarrow switched on her television set to watch.

The mayor had lent fifty voting machines to the union to expedite the counting and they had been placed in the basement of the Garden. Six thousand printers had turned up and they surged bitterly into the huge arena. Some of the bitterness stemmed from Elmer Brown's threat to stop strike benefits. The members were angry with their leaders. Not all the printers who came were employed by the newspapers, but ten thousand unionists were entitled to vote on the issue. The printers had always been a proud and clannish group. Printing jobs were regarded as a right, not a negotiable contract between an employer and an employee. It went way back to the old days of Caxton when, in a time of general illiteracy, printers were the educated men, the skillful men, proud of their craft and determined to guard their status. Of the ten thousand men who were entitled to vote, half that number worked in commercial shops throughout the city, eighteen hundred were pensioners, the rest were employed by the major newspapers.

Inside the Garden the arena was still set up as an ice rink, which had been used the night before for a game between the New York Rangers and a Canadian team. The speakers' platform had been placed far down behind a goal net. There were four mikes in the stands for members to speak into. A whole group of deaf printers was massed together in one stand with their interpreter in front of them. There were a number of women printers, Yarrow noticed with surprise, and some men carried babies on their shoulders. She was struck with a melancholy feeling of pity as she watched and listened.

At eleven o'clock the spotlights went on and flooded the speakers' platform with light.

Hinton began by saying that there would be four hours of talk before the voting began.

"We've had enough talk," shouted a young man. "Let's vote."

"I want to give everyone a chance to be heard," said Hinton to a chorus of boos.

In Yarrow's office the phone rang. It was Rifkin, calling from the Garden where he was watching the events. The Garden officials, he said, had told him the speeches would be cut because crowds were building up in the corridors leading to the voting machines.

"The men can't hear the speeches anyway. They're angry and just want to pull a red lever and go home."

"Call me back," said Yarrow.

Brown was pleading for acceptance of the proposal, but his words were met by a salvo of hisses. He could not hide his anger.

"Use your judgment and not your emotions. I've enough experience to have some idea of when you've reached the ultimate. Some of you may want to become professional strikers, but I think the vast majority of you don't. I've listened to loud mouths at union meetings yelling 'strike, strike,' and they were the first to leave town."

"This contract is an insult to our intelligence," said a voice from the crowd. Yarrow listened to the complaints from the floor as, one by one, people came up to the mikes. Some were for the strike, some were against. She wondered how her grandfather would have voted.

"If we have to accept this settlement, the strike wasn't worthwhile. We were told before the strike that the International would support us. Now we're told they won't. What kind of double-talk is this?"

"Be reasonable. Think of what will happen if you don't take it."

"When we saw this contract we were sick to our stomachs. I say let's go back for that fourth week of vacation, for five days' sick leave."

"The International wants to get New York off its books because we are costing them too much money."

"It's a shotgun contract."

"Don't desert the members who are paying your way. If you reject this, you may find yourself up a blind alley."

"Don't *you* desert us."

Hinton spoke up again from the platform.

"Take the contract," he said. "For the good of the union, take the contract."

The voting was indeed fast. On each machine was posted a sign: "Should the Newspaper Contract Be Adopted?" People only had to pull one of two levers, FOR or AGAINST.

The vote came in: For the contract by a three-to-two majority. The longest strike in the history of New York newspapers was almost at an end.

The *Times* and the *Herald* both announced immediately that they would increase their newsstand prices from five cents to ten cents. Yarrow was already selling the *Telegraph* at ten cents. There was a last hiccup when the photoengravers refused to ratify their agreement. They had a rowdy meeting in a school building, and Hinton said his men would not cross their picket line. On the thirty-first the photoengravers finally agreed; and on April Fool's Day the presses rolled again in all newspaper offices across New York City for the first time in 114 days.

On April 18 the *Telegraph* and the Big Six agreed to the same contract the others had negotiated. Yarrow sighed with relief when it was signed, and then she flew to Paris for four days with Elliot. Her cold had developed into bronchitis and she needed rest. In May Dryfoos of the *Times* died of a heart attack at the age of fifty. In October the *Mirror*, with the second largest circulation in the United States, went out of business. In March 1966, after further union problems, the hemorrhaging of the *Tribune* was temporarily stanched by its merger with the *World-Telegram* and the *Journal-American*. But the *World Journal Tribune*, or the "Widget" as it came to be known, was short-lived. The guild and the pressmen's union and the Big Six, all struck it. It came out late in September 1966, but it couldn't survive. On the fifth of May 1967, the death of the Widget was announced. Two thousand five hundred jobs were lost.

Yarrow clung to her tiny, leaking raft on South Street as it bobbed its way through the reefs of the sixties. It would survive, she said. She would survive. Outside New York she invested carefully and did well. However, success at the *Telegraph* was always marginal. Bu she wouldn't give it up. When nightmares woke her at night, she stared at the apple painting Elliot had given her and tried to figure it out. During the day, when anxiety rolled in her stomach like a pair of knotting hands, she lifted up the slug that acted as her paperweight and said silently to Jock, If only you knew. If only you knew.

She decided to take Eric's advice about Jock's cabin and rebuild a house there for herself and her mother. Over the years the house grew around the remains of the old cabin and became her escape from the world she had created.

CHAPTER 35

EVEN BEFORE ELLIOT'S SPECTACULAR PUBLIC FALL FROM GRACE in the presidential election in 1960, he had been a loner. He had always known that and thought it was a plus. He had been proud that no man could say they really knew him, that no man could say they owned him.

Although he had powerful friends in the Democratic party, none of them had rushed to his defense in the days after his reputation was slandered. No one outside his own committee for election had stood up for him. No one had spoken out and said the accusations were lies or half truths. His accusers met with a wall of deafening silence. In the years since, Elliot had recovered all the ground he had lost. But it was not without cost. He had gritted his teeth and determined to prove to the world, particularly to those people who had treated him like a pariah after his public humiliation, that he was better than they. He would work harder, he would be more successful, they would have to eat crow. One day they would all come begging to him to take on their business. And it happened as he had planned.

He had cultivated people he had never had time for before. They, he justified to himself, were his defense for the future. He was no longer the loner, the outsider, the one nobody knew. They were still curious about him, but now he was their secret ally, their confidant, their banker. He gave advice, he was flattering. Since he loved women, and they responded, a stream of wealthy widows crossed his threshold every week. Some of them would not buy an apartment until Elliot had checked it out first. He could talk to them about their jewelry and their art collections and their love lives, and while he was doing so he picked up gossip. But Elliot's greatest asset was his discretion, for although gossip and information came to him, he was a one-way street. He absorbed the information, filed it away and spent it as carefully as a miser at Christmas. Elliot Weyden, investment banker, became indispensable. His reputation soared. He was untouchable.

While pursuing his political ambitions, Elliot had let his business slide. His partners had valiantly soldiered on, but Phoenix and Company *was* Elliot; without him at the helm, the company lost its vigor and originality. It looked after its corporate clients, it gave out advice, it invested, but it did not grow. Not until Elliot came back and threw himself with a frenzy into his work did Phoenix burst into life again. In the seven years since the election, Elliot had turned Phoenix and Company into the star of the financial world. Hardly a week went by when a merger or acquisition involving Phoenix was not reported in the financial pages of *The Wall Street Journal.* To achieve this turnaround, Elliot had extended his working hours even beyond what they were before. His partners in Paris often found their telephones ringing as they walked into the office in the morning. "Where have you been?" he would ask. "I've been calling you for hours."

Elliot had opened a branch of Phoenix and Company in London and employed his brother-in-law, Clive Basingstoke (who had been knighted by an outgoing prime minister for services rendered). Elliot had found his sister's comment years ago, "Don't underestimate Clive," to be true. Clive's upper-class, self-deprecating manner hid a mind like an adding machine. Vivienne had always been shrewd about people.

Business absorbed Elliot. He devoured information; memos and messages poured across his desk detailing the minutiae of his business. He began going down to his office on Wall Street more and more. Afternoon visits to art galleries were no longer possible. Lainie could not cope with the work now flooding her desk at the Carlyle. He sent few letters himself; he preferred the telephone—direct, quick, final—but his desire to be in control forced him to keep up a frantic pace, compelled him to demand instant accessibility to every member of his company. He was not easy to work for, he was driven; and yet his people were devoted to him. His personality and enthusiasm shot off sparks like a Catherine wheel spinning like a dervish. He was able to push people to go that extra mile they would not walk for anyone else.

The number of people working for him in the Wall Street office had trebled. They could feel him approaching before they saw him. A restless hum preceded him and announced itself as a surge of excitement as he approached the swinging doors. The doors would open and there he would be, larger than life, his eyes sparkling, his mind twirling, asking questions, probing, throwing off ideas so fast that the more timid members of the firm quaked and even the others, more senior and longer-suffering, were not immune from moments of terror. If they couldn't come up with the answers, the black eyebrows would rise and one scalding phrase would sear across them and send them back, sweating, to their telephones and desks to rectify the oversight. In other things he was easy and sweet; he disliked being fussed over and to those in his good books he could be kind and charming.

Yarrow worried about him working too hard, but she kept her own counsel. She, too, had been busy. The sixties were good for her business. McLean Publishing was flourishing. She had bought out Schaeffer, and the magazine division was healthy and one hundred percent hers. New titles had been added, a television magazine, a magazine for boating enthusiasts, a men's quarterly. On other fronts, her company had bought a paper in Texas, a suburban weekly in Chicago, a radio station in Santa Barbara. So she never questioned Elliot. The last thing Yarrow wanted was him questioning her in return.

Nor did she ask him about Blanchette, or about marriage, though she knew Blanchette now lived half the year in London, where she had bought a large house in St. John's Wood. Meredith was at school at Godolphin and Latimer. Elliot still spent holidays with his wife and daughter; he had his own room at each of their homes. To outsiders, theirs was a perfect marriage, they were a compatible couple. Blanchette had recovered from Elliot's debacle as his good character became restored, and she supported and defended him against all criticism. It made it doubly difficult for Elliot to insist on the divorce he wanted.

"You're changing," said Yarrow one day in London as she heard him on the telephone berating some poor devil in West Africa about an aluminum company.

"The man's incompetent," said Elliot, banging down the receiver. "I should have gone there myself."

"Impatient and irascible," she said, walking to the door of her adjoining suite.

"Not with you." He gave her a flashing smile and then turned to a pile of reading on his desk.

"Then come for a walk with me. Talk with me. Look at this day." It was a perfect June day outside. The trees of Green Park shook softly in a thick dark green canopy outside the window.

"I can't, love. I have a meeting with the minister at four. I'm not properly briefed."

"One hour," she said, coming back to him and turning him from his labors. She held his arms above his elbows. She could feel how powerful his arms were under his fine wool suit. He exercised and played tennis. She was glad he at least took the time to do that.

"Elliot." He was still trying to read a report over her shoulder. "Will you look at me?" He laughed and gave her a quick kiss. "Elliot. I flew across the Atlantic to have this time with you. This is my first visit to England and all I've seen is the inside of this room."

"I thought you came to see me." However, he gave her a longer kiss this time.

"I want to talk to you," she said, "and get some air at the same time. Please."

He sighed and gave a last, longing glance at his work. "I'm yours," he said, "until three o'clock."

She picked up her cane—it had become part of her style, the way some women will always wear a scarf—and they left the hotel.

They walked arm in arm through the park, which was glorious with colorful borders of flowers and chestnut and elm trees. Hundreds of Londoners thought so, too; they sat in canvas deck chairs and turned their faces toward the sun. A group of office workers, their shirts off to expose pale chests, played football in a small dusty circle.

"I'm thinking of buying a newspaper here," said Yarrow as they stopped and watched the players. "I want Phoenix to negotiate for me."

"I knew you didn't come all this way just to see me," he said. "When did this happen? Who are you talking to?"

"Nothing's final yet. I'm meeting with the owners at six o'clock tonight. Will Phoenix act for me?" Elliot's company had handled most of Yarrow's financial affairs since she moved to New York. They had advised her wisely and set up a portfolio of stocks and shares for her. She had made a lot of money in real estate investments, and Phoenix had sheltered much of her income from taxes. The one serious row Yarrow had with Elliot had been over a bill that his company sent her last year which she thought was exorbitant.

"How can you possibly justify this on the amount of money you made on this deal?" she had shouted at him over the phone.

"It doesn't represent our fee for the money you made on this deal. It's payment for all the half-baked deals we *stopped* you from getting into." Yarrow had sent his firm half the amount they asked for and nothing more had been said.

"Of course we'll act for you. Clive would be good at that. He understands the ins and outs of the politics here." They walked a little further around the pond and watched some ducks that were making a great noise as passersby tossed bread at them. A pair of swans gracefully ignored the sodden dough on the water.

"We don't see enough of each other," said Yarrow.

"Whose fault is that?" He sounded very sharp. She glanced at him.

"Both of ours."

He stopped abruptly and took her by the shoulders.

"Then give it up," he said. "Sell your business and stay with me. I need you."

"You can't be serious," she said.

"Darling, you've proved you can run a company. You took over a sick business and you've built it into a large, successful one. Can't you stop now?"

"Could you?"

"It's not the same."

"Why isn't it the same? What would I do with myself?"

"Be with me. Travel with me."

"I'd be—superfluous." She couldn't believe what he was suggesting. She turned away from him and started toward Birdcage Walk. The sun flashed on her shapely legs under the knee-length tailored white suit she was wearing. Heads turned as she went by. He caught up with her.

"Yarrow, if you're complaining, you can do something about it. Listen to me."

"I don't want to listen to you, Elliot. It's as though you're telling me give up one of my children. I thought you were proud of what I'd achieved."

"I am proud of you."

"But you didn't think it would go this far? You didn't think I would be successful. You didn't think it would mean I would become independent." She waited for him to say something.

"I've always wanted your success but I'll be honest, it isn't easy at times loving you. I hate to see you moving out on your own—without me. I have to make an appointment to see you these days."

"*You* have to make an appointment to see *me*?"

"I want a woman in my bed, Yarrow, not another corporation."

"I thought you liked independent women, but you're just like other men, you want a clinging vine."

"That's not true."

"Then you're upset because I didn't talk to you about this London paper. I've been thinking about a move like this for months. I did mention it to you once, but you were too busy to listen.''

"I remember you asking me in a very offhand way if I thought you should enter the Fleet Street market and, if I recall correctly, I said no.''

"Then I did talk to you about it.''

"Not specifically. I thought you were talking about a hypothetical case. Besides, if you ask me for advice, why don't you damn well take it?''

"I don't have to take it. I make up my own mind.''

"Yes, I've noticed.''

"Anyway, I can't resist it. It's a challenge. Do you know what Fleet Street means to a publisher?''

A whole family of ducks had come out of the water and begun shaking their feathers in the sun. Drops of sparkling water flew onto Elliot's trouser legs. He glanced at his watch. "I have to go back. The minister will be waiting. Can we talk about this later?'' Yarrow looked at him with more sadness than anger. She shrugged. She knew she was being less than adult, but he had hurt her.

"Goddam it,'' he said, "this is a very important meeting.''

"Then you must go,'' she said. He hesitated for a moment, and then he turned on his heel and strode back through the park, scattering the ducks before him.

Yarrow sat on a bench beside a Norland nanny with a little girl strapped into a high, spotless perambulator. The little girl, in her smocked Liberty print dress, was placidly playing with a doll, while her brother, not much older, played on the steps at the edge of the pond. "Look, Nanny, look,'' he shouted as he ran up and down the slimy steps. The woman, who wore a gray felt trilby and a tie, kept smiling at him and nodding. "Clever Gregory,'' she kept saying.

Yarrow was miserable. She had so looked forward to this time with Elliot. She had bought new clothes, organized her own children's schedules to have this time with him. Buck had gone to a summer camp near Boulder with an Outward Bound group. Lily was working as a news researcher at KMZO in Denver. Yarrow wondered how long Lily's enthusiasm would last. John, now twenty, was spending his summer vacation from college working in the pressroom at *The Washington Post*. Hell, Yarrow had even had her legs waxed and her nails done before she came over to join Elliot. She had thought their time together would be romantic, intimate. Instead, they were bickering between appointments. Was he tiring of her? She had once prayed that he

could separate the woman from the publiser. Was he now showing that he was unable to do so? She couldn't bear to think that
she and Elliot were falling out of love with each other. She
wanted to hold on to their love the way it was, enshrined forever
in her memory as perfect and new. If it was coming to an end,
she decided as she walked toward Hyde Park swinging her cane,
she would finish it abruptly. She would cut it off like a surgeon.
She had never imagined that he would ask her to choose between
him and her career.

Yarrow was so involved with her thoughts that she stepped
onto the bridle path and into the path of a young girl cantering a
horse. The girl reined the horse expertly at the last minute, but
not before Yarrow had fallen to the ground. The girl pulled up
her panicky horse and came back to Yarrow, who sat shaking the
dust from her hair.

"Oh, I say, I'm awfully sorry. I thought you would see me
coming." Her diction was not quite clear.

"It was my fault," said Yarrow, looking up at her. She was a
young girl, about thirteen, with almost white hair pinned in a
tight little knot beneath her black velvet cap. The girl jumped off
her horse and put her hand on Yarrow's elbow to help her to her
feet. The girl had a pretty face except for a scar that ran across
her upper lip as though it had once been cleft. Yarrow found
herself staring into Elliot's eyes, dark and penetrating and worried.

"Are you sure you're all right?"

"Quite sure. Thank you."

The girl's face broke into a smile. "Oh, that's a relief.
Malone, my riding instructor, is always at me to be more careful. He'd like to see me on a rocking horse." She giggled. She
was really quite beautiful, thought Yarrow, once one got used to
the slightly odd-shaped lip and the not-quite perfect nose. She
had a way of ducking her head so that the lower part of her face
was in shadow.

A man came thundering up Rotten Row on a big bay. "Bloody
hell, Meredith, be more careful." He tipped his hat at Yarrow.

"Oh, shut up, Malone," said Meredith, hoisting herself back
onto her horse. "You're just a worry wart. Race you back to the
stable." She was off like a bolt, and Malone was unsure whether
to stand on his dignity or not, until she shouted over her shoulder
at him, "Fussbudget," and he gave in and kicked his horse into
a race.

So that's Meredith, thought Yarrow, watching them disappear
under the elm trees. No wonder Elliot was proud of her. She
seemed an independent girl. Elliot had said she wanted to be a

doctor when she grew up. Yarrow wondered if Meredith would
have the same trouble with her father as Yarrow was having now
with him. But then, men were inconsistent. What did they want
in a woman?

At six o'clock Yarrow was at a flat in Eaton Square to meet
with the Randolph family who owned the *Sunday Enquirer*.
Clive Basingstoke, as per Elliot's suggestion, was with her. Sir
Clive was in his sixties and his leg still clicked whenever he sat
down. He had a dry sense of humor, and Yarrow liked him
immediately. He knew the Randolphs socially, he said; he played
at the same golf course as old Bing Randolph.

It took some time for Yarrow to figure out which son was
which, which wife belonged to whom, which was the cousin
who worked in the business. She was unimpressed by them all.
No wonder the company was sinking when such nepotism went
on. She hoped she would never make the same mistake in her
own company. The Randolph business was ripe for a takeover; it
had underutilized assets and an incompetent board of directors.
The more they spoke, the more convinced she was that none of
them deserved their positions. She knew there was going to be
no business done this evening; they were checking her out.

It was immediately clear to Yarrow, sitting in the chintz-
decorated library that overlooked the square, that it was Lady
Randolph who was the power in the family. Her pale eyes were
as shrewd as any banker's.

"We are the subject of an unfriendly bid from Piers Molinski,"
said Lady Randolph. "Sherry?" She handed Yarrow a tiny
thimbleful of sherry in an etched glass. Yarrow had heard the
Randolphs were stingy.

"Bloody disgraceful," said Sir Bing.

"I guess that's why I've always remained a private company," said Yarrow, sipping the sweet sherry and then putting it
down on the black lacquered tray that served as a table.

"Institutional shareholders are a menace," said Sir Bing. "No
loyalty. No damned loyalty."

"We're a large family and the *Enquirer* was founded by Sir
Bing's grandfather," said Lady Randolph, patting her short,
curly gray hair in which not a tress was out of place.

"We are only in this situation because one of our family wants
to sell out. He doesn't have the interest, you see."

"No damned loyalty."

"We can't match the price being offered by this dreadful man
for those shares. Mr. Lipton, our banker, advised us to see you.

He says your credentials are excellent.'' And my credit, thought Yarrow.

"If we are to be forced into this situation we would like to pick our own bedfellows,'' said Lady Randolph. ''Don't you agree? Both our sons work for the company, my sister's son runs our mill division. But it's one of the other cousins, Sir Bing's nephew, who has never shown the slightest inclination to come into the business, who is causing all this trouble.''

"Used to play croquet with the little blighter,'' said Sir Bing, shaking his jowls. "Always getting in the rough, he was.''

"Where does he live, this nephew?''

"In Switzerland.''

"Tax exile,'' said Sir Bing.

"He's promised to sell his shares to Piers Molinski, providing Molinski gets fifty-one percent control. You must have heard of Molinski, Member of Parliament, Labor, of course, dreadful man.''

"My dear, he's a Socialist,'' said Sir Bing.

"Yes, a very rich one, I'm afraid,'' said Lady Randolph.

"They're the ones who can afford to be Socialists. But I'm not angry with him but with that young whippersnapper.'' Sir Bing's pink jowls began to become mottled.

Lady Randolph patted his hand. "At ten o'clock tomorrow when the stock exchange reopens, we are afraid Molinski is going to increase his offer. This is a wonderful opportunity for you, my dear, to join our company as a partner.'' Save the condescension, thought Yarrow.

"More sherry?''

"No thank you.'' Yarrow stood up. "We'll meet tomorrow with Mr. Lipton, your merchant banker, and see what's possible. I have to know what Mr. Molinski is offering.''

"Of course. Good-bye, Clive, we don't see enough of you these days.'' Lady Randolph got up, her eyes once again going over Yarrow from head to foot, and the audience was over.

They were in bed in his suite when the phone rang. They had made love to each other with only barely concealed anger. There had been no foreplay—it had even irritated her when he kissed her breasts. Get on with it, she wanted to say. It often surprised her what moods sex could encompass; anger, pain, passion, tenderness, humor. Tonight, even though they were angry with each other, the act itself had released them.

"Never let the sun go down on one's anger,'' said Elliot,

kissing the inside of her wrist. He could afford to be tender now because he was not afraid she would reject him.

"Who said that?"

He paused, "Mrs. Neil," he said. The pink glow of the bedside lamp lit his face. They had made love so rapidly that they had not had time to switch it off.

"Oh. *The* Mrs. Neil."

"Yes. She was a wise old bird."

"Don't talk about her. It makes me jealous."

"Good." He kissed her again, on her collarbone. The phone rang and she could tell the way he turned over and reached for his writing pad that it was important. It was Uruguay, or Peru, or the Ivory Coast, or Iran. She had given up trying to keep Elliot's deals separate in her head.

She lay and watched him while he spoke on the phone. She absentmindedly stroked his flank while he spoke. Well as she knew him, there was an undercurrent in him that she could sense but could not touch. It flowed along inside him, guiding him, driving him, and there were times she wanted to dive in and discover it, because then there would be nothing of his that was not hers. It would be the ultimate oneness, because it would destroy the uniqueness of each other. She imagined it, this subterranean flow, as a lagoon inside a dim limestone cave like the one he had visited with her children in Jamaica. But she was afraid, as she had been then, of diving in. The undercurrent might engulf her. Was he, she thought with a jolt, was he afraid of that within her, too? Afraid of her own undercurrent, which she sank into to find the strength to go on, to take risks, to fight when others might give up, did he perhaps feel that he wanted to destroy it, so that she too would be wholly his? Was there in each person such a cave which, desirable as it might be to others, must be left alone?

She was thinking, could I give him up? Could I live without him? It was not that he was presenting her with an ultimatum, me or your company, she saw that clearly now, but she saw that his unhappiness with their current situation left him vulnerable. She was afraid he would fall in love with another woman; a woman with more time, a woman who went to the hairdresser every week, and had her nails and legs done regularly, and who knew how to apply liquid eyeliner as all women did now. (Yarrow had never gotten the hang of it though Greta tried to show her.) Elliot wanted a woman to whom he would be all-important. I am forty-five years old, she thought. She was unaware of her own, real, ageless beauty. Like Freya before her, she was without vanity. How can I keep him? Her own vulnerability made her aware of his.

When he hung up they lay in each other's arms, deep in their own thoughts.

"I must get up," she said.

"Why? Are you leaving me?"

"No. I can hear the phone ringing in my room. I'll be right back."

It was Sandy, calling from Washington. She knew immediately something was wrong. She stood naked beside the phone and listened. His voice sounded heavy, humid like the weather he was experiencing.

"It's John," he said. "He's gone. He's gone to Canada to avoid the draft. I'm so damn mad at him."

"Oh, Sandy. What happened?" Yarrow sank onto the bed and pulled up a sheet to cover herself.

"He wanted to drop out of college. He's been doing so well. I told him if he dropped out, his *2-S* deferment as a student would stop. So he agreed to register for the next semester, but now he's changed his mind and left."

Yarrow listened to Sandy in silence. John was not an easy boy to deal with, but there was something Sandy wasn't telling her. It was unlike John to go off, half-cocked, without a reason. Even if you didn't agree with the reason, he usually let you know what it was.

"Did you hit him?" she said.

"I'm ashamed to say I did. But I'm more ashamed of him. Every time he started with this pacifism stuff, I'd get so mad. He doesn't even know what pacifism is. He's got your temper."

"Mine?"

"He said he wasn't going to fight for this 'lousy country.' He's a damn coward, that's what he is. You should see the stuff that comes into this house. All antiwar, anti-everything. They don't teach them the word 'patriotic' anymore. Student Union for Peace Action—'America, you bastard' is what they write. It makes me sick to think of him."

Yarrow could imagine Sandy glancing at his war decorations as he spoke.

"You shouldn't have hit him."

"Ach. He upsets Wilhelmina, he upsets everybody. I swear, Yarrow, if he comes back here, I'll turn him in myself."

"Sandy . . ."

"I swear it. I wash my hands of him."

Yarrow hung up softly.

"Are you coming back to bed?" Elliot stood in the doorway waiting for her.

"Yes, I'll be there in a minute," she said. He came over and put his hands through her hair.

"What is it, baby?"

"Oh, just family," she said. "Family business."

Later in the night, when the unfamiliar sound of a London fire engine woke her, she whispered to him, "Did you mean what you said about me giving up?"

"No, darling. I'll take you any way you are."

She curled into him and fell back into a deep, effacing sleep.

"A breakfast meeting?" sputtered Sir Bing as his wife pushed him through the door into their dining room. "Don't these Americans have any sense of decorum?"

Yarrow came forward with a wry smile. She had put on a classic, if somewhat dowdy, gray suit today. She thought it was more appropriate than the spring-yellow Courrèges suit that Elliot had picked out. Elliot always wanted to see her legs. He thought they were one of her best features. But today Yarrow wanted the Randolphs to think of other things. She was not going to be threatening, certainly not threatening to Lady Randolph or the other women in the family. They were all gathered this morning, standing around the mahogany table, waiting for the patriarch to sit down. Weak tea had been poured. Yarrow longed for a cup of strong thick black coffee. She almost choked when she swallowed some tea leaves. How American I must seem to them, she thought. She had been expecting tea bags to be used. She removed a black tea leaf from her tooth. The butler offered her some kedgeree, but Yarrow politely refused. The smell of the smoked haddock was too much for her so early in the morning.

Lipton, the Randolphs' banker, was a cross-eyed old rogue who looked as though he would be more at home on the poop of a pirate ship than running a distinguished banking house. His questions and answers showed him to be a realist. He shoveled rice and fish into his mouth without stopping. He knew there were no second servings at the Randolph table.

Clive had come up with a proposal of share-swapping that would enable Yarrow to take control of the company and also save face for the Randolph family. It was basically the same deal as Molinski was offering; it was up to the shareholders to decide which offer was worth more. There was going to be a proxy fight. A general meeting of the shareholders would be held in a month's time. Yarrow's plan was to inject a number of the McLean assets into the *Enquirer* company. Yarrow felt she was sitting pretty. Even if the Randolphs did not like the idea of her coming onto their own turf, they disliked the idea of Molinski coming onto it even more.

The bankers batted off each other for a while and Yarrow brooded, toying with her tea and a square of cold toast. A clock was ticking away on the wall above the Adam fireplace. She had very little sympathy for the Randolph family. Sir Bing, she mused, might once have been a power to reckon with—but no longer. A degeneracy of ambition and drive had left him a mere cardboard figurehead. Under his sons, the company was appallingly, sloppily run. She had had a quick tour around the premises of the *Enquirer* yesterday before meeting with the Randolphs. She thought the presses and the machine room were out of the dark ages. The sons told her with great pride that they knew nothing about the machines; in fact, one admitted, he hated walking through the pressroom altogether. Even the editorial floors were segregated from the administrative side by class walls thicker than any brick walls Yarrow had ever seen. Her egalitarianism was offended.

"I believe," said Yarrow, cutting across the talk, since it seemed to be going nowhere, "that in return for your interests in the *Platte City Journal-Record* and *Mollie* magazine, my company will have thirty-one percent of the *Enquirer*. Is that correct?"

"It is, my dear," said Sir Bing.

"In return, your company will be saved from Mr. Molinski's overtures and you, Sir Bing, will agree to remain as chairman, I hope."

"Chairman and managing director," said Lady Randolph with a smile.

"Oh, no," said Yarrow. "You misunderstand. I won't put my company and my reputation on the line unless I am sole chief executive."

Lady Randolph looked at Yarrow and then at her husband. "But that's out of the question. This is a Randolph paper."

Yarrow pushed herself away from the table. "Then, I thank you for breakfast. I've enjoyed my visit to England and I've lost nothing except my plane fare."

"Now don't be too hasty," said Lipton, leaning forward suddenly, his cross-eyes glinting at Yarrow through his glasses. "Why don't you leave us for a few minutes so we can talk about this in private?"

Yarrow knew in that moment that she had won. She looked at

Basingstoke, and they retired to wait in the next room. As they closed the door, she winked at Clive. "Not bad for a couple of old cripples."

They spent a long ten minutes waiting in the drawing room, listening to murmurs from the dining room. When the others came out, Lady Randolph was markedly icy. The board of directors would unanimously support McLean Publishing's offer for their company, and Yarrow would be named managing director. It was five minutes to ten. The stock exchange would be open for trading in five minutes. A statement would be issued in the next hour.

Yarrow couldn't help giving a little swagger with her cane as she left with Basingstoke.

"Thank God we don't have to go to Geneva," she said.

"Why Geneva?" Clive asked. The chauffeur pulled out, turned into Sloane Square and headed for the Embankment.

"If it wasn't going to work I was going to face down the errant nephew myself, hopefully waving a large check from your bank, my dear Clive."

Clive chortled. "I wish you had time to meet Vivienne. You'd both get on so well."

Until the proxy meeting took place, Yarrow felt there was nothing further that she could do. She was frantic about John's whereabouts. He had disappeared once he had crossed the Canadian border. He was probably living under an assumed name. He was such a fool, that boy, he didn't seem to understand that now he could never come back home, that if he did he would be liable to five years' imprisonment and fines. She wondered if he had a passport, she wondered if he would renounce his U.S. citizenship. She flipped through the magazines on the plane, but they all dealt with the war. There were pictures of boys dying, boys afraid of dying. It was an ugly war, and she did not want her son to die, but she wished he had gone out and met it and not run the way he had. Clara Russell, voting on the House floor years ago, she had run. The one who hadn't was the sole woman who voted no, Jeannette Rankin. She had stayed and taken her punishment. If John had accepted that, if John hadn't run away, Yarrow would have been proud. Now she was ashamed of him. She would always love him, but with sadness, for he was a disappointment to her. Guilt assailed her.

She flew back to New York, determined to find out what had happened to him, and landed in a crisis she had not seen coming.

CHAPTER 36

NEW YORK WAS AS HOT AND MUGGY AS A STEAMBATH. GRIT AND car fumes swirled around the streets. Hot air shimmered up from the baking concrete. The heat made everyone bad-tempered, and on the FDR Drive, where a taxi and a car had collided, Yarrow saw two middle-aged men in plaid shirts punching each other.

"It's good to be back," she said. Vasik drove around the contretemps with his usual phlegmatic skill.

Yarrow flung herself into her air-conditioned office with relief. She walked to her desk, slipping off her jacket and eager to attack the mountain of mail that usually awaited her, only to see a forlorn envelope lying in lonely splendor on her blotting pad. She looked around for Margaret, but Margaret had suddenly found this was the moment to disappear. Yarrow ripped open the envelope with her silver letter opener. It was a formal letter dictated by a lawyer. Ned Griffin was resigning. There was not a personal word in it. Yarrow turned over the letter, looked into the envelope to see if there were a note she had missed seeing. There was nothing. Ned Griffin was giving her two weeks' notice, and his lawyer would be in touch about his severance pay and so forth. Ned had never had a contract, it hadn't seemed necessary. Yarrow's stomach felt as though it had been kicked.

She sat down slowly at her desk and placed her head in her hands and rubbed her forehead hard. She looked at the cold, impersonal letter in front of her. They had grown apart, she and Ned and Mary-Ellen. Yarrow had moved on, her horizons had expanded. Ned and Mary-Ellen's had not. There had been a time when she could not wait to telephone Mary-Ellen to discuss with her something that had happened, relate some amusing story. And then, Mary-Ellen changed—at least, that was how Yarrow saw it—Mary-Ellen had become abrupt on the telephone, sarcastic. Yarrow found she was phoning less and less. Increasingly, when she was free and ready to have a quiet dinner with friends, she seldom called the Griffins—it was a strain to be constantly

426

wary of saying something that might be misconstrued or passed on. She had stopped trusting the Griffins and the Griffins had stopped trusting her.

Or was it about money? She had not thought about Ned's income; he never came to her about it, never asked, so she assumed he was content. How stupid of her not to see it coming. How stupid of her not to realize that what she had accepted as friendship had been replaced by an employee-employer relationship.

She got up. Nausea hit her and saline-tasting saliva came into her mouth. She went into the bathroom and was sick. She hadn't been sick like this since the early days when she took over the *Platte City Journal-Record* from Sandy and threw up every morning on the way to work. Then it had been due to fear and anxiety; this time it was due to betrayal by someone she had thought of as a friend. She wiped her mouth and gargled with some Scope, and then reapplied her lipstick carefully and sent for Ned.

He came in, as affable as usual, and kissed her on the cheek. Yarrow was in such a state of shock that her wits seemed to have left her.

"I see you got my letter," he said.

"Yes. I'm kind of surprised."

"Well, it was time for a change. I had to think about my future."

"I can't talk you into staying, I suppose?"

"No, Yarrow. I have another job lined up."

"Ah. Could you tell me who with?"

"They've asked me not to say. Other people are involved, you know."

"I understand." She paused. "How are the kids?"

"They're fine. You must come and see them one day. Sally's now a nurse. Young Malcolm is working as a reporter at the *Courier*."

"So I heard."

How empty their words were. They meant nothing.

They said good-bye with protestations of goodwill, and she watched him leave and then she called in Rifkin.

"I'll bet he's going to the *Courier*," she said. "I'll bet you anything."

They discussed who she would replace him with, and Yarrow asked the city editor, Andrew Rockman, to come up and see her. Gossip in a newspaper office travels faster than smoke through the air vents. Rockman already knew about Griffin's resignation.

He was delighted to take the job, but Yarrow wondered if she was pushing him too far too fast. Time would tell.

In the next few days a pall of gloom settled over the editorial floors. Ned had been popular and the editorial floor of the *Telegraph* had been a friendly, joshing place. Now a sort of black Irish wake seemed to be taking place. Yarrow asked Ned to leave early. There was no need for the agony to go on. She did not phone Mary-Ellen. She felt it was Mary-Ellen's place to call her. They, after all, were leaving her.

Yarrow found it impossible to understand why Ned had handled his resignation in this way. It was the way it was done that stung the most, and Mary-Ellen had to have known about it.

She was hurt more than she would admit by the Griffinses' defection. She saw it as a reflection on her and her company, because it showed that they thought something was wanting. It gnawed at her self-esteem, resurrected a timidity of ego that she thought she had long since buried.

A few days later, the *Courier* came out with a big front-page headline announcing with glee their successful poaching of the *Telegraph*'s editor. Yarrow's hurt turned to anger. Ned's son, Malcolm, whom she had bounced on her knee, was a reporter on the *Courier*. She had Rifkin make him an offer he could not refuse, and they also poached two of the *Courier*'s best sports writers that same week. When Yarrow flew back to London, the dust had settled somewhat, but she kept thinking about Mary-Ellen, her old school friend. Her mind kept repeating, like a refrain, "How could she, how could she?" It was as though two young girls, giggling over bowls of chopped onions and tomatoes, had forgotten to lift the needle off a Victor record long ago.

Five hundred shareholders turned up at the Lambert Rooms where the meeting to decide the future of the *Sunday Enquirer* was to take place. Piers Molinski and Yarrow appraised each other along the front row, and then the Randolph family came in and took their seats on the dais, and the shareholders applauded. Yarrow wondered why, since the company was doing so badly.

She knew little about Molinski except that he had come to England after the war as a displaced person and had made a fortune manufacturing pharmaceutical products in Bradford. He had been elected to Parliament four years ago. There were unsubstantiated rumors about his political allegiances, about the state of his business. Clive and Yarrow knew that Molinski's offer, which looked better on paper than their own, was falsely inflated. The value of the shares of Molinski, Ltd., depended on one's interpretation of his figures. His business, Clive said, was just a house of cards; no one could figure out where the inventory was, or what its value was. For example, how could you evaluate a shipment of rubber condoms that had been sitting on Indian wharves in the sun for the past twelve months? "Their offer is full of holes," said Yarrow.

The English press was riding with the story at full tilt; it made the American press seem pale by comparison. Without exception, the financial pundits had come out in favor of Molinski's offer over Yarrow's. A writ had been put out for damages for breach of their fiduciary obligations against the *Enquirer* directors. The trading of shares in the *Enquirer* company had been suspended by the stock exchange. A flurry of acrimonious statements was made by both sides. When trading was resumed, Yarrow's bankers accused Molinski of being the "mystery" buyer of one million shares when both sides had agred not to add to their own holdings. The board of trade had gotten into the act, the takeover panel had been summoned. The difference in price between Molinski's and Yarrow's offers was pointed out to be ten shillings and threepence. Lawyers had been huddling for weeks.

Molinski's people telephoned shareholders and asked them not to vote as their directors advised. The Randolphs and Yarrow were outraged. Then a rumor circulated that in Platte City, a rival newspaper was about to start up against the *Journal*. Yarrow shrugged the story off when she was asked about it. "I stand by my profit estimates," she said.

Molinski then stated that the *Enquirer* board "was asking shareholders to make a substantial financial sacrifice without precedent in the history of major public companies in this country."

"What a pompous ass," said Yarrow. But what got her really steaming was a statement Molinski had made that "Miss McLean cannot manage two dissimilar businesses with the Atlantic Ocean in between." McLean Publishing, the statement continued, "was the purveyor of salacious newspapers in New York and Colorado which are currently overvalued due to temporarily advantageous circumstances." Yarrow looked at the screaming headline of the current issue of the *Enquirer*, VICAR STEALS KNICKERS OF GIRL BELL-RINGERS, and wondered if Molinski had ever read the paper.

Yarrow fought back. She held a press conference as soon as she got to London. She challenged Molinski's figures and snapped back with her own; she demolished Molinski's attack on her newspapers and on her managerial abilities.

"My grandfather was born in Scotland," she said on BBC television that night, "and my grandfather and my father were

printers. I know a great deal more about newspapers than a man
who manufactures rubber duckies.''

Yarrow was incensed by Molinski's attacks on her. She was
convinced it was because she was a woman. At dinner in their
hotel the night before the proxy meeting, it was Elliot who
calmed her down. Elliot, known for his impatience and steaming
rages when things went wrong, was the understanding, soothing
partner she needed. He toasted her with champagne. ''You're
doing fine,'' he said. ''You're going to win tomorrow.''

''How can you be sure?''

He looked at her as she sat opposite him, the candlelight
throwing a warm glow on her face, an emerald-green velvet
gown, worn off the shoulder, showing her creamy skin.

''I only back winners,'' he said.

He had bought her a present, a pretty birch walking stick with
a gray horn handle and a silver collar. ''If all else fails, you can
beat them off with it tomorrow,'' he said. ''But you won't need
it. Molinski's a goner. As Jock would have told him, 'Don't pick
a fight with a gal who buys ink by the barrel.' ''

''You could have told him that.''

''Yes,'' he said, lifting her hand off the table and kissing the
palm, ''but I prefer to forget.''

Next day all the players were assembled in the crowded
meeting room. Molinski had made a last-minute bid to stop the
use of the pension-fund shares being voted today. The bid had
been rejected by a High Court judge. Yarrow breathed more
easily; if the vote was close, those shares would be important.

Sir Bing got up and, to loud applause, welcomed the appearance of so many of his shareholders. He looked haggard
after the legal battles of the last few weeks, but gave a brief
rundown of the takeover attempts, including the role of his
nephew who had started it all.

''Your board has decided that the Molinski offer does not
make any commercial sense at all. Editorial and management
skills are what we need and we believe we have found those in
the expertise of Miss Yarrow McLean. McLean Publishing is a
highly respected and dynamic company in the United States with
interests in newspapers, magazines, television and broadcasting.
We believe it is in your best interests, in both the short and the
long term, to vote for our company to join with McLean Publishing and to reject the offer proposed by Mr. Molinski.''

A great cheer went up; and then Sir Bing introduced Yarrow
and she stood up and faced the curious crowd with some em-

barrassment. She spoke modestly and kept it short. She thanked Sir Bing for his kind words.

"Much has been said about the assets of my company," she said. "I assure you they are first class and not inflated by artificial means. I intend to work hard for your company and I am absolutely confident that together we can embark on a whole new and exciting era in British and United States publishing."

Molinski got up to speak.

"State your name and how many shares you have," shouted a heckler. "Sit down," shouted another.

"May I make a statement in reply to your opening remarks, Sir Bing?"

"You may speak for exactly as long as Miss McLean, three minutes."

Molinski's voice and presence were more British than the British, but Yarrow could sense the hostility in the room.

"I'm amazed," he said, "at the remarkably spontaneous questions from your shareholders. I notice they are all listed on your board."

"They are not!" said Sir Bing.

"Withdraw," came a shout.

"Many of your editorial and production staff have been in touch with me that they were ordered to come here and pack this hall."

"I'm tired of listening to these half truths, Mr. Molinski," said Sir Bing, his jowls quivering.

"He is out of order," someone shouted.

"I seek the protection of the chair," said Molinski coolly. "I didn't interrupt Miss McLean. It seems lamentable to me and absolutely damning that the only way this board could save itself was to throw itself into the arms of Miss McLean and make her managing director."

"We are not being saved by Miss McLean. We are saving ourselves and I don't care a tuppenny cuss what you think of this board, Mr. Molinski."

"This is a disgrace," thundered Molinski. "If you support your board you are voting for a substantial fall in the market value of your shares."

At this Sir Bing rose to his feet and addressed the shareholders. "Do you wish to hear Mr. Molinski any further?"

A resounding NO came back.

"Then I call for a show of hands from those who support the board's decision to accept a merger with McLean Publishing." Everyone, except for about twenty people, stood up and raised their hands.

Yarrow sat back and watched while a poll with cards was taken. There was no need for her to say any more. Let the others do the fighting.

At the end of the meeting, when it was declared that the resolution had passed, there was one other disgruntled man besides Molinski.

"I'm not sure how many shares I have," he said, "but could I ask the chairman if the usual tea for the shareholders will be provided this afternoon?"

Yarrow watched with amusement as the chairman struggled to explain how expensive a tea for four hundred people would be.

"Absolutely not," said Sir Bing, rushing out to his own champagne. "Have you ever heard such balderdash?" Right to the end the Randolphs remained true to form.

She was at the *Enquirer* office in Fleet Street early the next morning. She had to wait until someone could find the keys to let her in. The place was like a mausoleum. There was not a soul at work except the security people and the cleaners. She wandered along the marble entrance hall, into the scratched and dirty elevators, the offices on mahogany row, the editorial floor with its partitions of wood, the executive dining room, the kitchen, the chairman's bathroom. She decided which office she would like for herself—and picked one right near the front door to the executive wing. She hated to waste time walking along the corridors, and she wanted to see who was coming and going. By the time the first people who worked on her floor drifted in about ten, the word was around that Miss McLean had been in the building for hours.

"My God, where is she now?" asked one of the young Randolphs of the security man.

"She said she was going down to the machine room."

"On her own?" No one had ever heard of such a thing. Young Randolph got terribly lost trying to find her. He did not know this part of the plant at all. When he finally unearthed her, she was leaning on an iron stairway, looking over the presses and the dirt and filth and ink of a hundred years.

"How many men work in here?" she asked, pointing with her cane.

He told her.

"That's far too many. How do they all fit in?"

"They don't. Half of them at any time are out on a 'blow.' "

"A blow?"

"They wait outside and come in when the other half go out."

Yarrow walked back up to her office with young Randolph following behind her. The place was totally empty at the moment. It was unnerving. For five days a week, nothing happened in this building. Yarrow knew how to rectify that. She was going to start a daily. But she didn't tell young Randolph that. It was none of his business. By the time she would be ready to move, none of the Randolphs would be around to be involved.

"How are you going to manage living on two continents?" asked Greta at the end of September. They were at Yarrow's house in the mountains of Colorado. Yarrow had sneaked away for three days' rest before going back to London.

"With some difficulty." Yarrow laughed. "Isn't it beautiful here?" She and Greta were sitting outside on a terrace that overlooked the bowl that Grandfather had fallen in love with when he was a boy. The "modest" house that Yarrow had started to build had grown over the years into a big, comfortable ranch house. She called the house Chipeta. The outside was constructed of split logs like the old cabin, but huge windows had been put in to bring the view indoors. Yellow aspens shook outside the windows against the deep green of the fir trees. Greta poured another glass of lemonade for Yarrow. The sun was bright and hot, but the breeze was cool. Within a month snow would again be on the ground.

"I'm going to spend half the year in London and half the year in New York. I have good people in both places. It's probably better for them to be more autonomous anyway. Buck's enjoying boarding school now and Lily doesn't need me. I wish she wasn't living with that young man, though. It's not right."

Greta raised her eyebrows at her sister, but said nothing.

"I just wish I knew where John was." Yarrow looked out at the mountains she loved and thought about her failure to locate her son. Lainie's son had died in Vietnam. Elliot had told her that Lainie had two boys in the war. It had been the most difficult letter for Yarrow to write. Lainie's son had sacrificed his life in Vietnam while her own was hiding across the border in Canada.

"How's the restaurant going?"

"Oh, great. Just great." Greta had taken up Eric's challenge and was now running one of the best restaurants in Galena.

"My pastry chef, Eduardo, is divine," said Greta, rolling her eyes.

"Oh, no."

Yarrow looked at her sister. Greta was forty-one, a full-bosomed blond woman with the face of an angel. She was wearing jeans and a sleeveless down jacket over a white cambric shirt. Even up here, Greta still looked as though she were ready to be photographed for the cover of a magazine.

"I'm not getting married again, don't worry. He's just a baby. I must admit though I find it very hard to go to bed with a man if I'm not married to him. Do you know what I mean?"

"No."

Greta laughed. "I'm sorry. I meant—well, I just fall into things. I don't plan them the way you do."

"Perhaps your way is better."

"I wonder." Greta looked at her hands, which now kneaded and chopped and stirred. There was a Band-Aid on her right thumb.

"I think I'm happier now than I've ever been. Sometimes I think of Palmer and his son, Shipam, and I think it isn't fair."

"I could never understand why you took him back."

"What about you and Sandy? You gave him so many chances."

Yarrow looked at her and said nothing. She tilted her chair back with her feet up on the terrace railing. She put her head back to get some sun on her neck.

"I'm getting a double chin," she said.

"What rubbish," said Greta. "You look better now than you ever have in your life. You used to look so 'hangdog' when you were married to Sandy."

Yarrow laughed. "I do feel good," she said. "You've changed, too, you know. You've got your act together, Greta."

"It took me long enough. It was all too easy for me when I was young. Things fell my way. I didn't work for my success the way you did. I got things because I was pretty—it was an excuse for me—and then—when I wasn't getting the jobs, I had nothing to fall back on, no reserves to help me. That was when I really fell into the gutter."

She abruptly changed the subject. "What are you going to do about the business?"

"I just told you. I'm going to spend half . . ."

"I mean later. Who's going to run it?"

Yarrow let the front legs of her chair down with a bang.

"I don't know. Stop trying to put me into an early grave. I'm going to be around for a long time."

Edith came out with a tea tray. She loved the mountains as much as they did. It had been decided that Freya would be far better off here than in New York City now that Yarrow was traveling so much. Freya said it was like coming home.

"Laura remarried," said Greta.

"No! Oh, I am glad."

"Her husband helps her with the business and George is now working for Eric. Eric says he hasn't had any trouble with his press since George joined him."

"Just like his father."

"*We* all got on. I wonder what will happen with the next bunch?"

"I wonder."

Greta broke off a piece of shortbread and placed the crumbs on the railing for some birds. A jay swooped down.

"Justice Hoggart is an interesting boy."

"He's fifteen?"

"Yes, a year older than Buck. He writes to me. I've become a sort of den mother all the children write to."

Greta would have been the perfect mother, thought Yarrow.

"He walks his own line," Greta went on. "I think John writes to him."

Yarrow sat up. "Do you know where John is?"

"No. Justice won't tell me, but I know he's living in a commune."

"In a commune? You mean a hippie commune wearing beads and bell-bottoms? Oh, my God."

"You're so conservative, Yarrow. Lots of your friends' children are going through the same thing."

"My God, he's into drugs and sex. I can tell."

"It may not be like that. I've told you more than I meant to anyway. I just wanted to tell you that John's OK. He was always angry, wasn't he? It strikes me as strange that he's the one who's not fighting. Remember that time he made a ship and Lily glued stars all over it? He went and glued all her books together."

"I would have been angry, too."

"I must go," said Greta, standing up. "I've got three crèmes brûlées to make before tonight."

"The mind boggles."

"You're becoming so English."

"Boggles?"

"Yes. Don't change too much."

Yarrow watched her sister stroll down to her car. Then she went into the house she had built "from scratch," as Greta would like her to say. Dark beams from the old silver mines held up the soaring roof, and the fireplace, constructed of river stones, could hold a log six feet long. Yarrow had placed her bedroom where the old cabin had been. She went up there now, over a bridge that hid a sauna and led to a swimming pool, and into her room where the head of the bed was made from the logs of the old cabin. Books and pictures and tapestries hung on the walls. It was certainly not simple, and the effect was warm and rich. She crossed to her desk and ripped open the express package that came every day keeping her in touch with her empire. Funny, she thought, stopping with the envelopes in her hand, it was the first time she had used that word to herself though she had seen it in business reports more and more in conjunction with her enterprises. She must watch it. Yarrow sat down to do three hours' work before having dinner with her mother.

But forty minutes later, a car drove up and she heard Lily calling her. She went downstairs and Lily came sobbing into her arms.

"He's left me," she said.

"Oh, the brute," said Yarrow, stroking back her daughter's fine hair.

"We had a terrible argument. I can't stay and work there anymore, Mom. He's a technician at the station. I feel so humiliated."

Yarrow got some ice for her daughter's swollen eyes. She let her talk on until the sobbing had stopped and she was calm.

"Can I stay here?"

"Of course you can. This is your home. But you'll have to go back to work on Monday, Lily."

"I can't do that."

"You must. You can't let people down. You hand in your notice, you work out your time and then you leave with dignity."

"Don't make me do it."

"Lily, pull yourself together. Come on." Yarrow took her daughter to her own room. "We can talk about this later. Tomorrow you can go into town and buy yourself something pretty and you'll feel much better."

Lily closed the door with a sigh and threw her overnight bag on the bed. Her mother was right. Tomorrow she would feel better. She would go into town and see Aunt Greta and buy something nice for herself. She hung up her slacks and blouses on the hangers. They were all new, the price tags still dangled from them. She had better cut them off before her mother saw them. And somehow, she thought as she used her manicure scissors, she would get out of going back to work on Monday, even if she had to pretend to be sick. Lily changed into a new outfit for dinner. When Yarrow complimented her on her outfit and asked, "Is it new?" Lily answered, "What, this old thing? No, I've had it for ages."

On the way back to New York, Yarrow stopped in Platte City to attend Miss Hines's retirement party. It was good to see old friends again. The company was well run, and she told the publisher that she wanted to ask Joe Bellini, his managing director, to come to London with her.

"I need him more than you do," she said. "Joe knows the rackets that go on, and I trust him."

Joe said he wanted to think about it, but he was flattered he'd been asked. He had a wife and two kids to consult. "Tell your wife she'll love London," said Yarrow. "I guarantee it."

Yarrow then went to Denver to visit the television station, sat through a couple of shows, commented on the ratings and took some of her executives out for dinner. She apologized to Tom Marx for Lily's absence; she had come down with a mysterious virus and was unable to return. Tom no more believed this than Yarrow did.

Cal had breakfast with Yarrow in the morning. He still loved her, he said, if she ever changed her mind, he was waiting. When he put her on the plane, he gave her a long, lingering kiss. She tried to avoid his lips, but he turned her chin toward him.

"Stay one night," he said. She knew he was lonely.

"I'm sorry, Cal. I can't."

She was fond of Cal, she thought as she buckled her seat belt, but she was never going to marry him. She had been single now for fourteen years. She doubted she would even marry Elliot now if he were free.

The next morning she flew to New York and, after a full day at the office, had Albert Hinton in for a drink at her house along with Marvin Rifkin.

If anyone had told her years ago that she would come to like Hinton, she would have thought they were insane. But it was true. Millie, who still found it difficult to speak to her and now ran the house without the effervescent Edith to guide her, placed a bowl of salted almonds on the coffee table and withdrew.

"This house is too big for me now," said Yarrow as Marvin made her a drink. "No more nuts, Marvin," she added as he went to take a handful. He sighed; his weight was something Yarrow always worried about more than he did.

"You and I have to stick together, Albert," she said, sipping her wine. She drank very little and one glass would last her the whole evening.

"That's right, Yarrow," he said, taking a good swallow of his

Scotch. They had moved on to first-name terms at their Chinese lunch during the '63 strike.

"Here's to the man in the moccasins," said Yarrow as she lifted her glass to him.

"You know we want to try to automate the composing room," said Rifkin. "But it will mean training."

"Yes, we talked about this the last time Yarrow was in New York."

"Have you given it any thought, Albert?" said Yarrow.

"Yes, and the answer's still no."

"Albert, be reasonable. I can't afford to keep running the *Telegraph* if I can't make economies."

"You found the money to buy into Fleet Street."

"That's different. I can borrow against that. I can't borrow against out-of-date practices."

"Have you seen the computer we've rented?" said Marvin.

"I have and it will need the same number of men on it as we have running the machines now."

"Albert!"

"I'm serious. I won't negotiate with men's livelihoods. Anything else, but not that."

"If we can't talk about manpower, then let's talk about those other things."

"What other things?"

"You just said we could negotiate on other points."

"Well, make me an offer."

"What about retirement then? Can we talk about natural attrition; that we'll put no more men in the machine room, and that as they retire or leave the numbers will come down?" said Marvin.

"I've still got a lot of printers out of work," said Albert. "I mean, that's quite a lot you're asking for."

"There won't be any work for them soon, Albert. I've seen these photocomposing machines. They work at fifteen times the speed of the traditional Linotype."

"Automation is here. It's only a matter of time until the printers are wiped out. Thirty people could produce a paper that takes nine hundred printers now," said Yarrow.

"I have a veto on automation."

"Yes, you have," Yarrow agreed. Yarrow also knew he had ordered the printers at the *News* to go at normal, slow and very slow last month. At the *Times* he had kept calling chapel meetings so that the printers spent nineteen hours out of every three-day shift standing around doing nothing.

"You and I are not unalike, Albert. We both love this industry."

"We might love it, Yarrow," he said, standing up, "but we're not alike. The answer is no, no and still no."

Yarrow showed him out, and then came back and said to Marvin, "He's impossible but I think he's lying. I think he knows what's coming and he's terrified. He's too smart not to be. I hope I'm here the day he gives us the green light. Not us, specifically, but the *Times* and the *News*. They're the ones he has to deal with."

"I saw a report where he said he's going to take out a lead pipe, unwrap it and beat the publishers over the head with it. He says he'll try not to kill them."

"And he seems such a gentle man, too," said Yarrow. "But I know I'm right. It's just a matter of time. I hope I can last."

Yarrow handed Marvin his hat. He took her hand instead.

"You look tired," he said.

"I am tired. I've got an early start tomorrow. I'm going to London."

"Do you want to have a light dinner with me?" Somehow in the way he stood there holding her hand, Yarrow knew that Marvin was sweet on her. She smiled and kissed him on the cheek.

"Thank you, but as our erstwhile friend just said, no, no and still no." She said it very gently, making a joke out of it.

"Good night, Yarrow."

Yarrow sighed as she went up to bed. Two propositions in one day was too much for her. Still, it made her feel that she was attractive. Why was that important to her? the publisher asked the woman. Oh, shut up, she said, and skipped up the last few steps and closed the door of her room with a bang.

CHAPTER 37

IN THE FIRST WEEK OF MAY IN 1970, WHEN YARROW WAS IN THE middle of negotiations to buy a paper in Boston, she read on the wires in London that four students had been shot to death on the Kent State University campus in Ohio. Justice Hoggart, her nephew, was a freshman there that year. Yarrow telephoned Nellie in California. Justice had not been injured, but Nellie was crying.

"How can you keep supporting Nixon and Agnew in your papers?" she shouted. "You have no idea what's going on here. It was a peaceful protest against the Cambodian involvement."

"Nellie, I'm not supporting Agnew or Nixon, and it was not peaceful." Yarrow was reading the wires as she spoke. "The students burned down a building. The governor declared martial law against the demonstrators."

"They're shooting our children. It's not enough to send them off to die in Vietnam. It could have been Justice."

"Thank God he's OK. Is he home?"

"No. He was arrested for trespassing. I told John."

"You spoke to John?"

"Yes, he called from Vancouver." Nellie gave a loud sniff. "I have his phone number if you want it."

Yarrow was humbled. "Yes, please."

Nellie gave it to her.

"Can I do anything to help Justice?"

"No. His father flew out to Ohio this morning. We're just fed up with politics in this country. And I'm fed up with your editorial line."

This was not a new tack of Nellie's. She had been disgruntled for years, and Yarrow dealt with it by ignoring it and Nellie kept accepting her dividend checks.

Yarrow called the number Nellie had given her, and a female voice answered. "Peace," it said.

John wasn't there.

"Could I leave a message?"

"Yes?" A waft of loud music blasted through the telephone.

"On second thought, give me your address, and I'll write to him."

Yarrow wrote down the address and hung up. She looked at her calendar. She could visit Vancouver in a month when she would be on the West Coast for a meeting in Santa Barbara at the radio station.

"Margaret," she said, through her intercom, "who do we know in Ohio? My nephew's been arrested at Kent State." Margaret came in with her blue book of contacts. Wherever she traveled with Yarrow, the blue book went with her. Yarrow got on the telephone to someone in the governor's office. She wasn't in the communications business for nothing.

Then she called her negotiating team in Boston. She hadn't

wanted to leave them, but had had to go to London for a meeting. The paper was hers, they told her, but the announcement would be delayed until she came back next week.

The limousine pulled up outside a small clapboard house in a seedy suburb of Vancouver.

"This must be it," said Yarrow, getting out and checking the number. There was no doorbell and the door was open. A big yellow sign reading "Dissent" hung in the hallway. There were a number of open doors through which Yarrow could see mattresses on the floors and crumpled bedding and clothing. She could hear a child wailing from the back of the house and she went in. At the back there was an open veranda and a few young people with long hair and flowered clothing were sitting on the floor. They looked up as Yarrow came through the door. One young man had a zither on his knee.

"I'm looking for John," she said, realizing that in this setting, in her sleek black suit and high heels, she was the one who looked ridiculous.

"Hello, Mom," said the man with the zither, uncurling from the floor.

"I didn't recognize you," she said.

"That's OK. I recognized you." He gave her that lazy, angry smile he always had that reminded her of Sandy. She looked at him. His hair was long and worn in a ponytail, and he had grown a beard and moustache. He looked thin and underfed. He had no shoes on. His feet were black with dirt and the toenails were like yellow horn.

"Come into the kitchen," he said. "Do you want a cup of coffee?"

"Yes."

She put down her crocodile bag and white kid gloves on the Formica table. John pushed away a carton of rancid milk and a plate with congealed eggs, and sat down opposite her while the coffee perked.

"You found me."

"Why didn't you write?"

"I was afraid Dad would turn me in. I like it here. I've reverted to my tribal past. Didn't the old Ute Indians play the zither, and didn't they chew the peyote button—mescaline to you? I've come home."

He did look Indian, she thought, with his dark hair parted in the center and his high, sharp cheekbones.

"You like this? You call this 'home'? This isn't living—it's squalid."

John's jaw worked and she could see his neck tightening. "I'm sorry," she said. "I didn't come here to argue with you. I admit I don't understand any of this. I don't understand you, John, or what's happening in this country anymore. We were a family once."

"You call us a family? With you always working? My father gone? Elliot Weyden always in the background?"

"We were a family, not perfect, but we held together. I always loved you, John. All the work I've put into the business, it was all for you and Lily and Buck."

He laughed. He did not believe her and got up and poured two mugs of coffee.

"The milk's sour."

"I'll drink it black," she said.

"I came here to get away. I hated what we were doing in Asia. It's not right. There's so much lying going on. America was the one place in the world that could be perfect and it stinks. I couldn't take it."

"You're not going to change it sitting here."

He looked sadder than she had ever seen him except when he was a little boy of six standing beside her bed when Buck was born.

"When you were five, you wanted to live in the woods. This was just before Zeb died. You told us that all you needed in the world was an ax—with that you could build a hut, make a bow and arrow. You would hunt for food and clothing. You had it all worked out when you were five years old. But Zeb told you it wouldn't work. 'Why not?' you asked. 'Because your wife won't like it,' he said. I remember to this day Zeb saying that.'' Yarrow smiled softly.

John's mouth remained tight, as though she were trying to trap him.

"I can't come home," he said. He tossed his hair back like a girl. She wondered if he had regrets. He said, to change the subject, "Your hair's going gray, Mom."

"Do you have a girlfriend?"

"I have a daughter."

Her mouth must have dropped right open. He laughed at the look on her face.

"Which one is she? May I see her? What about her mother?"

"These are all meaningless questions. They're all our children."

"You can't deny your own flesh and blood, John."

He shook his head. "We are truly all one family here."

"God, I hate this—this moral looseness you have. What do you kids call this—a sexual revolution? It's disgusting the way you live."

"Why? You got away with it."

"Elliot and I . . ."

"You're a bunch of damn hypocrites, that's what you are. You and your whole generation, you all lie. Nixon lies, you lie, Elliot lies. He pretends he's married. You think we're worse than you are. We're open about it. Christ, you can't see it, can you? You can't see what's different."

"I think you're fooling yourself. I think that stuff you're smoking is affecting your brain."

Zither music began playing from the group outside. Three bare-footed children ran into the kitchen and chased a kitten under the table. Yarrow wondered if one of the girls was his. He made no special acknowledgement of any of them. The kitten escaped into the hall and the children went after it.

"I have to go to work," said John. "I bring out a newsletter once a week for other American dissenters." She noticed he avoided the words "draft dodger."

"I wanted you to come and work at the *Telegraph*."

"I don't like its politics."

"I run a huge company, John. You're my eldest son. There are a number of positions that would suit you. Why am I working this hard if it's not to pass it on?"

"I don't know," he said.

"I don't understand you. You won't work for me, but you're working up here putting out a—a—propaganda sheet."

"But there's a difference, Mom. I'm doing this because I want to, not because I have to."

A faint smell of something she supposed was marijuana drifted through the doorway.

"John, come away from this," she said. "Face up to your life. You have a great future with me if you come. How many other young people have the opportunities that you have?"

He didn't answer, just gave her that same ironical look he had developed as though he were cynical about everything.

She stood up with a sigh. "What's her name?" she asked as he showed her to the door. "My granddaughter's?"

"Star."

"And her mother?"

"One of the girls."

"John, let me take her, please. This isn't any life for your daughter."

"My daughter, or your granddaughter? You don't own me, Mom. You don't own anybody. That's your whole problem—you and your generation, you think you do. Well, I'm not buying it, OK?"

Yarrow's eyes filled with tears as she drove away. How had she failed him? How could she ever put things right?

It was a though John had transferred his ambiguous feelings about her onto his country. Yarrow knew that she had loved Elliot more than she had loved her son. Could a five-year-old suffer from a broken heart? She had not been perfect, but she had tried; neither was his country perfect, his motherland. Why did he reject them both with such righteousness? Where had he earned that right? She was just one woman juggling to cope with family and business. Where had he gotten this idea that things must be perfect? Did he really believe that the "pursuit of happiness" guaranteed its capture without sacrifice?

Yarrow thought about it as she drove back through the Vancouver suburbs to her hotel. Was it affluence that had corrupted John's character? Was John angry because he had been asked to sacrifice some of his soft life for others?

Or was he a genuine conscientious objector? Yarrow tried to remember the little boy who wanted to live in the woods.

Or was he just a coward? That was Sandy's explanation, that was what made Sandy mad.

Or was it a combination of all these things that made John the way he was? But he was not the only one—there were thousands like him. Where had all the other parents gone wrong?

Yarrow telephoned Elliot when she got back to her hotel room.

"I'm a grandmother," she said and then burst into tears.

"Impossible for you, darling, to be a grandmother."

"It's true. Her name is Star and I have no idea what she looks like. He won't tell me which one she is."

Elliot made soothing noises.

"I need to hold her. How can I treat all those children the same? It's unnatural."

"He'll tell you when the time comes. Is he well?"

"He looks terrible. He has no—direction. Oh, I wish I had another chance—start again with him. Perhaps I could do better."

"What would you do differently?"

"I don't know."

"Don't blame yourself, darling. Never look back."

She blew her nose loudly on a tissue.

"So much for romance," he said.

"What are you doing?" she asked.

"I'm sitting at my window in New York thinking of you."

"Liar, but thank you. What are you really doing?"

"I'm actually writing a check to support McGovern's campaign. I'm hoping he'll decide to run for the presidency."

"Oh, you'll be the kiss of death to him."

"Yarrow."

"Stevenson, Weyden, Humphrey, how about Muskie? Your record is faultless."

"All fine men. I can't help it if the electorate doesn't know a good man when it sees one. I must go. I'll see you tomorrow in New York?"

He was gone. Yarrow wondered how many hours of their long-term, long-distance romance had been spent on the telephone.

Yarrow ate in her room and read through a bag of correspondence, ratings and budget reports, memos and letters, and copies of her publications. Her eyes ached but she kept on reading. She read through two weeks' worth of editorials in the *Telegraph* and then did a double-take. Andrew Rockman, the new editor, had completely flip-flopped on the *Telegraph*'s editorial policy about the war. Yarrow seldom interfered with editorials; she didn't have the time, and a certain degree of independence was mutually respected by the publisher and the editor. As Ned Griffin had once said to her, "I can't edit this newspaper with your elbow in my face." But this—Yarrow read the offending article again—was against any policy discussed between herself and Andrew Rockman. It called for an immediate cease-fire and withdrawal from Cambodia.

Yarrow reached him at home and woke him up. She was livid.

"Who got to you?" she asked, reading aloud the lines from the editorial that had incensed her.

"Nobody got to me," he answered when he grasped what she was talking about. "I talked to your sister and she said she had spoken to you and after the Kent State riots . . ."

"My sister? Nellie called you?"

"Yarrow—we just had a long talk about the situation on the campuses—and it seemed to me that we on the paper were shifting our ground anyway about Cambodia."

Yarrow swore under her breath. She had suspected that Andrew was still immature for this job. She had been forced to place him in that position when Ned left.

"You don't take orders from my sister. My God, Andrew, I find it hard enough to get you to take orders from me! This is my paper and I'll tell you what's to go into it. I don't want any surprises."

He was apologetic. She cut him short.

"Go back to sleep," she said. "I'll talk to you tomorrow."

In New York, Andrew Rockman was wide awake. He would never get back to sleep now. He swung his legs over the bed and sighed. He knew he should have checked out the editorial with Yarrow before running it. But Nellie Hoggart had so precisely expressed his own changing views on the current administration that he had run with it. He would go more easy tomorrow. This was no time to hit the throttle. Let the owners fight it out.

Yarrow telephoned Nellie.

"What do you think you're doing? You have no right to call one of my editors and dictate your terms. How dare you undermine me like that? Who gave you the right?"

"I own some of this company, too. May I remind you it isn't just yours—it doesn't say *Yarrow* McLean Publishing over the door."

"I don't believe we're arguing over this. If you have complaints about how I'm running the company, bring it up in the proper way. Get involved with it. But don't leave it all to me and then come in when the pie's baked and say, I don't like it."

"Oh, what could I do? Don't be so damn stupid. You won't listen anymore. We used to have discussions, now we get orders; you give them, we rubber-stamp them."

She's always resented me, thought Yarrow. But now it's out in the open. This isn't about editorial policy, it's about power and money. Yarrow felt sick at heart. She was glad her mother couldn't hear them arguing. Nellie continued to cry and harangue her about the paper, the radio station, about Justice's future and imagined slights that Yarrow had inflicted on her. Yarrow let her go on until she wound down like a clock.

"I'm sorry you feel this way," she said. "I'm truly sorry."

They ended the conversation on an unhappy, unsettled note.

She had made her sister a wealthy woman, thought Yarrow, as she got ready for bed. She had made them all wealthy. And where was the gratitude? Now, don't be silly, she said to herself, it's only Nellie venting her spleen. Greta and Eric were behind her one hundred percent. One person could not corrupt the closeness of their family business.

*   *   *

The next morning on the way to the Vancouver airport, Yarrow couldn't stop thinking about John's daughter. She felt agitated, as though her heart were fibrillating. Oh, hell, she thought, I'm not leaving Canada until I know.

"Turn the car around," she said to the chauffeur. "I want to go back to the house I visited yesterday."

The sun had come out briefly from behind some low clouds. Yarrow had the chauffeur stop at the far end of the street, and she walked up the concrete sidewalk where straggling weeds poked through the broken slabs. A young woman with a scarf tied around her head and wearing sandals was sitting with four or five children on the front step. She was waiting for the school bus; one of the older children had a knapsack on her back.

"Hi," said Yarrow.

"Hi." The woman was only about nineteen. She recognized Yarrow. "John isn't here today."

"Oh, too bad."

The young woman smiled and went on picking at her toes in her open sandals. When the bus appeared at the far end of the street, the woman got up and took the older child's hand to walk to the corner.

"I'll stay with the children," said Yarrow.

"Gee, thanks."

Yarrow sat on the step and looked at the four remaining children and they looked at her.

A little girl squatted on the steps and poked splinters through a hole.

"Star?" said Yarrow. One of the children looked up and clapped her hands. "Is your name Star?"

She was just a baby, with dark curling hair and dimples. She got up, came over and put her hands in Yarrow's. Yes, thought Yarrow, looking into the little upturned face, this one is John's. My first grandchild. Yarrow felt as though her heart would burst, such a mixture of emotion and tenderness and pity flooded in it. She stroked the backs of the little plump hands with her thumbs. The child wriggled away and went back to her companions and squatted down happily again in her dirty torn dress. Yarrow just sat and watched her playing until the young woman came back.

"Are you her mother?" Yarrow asked.

"No. Her mother doesn't live here anymore."

Yarrow walked to the car. I feel calmer now, she told herself, I've seen my grandchild. She looked a healthy, sturdy and happy little girl. What more could anyone want? Yarrow would not lose touch now. Star would have her own guardian angel; she would want for nothing, Yarrow would see to that.

The next year came and went, too fast for Yarrow's liking; it was as though she were in a race against time. Her wealth and influence grew apace. She was an astute investor. She borrowed carefully. In areas where she knew she did not have the expertise, she employed people who did. She drove her company with a light hand but an iron will; no one was in any doubt that Yarrow was the Boss. In her family, too, her influence grew. As Freya's health deteriorated, Yarrow became the matriarch. Gatherings were held at Chipeta, the house in the mountains, and the estrangements and reconciliations within the McLean clan ebbed and flowed like moon tides.

To celebrate Yarrow's fiftieth birthday in 1972, Greta and Lily organized a surprise party at Chipeta. Lily had given up her television ambitions and had gone to law school in New York. "That will be the death of her as a journalist," her father said, "but I'm glad she's doing something."

They booked rooms for the many guests in the inns around Galena. Greta's own restaurant supplied the food and Edith scrubbed and cleaned and polished the house until every window shone so that when the sun sparkled on the winter snow it was too bright to look at.

"Elliot," Lily said, when she embroiled him in the plan, "you have to get her there by nine o'clock, but don't tell her. We want it to be a surprise."

"I've never been able to lie successfully to your mother yet," said Elliot, "but I'll do my best."

"Why do you want to spend election night with me in Galena?" asked Yarrow as Elliot's jet took off from Teterboro Airport in New Jersey.

"You keep asking me to come see your house. I have a few days now in which to do that. Don't you want me to come?"

Yarrow looked across at him; his dark suit had picked up hairs from the mohair blanket the steward had handed him. He had put on glasses to do some paperwork.

"Of course I do," she said. "But I thought you'd want to be with the McGovern crowd." He had forgotten her birthday, which was not like him. She put on her own glasses and leaned across the aisle and kissed him as the small executive jet climbed steeply to forty-one thousand feet. Their glasses clinked. Yarrow smiled wryly; sign of the times, she thought.

A few hours later they were being driven up into the back

country above Galena. The road was good, the snow packed
solid. The night was "dark as the inside of a cow," an old
phrase of Jock's. Just at the final rise before the bowl fell away,
the car pulled over to the side of the road. "We change transpor-
tation here," said Elliot.

"What do you mean?"

"You'll see." A horse-drawn sleigh stood at the side. Yarrow
recognized it as belonging to one of the neighboring ranchers. A
cowboy she knew as Big Sky stood grinning and stamping his
feet to stay warm.

"Get in," said Elliot. "You'll need your hat and gloves." He
pulled his own sheepskin coat around him and put on a dark
brown Stetson she had given him once. It had pressed silver
dollars around the headband. "We're going to arrive in style."

They climbed into the seat of the sleigh and the driver covered
them with a blanket, stiff with frost and horse hairs. The car took
off down the road with their luggage, and Big Sky made kissing
sounds at his two horses and with a crunch and a lurch, the
sleigh's runners pulled free where they had frozen to the ground.
They set off with a soft jingle of bells across a track that led to
the meadow.

"This is the old road," said Yarrow with delight as her eyes
became accustomed to the dark. "I love it. Elliot, thank you. I
thought you had forgotten."

"Forgotten what?"

Yarrow was perplexed.

"Nothing," she said.

"Someone has to keep romance alive," he said and put his
arm around her. Her fur hat tickled his face.

"Remember when we came up here with Mama and she told
us the story about the owl?"

"I remember the time you broke your leg. I've hated cassoulet
ever since."

They laughed and she pulled the frozen blanket closer around
them. It was dark and iron cold. All was silent except for the
breathing and snorting of the horses, the jangle of the bells on
the harness, the crunching of the runners on the snow. It was
easy to imagine that it was just like this one hundred years ago.

They were silent, enjoying each other and the serenity when
they came in sight of Chipeta. Only a few lights of the house
shone out over the snow.

"I had no idea it was so big," said Elliot.

"I got carried away," said Yarrow as they pulled up in front
of the wide wooden steps. Salt had been scattered to melt the

ice. They hurried inside out of the freezing cold, and Yarrow called out, "Hello, I'm home," in the hallway as she took off her boots.

"Where's Edith?" she said as she walked to the huge double doors that led into the one central room. The room was in darkness, but the fire was lit, and then she saw a movement in the dark and the lights came on and a roar went up. "Surprise!"

"You sneak," she said to Elliot. A strolling band of musicians started up some country music and someone took her coat and she was engulfed by friends and family and presents and kisses.

"Don't ever do this again," she said to Elliot, kissing him on the side of the mouth as he nibbled a crab cake.

"It was Lily and Greta's doing," he said.

"Are you sure you didn't know?" said Lily. "I was sure someone would tell you."

Lily was wearing a turquoise and coral necklace that she had been unable to resist.

Yarrow touched the necklace with her finger but said nothing about it. "A complete surprise, Lily. How nice you look," and was swept off into another group of well-wishers.

Greta and her staff had arranged a buffet under the staghorn chandelier in the dining room. In the wide dining room fireplace, a spit turned a small roasting pig. The fat sizzled as it fell on the flames. There was a big black cookpot with fragrant chili con carne; there was a dish of spicy red beans, chick peas and lentils; and there were king crab legs and mountain trout, and crusty hot bread, barbecued spare ribs—black and sticky with molasses sauce—saddles of roast venison and lamb with currant jelly, scalloped potatoes with bubbling brown cheese, hash browns and onion rings, and apple and blackberry pies and a chocolate mousse cake that Yarrow knew, from eating in Greta's restaurant, put pounds on the hips before it was halfway down.

Yarrow had changed into a deep green silk blouse, jeans and cowboy boots. Elliot had put on a sweater and slacks. Yarrow was sure he didn't own a pair of jeans. She kissed her sister Greta, whose face was flushed but happy as she lifted meats and carving boards and stirred and supervised in a long white apron. "This is just the kind of party I like. Thank you." The violinist was fiddling up a storm while Yarrow helped herself to some champagne, and moved among her guests.

There were a hundred people in the great room under the cathedral ceiling. Above the blazing fire hung a large painting of

Chief Ouray and his tribe struggling on horseback through a winter pass. Yarrow had named the house after the chief's wife. Freya sat smiling near the fire with Edith beside her. Yarrow was struck by the similarity between her mother's face and that of Chief Ouray's in the picture above her. A group of political stalwarts of both parties huddled around a television watching the election results.

J. C. Calloway came up and put his arm around Yarrow. "Where's Elliot? We had a bet that Nixon wouldn't win. He owes me fifty dollars." Yarrow laughed. "I'll come with you. He owes me money, too, then."

Lily danced past in the arms of her new young man.

"I wish your mother liked me more," said David.

"She will one day, David. Don't be so afraid of her."

"She's beautiful for someone turning fifty. Not as beautiful as you, of course."

"Thank you."

"Who is the distinguished dark guy who keeps watching her all the time?"

"That's Elliot. I've told you about him. Elliot Weyden."

"That's Elliot Weyden? I thought he'd be much older. He's part of the mythology down on Wall Street. I expected him to have a beard like Moses. And the blond lady is?"

"Aunt Greta. She runs the best restaurant in town, America Hurrah. She's married to that man there. Hi, Eduardo." Eduardo, going by with another tray of Louisiana crab cakes, held one up for his niece to bite. "Bellissima," he said.

They swung past.

"He's so much younger than she is."

"Aunt Greta has a weakness for young, dark, handsome men. Why are you so worried about people's ages? He is her third husband after all. Aunt Nellie is the dark one who's very intense about politics; she's wearing the hand-crafted shawl. She and my mother argue all the time. She'll be miserable that Nixon won. There's Uncle Eric. He runs the paper in Galena. There's my father. I wasn't sure if he would come. That's Wilhelmina, his wife. Wilhelmina is very neat, isn't she? She's the White House correspondent for ABC."

"I'll never get your family straight. I read your father's latest book, *Hawks on the Potomac*. I liked it."

"It's number three on the best-seller list. I bet my brother John hates it. He's the only one not here. That's my cousin Justice, the one in the baggy clothes. Mother calls him the 'Tight-Rope Walker.' "

They bumped into Buck doing the Watusi with a pneumatic blonde. "This is my brother Buck, but we'll try to ignore him."

"When are we going to tell your mother that we're engaged?" said David.

Lily kissed him. "As soon as your daddy gives you a partnership in the firm." David groaned.

"You'll be on your board before I'm on mine."

Lily smiled and her cat's eyes narrowed. He was probably right, she thought, tossing her fine blond hair across her shoulder. One day the company might be hers. By all rights, she thought, it should be.

It was obvious that John was incapable of running it; besides, he couldn't come back from Canada. He'd really burned his bridges that time. Sometimes mother talked about what he was doing in Canada—she said he'd grown up a lot in the past two years. His daughter, Star, had been ill—nothing serious—but it had jolted John out of his "selfishness," as Yarrow put it. Lily tried to close her ears whenever her mother talked about John. She was glad he wasn't around for her to deal with. She and John had always been jealous of each other. Lily thought John was a moody, spoiled boy who used his mother's guilt to punish her. She felt she'd been right about John all along.

There was still Buck, of course. Lily looked at her nineteen-year-old brother making a fool of himself on the dance floor. Buck was just a ladies' man. Women flocked to Buckley Heartland. Lily couldn't understand it. He always had friends and yet Lily always thought that she, herself, was the infinitely worthier person. It was something about his eyes, she suspected. They always had a wicked gleam in them. He was outrageous. As if he knew what she was thinking, Buck gave her a big wink and leered down his partner's dress. "Oh, grow up," said Lily and left the dance floor, pulling David behind her. No, Buck wasn't interested in newspapers—only women, and he still wanted to be an artist. Lily shook her head as she led the way to the buffet table.

But Buck was having more trouble than his sister suspected with the young woman, Joanna, with whom he was dancing.

"Oh, where have you been all my life?" he groaned as some slower music began and he pulled her closer to him.

"With my mother."

"Do you ever get up to Harvard?"

"Seldom. I live in Denver. My father's the congressman."

"Oh, yes. We endorsed your father in the last election."

"You do keep up to date."

"I have to—my mother sends me all the papers and grills me on it later. She wants us all to go into the business."

"I thought you wanted to be an artist."

"I do. Do you know anything about—minimalism?" Buck couldn't take his eyes off Joanna's cleavage.

"No."

"It's the opposite to—maximilism. You must see my paintings."

"I'm not allowed."

"Figurative art, then. I could become a portrait painter. You could be my model. Did anyone ever tell you your eyes are very beautiful?"

Yarrow went by and said, "Buck dear, did you read last Thursday's column on Henry Kissinger? What did you think?"

"I agreed with it, Mom. Every word." He winked at Joanna. "See what I mean?"

Justice Hoggart, sitting on the floor near the fire, was picking at the ink under his fingernails. Justice's hair stood out all over his head as if he had had a bad haircut.

"Well, tell me about your idea," Eric said. He had grown a full set of whiskers and his red-blond moustache twitched under his long nose. Eric sat on a raised stone bench that ran the length of the fireplace.

"Well, it's a newsletter for young radicals."

"Radicals?"

"No one else is writing for us. Young people have changed, Uncle Eric. I want to write about the war and the drug scene, the riots, the civil rights movement. We'll cover the rock music scene. I've called it *Fortalice*. I can't get this ink off my fingers."

"It never comes off," said Eric, looking at his own. He moved a foot away from the heat of the fire.

Justice was a nervous, tall, thin person, like his father, but he had the big McLean head. He had a great look of Jock about him. Eric wondered if Yarrow had noticed it, too.

"Would I buy it?"

"It's not aimed at your age group. No offense, but it's not aimed at Buck's group either. They don't want to change the world. We're printing it on recycled paper. Mom's set me up with the old press my father used when they started their poetry magazine."

"Oh, yeah, is that still going?"

"Busted. But they did it all wrong. I'm going to start small;

besides I have another year to go at college. I've switched to UCLA.''

"I thought Yarrow wanted you to start learning the ropes of McLean Publishing?''

"Oh, yeah. Mom says I should go, too. But I want to do my own thing. What I want to do can't be done in a big conglomerate. Working for Aunt Yarrow would be like working for a corporation. They're too interested in the bottom line—that's their whole criterion for success. I want to control it—like writing a book, you know, just yourself and your words.''

He was silent, picking at his nails.

"Do you think Uncle Sandy would write an article for me?'' he asked.

"What on?''

"Anything—his name would be great on my cover.''

"He's hardly a radical.''

Justice laughed and ran his hands through his hair so that it stood up even more. "That doesn't bother me. I can get a dialogue going—get some sparks flying.''

"You can ask him, but take your earring off first, it might help.''

Justice put his earring in his pocket, unwound from the floor and pulled his collar straight. He slouched over to Sandy, and Eric watched him go with interest. If only, he, Eric, had had that enthusiasm when he was young. Yanna, his wife, came up with a can of Coors for him.

"Let's dance,'' she said and he swung her out to the music. No, he thought, as he held her, he had never had the will.

Justice's sister, Thimi, who was twelve and her cousin, Avril, nine, sat on the stairs like a pair of old maids watching the proceedings.

"What are you two laughing at?'' said Eric as he stopped dancing, came over and tweaked his daughter under the chin.

"Cousin Buck. He's funny.'' Buck was swooning at his partner's feet.

"Mommy's abandoned me,'' said Eric. "She says I step on her toes. Would you like to dance?'' He lifted up his daughter and placed her feet on his shoes. She giggled as they set off across the floor.

"Me next,'' said Thimi, hugging her knees. She wished *her* father would dance with her like that, but Jack never danced. He was huddling with some newspaper people from California talking about sludge disposal—he was deep into conversation, and gave lectures and talks on it—and Nellie, Thimi looked at her mother, was arguing about the death penalty with Deke Smith who was on the California state legislature. Didn't they ever have any fun? wondered Thimi, looking longingly at Eric and Avril stepping from side to side like dancing bears around the floor.

Albert Hinton and J. C. Calloway were in a corner with the governor of New York and a man who ran a shrimp farm down in Florida. The governor was wagging his finger at Albert. But Albert wasn't worried—away from the bargaining table, a euphemism if ever there was one, thought Yarrow as she joined them, he was as affable and gentle as a lamb.

"At least I know where my votes are," said Albert.

The governor winced. Yarrow revised her definition of Albert from a lamb to a scorpion; there was usually a sting in his tail.

The shrimp farmer spoke up. He hated to see a Republican governor put down by a union leader.

"You ought to see the *Miami Herald*," he said to Albert. "They have a new completely automated composing room, nonunion."

"Is that a fact? Can you get me in there?"

Yarrow was surprised to hear the seriousness in Albert's tone. She knew he had taken a delegation of union officials on a tour of *The New York Times*'s eleventh floor, where the most advanced automation for their industry was being tested. Albert, she was told, had not been very impressed. But the technology was improving more rapidly every day. For papers like Yarrow's *Telegraph*, the prospect of huge capital outlays for equipment that might be obsolete in a year was terrifying.

"I might be able to," said the shrimp farmer.

Laura, who had come to the party with her new husband and her son, George, came up to Yarrow and put her arm around her. Laura hardly looked a day older than when she had come to take care of the McLean children forty years ago.

"You son looks older than you do."

Laura laughed. "George is a thirty-year-old electronics freak. I don't know what he's talking about anymore."

"I'm getting like that at the office," said Yarrow. "We're trying to prepare for the coming of computers when that old buzzard over there"—she jerked her head toward Albert Hinton—"lets us install them."

"I think your mother's getting tired and would like to say good night."

"You've been a good friend to her," said Yarrow, as she and Laura walked through the room together, "to all of us."

"You were good to me."

Edith had Freya in a wheelchair, ready to go to her room. Freya's face was glowing from the fire. Yarrow held her mother's crippled hand in hers.

"This," said Freya slowly, "was the best night of my life. To see you all so happy together under one roof."

When Freya was put to bed, Edith came back and Yarrow saw her sitting quietly talking to George beside the fire.

Yarrow wanted to talk to one of her editors. They were deep into a discussion about Watergate when Elliot came over and took Yarrow away.

"I want to talk to you." He pulled her over to the dining room where the buffet table was much diminished and only the fire spat and sizzled in a deep orange glow. He slipped a ring on her finger. It was a large step-cut emerald set with diamonds. The stones were supported by a yellow-gold band on which leaves were etched.

"It's beautiful, but I can't take this from you, Elliot."

"You must. I want the world to know you're mine. Besides, I have the matching ring." He opened his palm and there lay a simple gold band. "I can't give this to you yet, but one day you will wear it. You haven't changed your mind, have you?"

Yarrow looked at this man she loved and knew that she could not say no to him.

"I am yours without it." He kissed her.

"Happy birthday," he said.

He came to her in the night, in the bed she had built with him in mind. She felt like Penelope waiting for Odysseus. She had lit the fire and lay on the bed under the paneled skylight and watched the moon appear as the clouds fled. The moon traveled across the panels. When she looked up once, with Elliot above her, she saw the moon as a Japanese lantern. He told her, later, when she was above him, that the moon was like a halo around her head.

"I see it, too," she said, lying peacefully in his arms afterward. "There's a rainbow ring around it. I must close the blinds or the sun will wake us up." She got out of bed. He watched her in the dim firelight.

"Leave it," he said. He watched her walk back toward him. Her belly was a little rounded. He liked it. He didn't want a woman with a concave belly whose hipbones jabbed into his, who was so fragile he couldn't thrust and feel her thrusting back. He put out his hand to her. "Come back. Don't ever leave me."

In the morning when she woke, he had left her bed. She could hear him downstairs in the pool churning through the water as he swam. She rolled into the long, warm furrow he had left in the bed. He had made love to her as though they were both still young. His body was good—it was hard and solid, thicker around the waist than it once had been, but when she held him, she was grateful that she had a man. This was no boy, nor an imitation of what a man should be. He could take care of her, defend her, yet know he could leave her and she would survive. He accepted the woman in her and the child in her, as she accepted the boy and the man in him. She acknowledged his fears, his desires in the deep darkness when they were joined, and held them to her, those secrets of his soul. They were gifts he gave her. She wrapped them in the paper of love and stored them away in her memory.

How perfect life is, she thought, savoring the moment. She listened to the noise of the water. And then it stopped. She heard Edith's voice and then Elliot came in with a towel around his waist. Water dripped from the black hair around his nipples.

"Yarrow," he said. "It's Freya. She died in her sleep."

CHAPTER 38

*T*HE YEARS SLIPPED BY LIKE BOW WAVES AGAINST A SHIP. *SOME*-times Yarrow was able to stop, lean against the rail, look down and see it happen. But mostly she was too busy with her life. Her family and her business intermingled in a series of births and deaths, marriages and divorces. Her hair turned white after her mother's death.

Albert Hinton did an abrupt about-face in 1974 and presided over the inevitable demise of the power of the printing union. She read about it at her desk in London one winter afternoon about four o'clock. It was dark and gloomy and she had already switched on all the lights. At a meeting with the *Times* and the *News* in New York, Albert had given the green light for automation in the composing room in return for lifetime job guarantees. He had also agreed to stop the practice of bogus. "Heaven

be praised,'' said Yarrow, getting up to close the window as a
great clap of thunder sounded. Outside, a hoist was lifting a reel
of newsprint into her building. The presses of the *Daily Enquirer*
would soon be shuddering beneath her feet. The unions in Fleet
Street might be the death of her, she thought, watching the
rain pouring down. If only they had someone like Albert to lead
them. She could see no way out of the imbecilic relationship
between management and unions on Fleet Street except through
the total destruction of one side by the other. It was a tragedy.

When Albert retired, and she heard he was going up to Canada
to see a married daughter in Vancouver, she asked him to look in
on John. Albert's remarks to her later were guarded. Her son
was doing fine, he said, working as an editor at a daily paper
owned by the Thomson organization. He'd also had some experience with management. Albert had checked that out with his
own colleagues. There was something though, some piece of
information that Albert was not divulging, Yarrow felt. Still,
Albert never had enthused. He was going to retire to Colorado,
he told her.

That same year, Lily married David. His father had at last
taken him on as a partner in his Wall Street firm. Lily wanted,
and got, a fancy wedding at the Pierre Hotel in New York. Her
dress came from Paris and caviar was on the menu. Yarrow
shook her head at her daughter's extravagant taste. She was
determined Lily would have no avenue to deplete the McLean
fortunes. Yarrow frustrated Lily's efforts to do this at every turn.
Lily kept badgering her for more power in the firm. Yarrow kept
fobbing her off with meaningless titles. Lily, pleading economic
difficulties, sometimes sent bills for expenditures to Yarrow.
Yarrow sent them right back. Only when Lily gave birth to
twins, Rose and Nigella, a year later did Yarrow soften and
increase her daughter's allowance.

Buck continued to charm and worry his mother. She brought
him over to London to work on the *Enquirer* after he finished
college. He was hopeless on the editorial side, he was as dys-
lexic as Eric had been. But where Eric's love of words had
overcome his disability, Buck grew frustrated and angry and
turned to women and drawing for solace. His charm induced
others to cover up for him. Whenever Yarrow sent for him and
he was not in the office, a flurry of lies came over the telephone.
''Oh, yes, he's here. We'll get him to call you back.'' And he
would, with some female voice whispering in the background.
His dalliances were notorious. In despair, she had him make

some illustrations, and the editor liked them and began to use them steadily.

In 1977 President Carter declared amnesty for "nonviolent draft resistors." Yarrow wept when she saw the news on the wire. She had seen John only once since that time in Vancouver. He had not made her welcome, but she had stayed in touch, sending letters and gifts for Star. Star would be eight years old now, she realized.

Yarrow had been waiting for this opportunity. "I want to offer you a job," she said when he called on her in New York. John had cut his hair and put on weight so his cheekbones were not so pronounced. He had married a Canadian woman, Patsy, who was critical of all things American.

"I want you to be publisher of the *Telegraph*. I've been waiting for a McLean to be ready to take over that position. I heard good things about your work in Vancouver. You're tough, they say."

"Tough enough."

"You'll need to be. The *Telegraph* isn't easy—we fight for every ad we get. Do you think you can do it?"

He leaned back in his chair, a confident smile on his face.

"I'm sure I can."

He accepted the job, but she was miffed at the offhand way in which he did so. There were men and women in her company who would die for that position. She thought she had been magnanimous; he accepted the job as though it were his right. I'm not going to start creating problems where none exist, thought Yarrow. Time will be the judge.

At the end of 1979 Elliot took off for an extended tour of the Middle East. His company, Phoenix, had been involved in a number of projects under the shah of Iran's protection. Now, with the Ayatollah Khomeini and his mullahs in charge, Elliot and his advisers set off to find out what could be salvaged—if anything.

"Please don't go," Yarrow begged him. "It's dangerous."

"There's no danger," he said. "This is a religious war and they still need bankers. Khomeini's not a fool."

"You're the fool!" she shouted. "Don't you even read the papers? Demonstrators overran the embassy in February! They even took hostages."

"Only for a few hours, Yarrow. The Iranian government intervened. I must go, don't you see? Millions of dollars are at stake, this whole project is in jeopardy."

He telephoned her once or twice while he was away and then,

on Monday, November 5, she heard reports that demonstrators had overrun the American embassy in Teheran and taken a number of hostages again. She couldn't eat or sleep for worrying. She wandered through the empty New York house with Millie following her, offering her herbal teas. No one knew anything. All her contacts had dried up because of the situation. The prime minister of Iran, Bazargan, seemed not to be in control of his government. Yarrow tried to find out if Elliot was numbered among the hostages. She watched Sam Donaldson on ABC television for clues, then switched from one network news program to another. There was nothing about Elliot or his team of advisers. They seemed to have dropped off the face of the earth.

On the second day she telephoned Blanchette in London. Yarrow was unsure if Elliot's wife would take the call, but she did.

"Have you heard anything?" said Yarrow.

"No."

"I will call immediately if I hear."

Blanchette hesitated for a moment. "Thank you," she said.

On the day it was announced that Bazargan had resigned, Elliot phoned Yarrow. He was safe. He was in Turkey.

He didn't talk much. His voiced sounded ragged with weariness. "I'm exhausted," he said. "But I'm OK. I was going into the Iranian foreign ministry when the embassy was seized. My friends smuggled me out." There were State Department people with him, he said. It was not until she read the news reports that she learned he had been shot in the arm in the demonstrations outside the embassy. She wept when she saw the news pictures of him with a stubble of a beard and his eyes rimmed with fatigue. But he was alive. He was safe. She thought about the others who were not. She told her editors to run hard with the story.

Elliot became a national hero. At a time when the Carter administration was unable to solve the hostage crisis, Elliot's escape appeared as the "possible." He represented the John Wayne figure that Americans wanted. The air of frustration among Yarrow's fellow citizens in New York was palpable. She felt it was all over the country. "Run with the story," she said. "Carter won't win another term."

One day the following year, Yarrow went down to the editorial floor of her London office to discuss a series they were publishing on the royal family. She was growing increasingly tired lately, and a visit to the newsroom always revived her. Sitting opposite the editor's desk, she was watching the activity of the newsroom through the open door when she saw a young man who looked familiar. "Who is that?" she asked. "That tall, good-looking boy?"

"That's Ship Truitt, an American. He's working on the subs' table during his break from Oxford. I'll introduce you," said the editor.

"Don't bother," said Yarrow getting to her feet. "I know his family well. I want him off the premises."

"Miss McLean, he's a very good young sub . . ."

"Don't argue with me. Do it."

She stumped out, banging her cane against the door as she left. Seeing Shipam had upset her more than she realized. He looked so like Palmer Truitt, it was uncanny. Palmer's paper, the *Courier*, and her own *Telegraph*, had been fighting to the death for years in New York. They were like the snakes Buck used to keep in a tank in his bedroom, their tails lashing at each other, as they fought over the same dwindling advertising market. Yarrow knew one of them would have to die eventually. She hoped the *Courier* had swallowed the tail of the fish, for if memory served her correctly, that was the one Buck said always lost.

Back in her office she worked through her correspondence, dictating to Margaret and signing letters.

"Miss McLean," said Margaret, "I'll have to retype this one. You've signed it in the wrong place."

"How silly of me. I'm sorry, Margaret." She had scrawled her signature across the text.

At the end of the day she sent Margaret home. Yarrow wanted another hour to do some reading before going home and changing for a formal dinner at Number 10 Downing Street. Elliot was in northwestern Australia looking at a cotton plantation that Phoenix had underwritten. Yarrow marveled at his stamina. She was fifty-seven and admitted to getting tired, Elliot had celebrated his sixty-first birthday by helicopter-skiing on a peak in New Zealand. He had never seemed so far away as when he was in the southern antipodes. It was always the wrong time to telephone, and Yarrow felt as though her lifeline to Elliot had been cut off.

There was a knock on the door and Shipam Truitt stood there.

"What do you want? I told them you had to leave." She was cross at being interrupted.

"I had always heard you were fair, Miss McLean. I thought you should hear me out."

"Why should I hear you out? Your father and your grand-mother brought nothing but misery to my family."

"That was all before my time."

"What are you doing here anyway? Spying on us?"

"I swear I'm not. My father doesn't even know I'm working here. I'm in the same college at Oxford as your editor's son. It just seemed natural to come here. I love this business and I wanted to learn sub-editing on Fleet Street. You've always said it's the best training for a journalist in the world."

"How do you know I've said that?"

"I read it in an interview. I've read all your interviews."

"I should learn to keep my mouth shut."

His dark eyes were ringed with lashes as Palmer's had been.

"My father told me you once saved him from drowning."

"There have been times I regretted that fact."

"Well, I for one am glad you did. I wouldn't be here otherwise."

"What else did he tell you about me? That I'm a soft touch for flattery? I'm not Greta, you know."

"He didn't say that exactly. Actually, he said you were tough." What his father had really said was that she was a tough old bitch, but he kept that to himself.

"All I want," he said, "is to show that I can do it on my own. I got this job on my own merits, nothing to do with my father. If you'll just give me a chance."

He must be about the same age as her niece, Thimi, she thought.

"How old are you?"

"Twenty."

"When I was your age . . ." she began and then stopped and bit back her words. When she was his age, she had gone to work for Larry Schaeffer in Denver. He had asked her the same question. "Are you spying on me?" Yarrow looked at the young man. He waited for her to speak. He was still standing halfway between the door and her desk, with his hands holding each other in front of him. He looked intense and miserable; not at all proud or arrogant like his father. He looked so damn vulnerable standing there, she thought, like one of her own. She knew her reputation in this building. They said she was getting crusty and autocratic as she got older. Neither of these was true, she thought, but she had become a remote figure to many of the people working for her. Of that she was aware and tried to overcome it. It had taken some guts for him to come up here on his own.

"All right then, you can stay. But if I hear one word about you . . ."

"You won't hear anything but praise. Thank you. I promise you, you won't regret it."

Yarrow went to get her coat out of the closet. He helped her put it on over her shoulders, handed her the birch cane, and then escorted her to the elevator. He waited politely until it came, saw her inside and then took off, bounding up the stairs two at a time.

"Hmmph," she said to herself as the doors closed and took her down. "Another ladies' man. Like father, like son. I'm surrounded by them."

At dinner that night with the prime minister, a dinner in honor of the American ambassador, she found her mind wandering off. She hadn't thought about Fabiana Truitt and her story about her father, Fabian Wallace Shipam, for twenty years. She missed what the ambassador, who was on her right, had said.

"Excuse me, you were saying?"

"I wondered if you'd heard the news about my replacement yet?"

The ambassador, an old friend, had been ill and had asked to be replaced.

"No, I haven't. Who is it?"

"Your friend Elliot Weyden. They made the announcement today."

"Good heavens," said a shrill woman further down the table. "Wasn't there a scandal about him some years back when he ran for president?"

The ambassador's hand slipped over Yarrow's under the table.

"I'd forgotten that," he said.

"Oh, yes." The woman went on. "All about his connection with some bootlegger and running a house of ill-repute. Oh, well, I suppose if your country can send us Joe Kennedy on the eve of our war with Hitler, they can send us Elliot Weyden in the eighties."

"Elliot Weyden is a hero," said the ambassador.

Yarrow's hand was shaking under the table as she fought to bring her emotions under control.

"Don't let them get to you," said the ambassador. "You and he will outlast them all."

Blanchette Weyden stood in the receiving line with her husband, the ambassador, at their residence, Winfield House in Regent's Park. She had not shared a house so intimately with him since their days at Coakley; she had not been a wife, mistress, or châtelaine in any form for twenty-six years. But not a year had gone by that they had not been together for Christmas or for their daughter's birthday at one or the other of their houses. She was still his wife, and when the announcement of his appointment as ambassador was made, she had been unable to resist the power, the glamour, the prestige of representing the United States at the Court of St. James.

In her yellow beaded dress and her white buttoned gloves Blanchette moved gracefully to her position as the diplomatic aides announced the guests. She stood between Elliot and Meredith, now finishing her residency at a London teaching hospital, and dutifully began shaking hands with six hundred people.

"Miss Yarrow McLean and Mr. Buckley Heartland," intoned the aide. Yarrow had not wanted to come, but Elliot insisted that her absence would be noted more than her attendance would be. She had picked a red satin and black velvet dress, and her white hair was done in a pompadour style. Diamonds gleamed from her ears and throat, and her gray eyes glistened under her dark brows. Yarrow knew she looked much younger than her years. Beside his mother, Buck thought, Blanchette looked like a "citron presse."

"Miss McLean," said Elliot. Yarrow blushed under his gaze.

"Mr. Ambassador," she said. Blanchette gave her a cold look and their gloved hands barely touched each other.

"Doctor Weyden," said Yarrow to Meredith and put out her hand. But Meredith managed to find that moment to turn and take a drink from a passing waiter. Yarrow ignored the snub and greeted a friend just ahead of her. Buck was too entranced with Meredith even to notice.

The house was enchanting, Yarrow thought, as she strolled through the rooms greeting friends. Blanchette was certainly a great hostess. Bowls of flowers sat on the polished tables and spilled out from vases and urns in every corner. In the yellow drawing room, where the burnished Chinese wallpaper gleamed under the lights, Elliot caught up with her. She was admiring one of Elliot's Impressionist paintings.

"I apologize for my daughter's behavior."

"I didn't notice."

"Where's Buck? Isn't he looking after you?"

"Now, don't you worry about me. Why, there's Deke Smith." She slipped her hand through Deke's arm. "Hello, you old rogue. What are you doing in England? A congressional trip? Deke, tell me all. You know I can keep a secret. Besides, you owe me." She waved to Elliot, who, relieved, went back to his duties.

"Do you remember me?" asked Buck, going up to Meredith just before dinner began. "We just met on the receiving line."

"I wish I could forget."

"Tut-tut, Doctor Weyden. Manners. What table are you at?"

"Not yours, Mr. Heartland. I made sure of that." Meredith turned away. She thought Buck was a very handsome young man. He was over six feet tall with the thick, red-blond hair his aunt Greta had. It curled onto his collar at the back and appeared as a down on the back of his big hands. He had his mother's wide gray eyes. Meredith had noticed all this in a second. His mother was more beautiful than she had imagined. But it pained Meredith to see them here, this night, of all nights, when it should have been her mother's triumph. How could her father have let this happen? Meredith had heard the rumors belowstairs about her father and Miss McLean. As a little girl it hadn't bothered her much. She assumed that other children's parents lived just as much apart as hers did. Not until she was older had she understood that her father's absences were because of *her*, Yarrow McLean. She watched Yarrow now, the center of an admiring circle in her bold, romantic dress and her dramatic upswept white hair. Yarrow had her head back and was laughing at something one of her companions said. Meredith saw the fascination her father had seen and fallen in love with. When she had asked her mother about it once, her mother had answered that Yarrow McLean was a witch, and that her father could not break away from Yarrow's spell. But Blanchette had promised her daughter that she would never give Elliot his freedom. Blanchette would protect Meredith from Yarrow McLean.

When the guests went in for dinner, Meredith found she was seated beside Buck Heartland.

"How did you arrange this?" she asked. He had wicked eyes; they seemed to see right through her and his eyebrows raised laconically each time he spoke. He picked up her evening bag where it had dropped on the floor.

"I changed place cards."

"That's outrageous."

"Not as outrageous as it might have been if I had to sit beside the Dowager Lady Hoban. The woman is totally deaf."

"You shouldn't laugh at people's afflictions."

"I'm not—I suffer from my own. Do you know that every artist believes that creativity and sexuality are inextricably intermingled? You have a lovely way of speaking, by the way."

Meredith was conscious of her voice not being quite normal. Years of speech therapy had cleared her speech as much as possible, but the glottal stop was still there when she forgot or was agitated—as now. Buckley Heartland disturbed her.

"Are you an artist, Mr. Heartland?"

"Right now, I'm an illustrator, a cartoonist for my mother's yellow journalism."

"You don't like your mother's papers?"

"Some of them less than others. I'm living in the wrong century. Here." He took out a pen and drew rapidly on her napkin. It was a likeness of her, with her soft blond hair, her dark brown eyes and heart-shaped face.

"You made me look too pretty," she said.

"Impossible." He was about to draw on the tablecloth.

"Don't do that," she said. "My mother will die if she sees you doing that."

"I believe," he said, putting his pen back in his pocket, "that—can I speak bluntly, you are a doctor, aren't you?—that for every orgasm I have, I lose a work of art."

Meredith burst out laughing so that the man on her right glanced at her.

"Haven't you come across this phenomenon before?" whispered Buck.

"No. I'm a pediatrician."

She turned and began conversing with her neighbor, and Buck turned to his left and spent most of the evening talking to the wife of an Indian diplomat about the Kama Sutra. But his ears picked up every word Meredith said.

After the toasts, Buck grabbed Meredith's hand. "I must see you again," he said. For once he dropped the bantering tone he usually used with women.

"That's impossible," she said.

"Just because our parents . . ."

"Please don't go on," she said. "I won't discuss this with you."

A short, agitated man came over and took her arm with a sense of propriety.

"May I introduce my fiancé, Dr. Howard Lawson?"

Buck shook the man's hand.

"Excuse us," she said. She and Lawson moved onto the dance floor, where she picked up the train of her rose silk dress. It was such an easy motion and the artist in Buck was entranced. He watched her dance. She was slim and pretty, and a fierce intelligence shone out of her eyes. He had never met anyone like her before. He had met and bedded many more beautiful women, but there was something untouchable about Meredith; something that made him want to know her better. He had listened to her conversation with her dinner partner when she talked about her work. Her dedication had shone through everything she said.

Meredith was conscious of him watching her and it flattered her, but she ignored him and chatted to her fiancé and swung her rose silk skirt a little more.

Buckley Heartland went to collect his mother, but all the way home he could not stop thinking of the slim, blond doctor with the scar on her lip.

"What are you thinking?" his mother asked as they sat together silently in the back of the Silver Shadow.

He turned to her soft, beautiful face, the luminous eyes that saw everything. I am thinking, he thought, that I have met the woman I want to marry. But he said instead, "How lovely you looked tonight, Mama."

CHAPTER 39

B UCK LEANED AGAINST THE WALL OF A BUILDING WATCHING THE exit doors of the Great Ormond Street Hospital for Sick Children. Visiting hours were over and people streamed out into the dark, dripping night. Buck pulled his collar closer, and then he saw her and ran across the wet, glistening roadway.

"Hi."

"What are you doing here, Buck? You're soaked." She had on a big tan-colored raincoat and her hair had frizzed up with the damp weather. She tied on a headscarf printed with red horses. She looked tired. She had been on duty for fourteen hours.

"I thought I could give you a lift home," he said, taking her elbow and guiding her toward his car.

"Buck, I told you yesterday, I don't want to see you anymore. I'm engaged to be married." A great gust of rain and wind blew across the road, and she abandoned her argument and ran with him for the shelter of his car. Inside, he leaned against the steering wheel and watched her take off her scarf and shake the pellets of water from her hair.

"You fascinate me, Doctor," he said.

"Buck, I don't want to be rude, but this is silly. You've been standing outside the hospital every afternoon since we met two weeks ago."

"Two and a half weeks."

"I'm engaged. Doesn't that mean anything to you?"

"Nope." He started the car engine and waiting for it to warm up, chafed her hands in his. "You're cold. You need someone to look after you."

She pulled her hands away. "I do not. I'm a doctor. I'm a very busy woman and you're acting like a lovesick cow around me. It's embarrassing. As for sitting up in Billy Simpson's bed when I was doing my rounds . . ."

"Billy thought it was a great joke. When you pulled back the curtains and saw me sitting up in his bed, he nearly died laughing."

"He shouldn't have been out of bed, he'd just had an appendectomy; and you shouldn't have been in it."

"Well, we thought it was funny and I wanted to give you some flowers."

"Thank you. Howard is getting annoyed."

"Howard is getting annoyed? What about me? I'm the one who's going to end up with no girl while he rides off into the sunset with you."

"Howard doesn't ride."

"Too big for his boots."

"He is a very serious young surgeon with a great career ahead of him."

"He's so pompous. How can you stand him?"

"Go left here," she said. Buck zigzagged through the streets behind Oxford Street to avoid the traffic. He turned into Edgeware Road.

"You haven't said you love him," said Buck. He took his eyes off the road and glanced at her quickly. Fatigue lines were drawn around her eyes. His heart lurched for her.

"I do love him."

Buck turned into a mews and stopped in front of the house where Meredith lived.

"I'm serious about his, Buck. I don't want you to keep pestering me."

"What's the matter with me? Most women like me."

"Some may. But you don't have enough substance, Buck. Who are you? What do you do? You're just playing at life. I'm working. Good night."

*   *   *

Lily asked Patsy, John's wife, to bring Star over to a birthday party she was giving for the twins in her apartment on Park Avenue.

"Not that same old magician again," said Star as the clown produced a stream of colored squares from his sleeve. The children were all sitting on the floor of the drawing room while the show was going on.

"Sssh," said Lily. "You mustn't spoil it for the younger ones, Star. They haven't seen it before."

The five-year-olds were rolling on the floor laughing. A few nursemaids sat against the wall giggling. Lily winced as she saw some chocolate cake being squashed into the rug.

"Why don't we have a quiet cup of coffee in the den while this is going on?" said Lily to Patsy and led her out holding her hand to her forehead as if she had a headache.

"How do you like it?" she asked, suspending the cream jug over her sister-in-law's cup.

"Oh, I'll have it any way it comes. I must say I've married into the nicest family. You've all been so kind."

Lily decided to put cream in.

"Have you settled in all right?"

"I've found it much easier than I thought it would be. New Yorkers are *nice*."

Patsy was a short young woman with shapely legs. She crossed them and went on.

"We had an office party this week and they were the nicest group of people, all very friendly and helpful."

"You had an office party?"

"Yes. John said we should do it more often. He has an undeserved reputation for being uninterested in people. It's just not true. John's very ambitious and he knows how he wants the company run. Now, some people may not like that. John says they have to like it or lump it and get out. The cook made . . ."

"You have a cook?"

"The cook from the office came over, she made a whole batch of . . ."

"John has a cook at the office now?"

"Yes. He says it helps wonderfully with entertaining advertisers. It saves him from having to go uptown every day. They come to him. It is so nice to be able to have someone available. Next week, when we have the magazine editors home we . . ."

"The magazine people? John has nothing to do with them— has he?"

"Oh, Lily, haven't you heard? It's the nicest thing. Your

mother named John vice-president of McLean Publishing. It was in the papers, I thought you knew.''

"No one told me anything.''

Patsy put down her cup, stood up, and tugged her skirt down. "I must go home. I'll send the car back for Star. Why don't you come and join us next week? You would be very welcome.''

Lily sucked in her feelings. She showed her sister-in-law to the elevator and then rushed to the window, pulled back the curtains, opened the window and looked out. There was a big, black stretch limousine with a chauffeur waiting for Patsy downstairs. Lily squeezed her lips together as she saw the chauffeur salute and Patsy climb in the back.

"And I can't even get John to pay my expenses,'' she fumed. "I'll show them who the patsy is around here.'' She pulled in her head and bumped it on the window frame. Slamming the window down, she rushed off to wash her hands in the bathroom and get some ice for the bump on her head.

"I have to think of the future,'' said Yarrow to Elliot one afternoon as they sat in the library of her London flat. "I hate to think of it. It's like making a will—it's a future without me.''

"Better than dwelling in the past, darling,'' said Elliot. He had his feet up on a velvet ottoman and he was reading news faxes from the machine. Through the window came the faint strains of marching music as the guards changed at Buckingham Palace. It was a Saturday and Elliot had escaped from his duties as ambassador for a few hours. She liked having him sit here, comfortable and sloppy without people around. She had sent her maid off and toasted some bagels for Elliot that she had brought over from New York. She watched him pick up a piece of one with cream cheese on it and lick his fingers.

"There's a hole in your shoe,'' she said. "Blanchette doesn't look after you.''

"Then buy me a new pair. I don't have the time.'' She didn't laugh and turned to the window again. Through the dotted voile curtains the whole world appeared to Yarrow like a halftone.

"I'm losing my sight, Elliot,'' she said. "I have glaucoma.''

He dropped the rolls of paper he was reading and came to her at the window and took her in his arms. "Darling, how long have you known?''

"Oh, some time. I've been missing a lot of what I've been reading lately. But it was the flashing pain and aching eyes that frightened me. I knew something was wrong. Don't worry, I have a very good doctor looking after me, but I'm in the reading business. How can I go on at this pace if I can't use my eyes?''

He kissed her eyes.

"I have to think about the future," she said again. She left his embrace and sat down on a linen-covered chair with a bold pattern of red ribbons and parrots. "I now own eighty percent of McLean Publishing. You know, over the years I've increased my stake, as the others wanted money to start their own businesses— Greta opened her restaurant, and Eric wanted to own the *Gazette* outright, and Nellie and Jack bought that ranch. They're hopeless managers. Hopeless." She shook her head. "I don't know what I'm worth anymore. Do you?"

"McLean Publishing must be worth some hundreds of millions of dollars, I guess."

"Yes, something like that. Of course, that's all on paper. Only by selling it would that amount of money be realized." She laughed. "I just remembered. I was sitting beside a friend of yours in New York and he had just bought a painting. I asked him what it was. He said, a Madonna by Correggio, or something grand like that. I said I couldn't afford that, and he looked at me, made a judgment and said, 'Ah, cash poor.' '' She laughed again.

He sat down and held her hand.

Then she was serious. "I've built up something that I would like to pass on intact."

"That's what I envy you for. You created something—your ideas built a vast chain of communication. You have something to leave."

"You have, too, Elliot."

"No. I've created wealth, perhaps some jobs. The only time I went into something tangible, real estate, I got my fingers badly burned. When I tried to go into politics, that didn't work either. I have nothing to leave but money."

"The boy who was going to be very, very rich."

"What did I know? I am the capitalist, you, the entrepreneur. I guess that's why the Iran deal was so important to me. I wanted to leave the name Phoenix on a great dam, on an irrigation project."

"We're all struck by the desire for immortality at some time or other. I guess it's the greatest urge."

They were silent.

"How do I hand it over to them without them losing everything in taxes?"

He thought for a minute. "It's not my field of expertise but you could recapitalize the company. It may be too late though."

"What do you mean?"

"You could have a preferred-stock recapitalization, but it should have been done years ago."

"And given up some of my control? Hardly likely. Who should I talk to?"

"We have a number of people who specialize only in that. I can arrange for you to talk to one of them."

"Damn. I don't want to do it. I'm still young. I want to do so many things yet, but this problem with my eyes—it's—well, it makes me think how hard it was for my father when he made his will."

She looked so worried, he squeezed her hand. "Darling, don't worry about the business. It's your eyes, your health that are important."

"My grandfather went blind, you know, Elliot. And when I stayed with Miss Hines when I worked at the *Globe*, I used to look at her father—he'd lost his sight in an accident, I think— but I used to look at him and wonder what it would be like." She burst into tears. "What will it be like not to see your dear face again?" He held her and she stopped crying.

"I have to think it through. I would like to talk to someone at Phoenix. And then I have to talk to the children. One of them has to be my successor. It's only fair to them and the company that I make that decision."

"You don't have to make it now."

"Yes, I do! Why put it off?"

"Have you made up your mind? Who will it be?"

She turned her beautiful gray eyes on him, in which he could not see any sign of disease.

"John," she said. "It has to be John."

"Why is John being named president of the company?" shouted Lily at the board table in South Street. Yarrow had just made her announcement and John was sitting back with a big smile on his face. Yarrow hadn't told them about her glaucoma. She was taking medication to relieve the pressure on her eyes. It helped the pain—she had eyedrops, too—but one embarrassing side effect was that she had to go to the bathroom a lot. She would not talk about her own problems; she hated to be thought a hypochondriac. She had merely announced that she was planning to give them stock and gradually hand over control of the company to the next generation. She had not put things in place yet. She was still talking to people. But she wanted her children to know what was on her mind. She was inviting them onto the board of directors and John would be president and CEO.

She looked at her thirty-six-year-old daughter. Lily was elegant in a cold way, the thin blond hair of her childhood was now permed into a chic, blown look. The frosted hair flew off her face as though a permanent wind were in front of her.

"I'm sorry if you're upset," said Yarrow.

"Upset! I'm not upset. I'm furious. John's been nothing but a burden since the day he was born. He flies off to Canada because he won't fight for his country and he walks back in here and three years later it's all his."

"Oh, shut up, Lily," said John with his arms folded. "I'm tired of your histrionics. Our mother knows what she's doing. You're going to be on the board. Why are you complaining?"

Lily stood up and grabbed her shoulderbag off the table and leaned forward toward her brother. "Because it should have been mine." She left the room without looking at any of them and slammed the door as she left.

"Frankly, I don't care," said Buck, who was lounging back in his chair.

"Do sit up," said Yarrow. Buck scooted his spine up about an inch. He was miserable. He had just heard that Meredith and Howard had been married in Bermuda. Meredith had wanted to avoid a fuss, his mother told him. She hadn't wanted a big wedding at the embassy with all her parents' stuffy friends. Buck thought that the truth was different. There had been an item about him and an actress in the London *Daily Mail*. He had been hoping to make Meredith jealous. He was a fool. The actress had meant nothing to him. Meredith had married suddenly because she didn't want to face him again. He slammed up to a sitting position. He knew she loved him. It was impossible that she didn't feel the same way he did. He had only kissed her once, taking her home from the hospital, but it had proved it. She wouldn't have responded the way she did if she didn't love him. Lips didn't lie, only words did.

"What about me?" he asked. "Have you decided in your wisdom where to place your errant son?"

"You are twenty-seven years old, Buck, and it's time you grew up. I've asked Bourget, the head of the design department at McLean Magazines, to take you under his wing."

"Thank you, Mama."

"There's no need to be sarcastic. Bourget is the best, but he also has a very sharp beak. He'll rip you to pieces if you fail him."

Buck banged the table. "I'm an artist."

"Then use your talent. Stop pissing it away on starlets."

Buck blushed. His mother seldom used coarse language. But then nothing escaped her notice either.

His mother went on calmly, pushing her black-rimmed glasses more firmly on her nose and peering at a paper in front of her.

"I've also asked Justice Hoggart to come up from Texas to run the suburban papers."

"He's not part of this reorganization, is he?" said John.

"He will not inherit any of my shares, but he and your cousins control twenty percent of the company. I've also appointed him to the London board. He can be the liaison between McLean Publishing and the London *Enquirer*'s public company. Any questions?"

Her sons sat brooding at each other across the table. Yarrow got up and they stood.

"Then I leave you to talk it over between yourselves."

"Why don't you quit, since you hate it so much," said John when his mother had left the room and they sat down again.

"What, and leave it all to you? Fat chance."

"Go to art school, you fairy."

"That I'm not. Take that back."

Buck grabbed his brother's hand and tried to force it down on the table. Beads of sweat burst out on their foreheads. Then John gave in—Buck was too strong.

"This is juvenile," said John. "We won't solve anything this way. I'll get your shares another way, little brother."

Buck stood up and kicked his chair out of the way and left the room.

Whenever Yarrow was agitated, she walked through her building. She was agitated now because she knew that John was not the perfect choice, but she hoped in making the decision early, she would be able to help him grow into the role. He was not doing too badly; he was a presence around the place; he was not afraid of hard work; his failing, she believed, was that he could be corrupted by power. She had seen it happen in other families; the scion is picked and his head immediately blows up out of all proportion.

She went now to the composing floor where the paste-up was in progress. She told the foreman that she just wanted to watch and they should ignore her. The composing room was automated now. Slanted tables for working on the page layouts were ranked along the sides. Each page had its own station marked off, one, two, three, four and so forth. Dummy sheets were taped to the upright pegboards at the back of each table. The dummy sheets, preprinted with column rules, were already marked with the spaces for display ads and photographs and copy. They acted as guides for the paste-up operators. The paste-up sheets themselves were of heavy-quality paper and were held in place by masking tape. The men worked with hurried grace. The deadline was near. Yarrow looked at the lighted board above them—the numbers of the pages that were still not finished were illuminated. Down below, in the reporters' room, a television monitor showed the illuminated board to the reporters.

The digital typesetting machine sat enclosed in its glass-walled booth in isolated, air-conditioned splendor. It received information from the main computer down the hall. The reporters and editors, through the video display terminals on their desks, had keyboarded this information to the computer. From that information, the computer had electronically transcribed the text—the column width, the length, the typeface and the size of type that was to be used; not only the text itself but the "woods" (the *Telegraph*'s term for headlines) were justified. This was then relayed to the typesetting machine, and a cathode-ray tube in the machine transferred the images onto photosensitive paper.

From the bowels of the typesetting machine, an operator removed an oblong black box that contained the photosensitive paper. The black box was put into a processor where the paper was developed and dried. Yarrow watched as the eight-inch-wide ribbon of paper was then extruded into the composing room with the text printed on it, and the paste-up operators cut it to fit the pages. It was so quiet, so clean, so clinical compared with the old days. Everything was white, the floors, the paper, the slanted benches, even the men's shirts were white. There was no ink or metal to be seen. The draftsmen used square rules and blue pencils and sharp razors to slice and splice the stories and headlines in position. The wax on the back of the ribbons of paper held the columns in place; sometimes, on narrow columns of classifieds, adhesive tape was used to hold down the edges. Like the blue pencils, the adhesive tape did not show when the negative was made. As each page was completed it was placed in its slot in a transfer cabinet ready for photocopying. When the page was photographed, the negative was sent down to the plate room to make the plate to go on the presses. The lead plates of the old stereo room had now been replaced by plates of photopolymer plastic.

"Photocomposition," thought Yarrow. "We are all technicians now."

She walked downstairs and through the reporters' room where the video display terminals hummed on every desk. Telephones still rang; that hadn't changed. Nor had the people. Along with the screen that showed the pages that still had to be done, a number of television monitors were switched to the news. A woman reporter ate a sandwich while she typed out a late-breaking story. She pressed FE for "Fetch," and the Harris VDT scrolled up a list of stories organized by author's name. She called up the one she wanted and the green words spilled across the screen. Yarrow watched while she brought up a split-screen image to compare what she was writing to what she had written before. The woman did not look up. She held up a Styrofoam cup with half an inch of coffee and a number of cigarette butts in it. "Refill," she said. "Regular."

Yarrow got it for her from a vending machine in the corner.

"Smoking's bad for you," said Yarrow, putting a fresh cup down beside her, "and 'success' has two c's." The woman looked up at the familiar low voice and almost choked on her sandwich. Yarrow smiled and left. She felt quite jaunty as she waited for the elevator. For a moment she was able to forget that the prognosis for her left eye was not good. She had left it too late, ignored the warning signs all those times when her eyes hurt. But the doctor promised he would do his best to save the other eye.

Each time the lawyers came up with a scheme to formalize the control of McLean Publishing, Yarrow drew back from it. She had never vacillated so much in her life. John kept badgering her about it and Lily complained and the more they did so, the more stubborn Yarrow became. She heard, through Greta, that there was so much bad blood between Lily and John now that they hardly spoke to each other. Yarrow was at her wit's end how to rectify it. If she planned a family dinner, one or the other of them would refuse to come.

At the end of the year, Yarrow sent for John and told him that she had decided to endorse Ronald Reagan for president.

"You can't do that," he said. "That's my decision as president of this company."

The look on his mother's face made John realize he had made a grave error.

"Until you pay the bills, this is my newspaper, and it will be my decision whom we endorse." The Telegraph was the first paper in the United States to come out for Ronald Reagan for president.

Lily argued with her brother about her expenses. Under her constant wheedling, her mother had put her on the board of

KMZO in Denver. Yarrow thought that might keep Lily and John apart. But John, building his own power base, had reorganized the company so that KMZO came under his jurisdiction, too.

He had returned the last bunch of requisition slips that she had sent in. "What does he want me to do?" she complained to David as she read his last missive. Even her brother's way of refusing her requests was offensive. "No" he'd scrawled over her expense sheet. "Does he expect me to walk to Denver for the board mueetings?"

"Or go business class," David said mildly.

"He's a pig," said Lily. "I hate him."

"Yes, dear." David had learned never to argue.

As for Buck, he came to admire Bourget and the work of his design team. But Buck was like a fish out of water. He was not interested in the look of a magazine, or how a page should be set up, or in typefaces. Talks about circulation and promotions and advertising bored him. He set up a studio for himself in Soho and worked at night on his own canvases. They were big, bold, abstract paintings that meant nothing to those who saw them because they meant nothing to Buck. He strove and worked and painted till his head swam with fumes and his arms ached. But the energy was still unchanneled. He would fall onto his mattress at the end of such a session with whichever woman was available. Buck was a big, blond, beautiful young man. His muscles rippled, his neck was thick. He had grown a beard and it had come in red-gold like his Uncle Eric's.

"I'm misunderstood," he would say, his large blue eyes swimming in tears, and the current woman would squeeze, bob, groan, thrust, lick, plunge to try to assuage his sadness. The big blond giant would come with a roar. He was like a lion. He would go on and on and on, and in the end, spent, he would subside into melancholia. He would pull on his jeans and go down to the coffee shop where his artist friends hung out. "My God," he would say sadly as he sat down, with his beard tangled and damp from lovemaking, "I've just lost another masterpiece."

The President of the United States named a new ambassador to the Court of St. James who was closer to his own political philosophy. The departure of the previous ambassador was amicable, and a round of parties and farewells took place in London before Elliot could leave.

Yarrow telephoned him to say she was sorry she would be unable to come to his last gala evening. She gave him the news that her medication had not alleviated the pressure in her eyes and that they would have to operate. She was terrified.

"Blanchette," said Elliot on the last day of his official duties as they drove away from Buckingham Palace, "up until now, I've yielded to you on the status of our marriage. I've treated you with respect . . ."

"You've slept with another woman . . ."

"I've been faithful to one woman for twenty-seven years. I asked you for divorce once and you refused. You said you needed me then. I acquiesced."

"Your daughter needed you."

"She doesn't need me now. You've never let me go, Blanchette. I've begged you to let me be with the woman I love without making a scandal. You wouldn't do it. She needs me now."

Blanchette turned on him with a fierceness he hadn't seen for a long time. She wore a big blue hat with an ostrich feather that quivered with rage.

"How can you ask this of me? Why do you blame me? I prayed to God to help me forgive you. But I couldn't. *I* did nothing. You broke your vows, you adulterer."

"I'm not asking you for forgiveness, Blanchette. I'm truly sorry for what we did. I never meant to hurt you. You've been a good mother to my daughter and for that I'll always be grateful. But you've made me pay for not loving you. I've paid. Over and above, I've paid."

It began to spit with rain. The windschield wipers of the Daimler squeaked. Elliot wondered how much of their conversation the chauffeur had overheard through the glass panel. He pressed a button and lowered the panel. "You can drop me off at St. James's," he said, "and then take Mrs. Weyden back to the residence." He pressed the button to close the panel.

"You're not coming back with me?"

"No." The car stopped and the chauffeur hopped out and opened the door for Elliot. He got out and put on his top hat. "Good-bye, Blanchette."

She turned her head away from him. The last he saw of her was the blue feather quivering in the back seat as the black Daimler with the diplomatic plates sped up the hill toward Piccadilly.

CHAPTER 40

*L*ILY HEARTLAND, NEWLY FORTY-ONE, SAT BESIDE HER BROTHER and listened to the speeches. She toyed with the poached salmon on her plate as Mario Cuomo, the governor of New York, was introduced. She and John were attending the American Newspaper Publishers Association luncheon at the Hilton Hotel in San Francisco. It was April 22, 1986. She knew the date by heart because it was her wedding anniversary. David was staying with the kids at home in New York and he had sent her a dozen roses. She had been in a fine mood until she sat down next to her brother at the luncheon and he had told her he was asking her to get off the board. She was incensed by this announcement.

"Why do you want me to resign from the board?" she whispered. John had grown corpulent since taking over as president of McLean Publishing. He polished off his salmon before he answered her, never taking his eyes off the speaker.

"Because I want to make room for outside directors. Shut up and let me hear this speech, will you? This man could be president one day."

"Oh, it's the same old speech he's made six thousand times. I won't get off, not without a fight." Her voice hissed at him.

"You'll have to. Buck and Justice will support me."

"What? Why?"

"Because you're too damn negative and you weren't loyal. You bad-mouth me wherever you go." He had raised his voice and people around shushed them.

The speaker said, "In this America, more than one child in every five is growing up in poverty—among black children, more than one in two."

Lily hissed in her brother's ear, "I suppose you'll want to put a black woman in my place, two minorities for the price of one."

John glared at her.

"Well, it won't happen." Chauvinist, she thought. Why didn't her mother pick her? Women should help each other. She sat fuming until Cuomo had finished speaking, and then when the luncheon broke up, she made her escape. Shipam Truitt stopped her on the way out.

"You didn't like the speech, I take it."

"I didn't. I disagree with everything the governor says, but I suppose John will praise his speech in the *Telegraph*. My mother would die if she read it, if she were still interested."

"Then you might like our editorial instead." Shipam had been editing the *Courier* since his father died six months ago.

"I heard you're making some changes at the *Courier*—all yuppies and dinks."

"Dinks?"

"Double income, no kids."

He laughed. If Shipam's father had looked anything like him, she could see why Greta had once fallen for him.

"Well, someone must like them. We've beaten you in circulation for the last two months running."

"Am I supposed to congratulate you?"

"No, but I offer my condolences."

She was about to leave when he said, "How's your mother? I heard she's lost sight in one eye."

"She's recuperating, thank you. Right now she's on a tour of the Pacific with Elliot. She's due in Hawaii today and then Fiji."

"Your mother has taken a vacation? I thought she never stopped."

"Like everything, she's combined this one with launching a business magazine in Australia. She should be here, not gallivanting off to new pastures."

"Will you give her my best?"

Lily nodded and pushed her way through the throng. You would have thought Shipam really liked her mother, the way he spoke. Well, she would pass on the message. She had a couple of messages to pass on—like, what John was doing with the company while their mother's attention was elsewhere. Lily knew the *Courier* was beating the *Telegraph* hand over fist. God, John was a fool. He thought he knew everything. He had begun to make changes at KMZO-TV in Denver and Tom Marx had resigned. There were stirrings among the magazine executives as John's heavyhandedness began to interfere with operations. Under Yarrow and Bourget they had enjoyed a certain amount of autonomy. Now John Heartland wanted everyone to report to him. Even Justice wanted out. Justice said he'd worked long enough for the McLeans; now he wanted to work for the Hoggarts.

Lily worried about her future. It was her inheritance John was in control of—if he messed up, she would suffer for it. Lily would have run the business differently from John. He was squeezing it too hard. Why, he even insisted that she show him her taxi receipts before she could be reimbursed! She was an equal shareholder! She was his sister! He sent her memos instead of letters! He was worse than her mother had been. Lily was going to talk to Buck—let's see if he really wanted her off the board. She felt sure John was bluffing.

Outside the hotel, in the afternoon sunshine, Lily passed Gump's department store and stopped. In the window there was a set of Limoges with a border of blue flowers. Lily had been looking for that exact color for months; it was perfect for the dining room in her apartment. Lily hesitated; she was already overdrawn this month. But she could already see the plates in her New York dining room. They would be perfect with her blue mats and napkins, the Christofle flatware, and the lupines on the wallpaper. Lily went into the store. She said to the clerk, "I would like to buy the Limoges dinner service in the window and have it shipped to New York. You do take American Express?"

The seaplane landed with a splash and a ripling series of jolts, and then turned and thumped over the waves to a long jetty that thrust out from the island like a finger into the sea.

"It's beautiful," Yarrow shouted to Elliot above the roar of the engine. He gave the thumbs-up sign. Yarrow seemed to have become completely adjusted to the loss of sight in her left eye. The operation on the right eye five years ago had been successful, but the left eye had been too far gone. Elliot still thought she was the most beautiful woman he had ever seen.

She ran her hand over his back. His shoulders were beginning to round, but his hair was as black as ever; there were more gray hairs in his eyebrows than on his head.

"Welcome to the most beautiful island in Fiji," smiled Timini, the manager of Elliot's copra farm, as he welcomed them.

Their luggage was unloaded and carried off by a group of Fijians, the women in colorful cotton dresses, the men in sulus, straight wrap skirts that stopped at their calves. Yarrow and Elliot walked behind them. They walked onto a beach of fine, white sand and up a flight of wooden stairs to their burra, a thatch-roofed bungalow that sat on a narrow saddle of land overlooking the jetty on one side and the open sea on the other. The surf crashed mightily on the windward side, and a hammock, strung from two trees, rocked continuously in the breeze.

The manager offered them some kava, a milky drink with anesthetic qualities, toasted them, and took his leave. Yarrow watched him descend the stairs with the others. None of them wore shoes.

"I love it," said Yarrow, kicking off her own and settling into a chair.

"There are no cars, no roads, no electricity," said Elliot.

"No telephone?" she said in mock horror.

"A radio telephone for emergency, but no one ever listens to it."

"I may find it hard to go back to civilization."

Yarrow was thinking specifically of the phone calls she had received in Hawaii. Her children seemed incapable of working together without conflict. Lily complained about John's autocratic behavior. John wanted her off the board, she said. He wanted to get rid of Greta and Nellie, too. Yarrow wondered when John would get around to asking *her* to resign. When she had called John, he had been defensive and belligerent. He needed people who could advise him on the board, he said. The nation's economy was sluggish, so of course the company profits were down; that was why he wanted directors who understood finance and business, not a bunch of female relatives whose only interest in the company was the amount of the dividend they received. Justice called Yarrow to say that the acrimony on the board was getting worse, and when was she coming back? Justice didn't take sides. Sometimes she wished he would. The only one who hadn't called her was Buck, but Yarrow ascribed that more to apathy than anger.

Even Shipam Truitt had called her, but only to inquire about her health.

At dusk she watched two women walking along the beach with lanterns swinging in their hands. It was like watching fireflies coming up to their room. The fireflies ascended the steps and settled on the doorstep, and the two women left. Soft guitar music wafted up to them from the jetty and Yarrow put a hibiscus flower in her hair, wrapped a sarong around herself, crisscrossing it at the neck, then she and Elliot took their lanterns and walked down to the main house for dinner. There were no other guests. They had the island entirely to themselves.

After dinner they relaxed under the trees near the water's edge. Bats squeaked overhead. The male cook was an Indian, and a group of dusky, beautiful children ran and played in the dark. The Fijian children with their thick, black, frizzy hair and shining teeth were more shy. They giggled in the dark around them.

"I've made inquiries about my divorce," said Elliot, lighting up a cheroot the manager had given him. Yarrow had never seen him smoke before.

"Blanchette still hasn't agreed to it?"

"No, and New York is one of the last states that doesn't have a no-fault law or statute."

"Which means you need grounds for divorce."

"And Blanchette has all of those—'adultery, abandonment, cruel and inhuman treatment,' but she doesn't want to use them."

"So where do you stand?"

"I may have to move to New Jersey." He said it so sadly that she burst out laughing.

"Why?"

"New Jersey has a no-fault divorce law, so after twelve months of residence there, I'd be eligible and we could be married. I'll be seventy by then," he said. "How would you like an old bridegroom?"

Yarrow looked at her emerald ring. She could only see the diamonds faintly in the dark. "I would like that," she said. But she said it more for Elliot's sake than her own. How could she explain that she felt their years together constituted an agreement more binding than any piece of paper? But—perhaps to be blessed by God—Yarrow nodded her white head in the dark.

"Meredith's getting a divorce, too," said Elliot. "There was something wrong with that marriage from the beginning."

"I'm sorry. What will she do?"

"She wants to come back and live with the children in New York. She'll continue to work. You know, she's been offered a job by the man who operated on her when she was a baby? He's in semi-retirement now, but he runs a clinic in New York. It's funded by the foundation I set up in Washington."

"I think Buck was fond of Meredith."

"She never said anything."

"No, neither did he, but I could see the way he looked at her. It was the way you used to look at me."

"I still look at you the same way."

"No, you don't. But I like what you do all the same."

Yarrow went on. "Lily and David bash along from one year to the next. They're not really happy, but they're happy in their unhappiness, you know? John says that's Lily's natural state."

"What about John?"

"Oh, John. What about John?" She was not really asking Elliot, she was asking herself.

"Of my three children I thought he was the best to run the

company. There's an anger in him that he can't let go. He was like that even as a baby. He threw a rock once into Buck's baby carriage, and when he used to hug Zeb, he'd hug him so tight he gritted his teeth. He said he was afraid he would squeeze him to death otherwise.''

Yarrow didn't want to think about John anymore. She was worried about her company. She had worked hard to put it in the position it was in today, and she wanted one of her children to run it. Hadn't she worked this hard for them?

"Tomorrow," said Elliot, as they walked along the beach with their lanterns, "we'll go out and dive for oysters. There's a spot near the coral where we anchor. Will you come in the boat?''

"I'd like that. Remember in Jamaica when you put me on your back and we swam in the sea?''

"We could try it again.''

"Oh, no—but it was lovely to feel so—supported.''

"And then," he said, "you swam off on your own.'' But of course he was not talking about the sea; there, she had kept her arms around his neck.

"It was a nice feeling," she said.

They spent the days lazing, sometimes on the hammock in the breeze, or fishing and swimming and collecting shells. One day Elliot went off with the manager to another island to see the new smokehouse for drying out coconut flesh. But Yarrow didn't want to see how copra was made. She felt almost somnambulant and stayed behind with a book. She lay in the hammock and watched the boat put-put around the point. She could see Elliot's big broad-brimmed hat for a long time out of her good eye. His brown back looked pale next to Timini's black one.

On Sunday they went over to a neighboring island in the boat to attend a Mass. Yarrow and Elliot carried their shoes in their hands as they waded in from the boat. Streams of people in Western clothes emerged from a village of huts and climbed up to the little chapel with them. The chapel bell tolled over the blue Pacific. All the women knelt on grass mats on one side of the wall-less chapel, and all the men knelt on the other. They swayed on their haunches as they sang the hymns. Little girls in straw hats and spotless white dresses giggled at the visitors sitting on chairs at the back. Yarrow wondered how the women laundered and ironed their clothes.

After the Mass was over and the priest intoned a blessing, the priest gave Yarrow a golden cowrie shell he had found near the oyster beds. The next day when she was packing her bag to leave, she picked up the shell, stroked its smooth, spotted gold dome, examined the ventral side with the tooth-edged womb, and dropped it in her pocketbook.

"Do you think it's true," she asked Elliot, as the seaplane took off for the main island, "that women put love first?"

He looked at her and smiled.

"Yes," he said and she nodded and looked away. The sun glinting on the sea made her eyes water. She put her hand into her pocketbook to get out her sunglasses and felt the shell. She kept looking out the window and holding the shell secretly in her hand. It was perfect, she thought, just perfect, like a blessing.

On the fourth of July the scent of the cottonwood trees drifted down over the valleys and hills around Galena. The scent was as green and fresh and aromatic as the grass itself. There was a softness in the dry air of the high country that often came at the end of the summer. The aspen trees shook and the grass bent down, flattened like breezes on a green sea. Dandelion heads, white and downy like fairy clocks, rimmed the edges of the meadows like salt crust.

Yarrow drove her three granddaughters twenty miles down to town to take part in the early morning parade. She had insisted that the whole family come to Galena this year for the holiday—she would take no excuse from anyone this time.

Nigella and Rose were dressed like pioneer women with mob-caps on their heads and shawls around their shoulders. Star, who had just graduated from high school, was dressed like a young boy with a tricorn hat and braces holding up her britches.

They all met at Eric and Yanna's house, where the pony that Avril used to ride was harnessed to a cart. The twins climbed in the back, Star shouldered the Stars and Stripes and Avril kept a firm grip on the lead line as her pony, beribboned and sulky, set off to join the parade. Yarrow had a lump in her throat as she walked behind the little procession with Eric and Yanna. They walked out the gate of the house that her father had been born in, down the road where new houses had sprouted up between the old ones. Laura and her husband, whose name Yarrow could never remember, came out of the old Brogan house and joined them. Laura put her arm around Yarrow's and whispered, "My George wants to marry your Edith," and Yarrow smiled.

"It's taken them long enough to make up their minds. Walk on my good side so I can see you."

They assembled with their other friends on Main Street, and then, with the local high-school band slightly out of key but making up for it with passion and charm, they all whistled and

piped and drummed their way into the old town square. The
veterans lifted their feet to the tune of "When Johnny Comes
Marching Home," and then, at the flag raising, when the children sang "Oh, say, does that star-spangled banner yet wave,"
goosebumps ran over Yarrow as she shivered in the sun.

That night, Eric and Yanna's house on Boomer Street and the
meadow behind was the gathering place for the celebrations.
They expected a hundred people to come and it made Yarrow
happy to see the old family home alive and full of people.

Elliot arrived with Meredith and her children. They had flown
in late, and Meredith and the children were staying at the old
railway hotel. Justice and his wife, Marla, an aspiring dancer
who spent most of her non-Broadway time teaching aerobics,
were staying in Yarrow's old room upstairs with their baby,
Kent. Justice carried the baby around in a sling across his chest.
Marla boogied, jived, or whatever the modern term was, to any
music that played.

Yarrow took Kent from his father and jiggled him on her
knee. She played a game with him, tapping on his forehead and
chin. "Knock at the door, peek in. Lift the latch and walk in.
Take a chair and sit down there. And wait till your daddy comes
home from the fair."

Buck came in the front door as Yarrow was wrapping a
blanket around Kent to take him outside to watch the fireworks
which would start soon. Buck kissed his mother. She heard he
was drinking heavily, but he refused a drink from his cousin,
Thimi, who came out of the kitchen to greet him.

"You look better," said Yarrow as they went out the back
door into the meadow. "You've lost weight. How's the painting
going?"

"Mother," he said, stopping her on the steps and not letting
her continue, "I know now what I want to do. I want to paint. I
should have made this decision years ago, but I didn't want to let
you down."

"You mean leave the company altogether?"

"Yes. Whatever you want me to do with my shares, I'll be
guided by you."

"Has this anything to do with John and Lily?"

Someone began to sing "Take Me Out to the Ball Game" and
others joined in.

"Yes and no. I hate going to board meetings. We fight about
everything."

Yarrow nodded. "There's someone here you might like to
see. Meredith. She's over there talking to Avril."

Yarrow watched her son's face. The big handsome features lit up and she knew she was right about his feelings. He hitched up his jeans and sauntered, casual as anything, over to Meredith and his cousin. Avril gave him a big hug and then she left. Yarrow watched her youngest son talking to Meredith. It was like watching a hulking bear being trained by a very small ringmaster. Yarrow smiled. She had made her decision about the future of her company coming back from Australia. There had been plenty of time to think on the airplane.

The singers had gone through all the old family favorites—"Yankee Doodle," "In the Good Old Summertime," "Jeepers Creepers," "Jimmy Crack Corn and I Don't Care"—when Elliot came up to her whistling.

People were sitting down on blankets they had brought to watch the fireworks.

"You want to canoodle with me on a blanket?" he asked.

"If I can bring my great-nephew along."

Kent gurgled in her arms as Elliot led her through the happy crowd of singing families. Eric, and Greta's husband, Eduardo, had gone down to the bottom of the meadow to light the fireworks they had set up. The first rocket went up to a great shout of appreciation from everyone. People poured themselves another beer, ate another slice of pizza, bit into another hot dog. Yarrow settled down beside Elliot and leaned against him with a smile on her face; then she heard Lily's voice. Lily was just behind her somewhere, she couldn't see her in the dark, but she could hear her arguing with John.

"I hear you've arranged to borrow some money and you're offering your future shares as collateral. You're ruining this company. Why our mother picked you to run it I'll never know. She must be getting senile."

"She did it because she knew you couldn't do it, Lily. You're a pain in the neck. Well, it's my company now and I want you out and I'll soon have the money to do it, not just off the board, sis, but O-U-T, out."

David's voice: "Lay off a bit, John."

"You jerk, you don't come into this."

"Don't you touch him," said Lily.

"Shut up, you bitch."

"I won't let you talk to my wife that way."

"John," said Patsy, "that's not nice."

"I don't need you defending me," said Lily to Patsy. "I'm warning you, John, the minute I get my hands on my shares, I'm going to sell them to the highest bidder, and it won't be you.

Buck will sell his, too, and you won't have a company to run.
You'll be a minority.''

"Hey, what's happening? You're spoiling everyone's fun,"
came Buck's voice.

"Stay out of this, asshole." There was a scream, a lot of
scuffling, panting. A whole series of rockets and flares went up
from the bottom of the meadow and showered down. Everyone's
attention was on the sky. Everyone oohed and aahed except
Yarrow and her children.

"Stop them, Elliot. Make them stop."

Elliot got to his feet, but Justice had gotten there first and
pulled John and Buck apart. Lily began kicking John on the
shins. "I hate you. I hate you."

"That's enough, Lily," said David, pinning her arms behind
her back. Yarrow rose to her feet. In the red glare of the next
rocket her three children saw her. They stood on the crumpled
blankets, the scattered picnic basket spilling out its contents,
rolls and apple pie smeared into the ground, bottles and glasses
tipped over.

"This has been the worst night of my life," said Yarrow.
They looked ashamed, defiant, troubled. She stared at them long
and hard and then handed Kent to his father. "Take me home,
please, Elliot."

She turned and left them standing there. A group of carousers,
stoked up on Coors, began a whole new medley of songs: "And
the Band Played On," "On Top of Old Smokey," "Indian Summer." The words hung in the air as Yarrow stepped across
people on blankets. Everyone so happy, all these families, she
thought, everyone except mine. The words of a song followed
her out of the house: "You see so many dreams that don't come
true/Dreams we fashioned when Summertime was new."

"Well, it wasn't for a lack of wanting," said Yarrow.

She could not put it off any longer. The next day Yarrow
locked herself in her bedroom and worked on the telephone,
which rang all day. Edith took food up to her on trays. Elliot
went for a hike with Meredith. When Yarrow's lawyers arrived
the following morning, the family had gathered together at Chipeta.

"I've called you all here this morning because I have something important I want to say. I address my remarks to my own
three children, but I want you all to hear this and understand why
I'm doing what I'm doing. I have been thinking of this course of
action for some time but I hesitated. I loved you. I thought you
would come to trust and respect each other. I thought that

responsibility would teach each of you humility. I was wrong. It taught you greed, and disloyalty and hatred. The disgraceful exhibition that I witnessed the night before last has convinced me that my course is right."

Yarrow picked up her cane with the silver collar and banged it down on the table in front of her. They all jumped.

"Your great-grandfather would have been ashamed of you. My father would have been ashamed of you. I am ashamed of you."

She picked up a piece of paper her lawyers handed her.

"I have decided for the sake of peace and harmony to sell McLean Publishing."

"You fool," said John, rising to his feet, his face flushed with anger.

She banged the cane down again. Edith winced when she saw the tabletop. "Shut up," said Yarrow. "Sit down."

He sank back into his seat, cowed. None of them had ever seen her in such a temper. But she was cold, not hot; cold and remorseless.

"You have no recourse but to accept what I'm doing. I own eighty percent of the company. You've counted your chickens too soon, John. So have you, Lily. As for the rest of the shareholders, it will be up to them to decide whether to remain with the new owners or whether to sell."

"What about us?" asked Lily, who had turned white when she heard what Yarrow was planning. "What about our children?"

"You should have thought of that before, Lily. You've bandied my company's name around, publicly complained about the way I've been running the company. How dare you!"

"It's rather a drastic solution, Mama," said Buck.

"You forced it on me. You never wanted to work at it, Buck. You wasted the first thirty years of your life, womanizing and carousing." Buck blushed as he heard her say this in front of the children.

"But you, John," she said, "You disappointed me more than the others because I expected more from you. I thought, even with our differences, that you would be the one to continue after me. I thought you left your country those many years ago because you loved something more. In a way, you did—you loved yourself. I didn't know you would split the family in order to increase your own power. You couldn't wait to get your hands on everything. It was ugly to see."

"I'll fight you," he said.

"Try it in Canada," she snapped. She put on her glasses and looked at the sheet of paper.

"Depending on your attitudes toward me and your public utterances about this development, I will undertake to set up trusts for your children. However, I am under no obligation to do so. It's up to each of you. No public announcement will be made about the sale of the company. I would prefer to do this quietly. However, at this very moment our company auditors are presenting our figures to a buyer in New York. Any questions?"

They all sat stunned. Some of the children were crying. Yarrow hardened herself. They must know, she thought, they must know, and understand for their own future, how important family loyalty is. It was harder to keep loyalty within the family than it was to keep love or money. She did not equate loyalty with love; the union of the family should have been enough. It was a hard lesson for the younger ones. She looked at Star, for whom she had high hopes, but Star wouldn't catch her eye, and when John lumbered to his feet and stalked out without saying a word, Star and Patsy rushed out after him. Lily was sobbing on David's shoulder. "It's so unfair," she cried. David and his weeping women left the room. Buck had been leaning against the wall with his arms folded and his chin on his chest. He looked up at his mother and his beard quivered.

"You're right," he said. "I could never get my act together. Perhaps, if I had, this could have been avoided. But you, Mama, aren't blameless. You never took my own ambitions seriously. I guess that's why I didn't either." He uncrossed his arms and came over to her. "I'm sorry," he said. Yarrow nodded. She felt as though her heart were breaking.

As Justice and Marla started to follow him out, Yarrow said, "Justice, would you take over the day-to-day running of the *Telegraph* until the new owner comes in? I'll be in there, too, of course."

"How can I refuse you? Sure." He paused. "Will you tell me who the new owner is?"

"No."

"It'd be a good story."

She smiled—always the newspaperman.

"You'll know soon enough."

She watched him leave with his parents and his sister. Greta and Eric and their families also left, and Yarrow shook hands with the lawyers and said she would see them the following day when she flew to New York.

Elliot sat in a big armchair with his feet up watching her. He was the only one left.

"Oh, my darling," he said, "that was grown-up."

"It hurt to see their faces."

"Are you really sure this is what you want to do?"

"Yes." She looked fierce for a moment and then came across and put her hands on his arm. "You look haggard."

"I was proud of you," he said. "Little Yarrow who told me on her swing she was going to make babies and wear gloves. Boxing gloves." They laughed together and then she said, "I wonder if Jock would have done the same thing."

"He would probably have straightened them all out a bit sooner."

Edith came in with a coffee tray and then went out again.

"I take it you've decided on this buyer."

"Yes," she said. She bit her lip and turned her head the better to watch his face when she told him. "I've agreed to sell McLean Publishing to Shipam Truitt."

He sat shocked for a moment, and then he put back his head and laughed.

"Oh, that's rich," he said, "that's rich."

She watched him, but he couldn't stop laughing. She pulled down the jacket of her suit more firmly—she had dressed in her business uniform to deal the coup de grâce.

"It made perfect business sense and I thought it had a certain appropriateness about it." She had long since shared the story of Fabiana's father with Elliot.

"Then Jock would be pleased," he said. "You're a woman after his own heart."

CHAPTER 41

"WILL THAT BE ALL, MR. AMBASSADOR?" ELLIOT'S MANservant hovered at the door of the library.

"Thank you. I'll have breakfast at the usual time."

"Yes, sir. Good night sir." The man withdrew. Elliot sighed and picked up the evening papers and sipped his sour-mash bourbon. He hated this mansion in New Jersey, hated this room with its dark paneling and heavy curtains. He was only here to satisfy the legal requirements for the divorce. He took another drink and he felt his heart give a little bump. He had had some angina pain before, but the doctor had said there was nothing to worry about, just take it easy. Elliot felt he had been taking it too easy this year. He had reliable people, talented people, in his offices around the world, but he knew they missed him when he was not around. He knew it revitalized them for him to be interested, to question, to make suggestions. But Elliot also knew he was slowing down. He had thought he would mind when that happened. But in fact, he did not. He wanted to enjoy simple pleasures with Yarrow—visit art galleries, take in some music at Carnegie Hall. If only Blanchette would divorce him, this charade could be over.

Elliot was tired. He had spent the day with his senior people on a complicated refinancing of a South American bank. There was a time when the more complicated the deal, the more Elliot liked it. He had found that the mathematics were always simple; what he enjoyed was finding his way through the maze of regulations and laws, motivations and profits. It had all been a game, and he had become very good at it.

Now he just wanted to resolve this ridiculous situation with Blanchette and make Yarrow his wife. It seemed so foolish at their age to be going through this nonsense.

He switched on the television and put the mute on. Yarrow was being interviewed by Ted Koppel at eleven-thirty P.M. on *Nightline* and he didn't want to miss her. She had been worried about how long it was taking to put the sale of her company through. It was unsettling for her and the people who worked for her. He had seen it happen in other businesses. It was bad for morale and bad for business. She hoped that the interview would allay some fears.

He worried about her. He hated to see her becoming thinner and her tongue sharper. He loved her. She had tried to keep it a secret that she was selling to Truitt. Sometimes he wondered if she would really go through with it.

Every name imaginable had been mentioned as a buyer; even the old Randolphs in London had been quoted in some ambiguous fashion, and Molinski, still hot for a newspaper property, had issued one of his usual bombastic statements. Yarrow feared that if she did announce who it was, the deal would unravel. Besides, her children would be furious when they found out. Better to let them deal with it when everything was completed.

The doorbell rang. He stood up and a spasm shot across his chest. He had felt that pain once before, too, and the doctor had told him it was because he was holding the telephone too tightly when he used it. Elliot rubbed his chest under his silk dressing gown and went to the door.

"I have to talk to you."

It was John, Yarrow's son. He stood in the soft snow holding his hat.

"Come in. I'm not doing anything."

They went back into the library and John threw his damp coat on a chair.

"Help yourself to a Scotch," said Elliot, turning up the sound of the television. Yarrow had come on. He thought she looked lovely but so nervous that his heart went out to her.

"Elliot," said John, throwing back his Scotch, neat. "You know who she's selling to? That goddam Shipam Truitt."

"Yes, I know." Elliot was trying to listen to Yarrow.

"But you've got to stop her."

"I can't stop her."

"She'd listen to you." John took Elliot by the shoulders and stood between him and the television set.

"Let go of me, John. I want to watch your mother."

John swung around and switched off the television. "Will you listen to me? She's selling her own children out. And for what—spite?"

"Put that show back on."

"Not until you hear me out. If you'd help me, I could raise the money. We could put together a consortium . . ."

"I'm not interested. Put that damn show back ON . . ." Elliot pulled away and switched on the set, while John struggled with him. John was a large, heavy man and Elliot could not make him budge.

"I just want you to hear me out . . ."

Elliot began to feel his ears pop. He was enraged at John. He was breathing very heavily. He couldn't hear what Yarrow was saying. He couldn't hear what John was saying. A steel band was tightening around his chest, and then he felt something burst inside him. He clutched at John's jacket, but it couldn't stop him from falling. He could see John's lips moving in concern, but it was too late. Elliot stared at the television screen as he fell. "Yarrow . . ." he said.

"Oh, my God," said John. Elliot had crumpled to the floor, one hand clawing at his chest. John knelt beside him and moved Elliot's head from side to side, but there was no response. The manservant came in. He had come up to check on who had rung the doorbell. He felt Elliot's pulse, put his ear to Elliot's chest.

"Ambassador Weyden is dead, sir," he said.

Buck stood beside his mother at the funeral service, and Meredith stood beside hers. The church was packed with the mighty and the powerful, the front rows taken up by dignitaries who had come to pay their respects. The eulogies were long and moving, though later Yarrow could not remember a word of them.

Yarrow could not believe she had lost her beloved Elliot. She could not believe he lay in that shiny wooden box with the thick brass handles under the blanket of roses. If only their lives had been different, it would have been she receiving condolences as his widow at the door. But she did not even have that comfort.

When the service was over, she had to pass Blanchette. Blanchette stood in the vestibule receiving murmurs of sympathy from the mourners as they left. Yarrow could hardly stand. If she had pained this woman, Yarrow thought, how much had this woman pained her? Blanchette was looking pale and pinched, but Yarrow could barely see her through her own black veil.

"You were the only one," said Blanchette, "the only one of Elliot's women I was afraid of." Yarrow ignored the sting.

"Why couldn't you let him go?"

"I prayed for the strength to do so. I did it for my father, but I couldn't do it for you."

"Why couldn't you do it for him?"

Buck led his mother to her car. She did not go out to the cemetery in Long Island. How she wished she could take Elliot with her to the mountains. At least there he would be free of Blanchette. Yarrow could then imagine they were together. But all this was denied her.

"Take me home, son, before I make a fool of myself," she said.

They put her under sedation, and Edith, who had come to the funeral, flew back with her to Chipeta. Edith and George Thringle, Laura's son, had married a few weeks before, but Yarrow could not take joy in their happiness.

Everything she looked at reminded her of Elliot. Every part of her own body reminded her of him; they had been one, she felt that they still were, that he was in her and would never leave her. How could Blanchette understand what it was that Yarrow and Elliot had shared? She had only known a part of it, and in suspecting what it was, had determined to make them suffer for it. Oh, God, Yarrow thought, if there is a heaven or a hell, keep him there until I can be with him.

Days went by in which Yarrow faded in and out of reality and Greta came and sometimes Edith and stayed with her in the big house though none could share her bed. He had left a nightshirt hanging on a hook in her bathroom; it still had his smell, and she took it to bed each night and wrapped it around her pillow. The snows came and one morning she woke and it still seemed to be night, for the skylight was totally blacked out with the night's heavy snowfall. Edith had brought the little picture from New York that Elliot had given Yarrow, the still life of apples by Cézanne. *Nature morte*. Yarrow lay and looked at it with her good eye, with her whale's eye, that morning. In the dim room, with the lamp lit, the little picture glowed. The colors of the appleskins promised summer, she could smell their sweetness, remembered how Elliot used to eat them, his strong white teeth leaving grooves in the white flesh. How she had loved him. She picked up the picture and held it close to her eye. Now she could see it clearly. She could see the basket where it lay on the table. She could see it from above and from the side as though the artist had given her two views of the same object. The picture was like Elliot; there were two views of him, the public one, the one she had to share with others, and the private one, the one that none of them knew. If anybody had reached that inner cave of his, it had been she. What a gift he had shared with her. How could she ever thank him?

Days later, Buck arrived at Chipeta. Yarrow was up, sitting beside the fire with Greta. Greta was brushing her hair.

"Everyone used to think that I had the pretty hair in the family," said Greta, shaking her short locks. "But I always liked your mother's better."

"Did you?" said Yarrow, "I never knew that." Greta brushed the white hair that fell past Yarrow's waist.

"Oh, yes, I always did. I wanted to be you. You always seemed to know what you wanted, I envied you that."

"I must have been tiresome." Buck smiled to hear his mother being more like herself again.

"Meredith gave me something for you," he said, taking an envelope from his pocket. "She said her father meant it for you." Yarrow felt the ring through the envelope.

"Yes," she said, "this is mine." She shook it out and into her hand, such a little circle of gold it was, and put it on her wedding finger.

"There was a slip of paper, too. Elliot was writing on it the night he died."

Yarrow took it from him.

" 'Ask Yarrow, was it worth it?' "

Yarrow folded up the paper and slipped it through her wedding ring. She couldn't look at Greta or her son. She looked into the fire. The flames were pillars and columns of orange and red and gold. They leaped over the white-washed logs. Yarrow felt that she and Elliot had been the flames—they had left the dying embers for others. Oh, yes, darling, she thought, it was worth it.

The warning bells at the railroad crossing clanged as the Amtrak train pulled into the Hudson station in upstate New York. The stationmaster placed some aluminum steps in front of the railroad car as passengers stepped down to the grade level. Yarrow scanned the faces of the people waiting as the conductor helped her down and handed her to the stationmaster. She took her cane and her small bag, and then she saw Edith rushing up to her, wearing a coat that wouldn't button over her stomach.

"I'm so glad you could come," said Edith, helping her into her station wagon. The car was an old model with manual transmission. Edith drove off with a clash of gear changes. "George is as crazy as a bandicoot about this. He and Justice have been slaving like mad for this day."

"It's good to see you, Edith."

"Oh, it's good to see you, too, Miss McLean. I've missed you." Edith gulped noisily.

"How is Justice's wife?"

"Marla? Oh, she's got all the local ladies jiggling around in leotards. She started a low-impact aerobics class."

"My, my," said Yarrow.

Edith maneuvered up the hilly main street of Hudson, which had once been an old whaling town. A sign with a big blue whale swung above a doorway.

"Are you coping all right without me? I was worried when George said we were moving. I miss Colorado."

"Oh, don't worry about me. Eduardo seems to have a constant stream of 'cousins' who come in to help me. You must always put love first, Edith. Nothing else matters."

"Well, you ought to see where George's main love interest is right now."

Yarrow glanced at Edith's figure, which had filled out somewhat.

"I can see where that is."

Edith blushed.

"I feel a right galah having a first baby at my age. Forty-five years old! It's indecent, isn't it? But I've had all the tests, amniocentesis, the lot, and mother and baby are fine."

Edith clashed the gears again and they reversed into a parking space in front of a shop at the top of the main street. Edith opened the door of the shop with a flourish and a little bell tinkled above the doorway.

"Da-dah," she said.

Justice came rushing out of the back, his hair sticking up all over the place. At thirty-five, he looked as gangly as he had when he was a boy. He gave his aunt a smacking kiss on both cheeks.

"Welcome to Desktop Publishing," he said. "All bought with Truitt dollars." His face was flushed with enthusiasm. He helped her into a chair.

"Tea for the lady. Where's my partner? GEORGE!"

George Thringle appeared through the door with ink on his nose. He was ten years older than Justice, but his face was ageless as his father's had been. He peered out shyly from behind his glasses.

"My boffin," said Edith, rolling her eyes and setting down mugs of tea while she fished out the tea bags with a spoon.

"What you are about to see is the democratization of printing," said Justice.

"Pagination," said George, "is the future. Up until now it's the pictures that have been the holdup."

"The graphics were always a problem," said Yarrow.

"Each dot in a photograph had to be scanned and then 'digitized,' " said George. "It's complicated, but we're getting there. Once we have the large microprocessor, all will be possible."

"Come and see," said Justice.

Yarrow went into the back room, where four computer terminals sat on desks. A young woman wearing a telephone headset was taking ads at one and smiled at her. Yarrow went to a desk where George punched up the computer screen.

"Now," he said, "we can compose the whole paper with this—this one machine, isn't that amazing? We can make up the whole page on the videotube."

"Electronic page makeup."

"It eliminates the composing room—no more waxing, no more guys with razor blades."

"No more scraps of paper."

Yarrow listened to their excitement. They used words she could no longer follow—"kerning" and "laser scans"—but she caught the gist. And when she pushed the button to start the Goss offset press, she understood even more. It was no different from the feelings she had had when she realized her mortality and tried to postpone it. Justice and George knew that here, in this way, as the printed words on the newspaper came off the press, their thoughts had been captured. Even when they, much younger than she, would be gone, those thoughts would remain. It was a form of immortality. It was something she understood better than anyone.

She took the first copy they gave her and tears filled her eyes when she saw the new masthead: *The Hudson Humdinger.* A humming bird and a whale were incorporated in the artwork.

"Why, it's just beautiful," she said. "I think it's one of the most beautiful things I've ever seen."

Buck had waited six months for Meredith to get over the loss of her father. He knew she grieved for him, and she had stopped working at the clinic. He had gone a few times to check if she was there, but now he could wait no longer and he decided to drive out to Long Island and see her himself. In the past few months he had been working hard on a series of paintings. He had one successful show at a downtown gallery and was encouraged by the interest in his paintings. The first check he had earned from his paintings meant more to him than any money his mother had given him. He packed some finished canvases in the back of his Toyota truck and set off, not knowing if Meredith would see him. After her father's death, she had asked him to convey some things to his mother. Since then he had stayed away though he longed to be near her. Now it was up to him. Buck was thirty-five years old. He didn't want a friend. He didn't want a "relationship." He wanted a wife. He wanted Meredith.

In Amagansett Buck got directions to a road that led into the potato fields. He remembered how happy he had been here as a boy on the summer vacations. Now it was April and a salty, stiff wind was blowing in from the Atlantic. He saw her children first, their fair hair standing out like beacons as they kicked a ball in front of the flat, open land that surrounded the modest frame house. That was another thing. Meredith was now an immensely wealthy young woman. Buck hadn't wanted to be the first suitor panting at her door. He thought the frame house was a bit like Meredith, a modest enclosure around a jewel.

She came to the screen door when his truck drove up. She

stood there with a kerchief around her head and her hand up to shield her eyes from the sun.

"What are you doing out here?" she asked.

"Hi. I'm trying to sell some of my paintings to those fancy art galleries in Southampton."

"Come in." He squeezed past her as she held open the door. He could smell that familiar scent of hers, the shampoo she used—Prell? VO5?—the Imperial Leather soap, the faint, underlying antiseptic scent, not Lysol surely. He had always assumed that came from working in the hospital. Now he wondered if he had imagined it.

"Have you sold any?

"What?"

"Paintings."

"Oh, well, one. But I'm here because I have an introduction to a gallery owner on Main Street. Windsor Artists?"

"Windsor's. Oh, I know them. Mention my name."

"I will. Thanks." They stood in her kitchen. He was unsure what to do. He was here but he didn't know what to say. She pushed the sleeves of her sweatsuit up above her elbows.

"You look busy," he said. "Am I interrupting something?"

"Spring cleaning. I'm turning mattresses upstairs. Actually you could help."

She led the way up the stairs. "I'm turning everything out," she said. "I used to have a nanny who did that. When things upset her she would turn the nursery upside down. It's therapeutic."

"Don't you have anyone to help?"

"I don't want anyone around."

He stared at her eyes over the top of the mattress as she shoved it over and he caught it. Then he held it while she vacuumed underneath the bedsprings.

She let the mattress down with a bang and laughed at him as he struggled with the unwieldy thing.

"I guess you've never done this before."

"No. Is that it?"

"That's the first one. We have five more to go."

Later, after he had turned mattresses, moved wardrobes, laid rugs, washed venetian blinds, and jostled a dresser down the stairs on his back, she declared she was satisfied.

Buck held his back and collapsed onto a kitchen chair. Meredith put her head out the door and yelled for her children to come in.

"Like some soup?" she said to him, washing her hands at the sink. She set the table deftly around him, and he watched her neat ways, her strong but pretty hands, the lock of hair that escaped from under the kerchief.

"You're seeing me at my worst," she said, noticing his attention. The children giggled. He took up so much room in the little kitchen. Outside a squall had moved in and the rain lashed at the window. The children groaned when they saw the rain, but Meredith said the sun would come out again soon.

They ate companionably and he listened to her little boy and girl talk, and he watched her. He did some funny drawings for the children on their napkins. When they were finished, the sun came out as abruptly as it had gone away.

"You see, I told you," she said as the children scampered outside.

"I must go," he said.

"Will you come back?"

"You mean this afternoon?"

She laughed. "Yes."

"If you want me to."

"I was wondering why you took so long to come."

"Meredith, you mean that?"

She stood with the dishcloth in her hand at the door of the kitchen. She didn't smile.

"Yes, I mean that, Buckley Heartland."

He let out a whoop, and ran to his truck. He started it up and then as she went back inside the kitchen, he came running back and peered at her through the screen door. He put his hand on the screen and she put her hand up and matched his on her side.

"When I come back," he said, "we'll pretend we never met—our parents never knew each other—we never had an argument."

"OK," she said. She watched him running back across the rutted potato fields to his truck.

"We'll begin," he shouted at her above the roar of the engine, "right back at the beginning."

ABOUT THE AUTHOR

ANNA MURDOCH was born and grew up in Scotland before moving to Australia, where she worked as a newspaper journalist. She has traveled extensively worldwide and lived in London for six years. In 1984, she completed her master's degree at New York University in the study of literature and mythology. In 1985, IN HER OWN IMAGE, Mrs. Murdoch's first novel, was published to great acclaim. She lives in New York with her husband, Rupert Murdoch, and their three children.